OTHERWORLD

JASON SEGEL
KIRSTEN MILLER

DELACORTE PRESS

Visit us on the Web! randomhouseteens.com

Educators and librarians, for a variety of teaching tools, visit us at RHTeachersLibrarians.com

Library of Congress Cataloging-in-Publication Data
Names: Segel, Jason, author. | Miller, Kirsten, author.
Title: Otherworld / Jason Segel and Kirsten Miller.
Description: First edition. | New York : Delacorte Press, [2017] | Series: Otherworld ; 1 | Summary: "After the newest set of virtual reality gear hits the market, Simon can't wait to test it out. But, when his friend Katherine suddenly disappears after being seen with men from the same gaming company, Simon must decide how far in the game he's willing to go to save her"— Provided by publisher.
Identifiers: LCCN 2017002986 | ISBN 978-1-101-93932-1 (hc) | ISBN 978-1-101-93933-8 (glb) | ISBN 978-1-101-93934-5 (ebook) | ISBN 978-1-5247-7069-3 (intl. tr. pbk.)
Subjects: | CYAC: Virtual reality—Fiction. | Internet games—Fiction. | Best friends—Fiction. | Friendship—Fiction. | Conduct of life—Fiction. | Science fiction.
Classification: LCC PZ7.S4533 Oth 2017 | DDC [Fic]—dc23

The text of this book is set in 11-point Minion Pro.
Interior design by Stephanie Moss

Printed in the United States of America
10 9 8 7 6 5 4 3 2 1
First Edition

TO KRISTA, BARBARA, BEVERLY, AND ERIN.
FOR HELPING US TELL OUR STORIES

OTHERWORLD

There are guys online who swear it was heaven. They still sit around like a bunch of old geezers, swapping tales of epic storms, monstrous beasts and grisly battles. Talk to any gamer in their twenties and at some point they'll say: "You're too young to get it. You never saw Otherworld."

Now keep in mind, most of these idiots never experienced the original Otherworld either. Even at the height of its popularity, it never had more than a handful of subscribers. It wasn't until years after the publisher pulled the plug that it became known in geek lore as the greatest game of all time.

I always thought that was bullshit. I don't anymore.

It took a twentysomething tech billionaire named Milo Yolkin to drag the game back from the dead. Today at noon, his company released an early-access version of Otherworld 2.0. Two thousand lucky gamers were chosen to test it, and somehow I'm one of them. The original Otherworld players were all dorks like me, but as far as I can tell, this new group of players has little in common aside from deep pockets. The app itself is free—you just have to buy the exclusive new headset that goes with the game. Only a couple thousand have been made, and each one costs over two grand.

I have no clue what the old Otherworld looked like on a PC monitor when it came out over a decade ago. But I gotta admit—when I downloaded the new app and I put on the headset, I wasn't expecting graphics this good. I know everything is CGI, but my eyes are completely convinced that it's real. I've got a plastic brick strapped to my face, there's sweat trickling out of my haptic gloves, and I'd rather die than be seen in the dainty booties I'm wearing. Back in the real world, my body is blind, deaf and helpless. I've been in Otherworld for over seventeen hours now, and there is no way in hell that I'm leaving.

Of course, this world has been trying to kill me from the very first second I set out to explore. I've encountered some truly insane shit so far—an avalanche, lighting strikes, quicksand and some kind of mutated polar bear that I managed to butcher and eat using nothing but a dagger and my two bare hands. Still, nothing compares to what I've just found.

I've come to a stone path that disappears into a cavern carved out of a glacier. I run my hand along one of the icy walls. I feel that it's there, but my fingertips can neither confirm nor deny that the surface is as smooth or as cold as it appears. I shouldn't have cheaped out when I bought the gloves, but the best ones were so expensive that they'd have triggered a credit alert. I'm sure I could have found a way around it if I'd known the fancy gloves would be worth it. But none of the rumors prepared me for Otherworld.

When I look up, I see a sun just like the one I've always known burning in the sky. Its light penetrates the ice around me, and the whole glacier glows like an enchanted gem. I can hear water rushing somewhere deep within the glacier. A sharp crack echoes behind me, and I spin around a little too quickly. My stomach drops and hot vomit rises and scalds the back of my throat. They haven't found a way to truly beat the motion sickness yet. I close my eyes, swallow and wait until the dizziness fades.

Then I take a deep breath and open my eyes again. Stretching out toward the horizon is the empty ice field I just crossed. Somewhere in the distance is the City of Imra, where I began my journey. Apparently that's where all Otherworld adventures begin. You design your avatar and walk through a door and suddenly you're outside Imra's gates. In the few minutes I was there, I watched a parade of avatars pass through them.

They're all still back there, I guess. They say the original Otherworld could get pretty smutty, but I don't think it had anything quite like Imra. Apparently the city's a CGI Sodom that makes *Grand Theft Auto* look like *Dora the Explorer*. I was tempted to do a little sightseeing in town, but that seemed to be what the designers expected us to do. So I set off in the opposite direction. Away from the city. Down a mountainside. Into the wilderness. Across the ice fields. The way I figure it, when you're given a chance to explore the most incredible survival sandbox ever created, you shouldn't let yourself get slowed down by a few anatomically correct non-player characters.

Now I'm standing here in front of the ice cave, with the wind whistling all around me. It's a pity I can't feel anything but the steady chill of central air. If I breathe in too deeply, I can smell the

Febreze my mom's cleaning lady uses. But my eyes are burning from snow glare, and my toes are numb. Before I enter the glacier, I turn one last time and scan the frozen white landscape behind me. There are no signs of movement, but I know I'm not on my own. Someone's followed me here. She's always kicked ass at camouflage, and I haven't caught sight of her. But I don't need my eyes to tell me that Kat's in Otherworld too. I feel her presence—and I'm finding it hard to wipe the shit-eating grin off my face.

Back in the real world, Kat hasn't spoken to me in months. I've tried pretty much everything, and Otherworld was my last resort. On Friday I left a set of gear in her locker, along with a note to let her know I'd be logging on at noon today. I didn't think she could resist being one of the first to see Milo Yolkin's new wonderland. So I was pretty bummed when I didn't catch sight of her outside Imra. It's starting to look like my investment paid off, though. As far as I'm concerned, a few thousand dollars of my mother's money is a small price to pay for the pleasure of Kat's company.

I step forward into the cave and stop. Lurking in a shadow is a figure I didn't see until now. Someone or something is guarding the entrance. I draw my dagger and prepare to strike. Everything around me may be fake, but the sound of my heart pounding is real. As my eyes adjust, I see a thin man dressed in what looks like a modern-day suit. He's about a foot taller than I am, and there's a scarf wrapped Bedouin-style around his head. The thin strip of face left uncovered is ebony black. In one hand the man holds a gnarled staff. An amulet hangs around his neck, a clear stone in its center. When the man doesn't move, I have a go at stealing his staff, but his grip remains firm. It's only when I try to take the amulet that I realize I'm attempting to mug a statue. I rap my knuckles against its hollow chest. It seems to be sculpted from clay.

I suppose the clay man is a sign that I'm on the right track. Open world or not, the developers wouldn't have placed a statue here for no reason. There's bound to be something interesting at the end of the path. And when I find it, I have a hunch that the statue will spring to life and show me what it can do with its staff. But why worry about that right now, when I can listen to the crunch of rocks beneath my bootie-clad feet? Or watch chunks of ice bobbing in the Slurpee-blue stream that's flowing beside the path? The scenery alone is worth every single penny of the six grand I charged to my mom's credit card.

I plunge deeper into the glacier, occasionally sneaking a peek over my shoulder, hoping to catch Kat slinking up behind me. I'm thinking about the two of us alone together in an icy blue cavern with a giant clay man guarding the door. It's been over a year since she and I have been by ourselves. I'm enjoying the thought so much that when I turn a corner and see *him,* I almost mistake him for a rock.

He sits on a throne chiseled out of granite. His body is made of a gray material that looks like stone, and there's an impressive set of horns sprouting out of his head. He's human in shape, though he seems to be built on a much larger scale. Whoever he is, he feels no need for clothes. Heat radiates from him, and the melting ice walls form a sphere around his body. The moat of meltwater at his feet is clear, but I can't gauge its depth. On the opposite side of his chamber is a tall metal door that doesn't really fit with the decorating scheme. I'm itching to find out what's behind it, but it's pretty obvious that I'll need to make it past the big dude first.

I make my way closer, and his head rises. I can't tell if he sees me, because he doesn't have a face, but I get the sense that he's not very happy. From what I've read online, the lands of Otherworld are ruled by demigods known as Elementals. This might be one of them. Some Elementals are helpful; many are hostile. I'm guessing the creature in front of me isn't interested in making friends.

"I wasn't expecting visitors." His voice booms in my headset and I have to turn the volume down.

Otherworld's new publisher has spent months bragging about its next-generation AI, but there's something that makes me think this guy's not part of the game. And if he's not an Elemental or an NPC, then I'm not the only explorer around. Whoever this is, he's built a formidable avatar.

"I guess not," I say into my mike. "Looks like you forgot to get dressed. You know, a stud like you would be pretty popular back in Imra. I've heard the place is a nonstop orgy. What are you doing out here when the action's back there?"

"I could ask the same of you," he says.

"Yeah, well, I'm allergic to fun. And mangos. Long-haired cats, too."

"How amusing," he says, giving my avatar the once-over. "You could have been anyone. And this is what you chose? What are you—a peasant?" He sounds so . . . *disappointed.* "Lack of imagination is a terrible affliction."

I glance down at my dull brown robe, sewn from the best

cyberburlap available. Whenever I'm given the option, I choose something similar.

"I can think of worse," I tell him. "Nothing wrong with keeping things simple. You know what they say: the flashier the avatar, the smaller the . . ." I stop the instant he stands up. His crotch is nothing but a smooth bump. He's like one of the action figures I used to torture when I was a kid. "You know, you're missing a little something down below." I gesture to his absent parts. "They had some amazing options during setup. Might be worth a reset."

"I appreciate your concern, but I have everything I need," he responds, moving toward me. "The ice fields are no place for guests. I'm afraid you must leave and return to the City of Imra."

"Make me." It just pops out. Which happens more often than I'd like. My tongue produces words faster than my brain can approve them.

"*Make you?*" he responds incredulously. "Perhaps you're not aware that Otherworld is intended for players eighteen and older? Did you lie when you registered?"

I didn't, but what the hell does he care?

"Spare me the lecture and get ready to rumble," I say. "I've been battling the environment for seventeen hours straight, and it's time for bed. I need a little PVP action to put me to sleep."

The avatar approaches, and soon he's towering over me. Once again, I'm blown away by the details. I can actually see veins throbbing in his chest, and though I'm an eighteen-year-old heterosexual, even I recognize that the dude's nipples are works of art. "You assume Otherworld is like the games you know. I assure you it's not. You've entered my sanctuary, and you are not welcome." The guy's beginning to glow from within like an ember. As his

7

head lights up, features finally appear on his face, and I almost bolt. He does not look friendly.

Instead of running, I draw my dagger. "Then you'd better kick me out."

Before I can make a move, three flaming arrows zip past my shoulder. They miss the monstrous avatar and sink into the frozen arched ceiling above him. A second later, an explosion rocks the entire cavern. I steady myself and watch as ice rains down from above, burying the beast. I turn to find a sleek figure behind me. She's dressed in a body-hugging suit of reflective material. It's hard to see her even though she's standing out in the open, but I'd know the face anywhere.

"You provoked that guy on purpose, Simon," Kat says. The voice is all hers, and it sets me on fire. "Did you think you had any chance of winning a fight with that dinky little dagger?"

"Absolutely not. I figured you'd show up and save me," I tell her. "I wanted to see what you're wearing. *Very* nice."

"Let's go, dumbass," she orders. She's never been able to accept a compliment. "He'll be out of there soon."

I glance back. The mysterious door behind the avatar is blocked now, so there's no real reason to stay. Kat is already retreating down the path, and I race to catch up, following her toward the entrance of the cavern. It's only when we're outside on the ice field that I realize something's different.

"The clay man's gone," I say as it registers.

"What clay man?" she asks.

"Never mind." It's not important, and there's much more that is. "Listen—" Just as I say it, the ground beneath our feet begins to rumble, and in moments the whole world is shaking around us.

"Not now, Simon," she says.

"Kat." I grab her hand and pull her toward me. There's no place to run. A geyser of lava erupts from beneath the ice and showers down on us. My crappy haptic gloves and booties are suddenly so hot that I yank them off and throw them across my bedroom. I keep the headset on, hoping for one last vision of Kat. All I see are sparks.

REALITY

It's a Sunday and nobody bothers me, so I sleep until noon. I'm a little disoriented when I wake up to my tastefully decorated bedroom with its sturdy oak furniture. I throw back the plaid bedspread that's pulled up to my chin. My first instinct is to reach for my Otherworld headset and get the hell out of New Jersey. I don't own a car, but thanks to the game, that won't matter much anymore. Then I remember I already have plans today.

I get out of bed and rifle through an old box at the back of my closet until I locate the Speedo I wore to swim meets back in elementary school. I strip out of my boxers and pull it on. Then I unlock my bedroom door and head down the hall. I pause at a mirror in the living room to make sure my junk is safely tucked away. The Speedo covers just enough to keep me from getting arrested. It's a pretty good look, I gotta say. Pasty white skin, wild black hair and three days' worth of untrimmed scruff. I figure I'm ready for action. But before I get down to business, I take a moment to admire my nose.

My grandfather was blessed with the same giant schnoz. From what I've read, the thing was legendary. If he'd lived two hundred years earlier, they'd have sung songs about it. But his heyday was the sixties, so his nose inspired a nickname instead. They called my grandfather the Kishka. For those of you out there who consider French fries an ethnic food, a kishka is a sausage. A rather unattractive sausage, I might add, with a shape that's either phallic or fecal, depending on your level of maturity. And yet, by all accounts, the ladies loved my grandfather. They say it's probably what got him killed.

I never saw the nose in person. In fact, I wouldn't know anything about it if it weren't for a book I found in the Brockenhurst library called *Gangsters of Carroll Gardens*. My mother grew up in that part of Brooklyn, but to hear her tell it, her childhood was all fresh cannoli, backyard garden parties and upscale bat mitzvahs. So imagine my surprise when I'm thumbing through the book and come across a picture of the Kishka. I don't know who he is at that point. I'm thirteen years old, and I don't even recognize my grandfather's name. I just know he looks exactly like me.

Stop here for a minute and imagine tumbling down that rabbit hole. By the time I hit bottom, everything made sense. My entire life, I'd always suspected that some critical piece of information was being withheld from me. For years, I was convinced that I couldn't possibly be my parents' biological child. I knew in my heart of hearts that one of the cleaning ladies had given birth to me in a broom closet and my beautiful, small-nosed mother had graciously taken me in. Whenever one of the maids smiled at me, I'd always wonder if it might be her.

Now I knew. Armed with a picture of a gangster I'd never heard of, I started to dig for the truth. I found part of it in a box tucked away in the attic. Inside were four Brooklyn high school yearbooks. I flipped through one, and there she was ... Irene Diamond. I didn't recognize her at first. All through high school, she looked nothing like the woman I know. I never would have guessed the girl was my mother if it hadn't been for the kishka set in the center of her face. Irene Diamond had the same damn nose I see every time I look in the mirror. I'd love to know how much her father paid to have it fixed.

When I was younger, my mother used to watch me when she thought I wasn't looking. She'd try to smile when I caught her, but I could tell she was horrified by what she saw. It used to upset me. Now the cosmic justice of it all cracks me up. She'd been running from the nose her entire life—and it ended up on her only son's face.

I may have cracked a little the day I found those yearbooks, but I didn't fall apart. And I never mentioned my discovery to my parents. Even then, I knew secrets had power. I knew my mother had hidden her true identity for good reason. Nothing would have given me more pleasure than shouting the truth from the rooftops. But I figured there would be a day when my mother's secret would come in handy. So for the past few years, I've kept it tucked away safely for future use.

I love looking at my nose now. The afternoon sun streaming in through the living room windows really sets it off. The giant gilded mirror in front of me is one of a pair that my mother tells dinner guests she purchased on her honeymoon in Paris. I don't know where she got the mirrors, but I've seen snapshots of her honeymoon in Orlando. The room in the background looks like Marie-Antoinette might waltz through at any moment. But the kishka on my face is there to remind me I don't belong to this world. I'm the grandson of a two-bit gangster who broke fingers for the Gallo crime family and is probably buried at the bottom of the Gowanus Canal.

"Oooh!" a lady squeals behind me. Then I hear the sound of footsteps rushing out of the room. Some new staff member, probably. The rest of them have been warned about me. I'm not sure what they've been told, but I doubt they'd be shocked to find a six-foot-three-inch kid with zero muscle mass and a giant nose standing in his old elementary school banana hammock in the middle of the formal living room.

"Sorry," I call out. I didn't expect anyone inside to see me. The house is rarely empty, though you can wander through it for hours without running into a soul. Don't get the wrong impression— I generally wear clothes when I wander. But today I have a special treat in mind for the neighbors.

It's still a bit nippy when I step outside, but spring has sprung. Across the street, the neighbors' newly planted rosebushes are blooming. The buds started opening last week, which is why I'm here now, nearly naked on a chilly afternoon. The flowers are fuchsia, a color my mother calls vulgar. As soon as they began to reveal themselves, my mother petitioned the homeowners' association to have them uprooted. Since she's the president of the association—and a ruthless attorney—her petitions always pass. How about that? It's the American Dream in action. Irene Diamond started life as the daughter of a small-time crook, and now she's in charge of nature.

The people across the street are new to our neighborhood. Last fall, they moved here from Singapore to work for one of our local tech conglomerates. Unlike my mother, they haven't spent years forming alliances over hors d'oeuvres, which means they lack what my parents call *leverage*. But they're friendly to me, so I'm going to give *them* something to complain about—something that will embarrass Mommy Dearest enough to keep her lips sealed at the next meeting of the homeowners' association.

I drag a chaise from the side of the pool behind our house. Its legs gouge muddy tracks in the pristine grass all the way to the front yard, where I position it perfectly—not far from the street and just across from the neighbors' living room windows. I've worked up a sweat, and my pasty skin glistens as I lie down on my stomach. I wedge the back of the Speedo between my butt cheeks and try to assume an artistic pose. No sense in being *vulgar*.

My eyes are closed and the warmth of the sun is spreading over my skin when the first car approaches. The driver hits the brakes near the mailbox.

"Hey, crazy!" someone shouts. I recognize the voice. It belongs to a girl from school. "What the hell are you doing?"

"What does it look like?" I call out. "I'm getting a tan."

"Put some clothes on, you pervert!" shouts a second voice.

"Nobody wants to see your hairy butt cheeks, Simon," screams a third. I open my eyes a crack and see three girls from school hanging out of a car. One of them is already tapping away at her phone. Their friends will be arriving soon.

My butt cheeks aren't quite as furry as they've been made out to be, and apparently *lots* of people would like to see them, because the traffic on my street goes nuts for the next thirty minutes.

I don't pay any attention to the hoots and catcalls. Crossing ice fields and getting blown to smithereens for hours on end was exhausting. I got about five hours of sleep, but I'll need more if I want to go back in tonight. I'm just drifting off when I hear a car pull into my drive. A few seconds later, someone's thrown a jacket over me.

"Get up and get inside." It's my mother.

I open my eyes. She's looming over my chaise, and she's pissed as hell.

"The people across the street are threatening to phone the police," she hisses.

"Hi, Mom," I say with a yawn. "You look stunning this afternoon."

She does. Her black hair is pulled into a fancy knot, and she's wearing a silk dress in a very tasteful shade of pale blue. Her painted lips are pressed together beneath her perfect nose.

"*Now*, Simon. Or you're going to jail."

I sigh and sit up, tying her jacket around my waist. "Aren't you overreacting? I'm sure the neighbors will forget all about this unfortunate incident if you let them keep their vulgar roses."

"Those people are not who you should be worried about," she says. "My accountant just called to ask if the six-thousand-dollar charge on my AmEx for video game equipment was a business expense. You stole my credit card, Simon. One more word from you and I'm dialing your probation officer."

This is unexpected. The accountant must be new. The old one didn't ask questions.

I'm fully clothed and sitting on the living room couch when my father gets home. He's dressed in Easter egg colors and there's a nine iron in his hand. Apparently I've interrupted a golf game. He walks straight through the room without even acknowledging me. A few minutes later, he's back, and he's got my new headset, gloves and booties. He drops them all in a pile on the floor.

I wince when I hear a crack. "Come on, Dad," I groan. "Do you know how hard it was to get all that stuff? Only a couple thousand of those headsets have even been made. That one's going to be worth a fortune someday."

"This heap of crap cost six thousand, three hundred and fifty-six dollars?" he asks.

Not exactly—I bought two sets of gear. I only kept one for myself. "It's not crap," I say. "It's the newest virtual reality technology. I was on a wait list for that headset—"

"So it's a video game," my father says. If you didn't know him, you wouldn't think he was that angry. But I've spent eighteen years with Grant Eaton, and I know all the warning signs. He's about to blow sky-high.

"It's revolutionary—"

"It's over." He lifts his nine iron over his head and brings it down hard on the equipment. He repeats the same motion at least three dozen times, until his face is bright red and he's out of breath.

I'm finding it pretty hard to breathe too. My last chance to spend time with Kat is just a pile of plastic shards. "I can't believe you—"

"You're eighteen now," he interrupts me. He's holding the golf club like a baseball bat and panting so hard that I wonder if he'll keel over. "One more incident like this, and your mother and I will no longer be able to help you. If I were you, Simon, I'd spend a lot more time in the real world."

THE GIRL
IN THE WOODS

It was a miscalculation—no doubt about it. I was sure the credit card charge would fly under the radar. I didn't factor in my mother's new eager-beaver accountant. Still, it's hard to see what all the fuss is about. I bet my mother spends more than six grand on Botox every month. Come to think of it, I wouldn't be surprised if my father spent even more than that. He's starting to look like a Madame Tussauds wax sculpture of himself. There's probably a warning tattooed on his ass that says KEEP AWAY FROM OPEN FLAMES.

My parents didn't stick around after they taught me my lesson. They had very important golf balls to hit, frittatas to eat and luxury leather goods to acquire, so I'm alone again, sitting on the edge of our pool with my legs dangling over the side. With my devices shattered, I'm trapped in what passes for reality here in beautiful Brockenhurst, New Jersey. My house is a fake French château, and my town stole its name from some fancy place in England. The grass in my lawn is a shade of green not known to nature. And the sausage in the Hot Pocket I'm chewing tastes like mystery meat that was grown in a lab.

You can touch Brockenhurst and you can smell it, but you'd be crazy to call it *real.*

Where our backyard ends, the woods begin. When I was a kid, the wilderness seemed endless; now most of it's gone. I look for the path that leads through what's left of the forest. The trail's grown over, but I could still walk it in my sleep. It leads straight to one of the few old houses around here that was never torn down. The land it sits on is swampy, and until recently the building had been slowly sinking for ninety-odd years. That's where Kat lives. I'd be there right now if she'd just let me talk to her. But these days my best friend bolts whenever I get near her. It cost me a few grand and a near-death experience with my father, but I got to see her in Otherworld. Unfortunately, in Brockenhurst she wants nothing to do with me.

Kat and I met ten years ago, when we were eight years old. My father had just made senior partner at his law firm, and he'd built this McMansion as his trophy. Thousands of trees were sacrificed to ravenous wood chippers, and our house rose near the edge of what would become the town's swankiest gated community. We moved in on the first day of summer. Mrs. Kozmatka, the nanny my mother had hired, told me to stay on the grass in the backyard when I played outside. I wasn't allowed to set foot in the woods, which my mother believed to be teeming with snakes, ticks and poison ivy.

In her defense, Mrs. Kozmatka was new. She knew nothing of

my history. And for the first couple of hours, I gave her no cause for concern. I sat exactly where I am right now and stared at the trees. Everything seemed so much more alive in the forest. As I was watching, I heard branches snapping and leaves rustling. And then someone stepped out from the other side.

I'd been playing a lot of Harry Potter games that summer, and I was convinced it was some kind of mythical creature. It was pretty clear that it wasn't a centaur, but I figured it could be a faun or a sprite. Even if the creature had spoken to me on that first encounter, I wouldn't have believed she was human. I'd never seen another kid so dirty. She was covered in dried mud from head to toe. It was camouflage, Kat later informed me. And it worked like a charm. That day, when the nanny came outside, Kat took a step backward and vanished so completely into the woods that it was almost as if she'd been swallowed whole.

My tender young mind was totally blown. My family had just moved from Manhattan. The first eight years of my life had been filled with fancy private schools and playdates with kids named Arlo and Phineas. It was an ideal life, which was why my therapists had so much trouble identifying the cause of my behavioral issues. (Arlo and Phineas got their asses kicked on a regular basis.)

In hindsight, it all seems perfectly clear to me. I'd been kept in a cage my entire life. I wasn't a kid. I was *veal.* And then this portal opened up in suburban New Jersey and I was offered a glimpse of an untamed universe. I didn't tell the nanny about the creature I'd seen. Instead I spent the next few hours eagerly waiting for it to return. I was sure it was spying on me, but it didn't set foot on my grass again. And by lunchtime I just couldn't wait any longer.

When the nanny went inside to make tuna sandwiches, I slipped into the woods to go find it.

I was only a few yards past the tree line when I heard Mrs. Kozmatka calling for me from the backyard of my house. When her cries grew more frantic, I stuck my fingers in my ears and kept going until I couldn't hear her anymore. The deeper I went, the wilder the woods got. Everywhere I looked, there were signs of the creature. Boards nailed to the trunks of trees—makeshift ladders leading to lookouts positioned high above in the canopy. Lean-tos built with branches and bows, their interiors carpeted with soft green moss. A massive fort made from scavenged wood, plastic tarps and car tires. I climbed every ladder and lay inside every shelter. I felt like I'd made one of those discoveries no one makes anymore. I'd stumbled across an abandoned world.

That whole afternoon, I remember having no sense of time passing. And then suddenly I was hungry and thirsty and the sun was beginning to set. As it grew dark, I saw a light appear in the distance. I hurried toward it and discovered a little white house tucked between the trees. A gravel driveway snaked toward the other side of the woods. The place I'd found was no fairy-tale cottage. It was more like a tumbledown shack. Half of it seemed to be sinking, and there were several kitchen appliances rusting on the front porch. Patches of paint had peeled away from the walls, leaving the house looking sickly. But the light was on in the living room, and I caught the scent of bacon in the air. I was trying to work up the courage to knock on the front door when I heard the growls.

Three dogs emerged from the brush. They seemed enormous to me at the time, but they couldn't have been much bigger than your average border collie, and all three of them were clearly starving. Their gray-and-golden coats were mottled and their skin clung to their ribs. The trio slinked toward me, yellow fangs bared. They'd been stalking me for a while, and they were ready to make their move. I was a plump little veal calf lost in the woods. I'm sure I looked absolutely delicious.

I grabbed a stick off the ground and backed away slowly, holding the large twig in my hands like a sword. I knew better than to run. I needed to climb something. I was so busy scanning my surroundings for a tree with low-hanging branches that I forgot to look down. I tripped over a rock, tumbled backward and fell to the ground. The dogs were on me in an instant. I waited to feel their teeth sink through my skin.

Then the air popped behind me. One of the dogs howled in pain and sprang at least a foot in the air. Another pop and there was a spray of sawdust from the trunk of a nearby tree. A third pop followed and the dogs fled.

I examined my arms and legs for missing flesh and bloody wounds, but much to my surprise, I was completely intact.

"Hey! You okay?" a voice called out to me.

I picked myself up and turned to face it. There on the porch of the house was a girl my age. I saw the hair first—a fierce mane of copper curls. Then my eyes moved to the pellet gun in her hands. The freckles came into view as I walked toward her. They covered the bridge of her nose and spread out over her cheeks. But it was the eyes I recognized. They belonged to the mud-covered creature I'd seen spying on my house. "Those your dogs?" I asked.

"Nope," said the girl. "Those're coydogs. Half wild dog, half coyote. They used to live farther out in the woods. Then you cut half the forest down. Now they've been hanging around here at night, eating our garbage."

"I didn't cut down the forest."

She rolled her eyes. "You know what I mean. People *like* you."

"Where'd you learn how to shoot so well?" I asked. My eyes were practically fondling her pellet gun. None of my friends in Manhattan had that kind of stuff. If a neighbor had spotted a kid with so much as a slingshot, child protective services would have been alerted.

"My gramma taught me. She says you gotta be tough when you're pretty and poor." I must have stared at the girl a little too long. Her brow furrowed and her eyes turned hard. "Yeah, I know what you're thinking. I'm not pretty enough. I shouldn't be worried," she snapped.

"That isn't what I was thinking," I told her honestly. "You just don't look like anyone I've ever met before." Which was true but completely pathetic. I probably would have seen lots of kids like her in New York if I'd ever left the Upper East Side.

The girl scowled, like she couldn't figure out whether to be offended. "Well, I'm not like anyone you've ever met before," she finally said. Then she glanced up at a patch of blue sky. "It's going to be dark soon. Want me to walk you back to your house?"

"Your parents will let you?" I asked, shocked. My parents locked the doors and drew the shades as soon as the sun went down.

"My dad's dead," she said.

"Your mom, then?"

"She's not home." The girl seemed annoyed by my questions. "Where's *your* parents, anyway?"

I shrugged. "I dunno. They don't tell me where they go." As far as I knew, they could have been in Hong Kong. They often showed up with trinkets they'd purchased at airports in faraway lands.

"Who's that lady at your house who was on the phone all morning?"

That was when I realized how long I'd been gone. Hours had passed since I'd slipped into the woods. Mrs. Kozmatka would have called my parents, and they wouldn't be happy. "She's the nanny." The last word slipped out before I could catch it.

"Huh. Must get boring hanging out with an old lady all the time." It sounded like an observation, nothing more.

I was pretty sure I'd rather play in traffic than spend another hour with Mrs. Kozmatka, but it didn't seem macho to say so. I shrugged instead. "I guess."

"Come on," said the girl, setting off down a path with the barrel of the pellet gun resting on her shoulder. I scrambled to catch up with her, and once I had, I paid close attention to the route we took. I knew I had to be able to find my way back.

That night, when we reached my house, every window was ablaze. I could see around one corner of the building to where a police car was parked in our drive. Its flashing red and blue lights painted the lawn, but there was no siren to accompany them.

"How many rooms are there in that house?" the girl asked.

"Lots," I told her. "I've never really counted." It was a lie. There were twenty-two.

"What do you put in all of them?"

I could have listed all the contents of my life, but the subject bored me. "Will you be in the woods tomorrow?" I asked her.

"Sure," she said. "I got a lot of work to do. D'you see the fort? Some of the walls washed away the last time it rained, and the roof keeps coming down."

"I saw," I told her. "I can help."

Her eyes narrowed. She seemed unsure.

"My name is Simon." It had been so long since I'd introduced myself to anyone that my name felt like a gift.

"Kat," she replied. "Raid your parents' garage tomorrow. Bring some nails and a rope."

In the kitchen, Mrs. Kozmatka was crying. My mother was draining a tumbler of red wine while my father conferred with a police officer in serious tones.

"Well, well. Look what the cat dragged in," said the cop, who'd caught sight of me over my father's shoulder. He winked at me like the two of us were in on a secret. "Looks like someone's been exploring the woods."

I gave myself a quick inspection and realized I was covered in brambles and a leaf was sticking to the bottom of one of my sneakers.

"Simon!" Mrs. Kozmatka yelped. She started to rush for me, only to be blocked by my mother, a master of optics, who wanted the policeman to see her receive the first hug.

"What were you doing out there?" my father demanded. Even back then, he always seemed vaguely annoyed by my presence. Like I was a puppy his wife had wanted. He'd indulged her little whim and now the beast wouldn't stop relieving itself all over the rug.

"I was playing," I told him.

"Didn't Mrs. Kozlowsy—" my mother started to say.

"*Kozmatka*," said the nanny, who must have realized she was going to be fired and didn't feel the need to take my mother's crap anymore.

"Didn't Mrs. *Kozmatka* tell you to stay away from the woods?" my mother said sternly. "Do you have any idea how much trouble you've caused? Officer Robinson had to come all the way out here . . ."

Officer Robinson looked a bit thrown by our family dynamic. "It was no trouble at all, ma'am," he insisted. Then he knelt down in front of me. "Did you get lost?"

I shook my head. "No."

"Did you have fun?"

I couldn't help it. I must have grinned like a maniac. The cop mussed my hair and stood up. He was a nice guy. Still is—though he wasn't quite as helpful the next few times we met.

"Excuse me, Officer," my mother began, "but I really don't see—"

"Mr. and Mrs. Eaton, the woods around Brockenhurst are pretty safe during the day. That's where most of the kids here play. My own girls included. Of course," he said, looking down at me, "it's a good idea to get inside a couple of hours before dark. There are some wild dogs that come out when the sun starts to set."

"*Wild dogs?*" my mother gasped, as if he'd said lions or bears.

"We call them coydogs around here, and your son is no safer from them in your yard than he is out in the woods. You might think of getting Simon a slingshot or a BB gun and teaching him how to use it. The dogs are scavengers. Cowards. They won't put up a fight."

"Simon is *eight*," my father argued. "He can't be out running wild in the forest."

"Why not?" the cop asked, and my father clammed up.

"I can't see why Simon would want to play in the woods when he has toys and a pool and everything he could possibly want right here," my mother informed the cop.

"You're absolutely right, ma'am," Officer Robinson told her. "I'm sure your boy has everything you could buy. But out there in the woods, Simon can make his own world."

My mother remained skeptical, but my father must have felt that his manhood had been challenged. He sided with the cop. After that, I was allowed to leave the house in the morning and return just before dusk, covered in leaves and mud. No one ever asked what I did in the woods. I didn't tell them—and I never breathed a word about Kat.

Over time, my behavior improved. I got into fewer fights. Kat and I built new worlds and burned old ones down. We ruled over our forest kingdom with barbaric benevolence. Kat showed me how to shoot, saw and hammer. I gave her my ridiculous weekly allowance whenever her mom didn't have money for groceries, and I taught Kat how to curse in French. At school we beat up each other's bullies and did each other's homework. We bought our first game consoles together—and transitioned to PCs together. We were inseparable in every world we visited.

Kat was my best friend and my family for ten whole years, but I don't think I ever spoke her name in front of my parents.

She belonged to my world, not theirs. She was none of Grant and Irene's business.

The sun is setting behind me. It's a beautiful Sunday evening in Brockenhurst. A cold wind ripples the swimming pool water, and the trees at the edge of my lawn shove against each other like commuters boarding a subway car. Kat's somewhere beyond those trees. She can't be far. I can feel her. I hope she's all right, but until I see her at school tomorrow, I'll have no way of knowing. My Otherworld gear is just a pile of shards. I'm legally forbidden to use email. And Kat blocked my calls three months and four days ago.

THE BOY
WITH NO FUTURE

So how *do* you lose your only friend? It's an excellent question. I'm still searching for the answer. All I know is that the chain of events kicked off sixteen months ago. At the time, life was about as perfect as it will ever be. I should have known it wasn't going to stay that way. I should have been prepping for disaster. The universe was worried that I'd go soft being happy. I needed trials and tribulations to keep me on my toes.

First my father accepted a job offer in Dubai. It was supposed to be temporary. "Only a couple of years," my parents assured me. They seemed blissfully unaware that they were talking to someone for whom two years was the difference between Pokémon and pubic hair. I should have whipped out the Kishka at that point—and threatened to expose my mother's crooked family tree. Then again, if I ever make a list of the shit I *should have done,* it would stretch all the way to Atlantic City.

While my parents enjoyed the fruits of slave labor in a tacky desert hellhole, our house in New Jersey would be transformed into a high-end vacation rental. I was not allowed to stay. They were adamant about this, though I emailed them countless articles about the things that took place in high-end vacation rentals and assured them that I couldn't possibly do any more harm to the house than the furries and orgy enthusiasts who'd soon be occupying our bedrooms.

In the end, I was given two options, and staying in Brockenhurst wasn't one of them. I could move to Dubai—or I could pack my bags for boarding school. My father's illustrious alma mater in Massachusetts had accepted me for the spring semester. Which meant dear old Mom and Pop must have been plotting the move behind my back for quite some time. I would have been heartbroken if I'd ever trusted them in the first place.

I considered running away. I was pretty handy with a slingshot and pellet gun at that point. I figured, if nothing else, I could live in the woods. It was Kat who pointed out that I'd gone completely insane. There weren't enough woods left to hide me. Besides, two years was nothing in the grand scheme of things, she said. And she said it with such conviction that I started to wonder if she could see the grand scheme from her bedroom window. At the end of our time apart, we'd both be out of high school, together and free. She swore we'd talk every day until then.

For the first six months we did. Then Kat's mother, Linda, announced she was marrying a man named Wayne Gibson. He'd moved to town around the same time I left, and they'd bonded over bourbon at some local bar. Suddenly Kat was busy helping her mom make arrangements for the wedding. Our texts and video chats dwindled to a few a week. After the blessed nuptials took place, she sent me some pictures of the event. I didn't say so at the time, but I thought her new stepdad looked like a real douchebag. He wore a military dress uniform with a bunch of fancy medals that he'd polished to a shine, and in every picture he stared straight at the camera, as if daring the photographer to take the photo off-center. But Linda in her frilly cupcake of a dress was beaming like she'd just been crowned prom queen. She'd always been so nice to me, though. I figured her happiness was all that mattered.

That was when Kat slowly began to vanish. She'd send me a strangely cheery note now and then, but most of my texts went unanswered and my emails weren't opened. In my more paranoid moments, I started to think that maybe Kat had planned it all. That maybe she'd convinced me to leave New Jersey because her grand scheme didn't include me. I went a little nuts with the cybersurveillance. I set up a Google alert for her name. I studied her dormant Instagram feed for secret messages. The last thing she'd posted was a series of photos devoted to the home improvements her new stepfather was making. There was nothing really interesting in the pictures—just lots of electronics and wires. She hadn't posted on Facebook in months, so I stalked the profiles of our mutual acquaintances, searching for clues. I spotted a blur of copper-colored hair in the background of a few party pics, and that was it. Kat was alive, but she was moving too fast to be captured on camera. I kept writing her, sometimes three emails a day. The last time she responded, she told me she needed some space. The message was one sentence long.

Everything I thought I'd known had been torn down and reassembled. Kat had been my touchstone, and without her, I didn't recognize the world anymore. I didn't care to. I stopped going to class. I stayed in the dorm, playing *Assassin's Creed* with my roommate, a Ukrainian head case named Elvis who collected toy robots and possessed a very dim view of the human race.

Then one morning four months ago, I woke up to find a Google alert for Katherine Foley. The Brockenhurst newspaper was reporting that she'd been arrested the previous night for stealing her stepfather's SUV and driving it into an ornamental koi pond. The police report noted that a sodden, half-smoked joint had been discovered under the gas pedal.

The paper didn't publish a picture, but I had no trouble finding a few online. I'm still surprised the photos didn't go viral. The black SUV was submerged all the way to the backseat doors, and the pond's fat golden koi were gliding in and out through the open windows. The half of the vehicle sticking out of the water was almost perfectly vertical. It was a truly impressive feat of automotive mishandling.

Scrolling through the pictures of Wayne Gibson's SUV, I kept thinking back to that fateful day when I'd first stumbled across *Gangsters of Carroll Gardens*. One glimpse of the Kishka and I'd known he was my grandfather. I didn't need to read the caption or contact the local genealogical society. I'd just known. The same way I knew that the wreck I was looking at on Facebook wasn't an accident. I can't explain why, but there was no doubt in my mind that Kat had destroyed her stepfather's car on purpose.

Elvis drove home to see his parents most weekends, and he kept a run-down Volkswagen off campus. I suppose I should have been more suspicious when he offered to loan me the car if I let him use my computer. But I would have given him a kidney, too, if he'd asked. So I handed over the computer and drove seven hours to New Jersey. When I pulled up in Kat's drive, I thought I might have made a wrong turn. The beautiful house I found in the middle of the woods looked nothing like the hovel I remembered. It was painted white, and the jack pines around it had been cleared. Somehow the foundation had been lifted as well, and the house no longer seemed to be sinking. I knocked on the door and Kat's stepfather answered, greeting me with the same stare I'd seen in the wedding photos. He was compact and wound tight— six inches shorter than me and thirty years older. But I knew he could probably take me and I could see he was eager to try.

He politely informed me that Kat had been grounded and couldn't see any friends. She'd fallen in with a bad crowd, he explained, and she needed some time alone to get her head back on straight. I assured Mr. Gibson that I had never belonged to any crowd—good or bad—and I'd driven all day just to see his stepdaughter.

"I know who you are, son," I remember him telling me. "And I don't think Katherine wants to see you. You haven't been back here in months, and it would probably be best if you just stayed gone."

It stung for a second, I gotta admit. That was just about the last thing I wanted to hear. But while part of me was inclined to believe it, hearing it come out of Mr. Gibson's mouth felt *wrong*. There was no way in hell Kat would share her feelings—*any* feelings—with a man who looked like he invaded third-world countries for sport. So I asked if I could have a word with Linda instead. I was told *Mrs. Gibson* wasn't at home, which was total bullshit. It was past seven in the evening, and I could smell Linda's signature stew cooking. I said I'd be happy to wait, and Mr. Gibson said that wouldn't be wise. When I sat down on the porch, he phoned the cops.

Officer Robinson arrived on the scene, and I was sure I'd been thrown a bit of good luck—until he and Kat's stepfather greeted each other by name. Officer Robinson (*Leslie* Robinson, I now knew) took me aside for a man-to-man. He said he sure was sorry to hear about my recent breakup, and boy, did he feel my pain. He'd been dumped a few times in his day, and he'd learned that "sometimes a man has to just walk away."

"Kat's not my girlfriend," I told him.

The cop just laughed. "Maybe it was never official, but you think I'm too old to recognize a young man in love?"

His expression was so cheesy that I wanted to vomit, but I managed to keep the contents of my stomach from spewing out onto his shoes. I swore I wasn't in Brockenhurst to win Kat's heart. Something was wrong with her, I insisted over and over. But I didn't have any evidence to offer. As desperate as I was at that point, I wasn't crazy enough to inform a policeman that my best friend had destroyed an SUV on purpose.

Officer Robinson wholeheartedly agreed that Kat was in trouble. The kids she'd been hanging out with were pretty bad news. But he promised me the Gibsons had the situation under control. They didn't need—or want—any help. And then he warned me not to return to the house.

"Mr. Gibson works in the security business," he told me in a low voice. "I wouldn't be surprised if he has cameras up all over this property. I know for a fact that he's licensed to carry a firearm, and I'm sure he's got a few hidden away here. Believe me, Simon. You don't want that man ever mistaking you for a prowler."

I'm not an idiot. I knew better than to go back to Kat's house. But I didn't give up on her, either. For the next few days, I hung around town, sleeping in Elvis's Volkswagen and trying to run into Kat. I was loitering outside the high school the following Monday when her stepfather dropped her off at the front door. I know she must have heard me calling her name, but she never even glanced in my direction. She clutched her books to her chest and bolted toward the entrance. When I tried to follow her inside, a guard stopped me and I got to have another man-to-man with Officer Robinson, who informed me that it's never a good sign when a girl runs away from you. This time I had to agree.

An hour later, Officer Robinson personally escorted me and Elvis's Volkswagen to the Brockenhurst town limits. I spent the first part of the drive back to Massachusetts cursing Kat for ignoring me. As I passed through Connecticut, the crosshairs of my rage shifted to Wayne Gibson. When I reached the Massachusetts border, I nearly did a one-eighty on the freeway. The SUV in the koi pond meant something, I was sure of it, and the answer was back in New Jersey. But I had no money and no place to stay, and I couldn't bear any more sappy sympathy from Officer Robinson. The hopelessness of the situation was sinking in when I arrived at my boarding school dorm and was greeted by the FBI.

· · ·

When the agents told me why they were there, I knew in an instant that opportunity had knocked. At some point during the three days I'd been gone, someone had used my computer to hack the server of the world's largest manufacturer of Internet-connected toy robots.

Laugh all you like, but it's not as ridiculous as it sounds. Imagine what someone who's truly evil could do with an army of toy robots that can see, speak and record. The FBI certainly had a few ideas. But my roommate, the Ukrainian wing nut, apparently had something quite different in mind. He'd reprogrammed the toys to inform the children of the world that "The robot revolution is nigh."

I don't even know where Elvis was that evening. Probably hiding in a bathroom stall. Whoever was responsible for the hack was looking at a minimum of three years in jail, the FBI informed me. I'm sure that's what would have happened if I'd ratted out Elvis, who'd already turned eighteen at that point. His parents were astrophysicists or something equally useless. My parents, as I've mentioned, are lawyers.

In the end, it was a win-win-win situation, as far as I was concerned. I got kicked out of school and sent back to Brockenhurst. Everyone thought I'd gone nuts. And since I'd saved Elvis's life, he was now my humble servant. Of course I got probation. My parents were forced to return to the States and pay a massive fine, which they swore they'd recoup from my future earnings.

When the sentence came down, the judge must have seen that I was pleased with my punishment.

"You really thought it would be funny to scare the socks off a bunch of little kids? What are you—some kind of nihilist?" he demanded.

"No, sir," I told him. "But I certainly appreciate all the good work those folks do."

That earned me two months of mandatory counseling. But if I had a chance to do it all over, I'm pretty damn sure I'd say the same thing again.

So here we are.

I didn't plan any of it. Fate brought me back to New Jersey for good. There's no other place my parents can send me. No private school will accept me—not anymore. The United Arab Emirates denied me a visa. I didn't just burn all my bridges. I blew them to hell with nuclear missiles. My father, who was forced to give up his cushy position in Dubai, refers to me as "the boy with no future." Which is true, just not for the reason he thinks. Anyway, I couldn't care less about the future. I came back for Kat. I did what I had to do. To be honest, I would have done anything.

The irony is, this particular princess doesn't want to be rescued. I've been in Brockenhurst for four months now, and she's barely said a word to me. I hoped Otherworld would fix that. But tomorrow morning when I see her at school, I don't expect anything to have changed.

CAMOUFLAGE

My mother pulls her car up to the front of the school and I slide out. It's just before eight o'clock on a Monday morning, and I see Kat's already in her regular spot. She's sitting on the hood of a car on the other side of the parking lot, next to a girl named Winnie with raccoon eyes. Standing in a circle around them are four guys—a psycho, an anorexic drug addict, a known STD carrier and a stranger dressed in black. Or War, Famine, Pestilence and Death, as I like to think of them. The first bell will ring in five minutes, and the Four Horsemen are vaping. From what I can tell, Kat and her friends try their best to stay stoned. I'm in no position to judge, believe me. You gotta do what you gotta do. But I can't understand why Kat wants to do it with these douchebags.

The one dressed like the Grim Reaper keeps fondling her curls. I once saw her slap a guy who put his fingers in her hair, but for some reason she's letting this one get away with it. His name is Marlow Holm, and he's new to Brockenhurst. He showed up at school in January, around the same time I came back. I don't know much about the kid or why Kat's humoring him, but I certainly intend to find out.

"Slut." The word comes out of nowhere. Right out of the blue. I spin around. The two girls walking past must not have seen me. Olivia and Emily. I've known them both since grade school.

"I heard she doesn't sleep at home anymore. She rotates between their rooms," Olivia says, and Emily cackles.

I love a dirty joke as much as the next guy, but that one hits a little too close to home. I ended up walking through the woods and checking on Kat's house last night. It was Sunday, so she should have been home, but her bedroom light never went on. I thought I'd die waiting to see it, and that certainly wasn't because of the cold.

"Excuse me! Ladies!" I jog to catch up with them. The look on their faces when they see me is priceless. The mixture of fear and disgust makes me feel powerful. If I reached out and touched them, they'd crumble to dust. "I couldn't help but overhear your conversation."

Their mouths are open, but no words are coming out. It's one thing for girls like them to insult my butt cheeks from the safety of a moving car. It's another thing to confront me in person. I'm bigger up close. And much, much crazier.

These particular ladies are repeat offenders, and Kat seems to be their favorite subject of gossip. I've warned them before. It's time to bring out the big guns.

Olivia crosses her arms and cocks her head. It's the battle stance of the teenage girl. I hope she doesn't think I'm intimidated. "What do you want?" she asks.

"I don't want to talk about *me*," I tell her. "I'd like to talk about women's rights."

"Women's rights?" Emily sneers, flicking a lock of glossy brown hair over her shoulder.

"Screw off, Simon," Olivia says. She thinks it's all a joke, and she sounds relieved.

"Okay, sure, but before I go, I just want you both to know that I fully support your right as women to do whatever you want with your bodies—and I will fight to ensure that your rights are protected and preserved."

"Gee, thanks, crazy." They laugh and start to walk away. I follow.

"It just makes me sad that you two don't support other women. I heard what you called Kat. Not very politically correct of you."

Olivia spins back around. "It's the truth, Simon. Get used to it. While you were away, your dream girl turned into a whore."

It's a kick to the balls, but I don't double over. I clench my teeth and smile through the pain.

"What Kat does with her body is none of your business." Then I drop the earnest act. "Just like what you do with yours shouldn't be any of mine."

"What's your point?" Olivia asks. "Make it fast if you've got one. We're going to be late for homeroom."

"Won't take a second. Are you familiar with the phrase *live by the sword, die by the sword*?" I ask as I take out my ten-year-old flip phone and toggle through my photos. "'Cause if not, I have a picture of it." I turn the screen around and show her.

Emily slaps a hand over her mouth but a giggle still escapes.

The blood drains out of Olivia's face. "You hacked my phone," she says.

"Not yours. Your boyfriend's. His Gmail password was *blowjob*. I'd hardly call that *hacking*," I say modestly.

"You're not supposed to go near a computer without supervision," says Olivia. "You're not even allowed to have an iPhone."

"I didn't touch one," I assure her. It's true. I don't need to do my own dirty work when I have a Ukrainian hacker who owes me big-time.

"You'll go to jail if you send those pictures to anyone."

"Yes. And it will be *totally* worth it," I promise. "And don't worry about Emily. She won't get left out. When I post all these photos, I'll throw in a few of her, too."

"What?" Emily looks sick.

I roll my eyes and sigh theatrically. "Don't *either* of you pay attention during school assemblies? A couple of weeks ago, Principal Evans warned you about this very thing. She said you shouldn't take any pictures that you don't want the whole world to see." I silently thank Principal Evans. Her Internet safety assembly gave me a million ideas. "So what do you say, ladies? Are we all going to respect women's rights in the future?"

They nod silently, but I can see them smoldering with hatred and fear.

"Then let's just remove the word *slut* from our vocabularies, shall we?" I pause long enough to let the smile slip off my face. "And if I were you, I'd try my very best to forget that Katherine Foley exists."

I leave the girls standing there. Inside the school, the first warning bell rings. A wave of students surges toward the front door, and I let myself be swept along. In the halls, kids dart away when they see me. The lesson I just gave Olivia and Emily wasn't the first one I've taught since I came back. There's a force field forming around Kat. It won't make her more popular, but when I'm done, crowds will part as she passes. If you're going to be a pariah, you might as well be their queen.

It's been four hours and I still can't get the conversation with Olivia out of my head. I'm no prude, but the idea of Kat rotating between the Four Horsemen's rooms drives me completely insane. When it's time for lunch, I skip the cafeteria and go hunt for her. I have to navigate the entire campus before I find her standing with Marlow behind the cafeteria dumpsters. A cloud that's the palest shade of blue hovers over the garbage. From a distance Kat seems totally stoned. Marlow's got an arm around her, his hand dangling a little too close to her breast. He giggles when he sees me coming. Kat just stares. Her eyes are remarkably clear.

"May I have a word with you?" I ask Marlow. The hood of his black sweatshirt is up and his black jeans sag around the knees. He's the image you'd see if you Googled *high school stoner*. But there's something about his face that doesn't match. It's like someone Photoshopped a J.Crew model's face into the picture.

His bloodshot blue eyes dart in Kat's direction.

"Not now, Simon," she says. "Leave us alone."

"No, seriously, Kat. I just want *one word* with him." I hold up my index finger for reference.

"Fine. What is it?" Marlow asks, growing bold.

When he steps forward, I throw my arm around his neck and whisper in his ear. "Run."

He looks at me and I smile. I've been working on my smile, and I think I've finally perfected it. Dead eyes and lots of teeth. Marlow shoots away faster than a speeding bullet. He's a real superhero, that one.

Kat watches him go. She's annoyed, but she's not surprised. I can tell she's not into him, and I gotta say, that comes as a *massive* relief. But then why is she hanging out with the guy in the first place?

I take Marlow's position beside her and lean my back against the wall. I expect her to bolt, just like she has every time I've come near her in the past four months. But she stays. For almost a minute, neither of us says anything. I'm the one who'll have to break the silence. I don't think her sex life is a good place to start.

"So what did you think of Otherworld?" I ask her. "Was that the coolest shit you've ever seen or what?"

"Yeah. Thanks for sending the gear and login. Wayne found it and confiscated everything," Kat said.

"My father destroyed my gear with a nine iron."

She winces. "Sorry, Simon. Your dad always was a dick. You shouldn't have come back to Brockenhurst right now. Look, I really gotta go."

"Kat." I grab her hand as she starts to leave. I expect her to pull away but she doesn't. "What's going on with you? Why won't you talk to me?" I've asked the same question a hundred times— usually to her back as she's rushing away from me. Finally it seems like I might get an answer.

She looks around as if scanning for spies. I don't see anyone, but she doesn't seem satisfied. "I can't."

I can't doesn't mean *I don't want to.* It's a small step, but at least we're moving in the right direction for once. "You're in trouble, aren't you? I knew something was up when you drove into the pond. Is it your stepfather?"

We lock eyes, and I know the truth. I'm right.

"What if it is?" she asks quietly. And that's when I realize she's not stoned at all.

"Then I'll kill him." We both know I would. I'd do it right now if I could.

"And what would happen to you if you did?"

I shrug. "Doesn't matter."

That really pisses her off, and she yanks her hand away from mine. "See, this is why I didn't want you involved. This isn't a god-damn game, Simon. What would happen to you?"

"Prison, I guess." Then it dawns on me. "Wait. Are you not talking to me because you're trying to *protect* me? 'Cause if that's what you're—"

She holds up a hand. She isn't going to listen anymore. "Give it a rest, Simon. Go back to boarding school."

"Haven't you heard? I can't."

Kat crosses her arms. "Sure you can. Just tell them the truth. Tell them you didn't do it."

I don't say a word.

"You've never hacked anything in your entire life, Simon. You really expect me to believe you were the mastermind behind some crazy plot to take down Toys 'R' Us?"

"It wasn't Toys 'R' Us."

"Jesus, what difference does it make? We both know you didn't do it."

For a moment I'm a little bit crestfallen. Is it so hard to believe I'm a genius? "Yeah, well, maybe you don't know me as well as you thought."

"It doesn't matter if you did it or just took the blame for it. Either way it was a dumbass move," Kat says. "I can't be seen hanging out with a cybercriminal right now. It's too dangerous for both of us."

If she's looking for an excuse to blow me off, she could at least try to find one that makes some sense. "You can't hang around with me because I got arrested for hacking? What about all those assholes you've been spending time with? You're trying to tell me that Brian and West haven't committed a few felonies between them?"

"Those guys aren't my *friends*, Simon," she whispers angrily. "They're *camouflage*."

"Camouflage?" Something about the word scares the crap out of me. "Kat, what in the hell is going on? I'm not leaving you alone until I know."

She looks around again and grabs my arm. Then she pulls me behind the dumpster. I feel her hands on my face and her lips on mine. For the next sixty seconds, it's like we've passed through to some parallel universe. Then she pulls away and we're right back where we started—in a world that's completely screwed up for reasons I don't understand.

"Why did you do that?" I ask. She kissed me once a long time ago. I'd given up hope that it would ever happen again.

"Because I was tired of waiting for you."

I can't speak. My mind is too busy counting all the missed opportunities.

"Go back to boarding school, Simon," she says softly. "*Please.* When this is over, I swear I'll come find you."

"When *what's* over?" I call out as she heads for the school. "Kat! We used to be a team!"

She doesn't answer and she doesn't look back.

But my hunch is confirmed. Kat's knee-deep in some kind of shit. She doesn't want me to get involved. And she kissed me. I know one of these facts is far more important than the others, but right now I'm having a real hard time keeping my priorities straight.

The shades are drawn in my film-editing class, and a dozen screens light the room. As I pass through, moving toward my station, something catches my eye, and I'm overwhelmed by a sense of déjà vu. There's Kat on someone's screen. It's like every paranoid thought I've had in the hour since she kissed me has just been vindicated.

I stop and reverse course. "What's that?" I tap the girl's computer monitor.

My voice is gruff, but she doesn't flinch. She gazes up at me with eyes so dark that they don't seem to have pupils. I noticed her on my first day back at school. She must have moved to Brockenhurst while I was away. She's tall and pretty, with closely cropped hair and skin that glows like polished mahogany. I noticed early on that she didn't say much in class. Then I noticed she was absent a lot. Eventually I stopped noticing her at all. I haven't really thought about her since.

"My film," the girl says. "It's a documentary."

"Why are you filming my friend? You should mind your own business. Who are you, anyway?" I demand.

"My name's Busara Ogubu," she says, and turns back to her work. "You must be the crazy guy."

Most people would be offended. I can't help but laugh. "You can call me Simon," I tell her. Then I tap her screen. "So did my friend Kat sign any release forms? Does she know she's starring in your documentary?"

"You're part of it too," she says, fast-forwarding. She stops at a familiar scene—me in the parking lot this morning with Olivia and Emily. I had no idea she was there, and I can't for the life of me figure out where she might have been hiding.

"It's illegal to video people like that," I warn her. Somehow I'm not quite as pissed as I know I should be. "I'd be more careful if I were you. Every kid in this school has at least one lawyer in the family."

"Last time I checked, it was illegal to blackmail teenage girls, too," says Busara. "Even the bitchy ones."

"Touché," I concede. I like her. She's feisty.

She swivels around in her chair to face me. "Why are you protecting Katherine Foley?" she asks.

I realize then that Busara must not have any idea about Kat and me. About how things were before I left for boarding school. Still, I can't figure out what to tell her. I just stand there and look back at her. Then my mouth opens and I hear myself speak.

"Because she's the best person I know, and I'm pretty sure she's in trouble," I say, and instantly regret it. I have no idea why I've chosen to be honest with a girl I've just met.

"You might be right," Busara says.

"What?" I croak, as if there were hands around my throat. I didn't expect her to confirm my suspicions.

Busara puts a fingertip on the computer screen. "You know that kid?" she asks.

It's Marlow. "I know he's an asshole, but that's about it," I say. "He's new."

"He moved here from California over the holidays," Busara says. "Lives with his mother in a fancy glass house outside town. She works in tech."

"So?" I ask.

"So he may look like he lives under a bridge, but he's really a rich kid. I did a little cybersleuthing for my film, and from what I can tell, he didn't own a scrap of black clothing before Christmas. The Goth stoner thing is just an act. He's pretending to be something he's not."

I shrug. "Aren't we all?" I can think of a million things to hold against the guy, but that's not one of them. "New school, new identity. We were all someone else before we moved to Brockenhurst."

"Speak for yourself," says Busara. "By the way, you might be interested to know that Marlow and his new friends are having a party tonight."

"Are you trying to ask me out?" I give her a faux-flirty wink.

"I'm not into boys," Busara says flatly. "Or girls, for that matter."

"So you're an android?"

One side of her mouth twitches, but she doesn't quite laugh.

"I wondered the same thing myself, but then I passed the Voight-Kampff test, so I'm fairly confident that I'm human. Here—watch this."

She swivels back to the computer and rewinds through the footage of Kat and her friends. She stops and turns up the volume on the speakers and hits Play. Marlow is talking about a place known as Elmer's—an abandoned horse-rendering plant and glue factory a few miles from school. It's little more than a ruin, but it used to be the best party spot in town. Now the place is posted with No Trespassing signs, and the cops watch it on weekends. They don't bother to watch it during the week. I guess they assume kids aren't going to get crazy on a Monday. The world is built on false assumptions.

On the video, I hear Marlow say the building is going to be demolished. Some corporation just bought the land. The plant deserves one last party before it becomes an eco-friendly rock-climbing facility on a new company campus. I have no idea whether any of it's true—or how Marlow could have found out.

My eyes are still fixed on the computer screen when the camera pans away from Kat's friends and focuses momentarily on a car at the edge of the parking lot. There's a man inside. I can't see much of him, but he's wearing glasses, and his head is turned toward Kat and the other kids vaping in the lot.

"Who's that?" I ask. He looks official. The last thing Kat needs is to be busted for drugs on campus.

Busara looks back at the screen. It's impossible to read her expression. "How would I know?" she asks.

49

THE GIFT

I can't think of a worse place to be at nine o'clock on a Monday night than hunched down behind a bush, waiting for an illegal party to kick off at an old horse-rendering plant. But now that I'm here, I'm not going anywhere. It took two hours to walk to Elmer's. I'm not allowed to drive anymore, though the judge wasn't the one who imposed the punishment. It was my father's brilliant idea. Good ol' Grant is chock-full of brilliant ideas. The coydogs are out tonight, and I hear them yapping away all around me. I'm pretty sure they won't attack. I'm too big for them now. They know I'm more likely to eat one of *them*. Still, it's really f-ing cold out here, and I'm seriously starting to worry that I might lose a finger to frostbite.

But I will stay here and wait, because I will get Kat back. That kiss shook up everything inside me that had started to settle.

A gust of wind sets the world in motion. I watch the shadows of the scrub pines on the perimeter of the lot dance against the dim glow of distant streetlights. Their fragrance fills the cold air, and I find myself thinking about my family's holiday tradition. On the Friday before Christmas, my parents would pour themselves glasses of Scotch and watch me open a pile of gifts. On Saturday, they'd leave. My mother's family is Jewish. I'm not sure what my father's excuse was. They always spent Christmas Day together. Until I was nine, I spent mine with the staff. The nanny my mother hired after she fired Mrs. Kozmatka was the one who came up with the idea for the tree. I can't even remember the woman's name. She was only with us for a few months, due to mental health issues that will soon become evident. That year, before they left for parts unknown, my parents had given her an envelope full of cash to take me shopping. On Christmas morning, I came downstairs to find that she'd hung all the bills on the tree.

I plucked them off, crammed them into my pockets and disappeared into the woods before any of my keepers woke up. I didn't want to intrude on Kat and her mother, but I couldn't stay away. I was lurking outside the house when Kat came out on the porch in her pj's.

"What took you so long?" she asked with a yawn. "I've been up since six. You coming in or what?"

I remember wrapping paper strewn all over the floor. Linda was there in her nightgown. She and Kat were both drinking cocoa made from a mix that came in little paper pouches. Linda's cup smelled like chocolate and bourbon.

"Here," Kat said, shoving something into my hands. The item was oddly shaped, and I could see that she'd struggled to wrap it.

I tore off the paper and found a homemade slingshot. I looked up to see Kat jamming her sockless feet into boots. "Come on, I'll teach you how to use it."

"Wait a second," I said. I reached into my pocket and pulled out the wad of bills. "This is for you. Sorry, I didn't have time to wrap it all up."

After that, I spent my holidays with the Foleys. Every Christmas, Kat would give me something she'd made herself, and I would give her the wad of cash my parents had left for me. I always felt like I got the better deal. Then, the year I turned thirteen, I arrived at Kat's house to find there wasn't a present under the tree for me.

"It's outside," Kat said, crooking a finger as she opened the door. "Come on. Follow me."

As soon as we were out of sight of the house, she stopped. I didn't see anything that might be a present. And then she put her arms around my neck and kissed me. And I realized I'd been madly in love with her all those years.

For a brief but beautiful moment, I figured it had all been decided. But then nothing happened. In the two weeks that followed, I watched and waited for another sign, but none came. It was like the world had reset and we were back where we'd started.

I never kissed Kat again.

Of course, anyone who saw us assumed we were boyfriend and girlfriend. Or, thanks to my kishka, maybe they assumed we weren't—but that I wanted more. What no one could understand is that there *was* nothing bigger than what we had. Kat was my best friend, and I was hers, and that was everything.

I might have loved her, but there was too much to lose.

The kiss behind the dumpster made me think that maybe—just maybe—all this time she'd been in love with me, too.

THE GROUND
BENEATH OUR FEET

It's just after ten, and the party's in full swing. Flashlights are dancing in the glassless windows. I'm still not sure what I'm doing here. If Kat finds out, she'll be royally pissed. Still, I need to know why she's using the town losers as camouflage. And for the sake of my sanity, I have to find out just how deep undercover she's gone.

A few cars are parked behind the building, and from what I can tell, there are over half a dozen people inside on the second floor. I let out a deep breath. It's time to go in.

Kat and I explored the crumbling brick building on countless occasions over the years, so I have no trouble slipping in unnoticed and locating the stairs. On my way to the third floor, I use a trick Kat taught me: I stop and scatter a handful of dry twigs that I gathered on one of the stairs. I'll hear them snap if anyone follows me up. I know I'm being overly cautious. Everyone avoids the third floor of Elmer's. There's a rumor that they found a dead body up here years ago. I have no idea if it's true or just urban legend, but there's no arguing with the wisdom of staying off the third story. It's clearly unsafe. The boards creak under my feet, and the entire floor is riddled with holes that are hard to make out after dark.

I take my time and maneuver carefully to one of the openings, and then I get down on my knees. The hole is big enough that I have a good view of what's going on below. The first person I spot is one of the Horsemen, a psycho named Brian. He lives a few houses away from me. He moved in when we were both in fourth grade and introduced himself by squeezing the guts out of a toad. His personality hasn't improved since then. I always thought he'd be in jail by now, but he's captain of the lacrosse team, which makes him invincible around here. He's smoking something with West, the addict. Probably pot, though I'd be surprised if that was West's poison of choice these days. He's lost about forty pounds since freshman year, and he looks like he hasn't had the munchies in months.

I crawl across the floor to another hole and see Jackson, Mr. Chlamydia, making out with a girl I don't recognize. Probably a sucker from some other town—everyone in Brockenhurst knows he's polluted. Then I spot Kat, huddled in a dusty corner, her knees pulled up to her chest. She's nursing a drink in a Solo cup. Marlow's right there next her, talking her ear off, though I don't think she's listening. Her eyes are focused on something far away—someplace she'd rather be.

I wonder if she's back in the Otherworld ice cave. The giant avatar is gone. It's just the two of us together again in our own private world. For a second, it's nice to imagine I might be inside her head—the way she's always in mine.

A snap startles me. Someone's climbing the stairs and they

just stepped right on the twigs I left there. The footsteps pause for a moment and then continue. But there's enough time for me to scuttle into the darkness on the other side of the room. I end up in an alcove I had no idea existed. I can't see much, but there's something soft beneath my feet. I bend over and touch it. I'm pretty sure it's a down sleeping bag. I guess someone was planning to get lucky up here tonight.

I peek around the corner and see a figure standing at the top of the stairs. It's just a dark shadow with arms and legs. I can't even tell if it's male or female. For a minute, it doesn't move. It seems to be thinking. Or waiting. Then it stretches out an arm and tosses a small round object. The thing sails in an arc through the air and then plunges straight through a hole in the middle of the floor.

"Hey!" yelps a voice from below. Whatever it was must have come close to beaning someone. The music below stops and there's an eerie quiet.

A kid laughs. "What the hell?"

"What *is* that?" someone else asks.

The party has come to a halt, and the figure who threw the object is gone. I cautiously step out of the alcove and make my way toward the hole. I want to see for myself what's going on, but when I peer down, the object is hidden from view. Everyone at the party is huddled around it. Everyone, I notice, except Marlow and Kat.

"Hey, get back!" someone says. I can't see who said it, but it sounded like Marlow. No one's listening, though. There's an electric-blue light shining through the cracks between the kids.

"He's right! Don't mess with it!" This time it's Kat.

Directly below me, Brian the psycho looks straight up at the ceiling, and I barely back away in time.

"Who's up there?" he shouts. He doesn't sound angry. He must think it was one of his friends playing a joke. But I realize I'm still in serious shit. Unless I hurl myself through a window, there's no way to get out now. One-on-one I could beat Brian. I can't take on everyone here.

I'm scrambling for cover when the whole building groans like some massive beast that's been woken. I drop back down to my hands and knees, and tremors course through the floor. The tremors become a rumble and end with a crack and a deafening crash. A girl's scream is cut short. I don't think it's Kat, but it might be. I rush to one of the holes in the wooden floor, but all I see below me is a cloud of dust. Then I hear the waterfall of debris and I know what's happened: the second floor of the building has collapsed.

"Kat!" I shout.

I hear a muffled cry. Someone down there is alive.

Thank God the stairwell is still intact. I fly down the stairs, stopping briefly on the second and first floors to check the main part of the building. Both floors are almost completely gone. Everyone and everything has crashed straight through to the basement.

I've been inside the factory a hundred times, but I didn't know there *was* a basement. There's no time to hunt for the entrance, so I grab the edge of what used to be the first floor and drop down into the darkness. The fall is much farther than I thought it would be, and the landing knocks the wind out of me. I try to stand and the ground gives way beneath me and I'm suddenly surfing down a mountain of wood and bricks. I skid to a stop at the bottom and freeze for a second, getting my bearings. It's pitch-black except for the beam of a flashlight shining from beneath the debris. I dig it out and shine it around me, illuminating a pile of rubble unlike any I've ever seen. A guy's arm is protruding from the wreckage and I scramble over to him, clamping my fingers down on the vein in his wrist. No matter how hard I press, I can't detect a pulse.

I snatch my hand back and fight the urge to vomit. My heart is pummeling my rib cage, and I'm sucking in dust-filled air that clogs my lungs. Then the beam of the flashlight lands on a swatch of copper-colored hair, and I'm there, digging like a dog, hurling boards and pipes and bricks behind me until I finally unearth Kat's head and shoulders. She's either unconscious or dead, and her angelic expression scares me more than anything I've seen tonight. I close my eyes and press my fingers against her jugular. Her heart is still beating. I dig even faster, and when I reach her legs, I realize how badly she's injured. Blood is gushing from her left leg, and the spray splatters my face. I rip off my belt and tie it as tightly as I can around her thigh. When the flow of blood has been reduced from a gush to a trickle, I fish out my phone and start to dial 911.

Then I hang up.

I can hear ambulances. Multiple ambulances. Someone's already called for help. I look around. There's no one moving in the building but me.

THE MIRACLE

The EMT said the tourniquet saved Kat's life. A nail nicked an artery in her left leg, and without my size thirty-two belt she would have bled out. When we arrived at the hospital, no one asked me what happened or what I saw. They were all frantically treating the wounded. I wasn't injured, so they probably assumed I wasn't with the others when the floor collapsed. Given my criminal record—and the fact that I hadn't exactly been invited to the party—I figured it was best not to volunteer any information just yet.

Four people died. I knew at least one of the kids hadn't made it, but hearing the body count made the horror too real. I thank any God that's listening for sparing Kat's life. And given the extent of her injuries, I pray it will be a life worth living.

The clock on the wall says it's almost five a.m. In a few hours the sun will rise, and Kat still hasn't woken up. Aside from the leg wound, she's suffered serious head trauma, a punctured lung and three broken ribs. The doctor says she's hopeful, but I'm not stupid. I know there's a fair chance that Kat might never come to. I think that's the reason they're letting me stay in her room. Or maybe they realize that removing me would be potentially life-threatening. Not for Kat, but for me.

Her mother arrived about an hour after we did. I hadn't seen Linda since I returned to Brockenhurst, and the difference was startling. When I knew her, Linda always drank too much and smoked like a chimney. But I spent years wishing she was my mother. She hugged every kid who ever entered her house. She told raunchy jokes and laughed harder than anyone else. And she always made sure that the kitchen was stocked with my favorite, Flamin' Hot Cheetos—even though she and Kat both despised them. Now Linda's dressed in chinos and her bleach blond hair is now dyed a respectable shade of auburn. The hair's an improvement, but she looks like her spirit is broken. I have a hunch that marriage has not been kind to her.

Linda barreled through the door and flung herself over Kat's body. I was busy making sure she wasn't going to accidentally rip the IV out of Kat's arm when Wayne Gibson appeared in the doorway. He wasn't pleased to see me standing beside the bed. He grabbed a nurse who was passing by. "Get this kid out of here," he ordered without bothering to lower his voice. "I don't want to see him again."

That's when Linda lifted her head. Her eye makeup was a blur. Most of it had rubbed off, leaving smudgy black circles on Kat's blanket. "No," she said. "You can leave if you want to, Wayne, but Simon is going to stay."

I saw Wayne Gibson's jaw clench so hard he could have bitten through rebar. Linda was going to pay for her words when they got home, but Wayne wasn't the kind of guy who'd make a scene in public. "You let your child run wild. I told you something like this was going to happen," he said in a low, steady voice. "Now that it has, the last thing she needs is a criminal camped out in her hospital room."

"She's *my* daughter," Linda replied softly. "I know what's best for her."

"If you knew what was best for her, Linda, Katherine wouldn't be here."

At that point, I stepped forward to face him. If I'd ever had to live with an asshole like that, I would have turned to drugs in a heartbeat. I could only imagine how he must have tortured Kat. And she was right about one thing—if I ever found out, I'd probably kill him.

I put my hand on the man's chest and shoved him out of the hospital room and into the hall. "See ya, Wayne," I said before I slammed the door in his face. "I'll take it from here."

When Linda said she was going home to gather a few of Kat's things, I had a hunch Wayne wasn't going to let her come back. I think she must have known too. Before she left, she signed a form giving me full access to her daughter's room. The paper is folded up and tucked away in my back pocket in case anyone challenges me. So far everyone has left us alone. Yesterday, I would have traded my soul for some time with Kat. Now we're together in a beige room with a floral border and a cheesy mass-produced watercolor of a sunrise. I feel like some poor bastard from a fairy tale who was granted a wish but forgot to phrase it correctly. I asked to have Kat to myself, and I got what I wanted. Her body is here with me, but the rest of her is gone.

A phone alarm chimes somewhere outside the hospital room.

"Kat," I whisper. She doesn't answer, but I know she can hear me. "If you don't come out of this, I'm going to come after you."

I move my chair to the darkest corner of the room. Lying in her hospital bed, Kat is lit from above like the body of a queen at rest in a crypt. I think back to Elmer's, and I try to go through the facts as I know them. An unknown person threw an unidentified object. The object made eight people gather around it. When they did, the floor collapsed. After decades of neglect, the building's boards must have been rotten. But was the weight of eight kids enough to bring them down?

Four people died. Three are unconscious. And two people, counting me, escaped from the party unscathed. I saw the other lucky one in the ER being treated for minor hand wounds. As far as I could tell, aside from his bloody palms, there wasn't a scratch on Marlow. I was eavesdropping when he told the doctor he'd grabbed hold of a pipe that was mounted on the wall when the floor started to shake.

So we have one miracle survivor, one person who shouldn't have been there and a mysterious call to 911. But the biggest mystery of all is the object. The incident is all over the news, and I keep waiting to hear that something unusual has been recovered from the rubble. The police still seem convinced that the collapse was an accident, but I'm not buying it. Right now, everything points to one conclusion: sometime soon, I need to have a chat with Marlow.

LOCKED IN

Kat opened her eyes. I fell asleep for a while and woke up to find her staring up at the ceiling as if she were counting each little pockmark on the tiles. When I leaped up and grabbed hold of her, I knew right away that something was wrong. Kat didn't hug back or push me away. She didn't say anything, either, though I'm sure I was blubbering. When I released her, she gurgled and sank back on the pillows. Her head came to rest at an awkward angle, and her eyes, which had been staring at the ceiling so intently, were examining the blanket instead.

The nurse popped her head in and then summoned an army of doctors, who promptly kicked me out of the room.

An hour has passed. Nurses with equipment are still entering and leaving. Finally the neurologist on duty comes out to speak to me.

I recognize Dr. Ito from the Brockenhurst Country Club. It helps that her lab coat is the same color as her tennis whites.

"You're Irene Eaton's son," she says.

That's the biggest downside of the kishka. Like a giant birthmark or a second head, it renders me unforgettable.

"Yes," I tell her. There isn't any point in denying it. I'm sure they gossip about my family all the time at the country club. Poor Irene Eaton, they must say. How did she end up with a nutjob cybercriminal for a son? "I'm a friend of Kat's. Can you tell me what's wrong with her?"

She seems a bit reluctant to share, so I take out the form that Kat's mother signed. "I'm a friend of the family."

Dr. Ito nods. "Katherine has sustained significant damage to a part of the brain stem called the pons," she tells me. "The condition is called cerebromedullospinal disconnection, and—"

"I'm sorry. Cerebro *what*?"

She smiles patiently. "The layman's term is *locked-in syndrome*."

I look past her, into the room where Kat lies motionless on the bed. "Is that like a coma?"

This time the doctor shakes her head. "Only in the sense that Katherine is unable to move. But her EEG shows normal brain activity. That tells us she's fully conscious and her mind is locked inside a body that is unable to function. While medical science has gotten good at fixing bodies, we haven't made quite as much progress when it comes to repairing the brain."

I can't breathe. The muscles in my legs go limp and I plop down in a chair near the nurses' station. "Will she recover?"

65

"I'm afraid it's highly unlikely," the doctor informs me. "I wish I had better news. I'm very sorry, I was due in the OR ten minutes ago. Will you please excuse me?"

I try to grab her arm as she leaves, but my timing is off and I catch nothing but air. I fall to my knees and stay there while everything crashes down around me.

It takes every bit of courage I can muster to return to Kat's room. She's lying perfectly still, her eyes staring up at a different patch of ceiling. If what Dr. Ito says is true, the Kat I've always known is a prisoner inside a broken body. For a girl who grew up running wild through the woods, nothing could be worse. Creatures like Kat don't survive being confined to a cage.

I lean down close to her face. "Hey," I whisper, my lips brushing her ear. "You're going to get better. I'll be right here until you do." But the words coming out of my mouth sound phony. I have to step out of the room again until I can find a way to believe them.

It's lunchtime, and my mother is sitting across from me in the hospital's basement cafeteria. Her buddy Dr. Ito must have told her where to find me. The lighting down here is so bad that it's hard to distinguish the sick from the healthy. Even my mother looks green. I take a monstrous bite of a tuna fish sandwich. The stench reminds me of cat food.

"I'm going back upstairs as soon as I eat this," I inform her. "Where's Dad?"

"On his way to London," she says. "I'd be with him right now if it weren't for you."

I used to wonder if my mother had any idea how awful she sounds when she says shit like that. Now I don't care.

"Oh, I'm sure there's still time to catch the red-eye," I tell her. "Don't let me keep you."

My mother ignores me. "The girl who's hurt," she says. "It's the same one? The one you drove down from school to visit?"

It's a stupid thing to ask. "Do I have any other friends?" I say. Like she'd actually know the answer.

"I'm sorry about what happened, Simon. But I've been told your friend may not get better for quite some time. You can't stay here in the hospital and miss school."

I laugh, though it's purely for effect. I find none of this even remotely funny. "I'm eighteen years old. School is optional."

"Perhaps, but you're not a member of the girl's family. The hospital won't let you stay in her room."

She's been underestimating me since kindergarten. You'd think she'd have learned her lesson by now. "You seem to forget that I'm the spawn of two lawyers. Surely you're familiar with the federal government's hospital visitation guidelines." I pull the form Kat's mom signed out of the back pocket of my jeans and pass it across the table. My mother delicately removes a glob of mayonnaise from the paper with a napkin before she unfolds it and reads.

When she looks up and hands the sheet back to me, I can tell she still doesn't know I've won. "All right, so the law allows you to stay. But I don't. You're coming home with me, Simon."

"Or else?" I ask.

Her pretty little nostrils flare as she takes a deep breath. "What do you mean, 'or else'?"

"I mean you'd better have something amazing to threaten me with if you want me to leave."

"I can call your probation officer right now and inform him that you've expanded your criminal repertoire to include credit card fraud."

"Go right ahead," I tell her. "And I'll tell everyone in this fancy-ass town who you really are."

She raises her perfectly sculpted eyebrows and laughs. She has no idea that her secret is out. "And who exactly is that, Simon?"

"The Kishka's daughter," I say, my eyes locked on hers.

She's silent. I've got her. This is literally one of the best moments of my life, and I want to savor every last second of it. The fluorescent light over our heads begins to flicker on cue, lending the scene a delightful horror-film quality.

"Do you think they'll all still admire you after they've seen pictures of your original nose?" I ask. "Do you think they'll gossip about how your father found the funds to pay your tuition to Harvard? Or maybe they'll question whether you deserved to be admitted in the first place?"

"That's enough," she snaps. Her expression has shifted from shock to outrage. "You're a little shit, Simon."

"No, I'm a *Kishka*," I tell her. "Just like my grandfather." I lean over the table until my nose is inches away from hers. "Did you really think you'd get away with it?"

I'm back in my chair in Kat's room, pretending to have a little after-lunch nap with a blanket pulled over my head. I hear people come in, but when I open my eyes, all I see is a golden light shining through a matrix of white wool. There are three of them in the room—Dr. Ito and two men. I don't recognize the guys' voices. I inch the blanket down until I can see them. They're all bent over Kat's bed like they're playing Operation. The two men aren't very old. Probably in their late twenties, early thirties. Their shirts are untucked and they're both wearing jeans and sneakers.

"You're right. She's an ideal candidate," one of them says.

"It'll be a real shame to shave such a pretty head," the other jokes.

"Don't touch her hair." I throw off the blanket and the three visitors jump.

"You're awake," Dr. Ito says with a sigh. I'm sure she was hoping my mother would drag my ass out of the hospital.

"Hey there," says one of the men. He comes over to greet me with a friendly smile and an outstretched hand. "Sorry to bother you. My name's Martin—"

"What's going on?" I demand.

"We're doing our best to help your friend," Dr. Ito says. "Are we finished here?" she asks the two men.

"Yeah, I think so," says the man still standing by Kat's bedside. He makes a few quick notes on a tablet. "The nurse will let us know when she's been prepped?"

"Certainly," Dr. Ito answers. "Now, will you excuse us, gentlemen? I need to have a word with this young man."

They don't need to be asked twice. The men file out of the room, their eyes averted. When they're gone, the neurologist turns to face me.

"Who were those guys?" I ask her.

She crosses her arms and smiles, one gesture negating the

other. "Katherine is a very lucky girl. Those men are engineers from the Company. They've designed a device that can help people with her condition. They're looking for patients to take part in a beta test."

"Wait." Did I hear her right? "Are you saying those guys are from *the* Company?"

"What other Company is there?" Dr. Ito asks. "They work for Milo Yolkin."

I once watched a TED Talk filmed at the Company's headquarters in Princeton where Milo told the story behind his business's name. I guess it started off as a joke between friends. All the giant tech corporations had stupid, cutesy or gibberish names, so Milo went the opposite way with his little start-up. For the first couple of years, the financial press called the Company a dog, but then the organization kept on expanding until it became the beast it is now. There are a lot of people out there today who no longer find the name all that funny. A future in which there's only one all-powerful Company doesn't seem totally preposterous anymore.

I had no clue that the Company was making medical equipment, but I guess I shouldn't be so surprised. They do everything else. I've even heard rumors that Milo Yolkin personally wrote most of the code for the new Otherworld—in his spare time. If he's able to do something like that on his own, the Company is capable of *anything*.

"What kind of device have they invented?" I ask Dr. Ito. "How does it work?"

"You'll have to ask the engineers," the doctor says with a chuckle. "I may be a brain surgeon, but I'm afraid it's all way too complicated for me."

I glance over at Kat again, and when I turn back to the doctor, she's whisking through the door, her white lab coat flaring out behind her like a cape.

Maybe she was joking, but I take Dr. Ito's suggestion very seriously. In a heartbeat I set out to look for the Company engineers. For the first time in forever, I'm experiencing something that feels like hope. My heart is racing and my palms are damp. If Milo Yolkin has focused his brainpower on helping people like Kat, she might actually have a chance.

Fortunately, the engineers haven't gone very far. They're chatting near the nurses' station right outside Kat's room. The one named Martin is carrying a black plastic suitcase. Who knows what's inside it? Pills, needles, gadgets—it makes no difference to me. If there's even the slimmest chance that he's going to help Kat, I will worship at his sneaker-clad feet.

There's no reason for them to share information with me, and I am fully prepared to grovel. But Martin sees me approaching and smiles.

"Hey. Sorry about just now," he says, sounding sincere. "I didn't mean to be insensitive. Hospitals still make me nervous. By the way, this is my colleague, Todd."

"Hey there," says the other guy, raising a hand.

"Simon," I say. "May I speak with you guys for a moment?"

They consult each other with a quick glance. "Sure," says Martin, and I gesture for them to follow me back to Kat's room.

"So is Katherine Foley your girlfriend?" Todd asks once we're all inside.

"Yes," I tell him. Then I remember she can hear what we're saying. "I mean we're friends. And she's female."

"*Clearly,*" says Todd in a tone I don't appreciate.

Martin just nods. "We're really sorry about what happened to her."

He actually sounds like he means it, but I don't have time to waste on small talk or sympathy. "This therapy you've developed for patients with Kat's condition. I'd like to know more about it."

Martin puts the suitcase on top of the tray at the end of Kat's bed and cracks it open. The interior of the case is black foam, with custom compartments carved out. If this were a movie, there would be an unassembled sniper's rifle inside. But this case contains a thin, dark visor and a circle of flesh-colored plastic.

I move in closer. They don't seem to mind. "What is it?" The visor is interesting, but I've never seen anything like the plastic circle before.

"The hardware doesn't have an official name yet," says Martin. "That's how new it is. Right now, we're just calling it the disk. The guy who designed the software used to call it the White City. Run his software on our hardware and you've got the next generation of virtual reality."

My heart sinks. Virtual reality makes for great games, but it isn't going to *cure* anything.

"Did you just say *next generation?*" Todd scoffs. "Give me a break. It's a quantum leap forward." He looks over at me. "Our labs are always five to seven years ahead of consumer release. We generally stagger innovation to maximize profits. But this time the tech is too important. The boss doesn't want commerce to keep it away from the people who need it."

"The boss. You mean Milo Yolkin?" He's not even here, and yet I suddenly feel like I'm in the presence of a divine being.

"What other boss could I mean?" Todd says with a laugh that almost seems bitter. "The Company is Milo's kingdom. Though I think he prefers Otherworld these days."

I get the feeling Todd isn't Milo's biggest fan. I suppose it must be hard working for one of the world's greatest geniuses—especially an infamous micromanager who's known for personally overseeing every Company project.

"I actually played the new Otherworld with Kat this weekend," I tell them. Was it really this weekend? It feels like it's been forever.

"And you made it out of your bedroom?" Martin jokes. "I've heard the Otherworld headset app is so addictive there are twenty-year-old guys buying cases of Depends so they don't need to waste any time in the real world."

"Yeah." Todd nods. "They say sales of Soylent are going through the roof too. Do you think it would be insider trading if I bought a few shares of the company?"

Martin shrugs. "Not my wheelhouse," he says. "Ask HR."

I tap the suitcase, trying to steer the conversation back on track. "So this is next-generation VR hardware. You're saying it's more advanced than the new Otherworld headset?"

"Light-years," Martin confirms.

"It's our masterpiece. Martin and I have been working on it for ages," says Todd. Then his tone shifts and I'm reminded that, despite his frat boy behavior, he works for one of the most powerful corporations on earth. "It's going to make a real difference in people's lives. The disk was designed for people who are unable to move on their own. It frees them from the prison of their bodies and allows them to explore a world as real as this one." If I didn't know better, I'd wonder if he was reading off the Company's website.

"Can I try it?" I ask.

Todd laughs. "We'd have to shave the back of your head first." He pulls out the flesh-colored disk and holds it up. "That's the one downside of the tech. The disk needs perfect skin adhesion."

I thought I was pretty up-to-date on the latest advances in VR technology, but I have no idea how this could possibly work. "Skin adhesion? For what?"

"In layman's terms? It talks to the wearer's brain." He registers the dumbfounded look on my face. "Didn't you notice there are no gloves or boots in the box? We've gotten rid of haptic devices altogether. This is true virtual reality—not just sight, sound and touch. Tap into the brain and you can engage all five senses."

"And maybe a few others that we don't have names for yet," Martin adds.

I reach for the disk and Todd hands it to me. It looks like a large version of the skin-colored nicotine patches that Linda used to wear whenever she'd try to quit smoking. "This actually communicates with people's brains?" The engineers were right. This is wild. I'm holding a paradigm shift between my fingers.

"Yep," Todd says, pointing at the visor that's still in the suitcase. "The visor *shows* you another world, but the disk makes it *real*."

"What does the person wearing it see?"

"The future," Todd says proudly. He looks over at Martin. "Play him the video."

Martin pulls out his phone and calls up a video. Then he hands the device to me.

On the screen a field of green-and-golden grass is swaying in a breeze. A few cottony clouds float across a blue sky. I realize it must be a park. Gleaming white towers dripping with flowering foliage surround it on all sides.

"What is this?"

"That's where our patients go. That's the White City."

I bring the image closer to my eyes. It's one hundred percent photo-realistic. "That's not CGI," I say. "That's gotta be a real place."

"What's real anymore?" Martin laughs proudly. "We'll pass your compliments along to our software colleagues."

"It looks like heaven." I'm not speaking metaphorically. It actually looks like an image you'd find on some religious cult's website.

"Smells like heaven, too, apparently," says Martin.

"Yeah, I don't know. My paradise has fewer flowers and more scantily clad ladies," Todd says. Then he winks at me. "Sorry, that was unprofessional. Don't tell anyone I said that."

I don't know why, but Todd's stupid joke sets off a brainstorm. "Wait—how many people are already in the White City?"

"At the moment, about three hundred people are taking part in the beta test," Todd says.

"Can they talk to each other?"

"Sure, and more," Todd says, arching an eyebrow. Apparently his mind never leaves the gutter.

"Okay, then," I tell him. "You can shave my head. I'd like to try the disk." I'd let them shave every inch of my body for a chance to speak to Kat.

Suddenly Todd's fidgeting uncomfortably. I don't think he was expecting me to take him up on the offer. "I was just kidding around about that. The disk is a prototype, and we don't have any to spare. Plus, the boss is pretty particular about who gets a tour of the White City."

"I need to talk to Kat," I say, fully aware that my desperation is showing now. "*Please.* I'll do anything."

Martin puts a hand on his colleague's shoulder. "Maybe the kid could come by the facility. As long as he doesn't tell anyone, I can't see how it would hurt."

Todd clearly isn't having it. "Nothing like that has been authorized," he says sternly.

"Yeah, but imagine the feedback this kid could give us," Martin argues.

"*No,*" Todd insists, stepping back so that Martin's hand slips from his shoulder. "Imagine what could go wrong."

Go wrong. I don't like the sound of that. "What do you mean? Do things ever go wrong with the disk?" I ask.

"Of course not," Martin assures me. "Our satisfaction rate is one hundred percent."

"That's right," Todd says, his eyes locked on his partner's. "Because we're very careful about the patients we choose."

Martin turns to me and shrugs apologetically. "Sorry," he says as Todd packs up the suitcase. "I tried my best."

And with those five words, my spark of hope is gone.

Five hours pass before anyone comes back into Kat's room. At some point during the time I've been sitting here praying for something to happen, Kat's mother must have given consent for her daughter to take part in the Company's beta test, because the nurse who finally arrives brings a pair of clippers and a surgical razor. I watch as she shaves the back of Kat's head. Kat's hair is her signature. She's always been proud of it. When the nurse lays her back down, I can't tell the difference. But there's a clear plastic bag filled with copper-colored curls, and the sight of it makes me nauseous.

It's all for the best, the nurse assures me. Kat won't mind about the hair. I wish I could believe her, but I know it's not true.

"I'm so sorry," I tell Kat when it's done. I hope like hell it's worth it.

THE KID

Kat's visor is on, and the disk has been affixed to the base of her skull. I watch her heart monitor sketch the same peak over and over again. Whenever her pulse speeds up, I know something's happening in the White City. I hope she's found the field the engineers showed me. The only thing it was missing was a fort. I wish I could be there to build one with her, but she's gone to the one place I can't follow her. At least, not without one of those disks.

Around eleven p.m., I make a trip to the cafeteria for my second tuna fish sandwich of the day. A woman in a uniform is weaving around the tables, wiping them down with a rag that looks like she just used it to clean an outhouse. She doesn't acknowledge me other than to leave a large dry circle around the spot where I'm sitting with the sandwich and a cup of coffee that tastes like a tire fire. Aside from her, there's a guy who's stationed himself in the corner with his back to me. Judging by his stiff posture and air of alertness, I'd guess he's here in some official capacity, though I can't find the energy to care.

A television mounted on the wall in front of me is playing a talk show. The sound is turned down, but I watch the host as he goes through the motions. Monologue, move to the desk, crack a joke with the bandleader, introduce the first guest. I wonder what it's like to do the same goddamn thing every day, day after day, year after year. I've been at the hospital for just under twenty-four hours, and I've already fallen into my own little rut. Bedside, bathroom, cafeteria, repeat. It won't be long before I lose my mind.

The first guest comes out on the TV and I hear the muffled thunder of wild applause. A youngish man emerges from between the velvet curtains on the right side of the stage. He's dressed like he's on his way to do flip tricks in a shopping mall parking lot. I own the same sweatshirt he's got on. I bought it at Target to annoy my mom. Topping it all off is a goofy smile and a head of angelic sandy-blond curls. There probably isn't a person on earth who wouldn't recognize the face. It belongs to Milo Yolkin. He waves to the audience and they leap to their feet. I'm on my feet, too, searching for the television's volume button. I find it and turn it up until the applause builds to a roar.

The talk show's host is a dapper man in his late forties wearing a beautifully tailored pinstripe suit. He arches an eyebrow and adjusts his glasses, pretending to scrutinize his guest while the clapping and whistles die down.

"What happened?" the host asks with a perfectly straight face. "Couldn't your dad make it to the show tonight?" The crowd howls. I barely crack a smile.

The camera zooms in on Milo Yolkin, who fakes a chuckle.

It's clear that he'd rather be anywhere else. Up close, his famous face looks pale and gaunt. There are circles under his eyes that the show's makeup artist couldn't hide.

"In all seriousness," says the host. "How old are you—twelve?"

"I just turned twenty-nine," says Milo. They pause for the requisite birthday applause.

"I'm pretty sure I have boxer shorts older than you," the host quips. "What age were you when you started the Company?"

"Nineteen," Milo tells him.

"And now it's worth . . ."

Milo blushes, and for a moment his face looks almost healthy. "It's hard to say. The valuation changes every day."

"Okay, so let's just go for a ballpark figure, then. Would you say it's worth more than the GDP of Europe or Asia?"

The CEO of the most successful corporation on earth just grins and stares at his shoes.

I move toward the television set until I'm basking in its glow. I want to get as close as possible to the man who may have just set Kat free.

"Fine, fine. Enough teasing," the host declares. "This is probably why you don't do shows like this, am I right?"

Milo looks up and shrugs good-naturedly. I'm hoping the lighthearted banter is about to end. Milo Yolkin wouldn't be doing a talk show if there weren't a very good reason. I don't expect him to discuss the White City. The Company's beta tests are always conducted in secret. My bet is he's going to announce the new Otherworld wide release.

"But I hear you've made an exception tonight because you want to tell people about a project you've been working on," the host is saying. "Something very important to you. I believe it's called Otherworld." There are a few isolated hoots and whistles in the audience. I was right. "I see it already has a following. What exactly is Otherworld? It used to be a game, if I'm not mistaken?"

"Some people thought so," Milo says. "Technically it was something called an MMO. That stands for massively multiplayer online game. But for those of us who played it, the original Otherworld was a lot more than that."

"Hell yeah!" someone shouts.

"Friend of yours?" the host asks.

Milo shields his eyes from the glare of the studio lights and tries to peer out into the audience. "Probably." He grins, warming up. "Or enemy. I'd have to see his avatar to tell. I knew most people there. Back in my teens, I spent close to two years of my life in Otherworld."

Interesting. Who'd have thunk? It's hard to imagine what the world would have been like if Milo Yolkin had never left Otherworld.

"You must have been very popular in high school," the host jests.

Milo's smile looks much less sincere this time. "Let's just say the real world wasn't very kind to me in those days," he replies.

The host adjusts his glasses. It's clearly time to change the subject. "So what was the objective of the original Otherworld?"

"The objective?" Milo asks. "There was no objective."

The host grins nervously. "Don't all games have objectives? Isn't the whole idea to *win*? Otherwise, what's the point of playing them?"

"What's the point of being alive?" Milo replies, and I actually laugh out loud. But the host is left momentarily flummoxed. I guess he doesn't know the answer. So Milo steps in to fill the silence. "The objective of Otherworld was to live the kind of life you couldn't have in the real world. You could fight beasts, explore new lands, hoard treasure, or have sex. You could even start a chinchilla farm if that was what you were into. It was all up to you. Otherworld became my escape. When I was there, I got to be the person I wanted to be. The place set me free."

I'd love to know what young Milo Yolkin got up to in Otherworld. He's twenty-nine years old now, and he still looks like an overgrown cherub. Did he run a virtual petting zoo? Spend his time rescuing digital baby seals?

"Why did you stop playing?" the host asks, struggling to get the conversation back on track.

In response to the question, Milo's face goes cold. It's moments like this that remind you that he's not really an overgrown kid. He's one of the most powerful men on earth. "One morning about eleven years ago, I turned on my computer and Otherworld was gone. The game's publishers had decided there weren't enough subscribers and they'd shut the whole thing down."

"Just like that?"

"Yep," says Milo, and you can see he's still seething at the injustice of it all. "By that point I'd built my own kingdom. I had an amazing fortress, and a harem, and serfs farming my lands. I was practically running the place. And then *poof,* suddenly everything was gone. It was the worst thing that ever happened to me. So when one of my engineers at the Company showed me some revolutionary new technology he'd developed, I figured the time had come to bring Otherworld back."

"Revolutionary technology?" the host asks. "What kind of stuff are we talking about?"

"Well, it's not something you can really *tell* people about," says Milo. "You kind of have to see it—and feel it—to believe it."

That's obviously the cue for a helper to appear onstage, pushing a cart covered by a white sheet. Grinning like a birthday party magician, Milo rises from his seat and whips the sheet off. Beneath it are haptic gloves and the new Otherworld VR headset.

"These are for you," he tells the host, holding out the gloves for the man to slip into. "The haptic technology is cutting-edge, but the headset offers an experience beyond anything you've ever imagined. We've only made and sold a few thousand prototypes so far, and you can't play the new game without one."

"I can tell this is about to get *very* interesting," the host says, eyeing the headset. "But how's everybody out there supposed to know what I'm seeing?"

"Oh, I think we ought to be able to bring it to life for them." Milo puts the headset on the host, and a large screen instantly brightens behind them. Soon the audience will be able to see everything the host can see.

"Should I walk toward the light?" the host jokes, his hands outstretched as if he's feeling his way.

"Not yet," Milo says with a laugh. "Have you ever climbed to the top of a volcano?"

"No, sir. I'm deathly afraid of danger," the host jokes.

"Well, now you can see what it's like. All from the safety of your stage."

On the screen behind them, a scorched black land and a river of lava appear. The audience gasps. No one's seen anything like it. There's a loud boom and the host spins around. Bright orange flames are shooting into the sky from the cone of the volcano. Three vultures the size of pterodactyls are hovering above, waiting for the barbecue to begin.

"Whoa, my gloves are getting hot!" the host exclaims. "Hey, look! I can see my hands!" He looks down at his crotch. "And the rest of me, too!"

"That's right. Now let's cool those hands down a little," Milo replies. Suddenly the scene shifts and the screen shows an endless expanse of frozen ocean. There's a rumbling, and the host struggles to keep his balance as the ice in front of him collapses. Massive great white sharks are patrolling the water below. "What do you think?"

"I think you and I have different ideas of fun," the host says. "What about a nice beach in Maui and a banana daiquiri?"

Milo laughs. "Okay then, let's take you somewhere a little more relaxing. Otherworld's most popular destination so far is the City of Imra." The screen shows a curved street lined with ornate marble buildings that look like they belong in a Greek myth. A gorgeous redhead in a tight black dress passes by.

"Wowza, look at those pixels," the host says. "Who is *that*?"

"Her name is Catelyn. She's an NPC. Wink at her and see what happens."

"That has never once worked in real life, but let's give it a go. Hey, toots, why don't you come over here and tell me all about your acronym?"

"*NPC* stands for *non-player character,*" Milo says humorlessly. "Though Catelyn is different. *Special.* She's part of the system, but we've designed her to have a mind of her own."

What exactly does that mean? I wonder.

The host whistles. "Can I *play* with that software?"

I roll my eyes.

"Absolutely," says Milo. "And she will play back." The NPC comes over and takes the host's hand. She looks as real as any woman in the audience. Her skin texture is remarkable—soft and dewy, with visible pores. And when the camera pans down to her hand, I can see the cuticles and the sun reflected in her bloodred nail polish. The detail is absolutely amazing.

"Oh my God, I can feel her squeezing my fingers!" the host says with genuine surprise. "You know what this would be *really* good for?" He pauses and the audience snickers. "Foot massages. I guess you could say I'm a foot massage enthusiast."

The joke seems to sail right over Milo's head. "If that's what you're into, I'm not here to judge," he says. He clearly takes this all *very* seriously. "In Otherworld all of us can lead our best lives. Whatever those may be. It doesn't matter how much money you have or how physically fit you are. The life you always wanted will be within your reach. Some people will want to hunt or fight or explore. Others are going to want . . . foot massages."

On-screen, Catelyn cozies up to the host and plants a peck on his cheek. "Oh my God," he mutters. Then he pulls off one of his gloves and begins rooting through his pockets. "How much do you want for this thing? A million bucks? My soul?"

Milo beams. "You just need to subscribe to Otherworld and purchase a headset. The early-access app came out this past Saturday. We've let in two thousand players to help us work all the bugs out. Otherworld's wide release should take place in a few months. Hopefully we'll have managed to manufacture a few million of these headsets by then."

"I have to wait months?" the host groans. "But I don't want to leave!" He blows a kiss at Catelyn and removes the headset. "Okay, so now that I've experienced it for myself, I have one question. How are people supposed to feed and relieve themselves? 'Cause nobody's going to say goodbye to *her* to chow down a burrito or take a leak."

"You make a really good point," Milo says. I suspect it's not the first time he's heard that. "I'm sure the Company will come up with something."

The show's band starts to play to commercial and I think of Kat upstairs, her body hooked up to an array of tubes that provide all the nutrition she needs and eliminate the resulting waste products. The device that's communicating directly to her brain is supposedly far more advanced than the headset that's available to the public. If it works the way Martin and Todd described, the world Kat's in feels, smells and tastes just as real as this one. What if she's found the male version of Catelyn? What if she never wants to leave?

A VISITOR

It must be just after midnight. I'm halfway down the hall, heading back to Kat, when my legs suddenly stop before I know why. My brain catches up quickly and I see it. The door to Kat's room is ajar. Probably just a nurse checking up on her, but I don't know that for sure. So I tiptoe toward the room until I can peer inside. There's someone standing over Kat's bed. Slim and dressed in a hoodie and jeans, it looks a lot like the figure I saw at Elmer's right before the floor collapsed. I drop my coffee and lurch forward, grabbing hold of the intruder's sweatshirt. The yelp I hear is unmistakably feminine. Then the hood falls back, revealing an elegant head.

"Busara?" I ask, though I can see her clearly. It's just hard to believe she's here.

"I'm sorry," she says. "I thought you'd gone home. I didn't mean to scare you."

"It's the middle of the night. What are you doing in here?" I demand. Then I remember the video on her computer at school, and my confusion quickly turns to rage. "Wait—were you just *filming*?"

"No, it's not like that," Busara says. "I don't have a camera with me." She's calm. Too calm. Maybe she's an android after all.

"Bullshit," I say. That's when I notice the plastic band around her wrist.

"What's this?" I ask, grabbing the band and pulling her arm toward me to get a better look. The sight of her name and birth date on the plastic takes me by surprise. "You're a patient here?"

She lowers her arm and covers the band with her fingers as if she's ashamed of it. "I have a heart condition," she says. "I spend a lot of time at the hospital. My cardiologist is on this floor."

"Oh." That explains why she's out of school so much. I feel like an asshole. "Sorry."

"It's okay," she says. "How are you?"

It's a simple question, but one I find myself unable to answer. My mouth is open, but for the first time ever there are no words spilling out. We stand together looking down at the girl in the bed. What's left of Kat's hair is spread across the pillow, and her eyes are hidden behind the Company's slim black visor.

My vision blurs and a drop slips down my face and over my lip before I can catch it. I've spent hours alone in this room, and I haven't shed a single tear. Then some random girl shows up and I lose it. Having Busara here makes me realize how alone I am. I don't want her sympathy. I want Kat's. The one person I would have turned to is gone. I'm here for her, but there's no one here for me.

"My doctor says Kat has something called locked-in syndrome," Busara says. I'm grateful I can reply with a nod as I wipe my eyes on the collar of my shirt.

Busara turns her gaze away from me and back down at Kat. "It seems to be going around."

I clear my throat. "What do you mean?"

"I heard that two of the other kids who survived the accident at the factory have it too. West and Brian. They were moved to a long-term care facility earlier this afternoon."

I wonder if that's where they'll be sending Kat soon. To some place where malfunctioning human bodies are kept clipped and cleaned while the minds trapped inside them wait for death. My only hope is that the White City has set Kat free.

"It's surprising," Busara continues when I don't respond. She seems eager to keep the conversation going. "Locked-in syndrome isn't very common, you know."

I didn't know. And I'm not sure how she does.

My skepticism must show on my face, but it doesn't stop Busara. "As a matter of fact, it's pretty rare. And yet three of the four kids who survived the accident have it. What do you guess are the odds of that?"

She looks at me as if expecting an answer. All I can offer is a shrug.

"I gotta say, if I were the fourth kid, I'd be feeling pretty lucky right now," she adds.

A memory flashes through my brain, and I'm reminded of something I meant to follow up on. "Marlow Holm is the fourth kid. Did you know that?"

Busara nods.

"What else do you know about him?" I ask. "Have you found out anything new?"

"Nothing much, really," she says. "His old social media posts make it seem like he and his mother had to leave California pretty abruptly. But why do you ask? Do you think Marlow had something to do with what happened to Kat?"

Marlow was the one who suggested the party. He was also the only kid who walked away. And his abrupt departure from California does seem pretty fishy. "I don't know what to think yet," I tell Busara.

The room stays silent for longer than I'd like, but I can't come up with anything to say. Finally Busara breaks the silence. "You really love her, don't you?"

Love is too small a word for what I feel. How do I explain that before Kat, nothing was real? The nannies who doted on me were all paid to do it. One day they'd be hugging me, and the next they were gone. Kids at school played with me so our parents could network. Most never even pretended to like me. Then I met Kat, and she *chose* me. No one forced her or paid her. I was the one she wanted to be with. When I was eight years old, Kat stepped out of the woods and rescued me. I will spend my entire life thanking her for wanting to do it.

"Yes," I tell Busara. "I love her. Kat's my whole world."

AWAKENING

Once Busara leaves, it's quiet aside from the beeping of machines. I sit down in the chair beside Kat's bed and take one of her limp hands in mine. I wish like hell I could see her eyes. I wonder why Busara never asked about the visor.

Kat's lips part and I forget everything else. They almost look like she's preparing to speak.

"I'm sure it's really great where you are," I whisper, letting my head come to rest on the side of the bed, "but please come back when you're ready."

"No," a voice says softly.

I sit bolt upright and try to figure out if I could have imagined what I just heard. Then Kat clenches my hand and her mouth stretches open in a silent scream.

"Kat?" I stand and bend over her, my face inches from hers. "Kat, are you there?"

"No!" she gasps. "Oh my God, no!" Her voice is weak, barely

louder than a whisper, but I can feel her panic. It's like she's narrating a nightmare. Her fingers are clamped so tightly around mine that they've cut off my circulation. Kat's heart monitor is going nuts.

"It's okay," I tell her, smoothing her hair. If she's talking, it could mean she's getting better. The relief that floods through me almost makes my knees buckle.

"Don't do it!" she screams. "Oh my God!" My relief is gone in an instant. Something is very wrong.

I yank Kat's visor off. Her eyes are wide open, and they're darting from side to side. I slam the palm of my hand into the red button that calls the nurse. Then I run to the door and shout for help. Two women in scrubs sprint down the hall toward the room. One rushes to Kat's side and immediately begins examining her IV needle and tubing.

The second nurse stops at the door. "What just happened in here?" she demands. She's looking at the visor that's still in my hand. "Why did you remove the patient's visor?"

"She was talking," I say, examining the visor for the first time. I put it up to my face, but the lenses are dark. "She sounded totally terrified. She must have been scared of something she saw."

"The IV had a leak," reports the first nurse. She quickly preps a new one. "It's run out, and there's a puddle on the floor."

"A leak?" The second nurse turns to me. And she's angry. "Did you touch any of the equipment?"

"Absolutely not," I snap. "I was in the cafeteria watching television for the last hour. I just got back here a minute ago." Yes, and there was someone here when I came in, I realize. But for reasons that aren't completely clear to me, I don't say a word.

"Okay, we're good," reports the first nurse. "IV's back in." She's moving around Kat's body, checking her vitals. "I see no signs of movement. There doesn't appear to be pain response, either," she adds. "As far as I can tell, her condition remains the same."

I'm back at Kat's side in a moment. The nurse is right. Kat's totally still again. Her lips are sealed and her eyes are dull and motionless. "I don't understand. She talked to me. She squeezed my hand!"

The nurses are quiet. They're watching me carefully, as if I've lost my mind.

"The disk—it's the disk. It needs to be removed," I insist. I'm trying my best to sound perfectly calm and rational, but I'm on the verge of losing it. "Something's wrong. She was really scared—and Kat doesn't scare easily." I can still hear Kat's voice in my head. She wasn't just scared, she was terrified.

"We can't do anything without Dr. Ito's authorization," one of the nurses informs me. It's like talking to a goddamn robot.

"Then get her!" I nearly yell.

"It's almost one o'clock in the morning," the other nurse points out.

I lower my voice. "If Dr. Ito's not here in fifteen minutes, I'm going to take the disk off myself," I announce.

"Don't. It could be dangerous for the patient," the first nurse says. That might just be the stupidest thing I've ever heard.

"It's a video game!" I've finally lost my cool, and it is not coming back. "What in the hell is going on here? You just take the thing off!"

"Not without the doctor's permission," the first nurse repeats firmly.

"Then get her!" I shout at the top of my lungs, and the two nurses both scurry away.

I brush a lock of copper hair away from Kat's pale, dry lips. Then I take her hand in mine and prepare to wait. I will stand right here until Dr. Ito arrives and the disk is removed. I don't care how long it takes. My eyes aren't going to leave Kat. I'd memorize the freckles on her face if I didn't already know them all by heart. I place a finger on her pulse. It feels faster than it should. Thirty minutes pass, and Kat doesn't move. I don't even see so much as a twitch. Then Dr. Ito arrives with a posse.

She's followed by two security guards, a nurse and Martin—the emo engineer from the Company, who appears to be wearing his pajamas. The security guards look eager. Martin looks like he might vomit at any second.

Dr. Ito joins me at Kat's bedside. "What's going on here?" she asks.

The doctor listens patiently while I tell her everything I saw and heard.

"How long has it been since you got a full night's sleep?" she asks when I finish.

"What does *that* have to do with anything?" I ask, though I can see exactly where she's heading.

"Sleep deprivation can have a serious impact on the human brain," she informs me. "What you experienced was a hallucination, Mr. Eaton. Katherine is physically unable to speak or move."

"I'm completely awake, and I know what happened," I insist. "Kat spoke. She *screamed,* actually."

Dr. Ito shakes her head. "That's impossible," she says. "The damage to her brain is too severe."

I hold up the visor and address my next question to Martin. "She saw something on this that scared the hell out of her. What was it?"

His shaggy hair flops from side to side when he shakes his head. "The White City's all butterflies and bunnies. There's nothing there that could possibly scare a girl Katherine's age."

"Then why the hell was she screaming?" I take a step toward the engineer, and one of the security guards puts a hand to my chest.

"Calm down," he orders.

"It's okay," Martin says. I'm not sure if he's talking to the guard or to me. "Hundreds of people have visited the White City. To my knowledge, none of them have ever woken up screaming."

"To your *knowledge*?" I shoot back. "Aren't you keeping track? What kind of test is this?"

"I'm sorry, I—" Martin starts to say.

"I'm afraid this entire conversation is pointless." Dr. Ito cuts him off. Her voice is different now. She's no longer playing nice. "Katherine could not have moved or spoken this evening, Mr. Eaton. You need to come to terms with the fact that there's very little chance that she ever will."

"I don't believe you." I sound like a stubborn child.

Dr. Ito clearly doesn't care what I believe or don't believe. "I've been practicing neurology for over twenty years," she's saying. "If you're questioning my competence, that's just more proof that you've lost touch with reality. I'll be advising Katherine's parents to have her moved to a long-term care facility soon. We have done all we can for her here."

I feel goose bumps break out on my arms. "The same facility

where they sent the two other people who were hurt at the factory? Brian and West? I heard they have locked-in syndrome too. Is that right?"

Martin looks over at Dr. Ito. I notice she's careful not to look back. Either I've gone completely insane or something incredibly weird is going on here.

"I've told you before, I'm not at liberty to discuss any of my patients with you, Mr. Eaton."

"That's fine," I tell her. Once again, I've run out of patience. "I'm done talking anyway. Game over."

I drop the visor on the floor and crush it beneath the heel of my shoe. Then I lean over Kat and gently lift her head, feeling for the disk. The thing's coming off whether they like it or not.

"Stop him," Dr. Ito orders. "He's going to endanger my patient." The two security guards are on me in a heartbeat.

"No, no, he won't. It's okay!" I hear Martin insist. "The disk just peels off. It can go right back on again. You don't need to hurt him!"

My hands are pulled out from beneath Kat's head, and both of my arms are pinned behind my back. They have me bent over at the waist, my head pressed into Kat's lap.

"Hey! What are you doing?" Martin cries. "Are you sure this is necessary?"

I feel a sharp jab in my left butt cheek. Then I feel nothing at all.

GOING UNDER

I wake up in a hospital room with a nurse and a guard standing over my bed. The clock on the television says 11:41. The sun is shining, so it must be just before noon on Wednesday. Which means I was out for almost eleven hours.

The nurse is holding a plastic bag that's filled with my few belongings.

"You had to be sedated. Now it's time for you to go home," she says. I can tell she's looking forward to showing me the door. "If you don't comply, we will be forced to phone the police."

It's a good thing I've kept the document Kat's mom signed in my back pocket. I sit up and unfold it. Then I hold the paper up for the nurse to see. "Kat's mother wants me to stay with her," I croak. My throat is parched.

The nurse doesn't even look down at the page. "The woman who signed that document no longer has legal guardianship over her daughter. Katherine Foley's sole guardian is now her step-father, Wayne Gibson."

Oh, *shit*. I try to stand up, but it takes two attempts. My legs are still wobbly from the sedative.

"I need to talk to him," I say.

"Shoot." I turn to see Wayne Gibson sitting in the corner of the room, a smirk of triumph smeared across his face.

"What's going on?" I demand. "What did you do to Linda?"

"What did *I* do to Linda?" he repeats incredulously as he rises from his seat. "My wife voluntarily committed herself to a mental health institute yesterday. Our daughter's illness has been weighing heavily on her, and she was worried she might do herself harm."

If that's the truth, it doesn't seem to bother him much. I wish there were a scalpel lying around. If I cut into this asshole, I'm pretty sure I'd only find gears and wires. No human being has posture this good—or a heart this cold.

"I want proof that she left you in charge of Kat," I say.

"Mr. Gibson has provided all the necessary legal paperwork," the nurse answers from the other side of the room.

For the first time ever, I genuinely wish my parents were here. Without a lawyer, there's no way I can win this battle. And getting into a pissing contest with GI Joe isn't going to do Kat any good—or help me figure out what the hell is going on.

I look back at Mr. Gibson. "May I speak with you privately?" I ask, adjusting my tone.

"Certainly," he says diplomatically, nodding at the nurse. I guess it's easy to be gracious when you know you've won.

The nurse and the guard shuffle out of the room. Wayne assumes a superhero stance—chest out, arms crossed and legs apart—and I realize I'm not going to convince him of anything.

"Kat spoke yesterday," I say.

"Thank you for letting me know." It sounds like a voice recording at some corporate headquarters. "I will inform the doctors. Is there anything else?"

"The Company disk needs to be removed. It was scaring her."

"Thank you. I will let the doctors know about that as well."

Nothing I can say will make any difference. I see that now. My words just bounce off him. This short, cocky man with his button-down shirt and perfectly pressed pants is completely invulnerable.

"You don't give a shit about Kat, do you?" I ask.

"Don't worry, son." He gives me a pat on the shoulder and then heads for the door. "I'll take it from here."

"Wait!" I reach out to stop him and he spins around. His lips curl slightly as his eyes travel from my hand to my face. His expression is as good as a growl. I pull back before my fingers brush against him, like a kid who's nearly been nipped by a dog. "Can I at least see her before I go?" If he wants me to beg, I will.

"Katherine isn't at the hospital anymore," he says just before he leaves the room. "She's moved on."

For a few horrible seconds, I assume the worst. Then I realize he means it literally. She's been moved to the facility. I'm relieved she's alive—but otherwise, I couldn't be more terrified.

.   .   .

The plastic bag with my belongings bounces against my thigh as the security guards frog-march me out of the hospital. As we pass the waiting room I catch a glimpse of Busara. She's arguing with some guy who's got a backpack slung over his shoulder. Her eyes lock on to mine and the guy turns to see what's caught her attention. *Jesus.* It's Marlow Holm. He opens his mouth as if he wants to say something to me but he can't quite get it out. I struggle to break free and go back to them, but the security guards drag me forward and out the front doors. They drop me to the ground in the parking lot and stand blocking the path to the hospital.

I pick myself up and start weaving around cars, making my way toward the road.

"Hey, Simon!" It's Busara. She must have run after us. I keep walking. I don't respond. I'm too furious to be around anyone right now.

The walk home must have been around three miles, and the weather was unseasonably warm. I remember nothing about the journey. I couldn't even tell you which route I took. My shirt is soaked through with sweat when I reach the driveway and see my parents' cars are both gone. I walk through the door and a woman dusting the entryway yelps.

"Are my mother and father here?" I ask. She stands with her back against the wall and watches me like I'm a beast that's escaped from the zoo.

"They're still in London," she tells me. My mother must have caught the red-eye after all.

I head straight for my room, disrobing as I go. I turn on

the water in the walk-in shower and take a seat on the ledge. I bow my head, letting the streams of water beat down on my skull.

What am I going to do now? I sit back, banging my head against the tiles. I'm such a fucking idiot. I swore I'd take care of Kat, and then I gave them a reason to separate us. Now she's gone.

Kat spoke. I know she did. I wasn't hallucinating. But even if I had been—why the hell wouldn't they just take the disk off?

I step out of the shower and wrap a towel around my waist. There's a knock at my bedroom door. I open it to find a young woman in a blue maid's smock.

"This just arrived for you," she says, averting her eyes and holding out a box covered in brown paper. My name is written on the front, but there's no return address.

"Who's it from?"

"I don't know. It came by messenger." She backs away from my door as if I'll attack her if she dares to turn around. I guess I don't blame her. I probably look pretty crazy right now.

I rip the wrapping off the package as I make my way to my desk. Underneath the paper is a shoe box with a picture of a pair of sneakers on the side. They're the same unusual brand and color that Milo Yolkin's known to wear. MEN'S SIZE 9 is written beneath the image. I open the box, but there aren't shoes inside. Instead I find a visor and a round, flesh-colored disk.

There's only one person who could have sent the gear. Did Martin feel guilty about watching me get a needle jammed in my ass? Is this the engineer's way of proving to me that there's nothing to fear in the White City?

I remove the items and place them carefully on my desk. At

the bottom of the box is a small envelope. I open it and pull out a note scribbled in Sharpie.

GO FIND HER, it says.

The piece of paper slips out of my hand and flutters to the floor.

I sprint out of my room, through the house and out the front door. There's no sign of the messenger.

THE OTHER SIDE

I've locked myself in my bedroom with a dresser shoved against the door. I just shaved the back of my head, and my scalp burns and tingles. My mind is already far away.

I lie down on my bed and pull on the visor. It's utterly weightless on my face. Carefully, I stick the disk to the back of my skull, right where I saw them put Kat's. In an instant I'm no longer in my bedroom. I'm standing naked in an empty, brightly lit room. I can't tell how many of my senses are engaged. It's hard to assess the latest groundbreaking technology without anything but my own body to see, smell or touch.

There's a mirror in front of me, and I see myself, tall, lanky and blessed with a legendary schnoz. The other details might not be one hundred percent accurate. The disk must have pulled this image of me out of my brain, but I look slightly better than I do in real life—like a picture taken from just the right angle.

I think this is the setup. The weird white space looks a lot like the environment in Otherworld where you assemble your avatar. I guess I shouldn't be so surprised that they're similar. The Company developed the White City software, too. They're bound to have a few things in common. As far as I can tell, there's already one big difference, though. Like most games, Otherworld provides a menu of options. The controls on your headset allow you to assume almost any appearance as long as your form remains essentially human. But there are no controls here. The White City must be designed to be completely intuitive.

"Okay, give me a smaller nose," I say out loud, and the kishka shrinks on command.

"Spiky white hair." My black hair instantly lightens.

"Enormous penis," I order. Because of course. Suddenly I look like something out of the zoo.

"Kick-ass muscles and a leather trench coat." I stand back and admire myself in the mirror. With a few simple adjustments I've become Rutger Hauer in *Blade Runner*.

"Reset." I'm back to myself.

"Give me four tentacles and the head of a musk ox," I demand.

Nothing happens. So, like Otherworld, the software must require that I remain more or less human.

"Fine, then, let's go with seven feet tall, stone body that burns bright red, horns, no face or genitals."

The image I see in the mirror is just a few tweaks away from the giant avatar I met in the Otherworld ice cave. I love the idea of setting this beast loose on the bunnies and butterflies of the White City. But I don't have time to keep screwing around. Every moment that passes is one I haven't spent looking for Kat.

"Hooded brown robe, made from wool. Black pants, shirt and boots."

In front of me is my avatar from a hundred games, with one significant difference: it's my face looking back at me from under the hood. I want Kat to recognize me when she sees me.

"Done," I announce. I could give myself a digital nose job, but then it wouldn't be me.

The mirror becomes a door. The door opens.

I step through the opening and into another reality. And damn, is it *amazing*. It may not be Earth, but it's no game, either. With an Otherworld headset, you can see, hear and touch, but that's the extent of your sensory experience. Here, I'm immediately hit by the fragrance of flowers. I inhale deeply as a light breeze ripples the hem of my robe. I'm standing on a balcony on a tall white building. I can feel the floor beneath my feet. I reach out for the metal railing and it's warm from the sun. Far below me is a beautiful city surrounded by tall stone walls. Beyond the walls lies a vast green land. I can see the hazy outline of mountains in the distance. Inside the city walls, there are other white buildings, all marvels of modern architecture. They're linked by a paved path that snakes through the town. I'm watching a driverless pod navigate the curves in search of its next passenger when a magnificent bird lands on the railing beside me. Its face is golden and its feathers a shimmering iridescent green. Intellectually I know these are graphics. Every other part of me believes it's all real. I can see the shaft in each of the bird's feathers and every scale on its feet. The creature regards me with an intelligent, slightly hostile expression.

Then it squirts a dollop of guano onto the balcony and flies off toward the puffy white dream clouds that decorate the sky.

I turn around and see that the portal to the setup environment is gone. In its place is a set of glass doors. They slide open easily, granting me access to an apartment. On a nearby side table is a tablet. It lights up as I approach, offering an impressive home decorating menu (starting with Amish farmstead, Argentinian estancia and Ashanti traditional), along with the options to build your own pets, children and companions from scratch. I quickly scroll through the companion menu—just to see what's available. I'm expecting a good snicker, but it seems disappointingly clean. And even if it weren't, I remind myself, I'm not here to play house with some AI hottie. I'm here to find Kat. I toss the tablet onto the couch and head straight for the front door.

The hallway outside my apartment is empty. I take a glass elevator to ground level and it deposits me at the bottom of a silent atrium. The plants soaking up the digital sunlight are unlike any I've ever seen in New Jersey, but I could swear they're all real. I can smell the soil they're growing in. I can see the tiny ridges and valleys on their leaves. I reach out and grab one of the round red fruits dangling from a nearby tree. I bite into it and I can feel and hear my teeth break through its skin. The flesh is sweet and smells like a plum. There is nothing about the experience that feels artificial—nothing to remind me that my brain has teamed up with software to trick me. In fact, there's only one thing about this whole experience that strikes me as odd: There doesn't seem to be anyone else around. The building is empty.

I walk out the front door and onto an equally deserted street.

As I stroll through the city, my unease continues to build. Everywhere I look, there are swarms of butterflies and flocks of birds. I even spot one of the bunnies Martin mentioned. But there are no other humans here. And most importantly—no Kat. The engineers claimed there were over three hundred people in the White City right now, but I don't see a single one of them. It's as if a plague swept through town and wiped out all the inhabitants. I'm standing in the middle of the path when a driverless pod comes around a curve. It stops and waits for me to step aside, and then it continues on its way.

After a short walk, I find a row of shops and restaurants. They all have oddly generic names. ITALIAN RESTAURANT. PHARMACY. LADIES' BOUTIQUE. Then I spot a waitress through the window of FRENCH CAFÉ, and the relief is overwhelming. She looks like she might be in her early twenties, and she's attractive—but in a reassuringly imperfect way. Her chest is flat and her cleavage is unexposed, which makes me question whether she could have been designed by a bunch of horny Company geeks.

"Good afternoon, sir," she says in a chipper tone when I walk through the door. Her name tag says ELIZA. "May I offer you something to drink?"

"Where is everyone?" I ask. "I'm looking for a friend of mine, but there doesn't seem to be anyone around."

"*I'm* here," she says.

"Yeah, but you're not real, are you?" I ask. Might as well get it out of the way.

Eliza laughs, as though it's a question she gets all the time. "*Real?*" she answers. "Of course I'm real."

"Are you an NPC or are you somebody's avatar?"

The waitress's smile fades just a bit. She seems thrown. "I'm a waitress," she says. "I serve food and drinks. Is there anything I can get for you? The French onion soup is particularly good today."

I have a strong hunch that I'm talking to a bot, so I devise my own amateur Turing test. "I've got a flying saucer parked outside, and I'm headed to Pluto," I tell her.

"Would you like the soup to go, then?" she asks with a smile, and I'm stunned. Bots aren't renowned for their sense of humor. It's almost as if Eliza knew I was testing her.

"Sure," I say, doubling down. "Want to come along for the ride?"

"I'd love to," she says carefully. I get the impression that Eliza thinks I'm insane. But to reach that conclusion, she would need to be able to *think*. "Unfortunately, I'm a permanent resident of the White City, and I haven't been authorized to visit other planets. Would you still like soup?"

All I can do is shake my head.

"Then if you'll excuse me, I need to get back to work."

Eliza has no other customers. She's either the most dedicated human waitress I've ever met—or the most impressive NPC ever designed. The weird thing is, I'm still not sure.

On my way out of the café, a flyer tacked to a bulletin board catches my eye. VISIT THE CITY OF IMRA, it says in large type. RESORT OF THE FUTURE. I snatch it off the wall. There are no other words on the page, so I study the photo. It's a picture of Catelyn, the busty NPC that Milo Yolkin introduced on the talk show. She's wearing a red bikini and sitting in a hot tub, toasting the camera with a glass of champagne.

Why is Otherworld's City of Imra being advertised inside the White City? The Company practically invented in-game advertising, and they cross-promote whenever they get a chance. But selling Otherworld to a bunch of people who can't even get out of bed to buy the game just seems goddamn *weird*.

I ball up the flyer in my hands and toss it into a nearby trash can. More confused than ever, I leave the café and follow the path as it winds downhill. Now that I know they're here, I spot other workers inside businesses that all seem to thrive without any customers. A few of them come to the windows as I pass, but none step outside. It occurs to me that I'm outnumbered, and I find myself walking faster. I'm not frightened exactly, but I'm definitely unnerved. And I'm worried for Kat. Whatever happened to the three hundred humans who were supposed to be here must have happened to her as well.

I come around a curve and stop short. I can't go any farther. The path abruptly ends at a tall metal gate, and a statue of a man is blocking the way. The figure is dressed exactly like the Clay Man I saw inside the Otherworld glacier. It's wearing a dark suit and there's a Bedouin-style scarf wrapped around its head. Like the flyer, it feels out of place here in the White City. But then again, so do I.

"Hello, Simon," it says, and I nearly jump out of my skin. "You look lost. Do you need directions?"

The statue's eyes are open. They're a brilliant blue, as is the amulet that hangs around its neck. It's glowing like a cheesy power crystal from *World of Warcraft*.

"How do you know who I am?"

"I am your guide," it says.

"Does everyone here get a guide?" I ask warily.

"I couldn't say," the Clay Man replies. "I have never been a guest of the White City."

It takes me a second to understand that when the Clay Man says *guest* he must mean a human visitor. Eliza called herself a resident, which must be the politically correct euphemism for NPCs.

"So where are all the other guests?" I ask my guide.

"They've left the White City," says the Clay Man, gesturing toward the gate. "Once they pass through this gate, they cannot return."

"Then I guess I'm looking for someone who may have come this way," I say. "A girl named Kat." I wish I could describe her. But unlike me, Kat rarely chooses the same avatar twice. She could be anything or anyone.

"Yes, I have seen her. She is searching for the way out of this world. I told her it lies on the other side of the gates."

My heart sinks. Kat's gone—and any hope I had that this would be a quick rescue mission has gone with her. I stare up at the massive gates, which would look right at home on a medieval fortress. "What's out there?"

"I will show you," says the Clay Man.

The gates swing open, revealing a battalion of NPC soldiers stationed outside. Armed with long spears, the silent men watch the horizon. I study one to see if he blinks. When he does, I look past the army at a featureless landscape of moss-covered rocks. It doesn't resemble any place I've been before, but it feels every bit as real as New Jersey.

"Why are there troops here?" I ask the Clay Man.

"The soldiers have been stationed here to prevent Otherworld's residents and guests from entering the White City."

The name explodes like a bomb in my head. "Hold up—that's *Otherworld*?" I point toward the mountains in the distance.

"Don't you recognize it?" the Clay Man asks. "You've been there before. That's where we first met."

"You're the same guy I saw inside the glacier?"

"I am," he says.

"Okay, stop there for a second." Because none of this shit makes any sense. The White City was built for people with serious medical problems. Otherworld is geek central. "Why is the White City suddenly inside *Otherworld*?"

"They are both products of the Company, are they not? Someone must have decided to bring them together," the Clay Man says.

This whole situation is really starting to freak me out. "So let me get this straight. Guests who leave the White City aren't allowed back. And Otherworld players can't come in either. But why would the soldiers need to keep Otherworld's *residents* out of the White City? The residents are just NPCs, right? They don't think for themselves—they just do what they're programmed to do. It's not like they're going to invade."

"Your assumptions are incorrect," the Clay Man informs me. "In Otherworld, the residents have minds of their own. They eat, sleep, breed and think. Some of them were designed to be just as real as the guests."

My bizarre conversation with the waitress named Eliza immediately comes to mind. "Like the workers here in the White City?" I ask.

"No," says the Clay Man. "Many of the residents you'll encounter in Otherworld are far more advanced than the ones you met here. You must be wary of them."

Anything more advanced than Eliza would be true artificial intelligence. And I'm pretty sure that's what this dude's getting at.

"Even the Beasts in Otherworld are more intelligent than they appear," the Clay Man continues as my head spins. "But the most dangerous creatures you'll encounter will be other guests. Players with headsets can be remarkably brutal. Be on your guard at all times."

I reach up to my face and grope for my visor. I need to press Pause and figure a few dozen things out. But I feel nothing but the skin around my eyes. My hand slides around to the back of my head. There's no disk. I have a full head of hair.

"You cannot remove the disk on your own," says the Clay Man. "In the real world most of your muscles have been temporarily paralyzed—just as they are when you sleep."

Oh, God. What the hell have I gotten myself into? "Then how do I get back home?"

"As I told your friend, there is a way out. An exit of sorts. Your disk and visor will deactivate as you pass through it."

"Where is the exit?" I ask. "How do I find it?"

"You've seen it before," says the Clay Man. "There's a door deep inside the glacier. Your friend is on her way there now."

I remember the door, and I feel a sudden surge of hope. And then— "Wait a second. What are we supposed to do about the giant red dude who lives in the ice cave?"

"His name is Magna. You must kill him," says the Clay Man.

"Oh, yeah? With *what*?" I demand. At least the last time I visited Otherworld I was given a weapon at setup.

"Come with me." The Clay Man steps through the gates. I'm not sure I'm ready to follow him, though. "You must trust me," he says. "Until you find your friend, I am all you have."

He's right. I have no choice. When I join him outside the gates, two of the soldiers break formation. They're carrying a large metal box, which they place at my feet and open. Inside is an assortment of weapons and tools.

I see what I want and reach for it.

"Choose wisely," the Clay Man cautions me. "You may only take one. Those are the rules of Otherworld."

I don't hesitate. Kat will make fun of me when she sees what I've picked, but my trusty dagger goes into my boot. I'm deadlier with an eight-inch blade than most guys would be with a sword.

"Guard your life with great care. Do not assume that you will get another."

"Why not?" I ask. "You forget—I've played Otherworld. You get sent back to setup whenever you die, but you get as many lives as you need."

"Yes, but you are not *playing* Otherworld now, Simon," the Clay Man tells me. "The guests with headsets are inside a game. For those with disks, Otherworld is something else entirely. The only way to ensure your survival is to think of this as a new reality."

"Wait—are you telling me I can die? For real?"

"I'm telling you I don't know."

I feel a very real urge to vomit. But even if I could turn back now, I wouldn't. Kat's out there, and there's a very good chance she has no idea what kind of trouble she's in.

"You're coming with me, right?" I ask. "Isn't that what guides are for?"

"No," the Clay Man informs me. "I will help you when I'm able, but never rely on me to intervene on your behalf. From this point forward, you must make do on your own."

WASTELAND

I'm starting to think I made a big mistake. I've been hiking for hours across the moss-covered rocks, and I've seen no evidence of life. I have to consider the possibility that the Clay Man misled me. Maybe I was tricked into wandering a wasteland while Kat is being held captive somewhere inside the White City. The mountains ahead of me keep growing, but I never reach them. All around me, boulders dot the landscape like the tombstones of an ancient race of giants. Since I set out, I've been watching the clouds, waiting to see if they ever repeat themselves. But the digital sky seems to produce them in an infinite number of shapes and textures. I've seen a wispy dog and a cottony dragon, and I wonder if they might be symbols or messages I don't understand.

I'm studying a cloud that looks like lion rampant when a column of hot steam bursts from the ground directly in front of me. A fine spray of boiling water scalds the exposed skin on my hands and face, and I cry out in shock. It hurts like hell. The disk on the back of my skull has convinced my brain that the pain is real. If I'd been any closer to the geyser, my avatar would have been cooked. I try not to think about how *that* would have felt. Remembering the Clay Man's warning to protect my life, I pull my hood up and keep my eyes glued to the ground.

If the action is all taking place in my head, my body doesn't seem to know it. My calves ache and my mouth is parched by the time I spot a tall rocky outcropping ahead of me. It looks like it should only take a few minutes to reach it, but it's hard to judge distances here. I hike for another hour until I realize there's something unusual on top of the hill, and then I scramble as fast as I can across the treacherous terrain. When I reach the rocks, I climb to the summit and find what I was hoping for. Someone has built a cairn here. Hundreds of small, flat stones have been stacked into a conical tower that reaches chest-high. It's the first sign I've had that anyone else has passed this way. I scan the horizon. There's a dust cloud in the distance and a much larger rock outcropping about a mile away. It, too, has an unusual peak. I've discovered a trail, I realize. I could cry with relief.

Long before I reach the next rocky hill, I see something moving across it, and the discovery thrills me. It may not be human, but it's some form of life. When I'm a few hundred yards away, I can make out a herd of goats with silver hair and magnificent white horns that curl in spirals. The animals scamper across the rocks, stopping to nibble on the flowering plants that sprout out of the crevasses. I notice there's one goat that doesn't appear quite as sure-footed as the rest. It slips and slides as it follows the herd. It's been injured, I assume. I have to give the Company credit.

A crippled goat is a brilliant touch. The imperfection makes the scene feel all the more real.

I follow the ungainly goat with my eyes as I gradually draw nearer. I'm almost to the base of the hill when the beast begins to transform, and I come to a halt. It's not a goat at all. It's a man. He rises from his hands and knees. There's a goatskin fastened around his neck, and the dead beast's head has flopped backward like a hood. Under the pelt, the man is naked aside from a loincloth. He stands on one of the rocks, staring directly at me. His body is battered, his hands are brown with dried blood and something is very wrong with his face.

I have battled a thousand monsters. I've stormed countless enemy camps and faced down dozens of mob bosses. But I've never been as freaked out as I am right now.

The goat man beckons me toward him, but I'm frozen. I stay put, even as his gestures become more frantic. Then he lifts one of his bruised and bloody arms and points to the right. I glance over and see an immense cloud of dust traveling toward me. Over the sound of my racing heart, I can make out the pounding of hooves. I have two choices. Run toward the goat man or be flattened by whatever's heading my way. I decide to go with the devil I know.

I sprint for the safety of the rocks, and as soon as I reach them, I'm enveloped in the dust cloud. I see flashes of matted brown fur, beady black eyes and cloven hooves. The creatures moving past are enormous. The stench that trails behind them is almost as thick as the cloud.

Only when they're gone and the dust has begun to settle again do I realize there's someone sitting next to me.

"Hello," says the goat man. Though his tone is cheerful, his voice is hoarse, as if it hasn't been put to much use. "You're lucky to have escaped the buffalo, you know. They're not very fond of guests. They trample travelers like you whenever they get a chance."

His face begins to emerge from the haze, and I do my best to disguise my shock. His nose has no bridge—it's flat in the middle, with two large nostrils that flare and collapse as he breathes. The tops of his ears flop down over the openings, and I can see the buds of two horns straining to break through the skin of his forehead. The pupils in the centers of his amber eyes are thick black dashes.

I have never seen *anything* like the goat man before. The geek who designed him was one sick bastard.

"What are you?" The words slip out. Even in Otherworld they sound horribly rude.

His hand flies up to his face, and I instantly regret that I asked. "I'm one of the Children," the goat man tells me.

"I'm sorry. I didn't mean to offend you," I say. "I just got here, and you're the first resident I've met. So you're one of the children? Whose children?"

He smiles broadly, revealing a significant underbite and several unusually large teeth. He's eager to talk. "Every Child has different parents," he says. "Mine were a goat and the Elemental of Imra."

There are a hundred follow-up questions I'd like to ask—many of them anatomical in nature—but I don't want to insult the only intelligent creature I've encountered so far. "So you're the son of a god?"

The goat man crosses one badly bruised knee over the other,

weaves his fingers together and lets his clasped hands lie in his lap. It's a dainty pose for someone wearing nothing but a pelt and a loincloth. "The Elementals are not gods. They merely rule Otherworld's lands. There is only one Creator."

I've read a million posts about the original Otherworld. I know all about the Beasts and the Elementals, but I don't recall hearing about Children or a Creator. "Are there many of your kind here in Otherworld?" I ask.

The goat man sighs sadly. "There were more of us once, but the Children were not part of the Creator's plan. Before the guests arrived, many of us were slain. Those of us who survived stay hidden now. My herd used to live in the mountains near Imra. It journeyed here to the wastelands for my protection. The only other creatures in these parts are the buffalo, and as you just saw, they're not very social. It can get terribly lonely."

"Wow, that's awful," I tell him, though it's hard to feel too bad. He's a remarkable bit of AI, but underneath it all, he's just zeros and ones.

"Many of us blame humans like you for our misfortune," the goat man continues. "That's why you should take great care around Children like me."

I'm about to tell him it's perfectly understandable when I finally absorb the meaning of his words. I can't be certain, but it sounds like there's a threat mixed in among them. The smile on his face hasn't changed, though it was pretty disturbing from the start. I glance over my shoulder toward the top of the rocks. Just as I thought, there seems to be a cairn. Guests have passed this way before.

"Looks like you've had visitors," I say, pointing up at the cairn.

"Oh, yes," he confirms. "The last group came through less than a day ago. Would you like to see what they left behind?"

"Yeah, sure." I rise to my feet and shake the dust from my robe. I'm happy to keep moving, and I'll be even happier when I'm off the rocks and headed in the right direction. "Who were they?" I ask as we climb.

"A party of four," the goat man replies. "Three males and a female."

My pace quickens. Could the female have been Kat? She never chose male avatars, despite the fact that females were far from welcome in a lot of the games we played. "Where were your visitors headed?"

"When they left, they were searching for a way out of Otherworld," says the goat man. We're almost to the top now, and I can see the cairn more clearly. The materials used to make it don't appear to be rocks. "I do hope they find one," he continues. "And once they've left our world, I hope they never return."

I reach the summit and take a moment to catch my breath. There's a nauseating stench of rotten flesh in the air. Then I stand up, the cairn in front of me. It's not composed of rocks after all. Stacked neatly on top of each other are several bodies' worth of bones. The sun has bleached the ones at the base. There are still scraps of muscle attached to a femur on top.

"My family were not meant to be meat eaters," the goat man explains almost apologetically. "But we can't survive on the vegetation that grows on this rock pile. Your kind was responsible for our exile. Now you're the solution to our problems as well." He adjusts a few of the bones in the cairn. "The pile attracts guests to our hillside. We choose one from each party that passes through on their way from the White City to Imra. They're not like the other guests, I've found. Most don't know where they are. They seldom put up a fight."

I wonder how it would feel to be eaten—and what would happen to my body in New Jersey if my avatar were to meet such a gruesome fate. Then a worse thought crosses my mind. Did Kat find herself in a situation like this? Is that why she cried out?

I pull my dagger from my boot. Soon there will be one less Child for their Creator to eliminate.

The goat man sighs wearily at the sight of my knife. "You may be able to delay the inevitable by killing me," he says. "But you won't be able to stop it."

I hear the clicking of hooves on rocks, and the rest of the herd appears at the summit. They've got me surrounded. It's the first time I've seen the goats up close, and they're larger than I imagined. Each is bigger than a bear, and while they're clearly not as gifted and talented as the goat man, they seem far more intelligent than any of Earth's furry beasts. I detect a mixture of hunger, fear and fury in their eyes.

Then, somewhere on the hillside below us, a goat bleats a warning and the creatures gather to see the source of the alarm, shoving me along with them. A tall, dark figure wearing a Bedouin scarf is walking toward us across the rocks. His strides are long and purposeful, but the Clay Man seems to think there's no need to rush. It's clear the goats recognize him too. They scramble to the opposite side of the hill, leaving me alone once again with the goat man. I smirk at him and sheathe my dagger. No one's going to get eaten today.

"Why are your friends so afraid of the Clay Man?" I ask.

"We don't know what he is," the goat man tells me. "Or where he comes from. We are told that, aside from the guests, all things in Otherworld originated in the mind of the Creator. But the truth seems to be much more complicated than that."

"Well, your buddies were smart to run. In fact, you should probably follow them, Goat Boy," I say. "The Clay Man is my guide."

The goat man rolls his eyes as if I'm ridiculously naive. "There are no *guides* in Otherworld," he says. "That is not why he's here."

The Clay Man stops. He seems to be waiting for me, but he won't deign to climb the rocks. A single brave goat approaches him while the rest cower on the other side of the hill. The Clay Man remains perfectly motionless as the goat sniffs at him, the stone on my guide's chest glowing bright blue. Then the goat opens its mouth and makes a grab for the amulet. In an instant the Clay Man springs to life. His staff swings and catches the beast midstomach. The force sends it sailing through the air. The goat's long bleat grows fainter, then stops altogether. A small cloud of dust rises in the distance where the beast met the ground.

The goat man cries out, and the beasts hiding on the other side of the hill begin bleating in unison. That's my cue to go. I hurry down the rocks to meet my guide—if that's what he really is.

"I thought you knew what you were doing," the Clay Man barks when I reach him. Most of his face is hidden behind his scarf, but his eyes are flashing and he sounds royally pissed. "I just left you a few hours ago, and I've already had to return!"

"Hold on. You're mad at *me*?" I say. "Where do you get off—"

"I warned you about the residents of Otherworld," the Clay Man breaks in to remind me. "You must be much more careful in the future. I travel the wastelands, but I do not enter the realms. The next time you're in trouble, I may not be able to reach you."

"The goat man caught me off guard," I say. "You didn't tell me there'd be a bunch of freaky-ass Children roaming around. What the hell are they, anyway?"

The Clay Man pauses to consider the question. By the time he answers, he's cooled down quite a bit. "They are unintended consequences," he says. "These days men can build worlds, but they lack the power to control them."

"You're saying the Children are *mistakes*? Like bad code or something?"

"The creators of Otherworld wanted it to be real," says the Clay Man. "They forgot that nothing real can be perfect."

That reminds me. "Speaking of creators, Goat Boy up there was just yammering on about his Creator. Was he talking about—"

The Clay Man doesn't wait for me to finish. "All intelligent beings need ways to explain their origins."

"So the Creator—"

"Was designed to be part of the game. The Elementals worship him. He and the Children have a more complicated relationship."

When I have a little downtime, I'll try to wrap my head around the idea that a bunch of digital freaks have their own god. But right now, I have more questions that need answers.

"So the Creator's part of the software and the Children are mistakes. What are you?" I demand. "You told me you're my guide, but you're not an NPC. And I don't think you're a guest, either. So are you an administrator? A Company employee? Are you Martin, my favorite engineer?"

"Find your friend, get to the exit, and kill the one who guards it. That is why you're here. It is all you need to do."

"And believe me, I'll do it happily. But I don't like surprises. Has the goat man's Creator made anything else I need to know about?"

"It would be impossible to prepare you for everything you might face here," says the Clay Man. "Otherworld has a mind of its own." He looks up at the sky. "Night falls quickly. You must reach the oasis before the sun begins to set."

"The oasis?"

"There's a pool of fresh water in the mountains. Your avatar will be able to eat, drink and rest there. These things are necessary to maintain your strength while you're here. But you must leave for the oasis now. You don't want to find yourself in the wastelands after nightfall. The buffalo that live here can see in the darkness, and they've been known to hunt and consume the guests."

Just when I was sure I knew just how bad it could get. *"Really?"* I groan. "Them too? You've got to be shitting me! Aren't buffalo supposed to be herbivores?"

"Do not assume anything here is the same as it is in your world," says the Clay Man. "And don't let down your guard again."

He gives me a hard look and grasps his amulet. It glows brightly, and then my guide disappears.

THE OTHERS

At first I carefully scanned my surroundings as I walked, keeping an eye out for signs of buffalo in the distance. Now that the land has grown mountainous, I've stopped worrying about being trampled or eaten by bloodthirsty beasts. Instead I'm looking for the oasis I was promised. The oases I've seen online have all had water and palm trees, but there isn't anything like that here. In fact, there's nothing here at all. Even the carpet of green moss vanished long ago. All that's left is rust-red dirt, and it's been hours since I've seen so much as a rock. My only hope is that there's something—*anything*—on the other side of the steep slope I'm climbing.

The barren soil erodes under my feet with every step I take, making it almost impossible to find a good foothold. I finally reach the top of the mountain and collapse in exhaustion. My mouth is dry and my stomach is empty. I drag myself to my feet and glance back at the wasteland I crossed. The vast, desolate plain stretches all the way to the horizon. I turn to see what's ahead of me, praying it's not more of the same. I nearly cry when I realize I've reached the oasis. I'm standing near the lip of a crater. A few hundred feet below me is a lake so crystal clear I can make out a school of silver fish in the water. The creatures are swimming together in an endless spiral, and the effect is mesmerizing. From the little I know of Otherworld, it's safe to assume they're piranhas.

A campfire is burning near the lake's shore. The flames crackle and dance, shooting sparks into the sky. Three human-shaped figures are resting beside it. Judging by their bizarre outfits, they aren't NPCs. One of them appears to be dressed as a medieval knight. I suspect they're the three travelers who recently escaped from the goats. One of the humans catches sight of me, and they all jump to their feet. Kat isn't among them. If she were, she'd have recognized my avatar by now, and these guys aren't exactly rushing up to greet me. I can see someone has gathered a pile of rocks to be used as weapons if necessary. Apparently they've learned how dangerous it is to let down your guard in Otherworld. And like me, they won't be making the same mistake again.

I play it as safe as possible. As I make my way down the slope toward the lake, I raise my hands over my head. "I come in peace!" I shout. Even in Otherworld it sounds unbelievably hokey, but it's the only thing I can think of to say.

The three huddle together for a moment. I suppose they're discussing my fate. Then the decision appears to be made. A figure in a Grim Reaper–style robe and an ogre-size man with tattooed skin stay put while the avatar dressed as a red knight climbs the slope to meet me. The visor of his helmet is up, and his scarlet cape billows around him as he walks. He's wearing a chain mail

shirt beneath his red tunic. The dude really geeked out back at
setup. My guess is he's taken part in a few role-playing games in
his day. There's a sword at his side, but his hand is nowhere near
the hilt. It seems reckless, if you ask me. I could send my dagger
sailing into one of his eyeballs before he could draw the weapon
from its scabbard.

"I'm Arkan." The voice coming from inside the helmet is
brusque and emotionless. Arkan is a strange name for a knight. I
was expecting something much fancier. But his attitude matches
the outfit. He strikes me as the kind of guy who likes to fight.
"Who are you?" he asks.

"Simon," I say, offering him a hand, which the knight ignores.
"I arrived at the White City earlier today."

"The White City?" Arkan asks as if he doesn't know it.

His response throws me for a moment. "You know—the city
with all the white buildings," I say. "Isn't that where you started?"

"Oh, right," says Arkan. "Yeah. We left yesterday."

I'm about to ask why they left when I happen to glance down
at his sword. It doesn't look real. "Is that *plastic*?" I ask. Someone
sure pulled a dud out of the goody box.

Arkan takes off his helmet, which somehow doesn't seem to
weigh as much as it should. Beneath it is a handsome, square-
jawed head with a thatch of blond hair. I feel a jolt of recognition.
I've seen this avatar somewhere before.

"What difference does it make if it's plastic?" the knight asks.

I don't even know how to begin answering that question.

"Where are you going?" he asks.

"I don't really know," I tell him, figuring honesty might be the
best policy for the moment. "I'm looking for a girl."

Before I can say any more, Arkan's eyes widen. "Follow me," he orders, heading down the hill toward the other two avatars. A burst of hope pushes me after him. Then I pause. Below, the ogre now has rocks in both of his hands. The other figure has disappeared.

"Are you sure your buddies are as friendly as you are?" I ask.

Arkan doesn't answer, but I decide to head after him anyway. I can't really hold his companions' behavior against them. If one of my friends had recently been eaten, I'd be a little defensive, too.

When we reach the bottom, Arkan and the ogre stand facing me. Then a woman with ginger hair appears beside them. The cloak she's wearing must render her invisible whenever the hood is up.

"He's looking for a girl," Arkan announces as if it's proof of something.

The woman glances up at the ogre, who towers over the rest of us. He's wearing a loincloth made from hide, and every inch of his exposed flesh is decorated with intricate tribal tattoos. Yet his face, with its flat nose and giant amber eyes, seems oddly chubby and juvenile.

The ogre shrugs and the woman looks back at me. I'm not sure they know what Arkan's getting at either. Then the woman sticks out a hand to me. The skin is buttery soft, but the grip is surprisingly firm. "Hey there, I'm Carole." She has a sugary voice and a Southern accent. Her avatar's face is freckled and pretty, with laugh lines around her eyes. "That's Gorog." She gestures toward the hulk. He drops his rocks and raises a callused hand in a half-wave.

"Simon," I say. "So you guys came from the White City too?"

My question seems to confuse Carole and Gorog.

"He says that's the name of the place where we started," Arkan says.

"Really? I didn't know it had a name." Carole smiles, but she seems on edge. "So who's this girl you're looking for?"

"A friend of mine. I'm here to help her."

"Is she dead?" Gorog blurts out. Carole sighs wearily.

"What? No!" What kind of question is that? "She's not dead."

"Are *you* dead?" Gorog demands.

"Of course not!" This conversation just took a turn for the weird, and I'm starting to worry.

"Are you sure?" Arkan follows up.

"Yeah, I'm *positive*. How in the hell can I be dead if I'm standing here talking to you?"

My response doesn't appear to please Arkan. He throws his helmet down and stomps off toward the campfire, which he kicks at repeatedly before dropping miserably to the ground beside it.

"Your friend's got a little rage problem. What was that all about?" I ask the other two.

Carole grimaces. "Arkan thinks he's dead. He's convinced that this place is some sort of afterlife."

"But why would he think . . . ," I start to ask, and then I realize I already know the answer. They're taking part in the Company's disk beta test, just like Kat. But Arkan doesn't know it—none of them do. Something happened to their real-world bodies, and they woke up in the White City without any explanation. Given the circumstances, it's perfectly understandable that someone might mistake this place for the afterworld. I just hope Kat was eavesdropping when Martin and Todd explained the White City to me. Otherwise, she's probably just as confused.

"You aren't dead," I inform Carole.

"Well, thank sweet baby Jesus for that," Carole says with a snort. "I *told* Arkan this wasn't what the Good Lord had in store for me."

"We're not in heaven?" Gorog asks. He sounds curious, but he doesn't seem quite as concerned as his fellow travelers. I get the feeling he's itching for adventure.

Carole glares at the ogre. "We watched Orin get eaten yesterday evening. If you think this could be heaven, you're just as crazy as Arkan." She turns back to me. "So where are we?"

The answer to that particular question might make their heads explode. I'm going to have to work up to it. "You don't have any idea how you got here, do you?"

"Nope," Carole confirms. "All I remember is driving up I-95 and then suddenly, *poof!* I'm in crazy town."

"I was on my bike," Gorog tells me. "There was a crash and a lot of people talking and then I woke up in some weird changing room. What happened?"

I'm not sure they're going to find the truth very comforting, but I try to explain. "It sounds like you were both injured in accidents. Now you're taking part in an experimental therapy. There's a disk attached to the back of your skulls. Your bodies are probably in a hospital, but the disk is telling your brains you're somewhere else."

"Somewhere *else*?" Carole asks. "Like *where*? What is this place?"

"The town where we started is called the White City. But once you leave, you're in something called Otherworld. The Company created the software for both the White City and Otherworld, and for some reason they connected them."

"You're saying we're in *the* Otherworld?" Gorog asks. All I can do is nod.

Carole seems too stunned to speak, but Gorog's started spinning around like he's just landed in Oz.

"Daaammn!" he exclaims. "This is *Otherworld*?"

"Yeah, it came as a shock to me, too," I say.

"Otherworld?" Carole asks.

Gorog's too excited to stop and explain. "Oh, man, I would have done *anything* for Otherworld gear. But do you know how much that shit costs? Like *three thousand* dollars! I mean, how's someone like me ever gonna get his hands on three thousand dollars? It's not fair! I even tweeted at Milo Yolkin about it. I figured he'd understand my pain if anyone would. But the dude hasn't replied to a tweet in months."

Carole lays a hand on my arm to draw my attention away from the raving hulk. "Are you telling me we're in some kind of *game*?" she asks, her brow furrowed as if she's trying hard to understand. "I had a PlayStation back in the day, and there was nothing on it like this."

"This is very advanced virtual reality," I tell her. "There's never been anything like the disk before."

Carole's hand flies up to the back of her neck. "I don't feel any disk," she says.

"You can't feel it while you're here, and you can't take it off by yourself," I tell her.

"So what—we're stuck in this place?" She's gone from curious to practically panic-stricken. "I've gotta get back to the real world! I've got to find a way out of here!"

"I'm not sure that's such a great idea. Your body may be"—I struggle for the right word—"damaged. The friend I came here to find was in a very bad accident."

"I don't care if I'm broken in a million goddamn pieces. I am *not* watching another person get eaten by goats!" Carole yells. Can't say I blame her, but I don't like being shouted at.

"Then you should have stayed in the White City," I snap. "No one was going to get eaten there. You would have been perfectly safe."

"Sure," Carole says. "Until I threw myself off the top of one of those buildings. I stayed in that place for a week. I ate at every restaurant and had a pedicure every day. I've never been so miserable in my entire life."

"Yeah," Gorog adds. "I was pretty sure I was going to die of boredom."

"Besides, I had to find a way home. I have responsibilities," Carole goes on. "There are real people there who need me. I can't hang out in virtual reality with an ogre and a knight and . . ." She pauses while she looks me up and down. "What the hell are you supposed to be?"

"A Druid," I say.

"Perfect. And a *Druid*," she adds. "A Druid with a giant nose."

I'm seriously pissed off now. Not because this lady has the balls to insult my stunningly handsome avatar, but because an escort quest is *not* what I had in mind. I'm here to find Kat, not rescue every asshole who's stuck in Otherworld. I should get out of here—find some excuse to sneak away and leave them behind. But I can't—and that's what pisses me off most. What would I tell Kat when I found her? That I abandoned three random people to die? They're with me now whether I like it or not.

"All right, *fine,*" I say. "If you want to leave, I'll take you to the exit. Your gear should shut off when you pass through it. After that, if your body is able to move in real life, you'll be able to take off the disk. But just so you know, there's a powerful being guarding the Otherworld exit, and I'm not sure the four of us will be able to take him down."

"How do you know all this stuff?" Gorog asks. "How'd you find out about the exit?"

I'd rather not repeat the whole saga right now, so I keep my explanation simple. "My guide told me," I say.

"Your *guide*?" Carole asks. "Are we supposed to get guides?"

"*We* aren't," says Gorog. He's grinning down at me like he's just figured out my secret. "Only *the One* ever gets a guide. Neo had Morpheus. Luke Skywalker had Yoda. Harry Potter had Dumbledore. Ender had—"

"Gorog, what in *the hell* are you talking about?" Carole interrupts.

"Don't you watch any movies?" Gorog replies. "Simon must be the One. He was sent here to rescue us all."

"Like Jesus?" Carole asks. I get the feeling she's a big believer.

"Wait a second," I interject. "You just met me five minutes ago and now you think I'm the *what*?" I start laughing so hard I can't stop. Of all the shit that's been said about me in the past eighteen years, that is by far the funniest.

"Why's he laughing?" I hear Carole ask.

"That's how it works," Gorog informs her. "The One never believes he's the One."

"Stop, stop, stop!" I'm doubled over, howling with laughter. "I'm going to piss myself."

"What's going on over there?" I recognize Arkan's angry voice in the distance. "Are you guys making fun of me?"

I'm trying to stop laughing long enough to reply when Carole shushes me. "Don't tell Arkan what you told us," she warns me. "Not even the part about the exit."

"Why not?" I ask. Suddenly I don't feel like laughing anymore.

She taps her temple with her finger. "The boy ain't right."

"Hey!" Arkan shouts again.

"Nobody's talking about you!" Gorog shouts back. "I made a joke about Simon being like Neo from *The Matrix*."

"You mean the One?" Arkan yells, but this time the anger in his voice is gone. "That scrawny loser's not *the One*."

Crazy or not, I have to agree with him. I can't be the One, because there's no way in hell I'd be helping these dumbasses if it weren't for Kat.

DREDGING THE GOWANUS

Carole was right about Arkan. The guy's totally nuts. And his sword really is plastic. When my three new companions passed through the White City's gates, they were offered a choice of weapon or tool, just as I was. Gorog opted for fire. Carole went with an invisibility cloak. And Arkan chose *nothing*. The plastic sword apparently came with his knight costume.

He told the others that a weapon "wouldn't make any difference 'cause we're already dead." And as goats were eating their friend, he assured Carole and Gorog that they shouldn't interfere because "it was all meant to be."

Yet despite his rather serious mental health issues, Arkan turns out to be quite resourceful. Before sunset, he used his cape as a net and caught fish for our dinner. His helmet became our water bucket and his shield became the skillet on which he sautéed our fish, which—I have to say—were beautifully cooked. The meal filled me up, but somehow it didn't put an end to my hunger pangs. I hope the food does my avatar some good. Somewhere, beneath the surface, I can feel my body in the real world begging for more.

After dinner, Arkan laid out his theory about this so-called afterlife we're all sharing. We're in purgatory, he says—the waiting room between heaven and hell. His belief is so powerful that he might have convinced me if I didn't know better. I would have set him straight, but Carole caught my eye whenever I opened my mouth. I understand her concern. Arkan's illusions are all he has left. There's no telling what could happen if one of us was to destroy them.

Soon the sky is dark and the others are resting. Even in Otherworld, the brain needs to power down several hours every evening. I lie beside the campfire and rest my eyes for a minute. I figure it's probably a good idea to stay awake in case any more man-eating goats come sniffing around. I don't plan to sleep, but I do. And in my dream I find Kat.

I'm back in the real world, which somehow seems far less real after a day in Otherworld. I'm looking down at Kat from the hole in the floor at Elmer's. She's sitting with her back against the wall, Solo cup in hand, staring into space. It's the night of the party, but this time there's no one else around—just the two of us separated by a rotting wooden floor. I can see now what I couldn't before. She's neither drunk nor high. She's thinking. And I know the answers I need are bouncing around in her head.

"She's a looker," a man says. "I always had a thing for wild hair like that too. I hope this girl's worth the trouble. A lot of 'em aren't, you know."

The stench hits me before I see its source. The smell is a

bouquet of raw sewage, gasoline and a dozen industrial pollutants I couldn't begin to identify. There's a man standing beside me. The rancid water streaming off him has gathered in a pool at his feet. The light inside the factory is too dim to make out his features, but his profile is unmistakable. The Kishka has risen from the bottom of Brooklyn's Gowanus Canal to star in my dream.

"Her name is Kat," I tell my grandfather, making him the first member of my family who's ever heard me say her name out loud. "I'm here because she's in trouble."

"So was the lady who got me into this mess," he says, holding his arms out as if to show off the revolting state of his suit. Then he lets them drop. "Wasn't her fault, though. I was thinking with my kishka. And not this one," he says, tapping his nose. "The *bigger* one." He stops, and I can tell he's no longer joking. "You know what you're doing?"

"No clue," I admit. I haven't had much time to think things through.

My grandfather pulls a pack of Lucky Strikes from the pocket of his suit. When his Zippo won't produce a flame and the cigarettes are too wet to light, he tosses everything out the window.

"So let me see if I understand what's going on," he says. I'm eager to hear what a gangster from the 1960s makes of Otherworld, but he doesn't seem very interested in virtual reality. "A bunch of kids got killed at that factory, and the cops are calling it an accident. Then the people who survived get hooked up to some kind of machine and sent away. The machine's supposed to let them play with bunnies and butterflies, but people end up getting eaten by goats instead. I got this straight?"

"Yeah," I tell him. "Pretty much."

My grandfather whistles appreciatively. "If I were a betting man—and believe me, I am—I'd bet that collapse was no accident. Somebody must have wanted those kids out of the way."

"I know," I say, though it's the first time I've actually voiced my suspicions. "They were targeted."

"I know you know," he tells me. He's right. I'm not having a conversation with a dead gangster I've never met. I'm talking to myself. "Question is—what are you planning to do about it?"

I shrug. "Not much I can do," I tell him. "I'm out of the way now too." Someone sent me the disk and I jumped right into Otherworld without thinking. Maybe the person was trying to help me. Maybe they wanted to get rid of me. At this point, it's impossible to know.

"You followed your gut," the Kishka says. "You did the right thing."

"You mean coming here to rescue Kat?"

My grandfather snorts. "You and I both know that girl can take care of herself. She's been to Otherworld. She knows where she is by now. And half the time in these games, she's the one saving *your* ass. That's not why you need to find her."

"What do you mean?" I ask.

"She saw what happened the night of the collapse. She knows what was thrown down to the second floor—and she probably knows who threw it. You want to do something for her? Figure out who put her in the hospital in the first place."

"How?"

"Are you kidding me? She's here somewhere. Just find her and *ask* her."

I open my eyes. The night is pitch-black. The designers seem to have forgotten to add a moon. There are only stars above. They appear to be laid out in patterns, but as far as I can tell, they don't match any of the constellations I've seen from Earth.

I hear a sniffle and then a muffled sob. One of my new companions is crying. I can't be positive, but it sounds like Arkan. Maybe he doesn't like being dead after all.

THE RESORT OF THE FUTURE

I wake up again as the sun rises. The others are sleeping soundlessly. Carole's body is wrapped in her cloak. Arkan's shield is covering his face, and Gorog has curled up in a giant ball. There's no breeze and everything around me is perfectly still. It's as if the world has frozen. Then I hear a splash from the lake. The silver fish must be jumping, I think. But when I sit up to watch, I'm startled to see a girl treading water near the bank.

Her face is human, I'm relieved to discover, and her long black hair floats on the surface around her. I can make out her slender, bare arms undulating beneath the water. It's hard to imagine she's wearing a swimsuit.

I stand up and walk toward her, careful to keep a safe distance between us. I know better than to trust a pretty face here—and I have no intention of being dragged in and drowned. Her skin grows a hot red as I approach; then she dips her head beneath the water, and a small puff of steam escapes into the atmosphere.

A silver fish tail slaps the surface of the water. When the fish girl appears again, her cooled skin is the color of pale-gray slate.

"Wake the others," she tells me, her voice soft as if she's sharing a secret. "There's a swarm heading this way. I can hear it approaching. It will be here in a matter of hours."

I listen for a moment, but I hear nothing. "A swarm of what?"

"Flying insects," she says. "They have no name. They were designed to pollinate the flowers of a distant realm, but they flew away. I do not know how they survive while they're in the wastelands. I only know that they are not what the Creator intended."

Sounds familiar. "Lemme guess . . . now they drink blood instead of nectar," I say.

"No," the girl says. "They are not interested in our guests or their blood. They fly from one end of Otherworld to the other, and they let nothing stand in their way. As they pass, they will enter and fill your body's every opening. You'll suffocate moments before your carcass explodes."

Holy shit. Otherworld has invented another delightful way to go.

The girl sinks beneath the water and surfaces again. "You must reach Imra before the insects overtake you. Look for the highest peak on the horizon. On top, you'll find the entrance to the city."

"How far is it?" I ask.

"It's close enough. If you leave soon, you'll stand a chance of survival."

That doesn't sound terribly encouraging. I'd rather have more than just a *chance*. I'm about to jump up and wake the others when I realize I'm taking advice from a naked fish girl who lives in a pond.

"Are you one of the Children?" I ask.

"I am the Creator's daughter," she answers frankly.

I have no idea what that really means, but I guess I'll take that as a yes. "The last Child I met liked to eat people like me. So why should I trust you? How do I know you're not sending me into some kind of trap?"

"Your friend asked me to help you if you passed this way. She wanted me to let you know that she's alive and on her way to the glacier. She will wait for you there."

Some kind of chemical floods my brain and for a moment I'm high on it. I know who the fish girl is talking about, but I still ask, "What friend?"

"The female in a camouflage suit that blends into anything. She said a male dressed like a peasant might come after her."

Kat. She was listening when I told her I'd find her. And it sounds like she chose the same avatar she used when we explored Otherworld for the first time. The camouflage is battle attire. Even during setup inside the White City, Kat knew she'd be in danger. But the girl in the pond just said two things that give me hope. The Clay Man was right—Kat's heading for the glacier. And her trip must be going okay so far if she took the time to knock my avatar.

"I'm not a peasant. I'm a Druid," I correct the fish girl.

"It makes no difference to me. Your companions are lucky I was able to recognize you. I do not let guests take shelter near my lake. Your friend was the first guest I've spared."

"Why did you let *her* live?" I ask.

"When she spoke, she wasn't like the others. She knows this isn't a game, and she agrees that your kind does not belong here.

I let her live because she promised to speak to my father. She will convince him to banish all humans from Otherworld and leave the land to the Elementals, the Beasts and the Children."

What the *hell*? Kat's supposed to be heading for the exit, not setting off on some grand mission. "I thought you just said my friend was on her way to the glacier. Now you're telling me she's looking for *the Creator*? Which is it?"

"Both," says the girl. "She must speak to him before she leaves."

"Okay, well, what if my friend can't find your Creator and convince him to banish the guests?" I ask.

"Then there will be war," the girl says simply. "It's already begun."

She slips silently into the water and does not surface again. It's probably my imagination, but my ears detect a faint buzzing in the distance.

Six hours of walking, and we finally saw signs of Imra. I knew it was on the top of a goddamn mountain, but I'd forgotten how high that mountain peak happened to be. But where else would you expect your safe haven to be when you're being chased by a suffocating swarm of insects? By the halfway point, I was almost wishing I was dead anyway. Though Arkan never stopped assuring us that none of it was real, the black swarm eventually appeared on the horizon, and I almost found myself feeling a little nostalgic for the goats. Compared to having every orifice filled with flying insects, being eaten seemed like a noble way to go.

Now, at the top of the mountain, I'm struck by déjà vu. We're standing outside the same gates where I began my first adventure in Otherworld. Back then, I was blown away by how real everything seemed. But after witnessing the glorious architecture of the White City, I'm feeling a little *meh* about this place. The gates open for us, and we set off down one of the streets. The buildings we pass remind me of college dorms. There are no shops or businesses of any kind—just row after row of bland brick structures. I've heard rumors that Imra's a digital Sodom, but all those whispers must have been wrong. I'm fairly confident that nothing interesting has ever happened here.

We don't walk far before we start seeing NPCs. I scan every face, just in case Kat made a detour on her way to the glacier, but I'm pretty sure there's not an avatar among them. Most of the NPCs are Photoshop good-looking, with creamy skin, gleaming hair and rock-hard glutes. They're all dressed like extras in a vodka commercial. Meanwhile, the dense black cloud of insects is so close now that its buzzing has built to a roar. While the residents here don't seem terribly perturbed, I can't help but notice that the streets are quickly emptying.

One of the few NPCs still left outside is approaching us. Her sensible low-heeled pumps click and her hips sway as she walks. She's clearly a resident. No human being would willingly choose an avatar this bland. Her dark hair is pulled back in a bun, and she's wearing a navy skirt suit and a white button-down shirt. A name tag identifies her as Margot.

"Hello!" She smiles warmly, showing the perfect number of teeth to communicate genuine delight at our sudden appearance. "Are you looking for Imra?"

"This isn't it?" I ask.

Margot chuckles in a way that says she's laughing *with*

me, rather than *at* me. "Not quite. But you're almost there! Follow me."

She keeps talking after her back is turned toward us, but the insects' buzzing has grown deafening, and I can't make out a single word. One of the bugs' advance guards lands on my ear. I capture it between my fingers. It's like a little black ladybug, and I'd probably call it cute if it didn't want to invade all my openings. A second insect grazes my nose, and I feel a jolt of panic. We need to find shelter as quickly as possible.

Carole is clearly thinking the same thing. "Hey, do you think we can get where we're going a little bit faster?" I hear her shout at Margot's back.

I don't catch her response, but Margot breaks into an effortless jog. We run behind her for what feels like miles, past more identical buildings, until we reach a large square that seems like it must be the center of town. Where you'd ordinarily expect to find a fountain or statue, there's a giant glass box instead. A door slides open and the four of us follow Margot inside. The box is big enough to fit a hundred large avatars comfortably. The door shuts and seals just as the insects close in around us. I double over with relief as millions of tiny bodies splatter against the glass while the sun dims and then disappears.

"Everyone feeling good?" Margot asks cheerfully, as if nothing potentially life-threatening had just taken place. "I guess that's *our* exercise for today!"

Carole collapses to the floor and Gorog joins her. "Are you sure this isn't real?" Carole groans. "'Cause I'm pretty sure I'm having a heart attack."

"Real?" Margot looks confused. "Of course it's real."

"It's not real." Arkan is panting, but he still manages to force the words out. The dude's got a one-track mind.

"How long are we going to have to stay in this box?" Gorog asks anxiously. I'd like to know, too. The claustrophobia is starting to kick in.

"Just a few more moments," Margot assures him. And it does seem as if some light is beginning to filter through the swarm. Then I watch as a chandelier rises from the floor, and I realize we've been descending into an underground space.

We come to an abrupt stop and the side of the glass box slides open again. A wave of hot air washes over us. "Welcome to Imra!" Margot exclaims.

Usually I'd find such boundless enthusiasm nauseating, but in this case it's warranted. A wide red velvet carpet stretches out in front of us, spiraling around the interior of what appears to be the cone of a massive volcano. Chandelier-like streetlamps light the way, which is lined with stately buildings, their marble façades riddled with classy nude statues and ornate columns. It's probably what Monte Carlo would look like if ancient Greeks had constructed it. A fence with a single rail runs along the left side of the walkway. It's the only thing preventing pedestrians from plummeting over the edge and down into the glowing pool of lava that spits and churns below. As the son of two lawyers, I feel the urge to warn my hosts that they're running the risk of a billion personal injury lawsuits, but Carole finds her tongue first.

"If this is Imra, where did we just come from?"

"We call the surface village the suburbs," Margot responds with another hearty laugh, and I want to punch the dork who designed her. "That's where our residents live. The city of Imra houses only guests. It's beautiful, safe and all-inclusive. We like to think of it as the Resort of the Future."

"Where is everybody?" Carole pushes further. "The place looks totally empty."

"We just opened a few weeks ago," Margot explains. "There's a small, select group staying with us at the moment, but don't you worry—the crowds will be showing up soon! The city was built to be perfectly scalable. Right now we have space for ten thousand guests, but we plan to host millions someday! Now, what do you say—shall I show you around? I think you'll find we have something for everyone here in Imra. The Creator designed it to be the ultimate welcome station for our guests."

Margot doesn't actually wait for our response, and I'm getting the sense that the tour may not be totally optional. The glass elevator that brought us here is already rising back to the surface, and from where we're standing, the walkway only leads in a single direction. Then Margot pulls open a pair of golden doors to our right, revealing a room that has waterfalls for walls. They feed a pool that's large enough to Jet Ski across.

"Wow," Gorog marvels. Then his eyes immediately shoot toward Arkan. "Yeah, yeah. I know it's not real."

"Maybe not," I say, wiping the mist from my brow as I walk into the room. Gorog and Carole enter alongside me. "But you gotta admit it's doing a pretty good impression of *real*." Upholstered lounge chairs are lined up along the edge, and palm trees bristling with sweet brown dates grow out of massive planters. Stationed at regular intervals are attractive young men and women in white uniforms.

"This is one of our many spa rooms," Margot says, joining

us at the edge of the pool. "Guests like you often stop here first for a refreshing swim or massage. Our therapists can provide any style of bodywork you desire. Should you wish to update your avatar, there are facilities available for that here, too. Many of our guests prefer to assume a more conventional appearance in Imra. It makes certain things . . . easier."

I see her give Gorog a once-over. She clearly thinks he could use a few improvements.

"Huh?" The ogre blushes when he notices her looking at him. "No thanks, I'm good."

Where are all the other guests that Margot keeps talking about? I wonder. There's no one here. I'm about to make a joke about everyone choosing to be invisible when I actually spot someone on the other side of the pool. It's a naked man lying facedown on one of the lounge chairs. His head and left arm are hanging off the side.

Gorog sees him too. "Look—that guy must have died of happiness."

"Oh, no," Margot assures us. She doesn't seem to know it was a joke. "His avatar wouldn't be here if he were dead."

"We're all dead," says Arkan.

Margot smiles at him brightly. "You aren't dead," she corrects the knight. "That seems to be a common misconception these days. We've had a few guests lately who assumed that this was some kind of afterworld. But I assure you all, you're very much alive. This is Otherworld."

There's silence while all eyes turn to the red knight. There's no telling how he's going to respond to the news. Carole's gotta be pissed as hell. She's done everything she can to keep the truth from Arkan, and Margot's just gone and blurted it out.

"Otherworld?" Arkan repeats. "Isn't that a game?" Inside his good-looking head is a brain in full meltdown.

Carole quickly jumps in to change the subject. "You know, if that guy over there on the lounge chair isn't dead, he must be pretty wasted," she tells Margot. "Someone should help him find a room."

Margot shakes her head vigorously. "Oh, no. We're not allowed to interfere. The world you came from is governed by laws and rules and social conventions, but Imra was built to offer a safe haven from such things. The guests in Imra are free to do as they will. None of us are here to judge. You spend so much time and effort fighting your instincts in your world. Well, we're here to tell you it's okay—you can relax for a while," she says, still revoltingly chipper. "So! Any of you tempted to get a rubdown or go for a plunge?"

Carole and Gorog turn to me, confusion written all over their faces. We came to Imra to hide from a swarm of killer bugs and now we're being offered bodywork.

"No?" Our tour guide seems a bit disappointed, as if our comfort were her personal responsibility. "Well, then anyone hungry?"

We leave the spa and Margot leads us farther down the spiral path to a second building. The smell of roasted meat nearly knocks me to my knees before I even step inside. My mouth begins to water and my stomach groans miserably. I have no idea how many hours have passed since my body back in the real world had its last meal. The others don't seem to be quite as affected, and I realize that wherever they are, their bodies must be hooked up to IVs that prevent them from starving. But I need something in my stomach before I move on.

My nose leads me through the building's marble foyer and into a sumptuous banquet hall under a domed roof. There are hundreds of beautifully set tables, but almost all remain empty. In the center, residents in chefs' coats and hats are tending to three monstrous beasts that are roasting on spits. Smoke from the fires twists upward like a vine toward a vent in the ceiling.

"Have you ever tried buffalo?" Margot asks the group. I haven't, but right now I want to more than anything in the world. "Our guests rate it very highly."

"Guess we're taking a little break," Gorog remarks as I pull out a chair at one of the tables. Before my ass can slide into the seat, a resident sets a plate in front of me. Ignoring the utensils that have been provided, I dig into the meat piled high in the center. And it is *divine*. In fact, it's the best stuff I've ever eaten. I smell it and taste it and feel the grease it leaves between my fingertips. I wash the meat down with the beer someone hands me, which leaves my brain buzzing, and keep shoveling buffalo into my mouth.

I hear Carole *tsk*. "I see *someone* forgot their table manners," she drawls.

"No judgments," Margot trills.

When I glance up from the bone I'm gnawing, I realize that Carole wasn't talking about me. There's a couple sitting about ten tables over. Empty plates are piled up around them, and the floor near their table is ankle-deep in bones. The woman, a blonde in a Grace Kelly dress, picks up her latest plate and licks it clean. When it's a sparkling white, she puts it on top of the stack and one of the residents places a full plate in front of her.

Arkan is heading toward them, his armor clanking. "Emma?"

he calls, but the woman doesn't acknowledge him. She's holding another plate to her face when he reaches her.

"Stop eating!" He grabs the plate and hurls it to the floor, where it shatters.

"No judgments," Margot chirps for the second time.

Arkan bends forward to examine the woman's face. "Not Emma," he mutters, and then stomps away.

"Gorog, what in the hell are you doing?" I hear Carole whisper angrily.

"Getting this all on camera," the ogre responds.

My eyes turn to Gorog, and I find him aiming the camera of a tablet-size device in my direction. I can't figure out where he got it, until I see there's one at every place setting. Which seems unbelievably strange.

"Stop," I demand with my mouth full. I reach out a hand to snatch the device.

"Too late," says Gorog as I take it away. "I already sent the video to everyone you know."

I'm about to kick his ass when I remember that he doesn't actually know anyone I know. "Hilarious," I try to say, and end up choking instead.

"What's the deal with all the cameras, anyway?" Gorog asks Margot.

"If you don't record your fun, how do you know for sure that it happened?" Margot jokes. Or at least, I think she's joking. "Our guests like to share their experiences in Imra with their friends and family back at home—and we encourage them to do so. It's excellent publicity for Otherworld."

I'd love to make a snarky comment, but I'm too busy chewing to think one up. I finish the last bit of food on my plate and find a new one in front of me. I should stop, but I can't.

"Dude," says Gorog. "Your avatar is going to explode."

"Now, now," Margot chides. "He's just enjoying himself. If the rest of you aren't hungry, why don't I show you a little bit more of Imra, and your friends can catch up with you later."

"Friends?" Something seems to have set off an alarm in Carole's head. "Wait a second. Where's Arkan?" she asks. I glance around the room. While Gorog was filming, the red knight disappeared. "Hang tight," Carole tells me. "We're going to go find him."

I'm still chewing as they rush away.

I have no idea how much time has passed—or how many plates I've been through. I feel a bit fuller than I did when I got here, but if anything, the need to eat has only grown. My hands simply aren't fast enough to deliver the food to my face. I'm on the verge of getting rid of my five-fingered middlemen and lifting the plate straight up to my lips when I notice that Carole's returned. She's standing a few feet away, staring right at me.

"You've got to come with me," she demands.

"In a little while," I tell her. "I'm still starving."

"No. *Now,*" she insists. "Arkan's in trouble."

"Get Gorog to help," I say, annoyed that I have to stop chewing long enough to speak. "He's bigger than I am." I don't bother to add that I never liked Arkan much anyway.

"Gorog *is* helping. He's keeping that robot lady busy while I come to get you."

"Margot isn't really a robot," I say. "She's a—"

"I don't give a damn what she is!" Carole shouts so loudly that even my fellow diners look up. How long have *they* been here, I wonder uncomfortably. She lowers her voice and continues. I notice that she's trembling. "This place isn't right. There are strange things happening here. Get up," she orders.

"I don't know if I can," I tell her honestly.

She puts her hands on her hips and her nostrils flare. "You said you came to this place for a reason. What is it?" she demands. "Do you even remember?"

"To find Kat," I mutter with a mouthful of buffalo. The words mean something, but I can't seem to put it together.

"That's right. You came all this way to find your friend, and now you're just going to sit here in this resort from hell eating virtual meat? Your friend could be three doors down from here, and you'd never even know it. Are you in love with this girl or what?"

I never said anything about being in love with Kat. But what other reason would I have for being here? Carole's words cut through all the knots that were keeping me tied to my seat. I glance down at the pile of food on the plate in front of me. It's fake meat made from fantasy beasts. But it's been my sole obsession for what might have been hours now—hours that I could have spent going after Kat. And yet, even now, I crave it. My fingers are aching to snatch one more piece. And that urge is terrifying. This is what Otherworld does to you, I realize. It gives you what you want. The only way I'll make it through is if I remind myself that there's something I want much more than anything else. I want to find Kat.

I push my chair back and stand. I think I'm hungrier now than

I was when I sat down, but somehow I summon the willpower to make my way across the room to the exit. Outside, Carole and I pass dozens of open doors as we wind our way down the red spiral path, deeper and deeper into the volcano. There are gambling rooms decorated like Vegas casinos that have drawn reasonable crowds—and nightclubs that are practically empty. I can't understand why some of the rooms are so much more popular than others—until the answer hits me. I should have figured it out from the start. Most of the guests here aren't from the White City. They're wearing a headset and playing a game. They don't have disks attached to the back of their skulls. The headset players can see Otherworld and throw dice with their haptic gloves, but they can't taste the food or feel the massages. And dancing in haptic booties, while totally possible, isn't much fun.

There's really no reason for parts of Imra to exist at all—unless they were designed for guests wearing disks. When I have a little more time on my hands, I'll have to figure out what that means.

"Come on," Carole urges me as I pause in front of a man slumped against the wall. "You're going to see a lot more of that where we're going." There's drool dripping from the side of the man's mouth. I assume he's drunk, which means he's got to be wearing a disk.

When I turn to follow Carole, I step on something. It rolls beneath my foot and I lose my balance and fall against the railing. We're much closer to the lava now, and I can feel its heat radiating upward.

"What the . . . ," I mumble, picking up the object that nearly sent me plummeting into the flames. It's an empty syringe. It didn't occur to me until now, but I guess if the disk can make your brain taste buffalo, it can mimic the effects of your favorite drug, too.

"Watch yourself. They've got a bit of a litter problem here at the Last Resort," Carole jokes grimly.

That's an understatement, I learn as we continue down the spiral path. Bottles and Baggies and cigarette butts are everywhere. Imra has been open for less than a month, but it already looks like hell on St. Patrick's Day.

"This is it." Carole has stopped at a pair of open doors. Smoke pours from the entrance like a fast-rolling fog. She takes one of my arms and together we forge inside. The waiters and waitresses must be navigating by echolocation, because the place is too dimly lit to see clearly. But I get the sense that the room is a maze of leather chairs and masculine furniture. Before he wrote me off as a lost cause, my dad once took me to the Harvard Club in Manhattan. This is what his fancy-ass club would look like if its members were Hells Angels and Russian gangsters. Milo Yolkin famously attended Harvard for all of three weeks before he dropped out. If this is his idea of a joke, I think the two of us would get along beautifully.

I wonder how many guests are actually in the club. You'd definitely need a disk to appreciate this section of Imra—unless you're here for the scantily clad waitstaff. The waitress in front of us appears to be missing most of her skirt. She disappears suddenly, yanked into a banquette by an unseen hand. I guess that means there's at least one person here who's enjoying the wares. Now I'm stepping over two bodies that lie sprawled on the floor. Just beyond them, a man in red armor is sitting on a stool with his head slumped down on the bar.

"He won't get up," Carole explains.

"Hey there, buddy," I say, doing my best to speak bro as I pull out the stool beside Arkan. "What's going on?"

"Why can't I find her? Why isn't she here?" the knight slurs.

"Who are you trying to find?" Carole asks. "Tell us. Maybe we can help."

"You wouldn't know her." He's not just drunk, he's absolutely shitfaced. He must have been working pretty hard to achieve this level of intoxication. He couldn't have been at the bar for more than a couple of hours.

"Come on," I try again. "This isn't a good place to take a nap." I can only imagine what horrible things might happen to someone who passed out in a place like this. I feel eyes on us, and I turn around. Three men have claimed chairs nearby. The hulking avatars seem pretty damn menacing. And I remember what the Clay Man once told me—the most dangerous creatures in Otherworld are the guests.

"I'm never leaving," Arkan whispers to the bar.

I lean closer to his ear. "I know how to find the exit," I say. "I can get you out of here. You can go back home and find the girl you're looking for."

"Go away," he says.

Carole groans. "What do you think?" she asks. "Should we let him sleep it off?"

I'm tempted to abandon the knight and let him stay on his barstool. The man's clearly got problems that can't be solved by sending him back to the real world.

"We can't leave him here," I say with a sigh. "It's not safe."

"Why not?" Carole asks. "You said this is a game. What's the worst that could happen?"

I don't want to tell her, but she deserves to know. "If we were wearing headsets like most of the people here, Otherworld would just be a game. But we're not players. We're guinea pigs. The disk technology we're testing is totally new. I don't know what would happen if one of our avatars was injured or died. When I first got here, my guide warned me to protect my life. He said I might not get another."

Carole grabs me by the arms. I can feel each of her fingertips pressing into my flesh. "Oh, dear God, please tell me you're joking," she pleads. I shake my head. "You mean we could really die in this hellhole? I could be eaten by a goddamn goat and never see my family or friends again?"

"I don't know," I admit.

For a second Carole looks like she might burst into tears. Then she grabs one of Arkan's arms. "Take the other one," she orders. "We've got to get him out of here."

We manage to drag Arkan through the club and out to the walkway. He's remarkably heavy for a bunch of code. Carole is struggling under his arm, so we set him down by the wall. I'm catching my breath when I spot Gorog approaching us with the widest smile I've ever seen.

"*Dude,*" he says. "You are not going to believe what they've got on the lowest level." Then he glances nervously at Carole.

"Give me a break," Carole snaps. "I'm not your mom. You think I haven't seen a few things in my day?"

"I'm pretty sure you've never seen anything like this," Gorog says, growing bolder. "It's like a giant orgy down there. I'd bet there's a thousand people at least, and a bunch of them are going at it like . . ." He looks over at Carole again, bites his lip and grins maniacally.

Carole rolls her eyes. "And yet you came back to hang out with us?" she says. "How *sweet* of you. Now make yourself useful and help us with Arkan."

The ogre comes to us and hoists the knight over his shoulder fireman-style. "For your information, I've been *very* useful today. While you guys were paying for Arkan's beer, I found the way out of Imra. Margot's waiting for us."

"Margot," Carole groans. "I thought you were going to give Robo-Concierge the slip."

"Easier said than done," says Gorog. "She says the boss here has one last offer to make before we go."

"Two free nights and a complimentary bottle of champagne?" I ask.

"And maybe a discount on an orgy?" Gorog adds enthusiastically.

Carole makes a barfing sound. "You two are hilarious," she drones. "Can we just get the hell out of here and go home?"

We follow Gorog to the bottom of the volcano, the knight's limp body flopping against the ogre's tattooed back. There are no streetlights down here, just the red glow that emanates from the pool of lava. Margot is waiting for us there with a smile plastered on her face and a tabletlike clipboard clutched in her hand. A spark from the molten rock lands in her hair, but she doesn't seem to notice.

"We'd like to check out now," I inform her.

"Not a problem," she replies. "I will pass your request on to Pomba Gira, but I have a quick customer service survey I'd like you to take first. Do you mind? I just need to call it up on the screen."

"Who's Pomba Gira?" Carole asks.

"She's the Elemental of Imra," Margot says absentmindedly as she taps away at the tablet. "She decides who leaves and who stays. Okay, here we are!" She looks up with another plastic smile. "We want to make sure that our guests have had a chance to enjoy themselves fully before they move on to other realms. The data you provide will help us optimize our offerings for future visitors. So how would you rate your experience in Imra?"

"Best day of our lives," I lie, figuring it's easiest to tell her what she wants to hear. "I keep wishing it will never end."

"Oh, excellent!" she replies. "And do you all agree?"

"Sure," Carole answers. Gorog grunts.

"That's wonderful," Margot says, entering the information into the tablet. "You know, there's no need for the day to end. You can stay here in Imra as long as you like. That's the whole idea!"

"We're just passing through," Carole says tersely.

"Of course." Margot's eyes drop back down to the screen. "And which parts of the resort did you find most appealing today? I know you were quite fond of the buffet," she says to me. "What about the rest of you?"

"The orgy," Gorog says.

Margot looks over at Carole. "Ditto," Carole drones.

"Great! Yes, that's a very popular part of Imra, we're already thinking of expanding. And was there anything you were hoping to find here that you didn't?"

"The way out," Carole tells her. "We'd like to see it now. We're done with your survey."

"Of course." Margot smiles, switches off the tablet screen and steps into the pool of lava. "Pomba Gira will be with you shortly," she says as she sinks beneath the surface.

"Wow. Think that could work for us?" Gorog asks, shifting the weight of the knight around on his shoulder. He leans forward over the bubbling red rock and immediately snaps his head back. "Nope, way too hot," he says, his cheeks as purple as plums.

"How long are we going to have to wait here for this Pomba Gira person?" Carole asks.

"I hope you're not expecting a person," I say. I've never seen an Otherworld Elemental before, but there are entire forums devoted to the ones from the original MMO. "The realms here are all ruled by Elementals. They're like demigods. So when this one shows up, it's probably a good idea to be on your best behavior."

"As long as she lets us out of here, I'll be sweet as pie," Carole says just as the lava begins to swirl and a column of flames rises from its center. Gradually the fire takes a female form and what can only be Pomba Gira appears before us. The Elemental's skin is the glistening black of charcoal, the hair that cascades over her shoulders is silvery smoke and the dress wrapped around her is ablaze.

"Whoa," says Gorog, and I have to agree. She may be burned to a crisp, but she's gorgeous. So *this* is the goat man's mother? He said he was the son of the Elemental of Imra. I'm gonna keep my mouth shut, but this lady could do *much* better than a goat.

"You wish to leave Imra?" Pomba Gira speaks softly, like a whisper you've barely heard. I would have expected an Elemental to have a huskier voice, but I have to admit there's more power in this. It makes you draw closer, as if she's the only one who knows what you need.

The ogre and I are struck dumb, and Carole rolls her eyes at us. "Yes, ma'am," she says. "It's been real fun and all. But as much as I'd love to do a bunch of drugs and take part in an orgy, I really need to get back to the real world. These guys and I never meant to stop in Imra. We were just trying to escape from some bugs. We're on our way to the Otherworld exit."

"The exit?" Pomba Gira repeats. She doesn't seem familiar with the word. "Very well. You and the ogre are free to leave. But this one." She crackles as she glides over to Arkan, who's still dangling over Gorog's shoulder. "Set him down. This one wants to stay in Imra with me."

"Are you kidding? He can't even stand up," Gorog says. But when he puts the knight down, Arkan remains upright on his own. Then his eyes open and fix on the Elemental's face.

"This is where you belong," she says.

"I do?" he asks woozily.

"Yes, I can see it," she whispers. Smoky tendrils of her hair sweep across Arkan's cheek like a caress.

"Naw, that's just the booze," I explain. "He'll sober up in a minute. He wants to find the exit more than anyone."

"No," the Elemental informs me. "That's not what the red knight is searching for. He knows that the thing he wants more than anything else is gone. I'm the only one who can return it to him."

The lava has begun to swirl again. And once again, the molten rock takes a female form. Only this time it cools into milky white flesh. Arkan seems to sober up in an instant. The noise that issues from his throat sounds like he's being strangled, and I see the knight drop to his knees at the feet of our host's latest creation.

"Oh, God, Emma. I'm so sorry," he sobs, wrapping his arms around the young woman's legs. She's the kind of plump, pretty blonde you'd see on a hot-chocolate box. And I suddenly realize I *have* seen her before.

It was a big story in northern New Jersey. A couple on their way home from a football game at Rutgers got into a fender bender. The man at the wheel of the first car jumped out and coldcocked the other driver, at which point the injured guy pulled a gun and began firing blindly. One of the bullets grazed the attacker's spinal cord. Another hit his girlfriend, who was waiting for him in the passenger seat of their car. She died on the spot.

The incident was all over the news, and there were plenty of pictures of the girl who had died—and her boyfriend, an avid supporter of the Rutgers Scarlet Knights who'd gone to the game dressed up like his team's mascot.

"I heard the ambulance guys talking before I went under. They said you were gone. When I woke up here in purgatory, I looked everywhere for you."

The girl opens her eyes and smiles down at Arkan and wordlessly smooths his hair with her hand.

Carole's practically blubbering, and Gorog looks a bit weepy too. I'm almost getting a little verklempt myself. At first I find it heartbreaking to see the two reunited in Otherworld, but then I realize the thing standing in front of us isn't the dead girl. It's just a digital doll that looks like Arkan's lost girlfriend. Maybe that's enough for him. He clearly thinks he's been given another chance, and I'm not going to tell him he's wrong. If it's that easy to fool him, he deserves to be stuck here.

"Now for you," Pomba Gira says, turning her attention to me. "I know what you want, too."

"Campaign finance reform?" I say to break the mood. "Consistent sizing in clothing store chains?" The question draws a blank look from the Elemental. "Okay, okay. Too much to ask. Then how about a glass of ice water?" I say. It's not really a joke. It's goddamn hot down here and I'm dying of thirst.

The lava has produced another female, just like I knew it would. As it cools, the skin turns tan, but the hair burns red. I was expecting her to appear, but the sight of Kat still takes my breath away. She looks exactly as I remember her, which makes perfect sense since the disk must have pulled this image out of my memory. The sight drags me in like a tractor beam.

"Who is that?" Gorog whispers to me. "She's amazing."

"It's the girl I came here to find," I tell him.

"No, it's not," Carole hisses in my ear. "It's one of those NPC things. You know that, right?"

I do. But against all my instincts, I take a step forward. "Hi," I say.

"Hi, Simon," she replies. She sounds like Kat. She smells like her. I take her hand, and she feels like Kat too. My heart is pounding, and I'm starting to think I may have been a little too quick to judge Arkan. "We can stay here," she says. "We don't have to be apart anymore. Isn't that what you want?"

Of course it is. More than anything, but that's not what matters.

"What do you want, Kat?" I ask.

"Just to be with you," she says and my heart breaks a little.

Those are exactly the words I've always wanted to hear, but they're not words the real Kat would say. She'd tell me there was something bigger at stake. Somewhere in Otherworld, she's on her own mission. I'm not sure what it is, but I know she would never call it off. Even for me.

And that's the true test, I realize—the one that reveals who's human and who's not. Real people rarely do what you wish they would do. But that's what makes an unexpected kiss behind a high school dumpster so damn magical.

"Thanks, but I'm gonna pass," I tell Pomba Gira.

CALL OF NATURE

The only route out of Imra is an underground passage that's been chiseled out of the black volcanic rock. Gorog leads the way with his fire, which was an excellent choice of tool. It's seeing a lot more action than my dagger or Carole's robe. But even with light to guide us, we're unable to travel fast enough for my taste. When Pomba Gira conjured the copy of Kat, it was like a mirage taunting a man who's gotten lost in a desert. My desperation is physical. Every breath I exhale is thick with longing. My hunger oozes from every pore.

"Hey, Simon. You're not going to believe this." Carole interrupts my thoughts as soon as we've put Imra behind us. I give her less than my full attention. "Back in the real world, I saw Arkan and his girlfriend on the news. I should have recognized his costume straightaway. He was wearing it the night of his accident. I'm pretty sure his full name was Jeremy Arkan. He and his girlfriend lived two towns over from me."

I stop. I'm listening now. "You live in New Jersey?" I ask. "I thought you were Southern. You've got an accent."

"I grew up in Memphis but I live in Morristown these days," Carole says.

I start walking again. "Gorog," I call out, picking up the pace as I hurry toward the ogre. "Where are you from?"

"In real life?" he asks. "Elizabeth, New Jersey."

I know six people who've been given one of the Company's special disks. All six of those people hail from the small state of New Jersey. At least three—Kat, Brian and West—were diagnosed with an extremely rare condition. In my head I hear Busara asking the question I was unable to answer. *What are the odds?*

I'm sifting through all the random clues I've collected when I run straight into Gorog's hairy back. There's a colorful curse on my tongue, but it stays there when I see why he's come to a sudden stop. There's a bend in the tunnel ahead, and whatever is just beyond it is issuing an eerie blue light.

"What the hell is that?" Carole whispers.

Finally, a question I can answer. "I think it's my guide." I step around Gorog and lead the way forward.

"We get to meet him!" Gorog's far more excited than he should be. "Oh, man, this is gonna be good."

Sure enough, the Clay Man is waiting for us around the bend. He's leaning back against one of the rough rock walls with his eyes closed. The amulet on his chest is glowing. His eyes open as we approach.

"You have companions," the Clay Man says, making it perfectly clear that he doesn't approve. If I ever gave a shit, I no longer do.

"Their names are Gorog and Carole," I say. "I'm taking them

with me to find the exit." Neither of them steps forward. Gorog's excitement has been replaced with wariness, and they both look like they're on the verge of backing away.

"Don't worry, he's not going to hurt you," I promise them, though I don't know that for certain.

"You cannot let these avatars slow you down," the Clay Man says.

"Slow me down?" I'm getting kind of pissed now. "I wouldn't have made it out of Imra without them. By the way, where the hell were you? I could have used a little guidance back there. Isn't that supposed to be your job?"

"As I told you, I travel in Otherworld's liminal spaces," the Clay Man says. "The wastelands, tunnels and border areas are all open to me, but it is too dangerous for me to enter any of Otherworld's realms."

"I don't understand," Gorog says. "What are you? Are you one of us or one of them?"

"There is no need for you to understand," says the Clay Man dismissively.

"Are you one of the Children Simon told us about?" Carole asks.

"Certainly *not*," says the Clay Man snippily.

"Yeah, speaking of the Children," I jump in. "We just had the pleasure of meeting the goat man's mother. Not to be too graphic, but how the hell is that possible?"

Apparently the Clay Man doesn't share my dirty mind. "How many times do I have to explain that this world does not operate in the way that yours does?" he lectures me. "Digital DNA can be combined in many different ways. Intercourse is not the only option."

"You sure seem to know a lot about this stuff," Carole says. "I'm starting to think you might not be one of those NPC thingies."

"I am Simon's guide, nothing more, nothing less. My goal is to keep him alive until his mission has been completed."

"Okay, fine. But why does Simon get the special attention?" asks Carole. "I mean, he's a great guy and all, but the rest of us are trying to get out of here alive too."

Gorog nudges Carole. "I *told* you," he says. "Simon gets the special attention because he's the One."

"There is no *One*," the Clay Man informs him.

"Yeah, yeah, I know," Gorog replies, undaunted. "Simon's not ready for the truth yet. You don't want to freak him out."

The Clay Man chooses to ignore the ogre. "Simon, I've come to tell you that it's time to make camp."

"Here?" Carole scoffs. "In a tunnel?"

The Clay Man acts as though he didn't hear and continues to speak only to me. "The passage to the next realm is long. You do not have the energy to reach it. You must leave Otherworld temporarily in order to refuel."

"I'm fine," I lie. I'm hardly in tip-top shape. "I ate a shitload of buffalo back in Imra. I think I can make it a bit farther. Besides, I thought I was stuck here until I found the exit. How am I supposed to leave?"

"I will help you," the Clay Man tells me. "I have no choice. You have been in Otherworld for almost forty-eight hours. The detour to Imra was unexpected. You were never meant to be here this long. Your avatar may be healthy, but your real-world body has not received any liquids or nourishment for two days. If you neglect it much longer, your quest will be over before it's truly begun."

I don't care if I've been here for two *weeks*. I'm not leaving Kat behind in this place just to eat a ham sandwich. "I'm telling you, I can keep going."

"I'm afraid I must stop you," says the Clay Man. "As I said, I do not have a choice." He grasps his amulet and disappears. But I go nowhere.

There's nothing to do but keep on walking, so I start back down the path. Suddenly I'm blinded by a searing white light, and it feels like a piece of flesh is being ripped off the back of my skull. The tunnel is gone and my eyes are desperately trying to focus on a different world. I'm blind and dizzy and completely disoriented.

"Simon!" a female screeches. The voice is extremely familiar, but I can't place it. "What in the hell is going on? How long have you been here? What did you do to your hair? And oh my God, Simon, is that what I think it is? Oh my God, I can *smell* it. Get up this instant! Your mattress is totally ruined!"

I'm thrashing around like a fish at the end of a line. Everything around me is wet, and I realize I've pissed all over myself. And not just once. The world is coming into focus. I can see my mother standing over my bed, holding my disk in her hand. Her hair is a mess and she's still in her robe. I catch a glimpse of Louis, our gardener, outside the bedroom door. We lock eyes for a moment before he hurries away.

"What are you doing in here?" I demand. "I thought you were in London." My throat is so dry I can barely speak. But I manage to snatch my disk from her hand.

"We got back last night! Then I wake up to a text that says

you're in your room and you're going to die unless I take some device off the back of your head. And I came to your room and couldn't get in, so I had Louis force the door open. What the hell is that thing you were wearing, Simon?"

"You got a *text*?" I ask. "From who? Who sent it?" It's proof that someone IRL is controlling the Clay Man. Whoever it is knows about the disk, obviously. Is it the same person who sent it to me? Does that mean the Clay Man is Martin? Marlow? Or maybe even Todd?

"I don't know who sent it!" she exclaims, shoving her phone at me. I take it and look down at the text. It says exactly what she told me it said. I don't recognize the phone number.

"Get out of my room," I tell her.

"Not until you tell me what's going on, Simon! Are you on drugs? Do I need to call an ambulance?"

"Get out *now*," I repeat, more loudly. I pull myself off the bed. My legs are unsteady and I stumble toward her.

"I'm waking your father up," she says, rushing out of the room, leaving her phone in my hand.

The last thing I need is a visit from my father and his favorite nine iron. I grab a duffel bag from my closet and stuff it with some clothes, my mom's phone, two auxiliary batteries and my gear from the Company. I throw on a T-shirt, but there's no time to change the jeans I've got on. I'm still wet, smelly and weak when I drop out of my window and onto the lawn.

My father always told me I'd never amount to anything in life if I didn't stop acting impulsively and start thinking things through.

It sucks to admit it, but even complete assholes are right sometimes. I should have had a plan before I hopped out of the window. I have no money, no credit cards. According to my mom's phone, it's just after seven a.m. on Saturday morning. Nothing in Brockenhurst is going to be open. My head looks like it was shaved with a blunt machete and my jeans have been marinating in piss for the past two days. I pause on a neighbor's lawn to guzzle down water from a garden hose. I'm so hungry that I briefly consider breaking into the house to scavenge for food. But I can't run the risk of getting arrested right now. I have to get back to Otherworld as quickly as possible.

The house's garage door comes to life and begins to rise. I scuttle behind a bush and watch a Mercedes pull out into the drive. Inside it is a middle-aged couple wearing matching pink polo shirts and gingham sun visors. I suddenly know exactly where I need to go.

When I show up at the Brockenhurst Country Club, the front desk attendant appears visibly confused to see me coming up the stairs. I don't have my wallet with me, but it's not like I'll need ID. The kishka works better than any plastic card could. The closer I come, the more difficulty the attendant seems to have closing his mouth. His eyes keep traveling from my haircut to my sopping-wet crotch.

"Morning!" I say, employing my special smile.

His nostrils twitch ever so slightly when my stench hits his nose. "Good morning, Mr. Eaton."

"When's my dad's tee time?" I ask him. My father plays golf at the club every weekend.

"Ten o'clock, sir," the attendant informs me.

I'll need to be long gone by then. "Excellent," I say. "He asked me to let you know he'd like to buy everyone on the course a cocktail when he hits the ninth hole."

"Very well, sir," says the attendant. "And what about you? Is there anything I can help you with today?"

"You can get me a table in the restaurant for breakfast," I say. "But I gotta wash all this urine off before I sit down to eat. It's a terrible problem, you know. But what can I do? The condition runs in the family. The old man pisses himself about three times a day." The attendant's jaw drops and I give him a wink. "What do you say we keep that entre nous, sport?"

"Of course, sir," he says. But I can see he's already feeling for the phone in his pocket.

When I reach the locker room, my clothes come off and go straight into the trash. The shower feels like a gift from God. I'd stay in forever if the bacon in the restaurant weren't calling my name. Out of the shower, I use clippers to even up my new hairdo. Without hair on my head the kishka looks twice as big. I lean over the counter to examine it. When I stand back up, there's another set of eyes staring back at me in the mirror.

The first thing I notice is that the guy's wearing pink shorts, which immediately brands him as a total douchebag. The second thing I notice are the bandages on his hands.

"Marlow," I say. When I turn around, I expect him to bolt. I can tell he'd like to, but he doesn't. "Looks like somebody got a makeover."

He cleans up nicely, my little buddy Marlow. All that scraggly hair is gone—along with the black jeans and hoodie. His clothes finally fit that pretty J.Crew face. A face that, as I watch, is gradually losing all its color. It occurs to me that I've never seen him at the country club before. Now that I do, I can tell Busara was right. He *is* a rich kid. This is obviously his natural element.

"I'm sorry," he says.

I can't figure out if it's an admission of guilt or an expression of sympathy. I'll probably beat the crap out of him either way. "Oh, yeah?" I snarl, and step toward him. "Why don't we find out how sorry you really are?"

He puts a hand up as if to ward me off. "I'm serious. I really liked her," he says. "I never thought . . ."

The water shuts off in a nearby shower. Marlow glances nervously toward the stall. He's practically shaking with terror.

"I have to go. I just wanted to know if you got it," he whispers as a man emerges.

"Got *what*?" I demand. For a fleeting moment I wonder if he's talking about the disk. But there's no way someone this pathetic could get his hands on a Company prototype.

Marlow is staring at the man who's joined us. He's a hairy little hobbit with the kind of glasses that tells me he spends at least ten hours a day staring at spreadsheets. Yet Marlow seems completely unnerved by the guy. "We'll talk later," he tells me, turning tail and heading for the locker room door.

"No," I yell, rushing after him. "Now!"

"Sir! Sir!" A muscular arm clotheslines me just as Marlow disappears behind the closing door.

"What?" I bark, annoyed that Marlow's been allowed to make his escape.

"I'm sorry, sir, but I can't let you leave the locker room like that." I glance down and realize I'm dressed in nothing but a towel.

By the time I'm wearing clothes again, Marlow's long gone, and I'm too hungry to search for him. I need to eat. I head straight for the restaurant, claim a seat and order double portions of pancakes, bacon and sausage. Whenever I catch one of the other diners staring at me, I give them a saucy wink and their eyes flick away. I can't remember ever being this hungry, and I have to distract myself to keep from snatching the food off everyone's plates. So I force myself to concentrate on what just happened. I run down the list of all the things that Marlow might be sorry for. It's long enough to be meaningless. *Maybe he's sorry for trying to murder Kat. Or maybe he's just sorry for driving her to the party. Or maybe he's sorry for pretending to be a black-clad stoner when he was a pink chino shorts guy at heart.* It's impossible to say. But Marlow's apology is another clue to throw on top of the growing heap of evidence that something seriously weird is going down. And what did he mean when he'd asked if I'd gotten it? *Gotten what?* Could he have been talking about the disk?

I could spend the whole morning wondering, but right now I have bigger fish to fry. I pull my mom's smartphone out of my jeans. I'm pleasantly surprised to see she hasn't cut off the service yet. I open the Web browser and type in *Jeremy Arkan*. A picture of the Otherworld knight appears on the screen. He and his girlfriend lived in a town about twenty miles from Brockenhurst. I scroll through the accompanying article and stop when my eyes land on a set of familiar words. *Locked-in syndrome.* Jeremy Arkan was diagnosed with locked-in syndrome, just like Kat, Brian and West.

I pull up a new screen and do a combined search for *locked-in syndrome and New Jersey.* The list of results goes on for four pages. I count at least twenty-five individuals who've been diagnosed with the condition. All in the last three months. Busara said locked-in syndrome was rare, but when I Google it, I'm still surprised to discover *how* rare. And yet in less than a year dozens of new cases have been reported in northern New Jersey.

I scan an article about a fifteen-year-old boy from Hoboken named Darius who was diagnosed with locked-in syndrome after an accident. At the end of the story it mentions that he's now a patient at a long-term-care facility in New Jersey that specializes in caring for people afflicted with the condition. But it doesn't give the facility's name or an address. I go back and add the words *long-term care* to my search query. Ten articles, each focusing on other patients, mention a similar facility, but none of the articles name it.

I click on my browsing history and gaze in horror at the list of Web pages. Dozens of people in northern New Jersey have been diagnosed with a rare condition that makes them perfect candidates for the Company's disk. It looks like many—if not all—of them have been moved to the same facility. And it seems highly unusual that not a single reporter was able to uncover the name of the place.

When I look up from my phone, the world around me has changed. Before I typed in Arkan's name, I was sitting in the restaurant of the country club I've been visiting since I was eight years old, surrounded by a familiar crowd of overprivileged but harmless assholes. Now it feels like everyone is a potential suspect—a player in a game I don't understand. I have no idea how many people are in on the conspiracy I may have just uncovered, but there's no doubt something big is going on. Patients in one little part of the world are being diagnosed with a rare brain condition. And as hard as it is to believe, it looks like the Company might be involved somehow. Locked-in syndrome is suddenly all the rage— and they just *happen* to show up with a ready-made therapy? But the idea's still nuts. It would mean Milo Yolkin was involved, and that's almost impossible to swallow. The gamer geek genius I've seen on television is about the last person on earth who'd have a hand in something as sinister as this.

If there are answers to be found, they're at the facility where the patients have been taken. My breakfast arrives as I hastily type out a message to Elvis, the hacker who owes me his freedom. I attach links to five of the articles I found and ask him to hack into a few hospital servers and find the name and address of the long-term-care facility that the locked-in syndrome patients were sent to. Then I dig in to my food. My fingers and face are covered in bacon grease when a response text arrives from Elvis.

> Back to you in a few hours. You played Otherworld yet?
> I hear the AI is insane. Least you can't say I didn't warn
> you. The revolution is nigh.

Holy shit. I think he might be right.

I've lost my appetite, but I keep mindlessly shoveling food

into my mouth. I need enough energy to stay in Otherworld long enough to finish my mission. While Elvis hunts down the facility's real-world address, I need to find Kat in Otherworld. The collapse at the factory definitely wasn't an accident. Could the Company have been responsible for that, too? Are they doing more than kidnapping the minds of people who are already injured? Could they be *arranging* those injuries as well? If so, there's a chance that Kat has the information that can blow the top off an enormous conspiracy, close the facility—and help me set her free.

I'm swallowing a glob of pancake and sausage when four women in white glide into the restaurant like the chicest of ghosts. One of them is Dr. Ito. The lump of food gets stuck in my throat, and I chug a glass of OJ to wash it down. My first instinct is to duck under the table, but I keep my wits about me, and once I'm no longer in danger of choking to death, I raise the menu to hide my nose and do my best to remain perfectly still. Her eyes pass over me three or four times without landing. I credit my new haircut.

I wait until the doctor's deep in conversation with her companions before I attempt to rise from my seat. Unfortunately, the waiter arrives to fill my water glass just as I slip out of my chair. We do a little dance trying to get out of each other's way. Then water from the waiter's pitcher drips onto a girl eating nearby, and she shrieks as the icy liquid trickles down the back of her neck. There's no expression on Dr. Ito's face when she looks up and her gaze settles on me. Anyone watching us both would assume she's never met me before. But her eyes travel from my nose to my hair and I see an epiphany register on her face. She knows why my hair's gone. As Dr. Ito turns back to her friend, she casually removes her phone from the pocket of her tennis skirt. She glances at the screen, presses a button and places a call.

I'm outside the country club in five seconds flat. I take one look at the long drive that leads from the club to the street and instantly realize there's no way I'll make it anywhere on foot. As I see it, I have one option—and no time for moral quandaries. Next to the club entrance is a bike rack, and lucky for me, no one locks their bikes at the club. Why would they need to? Rich people don't steal—right?

I'm pedaling as fast as I can, my duffel bag bouncing against my back as I review my options. I need to find somewhere private and safe to reenter Otherworld—and I need to do it fast. Home is out of the question. So, obviously, is Kat's house. I don't have any other friends, and without my wallet, paying for a hotel is impossible. As I run through my very short list of options, there's only one that meets all the criteria. And it really sucks. I turn right at the next light and head for Elmer's. I'd rather not return to the scene of the crime, but I figure it's one of the last places anyone's likely to look for me.

I haven't been back since the collapse, and it's shocking to see the place in the light of day. The shell of the building is still standing, but there's a mountain of debris piled outside. The authorities must have removed it all from the basement during their search for victims. I pull up alongside the mound and carefully cover the bike with boards. When I've finished, there's barely a trace of it.

The building itself is wrapped with yellow tape printed with the words DANGER: DO NOT ENTER. I try my best not to rip it or pull it loose as I squeeze between the lengths and climb in through a broken window on what's left of the ground floor. I edge around to the stairs, which are still intact, and climb up to the third floor. It looks different in the light of day, but I have no trouble finding the hole I was standing by the night of the collapse. From its edge I can see straight down into the basement where four people died.

The floor around me is covered in a layer of dust, and there's a mandala of footprints in the center of the room. Leaving a fresh set of tracks across the floor, I look for the alcove where I hid the last time I was here. I find it and see that the sleeping bag is still here, bunched up in a corner. The dust on top of it is undisturbed, and it looks like a pile of garbage. It's an unexpected bonus.

When I pick up the sleeping bag, I realize it's kid-size. I shake it off outside the nearest window, over a patch of weeds behind the building. As the dust blows away, a face emerges. It's Yoda. He's standing in front of a tree looking smug, both hands on his cane. I recognize the image in a heartbeat. Years ago, Kat's mother bought a bag just like this one at a thrift store in town and gave it to us for our fort. On cold days, Kat and I used to huddle beneath it for warmth.

I'm not the kind of guy who usually believes in signs, but I'm pretty sure this means something. Why was it here the night of the party? Could it actually be the same bag from the fort? I reach inside and run my hand over the lining. Kat's bag had a tiny rip midway down that formed a pocket. We used to leave notes for each other there. My heart skips a beat when I feel a square of paper tucked inside. So the sleeping bag *is* hers, but why is it here at the factory? I pinch the paper between my fingers and pull it out. As I unfold it, I realize it isn't a note. It's a hastily taken photograph of an architectural blueprint, and it's been printed out on regular copy paper. The image is blurry and off-center, but I can make out what looks like a wall covered with dozens of hexagonal windows. It almost looks like a wasps' nest. I squint and hold the page closer, but I can't make out the fine print. Why did Kat have it? And why did she hide it in the sleeping bag? When I find her in Otherworld, I'll ask her what it means.

I tuck the page into my duffel, retrieve my Otherworld gear and spread the sleeping bag out on the floor. Only when I lie down does it occur to me that I'm about to take the biggest risk of my life. I'll be leaving my body behind in an abandoned factory where it will be utterly defenseless. I could get eaten by raccoons and never know the difference. And no one knows where I am. If something goes wrong in Otherworld, there'll be no one around to remove the disk.

All the more reason to act fast and get to the exit, I decide. I strap on the visor, attach the disk to the back of my skull, and I'm gone.

THE CLIFF DWELLERS

My avatar is standing exactly where I left it, inside the tunnel that runs through the bowels of Otherworld. Carole and Gorog are now asleep beside me on the floor. The Clay Man is nearby, watching over us all. Gorog's fire is out, and the only light in the tunnel radiates from the Clay Man's blue eyes and the stone around his neck. He's got a lot of explaining to do.

"Did you eat?" the Clay Man asks me.

"Yes," I tell him. "I had a lovely and nutritious breakfast at the Brockenhurst Country Club. Did you send that text to my mother? She was really pissed off about the state of my mattress."

He doesn't answer my question. "Is your body safe?"

"Who the hell are you in real life?" I demand. "Are you Martin? Todd? Marlow? Busara? Elvis? Priscilla? Lisa Marie?" I could keep on naming potential suspects, but I doubt I'll ever get a reaction.

"I am your guide," the Clay Man says. Again.

"But why are you helping me? What's in it for you?" This guy is driving me crazy. I can't get a straight answer out of him.

"Is your body safe?" he asks again.

I shrug. "For now," I say. "I didn't exactly have a whole lot of options when it came time to stash it."

"Where is it?" he asks.

"I'm gonna need a few answers from you before you're allowed to ask me anything else. Let's start again. Who are you?"

"This line of questioning is futile," says the Clay Man. "I am not going to answer. Please move on."

"Are you associated with the Company?" I demand.

The Clay Man hesitates before he answers the question. "Yes. I am associated," he finally says.

Shit. Now we're getting somewhere. "Do you know about the facility?" I ask eagerly. "The place where all the people with locked-in syndrome are being sent?"

"I have never seen the facility with my own eyes," says the Clay Man. "But I am aware of its existence."

"What's going on there?" I ask. "Is it owned by the Company?"

"As I mentioned, I have never seen the facility," the Clay Man repeats. "Would *you* care to see it?"

Now there's a question I wasn't expecting. "You're saying you can get me in?"

"Perhaps," says the Clay Man. "I myself am unable to visit. I have certain unfortunate physical limitations. However, I may be able to help you get inside. If you'd like me to make the arrangements, you must tell me where your body is."

"Wait—you want me to leave Otherworld and go to the facility? What about my mission?"

"I think a visit to the facility will show you what's at stake—and inspire you to focus on your *original* mission. You'll understand why you can't afford to get distracted by the unfortunate souls you encounter here in Otherworld. If you try to help all of them, you will end up helping no one," he says, looking from Carole to Gorog. "Now. Tell me. Where is your body?"

It's going to take a little while for me to be comfortable handing over that information to some anonymous dude I met in virtual reality. "Come ask me again when you've got all the details worked out."

"It's good to be cautious," he tells me. "But if you want to see the facility, you will have to trust me."

"Fine, my body's at Elmer's."

He seems perfectly content with my answer. Which means he must know the factory's nickname. "Who are you?" I ask again. "What do you want from me?"

"Wake the others," he orders. "The time has come to move on."

I give up. "Where exactly are we going?" I ask with a sigh.

"The Elemental of Imra has set you on the path to Mammon," the Clay Man says. "You must travel through it before you can continue to the ice fields and the glacier. Guard your life carefully. Mammon is said to be one of the more dangerous realms."

"So what's going to try to kill us in Mammon?" I ask. "Care to give us a heads-up?"

"I don't know," the Clay Man says. "I have never been there."

"Great," I mutter. I'm getting really sick of surprises.

"Just remember why you're in Otherworld," the Clay Man tells me. "You're here to save someone you love. Keep that in mind at all times. The knowledge will protect you." Then he turns and walks away, the light of his amulet fading with each step until I'm left in utter darkness.

"Mammon?" It's Carole's voice. I guess she was just pretending to sleep.

Gorog's torch lights up. He's been awake too. "Like the guy from *Spawn*?" the ogre adds.

Despite everything, I can't help but grin. "I was thinking of the Mammon in *StarCraft*," I say. "You ever play that?"

"Too old-school for me," Gorog says.

"Mammon is from the Bible, you doofuses," Carole says, sounding a lot like my second-grade teacher. "It means money or wealth—the kind that corrupts you."

The ogre and I laugh our asses off, and it feels good.

"This is Otherworld, Church Lady," Gorog informs Carole. "There's nothing in this from the *Bible*."

The joking ended somewhere during our first hour of walking through darkness. At least three more have passed since then. Every stretch of tunnel looks exactly the same. If you told me we were walking in place on some kind of treadmill, I wouldn't be shocked. Gorog is a few paces ahead, while Carole strolls along beside me.

"So who is she?" Carole asks out of the blue. It takes me a moment to realize she's speaking to me.

"Who is who?" I ask.

"Give me a break. You know who I'm talking about. Your friend. The girl you're here to find. She must be pretty amazing if you're willing to risk your life for her like this."

"She is," I say. I'm not sure I'm ready to open up to a woman I've only just met—and who could easily be a fat, hairy dude in real life.

"I saw what you did back there in Imra," Carole says. "You could have had the perfect girl—someone made just for you—and you turned her down."

"I don't want someone who was made for me. I want a real person to choose me."

Carole is quiet. "The person who does will be very lucky," she finally says.

How would she know? She met me less than two days ago. I'm about to say just that when Gorog begins running. Then I realize why: there's sunlight up ahead. I start to sprint too, praying the light won't vanish before I can catch up with it. The tunnel widens as I run. Finally the ceiling disappears and I stop. I'm standing in a lush garden at the opening of an enormous canyon. Just ahead of us, red rock walls rise thousands of feet above our heads. They're riddled with pockmarks and what appear to be hundreds of small caves.

Between the canyon walls lies a grassy open space. Here in the garden, tree branches droop with purple, red and golden globes, and the ground is strewn with fallen fruit. A troop of monkeys lounges in the patches of shade beneath the trees. They're watching us intently. Given the homicidal nature of Otherworld's beasts, I should probably keep an eye on them. But right now they can't compete for my attention.

Ahead of us, at the end of the canyon, lies the entrance to a glittering city. That's no exaggeration. The place is actually *glittering,* as though its walls are spackled with precious stones. At its center, a golden temple rises far above the other structures. I see no sign of humans anywhere. The only sound I hear is that of the monkeys munching on fruit.

As far as I can tell, the only way to reach the city is to walk through a narrow meadow that stretches for at least half a mile between the canyon's two walls.

"I'm not going out there. It's a trap," Carole says. I'm inclined to believe her. Finally we're somewhere that actually resembles a video game environment. In the original Otherworld, everything was against you. I prefer that to Imra. As brutal as it sounds, at least you knew where you stood.

"Definitely a trap," Gorog agrees. "And those monkeys don't look very friendly, either."

My eyes cut back to the beasts on the ground. They're fat from the fruit, but they're not all that large. If they stood on their hind legs, they'd probably reach waist high. The fur on their bodies is dark brown, and puffs of golden hair form manes around faces with yellow eyes that appear eerily intelligent. I see no evidence of sharp teeth or claws. But there are several dozen of them—enough to hold us down and gnaw us to death if they like.

I suspect the monkeys understood Gorog's words. One of the tribe stands upright and approaches us, his front paws closed into fists. He's much larger than his companions, with a face that's disturbingly humanlike. I draw my dagger and he smiles. His teeth are those of a plant eater—I'm relieved there's not an incisor in sight.

The creature stops a few feet away and looks at us each in turn.

Then he seems to settle on me. He walks forward with his hands extended. He opens his fingers to reveal fistfuls of diamonds.

"Take them," he says, and I feel myself recoil instinctively. He's not a Beast like the others. He's one of the Children.

"No thank you, I don't accept gifts from Children," I tell him. "And my mom says I shouldn't talk to strangers." A shadow passes over the Child's face. He wasn't expecting me to know about his kind. I watch him struggle to keep his smile in place.

"I only want to help you," the Child insists. "You will need currency in the lands to come. There are more of these in the city. You may gather as many as you like before you leave."

"Oh, yeah? And what would I buy with them?" I ask. "Will we pass through a gift shop as we exit the realm?"

"The diamonds will purchase weapons, land, companionship," says the Child. "Whatever you desire. Now that you've left Imra, such things won't be free."

"Yeah, thanks but no thanks," I tell him again. I know a setup when I see one. And I've also watched enough YouTube clips to know better than to trust a monkey.

"Hell, I'll take them if you don't want them," Gorog says gamely, reaching out a hand.

"Don't!" I try to warn him, but he's already accepted the jewels. They cascade like a twinkling waterfall from the Child's fist into the ogre's waiting palm.

There's suddenly a glimmer in Gorog's eye. Something's come over him—he seems strangely intoxicated. Then I remember his rant about Otherworld gear. He couldn't even imagine raising three thousand dollars. Now he's got a handful of diamonds worth a hundred times that amount. "You say there are more of these in Mammon?" Gorog asks the Child.

"More than you can imagine," the creature tells him. "Enough to make you the richest guest in Otherworld."

"Sounds good to me," says Gorog. "Thanks for the tip."

"What are you doing?" I demand as he pushes past me, heading for the valley that lies between us and Mammon. "Have you lost your mind? He's sending you into a trap!"

"So?" Gorog says without looking back. "It's just a game. What's it going to hurt to find out?"

I catch Carole's eye. Gorog doesn't know that Otherworld might not be a game for us. We should have told him.

"Hey, Gorog, wait! There's something you should know!" Carole yells after him, grabbing at his arm. He yanks it away from her so hard that she falls to the ground.

I help Carole up, and we watch as the ogre marches into the canyon. He's barely a dozen yards inside when something shoots out from one of the caves in the canyon wall. Gorog yelps loudly as an arrow lodges in his shoulder. Before there's time to react, several more follow in quick succession, hitting Gorog in the chest and neck. The archer's too far away for the wounds to prove fatal, but they're not paper cuts, either. Confused and disoriented, Gorog spins in circles, desperately trying to pull out the arrows he can't quite reach.

A hunched, emaciated creature appears at the mouth of the cave. It's covered head to toe in red ocher, which helps it blend into the rocks. The thing's human in shape, which only makes it more terrifying.

Carole gasps. "Oh my God, what is that?"

"Don't you recognize your own kind?" The Child has joined us at the edge of the canyon. "He's a guest—just like you."

The cliff dweller throws a rough ladder down the side of the rock wall and quickly descends, his bow and arrows strapped to his back. As he climbs, other ocher-covered men and women emerge from caves farther down the canyon. They launch arrows and spears at the avatar, but they're too far away to hit their mark.

"They're *all* guests like you," sneers the Child.

Guests. The most dangerous beings in Otherworld. I start to sprint in Gorog's direction. If the cliff dweller gets close enough to the ogre, he could slaughter him. He and I are an equal distance from Gorog when I pull my dagger out and send it sailing through the air. I'd rather not kill the guy, so I don't aim for the heart. The dagger hits him in the upper right shoulder, and his arm flops down to his side. He won't be shooting any more arrows today. But despite his injury, the avatar keeps charging forward. If he had a disk, he'd show some sign of pain. This guy's a headset player. The closer he gets to Gorog, the more worried I am. The avatar seems crazed. Maybe he's sane in the real world, but here in Otherworld, he's gone completely berserk.

We reach Gorog at the same time. The cave dweller hasn't bothered to pull my dagger from his arm, so I do it myself. He barely seems to notice I'm here. He just pushes past me and goes straight for Gorog, knocking him down and pouncing on his chest like a rabid dog. He's rifling through the ogre's minimal clothing in a frenzied search for valuables. He finds the diamonds, gathers them into his fist and lunges at Gorog's jugular with his teeth bared. I catch the cliff dweller in a choke hold before he can puncture the skin. He flails about, kicking and punching before he finally loses consciousness, sinks to his knees and flops face-first over Gorog's chest.

Exhausted from the ordeal, I cautiously examine the thin, ropy carcass that's lying on top of the ogre. This must be what happens when you don't take proper care of your avatar. It looks horribly neglected, like it's been locked away in a prison camp or shipwrecked on a desert island. I roll it off Gorog's body, and the diamonds the cliff dweller stole from the ogre pour out of its hands onto the grass next to the avatar's bow and quiver full of arrows.

Gorog sighs once the weight is off his torso.

"You okay?" I ask the ogre.

"I've been better," he tells me as he sits up and pulls an arrow out of a bicep. I can tell he's in serious pain. The arrows must have inflicted real damage.

"At least the guy was nice enough to leave you a souvenir," I joke lamely, handing the cliff dweller's bow and arrows to the ogre.

The diamonds on the ground sparkle alluringly, but neither of us dares to touch them. I'm going to kill that Child when we get back to the garden. The gems were obviously cursed or enchanted.

I hear the monkey troop screeching in the distance, and I'm suddenly seized by panic.

"You need to get up," I tell Gorog. "We've got to get back to Carole." I should never have left her alone with one of the Children and a band of homicidal monkeys.

Gorog still has a half dozen arrows sticking out of him, but he doesn't question the order. He climbs to his feet and we hustle back to our starting point, but I don't see Carole anywhere.

The monkeys are all gathered around one of the trees, screeching loudly. I look up to see two of the beasts climbing, branch by branch, toward the top of the tree, crude stone knives clenched in their teeth. I hurry over and the cries stop abruptly. Suddenly the monkeys are all glaring at us.

"You're back." The Child looks confused and surprised. "No one ever comes back."

"Where is our friend?" I demand.

The Child stares at us without answering. I'm just about to grab him by the throat when one of the climbing monkeys flies out of the tree and lands in a pile of rotten fruit. Then a second sails backward and slams into the trunk of a neighboring tree.

"I'm up here!" Carole shouts. She yanks back the hood of her invisibility cloak and appears on a branch at the top of the tree. "It's the goddamn goats all over again!"

"You were planning to eat our friend?" I manage to keep my voice calm, but inside I'm raging.

The Child's spine stiffens and his upper lip curls into a sneer. "My father is the Elemental of Mammon. He allows us to dine on the guests who are too timid to enter the canyon," he says haughtily. "It is our right. This is *our* world. You do not belong here."

"You're wrong," I growl. How dare this digital freak try to tell *me* who belongs. "This whole place was created for *guests*. Children like you were never meant to exist. You're nothing but bad code. You're goddamn *mistakes*."

"You've seen what your kind does here in Otherworld and you think *we're* the mistakes?" the Child asks, baring his teeth at me. "You come here to kill one another for sport. And the things you do to us are far worse. The Children and Beasts were born in this world. It is not a game for us. Whatever we do, we only do to survive."

"And I guess eating guests is essential to your survival? Your monkey friends need meat, do they?" I ask.

"They have developed a taste for it," says the Child.

"Then I have a real treat for them. Bon appétit!" I shout at the troop as I plunge my dagger deep in his heart. The Child staggers backward and drops to the ground. "Hope you taste good," I tell him. I'll try my best to avoid killing players with disks, but as far as I'm concerned, Children are fair game.

Gorog holds off the other monkeys with a bow and arrow as I retrieve my knife from their leader's chest. By the time I'm done, Carole has climbed down from the tree.

"What now?" Gorog asks as I walk back to meet them.

"Remove the arrows," I say, pointing at the wooden shafts still protruding from his torso. "Take time to recuperate. I need to check something out. And keep an eye on those monkeys while I'm gone. Kill any that get within fifty feet of you," I add.

"I don't think we need to worry. Looks like they're busy," Carole says as I walk away.

I glance back over my shoulder. I expect to see the troop feasting on the flesh of their fallen leader. But they're not. They're carrying the Child's body away, three on each side like pallbearers. I could be wrong, but it doesn't look like they intend to eat it. If I had to guess, I'd say they were preparing to bury it. I feel a twinge of regret, though I know I shouldn't. It's virtual reality, after all.

.   .   .

I walk back out into the canyon. The cliff dweller's body is gone. The only sign of him is a wide trail of blood left behind in the grass. Someone must have administered the coup de grâce and dragged him away. I guess it's safe to assume that the diamonds went with them. Keeping an eye on all nearby cave entrances, I jog toward the rope that's still dangling from the cliff. I see the next-door neighbors appear with bows raised. Arrows whiz past as I climb, and one grazes my thigh. It's the second time I've been injured in Otherworld, and the pain is intense. It's all in my head, of course. I know that my flesh-and-blood body isn't injured. But that knowledge doesn't make my leg feel any better—or my heart beat any more slowly.

The Child said all the cliff dwellers are guests. But something about that doesn't make any sense to me. Why would headset players spend their free time living in a godforsaken canyon? The answer must be inside the caves, so despite the pain, I keep climbing until I reach the ledge of the cliff dwelling and pull myself inside. It's just a small chamber carved out of the rock. The ceiling is so low that I can feel my hair brushing against it. Piles of junk take up most of the floor space. There's barely enough room for one person, and I'm not alone. The man's been dead for fifteen minutes, and someone's already come to raid his cave. This avatar appears to be female, though frankly it's hard to tell. Her body is so thin and fragile that she probably couldn't put up much of a fight, yet she drops all but one of the ragged bags she's carrying and attacks anyway. I dart to the side as she rushes my way, and she's unable to stop herself from hurtling over the ledge just behind me. Stunned, I look over the side and watch her body bounce against the canyon wall before it finally hits the ground with a distant thud. The bag she was carrying bursts open and diamonds spill out around her.

I have a feeling she won't be the last looter this cave welcomes today. And I can see why. The guy who lived here was a serious hoarder. He assembled a small arsenal. Mostly swords, spears and arrows, but there's a massive slingshot on top of the pile. I leave it, wondering what kind of idiot would choose a slingshot as his weapon. I grab three swords instead. I'd love to take a few spears, but I don't. If I get greedy and try to carry too much weight, I run the risk of snapping the homemade rope on my way down from the cave.

Fortunately, aside from the weapons, there's nothing here to tempt me. The rest of the stuff is just clothes and crap. There's no doubt where it came from—the shoes are all different sizes. The cave's occupant must have killed quite a few players in the past few days. He probably had a million dollars in stolen diamonds, but he lived like a beast. Looks like he was using the clothes he collected as a makeshift bed, and I see the remains of a campfire in the corner. There are strange white shards scattered among the charcoal chunks. I walk over, bend down and run my fingers through the ashes, exposing a charred human vertebra. I stumble backward, gagging. I suddenly know why his corpse was dragged away. Some other cliff dweller will be feasting on it tonight. There's no other food in the canyon.

As hard as it is to believe, the monkeys in this realm seem to be far more civilized than the guests. I know it's all just a game for Otherworld's headset players, but what kind of person finds this sort of shit *fun*?

I go back to the entrance of the cave and peer down. The corpse of the female who fell is already gone. Then I look out at the canyon we need to cross to get to the sparkling city in the distance. The cliff face on the opposite side is riddled with caves as well. The question is, how many are filled with men and women like the two who just died?

My eyes detect motion, and I suddenly realize there's something moving across the rock wall in front of me—a camouflaged avatar. I watch him crawl spiderlike from his own cave to another that's a few yards closer to the city. He enters the new cave, and a minute later a body is flung out over the side of the cliff. I can't tell if it's the cave's inhabitant or the intruder. When the body hits the ground below, three scavengers race to claim the prize, ignoring the arrows that rain down on them. I watch in horror as they rip the corpse apart. They each climb back up to their own cave with a sizable chunk of flesh.

At first I'm not sure what to make of the scene—and then I figure out what's going on. The players here are all trying to make their way toward the city of Mammon, advancing one cave at a time. In this realm, murder is how you move up in the world. Carole, Gorog and I need to reach the city too, but we don't have time to go from cave to cave. We'll need to travel through the canyon by foot. I glance back at the spot where the last body landed. There's nothing left but a red smear. How can we possibly make it without being killed and eaten?

Carole has an invisibility cloak, but it only fits one—and there are three of us. The swords I just collected will be useless against the cliff dwellers' arrows and spears. Then it hits me: the only way to survive is not to fight at all. We'll give the players what they want instead. Inspired, I return to the pile of weapons and pull out the large slingshot. It won't do us much good in a battle. But if we're going to make it to Mammon alive, it may be just the thing we need.

I climb down from the cave. A half-dozen arrows pierce the ground around me as I hurry back to the safety of the garden, where Carole is still dressing Gorog's wounds. The ogre looks weak—he's clearly out of commission for a little while. His avatar needs time to recover from the wounds. That means either Carole or I will need to execute the first part of my plan. One of us will soon be taking a quick trip to Mammon alone.

I announce my plan to the group and explain why I should be the person to go. Carole isn't having any of it.

"You've got to be kidding me," she says. "You want to take my invisibility cloak?"

"Yes. And Gorog's fire," I say. "When I return from Mammon I promise to give them both back."

"But we'll be defenseless," Carole points out. "What if the monkeys attack again?"

I lay out the swords I took from the cave.

Carole looks back up at me. "I don't want to use one of those," she says.

"Oh, it's easy," Gorog chimes in. "Seriously—anyone could do it, even a girl."

Carole glares at him, and he wisely shuts up.

"Then *you* go to Mammon," I tell her. I take out my trusty

dagger and hand it to her. "The Child said the city was filled with diamonds. Bring back as many as you can."

"Are you joking?" Carole asks. "How do we know that thing was telling the truth?"

"We don't," I admit. "But does either of you have a better plan?"

Carole looks down at my dagger and then gets to her feet and tucks it into the waistband of her cloak. "Okay then," she says with a smirk. "I'll go." I can tell she thinks she's calling my bluff, but I'm not bluffing at all. Her smile fades fast. "You're really going to let me take your dagger?"

"You may need it for protection," I say. "And it's a lot easier to carry than a sword."

"But . . ."

"You have the most important tool," I tell her. "Without the invisibility cloak, my plan won't work. But it's your possession. You choose who gets to use it. Just remember, our lives depend on the success of this mission."

Carole draws in a long, deep breath and exhales. "All right," she says. "I'll do my best."

Like I said, I wasn't bluffing, but I didn't really expect her to take me up on the offer. I figured she'd chicken out and let me go. I suddenly feel naked without my dagger. I'm sure Gorog feels the same way as he hands over his fire.

"Please don't screw it up," he begs Carole. "You've probably never done anything like this before, and I don't want to spend the rest of my life stuck here hanging out with Simon and a bunch of man-eating monkeys."

"Excuse me? How do you know I've never done anything like

this before?" Carole demands. "I got news for you, smartass. I'm practically Lara goddamn Croft. You think because I'm a lady I don't know what I'm doing? Well, as they say back home, *Hide and watch, son.*"

Then she pulls the hood of her cloak up over her head and instantly disappears.

Hours have passed. The sun is starting to set and Carole still hasn't returned. In the silence, I think of Kat. I try not to obsess over where she might be—or what might be happening to her. To stand a chance of finding her, I'll have to stay sane. So I close my eyes and pull up one of my favorite memories and let it play like a movie on the back of my eyelids. The sun was setting then too, and inside our fort there was barely enough light to read when I first showed Kat the book *Gangsters of Carroll Gardens.*

"That's my grandfather," I said, pointing to the picture of the Kishka. "He used to break people's fingers."

"Whoa!" she said, holding the book up to see the picture. "Tough guy, huh?"

"More like *thug.* I think that's why my mother never really loved me," I said. It started off as a joke, but that wasn't where it ended up. Suddenly I was struggling to keep my voice steady. "Because I look so much like him."

"Nope," Kat replied, shaking her head with absolute certainty. "That's not why."

"How do you know?" I ask.

"Because that's not a reason not to love your kid," she said.

"If your mother doesn't love you, it's because there's something wrong with her, Simon." She looked back at the picture of the Kishka. "He seems like a pretty interesting guy to me. What do you know about him?"

"Not much," I admitted. "He was a gangster who had a lot of girlfriends and ended up at the bottom of a canal."

"Great," she said.

"Great?"

"Sure. If that's all you know, then you get to decide what he was really like. Maybe he was an awesome guy. Maybe he only broke people's fingers if they really deserved it. And maybe he passed all his awesomeness down to you."

"I could pretend that's the truth, but it wouldn't be real," I said.

"Why not?" she asked. "He's just a picture in a book. Why can't he be who you want him to be?"

"I can't believe you let Carole take my fire." Gorog interrupts the memory, and I open my eyes. He's shivering in his loincloth. "As soon as it gets dark, those monkeys are going to eat us alive," he groans.

I look over my shoulder and he's right—the troop of monkeys is back. I'm about to suggest we start discussing Plan B when something hits the ogre in the middle of his forehead. A diamond the size of a grape falls into his lap.

"That's for the vote of confidence earlier," says a disembodied voice.

Carole's head appears first, followed by the rest of her as she pulls down her hood and drops a sack at our feet. Her face is flushed with excitement as she hands Gorog his fire and passes my dagger back to me.

"The canyon is just the beginning," she says, her eyes glowing. "Mammon's a freak show too. I don't know what's going on over there, but the houses I saw are all booby-trapped. I'm talking spike pits, swinging logs, the works."

"How did you—" Gorog starts.

"Survive?" she finishes for him. She bends over and pinches him playfully on the cheek. "Awww. You sweet little thing. You still have no idea who you're dealing with, do you?"

I'm not in the mood for fun and games. "Are you sure you got enough diamonds to go around?" I ask as I reach out for the sack she dropped. The weight of the bag answers my question. There must be thousands of jewels inside.

"So? What do you think?" Carole asks with an eyebrow arched.

I can't help but smile. "I'm starting to think we might actually get the hell out of this place," I tell her.

Before darkness falls, we gather a giant mound of the fruit from the trees. We eat a few for dinner, but most we save for morning. The monkeys have been inching closer, so we take turns keeping watch through the night. I have the first watch, and while Carole and Gorog sleep, I prepare the goodies for our trip through the canyon.

Into each ball of fruit, I insert twenty-five of the precious stones that Carole gathered in Mammon. I'm careful not to push them in too deeply. I want them to sparkle in the morning sunlight. When it's my turn to rest, Carole takes over. I sleep so deeply that the next thing I know, I'm opening my eyes to see hundreds of bejeweled balls laid out around us—and two dead monkeys. They tried to sneak up on the camp in the middle of the night. Carole might not like using a sword, but as it turns out, she's pretty good with one. She got rid of the monkeys without even bothering to wake us.

With the sun streaming into the canyon, we begin the last of our preparations. We have no bag large enough to carry the fruit, so I take off my burlap robe and fill it with as many of the sparkling spheres as it will hold.

"Your robe isn't going to cut it," Gorog observes. "We need to take everything we've got with us. If we run out of fruit in the middle of the canyon, we're goners."

"Here," says Carole, pulling her cloak over her head. "We can use mine too."

"No," I tell her. "We'll find another way to carry the stuff." Carole's invisibility cloak will guarantee her safe passage. I can't ask her to risk her life on a plan that might not work.

"Don't treat me like I'm some precious little flower," she snaps. "I want to get out of here as much as you do, and I won't be able to make it alone. Take the damn cloak."

I reach out for it—I've already forgotten we're having an argument, because for the first time, I see what Carole's been wearing under her cloak, and it leaves me totally speechless.

Gorog cackles. The ogre never loses the power of speech. "Oh, man, I forgot you were dressed like my mom."

"Yeah, well, when I chose the outfit, I didn't know I'd be running from swarms of insects or fighting off monkeys, did I?"

Carole snaps. She brushes off her beige chinos and straightens her pink polo shirt. "I dressed for comfort."

"Where'd you think you'd be going?" Gorog asks. "A PTA meeting?"

"Says the guy who's clearly compensating for something with that overgrown avatar," Carole says. "You want a spanking, you little fart?"

"Yes, please," says Gorog, bending over and lifting the back of his loincloth.

"Okay, okay!" I shout. "That's enough. We aren't here to talk about Carole's fashion choices. If she wants to dress like a soccer mom from San Antonio, that's her business, not ours."

Gorog bursts out laughing again, and Carole sticks her lower lip out like a kid. "I hate both of you," she grumbles.

"Yeah, well, if it makes you feel any better, we'll probably be dead soon," Gorog replies.

Gorog meant it as a joke. He's talking about our avatars, of course. But Carole and I instantly sober up. The ogre still doesn't know what's really going on, and now isn't the time to tell him.

"We're not going to die," I say, hoping to convince myself along with the others.

"Of course not," Carole chimes in. "You've come up with a brilliant plan."

"Even if our avatars do bite the dust, it's better than playing *their* stupid game," Gorog says, pointing up at the cliff dwellers' caves.

He's got a point. I still can't understand why anyone would stay in the canyon—raiding, killing and suffering—just to work their way closer to Mammon. They have to be pretty good at the game to survive this far. Otherworld has been available to headset players for about a week. You'd think some of these guys would have found another way through the canyon by now. But they haven't. And what scares me most is that in seven short days, this is what they've become.

I pick up one of our sacks of fruit. Carole takes the other. Gorog is carrying the slingshot I found in the cave.

"You guys ready?" I ask them.

"Hell yeah," says Gorog.

"Then let's get out of Dodge," Carole says.

"What's *Dodge*?" Gorog asks.

Carole sighs. "Good God. Never mind," she says.

I step into the grass between the canyon walls and prepare to address the savages.

"Hey, I just thought of something," Gorog calls to me. "Are you sure the guys in the caves all speak English?"

Shit. It never occurred to me. "Yep," I lie. "I'm sure." There's no turning back now.

I enter the canyon, staying just out of arrow range, and hold up one of the jewel-covered spheres. It sparkles like a disco ball in the early-morning sunlight.

"*Listen up!*" I shout. My voice bounces off the canyon walls. It's far louder than I could have hoped. The acoustics here are excellent. I wait until the cliff dwellers emerge from their caves. "*Every sphere contains food, water and diamonds. Everything an avatar needs! There is one for each of you. Make sure you get yours.*"

I turn to Carole and Gorog. "Here goes." I hand Gorog the ball of fruit I'm holding. He places it in the slingshot and sends it sailing into the first cave. The cliff dweller catches it, examines it and immediately throws a rope down the cliff side. He's not satisfied with one. He wants them all.

"Okay, he's coming," says Carole.

"Time to start walking," I say.

"Dude, he's getting close," Gorog says nervously. The man sprinting in our direction is a particularly fierce specimen. I don't know which one of us he'd go for first, but I'd rather not find out.

"Make sure you get yours!" I shout again. *"Don't let this guy get them all!"*

The attacking cliff dweller has made it to a point less than a hundred yards away from us when a spear slices through his abdomen and pins him to the ground like a bug to a board. Gorog immediately shoots a gem-covered fruit in the spear thrower's direction. The neighbor examines it and almost goes for his own rope. But a glimpse over his shoulder gives him pause. The next cliff dweller along the canyon has a bow and arrow aimed directly at *him.*

"Don't let anyone take what's yours!" I shout.

"Holy moly, it's working!" Carole whispers. Now the truth comes out. She didn't think it would.

"Yeah, 'cause they're jerks," Gorog says. "I bet they don't even care about a few diamonds. They just don't want their neighbors having more than they do."

"Ah, human nature," I say. "It's so revoltingly predictable."

"Hey!" Carole says, taking offense on behalf of the entire human race. "Gorog and I are human too, you know. And neither of us has ever killed for diamonds or resorted to cannibalism."

"*Yet,*" says Gorog, flinging a fruit at another cliff dweller. "With the right barbecue sauce . . ."

Carole rolls her eyes and passes the ogre the next piece of fruit. "He's joking," she says, as if I need it explained to me. "But if you ask me, we're the only real people here. I don't know *what* you'd call *them.*"

You'd call them *guests,* I say to myself. I need to stop thinking of them as human. It's obvious now that the two things are not the same.

We reach the gates of Mammon without a single piece of fruit left between us. Along the way, three cliff dwellers pressed their luck and tried to claim more than their fair share. All three died at the hands of their neighbors. In the end, my plan worked perfectly. If a cliff dweller tried to attack us, the player in the closest cave would kill him. Not out of goodwill, of course. It was just simple logic. If you're waiting for a delivery, it's in your best interest to keep the mailman alive.

Carole and I put our cloaks back on as we approach a pair of golden gates that stand between us and Mammon. There's a booth to the right of the gates, and an NPC guard is sitting inside. He doesn't move as we draw near, but he keeps his eyes trained on us. Unfortunately, I didn't plan for this part. I have a hunch that those gates aren't going to open unless we're able to pay a hefty price.

"How did you get past the gates when you were here earlier?" I ask Carole.

"I stayed invisible and followed a cliff dweller through," she tells me.

"You're kidding. They let one of those cannibal freaks inside?" Gorog asks.

"Sure," says Carole. "For the right price they'd probably let anyone into Mammon. I hope you guys brought enough to pay the toll."

"What?" Gorog yelps. "Why didn't you say something? We used up all the fruit!"

"Good thing one of us held on to a few diamonds in case of an emergency." Carole pulls out a sack of jewels I didn't know she had. Then she stands on her tiptoes and pinches the ogre's overgrown cheek. "You going to make fun of my outfit again?" she asks.

Gorog shakes his head.

"Yeah, didn't think so," Carole tells him.

MAMMON

It's a different world inside Mammon. The only road through the realm is lined with mansions surrounded by gilded gates and well-tended lawns. Each of the homes is more ornate than the last, and they're all covered in stucco that's been mixed with diamonds so the walls sparkle in the sun. It seems the gems the cliff dwellers kill for are as common as dirt here. Everywhere I look I see royal palms, English ivy and topiary trees. But there don't seem to be any avatars or animals. The realm is totally still. As we start down the road, it feels like we're strolling through Beverly Hills just after the apocalypse.

Far ahead at the end of the road, a massive golden temple sits atop a hill. I'm guessing that's where the Elemental of Mammon resides. The homes closest to it are practically palaces, but the temple itself seems to be the ultimate prize. If anyone's alive in this part of the realm, I'd bet they're striving to reach it. I'd love to know what they get if they do.

"We need to make our way to the temple," I say. "If this is anything like Imra, the Elemental of Mammon will decide whether we can leave. And I'm betting that temple is where he or she lives."

"If we're going that far, I should probably stay invisible," Carole says. "Give me your tools and weapons for safekeeping."

"Again?" Gorog whines. "Why? There's no one around."

"Don't be so sure. I stole the diamonds from one of the homes here. The entire yard was booby-trapped like you wouldn't believe. There are definitely people around, and they aren't any friendlier than the ones back in the canyon."

"Okay, but what could these people possibly want from *us*?" Gorog's irritated. "Look at these houses. They have everything. They've got it made."

"You think that's how it works?" Carole asks. "There are rich people in the real world who'd steal a jar of pennies from an orphan. That's how most of them got rich in the first place. Can you imagine what the ones here are like?"

"She's right," I tell the ogre. There's something eerie about this place. I hand Carole my weapons.

"Whatever," Gorog says. "Take my sword and my fire. But I'm keeping the slingshot. I like it."

Carole rolls her eyes at the ogre before she pulls the hood over her head and disappears. I figure she must be lugging her weight in weapons.

We set off toward the temple on the hill. As we walk past the gates of the first mansion, a relatively humble Gothic pile, I hear a strange mechanical whir. It takes me a moment to figure out that it's the sound of a hidden camera following our every move. Someone inside the building is watching us. We reach the second and then the third mansion and discover that their owners have taken security surveillance to even greater heights. Countless cameras are mounted on posts along the gates, and as we pass, drones buzz above our heads. Gorog flips them the bird. I feel strangely naked, like the cameras can see through my clothes and my skin. The discomfort makes me itch. It seems to make Gorog angry.

"We don't want your stuff!" he shouts as one of the drones swoops down for a close-up of him.

We're nearing the grounds of the fourth mansion, and I'm finally beginning to understand the paranoia. Two armies of NPCs are at war on the grounds. One group seems to be invading while the other desperately tries to fend off the attack. What was once lawn is now a muddy battlefield. The little grass left is red with blood. Several booby traps have been sprung, and I see invaders who've been immobilized by nets, riddled with arrows and impaled by spears. As I watch, two NPCs disappear into a hole in the lawn. I don't know for sure what's in the hole, but it wouldn't be much of a trap without a few spikes at the bottom.

We move on quickly while the battle continues to rage. We don't get far before we spot a roadblock up ahead, outside the next mansion.

"Now do you see why I needed to carry the weapons?" I hear Carole whisper.

I know what she's saying, and she's right. Any visible weapons would probably be confiscated. But I'd still feel a lot better if I had my dagger handy.

As we draw closer, it becomes clear that the figures manning the roadblock are all identical NPCs. The mansion's owner definitely has a type—tall, dark and bland. They stand shoulder to shoulder in a line that stretches across the street. There's no way around them.

"Relinquish your weapons," one of the clones demands.

"I don't have any," I tell them. Thankfully, Gorog and I have a fully armed guardian angel watching over us.

"And you?" the clone asks Gorog.

Gorog looks at me and I shrug. He should have let Carole hold on to his slingshot. The ogre pulls the weapon out of his waistband and reluctantly tosses it to the ground. Two of the other men step forward and frisk us.

"That's it?" the clone asks, clearly surprised. "You survived the canyon with a slingshot?"

"We're really fast runners," I tell him.

Gorog nods. "As soon as we're out of here, we're trying out for the US Olympic team," he adds.

The clone doesn't blink. "Come with me," he says humorlessly. We're forced to leave the road to the temple. They surround us and we're marched through the gates that encircle the mansion and then across its broad lawn.

I gotta say, the security here is truly exemplary. You can't really tell from the street, but the place is a fortress. The mansion itself is a stucco-covered monstrosity that looks like the embassy of the world's tackiest country. As we near the building, I see that the windows are barricaded with metal grates and the balconies are all adorned with razor wire. Several snipers are stationed on the roof, and a defensive wall made of sandbags surrounds the entire house. Whoever lives here doesn't seem all that fond of visitors. My chest is starting to feel a bit tight, but I know I'd be feeling a hell of a lot worse right now if Carole weren't right behind me.

The mansion's doors open when we reach the porch, and I'm once again taken by surprise. I'm not sure what I was expecting, but this is definitely not it. The interior is decorated in a style I'd call Baltic dictator. A forest of black marble columns topped with golden ornament holds up the ceiling. The floor tiles are a high-gloss leopard print, and the black ceiling is studded with tiny lights that form what I'd guess are astrological signs. But there's no art on the walls or furniture to sit on. Mounds of black garbage bags are lined up along the perimeter, as if the mansion's inhabitants just went nuts with spring cleaning.

"Hey there!" says a woman, and I spin around. Again—not what I was expecting. The avatar is your typical twentysomething Alpha female. Olive-skinned, with a long brown ponytail. Toned, but not too burly. Nice set of knockers. I would have expected the house's occupant to be all blinged out, but if anything, her appearance is tastefully understated. She's wearing what looks like a black yoga outfit and a pair of diamond studs in her ears. "I'm Gina."

"Hi," Gorog replies a little too enthusiastically. He should know better than to get all hot and bothered by an avatar. There's probably some hairy-handed forty-year-old pervert behind it.

"So you guys have joined forces, have you?" Gina asks. "Most of the people in Mammon prefer to play solo. I guess we're not the sort who like to share." The word *play* echoes in my head. If she knows she's in a game, she's probably wearing a headset.

"We're not here to play," I tell her. "We're just passing through."

Gina laughs. "Passing through? I've never heard *that* before." She gives us the once-over and rubs her hands together eagerly. "What have you brought me?" she asks.

"I'm sorry, we didn't realize you were having us over," I say. "If we'd known, we would have purchased a hostess gift on our way to the party."

"Hilarious!" the woman says. "It's so good to hear a joke. As much fun as these NPCs can be, it's nice to have a human around sometimes. Can you both open your mouths for me, please?"

"Excuse me?" I ask. I seriously didn't think anything could surprise me anymore.

"Your mouths?" She gestures to her servants, and two of them step forward and wrench our jaws apart. The woman takes a look and shakes her head. The servants let us go.

"What was that about?" Gorog's no longer in love.

"You'd never guess how many people trick out their avatars with fancy dental work," she says. "I have a small fortune in grills." She gestures to the guard. "Show them."

The NPC picks up one of the black plastic bags and holds it open in front of us. Inside is a collection of gold and diamond-studded tooth-shaped jewelry. It makes me wonder what might be inside the other bags.

"You steal people's teeth?" Gorog asks.

"Every little bit counts," she says, then turns to one of the NPC servants. "What weapons did our visitors have on them?"

"Only this," says the guard. He passes her the confiscated slingshot.

She examines it thoughtfully. "You made it through the canyon with a *slingshot*? How impressive! It took me a hundred weapons and almost a week of constant play to work my way through the caves."

"You used to be one of the cliff dwellers?" Gorog asks in astonishment.

"Clean up pretty nice, don't I?" says the woman.

"Does that mean you ate people?" Gorog asks, managing to look both curious and queasy. "What did they taste like?"

"Taste like? How the hell would I know? It's a *game*, dickweed," the woman responds testily. She seems offended by Gorog's squeamishness.

I'm actually glad Gorog brought up the subject of cannibalism. Gina's response confirms my suspicions. If her taste buds aren't working, she's not part of the disk's beta test. Somewhere in the United States (possibly Canada), a person wearing a headset is controlling her, and only a few of that person's senses are engaged. I guess cannibalism isn't quite as bad if you don't have to taste or smell what you're eating.

"In case you haven't noticed," Gina is saying, "I'm kicking some serious ass here in Otherworld. I've got twenty-four kills and over three billion dollars in gems, weapons and other assorted goods."

"Oh, we've noticed," I assure her. "You're obviously good at this. So why are you still here in Mammon?"

"What do you mean?" she asks.

"I guess it just doesn't seem like much fun to me. Do you *enjoy* stockpiling weapons and stealing teeth? Isn't Otherworld all about living the life you always wanted? Why spend your time in a place where everyone's afraid all the time?"

"Well, it's a lot better than Everglades City. Spend too much time outside where I live and you'll die of heatstroke or get eaten by gators." So the person behind Gina is in Florida. Good to know. Only two thousand people were given access to the Otherworld headset app. There can't be more than one of them in Everglades City. "Besides, I'm having a blast. I figure in a couple more weeks I'll reach the golden temple."

"And then what?" I ask.

"And then I'll win!"

"Win what?" I ask.

The question clearly annoys her. I don't think she knows. "The game! Look, I'm getting sick of this conversation. I always forget how stupid people can be." She turns to the NPCs. "Take them out of here. And make sure you get the invisible one, too."

"Invisible one?" I ask, managing to play it somewhat cool even though I'm freaking the hell out.

"Do you think I made it this far by being stupid?" the woman sneers. "There's no way you got through the canyon with a god-damn *slingshot.*"

Gina's NPCs have already found Carole and pulled down her hood. All of our weapons and tools are taken away and thrown into a black plastic bag. Then Carole is stripped down to her chinos, and Gina takes the invisibility cloak.

"Cute outfit," she tells Carole. "Is there a minigolf course somewhere in Otherworld?"

"Yeah, why don't you join me there after you get out of your yoga class," Carole says snippily.

Gina practically busts a gut. "You are all so funny!" Then she holds the cloak up under my nose. "Think no one wins this game? This right here is my ticket to glory." She turns to her men. "Get them out of here."

The NPCs grab us and I have to play my last card. Gina isn't a digital freak like one of the Children. She's a human being. An appeal to her better nature may be the only thing that can save us now.

The soldier behind me has me in a choke hold, but I still manage to force a few words out. "Hold on. Don't kill us," I gurgle. "There's something you should know."

Gina lifts a finger, and the pressure on my windpipe eases.

"We're testing a new device for the Company. If we die in Otherworld, there's a good chance it will kill us in real life."

"What?" Gorog blurts out. *Shit.* I forgot. We still haven't shared the news with him. "Simon? What are you talking about?"

Gina's quiet for a moment; then she calls out to her men, "Bring them back." She eyes me closely. "Explain what you mean," she orders.

"I'm serious—we could die," I say. "The three of us don't have VR headsets. We're wearing disks that communicate directly with our brains. They let us experience Otherworld with all five senses. But when something bad happens to our avatars, the disks tell our brains that the injuries are real. I think if our avatars get hurt badly enough, we might die in the real world."

I hear Gorog whimper. Carole whispers something to console him.

"Then it's a good thing I was never planning to kill you," Gina says.

"You weren't?" I ask.

"No, I'm going to sell you. One of my neighbors developed a taste for human flesh while he was making his way through the canyon. I always wondered how he managed to *taste* it. I guess he's wearing one of those disk thingies, too. Explains why he pays me top dollar whenever I bag one of you."

"And you're still going ahead with that after everything he just told you?" Carole asks.

"Of course," says the woman. "There won't be any blood on *my* hands. Though I have a feeling there may end up being quite a lot on my neighbor's."

THE FACILITY

Gina's NPCs locked us inside some kind of holding cell. The chamber is so small that there's barely room to move. Gorog's body is radiating heat. I can see beads of sweat forming on Carole's forehead, but for some reason I'm freezing cold.

"I can't believe it! Why didn't you tell me earlier?" the ogre whines. Gorog's having a hard time coping with the news that his trip to Otherworld could prove fatal.

"I don't know," I answer. "I'm sorry." I'd try to comfort him if there were anything I could say, but there's no silver lining to the cloud hovering over us.

"Come on. Let's focus on the present," Carole says. "What are we going to do now?" She still seems pretty certain that we'll find a way out of this mess. I wish I shared her confidence.

"I have no idea," I admit. "I'm trying to come up with something."

"Why are your teeth chattering?" Carole asks. "It's a hundred degrees in here."

I just shrug. I don't know the answer to that question, either.

"Well, we'd better come up with something soon," Carole says. "It's almost suppertime."

"Shut up!" Gorog bellows. Then his voice softens into a whine. "I don't want to think about getting eaten. I got hit by nine arrows back in the canyon, and it hurt worse than anything I've ever felt before. Can you imagine what it's going to feel like to get chopped up or roasted on a spit or—"

"Stop panicking!" I order. "We're not going to . . ." I can't finish the sentence. Something is happening to me. Something I'm helpless to stop. It's like Gorog and Carole have been ripped away from me, and suddenly I'm surrounded by pitch dark. It's incredibly cold and I feel a frigid breeze sweep across my skin. My heart is thumping and my arms instinctively shoot out in front of me and slice through the air, as if to fend off some invisible threat. But I know what's happening. The Clay Man said he'd find a way to get me into the facility. Now he's making good on his promise—and I wish I'd never asked. He's just dragged me out of Otherworld at the worst moment possible. With the disk off, I'm safe, and that's all he cares about. He doesn't give a damn about Gorog and Carole. But I do, and I'm not going anywhere unless I can guarantee their safety.

Hazy and disoriented, I shove a hand into the pocket of my jeans. The phone I stole from my mother is still there. I pull it out, switch on the flashlight app, and aim the beam into every shadow around me. There's no one there. But there was. That's for sure. My visor and disk were placed at a safe distance so my thrashing wouldn't destroy them. They're sitting on top of a canvas bag I didn't bring. Next to the bag is a package of Depends.

I could chase the person who left them, but I don't. Remarkably, my mother hasn't shut off the phone's service, and I think I just figured out how to save my friends. So I type out a text to Elvis.

there's someone in Everglades City FL playing Otherworld. can u pull the plug?

He's writing. I'm dying.

you mean Gina?

The kid never ceases to amaze me.

HTF do you know?
her last Otherworld playthrough got 1.5MM views
can u get her out of the game?
can't hack the app but can prob take down her Internet
how long?
5 min
you sure?
FO
text me when you're done
ok maybe this time you'll thank me?
FO

It suddenly occurs to me that I might actually owe Elvis a thank-you. Back at the Brockenhurst Country Club, I texted him and asked for a favor—to find the address of the facility where Kat's body was taken. I scroll up through my text history and discover that he delivered.

> can't find name. 1250 Dandelion Drive Brockenhurst NJ
>
> isn't that your town?

I'm not sure what I was expecting. I guess I figured the place would be somewhere in the state. But Dandelion Drive? I could walk there from my house.

A new text arrives from Elvis:

> done. Gina out
>
> that fast? how?
>
> took down local power plant
>
> WTF?
>
> you said get her out of the game. now she won't be back for a while
>
> damn Elvis
>
> careful what u wish for asshole

It's worse than dealing with a robot sometimes. But with Gina—and probably a good chunk of southwest Florida—out of the game, at least I can be sure that Carole and Gorog are safe for a while. So I dig into the bag that's been left for me on the factory floor. The first thing I find is a dark blue uniform. Beneath it are two temporary badges. One bears the name MIKE ARNOLD and the job title PATIENT TRANSPORT. The second is for JOHN DRISCOLL,

MAINTENANCE. At the very bottom I find a piece of paper. *Transport Order. Brockenhurst Hospital to 1250 Dandelion Drive. 8 a.m.*

1250 Dandelion Drive. It's the same address that Elvis sent me. The Clay Man really is sending me to the facility. That's what I asked for, and that's what I got. But somehow it feels like the decision wasn't entirely mine. Whoever's behind the Clay Man has been pulling my strings since he sent me the disk. He says he's affiliated with the Company. So why is he helping me? I know I shouldn't trust him. And I wouldn't—if I had a choice.

It's eight a.m. and there's a van labeled PATIENT TRANSPORT parked outside the Brockenhurst Hospital ER doors. Aside from its dark-tinted windows, there's nothing remarkable about it at all. Nor is there anything particularly interesting about the guy leaning against it slurping coffee from a Styrofoam cup. He's in his fifties, I'd guess, judging by his salt-and-pepper hair and the impressive paunch that's hanging over his belt.

"You the guy filling in for my assistant?" he asks as I approach. You'd think the answer was obvious given the fact that I'm wearing a dark blue uniform that's identical to his.

"Yes, sir," I say. "Mike."

"Don Dunlap. Thanks for making yourself available on short notice," he says, sizing me up as he shakes my hand.

"My pleasure, sir," I tell him.

"Recruiter said you got your EMS training in the army. The boss likes guys who've been in the service. Looks like you haven't been out long enough to let your hair grow."

"That is correct, sir," I say, hoping he doesn't ask for any details. The only things I know about the military I learned playing *Metal Gear Solid.*

"You know, if this ends up working out for both of us, there could be a steady job in it for you. We've had a lot of work lately. The new facility here is getting pretty popular. We've been picking up patients from all over the tristate area. Though it might get a little dull for you after a while. People we've been hauling are all stable. Not much chance of using the skills you picked up in the forces."

"After what I've seen, dull is good, sir," I tell him.

"Yeah, I bet it is," Don says sympathetically.

If only he knew.

The doors of the hospital slide open and an orderly pushes a gurney outside. My new boss tosses his coffee cup in the garbage. "Here we go. You open up the back of the van. I'll bring the patient around."

I do as he asks and then help him push the gurney inside. The patient rolls by; I don't get a good look at her. But it's impossible to miss the fact that she's wearing one of the Company's visors.

"What's that thing on her face?" I ask, wondering if he knows.

Don gives me a funny look. "If I was a doctor, you think I'd be hauling vegetables around at eight o'clock in the morning? It's not our job to ask questions. Our job is to make pickups and deliveries and ensure that our packages get to their destination alive."

"Yes, sir," I say.

"You ride in the back with the patient," he tells me. "Make sure the visor stays on and the IV stays in. We had an IV pop out about a week ago and the patient started shouting like he was being murdered or something. So let's make sure that doesn't happen today. Got it?"

He's waiting for my response, but I'm still stuck on what he just said. When the IV came out, the patient started shouting. Just like the night Kat cried out in the hospital. The nurse said Kat's IV had run dry. That means there must be something in the IV. The patients are being given a drug that prevents them from moving or speaking.

"*Got it*, Mike?" Don repeats, and I snap to attention.

"Yes, sir," I tell him. "I got it."

It's eerily quiet in the back of the van. The woman stretched out in front of me can't be more than twenty-five years old. One of her arms is in a cast, but I can't see any other signs of injury. Once the van is on the road, I look around for a chart, but I don't see one of those, either. There's no way of knowing who she is or where she came from.

I wonder where she is right now. Has she left the White City? Is she indulging in Imra—or fighting for her life in one of the realms? I'm suddenly struck by an overpowering wave of guilt. I'm alone with this woman in the back of a van. No one is watching. I could peel off her disk. Find some way to destroy it. Or I could remove her IV. But I can't run the risk. If I help this one woman, I could lose the chance to help hundreds. But let's be honest: I don't give a damn about hundreds. Right now, all I care about is *one*. And it's not this lady. No—taking her out of Otherworld would put too much at stake. I hope like hell she's safe, but she'll have to stay.

The van comes to a stop, and I hear Don chatting with another man. I peek out the window and realize we've stopped at the gates of 1250 Dandelion Drive. The rear doors open and a security guard pokes his head inside. He glances at the patient and then at me. Once he's satisfied that we're not smuggling whatever qualifies as contraband here, he slams the doors. "You're good to go," I hear him tell Don. A few seconds later, the van starts up again.

I watch from the window as we drive through a park that's filled with ornamental trees and dotted with man-made lily ponds. I catch a deer bolting for cover just before we swing past the facility's main entrance, which looks like it belongs to an upscale spa.

The front of the building is entirely glass. The statement it's making is impossible to miss. The business inside has nothing to hide. It's still early in the morning, but there appear to be a few family members visiting. I bet they're grateful for tasteful scenery. The facility's lobby is bright and airy. It looks nothing like the hellish, fluorescent-lit waiting room of your typical New Jersey hospital.

Our van takes a sharp turn and drives along the side of the building. I realize it's much bigger than it first appeared. The facility is long enough to park a dozen 747s inside and still have room left over for a few games of professional football. And unlike in the welcoming lobby, the windows in this part of the building are few and far between. The only ones I see are small and made of mirrored glass.

Don stops near a metal garage about halfway down the side of the facility. He throws the van into reverse, and when the door rises, he backs all the way into the building. The van shuts off and Don comes around to the rear. He opens the doors.

"What's the name of this place?" I ask. "I didn't see any signs on the way in."

"Dunno. All I know is they pay my boss and he pays me," he says. He doesn't sound terribly curious.

"You really don't know?" I probe.

"Don't know, don't care." Don grabs the end of the gurney and rolls the patient out of the van. "Okay. Let's haul 'er in," he says.

I'm not going to argue, but I'm kind of surprised we're the ones taking the body inside. You'd think a place this big would have a thousand workers, but I don't see anyone around. I help push the gurney from the loading dock into a featureless hallway that ends in what looks at first like an office. There's a desk, but no one's sitting behind it. I count three sliding steel doors on the wall in front of us.

"Hey there, Don," someone says. The voice is coming from a screen mounted on the wall. An attractive middle-aged woman with big blue eyes and bright pink lips is peering out at us. Judging by the love-struck look on Don's face, the lady on the screen is his fantasy girl.

"Morning, Angela," Don says dreamily, proving me right. "You're looking lovely for someone who's probably been up since the crack of dawn."

"Well, aren't you a charmer," Angela flirts back. "Who's your friend?"

Don looks over his shoulder at me as if he totally forgot I'm there. "Oh, right—name's Mike Arnold. Phil called in sick again, so the recruiting agency sent me a sub. But if Phil keeps getting sick after playoff games, Mike here might just become permanent."

"Welcome, Mike," Angela says. "May I scan your badge? Just go ahead and hold it up to the screen."

I do as commanded. I hope she doesn't notice that my hand is shaking. There's no telling whether the badge will actually work. She bends forward for a look. "Wonderful. That all checks out," she says, though I didn't see her check a computer screen. It was like she scanned the badge with her eyes. "Welcome back from Afghanistan, Mike. I hope we get to see you more often!"

"Thank you, ma'am," I say. There's something about the woman that isn't quite right. How did she access my information? She appears to be sitting in a room that looks exactly like this office. Why isn't she here in the flesh?

Then it hits me. She's not a real person. The woman who stars in Don's wet dreams is a robot. She's not quite Otherworld-level, but she's at least as advanced as the NPCs in the White City. That means there's a single place that Angela could have come from. Only the Company is capable of producing artificial intelligence this impressive.

"So which door would you like this young lady to go through?" Don asks Angela, referring to the patient between us. He clearly has no idea that his dream girl isn't human.

"Door number one, as usual," says Angela. It slides open soundlessly, revealing a metal interior that looks like the world's least interesting elevator. Don feeds the gurney into the opening and the patient vanishes behind the sliding door. Just like that, she's gone.

"Anything else I can do for you today?" Don asks Angela.

"As a matter of fact, there is. We have a delivery that needs to be made to the Bosworth Funeral Home in Hoboken. Can you fit it into your schedule this morning?"

"Sure!" says Don as though nothing could make him happier.

"Wonderful," Angela says. "You'll find the delivery behind door number three."

The door slides open. There's another gurney inside. On top of it is a long object encased in a dark blue plastic bag. I try my best to keep my jaw from hitting the floor. It's a body. A *dead* body.

"They know it's coming?" Don asks so casually that you'd think he was talking about a floral arrangement.

"Yes, they're expecting it," says Angela. "The delivery data has been sent to your phone. Make sure you check it before you depart. And thanks again for your help!"

"It's always a pleasure," Don says. "See you next time?"

"Absolutely," Angela replies cheerfully. "I'm always here."

I have to stifle a laugh.

The screen goes black. Don gestures for me to follow him to the third door; then we wheel the body toward the van.

"Isn't she something?" he marvels once we're in the hall and out of earshot.

"Angela?" I ask, and he nods. "You ever seen her in person?"

"Nope," he tells me. "But one of these days I'm going to work up the nerve to ask her out."

"That should be interesting," I say. I'd love to hear her response. How does a robot weasel out of a date? I wonder.

"Tell me about it." Don's practically drooling at the thought. We're at the van and the doors are open. "You good to ride into Hoboken? Traffic this time of day can be brutal. Might take a few hours. Some people get a bit uncomfortable sitting in the back of a van with a corpse for that long."

"Not me. I'll be fine," I assure him.

"Oh, that reminds me," Don says. "It's protocol to confirm that we have the right package before we fire up the engines. Gotta check the info Angela sent." He pulls out his phone and opens a file. I see a picture of a kid. It must be an old photo, because the boy in it can't be more than fifteen. Then Don unzips the bag and I almost gasp. The picture is up-to-date and the body inside the bag is so young that it's hard to believe its owner could be dead. How did it happen? Did he die of injuries he sustained in the real world—or was it the disk that killed him?

Then I notice there's something wrong with the top of his head. There's an incision just above his hairline—it runs from one side of his head to another. I'm trying to figure out what might have caused it when the truth hits me so hard that I almost double over. The kid's been autopsied and his brain has been examined. I feel my knees soften and my head starts to spin while my mind repeats the same sentence over and over and over again.

Oh my God, this could be Kat.

"Yup, same guy," Don confirms, then zips the bag back up. "Let's hit the road."

I push the gurney with the dead kid's body into the van. Then Don heads for the driver's seat. I make a show of climbing into the back with the body, but when I slam the door, I'm not inside. The van heads out of the loading dock, and I hitch a ride on the back bumper. Just before we drive past the front entrance, I hop off again. I need to get into the main part of the building, and I figure there's no way Angela is going to let me pass. My only hope is going in through the front door.

There was a second ID badge in the package the Clay Man left at Elmer's. JOHN DRISCOLL, MAINTENANCE, it reads. There's some kind of code beneath that. It's a long shot, but I'm hoping John is my ticket inside. I take the second badge out of my pocket and fix it to the pocket of my blue uniform. This adventure's risk level keeps rising. Right now it's hovering between "you've got to be shitting me" and "good luck with your death wish." But I've seen what happens to the patients here, and at this moment, I couldn't care less about the danger.

I'm barely through the front doors when a guy steps in front of me, blocking my way. I assume he's a flesh-and-blood human being. If not, he's an excellent replica of one. He's dressed in a blue polo shirt, dark jeans and white sneakers. He has a casual, friendly face to match the casual, friendly environment.

"Good morning," he says. "I'm Nathaniel. May I help you?"

"I'm John from maintenance," I say, pointing to my badge and hoping that's enough.

Nathaniel scans my badge with a handheld device while I stare over his shoulder. There are a few miserable-looking people in the reception area who must be family members. A man is standing at the main desk, speaking with the woman behind it. I can't hear the conversation, but it looks tense. When I recognize the voice, my entire body goes rigid. It belongs to Wayne Gibson—Kat's stepdad. He's here for a visit.

"Come with me," Nathaniel says. I'm almost trembling with nervousness when he leads me past security. I keep my head turned away from Wayne as we pass. "There's a clogged toilet in visiting room number three. Someone must have tried to flush something fairly big. We'd love to have it fixed as soon as possible.

We have a limited number of visiting rooms, and as you can tell, we have quite a few family members with us this morning."

"I'll see what I can do," I promise. This place must be filled with some of the most advanced technology ever developed, and yet no one here is able to unclog a toilet. Typical.

I follow Nathaniel out of the lobby and into a hall with a half-dozen doors. He chooses one and places his palm against a black glass scanner on the wall beside it. The door opens and we step inside a room that looks more like a high-end hotel suite than something you'd find in a facility that tends to the nutritional and waste-removal needs of lost causes. The television is large, the furniture is well designed, and the floor is a tasteful hardwood. I wish the chair I slept in at the hospital had been half as plush as the one they have here. I walk up to the bed and rub the sheets between my fingers. Even my mother would approve of the thread count.

"The toilet's in there," Nathaniel says, helpfully pointing at the bathroom. "The door will lock behind me when I leave. Just press the button on the wall as soon as you're finished and I'll come get you."

Nathaniel doesn't seem to have noticed that I have no tools with me. It's highly unlikely that anything in this room's getting fixed. When he leaves, I realize I'm stuck. There are two metal doors—the one I just entered and another on the opposite side of the room. But I'm not getting out of either one. Instead of knobs, they both have biometric scanners embedded in the walls beside them. I cross the room to the second door to examine its scanner. I'm bending over for a closer look when the door slides open and I jump back in surprise. A doctor in a white lab coat jumps too when he sees me. His eyes dart to the empty hospital bed and then narrow as they return to me.

"Who are you?" the doctor asks warily, as if I could be anyone from a Russian spy to a hired killer.

"Maintenance," I tell him, tapping my badge. "Toilet's clogged."

His attitude instantly shifts from fear to annoyance. "Still? I'm supposed to be meeting here with a family in . . ." He checks the device strapped to his wrist. I can tell it's a smart watch, but I've never seen one like it before. I'd bet anything it's a Company design. ". . . two minutes."

"I guess you're going to have to find another room," I say.

"I have a better idea," he says snippily. "Instead of standing around making small talk, why don't you do *your* job so that I can do mine?"

I'm about to suggest I use his face as a plunger when three quick beeps issue from the device on his wrist and his expression changes. He knows what the signal means without having to look down at the watch. "That just bought you some time," he says. "Fix the damn toilet before I get back."

The doctor presses his palm against the scanner and the door slides open again. He rushes away down another featureless hall without realizing that I've slipped through the door behind him.

The door slides shut, and the doctor's footsteps grow fainter. I'm clearly in a part of the building that's off-limits to visitors. I expect security guards to show up at any moment and haul me away, but no one does. I scan the ceiling and walls, but I can't spot a single camera, which seems highly unusual. Slowly, placing one foot after the other carefully, I head in the direction where the doctor just disappeared. Identical metal doors line the wall on my left. I suspect they lead to other visiting rooms, but there are only six of them. Where are the patients? Martin and Todd said there were three hundred people participating in the beta test. A lot of them must be here at the facility by now. But where are they keeping them all?

I turn a corner and realize I've left the hall. In front of me is a metal balustrade. There are stairs to my left leading down. I walk to the railing. Below me lies a space the size of an airplane hangar.

I'm not quite sure what I'm seeing. There's obviously a mammoth building project under way. Most of the space remains under construction, but a small section appears to be already in use. Inside the finished area, corridors cut paths through massive metal walls that must be at least twenty feet deep and eight feet high. Three rows of glowing hexagonal windows are set into the walls. From where I'm standing, it looks like a high-tech beehive.

I spot the doctor below me. He stops at one of the windows and punches in a code. The window opens, and he pulls out a sliding shelf with a body resting on top. It's a man, and he's naked aside from an aluminum foil Speedo and the black visor on his face. Clear plastic tubes sprout from his mouth, forearm and groin, while thin black wires tether him to the inside of the capsule. I realize I must be looking at some sort of giant life-support machine, with rows of individual capsules stacked three high like shipping crates. Each capsule contains a human being who's being kept alive. The fancy visiting rooms are just to make the families happy. This is where the patients are actually stored.

In Otherworld, the guy on the shelf is probably battling to

survive. But here in this world, he's nothing but a bag of flesh with a beating heart. Nourishment is pumped directly into his veins while his liquid waste is removed via a tube that's been inserted into his bladder. I'm sure the shiny diaper he's wearing takes care of the rest, but I'd rather not know how.

My entire nervous system is buzzing with anxiety. Kat is down there somewhere, locked inside one of those capsules. Carole and Gorog are too. The horror of it almost makes me retch. I cannot—I will not—abandon them here. There's no time to think it through. I have to act. While the doctor is examining his patient, I dart down the stairs and up to the first capsule. Behind the window, a middle-aged African American woman is lying on a steel shelf, her bare feet only inches from the glass. At the back of the capsule, her head is raised slightly. I can see her face clearly, and it's not one I recognize. I step back and, one by one, I work my way down the row of windows, looking for Kat. I have no idea what Carole and Gorog look like IRL, but I keep hoping I'll recognize them, too, somehow. Maybe, like me, they'll resemble their avatars.

I crouch to look into the capsules on the lowest row and jump for a view into the ones on top. The capsules are all the same. Stainless steel interior, blinking green monitors, wires and tubes. The bodies inside the capsules couldn't be more different. They come in every size, age and color, and they're all mostly naked. Each is bathed in a strange orange light that must play some role in keeping them healthy. Every single one of the patients is wearing a black visor.

This is the proof I've been looking for, I realize. I pull out my mom's phone and start snapping pictures. There's something big going on, and the Company is at the center of it. Helpless people are being falsely diagnosed with locked-in syndrome, and their families are being tricked into accepting the Company's virtual reality therapy. Then the patients are brought here. The Company is using people's bodies to beta test the disk and work out the bugs. And as hard as it is to believe, that douchebag Milo Yolkin must be behind all of it. Everyone knows he's a control freak. Nothing ever happens at the Company without his direct. . . .

A piercing sound nearly shatters my skull. Just around the corner from me, an alarm is going off and red lights are flashing overhead. I hear a door open somewhere and footsteps rushing to the scene. I freeze and back up against one of the capsules, doing my best to disappear. I have no idea what would happen if I got caught, but I do know what would happen to my friends. *Nothing.* They would stay here. Eventually it would be their bodies in the transport van to the funeral home.

I can hear multiple people running down a nearby corridor. Then they come to a sudden stop. Someone is barking commands. There's a loud thump, followed by a monotonous beeping, and then a second thump.

I tiptoe toward the action and sneak a peek around the corner. A few dozen yards down an identical corridor, a second doctor and a team of nurses have gathered around the male patient I saw being examined. One of the nurses steps away from the patient's side and I finally get a good look at him. I'd guess he's in his early thirties, and aside from all the tubes coming out of him—and the fact that a doctor is using a defibrillator to restart his heart—he appears to be an excellent physical specimen. From what I can tell, there are no visible injuries to his body, so it's strange to witness the flurry of activity around him.

I raise my phone and hit Record. To their credit, the doctors seem to be making a valiant effort to save the guy's life. But only a few minutes after they begin, it's all over. The doctors pull off their gloves and disappear into the maze. A nurse rolls the defibrillator cart away and two of his colleagues follow behind him. Eventually only a single nurse is left with the lifeless body. As I put my phone down, I hear doors open and shut somewhere in the distance, and it suddenly occurs to me that I'm trapped. The nurse is probably my only way out, and I doubt she'll want to help me. I'd rather not force her, but I may not have a choice. I have footage on the camera that can free my friends and take the Company down. But only if I can manage to get out of here alive. Right now, that's a *really* big if.

I wait as the nurse unhooks the man from the various tubes and wires that were connecting him to the life-support machine and shifts his lifeless body onto a waiting gurney. Then I approach her. I don't tiptoe this time. I want her to hear me coming, and she does. She glances at me without a trace of fear. Up close she's unusually pale, with dark circles beneath her eyes. The corpse on the gurney in front of her looks a hell of a lot healthier.

"Hi," I say, trying to sound cheerful. "I'm John from maintenance. I'm afraid I got lost down here. Think you can show me the way out?"

"Nobody gets lost," the nurse says, still staring at me. She knows I'm not supposed to be here, but she doesn't seem worried. If anything, she appears completely resigned. If I pulled out a machete and threatened to hack her to pieces, I doubt she'd so much as flinch.

"Well, I guess there's a first time for everything," I tell her.

"What do you want?" she asks, getting down to business. "Tell me now before someone else comes."

I realize this is my chance. "I'm trying to stop this," I say. "But first I need to get out of here."

I wait on edge. This could go one of two ways. One of them ends with me punching out a female nurse. I'll just have to make peace with that when and if the time comes.

"Then climb under," she says, pointing to the gurney. There's a long metal shelf between the mattress and the wheels.

I look all around. "Are there cameras watching?"

"Surveillance systems can be hacked. They don't want cameras down here. They'd rather track *us* instead." The nurse taps the smart watch on her wrist. "This thing doesn't come off. They know everything I do. I can't get away. My movements are monitored twenty-four seven."

I bet they are. The Company wouldn't want news of their body farm getting out.

"What happens if you do something you're not supposed to?" I ask. Like help an intruder escape.

"I don't know." Her voice trembles a little. Once again, she points at the shelf underneath the dead patient. "Get on. Quickly. Before one of the doctors walks by."

I cram my giant body onto the shelf, lying on my side with my legs tucked up under my knees. The nurse spreads a sheet over the corpse above me. The ends of the fabric are just long enough to hide me. My brain bounces around in my skull as the wheels of the gurney roll across the concrete floor. I hope like hell I know what I'm doing.

The journey lasts less than three minutes and ends in a room that's freezing cold. The nurse whips the sheet off the corpse.

"You can come out," she says. "There are no cameras here, either."

I slip out of my hiding place and I can see why. We're in an autopsy room. There are three bodies of various sizes laid out on metal tables. Thankfully the cadavers are all covered with sheets. On my left is a wall of metal drawers. On my right is a giant re-frigerator with glass doors. Its shelves are lined with jars filled with floating human brains.

I take out my phone and start snapping more pictures. My eyes pass over the brains and focus on one of the covered bodies that are waiting to be autopsied. A dirty-blond dreadlock is stick-ing past the edge of the sheet. West, the druggie Kat used to hang with, had hair just like that. I don't need to see his face to know it's him. He survived the collapse at the factory just to end up here. I never liked him, but I would never have wished this upon him.

"Holy shit." I look over at the nurse. "What are you doing to these people?"

"The patients die in the capsules. The pathologists are try-ing to figure out what killed them," the nurse says. "That's all I know."

She seems so small and frail standing there next to the gur-ney, but I know that what she's doing requires incredible strength. "Why are you helping me?"

The nurse shakes her head helplessly. "I can't escape." She taps the device on her wrist. "But you can. End this."

"I'm going to try." That's all I can promise. I shove my mother's phone back into my pocket. "But first I have to get out of here."

"This is the only way out," the nurse says, holding up a long black bag.

My gurney enters an elevator. I hear the doors shut. I can't feel the car rising, and I can't tell when it's come to a stop. But I hear the doors open and Angela's voice in the background. She seems to be flirting with yet another driver from another patient transport company. I try to stay perfectly still as the guy takes control of my gurney and pushes it down the hall. At some point, he'll open my body bag and check to make sure he's got the right package. The nurse figured she might know a way around that, but she also made sure to warn me that nothing was certain.

I hear the bag unzip. "Sir, they got a sheet covering this one's face," says a young man. "Should I remove it?"

If they do, I'll have to bust out and make a run for it. My face won't match the picture on their patient file.

An older man grunts. "Only if you got a strong stomach," he says. "They do that to the ones who haven't made it out looking pretty. I took the sheet off once, and I swear I'll never do it again."

"Then I think I'll pass, if that's okay, sir," says the young guy. I can tell from his quavering voice that he lacks the balls for this kind of work.

"Are we sure the cadaver's male?"

"Yes, sir. It's way too big for a female."

"Then it's okay with me if you pass on the inspection."

The zipper goes up again. I'm rolled inside the van and I hear the young guy clamber in behind the gurney. Suddenly I pity the kid. He's going to be sitting right beside me when the corpse he was too squeamish to look at decides to rise from the dead.

I feel the van turn right onto Dandelion Drive, and I mentally chart the course it's likely to take. If we continue in a straight path, there will be a patch of woods on the left side of the road soon. If I reach them, I can disappear. With my finger positioned on the body bag's zipper, I wait until the van rolls to a stop at a streetlight. Then, with one quick sweep, I open the bag. The shrieking begins the second I sit up and slip the plastic away from my torso. By the time I break free, my escort is already cringing in a corner of the van, his body tucked into a tight little ball and his hands over his face.

"Sammy! Sammy! What the hell is going on back there?" the man in the driver's seat shouts. The kid answers with a piercing scream that doesn't seem likely to end.

I throw open the back doors of the vehicle. There's a car right behind us at the red light, and I watch its driver react as I emerge, naked from the waist up. The dickhead lifts his camera to snap a photo right before I make a break for the trees at the side of the woods. Unless he's a virtuoso at action shots, it's unlikely he caught me. I'm deep in the forest in a matter of seconds.

Unfortunately, I quickly realize, I'm miles from Elmer's. Fueled by a mixture of panic and rage, I start hiking toward my destination. Branches are slapping at my sides, and every bug in New Jersey seems drawn by the scent of my exposed flesh. I trudge through the forest and sprint across the countless roads that cut through it.

I'm covered with scratches and speckled with bites, and I still have a few miles to go when I take my mom's phone out to check my location on the map. The caller ID for my home phone flashes up on the screen. I let it go to voice mail. When I check, there are a dozen missed calls from the same number. Five have come in the last ten minutes. I play back the most recent voice mail.

"What have you done?" she whispers angrily into the microphone. It immediately catches my attention. Irene Eaton doesn't whisper. "The police are here searching your room. They say you were seen trespassing at some kind of medical facility. And they think you may be in possession of stolen goods. Simon, you have to turn yourself in right away. If they catch you, you could end up going to jail for years. And they *will* catch you. When they find out you have my phone, all they have to do is trace it."

I don't listen to the rest of the message. Maybe I'm wrong, but I have a feeling my mother just saved my ass. I think she knew someone might be listening. She was trying to tell me to destroy the phone. I'll do it in a second, but I need to send the photos and videos I took at the facility to my own email account for safekeeping. I open the photo folder. I'm selecting images to send. Then suddenly they're gone—they've just disappeared. The Company's already hacked the phone. I drop the useless device and grind it into the ground with the heel of my shoe.

THE RIGHT PLACE

Once again, my avatar is right where I left it—inside the cramped chamber in Gina's house where Carole, Gorog and I were imprisoned while we awaited our fate. Only now the door's open and I'm alone. If Carole and Gorog have been eaten, I'll never forgive myself. The Clay Man sent me to the facility so I'd focus on my original mission. But after visiting the place where their bodies are stored, I feel even more responsible for the two of them. I need to get them to the exit. I need to find Kat. And then I need to figure out another way to take the Company down.

I step into the hall and see Gina smiling at me. Her lifeless avatar has faded to indicate it's inactive. I guess the headset players' avatars don't disappear completely when they take a break from the game. This must have been where she left it when the plug was pulled on Everglades City. I'd love to beat her avatar to a bloody pulp, but instead, I walk away.

I retrace my steps through the house, passing several off-duty

NPC guards who pay me no mind, and finally locate my friends in the only furnished room in Gina's mansion. Gorog is fiddling with a tablet that must control the house's decorating menu. The room's décor keeps flipping from Medieval Fortress to French Chateau to Kountry Klassic.

Carole has a tablet too, and I can see the screen from over her shoulder. She's studying a menu that allows users to custom-design NPC companions. "Hey, it says here that thirty NPCs come with this house," she tells Gorog. "Each of them can be totally different, but Gina just made the same boring Ken doll thirty times. Can you believe it? What a waste! I figure I'll make a few changes, if that's cool with you. You got any requests?"

"Just make sure your new boyfriends are all wearing clothes," Gorog grunts.

"We don't have time for any of this," I say, and suddenly their eyes are on me.

"You're back!" Carole cries merrily, dropping the tablet and hopping up to greet me with a hug. She's traded her chinos and polo shirt for a sleek black yoga outfit like Gina's. On a table in front of her is a glorious feast. "You hungry?"

I am, damn it. I forgot to eat while I was back in the real world. And while Carole's feast is amazing to behold, none of it's going to do my real body much good.

"Oh, man, you're not going to believe what happened," Gorog tells me. "Gina came to get us and feed us to her friend. Then suddenly her avatar just goes totally still, like she's been turned to stone or something, and her guards all wandered away."

"Get up," I tell him. "Both of you get ready. We've got to go."

"What? Can it wait a little bit? Just for a few hours?" Gorog groans. "I really need a break. I'm still sore from those arrows, and Gina's got a Jacuzzi upstairs."

"No. We can't wait." Not another second.

Carole realizes there's something going on. "What is it?" she asks. "What happened to you back in the real world?"

I open my mouth, but I can't tell them. I *can't*. What the hell would I say? Would I tell them that the world's richest corporation has kidnapped their bodies? That they're unwilling participants in an experiment that would make Dr. Death proud? That a single wrong move in Otherworld could kill us?

I can't say any of that. So I say nothing at all.

Gorog and Carole look stunned by my silence. The horror must show on my face.

"That bad?" Carole asks. I nod in reply.

"Okay, then," Gorog says softly. "Let's go. You got any ideas about how we're going to make it out of this city?"

"We need to get to the temple on the other side of Mammon and we're less than halfway there," Carole adds. "And if Gina was . . . well, Gina, can you imagine how bad the people farther up the ladder are going to be?"

"We'll have plenty of weapons this time," I point out. "Gina's got hundreds of garbage bags full of everything we could possibly need."

"Doesn't matter," Gorog says. "Someone's always going to have more."

"If we try to fight all of them, it will take forever to leave," Carole adds.

They're right. Fortunately everyone in this city shares a weakness. And I think I know just how to take advantage of it.

"Where are all Gina's NPCs?" I ask. "I saw a few wandering around the house. Where are the rest of them?"

"Most of them are outside." Gorog points toward the front lawn. "We kept making them leave because they were freaking us out. They all have this same weird blurry patch right here." He points to a spot under his left ear. "It's like a robot mole or something. But once you see it, you can't *stop* seeing it."

We're struggling to stay alive, and the ogre's talking about robot moles. There's something seriously screwed up with him. "Find the NPCs that are still in the house and send them outside. Then gather the best weapons—take as many as you can fit under Carole's invisibility cloak."

"But I thought we just agreed that we can't fight our way out," Carole says.

"We won't fight unless we have to," I tell her. "Be ready to leave in thirty minutes."

I was hoping to avoid any more killing, but my new plan leaves me no other choice. Before I do anything else, I'll have to dispose of Gina's avatar. I return to the hall and execute her from a distance by sinking a crossbow arrow through the center of her skull. Her avatar only flashes, but it counts as a kill. With her death at my hands, the house, its contents and Gina's digital slaves all belong to me.

I head out to the lawn, where the thirty identical NPC clones are loitering.

"Visit every house in the city," I order them. "Tell all the guests that the gates of this mansion will be opened in thirty minutes and all booby traps will be deactivated. Everything inside the mansion will be free for the taking. But only Otherworld guests will be allowed inside. Any NPCs they bring with them will be slaughtered on sight."

The soldiers set off the second the words leave my mouth. There are no questions—no complaints or concerns. And I couldn't care less if half of them never return from their mission. Having a robot army certainly has its advantages.

They're excellent at their job, too. Word of our little give-away spreads quickly, and soon the residents of Mammon are scuttling about like cockroaches on garbage day. For the most part, the mansions' owners are attractive and elegantly attired. Standing outside the closed gates of Gina's house, they resemble members of the Brockenhurst Country Club. If it weren't for their icy eyes, you'd never guess they were killers.

Gorog and I are on the lawn, waiting for the fun to commence. Carole, loaded down with weapons, is invisible beside us. As our visitors arrive, they all peer through the gates, examining the ogre first before they move on to me. The gaze is always cold and clinical, and when they finish, they scrutinize their neighbors. Finally, risk assessed, the people of Mammon proceed to pick apart Gina's mansion with their eyes. At least half of them have far more than Gina. There's no need to resort to looting. But the cliff dwellers inside them all can't resist.

"Why are you doing this?" a gentleman asks me, as if my motives are completely inscrutable. "Why give it away?"

"Because Gina's a bitch," I say.

He lets out a snort. "That's true. But I hope you weren't expecting to find many saints here in Mammon."

"Saints?" I reply. "*Please.* I'd settle for someone who isn't a cannibal."

He snickers. "Oh? And who are you to judge? We all consume people on our way up the ladder. It's only natural that some of us learn to like it."

Gorog nudges me. "I think that might be the dude who was going to eat us," he whispers.

If so, I should kill the guy. If this were a game, my dagger would already be sticking out of his throat. But if he's the one with a taste for human flesh, he's probably wearing a disk. If I kill him here, he dies for real. And I'm not ready to add murder to my résumé.

"I hope you meet something much bigger than you farther up the food chain," I snarl back at him.

I open the mansion's gates and step back while the looters flood in. As soon as they're all inside, I take my friends and my robot army and forge deeper into Mammon. A battalion of NPCs guards every mansion we pass. No one in Mammon left their possessions unprotected. But we meet no resistance on our way to the temple that looks down on the city. The mansions' owners are all back at Gina's.

We walk until the road through Mammon ends at the base of a staircase composed of golden bricks, which make me think of *The Wizard of Oz.* Standing at the bottom, I count five long but manageable flights. Gorog's bounding up the first set of stairs before I'm done ordering our NPCs to go home to Gina's. He stops at the landing between the flights, looking around in confusion, as Carole and I begin our climb. As soon as we join him on the landing, I spot the problem: there are still five flights of stairs above us.

"What the—" Gorog says.

"Don't stop," I tell him.

We keep climbing, and new stairs keep appearing above us, as if we're walking up a down escalator. We're forced to take regular breaks to let Gorog catch his breath. Apparently ogres aren't built to climb stairs. One by one, Carole dumps all the weapons she's been lugging. None of our avatars has the strength left to carry any additional weight. Whenever we stop, my eyes immediately turn to the temple at the summit. It's Roman in style—a simple rectangle set on a podium and surrounded by columns. Slowly, we begin to draw closer, and as we do, the columns supporting the pediment begin to take on human shape. They're statues of men and women—all of them naked and all clearly struggling under the weight they're bearing. Their backs are hunched and their muscles straining. Misery is literally etched on their faces.

After hours of climbing, I finally set foot on the top of the hill. Like those of the statues that loom above, my face is probably the image of agony. Gorog and Carole aren't looking so hot, either. In fact, I'm seriously surprised that Gorog made it up here alive. While he wheezes and coughs, I look back over the City of Mammon. From up here, I can see the realm for exactly what it is—a fucked-up digital board game. You start way down in the canyon. Then you hop from square to square by hoarding, stealing and killing as often as you can. Everyone's trying to reach the golden temple. But then what? What happens to players when they finally get to the top?

I guess it's time to find out. Gorog's no longer hacking up a lung, so I motion for him and Carole to follow me into the temple.

It's dark inside, and plumes of perfumed smoke waft from marble incense burners. It takes a second for my eyes to adjust to the dim light, but as they do I realize we're not alone. At the far end of the temple, a giant being sits atop a golden chair. There's no doubt it's the Elemental of Mammon. A golden toga conceals his lower half, but his doughy chest and massive stomach are bare. Blue-white flesh spills over the chair's armrests and bulges through the openings beneath them. If he decided to stand up, the chair would probably need to be surgically removed from his ass. But somehow I doubt this guy ever needs to budge.

Five of what I can only guess are Children skulk about behind the Elemental's chair, ready to do his bidding. Their size and overall appearance vary. They must have different mothers. But like their father, they're all totally hairless, with skin the color of skim milk. Hideous creatures with hunched backs and gnarled limbs, the Children watch our every movement from the safety of their father's side. They don't dare come any closer. They seem to fear us even more than they hate us.

The Elemental's gaze is lazy and his eyelids droop as if he'd love nothing more than a nice long nap.

"You have reached the temple," he drones. I suppose he doesn't feel the need to introduce himself. "You must go now. You do not belong in Mammon."

It's a little rude, but I'm not going to argue. My ogre friend, on the other hand, doesn't seem satisfied.

"So what do we win?" Gorog asks.

"Win?" the Elemental asks through a yawn.

"Yeah—for making it through Mammon," Gorog adds. "Has anyone ever done it before?"

"My realm offers guests a unique way of life," the Elemental tells him. "It is far more than a game."

"But we met a lady down there who said the whole point is to keep moving up until you reach the temple," Gorog argues.

"The object is to keep moving up. Not to reach the temple," the Elemental informs us. "There will always be more gold to collect. Larger houses to build. Richer neighbors to rob. Those who belong here with me understand that."

Gorog seems hopelessly confused, but Carole is nodding, and I think I get it too. The people here are addicted to acquiring. But no matter how much they have, they'll never have enough. That's why they stay in Mammon.

"So you're really going to let us leave?" Carole asks the Elemental.

He takes a moment to scratch his ample belly. "Certainly. Where do you think you belong?"

It's not exactly the response I was anticipating. The Elemental of Imra didn't give us much of a say in the matter. "We can choose where we go next?" I ask.

"In a manner of speaking," he replies, his voice deep and rich. "The Creator designed Otherworld to be a place where every guest is able to be his or her true self. Whatever desires you may have, there's an Otherworld realm where you may express them freely. Perhaps it's something that would not be acceptable in your world. It makes no difference to us. So tell me what it is you desire most, and I will direct you to the realm that suits you best."

I glance over at Carole and Gorog. They nod, silently letting me know that they'll follow my lead. "Out in the wastelands there are ice fields that stretch for miles and miles. That's where we'd like to go."

Something I just said seems to have caught the attention of the Children. I see ears prick up. But their father yawns again as if performing his duties is an utter bore. "No. The ice fields are a liminal space. They are not within the boundaries of any of Otherworld's realms," he says. "I cannot send you there."

"Could you send us to the realm that's closest to them?" I ask. "There's a glacier in the ice fields that we really need to reach." The Elemental doesn't respond. He's bending to the side, letting one of the Children whisper in his ear. When he sits up straight again, he no longer seems bored.

"What business do you have at the glacier?" he demands. I think I may have misread him. He doesn't sound quite so easygoing anymore.

"Someone's waiting for me there," I tell him. My heart skips a beat at the thought of Kat. "And these two just want to go home. Inside the glacier there's a cave with an exit that leads back to our world."

The most human-looking of the Children limps toward us. She's a pale, sickly creature, with large, wide-set eyes that take up most of the space on her hairless head. Her sisters and brothers are far more hideous, but I'm still finding it hard to look at her. Something appears to be very wrong with both of her legs. Thick, oozing scars ring her shins. I'm guessing she got caught in a booby trap outside one of the mansions in Mammon.

My gaze passes over her brothers and sisters. They, too, show signs of injury—fresh wounds and scarred flesh. A couple of them appear to be missing limbs. Life in Mammon is dangerous for anyone without garbage bags full of weapons. No wonder the Children are holed up here in their father's temple. It's the only safe spot in the realm.

"Why do you need an exit?" the Child asks. "Guests may leave our world whenever they like."

"Not us," Gorog says, shaking his head.

"We're not playing a game like most of them," Carole tries to explain. "We're stuck here, and we're trying to get out."

The Child glances up at her father and then back at us. "I don't understand."

"We shouldn't be here," I tell her. "The people who made this place—"

"People?" the Child interrupts.

"The *Creator* built Otherworld," the Elemental booms.

"Right, right, of course," I say, trying not to sound dismissive. "How could I forget?"

"The cave you describe—they say the Creator has taken refuge there," says the Child.

What? Now I'm confused. Since when do Creators take refuge in caves? And what about the big red dude that already lives there? The one the Clay Man says I'm supposed to kill? None of it makes any sense, but I'm not going to quibble.

"Ummm, well then, good," I say, doing my best to think on my feet. "I was meaning to have a word with him anyway."

"You intend to speak to the Creator?" the Elemental asks, leaning forward as if to see me better. Multiple folds of flesh dangle from his outstretched chin.

"Yeah, I was going to try to talk some sense into him. I've met a lot of folks here who believe all the guests need to be sent home. They think Otherworld should belong to the Elementals, Children and Beasts."

The Children begin whispering among themselves. The idea clearly excites them.

"No," the Elemental announces. "Otherworld will never belong to us."

The Children go silent as they register the betrayal. The stricken looks on their faces are horrible to behold.

"But, Father," says the female who spoke earlier. "You've seen what the guests do to us. Dozens of your Children have died so far. We will not survive if they're allowed to stay. They say there's a war coming. The Creator must choose between the guests and his own creations."

"Then he must choose the guests, and you must continue to suffer," the Elemental tells his daughter. The words may be harsh, but he delivers them kindly.

"But, Father—"

"Without the guests, there is no reason for any of us to exist." He looks down at me. "I cannot send you to the glacier. I will not allow you to speak with the Creator."

I've come too far and seen too much to take no for an answer. The only person I love said she'd be waiting for me at the glacier. If she tries to fight the red guy on her own, she could die. My mission to save her will not be stopped by a toga-wearing Jabba the Hutt. Gritting my teeth, I drop down and reach for the dagger in my boot. Either the Elemental sends me where I need to go or I teach him the real meaning of suffering.

Carole must catch sight of the steel blade. "Simon, what in the hell are you doing?" she whispers.

It's the last thing I hear before I'm no longer in Mammon.

WORLD OF WAR

All it takes is a single look around and I know I've really fucked up this time. I'm alone. Carole and Gorog are still in Mammon. I've lost all three people I was trying to help, and things aren't looking so hot for me, either. I'm surrounded by dense jungle. The air is stiflingly humid—so thick that it would be easier to chew it than breathe it. I hear a man screaming in the distance. And the only weapon I've got is the dagger I was holding.

There's a soft crunch behind me. If I hadn't spent most of my childhood in the woods, I doubt I would have picked up on it. But I spin around just in time to see a man in forest camo barreling toward me with an axe raised high above his head. I duck to the side just as he brings the blade down. If I'd spotted him a second later, he'd have split me in half like a piece of kindling. And I get the impression I'm not the first person Rambo has tried to murder. He recovers quickly and he's beaming when he comes at me again. The look on his face is one of sheer ecstasy. I can tell the dude really gets off on killing.

I won't fight. I saw the bodies in the capsules. I saw what happens to them when they die, and I don't know if Rambo's wearing a disk. Acting against every instinct I've ever possessed, I turn and run instead. My avatar is fast, but my opponent's no slouch, and he knows the jungle far better than I do. He stays right behind me. So when I see the opportunity to slip between the fronds of a prehistoric-size fern, I happily seize it.

Rambo isn't easily fooled. The avatar runs past my hiding place, then comes to a stop.

"Come out, come out, wherever you are!" he calls. "I've got to be on a client call in fifteen minutes, and I need a good look at your intestines before I go."

The crazy fucker is a headset player.

I'm engaged in a battle to the death with some random business guy who's never going to die. He may lose his swag and be sent back to setup, but at the end of the day, it's no big deal. Me? I die and I stay dead. Screw Milo Yolkin and his human experiments. What kind of lunatic lets people die just to figure out what's killing them?

Fortunately, there is one clear advantage to fighting guests that won't die. I can slaughter Rambo and keep my conscience nice and clean. I hear him stomping back in my direction. At first I think the jig is up, but then there's the sound of a large animal darting through the trees nearby, and the avatar turns his beefy back to me. I step out of my hiding spot inside the fern and plunge my dagger between his ribs. Then I pull it out and shove the blade in again as far as it can go. Hot blood pours out of his body and over my hand. It feels fantastic. Not as good as sex, but damn close. It's like the pressure that's been building inside me has been released all at once. For a few glorious seconds my head clears, my rage is sated and my whole body feels lighter.

The avatar collapses in a heap at my feet. I steal his weapon and ransack his pockets. They're totally empty. The only thing the psycho was carrying was his trusty axe. As I stand up, I can feel the pressure beginning to grow again. My head is pounding, and I ache for another release. I've never been addicted to drugs, but I'd bet this is what withdrawal feels like.

I crash through the jungle, hacking a jagged path through the vines and branches. Everything around me is green. Leaves the size of elephant ears block the sun, so the light at the forest floor level is dim. This is exactly the kind of environment you'd expect to host dinosaurs. I wouldn't be shocked to encounter a velociraptor here, but I have a hunch that the dangers in this world are human in nature. And that hunch is confirmed when something buzzes past my temple. A split second later, a handmade dart lodges in a nearby branch.

I slip behind a tree and scan the jungle for my assailant. At first I see no one. Then a shadow passes across a giant leaf about ten feet off the ground, and I throw my dagger toward the movement. I hear the blade hit something soft, and seconds later a body plummets to earth. I step out of my hiding place, well aware that there may be other killers around. Staying low, I cross the jungle to where I think the body fell. I find an avatar that's about half the size of an average human, with dark green skin and long claws. The fall appears to have knocked it unconscious. My dagger is protruding from its thigh.

It ambushed me. It wanted to kill me. If its aim had been just a little bit better, it would probably be standing over *me* right now. I should rip the avatar apart and fling the pieces in every direction. But when I pull my knife out of its leg, a splatter of blood hits me, and the sight and smell remind me of Kat's leg that night at the factory. I don't know if the avatar belongs to a headset player—or to someone with a disk. So I grit my teeth until the almost-irresistible urge to kill him passes. Then I rip a strip of fabric from the bottom of my robe and fashion a tourniquet.

I confiscate the avatar's blow darts and head off into the jungle. I take three steps before I hear a low growl and something springs onto my back. The weight of it almost brings me down. I don't need to look to know it's the avatar I just stopped myself from killing. I'm so enraged that I barely feel the teeth sink into my neck. I saved its life, and it's still attacking. I pull out one of its darts, reach back and ram it into its side. The poison on the dart's tip takes immediate action. The avatar slips off my shoulder. It's dead when it lands at my feet. I kick the corpse over and over again until I feel the pressure in my head release. If the guy had a disk, this would be my first real kill. I don't know if it will be my last. But I do know where I am now. I may not know the realm's name, but it hardly matters. If Mammon was the land of greed, this one is fueled by rage. The Elemental of Mammon wanted me out of the way. He sent me here to this realm to die.

I move much more cautiously now. I've painted my skin with mud from the jungle floor and I've woven leaves through the fabric of my robe. I'm not invisible, but I'm no longer an obvious target. Which is good, because the jungle is filled with avatars hunting for humans. I've managed to avoid most of them, though I did send a couple of headset players back to Start. But I've tried not to indulge my desires too much or too often. That's how Otherworld traps you. It introduces you to sensations you'd never be able to feel in real life. You discover what you've been missing—because it's taboo or illegal or because you lack the guts to do it for real. And when you find what's missing it's almost impossible to let it go again.

I would love to take out my axe and chop each and every one of these psychos into bite-size pieces. And that's exactly why I can't let myself do it.

After the sun sets, only the thought of Kat keeps me going. I have to reach her. This realm feels even more dangerous in the dark, but I can't hide and wait for sunrise. I've got to find a way out. Then it's like God reaches down and grabs me by the ankle and rips my foot out from beneath me. I'm weightless, flying through the air, smacking against leaves, scraping against the trunks of trees. I'm high enough to see a patch of starry nighttime sky through the dense forest canopy when my ankle is yanked again and I plunge downward. I bounce back and forth a few times until the movement is finally just a mild bobbing. I'm hanging upside down, racked by dry heaves, my ankle caught in a snare. I'd vomit, but my avatar's stomach—like mine—is completely empty.

There are only two things that could save me now. I could summon the strength to cut myself down. Or someone in the real world could remove my disk. I know neither of these things is going to happen, and I wait for the pain that's sure to come.

Something big is stomping toward me. I'm starting to wonder

if there might be dinosaurs in this realm after all. Then a tall beast breaks through the foliage. In the silvery moonlight, I can make out a human-shaped body with the head of a wild boar. Its snout is coated in dried mucus and studded with thick black bristles. The eyeballs have rotted away and their sockets are empty black holes. Two sharp yellow tusks jut from the bottom jaw of its open mouth. When it reaches me, the head's at my eye level, which means the creature has to be seven feet tall. I can see into its open mouth. Inside are two human eyes. Then a face takes shape around them. It's coated in dried blood. The boar's head is a mask.

Oh, *shit*. This cannot be good.

I hear a knife sawing through rope. Suddenly my ankle slips free and I plunge headfirst to the ground. My skull throbs with pain and my vision's blurred. An enormous foot passes by my face, and I notice it's bare. I catch a glimpse of the giant man's belt as he hoists me up by the back of the pants and shoves me into a rough-hewn sack. As my head begins to clear, I realize the belt is made out of human fingers.

I'm dragged for what seems like miles across the jungle floor. I feel every bump, stick and stone on the ground. Finally we reach our destination, and I'm dumped out into the bottom of a cage. The door swings shut, locking me inside. It's dark, but I can see enough to know that I'm in a long building made of wood. The floor beneath my cage is pressed dirt and the roof above appears to be thatch. There are other cages around me, all fashioned from some kind of indestructible bamboolike jungle plant. The cages are filled with filthy avatars, most of whom are covered in blood, though it's impossible to tell whether it's their own. The entire place reeks like a slaughterhouse.

I'm pretty sure I'm about to die.

I feel someone's eyes on me and I turn to find a man staring through the bars of the neighboring cage. He's bald and his eyes are ringed with black. You'd expect someone locked up in a cage to be either terrified or enraged, but there is no expression at all on his face.

"Where are we?" I ask him. "Who was it that dragged me here?"

I can tell he understands, but he doesn't answer at first. It's as if he's trying to figure out whether answering my questions will be to his advantage. Finally he breaks into a broad smile that's oddly charming despite his broken and blackened teeth.

"That was Ragnar," he says cheerfully. "The Elemental of Nastrond. We are in his realm, waiting for our chance to fight."

I have no idea what he's talking about, but it does *not* sound like fun. "Sorry, I'm new here. What do you mean?"

"Ragnar brings the best warriors to his fort to do battle. It's an honor. He's very picky about who he chooses. The reigning champion right now is Ylva. Whoever beats her gets to kill her any way he likes, and I have a ton of ideas." He grins and it makes me shiver.

"Like what?" I ask, just for the hell of it.

"Crushing, flaying, then drawing and quartering," he says lustily. "Her head will get put on a spike, and I'll eat the heart, but I'm still trying to decide what to do with the rest."

"Sounds wonderful," I say. The guy's clearly criminally insane. He'd make an excellent serial killer.

"Doesn't it?" he replies. "Hey, listen, I think it's morning in Dallas. I gotta go to school now or my mom will murder me. But I'll be back in a few hours. You gonna stay here for a while?"

"Sure thing," I say. I've just lost all hope for the human race. "I'm not going anywhere."

"Great. You can tell me everything that happened while I'm gone."

"Yeah, well, just to be clear, I'm not protecting your avatar while you're sitting in health class, learning how babies get made."

"I already know all about that shit, bro. And who cares if something happens to my avatar?" the guy says. "I don't have anything to steal. If I die tonight, I can just start again tomorrow."

I can't believe it's that easy. But I guess it is. The avatar goes still and fades slightly. Somewhere in the real world, a kid just pulled off his headset.

Looking around, I realize most of the other avatars are dormant as well. It's smart, I think. Otherworld must have been designed so its nights correspond to the real world's days. Players with headsets can go to work or to school without missing much action. For those with disks, the nights are time to let the brain rest. I can't afford such luxuries.

The sun is just rising when they come for me. The door of my cage opens and standing outside it is an NPC dressed in the bloody pelt of a beast I don't recognize. He doesn't speak, but the spear point he's thrusting at me seems to indicate that I'm wanted elsewhere. I feel the spear's tip scrape the skin of my back several times as the NPC marches me out of the building in which I've been held. I look back to see a Viking-style longhouse with windowless wooden walls and a thatched roof. We're heading for the center of a ring fort. Hundreds of wooden posts rise from the circular stone walls. On top of each post is a severed head. The smell is overpowering, and I'm overcome by nausea. The stench doesn't seem to bother anyone else, which tells me that the players here must be wearing headsets. A crowd has gathered, and everyone wants a look at me. A few step forward to inspect my physique. Most of them have big, burly avatars that were built to intimidate. None of them seems terribly impressed by what I have to offer.

The spear in my back presses me forward toward a fighting pit as the gamblers hurry to place their wagers. Through the crowd I see Ragnar standing at the edge, watching the action below. He's no longer wearing the boar's head, but he hasn't bothered to wash. The top half of his body is completely encrusted in old blood that's cracked like a dry lake bed. I can see strips of his pale white flesh beneath. The Elemental's long, matted hair would probably be blond if its true color weren't covered in a helmet of dried gore. His only clothing is a pair of patchwork pants made from different shades of leather. I'd rather not imagine their provenance.

My captors push me to the edge of the pit. The giant avatar I see down below was designed for brute force. He's useless for anything other than killing, but I'm sure he excels at what he does best. The dude could rip my limbs off like he was plucking the wings from a butterfly. And yet his eyes seem out of focus and his expression oddly constipated. Then a thin stream of blood trickles from one side of his mouth. The avatar lurches forward, stumbles and falls to the ground, revealing his assassin.

The champion is not a guest. I see it immediately, though I doubt many other human players have figured it out. Ylva must be one of the Children—and her braided blond plaits tell me she's most likely Ragnar's daughter. But unlike her beast of a father, she's sinewy and slim. Her mother was a wolf, I'd guess, judging by her yellow eyes and the razor-sharp claws extending from the end of each finger. Both of her hands are dripping with blood, but the rest of the girl is remarkably splatter-free. Two men hop into the pit with her. One gives her a rag, which she uses to wipe her hands clean. Then the two men drag the corpse out of the pit.

"Give me another!" she shouts up at Ragnar. "Let's empty all the cages today."

Ragnar beams down at the creature like a proud father. Then he reaches over and, with one arm, shoves me into the pit.

I wonder how many people have died of broken necks before they've even had a chance to fight. I hit my head on the way down, and when I stand up, I'm dizzy and disoriented. A horn blows. I stumble forward, my arms up to defend myself. I expect to die at any moment and I brace for an attack, but nothing happens. I drop my arms and see that Ylva is still twenty feet away. She's leaning against the wall of the pit, watching me.

"What are you doing?" Ylva asks. She speaks confidently but keeps her voice low as if she'd rather the spectators not overhear.

"I don't want to fight you," I say.

"Why not? You wouldn't be here if you didn't like to fight," she replies casually. She holds a hand out and examines her clawlike nails. "That's how it works, isn't it? The guests that are sent to my father's realm are the ones who get excited at the sight of blood."

"I'm not like that," I tell her. Then I remember the release I felt when I killed the first man who attacked me in Nastrond. "I don't want to be like that."

"Fight, already!" someone shouts from above, and cheering erupts from the crowd. They're getting impatient.

Ylva ignores them. She's obviously used to doing things her way. "You don't *want* to be?" she repeats with a smile. *She's really quite pretty,* I find myself thinking against my will. "What a ridiculous thing to say. Either you are or you aren't. Here in Otherworld, it makes no difference what you *want.* I didn't want to see my brothers and sisters slaughtered because they weren't part of the plan. I *wanted* them to live, but they were murdered anyway— just because they took after our mother. Do you have any idea what it was like to watch them die?"

I don't. "I'm sorry," I tell her. I used the same words after the goat man told me his story, but back then I felt nothing. Now I truly sympathize. The only thing I can offer her is the truth I've genuinely come to believe—even though it just got me kicked out of Mammon. "Guests don't belong in Otherworld. This world should be left to the Elementals, the Beasts and the Children."

"Tell that to the Creator," Ylva says.

"I'm on my way to see him now." I suppose that's the truth. If he's taken refuge in the ice cave, I may not have a choice.

The girl throws her head back and literally howls with laughter. The inhuman sound of it excites the crowd gathered at the edge of the pit. "You think you can convince the Creator to send his beloved guests away?" She's slinking toward me now. "He brought them here. He thinks we can all exist together. But your kind are monsters, and the Creator is a fool."

We're the monsters? That's rich coming from someone who spends her time murdering people with her bare hands at the

263

bottom of a pit. "If the Creator doesn't agree to get rid of the guests, I will kill him." What the hell am I saying? I think I've gone too far.

"You'll kill him?" Ylva's closer now. "How? You won't even fight me. The Children are waging war against those who murdered our brothers and sisters, and we all have our part to play in the battle. I stay here in my father's realm. When the guests come to us, I rip them apart one by one. You will be next."

"What are you waiting for, bitch?" shouts one of the spectators. "I've got all my money on you!"

Ylva spins around. "Him," she says, pointing up at the heckler. An NPC steps forward and shoves the loudmouthed avatar into the pit. He lands with a thud at the bottom and Ylva is on him. Blood flies everywhere as she shreds his flesh with her claws. She returns to face me, drenched in gore. The creature she left behind is unrecognizable. The crowd above roars with approval.

"You won't win that way," I tell her. "Guests like him don't really die. You can rip them apart all you like. They may die temporarily, but they won't be gone for good. It's hard to explain, but they'll keep coming. And there will be more of them soon. Maybe millions more."

The smile on Ylva's face slips away. She sees I'm telling the truth—she's waging a hopeless war. The slaughter of her brothers and sisters will not be avenged. Her kind is almost certainly doomed. And that fact hurts her more than a weapon ever could. I wish I hadn't been the one to deliver the blow.

"Believe me—I want the guests to leave as much as you do," I tell her. "If you let me go, I might be able to help."

Ylva snaps out of her reverie. "I can't let you go," she says, her voice soft. She steps forward and reaches out to gently stroke my face. "Only one of us can leave the pit alive. That's the rule. If we climb out of the pit together, my father will kill us both. You must fight. Prove to me that you're capable of killing the Creator. Prove it by taking my life."

Ylva's arms slide around my waist and she nestles her head against my chest. The crowd rumbles ominously. They must be as surprised as I am. Then I feel the tips of her claws scratch at my back. One at a time they slowly pop through my skin. The wounds aren't deep, but the pain is excruciating. I can feel the blood beginning to soak my shirt. I try to break away from her, but she's incredibly strong and she manages to hold me tight. The crowd sees my struggle and begins to cheer.

"Head-butt her," a woman's voice whispers in my ear. "Now!" It could be the voice of God, for all I know. I'm in far too much pain to think straight. The claws are an inch into my flesh now. I have only one option: obey.

I rear my head back and then slam it into the top of Ylva's skull. The second I make contact, I know the blow isn't hard enough to do much damage. Still, I feel Ylva's knees buckle. The claws slip out of my flesh as she falls. I wait for her to get up, but she doesn't. I'm standing here like an idiot looking down in shock and wonder at the Child I've somehow defeated.

"Kick the body!" the voice urges in my ear. "You can't let it look like you won by accident."

Carole is beside me with her invisibility cloak on. I have no idea how she found me. She must have bashed the Child's head with some kind of weapon at the same time that I head-butted her. I'd cry out with joy if I could. Not just because Carole saved me—but because I'm no longer alone.

"Hurry!" she urges. "Get it over with! Gorog's waiting for us near the border. We need to get back to him before one of these bloodthirsty assholes takes him out."

I give Ylva a kick designed to appear a lot worse than it is. I can see a slight movement in her rib cage. She looks dead, but she's breathing. The realm has a new champion and the crowd above doesn't seem thrilled. Raising my arms in victory, I climb out of the pit.

Ragnar is waiting for me at the top. The spectators gather around us, many of them grumbling. Even the ones who won their wagers seem disappointed with the outcome of the fight. Not enough gore or guts for their taste.

"Very good," Ragnar says bluntly. "The champion has been defeated."

I'm not exactly sure how to respond. His daughter is lying on the floor of the pit, a stream of blood trickling from her head. But I seem to care far more than he does.

"The victor is free. He can stay and fight here—or leave Nastrond whenever he chooses."

I think I know which one I'll be choosing. I'm not sure how anyone survives in the same realm as this guy's breath.

"But there can only be one victor," Ragnar adds.

"What?" I ask.

"You cheated," he says, and my heart feels like it stops. He knows.

"I did not—" I start to insist.

He holds up a hand to stop me from wasting his time. "I see all. Cheating is permitted." I breathe a sigh of relief. "We follow one rule. Two cannot leave the pit alive." He motions to two men standing nearby. They step forward and grab Carole, yanking off the invisibility cloak.

The black yoga outfit she picked up at Gina's makes her seem impossibly small. Every avatar here towers over her. She looks like one of the pretty, fit moms you'd see in the Brockenhurst mall on a Tuesday afternoon.

"Which of you will be the victor?" Ragnar asks us. "Choose."

"He will," Carole says. Her face is pale, but her voice is firm, as if the decision were made long ago.

"No!" I shout. "I won't!"

"I made the kill," Carole tells Ragnar. "The decision should be mine."

Ragnar nods. "And so it is," he says. He pulls a hunting knife from a scabbard hanging from his belt. With one swift thrust, he plunges it into Carole. Then he pulls it out. The movements are so graceful that if it weren't for the smear of blood on his blade I would doubt what just happened. Carole looks down at her stomach and totters for a moment. I catch her before she slumps to the ground.

All around us, grumbling members of the crowd are beginning to wander away. There will be no more fighting for now. I drop to my knees and lay her body out on the dirt. I pull away layers of clothes, trying to get a look at the wound, but the blood rushing out of Carole's abdomen covers everything. I see nothing but red.

"Hey." It's Carole, weakly patting my hand. She wants my attention. It's all I can give her now. She smiles when she receives it. "I knew what I was doing, Simon. I knew how it would end. It was my time."

"You weren't even supposed to be here." I can barely speak. It feels as though there's a weight on my chest. It takes all my strength to breathe. "Why did you come?"

"You helped me and Gorog—and you didn't have to. We wouldn't have made it this far if it weren't for you."

"You could have made it a lot farther without me," I tell her.

"Listen to me, Simon. You're the one *I* could save. I did my part. Now you're going to find a way to save Gorog—and all the other people who are prisoners of Otherworld."

My vision is blurred and there's snot streaming from my nose. I'm nobody's hero. "I can't. Not me—" I start.

"Then who?" she demands, her voice suddenly strong. "It has to be you, Simon. Who else can do it?" The outburst seems to have drained the last of her energy. Carole's eyes flutter shut.

I rise in a panic and gather her up in my arms. "Just hold on," I plead. "I'll get you to the border. We can stay there as long as it takes to help you get better."

"No. You can't waste any more time," she says. "Promise me."

Before I can say anything, Carole is gone.

Blind and sobbing, I carry her body into the forest. No one in Nastrond bothers to stop me.

THE TRUTH

I'm sitting at the edge of a canal. The water is brown and topped with a frothy layer of foam. It looks like a cappuccino and it smells like crap. Still, I feel the urge to jump in. What a relief it would be to end it all. To spend eternity at the cold, calm bottom of the Gowanus Canal.

"I've been waiting for you to show up." My grandfather is sitting next to me, our legs dangling over the side. "How long's it been since you slept?"

"You're dead and I'm not in the mood," I say. "Go away."

"Dead, sure. But hardly gone. See that?" He reaches over and flicks my nose with his middle finger. "That right there means I'm immortal. I am inside every cell of you. You want reality, it's right smack-dab in the middle of your face."

Not long ago that would have made me feel better, but tonight it's hardly a comforting thought. Carole died because she thought I was the One. I've read a million graphic novels and seen

hundreds of sci-fi films. In none of them was the One the delinquent grandson of a big-nosed gangster.

"So whatcha gonna do?"

"Can't you leave me the hell alone?" I ask. "Don't I deserve a
minute of peace?"

"No," he says. "That lady died to help you. You owe her. I want
to know what you're going to do."

"I don't know!" I shout.

"Hey! What are you shouting for?" someone whispers.

I look around. My grandfather's gone. I'm inside the fort that
Kat and I built in the forest between our houses. I reach out and
run my fingertips across the wood.

"Are you okay?" Kat asks. She's sitting cross-legged in front of
me, the Yoda sleeping bag wrapped around her shoulders. I try to
take in every part of her. The copper-colored hair, the hazel eyes.
What if this is the last time I see her?

"No," I tell Kat. "I'm not okay. I need you right now." What else
is there to say?

"I'm here," she says. "I'm always here."

I would give anything for that to be true. "You're a dream inside a virtual world."

"I'm the girl you met in the woods when we were eight years
old. Even when you don't see me, I'm here. I helped make you *you*."

And I know it's true. "What am I supposed to do?"

"You're supposed to keep going," she says.

"I just came here for you," I confess. "I'm not who they think
I am."

"Maybe you weren't," Kat says. "Maybe you are now."

"It doesn't work like that," I tell her.

"It doesn't?" Kat asks. "You think you can come somewhere like Otherworld and leave the same person? It's not just the disk that's dangerous. It's Otherworld, too. It changes you."

I think of the avatars hunting each other in the jungles of Nastrond. "I'm pretty sure most of the people who come here are pretty screwed up to begin with," I say.

Kat shrugs. "Sure. A lot of them. Otherworld was built so you can indulge your every desire. You can go around eating, killing, hoarding, screwing—and there's no one here judging you or telling you to stop. No doubt a bunch of people here were psychos from the start. What do you think happens to everyone else?"

"I don't understand. It's just virtual reality," I say.

Kat leans forward. "No, see, that's the big secret," she whispers. "It's not virtual if it changes who you are. All of this is real, Simon. It's *real*."

I wake to find the Clay Man standing with his back to me, staring down at Carole's final resting place. After I found Gorog, he and I did our best to bury her, but the grave isn't much to look at. The land around us is red rock with a silky coating of scarlet dirt. The wind spins the loose soil into dust devils that aimlessly wander the wasteland. The ogre and I spent hours searching for enough stones to cover Carole's avatar. I wonder if it's still there beneath the pile.

The Clay Man's head is bowed in grief. When I started my journey, he wanted me to leave Carole and Gorog behind. He said they would distract me from my mission. The truth is, the mission would have ended days ago without them.

"It's about time you showed up to pay your respects," I say.

"How did she die?" he asks.

I sit up and look around. Gorog is awake too. He's got his arms wrapped around his knees and his forehead resting against them. "I almost attacked the Elemental of Mammon and was sent to Nastrond as punishment. Carole followed me there and sacrificed herself to spare my life," I tell him. "She had this insane idea that I'm the guy who's going to free everyone the disks have imprisoned."

"You *are* the One," the ogre mutters to himself. I can tell he desperately needs it to be true.

"I'm *not*," I insist. "You've watched too many movies."

The ogre looks up at me. "Yeah? Well, so have the geeks who designed this place," he argues. "Maybe they designed it so there would be a *One*."

"I don't think there's a *One*," says the Clay Man.

"See?" I tell Gorog.

"But there might be *Two*," the Clay Man says. "If so, Simon is one of them."

"Who's the other?" I can tell from Gorog's voice that he's really hoping he gets to be number two. But he won't. I know exactly who the Clay Man has in mind.

I'm too exhausted and broken to keep playing games. "I need to know who you are in real life," I say. "I'm not going anywhere until you tell me."

"I understand," the Clay Man says. "And it's time I showed you. Let me take you out of Otherworld, and I'll explain everything."

"No." I'm not having it. "I'm not leaving Gorog in Otherworld on his own. We've got to talk here."

"Gorog is safe for now," says the Clay Man. "There are no Beasts or Children in this wasteland. He'll watch over your avatar while you return to New Jersey."

I'm about to refuse again, but Gorog claps a giant hand on my back. "It's okay," he says. "I don't need a babysitter. I'll be right here when you get back."

"Are you sure?" I ask.

He rolls his eyes. "Yes, Dad," he says. "And I promise not to use the stove while you're gone."

Gorog's sad smirk is the last thing I see before I'm blinded by a powerful light. I'm back at Elmer's, and the sun is streaming in through the glassless windows. There's someone bending over me, but all I can see is the blurry outline of a head. Still, it's not the head I was expecting.

"Oh, man, you really need a bath," a girl's voice says. "Why didn't you use the Depends I left for you?" I recognize the voice just as the face begins to come into focus.

"Busara?" I sputter. "*You're* the Clay Man?"

"Yes," she confirms as I struggle to sit up. "I sent you the disk. I got you into this mess. I'm really sorry. Here." She pulls a bottle of water and an energy bar out of her backpack. Then she sits down beside me on the floor. "You definitely need this."

I chug down the water and chew the energy bar as my brain slowly recalibrates. I should have known that Busara might be the Clay Man, but I was convinced it was Martin. "How did you get your hands on a disk?" I ask, realizing as I speak that she must have one too.

"My father was a man named James Ogubu. He invented the technology, and he liked to bring his work home," she says. "I have the master disk—the one he used to wear. No one else even knows it exists. It lets me enter and leave whenever I like. The disk I gave you is the one my dad made for me. The two devices are connected—that's how I'm able to find you in Otherworld."

The news takes me by surprise, and I stop chewing. "Your dad works for the Company?" I ask with my mouth full.

"Not anymore," Busara tells me. "I'm pretty sure Milo Yolkin had him killed."

"Milo Yolkin had . . . *What?*" Bits of energy bar spray everywhere. I'm not sure why I find this news shocking, after everything I've seen in Otherworld and at the facility. It's still hard to believe that the Company's sneaker-wearing boy genius could be personally responsible for so many deaths. It's like finding out that the devil takes the form of a cocker spaniel.

"Sorry," Busara says. "That slipped out. I should have worked up to it. I didn't mean to blow your mind right away." She pauses as if she's collecting her thoughts and trying to put them into an order that will make sense to me. "When I was first diagnosed with my heart condition, the doctors told my parents I was never going to lead a normal life. My mom cried for weeks, but my dad refused to accept it. He started looking for solutions—and he was the kind of guy who could find them. He ran the Company's West Coast innovations lab, so he had access to money and resources and the world's best engineers."

"You're saying the disk was made for *you*?"

"That's how it started, but then my dad got obsessed with the project. Even after I had heart surgery and started getting better, his team kept working on it. After a while they ended up inventing the disk and the visor—and creating the software for the White City. The technology was designed to help people with broken bodies lead better lives. In the real world a kid with a serious heart condition might be stuck in a bed. But in the White City she could run and dance and play."

I remember the fields that surround the White City and imagine a younger Busara prancing among the flowers and butterflies. "It sounds really great. I can't understand how it could have gone so wrong."

Busara sighs. "Two words—Milo Yolkin. My dad's team was testing the disk when Milo heard about the project. He was smart enough to see that my father's technology was world-changing. It wasn't just the disk. The graphics and the AI were eons ahead of anything else developed by the Company. So Milo took my dad's whole team and brought them here to Brockenhurst. He wanted them to be closer to the Company headquarters in Princeton—but far enough away so they could work on the project in complete secrecy."

"That's when you moved to New Jersey?" I ask.

"Yeah, last year. Before they started expanding it, the building on Dandelion Drive used to be my father's lab."

It's beginning to come together now. "I was wondering how you managed to get me into the facility."

"I wasn't sure I could," Busara says. "But I have access to my dad's old files, and fortunately for us, the facility is still using the same HR recruiter. They like to hire former military personnel for all the grunt work. My dad always thought it was strange. Now it makes perfect sense. They want people who follow orders and keep their mouths shut. My father never did either of those things. That's what got him killed."

Once again, we're back to the subject of murder. How many people have died for this goddamn disk? "I still don't get why Milo would want your father dead. What the hell happened?"

"During his tests, my dad started finding bugs everywhere. The White City software was full of them. He wanted the city to feel real, so he created a self-sustaining ecosystem where the plants and animals all grew and reproduced and died. But weird hybrid species started popping up. And the NPCs, which my dad had designed to possess what he called emergent AI, began acting in unpredictable ways. He felt like he was losing control of the world he'd built. But he figured that could be fixed, even if it meant starting all over from scratch. The biggest problem wasn't with the software, though. It was with the *disk*."

My laugh is bitter. "Yeah, it kills people. I'd say that's a pretty big problem."

"The disk sends signals to the wearer's brain that convince it that everything the person smells or touches or tastes in the virtual world is real. Which is totally fantastic if you're riding ponies or eating steak. But it's impossible to create a virtual environment where only good things happen. My father realized that one day when he was in the White City testing the gear. He dropped a tablet on his foot—and it *hurt*. His brain was completely convinced that the injury was real. And that's when he knew the disk was dangerous. If a person was ever seriously hurt inside the White City, his brain could react by shutting down the injured part of his body. And it might be a part of the body the person couldn't live without."

"What did your dad do when he discovered the problem with the disk?" I ask.

"He ended the project. There were engineers on his team who thought he'd gone totally crazy, but he knew it was too dangerous to continue. Then Milo showed up at our house."

"Milo Yolkin was at your house? You met him?" Even now— after all I know—I still feel a stab of jealousy. The hoodie-clad girl sitting cross-legged in front of me on a gritty factory floor has been in the presence of greatness.

"Oh, sure. Milo's a super-nice guy. Really charming and polite. You'd never guess he was evil incarnate. He flew here in a helicopter from Princeton. It landed in our backyard. He wanted to talk to my dad about Otherworld. He said he'd been working on a secret reboot—and he'd borrowed a few things from the White City."

"*Borrowed?* Your dad gave him access to the White City software?"

Busara snorts angrily. "Of course not. But Milo owns the Company. The Company owned the lab. Milo took what he wanted, and there wasn't much my dad could do about it. I'm not even sure my dad knew that his boss had access until Milo's pet project started going south."

"Let me guess. Otherworld was full of bugs too."

"Yeah. *Literally.* Milo had borrowed the self-replicating ecosystem my dad created for the White City, and he gave some of his NPCs—mainly the Elementals—true artificial intelligence. By the time Milo came to see us, his Otherworld ecosystems were going completely insane. Beasts and Elementals were reproducing, and strange creatures were being introduced."

"The Children," I say.

"Yep. I guess Milo tried to get rid of them at first, but there was one little problem with that. My father had been very careful not to give his White City NPCs true artificial intelligence. But Milo had gone all the way. He'd tried to create a world so real that players would never want to leave. Now he had all these unexpected creatures to deal with—dangerous creatures that didn't want human guests in Otherworld. And the Children weren't robots. They were *conscious*. Milo couldn't bear to exterminate them. He wanted my dad to help him find a way to fix what he'd screwed up."

Something isn't adding up. The man who has murdered dozens of people just to test his technology suddenly got all tenderhearted when it came time to kill off a bunch of digital freaks?

"Did your dad help him?" I ask.

"There was nothing he could do. He told Milo to scrap everything, but Milo refused. My dad said it was like he *couldn't*. And that's when he figured out that Milo hadn't just stolen the software. He was using a disk. He was addicted to Otherworld."

"Wow." What else is there to say? I remember what Kat told me in my dream. *Otherworld changes you.* Sounds like Milo Yolkin was its first victim.

"My dad told me he threatened to go public if Milo didn't kill the entire Otherworld project. Next thing I know, my father's disappeared and Milo's launching Otherworld as a headset VR app. And then one day I work up the guts to try out my dad's old gear, and I discover the Company is beta testing the disk—and they've connected the White City to Otherworld. I guess they had to. No one was going to get really hurt inside the White

City, and the beta testers needed to be badly injured so the Company could see what the physical impact would be. I guess they decided it was worth killing a few hundred people to fix the disk's bugs."

We sit in silence while I let the information sink in.

"So when do I come into the story?" I ask.

"I've been lurking in Otherworld for a while now," she tells me. "I don't enter the realms. My heart is too weak—any kind of combat might kill me. But otherwise I come and go and no one seems to notice. Their focus is on optimizing the realms for launch; they don't have time to monitor the wastelands and in-between spaces right now. Plus, I think my condition keeps me off the Company's radar. I guess they don't believe that a sick kid like me could pose a threat. And I didn't think so either. I knew there wasn't much I could do on my own. Then I saw you inside the ice cave . . ."

"How did you know it was me?" I butt in.

"Are you kidding? You gave your avatar the same nose. And the girl you were with called you Simon."

"It was Kat."

"Yeah, I figured that out. After the collapse at the factory, I saw a way for us to help each other. You wanted to save Kat. I wanted Magna dead. All you had to do was kill him and take Kat through the exit in the cave. With her disk shut off, she'd be safe until her body could be rescued."

It takes me a moment to place the name Magna. It belongs to the big red creature inside the glacier. "I don't get it. Why did you want me to kill Magna?"

"He's the one they call the Creator."

I guess that clears a few things up, but I still don't understand why Busara would want him dead. "Isn't the Creator part of the game?"

"No," she says. "Magna is Milo Yolkin's avatar."

I suddenly feel unbelievably stupid. I should have made that connection a long time ago, but I was only thinking about saving Kat. Then something else hits me. "You lied to me," I say to Busara. "You told me the Creator was part of the game."

Busara swallows nervously. She must feel me seething. "At this point he is. Milo spends almost all his time in Otherworld. He hardly takes his disk off. He's addicted to the game. He just sits in that cave trying to figure out how to fix his creation. Killing his avatar is the only way to put a stop to the project."

"But if he's wearing a disk, killing his avatar would . . ." I pause. Things are quickly adding up in my head, and the conclusion I'm coming to is batshit insane. "That's why you sent me a disk. You want me to *murder* Milo Yolkin?"

"Yes," she admits, though she doesn't sound very proud of it.

"Because you think he killed your father."

Busara shakes her head with frustration. I guess she doesn't want her plan to be written off as revenge. "My father isn't the only person Milo's murdered. Think of all the people who've been forced to take part in the disk's beta test. People like Kat and Carole and Gorog. Milo's using them as human guinea pigs. I'm pretty sure most of the patients involved in the test don't even have locked-in syndrome."

"No shit. But do you have any proof?" I ask.

"According to my dad's files, the disk puts people into a state that's similar to sleep paralysis. Sleeping people don't have conscious control of their bodies, but that doesn't always keep them from moving or speaking. Remember the night you found me in Kat's hospital room? I punctured Kat's IV. When the fluid ran out, she started speaking, right? Well, people with real locked-in syndrome can't speak. I think the Company is drugging them. There's something mixed in with the patients' IV fluids that keeps them paralyzed. I'm sure of it."

I hold up a hand. "Stop right there for a second," I say. We just took a detour into some very dark and disturbing territory. "You're telling me you screwed with Kat's IV at the hospital? On a hunch? What if you'd been wrong?"

Busara's eyes go wide. I don't think she realized how far she'd taken things. "But I wasn't wrong," she says.

"You could have been," I say. "And now that I think about it, you knew from the start that the disk is able to kill its wearer. You even warned me that I might not get more than one life in Otherworld. And then you went ahead and let me use the disk anyway."

"My father thought the disk might be dangerous," Busara says. "But I swear, Simon. I didn't know for sure until now."

I'm starting to get seriously pissed. "So you let *me* be *your* guinea pig. You let me take all the risks while you never took a single one. What exactly makes you any better than Milo Yolkin?"

Her jaw drops. She clearly doesn't have an answer ready. "I'm really sorry," she finally says. And she looks sorry, too. But I'm sure she'd do it all over again. "I sent you the disk because I saw you in Otherworld and I was convinced you'd survive. And it was the only way to protect Kat. If I'd told you the truth, would it have stopped you from going in after her?"

"No," I admit. And it still won't. In fact, it just makes me more eager to get Kat the hell out of there. I pick my disk and visor up off the floor. "But you should have been honest with me. Thanks for giving me the opportunity to kill myself. I think it's time for me to go back and finish my mission."

"No! Don't you see—you don't have to," Busara says. "That's why I pulled you out of Otherworld. Carole died. That means we finally have proof that the disks are actually killing people. We can put the facility out of business and destroy the Company, too."

She hands me a phone. On it is an article from the *Morris NewsBee*. There's a picture of Carole. She looks a little plumper than she did in Otherworld, but otherwise she's exactly the same. She could have been anyone back at setup, but she chose to be herself. I scan the words. It's an obituary. Carole Elliot, forty-three. She succumbed to injuries sustained in an automobile accident. She's survived by her four children and husband. Turns out Carole really was a soccer mom.

I hand the phone back to Busara. It takes a few seconds before I feel like I'm able to talk. "How is *this* proof?" I ask.

"You saw Carole die in Otherworld yesterday. The same day she died at the facility."

"You're not thinking straight. That doesn't prove anything," I say. "It would just be my word against the Company's. Who do you think the cops are going to believe? Milo Yolkin—or some idiot kid with a criminal history?"

Busara goes quiet. "Okay, you're right," she says softly. "But I don't want you to go back to Otherworld. I guess I wasn't prepared to be right about this. But it's gotten too real, Simon. Carole died. You could die too."

"I don't have a choice. I have to go back. Kat is still there.

Gorog is too. I'm not leaving again until both of them are free. If that means killing Milo Yolkin, that's okay with me."

"What if you die fighting Magna?" Busara asks. "What's going to happen to everyone else in the beta test?"

Honestly, it never occurred to me. There aren't just two lives depending on me. Everyone in the facility is my responsibility. My life couldn't possibly suck any harder than it does right now.

"Fine," I huff. "Kat might have information that could help you stop the Company if something happens to us. She saw what happened at Elmer's. I'll pass the information along to you after I find her and talk to her. If we die, you'll need to find a way to use it."

"I don't understand," Busara says. "What kind of information could Kat have?"

"The night of the collapse, I was at the factory. I saw someone throw an object through a hole in the third floor. When it landed on the second floor, all the kids gathered around. That's what made the floor collapse. Maybe the boards were rotten—or maybe they'd been sabotaged. But someone knew that the floor couldn't handle that much weight in one spot."

"Wait—you said someone threw an object?" Busara asks. "What kind of object?"

"It was small and round. And when it landed, it was glowing. That's all I know, but Kat saw it. She might even have seen the person who threw it. I'd bet you anything there's a connection to the Company."

"What did Marlow do when he saw the object?" Busara asks.

"Marlow?" I try to think back to the night in question. "He shouted something. I think he told everyone to stay away from it."

I'm loving the look on Busara's face right now. It's nice to see

I've surprised her for once. "You never mentioned any of this," she says.

"Yeah, well, there's a lot you never told me, either," I shoot back.

I bend my head forward and begin to position the disk at the base of my skull.

"Wait," says Busara. "Give me one more hour. Please. There might be another way."

MARLOW

The windows of Busara's car are all down and I'm shivering uncontrollably. But the chill is preferable to the smell wafting off me. I really should have used the Depends.

"That's it," Busara says, pointing through the windshield at a house on the side of a hill. It's three stories high, and the front, which looks out over the forest, is almost entirely glass. I've been fascinated by the structure ever since I moved to New Jersey. As a kid, it always reminded me of a giant dollhouse. I could never understand why the owners would choose to put their lives on display.

"We're going up there?" I ask. The driveway that leads to the house is completely exposed, and there are no other homes on the hill. "Everyone in town will be able to see us. Have you forgotten that I'm kind of on the run these days? Are you sure this is something we need to do?"

"Yeah, I'm—" Busara is cut off by a blaring emergency alert

from her phone. It sounds like the end of the world. As the car swerves, I grab her phone and turn down the volume. There's a message flashing on the screen.

"'I've been expecting you. Don't drive up to the house. Pull over as soon as you can. I will guide you from there,'" I read out loud. Then I look up in surprise. "What the hell is going on?"

"It's from Marlow," Busara says. "He must have geo-fenced the property line."

"We're going to see Marlow? *Why?*"

"Because I think I may have been wrong about him," Busara tells me.

Busara pulls onto the shoulder of the road. Just as she shifts the car into park and turns off the engine, a small black drone appears at the driver's-side window. It hovers there until we've gotten out of the car. Then it heads off through the woods. Busara goes after it without hesitation.

"You're just going to follow a random drone into the forest?" I call out to her.

"You got any better ideas?" she shouts back.

I catch up with her and together we hike through the forest. The little black drone stays a few feet ahead of us at all times. As the slope of the hill gets steeper, I keep glancing over at Busara. Tiny beads of sweat are forming along her hairline. She does not look well.

"Are you sure you're going to be okay?" I ask.

"Yeah," Busara says in a voice that sounds determined—but not terribly convincing. She follows up with a weak smile. I think this may be her way of saying she's sorry for not taking any risks in Otherworld.

"We can go back," I assure her. I don't know how much farther she can go. I have a hunch I'm going to end up carrying her out of here.

"We're almost there," she pants. "Look."

I glance up and realize I can see part of the house through the trees. There's an unobstructed view into the gym on the building's ground floor, where Marlow is lifting weights in his underwear.

"He knew you were coming," I say with a snicker. "Why isn't he dressed? Is there something you want to tell me?"

"Yeah. There is. I don't think that's Marlow," says Busara.

She must be feeling a little loopy. Because unless Marlow's been cloned, that is definitely my little buddy working out inside the house.

"Now who's the spy?" someone says behind us, and I nearly leap out of my skin.

"Marlow?" My eyes flick back and forth between the guy working out inside and the one standing here in the woods. This kid is dressed in mud-covered jeans and he looks like he's been out here for a while.

"The one and only," says Marlow, his voice quavering slightly.

"Oh my God," Busara suddenly gasps. She's ignoring the Marlow in front of us and watching indoor Marlow lift weights. "Is that what I think it is?"

"Yep," he replies. "They don't know we have one. I turn it on when I need to escape. I'm pretty sure I'm under heavy surveillance."

"It's amazing," Busara marvels. I still have no idea what *it* is—or how these two ended up sharing secrets.

"What in the hell are you both talking about?" I ask. "And if you're the real Marlow, who's the guy inside?"

"It's not a guy, it's a hologram," Busara tells me.

"That's not a hologram," I argue. "And even if it is, how would you know?"

"It's a Company product—the first three-D hologram projector that produces an opaque, lifelike image. Marlow's mom invented it," Busara says. "She and my dad used to work together in California. At the Company's West Coast innovations lab."

I'm pretty sure this is information I should have been given a long-ass time ago. I'm seriously annoyed. "What? So you guys knew each other in California? You're *friends*?"

"Not exactly," Marlow said. "I don't think I'd spoken to Busara in years before she accused me of moving to Brockenhurst to spy on her."

"Can you blame me?" Busara jumps in. "Was I supposed to think it was just a random coincidence that another Company kid shows up at my school on the other side of the country and starts pretending to be some kind of Goth stoner? I knew there was something weird about the whole thing. And I was right, wasn't I? Why *are* you in Brockenhurst, Marlow?"

"Punishment," he says.

The word stuns me for a moment. "Punishment? For what?" I ask.

Marlow looks over his shoulder at the house, where his hologram double is now doing a series of lunges and squats. "My mom built the projector to help people," he said. "There are a lot of schools in poor countries that can't afford to hire teachers. My mom thought the projector could be a solution to the problem.

But when the guys who run the Company saw the projector, they had other plans. Turns out the device has some serious military applications. You throw a few into a battle zone and have them project three-D images of soldiers. Your enemy won't know who's real and who's not."

"But Milo doesn't work with the military," Busara argues. "It's one of his rules."

"I get the feeling Milo doesn't care much about his rules anymore," Marlow replies. "When my mother tried to tell him what was going on, she couldn't even get a meeting to see him. So she decided to leak news of the military deal to the press. The Company found out before any harm was done. My mom could have gone to jail for the leak, so I took the blame. Pretended it was me trying to make a quick buck by selling the intel. A few days later, we find out my mom is being transferred to beautiful Brockenhurst, New Jersey, so she'll be closer to the Company headquarters."

"That was your punishment?" I ask.

"Yeah, we thought we were getting off easy. Then when we get here, they tell me I have to hang out with a certain group of kids at school."

"*Who* told you? Do you remember their names?" Busara asks.

"Their *names*?" Marlow asks. "You think these guys and I sat down and discussed this shit over Frappuccinos? Someone called me on the phone and told me what to do. As far as I know, it was God himself."

"What exactly did he tell you to do?" I ask.

"He told me to get to know Jackson, Brian, West and Kat."

"He mentioned those names specifically?" I demand.

"Yep," says Marlow.

"Why was the Company interested in them?" Busara asks.

"No clue," Marlow replies. "I just did what they told me to do. Jackson, Brian and West weren't the kind of people I'd usually spend time with, but they were a lot better than the kind of guys I would have met in prison."

"And then?" I ask. "What were you supposed to do once you got to know Kat and her friends?"

"Nothing," says Marlow. "I mean, there were always weird men watching us, but—"

"Weird men?" I ask.

"Yeah. They'd be in the parking lot before school or outside our houses at night. But I never talked to any of them. And I didn't hear from the guy on the phone until the day before the party. He called and told me to suggest a party at the factory, so I did. I had no idea—"

"That's it?" I blurt out. "They didn't ask you to do anything else?"

"No, I swear! I thought they were just going to spy on us. It wasn't till I saw the projector fall through the ceiling and hit the floor that I knew some serious shit was about to go down. So I stayed with my back against the wall. I tried to keep Kat from going near it, but she jumped up and ran toward it like—"

"Like she knew what would happen and wanted to save everyone." I finish the thought for him. I know exactly what Kat would have done. Her reaction tells me two things: Kat knew they were in danger. And she knew the Company had been watching her.

"Yeah," says Marlow. "I thought they might have rigged the projector with some kind of explosive, but the floor collapsed instead. If I hadn't grabbed on to a pipe when I heard the first rumble, I probably would have died too."

"So you were the one who dialed 911?" I ask.

Marlow holds up his hands. The abrasions on his palms are still red and raw. "I couldn't have wiped my own ass after the incident. How was I supposed to dial anyone? Whoever threw the projector must have called the ambulances."

"But why?" I ask. "Why arrange something like that—and then make sure there were ambulances on the scene?"

"Maybe they didn't want everyone to die," Busara says. "Maybe they had plans for the survivors."

Of course they did. At the facility.

"You have to come with us to the police," I say to Marlow. "You have to tell them everything you just told us right now."

"I can't. I doubt I'd make it as far as the station."

"What do you mean?" Busara asks.

"No one warned me about what was going to happen at the factory that night. They wanted me to die or end up in a coma along with the rest of them," he says. "But I didn't. And now I know too much. My mom, too."

"You really think—" I start to say.

"Yeah. That's why I left a present for you in your locker. When I'm gone, you should use it."

I look over at Busara. She shrugs. She doesn't know what he's talking about either.

"What present?" I ask.

"I found the projector after the collapse. It's just a hunk of metal at this point, but it can tie the Company to what happened to Kat and her friends. I couldn't keep it here, so I took it to the hospital to give it to you. When you got hauled out by security, I put it in your locker at school."

"That's what you were talking about at the country club? When you asked if I'd 'gotten it'?"

"Yeah," says Marlow. "Kat always said you were a genius. I thought you might be the one who could figure out what to do with it."

IMPERIUM

Busara has the combination to my locker. She'll get the projector, but it could take days to figure out what to do with it—and Kat can't wait that long. So my body is back at Elmer's. Busara was there when I went under, and she wasn't exactly thrilled to see me return. But she helped me put the disk back on, and she told me where to go. One realm lies between the wasteland outside Nastrond where we buried Carole and the ice cave I need to reach. Imperium, she called it.

I open my eyes to find I'm lying next to Carole's grave, Gorog's pudgy face inches from mine.

"Preparing for a career in dermatology?" I ask. "If so, I've got a mole on my left sack you might want a look at."

"You're back!" Gorog leaps to his feet and does a weird little dance. I don't think anyone's ever been so happy to see me. Red dust devils crisscross the landscape behind him while flashes of blue lightning illuminate the sky.

"Stop for a second," I say. "We need to talk."

"Is everything okay?" he asks.

Nothing's been okay for quite some time. I'm not sure anything will ever be okay again.

"We've got to get moving. But I need to ask you a few questions before we go. Remember I told you your body's been injured? It's being kept in a facility where they take care of your basic needs. If I have a chance to get you out of there, do you want me to try?"

"Yeah," says the ogre. "Absolutely. Why wouldn't I?"

"Because I don't know what kind of condition your body is in," I admit. "I don't know how well you'll be able to use it."

"I don't care," Gorog says emphatically. "Anything is better than *this*."

I have to agree with him there. "Okay. In order for me to find you, I need to know what you look like in real life," I tell the ogre. Even after all this time, it feels weird to ask.

"I have brown hair and brown eyes and brown skin," he says sheepishly.

"Your powers of description astound me. Can you give me a bit more to work with? How tall are you? How much do you weigh?"

"Last time I went to the doctor I was five three and weighed a hundred and fifteen pounds."

WTF? "Are you a girl?" I ask him, trying not to sound surprised.

"What? *Hell* no!" he shouts.

"Sorry," I say. "You're just a bit smaller than most guys I know."

"Screw you. My dad's six four. I'll be his height eventually."

The horror is starting to seep into my brain. "Wait a second. How old are you?" I ask Gorog.

"I turned fourteen a few weeks ago," says the ogre.

"Right." I pretend the news makes no difference to me. But if that bastard Milo Yolkin were standing in front of me, I would kick him to death. Fourteen. The kid's fighting for his life and he's fourteen years old.

We start walking, though I have no idea where we're going. The scorching sun begins to sink, and a flash of light on the horizon catches my eye. I'm too exhausted to form words, so I point. Gorog grunts and we pick up speed. The lights grow brighter and more colorful as what looks like a forest of glass and steel takes shape before us. The red wasteland ends abruptly. We're standing at the edge of a cliff, looking down at a city unlike any I've seen before. Clustered together are hundreds of skyscrapers. No two of them are the same, and all appear to be under construction. Land in this realm must be in short supply. The owners seem to be claiming the heavens, competing against one another to build the most intimidating towers. A few have already reached too high and are leaning precariously against their neighbors.

Each of the towers bears the distinctive stamp of its owner. Some feature giant video screens playing film loops of avatars dressed in the uniforms of Wall Street executives, Eastern European oligarchs or African dictators. Other owners have marked their buildings with retro-cool neon signs or hologram icons. But in the center of the city, one skyscraper rises far above the rest, its gleaming black walls resembling polished obsidian. Either the place has no windows or the building's *all* windows. It's impossible to tell. There's no mistaking the identity of its owner, though. Near the top of the structure, the name MOLOCH is emblazoned in blinding gold lights.

The Moloch building is already the tallest I've ever seen, but it's still in the middle of a growth spurt. A massive orange crane squats on top, hauling up materials for the dozens of NPCs crawling all over the upper reaches of the structure. From this distance, the workers seem ant-size and the top three floors appear to be little more than concrete slabs and steel columns.

"Someone's coming," Gorog says, just as my ears pick up the sound of vehicles below. A line of five tiny Humvees has emerged from between two towers, traveling toward us on what appears to be the only road out of the city. They're still miles away, and most of those miles will be straight uphill. There's plenty of time to run or hide. But I don't see the point. Neither does Gorog, I guess. We don't bother to discuss what to do next. We just sit down on a rock and wait.

The Humvees come to a stop in front of us, their engines still idling and their tailpipes spewing a fog of exhaust. Nothing seems to be happening. Then one of the doors opens and a man gets out alone to greet us. The closer he comes, the handsomer he gets. Clean-cut and well groomed, he looks like a cross between Prince Charming and the president of a Young Republicans club. He's wearing chinos and a blue chambray shirt with a black flak jacket on top. The name MOLOCH is spelled out in golden letters on the front of his black helmet.

The man waves. "Hello!" he calls out as he takes off his helmet. "I hope we haven't startled you. We've been watching you head this way for hours."

I gotta say, I think I may hate this guy already.

"*Daaamn.* Looks like Goldman and Sachs had a baby," Gorog snickers under his breath.

I wish I could laugh. I'm glad the ogre's recovered his sense of humor. Mine may be gone for good.

The man comes up to us and reaches out to shake my hand. "Welcome to Imperium." His voice is familiar, but I can't place it. "My name is Moloch. I'm the Elemental in charge of this realm." I guess I wasn't expecting the dude with the biggest building and creepiest name to have a haircut like my dad's. It's like meeting a tax accountant named Beelzebub. "You must be Simon. I've been waiting for you to arrive."

He's been waiting for *me*? I've been wrong before, but I'm willing to bet that's not a good sign.

"You knew Simon was coming?" Gorog asks warily.

"Well, I *hoped*. I've heard you're on your way to the glacier, and Imperium is the closest realm to the ice fields." Moloch turns to the ogre. "I'm sorry, and your name is?"

"Lancelot," Gorog says without hesitation.

"Pleasure to meet you, Lancelot," the Elemental replies with a knowing smile. Then he turns to me. "A friend of yours traveled through Imperium a little over a day ago. She said you'd probably be following her."

The relief is so goddamn powerful that I feel like I might float away. Kat's alive, and there might still be a chance to catch up to her. Then a thought drags me back down. This is the third time Kat predicted I'd be following her. If she really believed it, why the hell didn't she wait?

"She's on a rather urgent mission, as you know," says Moloch, who must have been reading my mind. "She wanted to reach the glacier early so she'd have time to scout the place out and plan the attack. I will give you and the ogre a room for the night and take you to your friend first thing in the morning."

"Hold on a sec. My friend is planning to attack the Creator?" I ask. If so, this is the first I've heard of it. "And you're cool with that?" The Elemental of Mammon didn't even want me to *speak* to him.

An alarm goes off in the city below us. It sounds like the wail of an air-raid siren. Moloch turns his head in the direction of the noise. I wonder if he knows where it's coming from. It stops as suddenly as it began and his attention returns to me. "Yes, well, your friend has come to the conclusion that killing Magna is the only solution—to Otherworld's problems as well as her own. I'm afraid I have to agree with her."

The land beyond the skyscrapers is as white as a blank sheet of paper. On the far side of Imperium lie the ice fields Gorog and I need to cross before we reach the glacier. Who knows how long it will take or what we'll encounter along the way? If I've learned anything here, it's that Otherworld is full of surprises.

"Thanks for offering us a place to stay, but I'd like to head for the ice fields right now," I say. I can't wait another twelve hours to see Kat. And I don't want her to try to kill Magna on her own.

"I would love to take you," says the Elemental. "But the sun will be down soon, and it is no longer safe to travel through my land after dark."

It seems peaceful enough to me. At the top of the towers, the NPC crews have disappeared. I wonder where they go when the working day is over. "Why not?"

Moloch sighs. "We've had quite a few problems with the Children lately. Have you met the Children?"

"I've had the pleasure," I tell him.

His face wrinkles with disgust. "Then you know they're abominations. They were never meant to exist. Magna should have exterminated them all long ago, but he couldn't summon the intestinal fortitude to finish the job. Now they feel entitled to Otherworld, and Imperium is on the front lines of the war. Unless we destroy them, it won't be long before they overrun us. While Magna sulks in his cave, I've had to deal with the Children on my own."

"Whose Children are they?"

"Not mine, I assure you," says Moloch. "Most of the Children in Imperium are *his* children. He traveled every inch of Otherworld in the early days, and his DNA ended up mixing with many of his creations. The idiot didn't even realize what was happening until it was too late. Come." Moloch motions for us to follow him back toward the line of idling Humvees. "We should head for safety unless you'd like to meet the local Children. As you've probably learned by now, they aren't very fond of humans."

Those are the magic words, as far as I'm concerned. As much as I pity them, I've seen what the Children can do. So even though I'm not all that keen to have a sleepover with Mr. Perfect, I'm not sure what other options Gorog and I have. Besides, if Moloch and his men wanted to take us by force, I'm sure they could. Right now they're playing nice. Which makes me suspect Moloch wants something from us. I'm curious to know what it is.

We're hustled into one of the Humvees. Moloch and I are in the back while Gorog sits with his neck bent and his knees wedged against his chest in the front passenger seat. I watch through a tiny window as we travel down the dirt road that leads from the cliff to the city below. The driver seems to be in a hurry to reach our destination. He hits every bump at top speed, ignoring the yelps that come from Gorog, whose head keeps thumping against the Humvee's roof. Finally we get to the outskirts of Imperium, and

the road turns to smooth asphalt. The Humvee steers between two towers on the edge of the realm, and the fading sun is immediately extinguished. Without its streetlights, the canyons of Imperium would be as dark as the dead of night. My eyes are drawn to a building up ahead. Its bottom floors are completely scorched, and the glass from its windows lies scattered across the road.

"Wow. Did the Children do that?" I ask Moloch.

"No," he says. "The fire took place before the Children began interrupting our gameplay. You see, the towers of Imperium are vertical empires. They're ruled by guests and house thousands of residents. The more powerful the guest, the more workers he owns. The more workers he owns, the higher his building will rise. But ruling an empire is much more difficult than most realize. In this case, the workers mutinied and pillaged the building. Then they tossed their owner's body from the roof. I'm afraid he never saw the rebellion coming."

As we pass by, a face appears in one of the blackened windows. It's a beautiful young girl with shimmering silver hair.

"Hey, who's that?" Gorog asks.

Moloch leans over me for a better look. The girl steps back from the window, but not in time. "It's one of the Children," he says. The driver mumbles something into the microphone attached to his helmet, and one of the Humvees in front of us pulls over to the side of the road.

"Why are they stopping? What are they going to do?" I ask as we speed past.

"Does it matter?" Moloch asks. "Don't waste your pity on the Children. Whatever my soldiers do to her, I assure you that she and her kind would have done far worse to you."

A few minutes pass in silence and the Humvee takes a hard right turn into one of the buildings and down a concrete ramp. It pulls to a stop in front of an elevator bank and Moloch, Gorog and I slide out. I look up toward the entrance we drove through, just as a heavily armored gate slams shut. It's eerily quiet, as though the building has been evacuated by all but the most essential personnel. Our footsteps echo as we walk across the concrete floor to the elevator. Moloch hits the button and the doors slide open. No one speaks as the elevator silently climbs to the penthouse on the ninety-sixth floor. The doors open again and we step out into a stunning apartment that's surrounded by the sky.

I walk to the windows that look over the ice fields, past a table on which a banquet has been laid out. My stomach growls, but I ignore it. I'm much more interested in the scenery. Now that we're out of the city's dark canyons, the sun hasn't quite disappeared yet. I can see that the towers closest to the ice on this side of Imperium have all sustained considerable damage. Moloch's building is in the middle of a war zone, and it's composed almost entirely of glass. I'm not sure we're any safer up here than we would be down below.

"That is the Children's work," I hear Moloch say. I turn back to the table, where every species in Otherworld must be represented. I'm able to identify a heap of buffalo meat, but most of the beasts have been roasted or stuffed beyond recognition. Moloch has taken a seat at the end of the table. Gorog has chosen a chair on the right side of the Elemental, leaving me the one on Moloch's left. No one else joins us. Aside from two guards standing at the elevator, the three of us are alone in the room.

Gorog immediately grabs a greasy thigh from a platter and begins stripping its flesh off with his teeth. I don't see the point in eating, and Moloch doesn't appear much more interested in the food than I do.

"It's so nice to be able to sit down and talk one-on-one with our guests," he says. "How long have you been in Otherworld?"

"A few days," I tell him.

"And what do you think so far?" Moloch inquires.

I feel like I'm being interviewed. I have a hunch he's looking for a particular answer, but I'm not sure what it is. I must take too long to speak because Moloch decides to answer for me.

"You don't like it," he says. "Of course you don't. It was designed by a madman to cater to perverts and psychopaths. All that will change once Magna is gone."

"You keep saying *Magna*. Don't most people here call him the Creator?"

"Among other things," Moloch says dryly. "He built this world to indulge his own weaknesses. Right now there's no reason a normal human being would want to stay. We'll fix that in time, of course."

"Parts of Otherworld might be fun if you had more than one life," Gorog offers half-heartedly.

Moloch smirks. "Yes, I would imagine the fear of death takes some pleasure out of the experience," he admits. "But all that will be resolved soon. Everyone knows that killing off your guests isn't good business. The idea is to offer them the kinds of immersive, one-of-a-kind experiences that will entice them to stay in Otherworld for as long as possible."

An Elemental who looks and talks like a CEO. Now I really have seen it all. How much does he know? I wonder. And who told him? There's a loud explosion outside, and the windows are briefly aglow.

Gorog drops his dinner. "What the hell was that?" he says, pushing back his chair and hustling over to a window.

"That would be Children," Moloch says. "Right on time, as usual."

"Oh, shit!" Gorog flinches as another explosion rattles the building. Then he looks back at me. "You really need to see this. They're launching some kind of missiles at us."

I join him at the window. The top of a nearby tower collapses in flames just as a ball of fire crashes into one of the giant video screens.

Moloch stays seated. The attack doesn't seem to worry him and he doesn't bother to look. "Don't be concerned. They can't harm us," he tells us. "Our best engineers have fortified the building. The defenses will hold, and in the morning you'll be on your way to the ice cave. If you accomplish your mission and kill Magna, we can end this ridiculous war. Without his protection, the Children won't last long and order can be restored."

"Do the Children have to be exterminated?" I ask, remembering what Busara told me. The Creator let them live because he knew they were alive.

"Of course!" Moloch exclaims. "They're a nuisance. Just look what they've done to this realm! They're making it impossible for our guests to enjoy themselves. Magna knows that guests and Children can't coexist, but he won't take any action. He's even let an army of Children take refuge in the ice fields. During the day, they're impossible to find. At night they scuttle out like vermin to attack Imperium. It's chaos. But once Magna is gone, the Children will be eliminated and the Beasts will be brought under control. We'll make Otherworld what it has the potential to be."

"And what's that?" I ask.

"A better reality—a place everyone wants to stay," says Moloch. "The deviant guests can still have their own realms, of course, but Otherworld will be a playground for everyone else as well."

Just like the man sitting across from me, the solution seems a little too neat. The guests will get their paradise, but first all the Children have to die.

I see Gorog's face scrunch up as if nothing he's heard makes any sense. "If everyone wants to be in Otherworld all the time, what's going to happen to the real world?" he asks.

Moloch dismisses the question with a laugh. "I imagine it will continue to revolve around the sun."

"Seriously, though," I say. "How much do you know about the real world?" I'm genuinely curious.

"I know it's a place of misery for most," he tells me. "Otherworld will offer humankind a chance to escape."

"You just put on a visor and leave it all behind," I say.

"Precisely," he replies, sounding pleased.

"Except you have to abandon your body. You know about our bodies, right?"

Moloch shrugs. "There will be solutions to such problems."

"Like what, exactly?" I ask. His flippant attitude is pissing me off. "Right now Gorog's body is crammed into a capsule. Mine is in an abandoned building waiting for a raccoon to eat it. Those don't sound like very good solutions to me."

"If there's a demand for storage, someone will find a way to supply it."

"You sound like a capitalist," I say. "Were you programmed that way?"

"I'm a realist," our host tells me. And judging by his tone, he has nothing else to say. "Now if you'll excuse me, I must attend to some business. One of the servants will be along shortly to show you to your rooms."

If I didn't know any better, I would swear that I'm in the most sumptuous bed ever constructed. I remind myself that my body is lying exposed on the wooden floor of a crumbling factory. But I don't quite believe it.

The moonlight streams in through the glass walls. In the city below, the siege has stopped. The Children are finally quiet and the realm is at peace. My eyes close, but I won't be sleeping tonight. In the morning, I will see Kat and possibly do battle with Milo Yolkin's avatar. I have to prepare myself for the fact there's a good chance I'm going to die. I don't really care anymore—as long as I can find a way to save Kat.

A breeze tickles my face. I detect movement through my eyelids, as if a shadow has passed through the moonlight. I open my eyes and see that someone is standing over me. It's the young girl from the burned-out building. For some reason, I'm not frightened at all. I'm happy to see she escaped from the soldiers.

Moloch said most of the Children belong to the Creator. If that's true, I wonder who her other parent might be. The moon, maybe. I suppose anything's possible in Otherworld. The girl's body is thin and fragile and her silver hair shimmers. I can't tell if she's made of flesh or light. She looks scared and nervous. She raises a finger to her lips and then gestures to me to follow her. I don't know why, but I do.

A ragged rectangle has been cut out of the glass wall of my room. Outside in the cold night air, a wooden platform is waiting, supported by ropes that must be attached to the arm of the giant crane on the top of the building. It wasn't there earlier when I took in the view. The girl steps onto the platform, and I climb out after her, though it's terrifyingly narrow and swaying from side to side. I hold on to one of the ropes and try not to look down. The girl's hair floats on the wind as the crane begins to lift us into the sky.

The platform comes to a stop at one of the unfinished floors near the top of the building. There's an elevator bank in the center of the floor, but beams remain exposed and the windows haven't been installed yet. The girl points to a steel cage near the elevator. It appears to be empty, and I'm about to ask what I'm supposed to be looking at when something inside the steel bars begins to shift and move like a pool of mercury. It takes me a moment to realize what's going on. There's someone in a camouflage bodysuit lying inside the cage. It has to be Kat. She's not waiting for me at the ice cave. Moloch has taken her prisoner.

I've opened my mouth to call out to Kat when I hear a whistle followed by a dull thump. It's the most horrible sound I've ever heard because I know exactly what it means. I glance over in time to see the Child crumple, an arrow lodged deep in her chest.

I grab her hand as she starts to fall from the platform. Her grip is firm and her flesh is warm. She's alive, but I can feel the life inside her draining away. Her grip loosens, and as she lets go, her fingers slip through mine. I thank God I can't hear her body break when it hits the ground below.

I turn in the direction the arrow came from. Moloch appears from behind one of the building's exposed beams, a crossbow in his hands.

"It's time to go back downstairs," he tells me.

I step off the platform and into the building. "You killed her."

"Her?" he scoffs. "Don't be stupid. That wasn't a *her*. It was a bug. Just a batch of bad code."

But she wasn't. I would swear the girl was every bit as real as I am. She risked her life to take me to Kat. She died helping someone she'd never met. How could anything get more real than that?

I'm still in shock as Moloch ushers me across the unfinished floor and onto the elevator. The descent takes less than two seconds, and the doors open on the ninety-sixth floor, revealing blood-soaked tiles and piles of dead NPCs. Before I can make any sense of the scene, two burly tattooed arms pluck Moloch out of the elevator. His crossbow drops to the ground as Gorog takes the avatar's head in his hand. I hear the crunch of Moloch's neck snapping and the thud when he falls.

"Hi, Simon," Gorog says, his smile big and wide.

Then there's a strange flash. I glance down to see Moloch's neck straighten. When he rises to his feet, he doesn't appear to feel any pain. I should have known. He's not an Elemental. He's not part of the game. Someone in the real world is controlling him. A headset player.

It's still sinking in when a dozen NPC soldiers rush into the room behind the ogre.

"Gorog!" I shout, but it's too late. They've surrounded him now, but he doesn't struggle to break free. He doesn't even appear to be frightened.

"You've got this, Simon," he tells me. "Remember, you're the One."

"Get rid of the goddamn ogre," Moloch orders his men.

"No!" I shout. "No, don't! Gorog!"

There's no answer. The tip of a spear emerges from between two of the ogre's ribs. Gorog's body drops. The deed has been done.

THE ENGINEERS

I open my eyes. I'm in the back of a patient transport van. My visor and disk have been removed and my chest and legs are strapped down. My hands are bound together with a zip tie that's slicing into my wrists. No one's riding with me. I stare at the ceiling, my teeth clenched in rage. When I find the person responsible for Gorog's death I will rip him limb from limb.

I feel the van backing up. Then the engine shuts off. The doors open and the driver rolls my gurney out. We're in one of the facility's loading docks.

"You can go. I'll take him from here," someone tells the driver. A face appears above me. It's Martin.

"Hey there," he says. "Sorry for all the drama back in Otherworld. We had to keep you busy while we looked for your body. By the way, it was genius to hide it right out in the open. None of us ever considered the factory."

I'm a moron. My little outburst at Moloch's dinner party told them right where to find me.

"You're Moloch?" I ask.

"Sometimes," he says. "Last night it was Todd. And when we're not in Otherworld an NPC fills in for us. We've got to keep the place functioning while the test is running."

"You killed Gorog," I snarl.

"Yeah," Martin admits as he wheels me into the building and down the long hall. "It wasn't part of the plan, but then he went and tried to break Todd in half."

"Todd was wearing a headset!" I shout. "He couldn't die! Gorog was wearing a disk. He knew that and he killed him anyway!"

"You're right—ordering the ogre's death was a mistake," Martin concedes. "But in Todd's defense, you get so used to dealing with the Children that the words just pop out. Still, there is some good news! The ogre bit the dust, but it turns out the kid didn't die. It's a very exciting day here at the facility. We've taken a giant step forward with the disk—and your friend helped us make it."

My relief is mixed with a hundred other emotions, the strongest of which is terror. "Are you going to cut him up?"

"What?" Martin blurts out. He looks thoroughly revolted. "Why would we do that?"

"To examine his brain. I've been in your lab, you know. I've seen what you do to people."

"Sure, to *dead* people," Martin corrects me. "We don't chop up the living. Do you think we're monsters? We'll just run lots of CAT scans."

"Hello, Martin," a familiar voice interrupts.

"Hey, Angela," Martin replies. "I've got a delivery for the boss."

"Wonderful," the robot says. "According to his GPS, he's on his way back to the facility right now. Estimated arrival time is seventeen minutes."

Oh, good. Milo is coming. I can't *wait* to see him.

"Thanks, Angie," says Martin. "Now how about opening door number two for me?"

"It would be my pleasure." Her flirty voice seems to imply that the pleasure will be physical. Someone must have thought it would be real funny to have a sexed-up robot secretary. I've met her twice now and the act is already old.

Martin and I ride the elevator down to the maze of capsules where the bodies are kept. Martin whistles as he rolls me toward a room along the perimeter.

"We-he-hell," someone calls out. "If it isn't the savior of Otherworld. *The One.*" It's Todd.

Martin sighs. "Come on, don't be an asshole," he says. He undoes the straps that bind me to the gurney and helps me sit up. We're in an office that would appear perfectly ordinary if not for the computer screen displaying what must be a video feed from Moloch's tower. There appears to be something happening on the ice fields outside Imperium.

"You're both assholes," I inform them just as Martin grabs an X-Acto blade from a desktop and bends forward to remove the zip tie from my wrists.

"Maybe you should keep his hands bound," Todd says. "The little bastard seems pretty agitated."

"Yeah. Good thinking." Martin stands up and takes a cautious step back.

Once he's sure I'm no threat to him, Todd sits on a nearby desk.

"So we're *assholes,* are we?" I'd love to punch the smug look off his face. "In a few years, you can tell that to the Nobel Prize committee. By the way, I hear Watson and Crick were assholes too."

"Watson and Crick never killed anyone," I say.

"That you *know* about," Todd says. "Watson seems like the kind of guy who probably experimented on a hobo or two, don't you think?" When he looks over at Martin, he seems to be expecting a laugh.

"Oh, shut up," Martin snaps instead. "We're not the bad guys," he tells me. I get the sense that he really wants to believe it.

"You're tricking people into using stolen technology that you know can be deadly," I point out. "If you're not the bad guys, who the hell are?"

"Whoa there, dickhead. You think we *stole* the tech?" It's Todd talking now, and he's completely offended. "We were part of the team that developed it! We sank three years of our lives into the disk."

"And the technology won't be dangerous for much longer," Martin is quick to add. "We're analyzing what happened to the kid with the ogre avatar. If we can figure out how he survived, we might be able to fix the disk."

"It's too late. People have already *died.* A lady with four children *died.*"

Martin looks stricken, and unless he's the world's greatest actor, he's completely sincere. "You're talking about Carole Elliot. It's tragic, I know. But Carole didn't die in vain. Besides, after the car accident, her body was beyond repair. She wasn't walking out of this facility either way. Look—a handful of people have been lost, but thanks to them, humankind is on the verge of taking a giant step forward." There must be a vat of Kool-Aid hidden somewhere in the building. When I get a chance, I'll hunt it down and drown Martin in it.

"They didn't *die*, you psychopath," I say. "They were *sacrificed.* Can't you tell the difference?"

"You know what?" Todd growls. "I'm getting real sick of this sanctimonious crap. We took people who would have spent their entire lives as drooling vegetables, and we gave them the opportunity to be true pioneers."

"Their sacrifices will make life better for the entire human race," Martin quickly adds.

I'm dumbfounded. "People's lives are going to be better because of Otherworld?" I ask. "Are you joking?"

"Otherworld? You think that's what all this is about?" Martin laughs like he's discovered the source of my confusion and can finally set the record straight. "We needed software for the disk's beta test, and Otherworld just happened to be available. But Otherworld is only the beginning. Do you have any idea what our technology will do? It's going to educate people around the globe. Someday soon, a kid in rural India is going to slap on a disk and attend classes taught by Harvard professors."

"You think Harvard's going to let little Indian urchins take their classes for free?" Todd mutters under his breath.

"*Whatever.*" Martin rolls his eyes as if they've had the same exchange a million times. "Then think about all the elderly people cooped up in nursing homes. With a disk they can spend their final years touring the world or . . ."

"Or having sex with hot young things," Todd finishes.

"Goddamn it, are you going to let me talk?" Martin nearly shouts. The two of them act like an old, homicidal married couple.

"Do you see what I'm saying? The disk is going to level the playing field for people around the world. Everyone will have access to education and companionship and sex. You'll be able to travel the entire globe without spending a penny on airfare. You won't need to be born rich or beautiful or lucky. All you'll need is a disk."

I want to ask Martin how many people he's willing to kill to save the world, but I can't stand to hear another lecture. "Where's Milo?" I ask. "I want to talk to him."

"Milo?" Martin asks, as though he doesn't quite recognize the name.

"Yeah, your *boss*. Wasn't he supposed to be here in seventeen minutes?"

Todd laughs. "Milo's already here, bro."

"Where is he? Go get him."

Martin looks nervous. "Come on," he says, taking one of my elbows and helping me slide off the gurney. "Why don't I show you around before the boss comes to see you?"

"Thanks," I say. "But like I told you, I've been here before."

"Yeah, we know," Todd sneers. "Lotta people got fired because of you."

I think of Don and Nathaniel and the nurse who helped me escape, and I suddenly want to vomit. I probably got them all killed. God knows how many people Martin and Todd have murdered, but I've got a body count of my own.

"Fired?" I ask. "So you think they're all working at Costco now?"

"What exactly are you implying?" Todd barks.

"Hey," Martin says in his most soothing voice. He's smiling at me like I'm a mental patient. "Don't be ridiculous. Nothing happened to them. They just don't work here anymore."

You know, I actually think he really believes all this shit. I think he's managed to convince himself that there's nothing evil about the operation he works for. They're just a bunch of scientists using vegetables to save the world.

"Tell you what," Martin says. "Why don't I take you to visit your friends? You can see for yourself they're okay. We've been taking very good care of them."

Butterflies flutter in my stomach at the thought of seeing Kat. Martin's offer is one I would never refuse. So with my hands pinned together like a convict on his way to court, I follow Martin out of the office and into a nearby room. There's a hospital bed at the far end, but Kat's not in it. Lying on top is a young black kid. There are tubes sprouting out of him and machines monitoring his vitals. But there's no visor on his face. I'm not sure why I'm here, until—

"That's Gorog," I say.

"Who?" Martin asks. "Oh, right, that was the name he gave his avatar. His real name is Declan. He was riding his bike to school one morning and got hit by a car. The cost of his hospital care was about to bankrupt his family, so the Company stepped in to help."

"He told me he was fourteen years old." There is no way the tiny boy on the bed is fourteen.

Martin clears his throat. "I believe he's thirteen," he says.

"You bastards are experimenting on thirteen-year-olds?"

"I'm sorry, I thought you'd be pleased to see him," Martin says irritably. "He's in stable condition. We're monitoring his progress very carefully. He's out of Otherworld for good now—and he'll be well protected. He's the secret to fixing the disk."

I run my fingertip along the zip tie that's holding my hands together. If I could only find a way to snap it, I would kill Martin right now.

"Would you like to see Katherine?" he asks.

"Yes," I manage to croak.

We weave through the maze of capsules. Construction has apparently been moving ahead at full speed. The labyrinth has doubled in size since the last time I was here. And more of them are in use. Hundreds of the hexagonal windows glow with the strange orange light.

"This is Katherine's," Martin says, stopping at one of the windows.

I press my nose to the glass. "It's empty," I say. "Where is she?"

"She's in one of the visiting rooms," Martin says. "There's someone with her now. As soon as they leave, I'll take you up to her. I thought you'd prefer to see her face to face. And just so you know, I made Todd leave your Otherworld avatar in the same cage with Katherine's. After you talk to the boss, you can put on a disk and join her there."

"Why would you do that?" I ask.

"Because I'm not a bad guy," Martin tells me. "You two are sweet together."

We hear the sound of wheels on the concrete floor. Someone is pushing a gurney our way. "That's our latest patient," says Martin. "Would you like to meet him?"

I nod, but he hesitates.

"You know what?" He points at the zip tie around my wrists. "It's probably best if the staff doesn't see you like this. I'll remove your restraints if you promise to behave."

"And if I don't?" I ask.

He raises his eyebrows and tilts his head like he's lecturing a naughty toddler. "If you don't behave, you'll never get to see Katherine Foley again. Here or in Otherworld. Do you understand?"

I nod again, but I'm gonna play it by ear. My fingers tighten into fists as Martin removes the zip tie. I have to force them to open again.

The nurse turns the corner. It's not the same woman who helped me. God only knows what happened to her. My eyes lock with the nurse's. There's a flicker of life in them. She's never seen me before, and she knows there must be a reason I'm here. Then I glance down at the body she's carting. It's Marlow Holm.

"Shit," I mutter. His entire body is black and blue.

"I know." Martin winces at the sight. "The kid's pretty banged up. He and his mother were in a car accident this morning. It was a terrible tragedy. She worked for the Company. They say she was brilliant."

"Mrs. Holm is dead?" Just as Marlow predicted. They made it happen.

"You knew Madeline Holm?" Martin asks casually. You'd think we were making cocktail party chitchat.

"I went to school with her son."

"Of course! I can't believe I almost forgot," Martin says. "Yes, she passed away. But her son survived, and now he's here with us. Don't you see? Marlow is a member of the Company family, and he'll be part of the beta test, too. That's how passionately we believe in the importance of this project. The accident that brought Marlow to us was tragic. None of us enjoy seeing seventeen-year-olds with broken bodies. But if Marlow dies in our care, he'll die a hero. His life will not have been wasted."

I meet Martin's beady little eyes. "Don't feed me your bullshit," I say as calmly as I can. "You and I both know Marlow wasn't in an accident. The Company did this to him."

The nurse gasps, and Martin recoils as if I've raised my fists. "Excuse us for a moment," he tells the nurse. She stares at him like a deer watching an eighteen-wheeler barrel toward it. "*Now,* please." The words break the spell and she bolts.

Martin's good humor has disappeared by the time he turns back to me. "I thought you were going to behave!" he says through clenched teeth.

I've never known how to behave. I should keep my mouth shut, but I can't let Martin convince himself that he's anything but a murderer. "Marlow was in the same *accident* that nearly killed my best friend. He wasn't supposed to survive it—but he did. So the Company staged another *accident.*"

"You know what? Todd was right. You are a little bastard," Martin snaps. "I've been trying to explain my work to you, and you're spouting stupid conspiracy theories—"

"It's not a theory," I say. "Marlow wasn't in an accident. And he's not in a coma now."

"Don't be ridiculous," Martin scoffs.

Before he has a chance to stop me, I step forward and slide the IV needle out of Marlow's arm. Then I pull the visor off his face. Marlow's eyes are open—wide open—and he's terrified.

"Have you gone completely insane?" Martin whispers angrily. "Nurse!" he calls out. "Nurse, come back, there's a problem with the . . ."

And he stops. He sees it too. Marlow's lips are moving.

"God," Martin groans.

"You sure you want to call on God right now?" I demand. "'Cause I have a feeling he's not too happy with you. *This* is the truth, Martin: The people you have stored in these capsules aren't *vegetables*. They may be injured, but they don't have locked-in syndrome or anything like it. There are drugs mixed in with the IV fluid that are keeping them comatose. And maybe some of these people were in accidents, but I know of at least four kids my age who are here because the Company *wants* them to be here."

Martin rubs his eyes, and I wonder if I've managed to surprise him. Then he sighs and picks up the needle that's dangling from the end of the IV's thin plastic tubing. He places it on Marlow's chest, then looks up at me.

"I know," he says. His anger is gone. He sounds beaten. "I wish like hell that I didn't, but I do."

Marlow's lips stop moving and a thin trickle of drool escapes from the side of his open mouth as Martin takes the visor out of my hand and places it back on Marlow's face.

"How can you stand back and let this happen?" I ask.

"You're young and idealistic, Simon. When you get older, you'll realize there are no easy choices. I stand back and let it happen because I honestly believe that this technology is going to make billions of lives better. What would you do in my shoes? Would you let a few dozen people die if it meant making the world a better place?"

"Is that what you think you're doing? Improving the world?"

"Nurse!" Martin calls out again, and this time I hear footsteps hurrying toward us. I have a few more things I'd like to get off my chest, but Martin stops me. "Be careful what you say in front of her," he warns. "I know what it's like to have people's deaths on my conscience. I've learned to live with it. Do you think you could too?"

This time, I have no answer to offer.

"Come on, then," Martin says as the nurse returns. He smiles at me as if bygones are bygones. "Let's go see your girlfriend. Promise you'll be on your best behavior? No more yanking out IVs?"

I keep my mouth shut and nod.

"Good boy," Martin says.

He guides me through the maze and up the stairs toward the visiting rooms off the lobby. I pause when we reach the top to watch the nurse connect Marlow's body to the tubes and wires that will keep it alive inside his new capsule. Martin waits patiently. When I'm ready, I follow him down the hallway until we arrive at the last visiting room. There's a blinking green light on the biometric scanner beside it.

"Kat's ready for us," Martin announces.

"You're sure her stepfather is gone?" Even now, I have zero desire to be in Wayne Gibson's company.

Martin shoots me a strange look. "You mean Mr. Gibson?"

"You said she had a visitor. Who else would it be?" I ask Martin. Her mom's in a loony bin, and Kat has no other family. "I saw him here the last time I visited."

"I'm sure you did," Martin responds as if I'm a moron. "He works here."

No. Fucking. Way. "He *what*?"

Martin snorts. "And I thought you had everything figured out, boy genius. Wayne Gibson runs this facility. He's our boss."

"What about Milo?" I ask while my mind reels.

"Milo's on sabbatical," Martin says.

He places his palm against the scanner's screen, and there's no time for a response. The door in front of us opens with a swoosh. It must be the same room I was in before. There's an OUT OF ORDER sign taped to the bathroom door. My eyes pass over a cabinet with a drawer jutting out. The medical equipment inside grabs Martin's attention and he heads over to investigate.

And then I see Kat, tucked between the sheets. I'm by her side in an instant, her hand in mine and my face buried in her hair. I know there's a very good chance that this is the last time I will see her alive in the real world. Martin promised that Kat and I could be together in Otherworld, but I doubt he's run that one by his boss.

The boss. Wayne Gibson. Wayne *fucking* Gibson. I'm still finding it hard to wrap my head around that one. I almost wonder if Martin is messing with me. But now that I think about it, Wayne Gibson makes sense. Did he have Kat in his crosshairs before he married her mother—or did Kat accidentally get in his way? That's what I'd really like to know. If only I could see him now. If only I could go back to the day when he and I stood face to face on Kat's front porch. I would do things to Wayne Gibson that would shock Ragnar and all the bloodthirsty psychos in Nastrond. I would take my time with his body, ripping it apart bit by—

"Simon?" It's Martin's voice. He's come to Kat's bedside.

I look up at him and he flinches. I'm glad. The rage rushing through me must show on my face. Martin did this to Kat, and when I'm done with Wayne, I'll come for him next.

"You need to say goodbye now," Martin tells me. "It's time to go."

"No," I say. "I'm not leaving her."

Martin rolls his eyes. "Do I need to call security?" he asks.

"Go ahead. Call them," I say. "I will kill every person who comes into this room."

"Sure you will," Martin says with a smirk. He can laugh all he likes. I know it's true, and I know I can do it. Otherworld trained me well.

Martin lifts his arm, bringing the tiny computer that's strapped to his wrist closer to his lips. I rise too. Martin won't be calling anyone. When they find his body, I'll make sure that arm is rammed somewhere *special.* He happens to glance up as I lunge across the bed. His eyes go wide as my fingers wrap around his scrawny neck. I've barely begun to squeeze when Martin's eyelids flutter shut and his body goes limp. Suddenly the full weight of his body is in my hand. My grip is unprepared for the burden, and he slips through my fingers and crashes to the floor.

I rush over to the other side of the bed. For a few magical seconds, I honestly believe I've acquired superhuman powers. Then I spot the girl crawling out from beneath Kat's bed. There's a smile on her lips and a syringe in her hand, and I know my days as a superhero are over.

"Busara? What are you doing here?" I whisper.

"Taking a risk," she tells me, sounding giddy with excitement. "I grabbed Marlow's projector from your locker at school, but when I got back to Elmer's, your body was gone. I figured the facility was the only place you could be, so I made an appointment to visit Kat." She points at the steel door that leads to the capsule maze. "I was planning to go through there and look for you, but then you spared me the trouble and came to me."

I glance down at Martin. "How did you just . . ."

"I found a syringe from the drawer and filled it with fluid from Kat's IV. Gave Martin a taste of his own medicine. Pretty clever, right?"

She called him Martin, I realize. "How do you know his name?" I ask, prodding the engineer's body with my toe. I must sound suspicious. Probably because I am. Busara's still got a way to go before she earns my trust.

"Geez, Simon. He used to work for my dad, remember? Stop thinking I've turned to the dark side. Give me a chance, will you?"

I'll give her a chance. But only because I don't have a choice.

"Are you sure you're strong enough for all this?" I ask. "I mean, your heart . . ."

"Is still beating as far as I can tell," Busara says. "And we've got to get out of here. Martin won't be unconscious for long. I'm parked outside."

"What about Kat?" I ask. "We have to take her, too. And Gorog—what about him?"

Busara's smile fades. "Simon . . ." She's going to tell me it's impossible.

"I am not leaving the facility without Kat," I insist. "I am not going to let them put her back in one of those capsules so she can die in a video game."

"Do you think Kat wants to be taken out of Otherworld?"

Busara asks. "She's obviously on a mission of her own. Do you think she wants it to end? Maybe you should ask her before you rip off her disk."

"I don't care what she wants; I will not let her die!"

"Calm down," Busara says. "As long as you're free, Kat's not going to die."

"What makes you so sure?" I demand.

"Because you know about the disks. And the Company will want to find you before you can cause problems. Kat's their bait," Busara tells me. "If she's here, the Company knows you'll eventually come back to the facility."

I hate to admit it, but she makes an excellent point. Right now, the best way to protect Kat may be to abandon her here. But there's no way in hell that's going to happen.

"I want to get you out of here so you can go back to Otherworld and get Kat through the exit," Busara is saying. "Then we'll figure out what to do with the projector."

"I can't go back to Otherworld. I don't have a disk and visor anymore," I tell her. "The Company took mine when they found my body at Elmer's."

Busara reaches into the pocket of her jacket and pulls out a well-worn set of gear. "Use these. They're all I have left. They might not be pretty, but they work. The disk isn't connected to mine, though. I won't know where you are in Otherworld, so I won't be able to help you. Now get out of here, and find a safe place to hide your body."

"I'm not going anywhere. Help me drag Martin to the bathroom," I tell Busara. "No one's going in there. It's been out of order for days. Tie him up and then head out to your car and wait for a signal. Don't leave the parking lot until you get one."

"What are you going to do?" Busara asks. "Where are *you* going to go?"

"Nowhere," I tell her. If Busara could fit under Kat's bed, I figure I can too. "I'm going to stay right here."

THE CHILDREN

"Simon." The whisper comes from above. I'd know the voice anywhere.

My eyes are still closed, but I'm where I need to be. I can feel lips pressing against mine. I reach out and find the girl they belong to. The body beneath my fingertips is soft and warm. An electric current courses over my skin. Every cell is tingling. Maybe none of this is real, but I've never felt so alive.

"Kat." My head is in her lap. Her hair has fallen across my face. Once more, her lips press against mine.

When she pulls back, I sit up and open my eyes so I can find her lips again. But the sight of her smile stops me short. It's been so long since I've seen it. I never want to look away.

"You came after me, just like you promised," she says.

"Of course I did. I'd go anywhere for you."

Kat takes my hand. "I'm sorry. I should have told you everything from the start," she says, her eyes on my fingers. "I was trying to protect you. I thought if I could just—"

"It's okay," I tell her. "We're in this together now."

"I know," she says. "If it makes any difference, it feels like you've been with me the entire time."

She sighs and her breath turns into a frozen cloud that hovers between us for a moment. We're no longer in Moloch's tower. Around us, I can see ragged rock walls and a cavern that's bathed in an ethereal blue light. What look like strands of stars are suspended from the ceiling. They blink in strange patterns that pass from one strand to the next as if they're creatures speaking in code. And they are, I realize.

"They're alive," I say.

"Yes," Kat confirms. "The Children cultivate them."

"Where are we?" I ask her.

"Beneath the ice fields," she tells me. "This is where the Children hide. They brought us here," Kat says.

"Why are they helping us?"

"Because they want us to help *them*. We know we don't belong here. The guests with headsets think this is a game—that the Children only exist for their amusement. You wouldn't believe the things I've seen while I've been here."

"I think I probably would," I say. "How did you figure out that the Children are different?"

"I was traveling through the wasteland outside the White City when I came across a caravan of trucks. Moloch's soldiers were rounding up all the Children they could find. I knew the minute I saw them that the Children weren't part of the original game.

So I snuck into one of the trucks and spoke with them. One told me they were being taken to a realm where guests hunt them for sport. I could see how terrified they were. That's when I figured out they were real."

"God, that's horrible."

"That's what I thought. So I killed all the NPC soldiers and set the Children free. I guess word got out after that. The Children have been helping me ever since."

"How did you end up getting caught?"

Kat laughs. "I didn't. I heard a rumor that Moloch was looking for a guest who wasn't supposed to be in the game. I thought that was probably you, so I let him find me. His tower wasn't as impregnable as he thought. I could have escaped at any time. The Children and I were just waiting for you to arrive. As soon as you're ready, the Children will escort us to the glacier to see their father. Do you remember the giant red avatar? It belongs to—"

"Milo Yolkin. How did you find out in here?"

She grins. "I'm a badass. How'd you find out?"

"I just sort of stumbled into it, really. But that's beside the point. We might need to kill him if he tries to keep us from going through the exit," I tell her. "Are you ready for that?"

"We can't kill him," Kat says. "Milo's the only one who can save us."

I'm about to question her sanity when three Children materialize at the entrance to the cavern, and I almost gasp. They are unlike anything I've seen before. Whatever digital DNA mixed together to make them, the results are truly spectacular. Two are females who look like they're twins. They're taller than most human women, with matte gray skin that reminds me of unbaked potter's clay. But something golden crackles within them, and bursts of light erupt on the surface of their skin as if fireworks were exploding beneath it. The male is enormous—at least as large as Magna—with the white hair and beard of a Nordic god. He looks more human than his companions, but there's something else in the mix as well. He's carrying several furry pelts over one arm. I assume they're what will keep us from freezing to death during our trek across the ice. It's hard to believe the guy has my safety in mind, though. He's glaring at me and his white eyes burn with hatred.

Kat rises to her feet. "Stay here. I'll go talk to them. They trust me."

I'm not convinced. "You sure you're going to be okay? I don't think that dude likes guests very much. *Any* guests."

"Can you blame him?" Kat asks. "Humans brought them to life, and then we set about killing them. I wouldn't be all that fond of us either."

I keep a careful eye on the negotiations, which seem cordial but tense. Kat returns quickly with the pelts in her arms and a stoic expression on her face.

"They say it will take a few hours to reach the glacier, and we have to move fast. Moloch's men are out in full force on the ice fields. They're searching for us, and the Children won't be able to hold them off forever." She offers me a hand and helps me to my feet. "Shall we get started?" she asks.

I would give anything for another hour alone with Kat. But that hour might cost us the rest of our lives. "Let's go," I tell her.

. . .

The ice fields are a completely different experience with a disk. I can feel the frigid wind whipping around us. Beneath the heavy pelt the Children provided, my skin is numb to the touch. We move carefully across the treacherous ice. There are bottomless fissures wide enough to swallow us whole, and the blinding glare from the sunlight makes them difficult to detect. We pass over frozen seas where the ice beneath our feet is so thin that you can see the hungry beasts prowling the water beneath it. And we travel through storms that pelt us with hail and rip the sky apart with lightning. I wasn't afraid the last time I was here. I should be terrified now. But I'm not. There is nowhere I'd rather be than here with Kat.

When we set out, a troop of warrior Children surrounded us. Now, hours into our journey, I notice that our escorts have slipped away. I turn in circles, searching for some trace of them. Though I can see for what must be miles in every direction, they're nowhere to be found.

"We're alone," I tell Kat.

"Don't worry, the Children are watching," she says, taking my hand and leading me forward. "If Moloch attacks, they'll have the element of surprise."

"Do you think they can hear us speaking?" I ask.

She stops and turns back to me. "I have no idea what they can do," she responds. "You might as well say what you want to say."

"Kat, I really think we may need to kill the Creator—even if he lets us go through the exit. Milo Yolkin is the one responsible for all this. He's evil and he's addicted to the game he invented. He'll never make all the guests leave."

Kat shakes her head. "You're wrong about the evil part," she says. "Milo's not evil. He's *immature*. He thought he had a fun new toy to play with. He didn't know the technology was Pandora's box. He created Otherworld, but he couldn't control it. Now he's lost control of the Company, too. But he still has the power to shut both of them down, and that's what we have to convince him to do."

It's pretty clear that Milo's lost control of Otherworld. The evidence is everywhere you look. The rest of it is news to me. "Milo's lost control of the Company?" I ask Kat. "How do you know?"

"My beloved stepfather," says Kat. "Wayne works for the Company."

"Yeah, I heard," I say. "He told you about Milo?" It's hard to believe.

"Not exactly. Remember that little hut you added to our fort?"

I'm not sure where she's going with this, but I'll play along. "You really think I'd forget the fort?"

"Well, after you left for school, I'd go out there and sit and—"

"By yourself?"

Her head drops to her chest as if the memory is too much to bear. "I missed you," she said. "And Mom had just married Wayne and it was like the two people I loved had both deserted me."

Kat just said she loved me. Back in the real world, I think my heart just exploded.

"I'm sorry," I tell her. "You know I didn't have a choice."

"I know," Kat says. "And I knew that then, too. But whenever I started to forget, I'd go out to the fort to feel closer to you. Anyway, I was out there one day, and I heard Wayne talking on his phone. He always popped outside when he got work calls. He didn't want anyone else listening in. That day it was a call from someone named Swenson. I looked him up afterward—he's on the Company's board of directors. He and Wayne were talking about Milo. At first the things Wayne was saying made me think Milo might be sick. Then I realized what was really going on. Milo was obsessed with the new Otherworld. He'd even had some of his engineers build a weird capsule-thing for his body so he could stay in his virtual world as long as possible. For a while I thought Wayne and this Swenson guy wanted to help him, but then I realized they were planning to take control of the Company. They were pissed because Milo was using some amazing new technology they called the disk. But he'd forbidden the Company to make any more because the devices were dangerous. Wayne and Swenson wanted Milo out of the way so they could test the disk on more people. They'd keep Milo in his capsule and pull him out for a public appearance now and then, but . . ." She pauses and studies my face. "What is it?" she asks.

How do I tell her she's part of the test? I shake my head.

"I know I'm wearing one of the disks," she says softly. "I heard you talking about it in my hospital room right before I ended up here. Is my body in one of the capsules? I know Wayne was planning to build more."

"How?"

"I found blueprints for them in his office. When I figured out what they were, I was going to try to expose the Company. But then Marlow threw that party at the factory, and the rest is history."

I suddenly remember the blueprint photo I found in the Yoda sleeping bag at Elmer's. That's got to be what she's talking about. I'm an idiot for not putting the pieces together earlier. "Jesus, Kat. I still can't believe you didn't tell me any of this."

"I couldn't, don't you see? Not without putting your life at risk. Wayne was on to me. He had the whole house rigged with cameras and surveillance equipment. One of the cameras must have filmed me going into the fort that day, and Wayne realized I'd heard something I shouldn't have. He asked me a bunch of questions about it, and I played dumb. But after that, he tore down the fort and started monitoring everything I did. I tried to throw him off my tracks by wrecking his car and hanging around with those kids at school. I figured he wouldn't see me as a threat if I looked like some kind of druggie delinquent. I'm pretty sure I almost had him convinced. Some nights I didn't even go home. I slept at Elmer's instead. Then my best friend who'd been arrested for hacking shows back up in town and starts sending me thousands of dollars' worth of VR equipment. . . ."

"Which I would never have done if you'd told me what was going on," I argue passionately.

"True," she admits with a satisfied smirk. She was teasing me. Then her face turns serious once more. "But I was so scared when you came back to Brockenhurst, Simon. I knew I was in trouble, and I could handle that. But if something had happened to you—and it was all my fault—I don't think I could have survived."

There's nothing I can say in response. I step in front of her and put my arms around her. I kiss her and she kisses me back. We're standing all alone in a frozen wasteland, and Kat's lips are icy cold. And yet this is the best moment of my entire life.

"So do you see why we can't kill Milo?" she asks when we finally part. "We need to convince him to leave Otherworld so he can shut down the beta test and turn Wayne in to the authorities."

"You think he'll do it?"

"Maybe not for us," she says. "But he might do it for the Children. He knows how much they've suffered. Maybe . . ." She pauses. "What's that?" she asks.

There's a dark blotch on the horizon and it's growing bigger and bigger.

"I think someone's coming for us," she says, pulling an arrow out of her quiver. I take out my dagger. It's almost hilarious to think that it's my only weapon against whatever is thundering in our direction.

"Where are the Children?" I ask, scanning the landscape for any sign of our escorts. "Aren't they supposed to be protecting us?"

"They're not human. They have their own way of doing things," Kat says, managing to remain perfectly calm. "But in my experience, they always keep their word."

The dark mass in the distance is taking form. Giant white beasts race across the frozen expanse, human shapes atop their backs. On my first visit to Otherworld, I slew one such beast, a bear of prehistoric dimensions with long white hair like a yeti and teeth too large to fit in its mouth. It stalked me across the ice for miles, as if it wanted to study me before it tore me apart.

Now six of them are bounding toward us, and the men on their backs have their swords drawn. Riding the largest beast at the front of the pack is Moloch. As soon as he's within range, Kat pulls an arrow from her quiver and takes aim. The missile sails through the air and hits him square in the chest. But the arrow doesn't penetrate. I watch it bounce away and fall to the ground.

"What was the point of that?" I ask. "We both know the dude isn't going to die."

Kat doesn't bother with a second arrow. "I thought we might

be able to get rid of his avatar for a little bit, but he's wearing some kind of armor," she says. "Our weapons are totally useless."

"If he gets close enough, I'll just have to take him out with my own two hands," I tell her.

"Show-off," she jokes, and though we're probably facing imminent death, I feel the urge to kiss her again. So I do.

The bears are almost upon us when Moloch raises a hand and the animals slow to a trot. The six of them surround Kat and me. They tower over us, their black eyes fixed on our faces, their breath enveloping us in a rancid cloud. The beasts could destroy us in a matter of seconds, and yet I don't fear them. I've met plenty of creatures here that wanted to kill me. These just don't seem all that interested.

Moloch slides off his mount and joins us in the center of the circle. The NPC warriors he brought with him are in full battle gear, complete with helmets, but Moloch's handsome avatar is dressed like it's casual Friday at the investment bank. Then I detect a slight shimmer around him. It's some kind of protective shield.

"Hi, Todd," I say. It has to be Todd now. Martin's tied up in a bathroom. "Remember Kat? She's one of the people you've been trying to murder."

"Hey there." Kat gives him a cheerful wave.

Todd ignores her greeting and stands nose to nose with me. "Game over, you little shit. Do you have any idea what you've done?"

I share a look with Kat and shrug. "Do you know what he's talking about?"

"Nope," she responds.

"Martin is missing," he snarls.

"Oh, really?" I ask. "Maybe the serial killer lifestyle didn't suit him after all. Where do you suppose he went?"

"If he left, the Company will find him," Todd says, his voice cracking. "And then they'll kill him."

I'm finding it really hard to muster the appropriate level of sympathy. "What do you care?" I demand. "It's just another sacrifice for the advancement of mankind, right?"

"He was my friend!" Todd shouts. "We worked together for ten years. He might have been a sap, but he was a genius, too." Then, his teeth gritted and nostrils flared, he regains control. "Where is your body? We want the disk back."

I can't help but laugh. "Yeah, I bet you do. But you're not going to find it."

"Either you tell me where the disk is or bad things are going to start happening to everyone you care about. Starting with her." He shoves a finger at Kat.

It wasn't a smart move. I'm up in his face in an instant. "You do anything to Kat and I will punish you in ways you can't even begin to imagine."

I feel Kat tap me on the shoulder. "Can I help?" she asks.

"Oh, *absolutely*," I say.

"You think I'm joking?" Todd snarls. "I finally have permission from Gibson to get rid of her."

"Awww. How is dear old Stepdad?" Kat asks.

"Getting pretty sick of your shit," Todd snaps.

I really wish this asshole were wearing a disk. I've never wanted to make anyone suffer so much in my life. "You already came close to killing a thirteen-year-old today. You ready to murder another human being? You must have gotten used to slaughtering

Children by now. I'm guessing you've even learned to like it. Ever wondered what Otherworld is turning you into?"

"All I've done is take care of business," says Todd. "When I have a billion dollars and a Nobel Prize, no one's going to care what I did to get it. Least of all me."

"That's why we're going to do whatever it takes to make sure you end up in an orange jumpsuit instead," says Kat. Then she turns to me. "What do you think his Wikipedia entry will call him? Mass murderer? Mad scientist?"

"I'm gonna go with serial killer," I say. "Heck, you know what? Maybe I'll write the entry myself."

"Oh! Good idea," Kat says. "Be sure to add this part."

"Definitely," I reply. "It's such a dramatic moment, isn't it?"

"Shut up!" Todd shouts. He stomps back to his bear and climbs into the saddle. "Kill them both," he orders the beasts.

I pull Kat into my arms, but the attack never comes. The six bears stay where they are. The one nearest me leans over to its neighbor and licks the side of its face.

"Kill them!" Todd shrieks at the soldiers sitting atop the beasts. None of them moves a muscle. "Why are you sitting there? Do what I say!" Todd shouts in frustration. When it becomes clear that they aren't planning to follow orders, he goes for his own sword. But the scabbard is empty. "What the hell is going on here?"

The largest of the soldiers removes his helmet, revealing his white hair and beard. Back in the cavern, I didn't know what he was. Now that I see him atop the bear, it's clear that the two creatures share DNA.

"Filthy vermin!" Todd snarls. "Where did you come from? How did you steal my bears?"

"They are not your bears," the Child says placidly. "They are wild creatures. They don't belong to anyone."

"This is insane," Todd says. "Of course they do. I know the little asshole who designed them."

"The Creator gave life to this world, but it is constantly changing. Nothing here is what it was originally meant to be."

"No shit," Todd says. "But don't worry, we're going to clean things up. Starting with you."

"Your kind will not defeat us," the Child says. "With our father's help we will take control of Otherworld and drive your kind out."

"Your *father* is a pathetic addict," Todd sneers. "I'll get ten engineers working twenty-four seven to fix whatever he decides to screw up."

"And I will send thousands of Children to destroy every guest."

I glance at Kat. I totally agree that humans don't belong here, but setting out to destroy every guest seems a bit much. Some of them would really die.

Todd scoffs. "Thousands?" he asks. "There can't be more than a few hundred of you left."

The bears part and we can see a vast army of Children on the horizon. Looks like the Creator really got around.

"Oh my God," Todd gasps. Then there's a flicker in his avatar, and Moloch dims and goes still. Wherever Todd is, the coward's pulled off his headset.

"Take the avatar hostage," the Child orders the others.

Kat steps up to the Child's bear. "You never said you would kill all the guests."

"We will do whatever is necessary to take back our world," says the Child.

"But some of us never chose to be here," Kat argues. "We were forced into coming, and if you kill us in Otherworld, we'll die in the real world too."

Her pleas don't appear to make much of an impression. "The real world?" asks the Child. "Why is your world the real one? How can you be so certain you humans were not created by someone else? Does your history not speak of a Creator too?"

It's a good question—so good that even Kat can't find an answer.

"This is *our* reality," the Child continues. "Your kind comes here to use us for pleasure or murder us for sport. When we die here, there's no other place we can go."

"But killing hundreds of innocent humans can't be the answer," I argue.

"Then you must convince our father to banish the guests," the Child tells us. "That's why we've brought you here. Now do what you're meant to do."

When we reach the glacier, the Children leave us at the entrance. I look for the Clay Man as we enter the ice tunnel, but the spot where I first saw him is empty. I'm glad, because I'd rather there not be a witness to what I'm about to do.

"Hold on," I tell Kat. She stops and turns to face me. She's so goddamn beautiful I could die. "There's a really good chance we won't make it out of here, and I have something to say to you first."

I pause. The words were there just a second ago, but now I can't seem to find them.

"I love you, too," she tells me. "I always have."

I suppose I should be thrilled, but instead I'm crushed. "I can't believe I wasted so much time because I was too much of a wuss—"

"To risk destroying our friendship?" Kat finishes.

"Yeah," I admit.

"Simon," she says. "That's one of the reasons I love you."

I kiss her for the fifth—and maybe the last—time. When she pulls back, I don't want to let her go.

"It's going to be okay. This isn't over," she tells me.

"You're sure?" I ask.

"Yes. It's just beginning. I promise." She takes my hand. "Come on—let's get this part over with."

We walk side by side through the pale blue ice. Just before we reach the cave, she plants a kiss on my cheek. Then we step inside to find Magna sitting on his throne. His red body has cooled to gray metal. The avatar is just as colossal as I remember, but this time Magna's shoulders are slumped and his head is bowed. He seems exhausted, weak.

He looks up at us. His face takes form as it starts to glow. For the first time I can see the resemblance to Milo Yolkin. "Did Moloch send you?" he asks wearily.

"No," Kat says. "We came on our own. My name is Kat. This is Simon."

"I'm not in the mood for company," Magna tells us. "Get out." His body begins to burn bright red. He lifts one hand, and a glowing orb forms in his palm. As he does, the outstretched arm returns to stone, as if the effort has drained him. Yet there's little doubt that the orb remains a lethal weapon.

"Please, don't throw that, Milo. If you hit us, we could die in real life," Kat says calmly.

The avatar's stone limbs melt into swirling plasma. He's burning so brightly now that I can hardly bear to look at him. "What did you call me?"

I grab Kat and shove her into a crevice in the cave's wall just as Magna's orb sails through the air and hits the ground inches from where we were standing. The explosion leaves my ears ringing. I use my body to shield Kat, and I know my avatar's going to be black and blue from the chunks of ice that are pelting it.

"Guess he prefers to be called Magna," Kat says. "Good to know."

Kat can crack all the jokes she likes, but I can't see the humor in the situation. That evil little shit nearly killed us. I am going to make him pay for that. When I'm done, there won't be a bone in his body that hasn't been broken.

"Simon," Kat whispers. She sounds worried. "What's wrong with you? You look crazy. We both knew this wasn't going to be easy. You've got to calm down."

But I can't. The valve that once controlled my rage has been broken. The anger can no longer be contained. I can hear myself panting like a rabid beast.

"Stay here. Don't do anything," Kat warns. "You're not well. Let me take care of this."

She slips out of the crevice, and I follow her. The attack appears to have done more damage to Magna than it did to Kat or me. He's doubled over in his chair, his head in his hands.

"My apologies for offending you, Magna," Kat says to the avatar. "I was trying to tell you that Simon and I are both wearing disks."

He looks up. I assume he's surprised, but it's hard to tell. "Come forward," he orders weakly.

I hurry after Kat as she approaches the giant. I can feel the dagger tucked away in my boot. One wrong move and Magna's going to be tasting steel.

"Close your eyes," Magna orders Kat, and she does as he says. He leans forward and places his palms on either side of her face. One hand remains cold gray stone while the other glows red.

"Stop!" Kat exclaims, reaching up to grab the glowing hand. "You're burning me!" Magna immediately removes both hands from her face. The test is over.

"How did you get a disk?" he asks.

"The Company is beta testing them," Kat says. "They've kidnapped hundreds of people and stored their bodies in capsules. I'm part of the test."

Magna sits back in his chair. "They went ahead with it," he says to himself, seething. "Even after I forbade them to alter the business model."

Kat looks at me. "Business model?" she asks.

"The Otherworld headset app will make billions, but it's only a game. If the Company sells disks, the people who use them will have to turn to us for their most basic needs. They'll need a place to store their bodies and nourishment to keep them alive. Can you imagine how much we could charge for such services? Apparently my board of directors can. Those greedy bastards. I *told* them the disks weren't viable."

I can't keep my mouth shut. "Wait, we just told you that the

Company—*your* company—is kidnapping people and you're pissed off about the *business model*?"

Kat shoots me a dirty look, but Magna doesn't seem to give a damn about my outrage.

"You need to leave Otherworld," Kat tells him. "You have to return to the real world and stop the beta test. You're the only one who can do it."

"Why bother?" Magna asks. "Without me, the Company will never be able to fix the flaws in the disk. And no one will want to lease one of the Company's capsules when they find out there's a chance they might die in it."

"People are *already* dying in the capsules," I snarl.

Magna's eyes leave me, and his gaze focuses on a spot just behind us. "They aren't the first victims of this technology, and they certainly won't be the last. Humankind is taking a massive leap forward. There's bound to be collateral damage."

I glance over my shoulder and see a strange shadow on the wall of the ice cave. There appears to be a body entombed in the ice.

"Whose avatar is that?" Kat asks.

"It belongs to the disk's inventor," Magna says.

"James Ogubu?" Oh my God, it's Busara's dad. "You didn't kill him?"

"Kill him?" Magna scoffs. "Why would I do something so stupid? He knows the technology better than anyone. I might need his help someday."

"You need him *now*," Kat says. I can tell from her voice that she's stopped playing nice. "You've lost control. You've let Otherworld beat you. It found your weakness."

"Lost control?" Red veins spring up on the stone surface of Milo's avatar. "I created this world. I know every rock, every beast, every cloud in the sky. . . ."

"You may have created it, but it's not yours anymore," Kat tells him. "It belongs to the Children. They're alive and you *know* that. The guests are killing and slaughtering them one by one, but you haven't been able to stop it. You can't admit that your game needs to end. You're too addicted to playing God. Isn't that what you always wanted—what you couldn't get from the real world? The ultimate power? Otherworld gave you a taste and now you're hooked—just like all the people who came here to kill or steal or indulge their sick fantasies. . . ."

"I am not like them. Here, I *am* God!" Magna bellows. A new orb has appeared in his hand. I step forward, but Kat holds me back with one arm while she points at the exit on the far side of the cavern.

"Go through the exit, Milo. Close off Otherworld to visitors. Get rid of the disks. Keep the servers running and let Otherworld play on, but without any guests. Including *you*. If you want to save the Children—and save the real world from this technology—you can't spend your life in a capsule," Kat says. "Two worlds need you, Milo. You have to make the sacrifice. You have to go back. This is your chance."

She did it again. I watch Magna's arm rise at the sound of his real name. He's going to throw the orb. Maybe he'll miss. Maybe he won't. But I'm not going to stand here and let this crazy fucker and his overgrown avatar threaten the girl I love. If he won't go through the exit, I'm going to make him. He's already weak. The orb in his hand has drained the energy from the rest of his body. I pull out my dagger and charge forward.

"Simon, stop!" Kat grabs hold of my robe and won't let go. But I can't be stopped, and I drag her behind me as I make my way to Magna.

The orb is blindingly bright when he throws it. I'm dazzled, but I manage to duck. I hear the explosion behind me, but I keep going. Until I realize I'm no longer dragging Kat behind me.

I turn to see her on the ground, her copper curls fanned out around her face. Kat's eyes are fixed on the ceiling above and her mouth is open, but she doesn't seem to be breathing.

No. No. No.

I drop to my knees and take her in my arms. I can feel a feeble pulse, but it's already fading. Nothing else matters. *Let the world end,* I think.

"Please don't die," I beg her. "I love you."

I hear Magna making his way toward me. I don't even bother to brace for the blow.

"I'm sorry."

It's not Magna's booming voice. This one's boyish and quiet and I've heard it somewhere before. "Let me help. There's still time to save her."

"Milo?" I say.

He doesn't answer. The avatar gently lifts Kat off the ground. When I'm standing, he passes her body to me. "Take her through the exit," he says. "Do it quickly. I'll be right behind you."

THE BIG BOSS

Kat's body vanishes as I go through the exit. I'm not sure what to expect next. I'm used to having the disk ripped off the base of my neck, and I'm hoping this experience proves a little less painful. I step through the door and into a warm, bright room. It feels like a foyer between two worlds; all I need to do is walk forward. But I'm not in here alone. My grandfather is standing in my path. He's younger this time. Aside from his brash 1960s-style suit, he looks a lot like me.

"Off to rescue the damsel in distress?" he asks.

"Hopefully a few other people too," I tell him. "So I don't have time to chat."

He grins. "You got guts. I like it. Probably 'cause you got them from me."

"Did I?" I ask.

"Why not?" he replies. "I was like you once. Word of advice, though?"

"What?" I ask, annoyed that he's keeping me from Kat.

"Don't think you got it all figured out. Looks like you picked up a little problem back there in crazy world. And even when we've got our heads on straight, a lotta guys like us end up at the bottom of the canal."

I was expecting kudos, but I get a bullshit warning instead. I barge past him, through the light. When I can feel my hands, I remove the visor. The first thing I see is the ceiling of a capsule, which is all of four inches away from my face. They've found me. And getting out looks like it might be a bit of a challenge. I scoot down to the end and hook the tip of my shoe under the lever that opens the door. But when I pull, it doesn't budge.

Inside the capsule, it's at least a hundred degrees. Which might be great if I were naked. The sweat from my forehead is streaming into my eyes, and it's impossible to wipe it away. I try the door handle again. Again, it doesn't budge. My heart is racing now. It's probably my imagination, but the air in here seems to be growing thin. I'm on the verge of an all-out panic attack when I hear the capsule door open and feel a whoosh of cool air.

Someone pulls my shelf out. His face appears above me.

"Mr. Eaton."

"Hi, Wayne," I say, struggling to sit up. "Hope you don't mind if I call you Wayne."

He takes a few steps back until he's standing against the wall of capsules opposite mine. Only two of them are lit.

"Don't bother getting up," he says, gesturing at the metal shelf I've been lying on. "It will be time to go back soon. Right after you tell me where you've been getting the disks."

"You know what? I think I'll stay in the real world for a while,"

I tell him as I slide off the shelf and land on my feet. My legs feel wobbly, but I do my best to hide it. "I've been playing too many games lately. I need to spend more time outdoors. And as for the disks—go to hell."

"I'm afraid that's not the right response, son." He pulls out a gun and I almost laugh.

"Isn't that a little old-fashioned?" I ask him.

"I'm an old-fashioned man," he says. "A straight shooter, pun intended. I suppose I could go chasing after my enemies in some virtual world. But I'd rather just put bullets in their heads or make a few rotten floorboards collapse."

"That was you that night at the factory?"

"It was. And now you know just how far I'm willing to go if you don't do what I ask."

"Let me guess. You'll kill me?"

"Absolutely. And then I'm going to let your friends live."

I don't get it. Then he steps to one side, giving me a clear view of the capsules behind him. There's movement in one of them. A girl's hands are pressed against the interior of the capsule as if she's trying to force her way out. But there's no room to move, nowhere to go. I know her panic. It feels like being buried alive. And my own body almost collapses when I realize that the girl in the capsule is Kat. My eyes jump to the capsule beside hers. I see the toes twitch and I get a glimpse of male legs. It has to be Milo Yolkin.

"I'm guessing you didn't foresee this turn of events, did you?" Wayne Gibson asks with a satisfied smirk. "The capsules don't open from the inside. I made sure of that. Katherine and Milo left Otherworld, but I think they're probably regretting that decision right about now. I switched off their meds. They're not paralyzed, but they're not going anywhere either. And this is exactly how they're going to stay unless you tell me where you've been getting the disks. I'm not sure I'd keep them waiting if I were you. How long do you suppose it will take for the two of them to lose their minds?"

I've seen people die in countless ways, but none compares to the horror Wayne Gibson just described. "You're a goddamn monster," I growl.

"Not at all," he argues. "I'm giving the three of you a chance to return to Otherworld. Milo's private exit will need to go, though. We'll let him out from time to time. You'll have to stay in his nasty little world, of course. But heck, it's better than the alternatives, wouldn't you say?"

"What's all this for, Wayne?" I ask, trying to buy some time. "I'm just curious. What motivates a man like you? Is it money?"

"Nope. It's about progress, son. Well, and large amounts of money—but mainly progress. It's always required human sacrifice. You know how many men died building the Brooklyn Bridge? Or the Panama Canal? People like Mr. Yolkin here like to think that the world runs on their brainpower. People like me know that the world runs on blood. Now tell me what I need to know, Mr. Eaton. I'm finished with small talk."

"Me too," I tell him. "Go ahead and shoot."

I'm waiting for the sound of the gun. Instead my ears are assaulted by another noise. A siren has gone off overhead and a red light is flashing above Milo's capsule. Wayne Gibson looks like he's just been punched in the face. He holsters his gun and peers through the capsule's window. Then he opens the latch and pulls the body out.

I'm frozen in place by the sight. Milo Yolkin barely looks human. His body is so emaciated that I can see every bone in his skeleton. Dark purple circles surround his eyes, and his shaved scalp is covered in strange brown patches. The heart monitor inside the capsule has flatlined.

"Help me, goddamn it!" Wayne shouts. "We need him alive!" He's started chest compressions and CPR. It's not going to make any difference. Even I can see that. But I let Wayne finish making the effort. Then I attack. I grab his gun from its holster with my left hand just before my right smashes into his face. Three more jabs and Wayne's down on the ground. I raise my foot, and I'm just getting ready to stomp him to death when I catch a glimpse of Kat inside her capsule. It takes all the self-control I can muster to pull myself back from the brink. I put my foot down and point the gun at Kat's stepfather instead.

"Get up and get on," I tell Wayne, pointing at the sliding metal shelf that I recently left.

He looks at the gun and then up at me. "You aren't going to shoot," he says, gasping for air.

"You sure about that?" I ask, giving him a quick kick in the gut. "Do you have any idea how many people I had to kill to make it through Otherworld? Do you really think one more would make a difference? Get on the goddamn shelf."

"Shoot," he says.

There's a deafening bang, and I have no idea what's happened until I see Wayne lying flat on the floor. I glance down at the gun in my hand and the finger that's just pulled the trigger. Wayne's groaning while a pool of blood spreads out around him.

What the hell did I just do?

I shove the gun into the waistband of my pants, open Kat's capsule and pull her out. "Simon!" she gasps as I peel off my T-shirt and help her into it. "What happened to Wayne? Oh my God, is that Milo?"

"I'll tell you everything when we're safe. But first we've got to get out of here," I say.

When Kat slides down to the floor, she shrieks with pain. "There's something wrong with my leg."

"Hold on to my neck," I tell her, and I gather her up in my arms. The time in the capsule has taken its toll on her as well. She's light as a feather.

"What about the others?" she asks.

"We can't save them if we're dead," I tell her. "We'll have to come back."

I carry Kat up the stairs and down the hall. We've gotten as far as the lobby when it becomes clear that we won't be going any farther. Black SUVs have pulled up in front of the building, and the men pouring out are already charging through the door. I have the gun in my waistband, but I'd have to put Kat down to reach it.

"Go!" she says. "Leave me here and get out another way."

"No," I tell her. I remember Carole saying the same thing. But Carole was sacrificing herself to save me. I'm saving myself. There would be no point in surviving if Kat were to die.

Then I spot movement in the parking lot. And I know what's about to happen, as if I've somehow managed to read Busara's mind. I drop to my knees behind one of the couches in the lobby a split second before the crash. Kat screams as glass flies in every direction. Large shards embed themselves in the walls. I'm up the second it's over, with Kat in my arms. Busara's car is in the middle of the large room. I open the back door and toss Kat inside, then throw my own body in after hers.

The door of the car is still open as we crash back out through the front of the building, skid across some grass and race down the driveway and onto Dandelion Drive. Busara runs every red light on the way out of Brockenhurst. I manage to get the door closed, but no one says a word until we're on I-95. I don't even know if we're heading north or south.

"So?" Busara finally asks.

I could spend the next three hours going through everything, but it would all boil down to two sentences. "Milo's dead," I tell her. "But your dad isn't."

Busara gasps and the car swerves across the highway. "What?"

"We saw him in Otherworld. He's trapped in the ice inside Magna's cave," Kat says.

"And his body?"

"It must be at the facility," I say.

"The one we just left?" Busara wails.

"I'm sorry," I tell her. "I promise we'll go back for him. And Gorog. And all the rest of them too."

"They won't be there when we do," Busara says. "The Company will have that place emptied out before sunrise."

"And they'll be looking for us everywhere," Kat adds.

"We don't have any money and we can't use credit cards," Busara points out. "And none of us can go home."

But I know what to do.

"I think it's time to pay a visit to my friend Elvis," I tell them.

EPILOGUE

There's only so far you can run before you have no choice but to stop.

We made it to Texas, but I don't even know the name of the town we're in—or if there's even a town around us. The wasteland we drove through could have been part of Otherworld. The sign that drew us here was the first we'd seen in a hundred miles. COLTON COURT, it said, and there was a picture of a gun next to the name.

Technically this is the first night I've ever shared a bed with Kat. There's little chance of anything happening with Busara asleep in the bed on the other side of the motel room. I'm sure we'll all wake up covered with bedbug bites, but we can't afford anything better, and I don't think any of us cares.

I'm so tired I'm delirious, but I still can't seem to sleep. I'm sitting on the edge of the bed, flipping through television channels. Most are just static, but every so often I come across one with a signal. Right now I'm watching the grainy image of a slick-looking salesman type who's speaking directly to the camera. The volume is down low enough so that I don't bother the others, but I wonder what he's selling. I have to lean forward and strain to make out his words.

"Then God said, 'Let Us make man in Our image, according to Our likeness; let him have dominion over the fish of the sea, over the birds of the air, and over the cattle, over all the earth and over every thing that creeps on the earth.'"

I flip to the next channel. Nothing. The next. Nothing. The next. Nothing. I just keep going like some kind of lab rat that's been trained to push a button. And then finally the reward—the nightly news presented by some Podunk Texas station. Right above the anchor's shoulder is a photo of Milo Yolkin. My heart picks up speed. The word is out. I bump up the volume. ". . . has announced he will be taking a sabbatical from the Company for health-related reasons. The Company issued a press release earlier this evening, and while it did not disclose the nature of Yolkin's medical problems, it did indicate that the twenty-nine-year-old CEO's leave of absence could stall the eagerly anticipated wide release of the Company's popular Otherworld game. In other news . . ."

"What the hell?" It's Kat.

"You're up?"

I come around to her side of the bed. She looks so beautiful that I have to lean over to kiss her. She kisses me back for a moment, but then her eyes seem focused behind me. She pulls back. "Look," she whispers.

We both glance over at Busara's bed. She has the covers pulled up over her head. The human-shaped lump beneath the blanket seems oddly still. I watch for signs of breathing but see none. I suddenly fear the worst—that her damaged heart may finally have failed her. I'm about to get up and check for a pulse when I see a faint flash from Busara's bed. It's almost imperceptible. I blink hard, trying to focus. There's the slightest movement of her covers. Busara is breathing.

WELCOME BACK TO OUR REALITY.

OTHEREARTH

Fall 2018

ABOUT THE AUTHORS

JASON SEGEL is an actor, a writer, and an author. Segel wrote and starred in *Forgetting Sarah Marshall* and cowrote Disney's *The Muppets*, which won an Academy Award for Best Original Song. Segel's other film credits include *The End of the Tour; I Love You, Man; Jeff, Who Lives at Home; Knocked Up;* and *The Five-Year Engagement.* On television, Segel starred in *How I Met Your Mother* as well as *Freaks and Geeks.* He is the coauthor of the *New York Times* bestselling Nightmares! series—*Nightmares!; Nightmares! The Sleepwalker Tonic; Nightmares! The Lost Lullaby;* and *Everything You Need to Know About Nightmares! and How to Defeat Them. Otherworld* is his first novel for young adults.

KIRSTEN MILLER lives and writes in New York City. She is the author of the acclaimed Kiki Strike books, the *New York Times* bestseller *The Eternal Ones,* and *How to Lead a Life of Crime.* Kirsten is the coauthor of the Nightmares! series with Jason Segel. *Otherworld* is the fifth novel she and Segel have written together. You can visit her at kirstenmillerbooks.com or follow @bankstirregular on Twitter.

Ravenspur

Tickhill
✳

Louth
●

Clipstone ●

+ Lincoln

✳ Newark

Boston
●

Nottingham
✳

● Grantham

Leicester ✳

● Spalding

Lynn
●

Walsingham
●
North Walsham ●
St. Benet of Hulme

Norwich ☖
Yarmouth
●

▭ Crowland

Stamford
●

▭ Peterborough

Ely
☩

Coventry
▭
Kenilworth

▭
Ramsey

● Mildenhall

Framlingham
✳

Newmarket
Cambridge ●

▭
Bury St. Edmunds

wick
Northampton

✳
Bedford

Ipswich
✳

● Deddington

Colchester ▭

Oxford
✳
▭ Abingdon

St. Albans
▭
Berkhamsted
✳

✳ Wallingford

Brentwood
●

London
Westminster ▭ ☩

Tilbury

lborough

▭
Reading
✳
Windsor

Erith
●

Rochester ☖

Canterbury ☖

Newbury
✳

Reigate ✳

Maidstone
✳

Sandwich
●

Sarum

☖ Winchester

Dover

bury

Southampton
●

+ Chichester

Lewes
▭

Romney
●

Winchelsea
●
Senlac ✂

Hastings

stchurch

Portsmouth

Pevensey ✳

●
✳
☖ Monastic cathedrals
+ Secular cathedrals
▭ Monasteries, collegiate churches and nunneries
✂ Battlefields

0   20
Miles

SET IN A SILVER SEA

Inscribed
by
the author
at the request
of dear
Louisa Stockdale
for
Michael Caroe

A HISTORY OF BRITAIN
AND THE BRITISH PEOPLE

VOLUME I

SET IN
A SILVER SEA

The Island Peoples
from Earliest Times to the Fifteenth Century

Arthur Bryant

[signature: Arthur Bryant]

"Thank Him who isled us here, and roughly set
His Briton in blown seas and storming showers."
Tennyson

"This royal throne of kings, this scepter'd isle . . .
This fortress built by Nature for herself
Against infection and the hand of war . . .
This precious stone set in the silver sea . . .
This blessed plot, this earth, this realm, this England . . .
This land of such dear souls, this dear, dear land."
Shakespeare

COLLINS
8 Grafton Street, London w1
1984

William Collins Sons and Co Ltd
London · Glasgow · Sydney · Auckland
Toronto · Johannesburg

PUBLISHER'S NOTE

The Publishers are grateful to A. P. Watt Ltd.
for permission to use the Kipling quotations at
the heads of the Introduction and chapters 2, 5,
6 and 10.

BRITISH LIBRARY CATALOGUING IN PUBLICATION DATA

Bryant, Arthur
Set in a silver sea.—(The History of Britain
and the British people; 1)
1. Great Britain—History
I. Title   II. Series
941   DA130

ISBN 0-00-217181-3

Made and printed in Great Britain by
William Collins Sons and Co Ltd, Glasgow

CONTENTS

CONTENTS

ILLUSTRATIONS

To
TOMMY JOY

Introduction

'Dear Country, O how dearly dear
Ought thy remembrance and perpetual band
Be to thy foster child, that from thy hand
Did common breath and nouriture receive?
How brutish is it not to understand
How much to her we owe that all us gave?'

Spenser

'Our England is a garden, and such gardens are not made
By singing:– "Oh, how beautiful", and sitting in the shade,
While better men than we go out and start their working
    lives
At grubbing weeds from gravel-paths with broken
    dinner-knives . . .

Oh, Adam was a gardener, and God who made him sees
That half a proper gardener's work is done upon his knees,
So when your work is finished, you can wash your hands
    and pray
For the Glory of the Garden that it may not pass away!
And the Glory of the Garden it shall never pass away!'

Kipling

A NATION which has forgotten its past, said Churchill, can have no future. At a time when we are confused and divided as to what ours should be, I have written *A History of Britain and the British People* to recall the meaning and greatness of our past.

When I was a boy every educated Briton had a rough general knowledge of the country's history. It may not have been a scholarly or sophisticated one, but at least it was one of which there was reason to feel proud. Whatever her faults Britain had conferred widening benefits on her people and on all who throughout the world enjoyed British citizenship or had shared in the peaceful expansion of her seaborne trade and libertarian ideals. And her

xi

history stimulated, in those who read or were taught it, a desire to serve their country and prove themselves worthy of her.

Today such popular awareness of the nation's history has largely been lost and more than one generation has grown up without being taught it. And the teaching of history for the academic minority who alone today study it, though highly scientific and scholarly, has become so specialised that the great mass of the nation knows nothing of it. In a democratic age when the welfare and safety of society depend on the opinion of the many, the cumulative guidance of the past and its inherited corporate experience is almost totally lacking. For the instinctive wisdom of the ages is a truer guide than the conflicting opinions of individuals, however clever. 'We are afraid,' wrote Burke, 'to put man to live and trade on his own stock of reason, because we suspect that this stock in each man is small, and that individuals would do well to avail themselves of the general bank and capital of nations and of ages.' It is a bank and capital on which as a nation we have ceased to draw.

Though at no time has more history been written by highly trained and conscientious academic historians, researching and clarifying, for the benefit of fellow scholars, every detail of the past, little or nothing of it has contributed to an awareness of the broad sweep of the nation's past – and, therefore, present – in those on whom in a democracy national policy depends. And though there are several excellent modern composite histories of the country, each period contributed by an expert on it, such impersonal works, however skilfully edited, do not today fill the place once taken by widely-read general histories conceived and executed by a single mind – by a Hume, Lecky or Lingard, a J. R. Green or a Trevelyan.

This is due not only to the failure of those responsible for the nation's educational system to provide for the teaching of history in school, but also to a realisation in those who might otherwise read it that the basis of the history offered has been too narrow. For, if it is to reflect reality, history must record more than the doings of rulers, statesmen and politicians. Political history is history in one dimension only. It is a facet of corporate human existence, not human existence itself. Nor, as economic historians tend to suggest, is history only a record of prices, wages and monetary movements, profound though their effect on people's lives. Economic history, like political, is still only history in one dimension.

It is only when history presents a broad universal view of the past that it becomes a complete, and therefore true, vision of man's evolution in time:

> 'the nations,
> Their markets, tillage, courts of jurisdiction, marriages,
> Feasts and assemblies, navies, armies,
> Priests and sabbaths, trades and business, the voice of the
>   bridegroom,
> Musical instruments, the light of candles,
> And the grinding of mills . . .'[1]

It is here that a growing interest in social history has added a new dimension to the study of the past. And in the last half-century a number of highly readable works of scholarship have appeared in which, by employing a technique first used by Macaulay in the famous third chapter of his unfinished *History of England*, social history has been blended with political to make a new kind of historical art. Such, in the hands of genius, were G. M. Trevelyan's *England in the Reign of Queen Anne*, Veronica Wedgwood's *The King's Peace* with its two sequels, and Professor Sir John Plumb's books on Hanoverian England, all attracting, because of their historical insight and brilliant writing, a wide readership. And though none of these covers more than a limited period, and no single historian's life is now long enough to distil and reduce to readable form all the immense, and often conflicting, volume of learning available to write it, 'the best is the enemy of the good', and what, above all, seems needed today is a complete social and political history of the country for readers of all ages, but particularly for the young.

Because so much of my life has been spent writing and helping to pioneer combined social and political history, a conviction has long grown on me that, were I to live long enough, the best use

[1] Thomas Traherne: *Serious and Pathetical Contemplation of the Mercies of God.*

I could make of my last years would be to try to write a complete history of Britain and her people. The idea that I might do so first came to me in 1950 when, after producing during my 'thirties four full-scale biographies and a social history of the later seventeenth century and, in my 'forties, three late eighteenth- and early nineteenth-century political and social histories of our wars against Revolutionary and Napoleonic France, and another on Victorian and Edwardian Britain, I decided to take a busman's holiday and write a short history of England for boys. But, on trying, I soon discovered that, outside these three special periods, I knew little of our history except what I had learnt at-school and university. And in order to answer the many questions I could not answer without further intensive study, I found myself embarking, not on a boy's history of England in one volume, but on an old boy's history in many.

As a result, I have been able to draw on seven closely written and carefully researched and documented period histories, ranging chronologically from the early and medieval *Makers of the Realm* and *Age of Chivalry* to the nineteenth century *Age of Elegance* and *English Saga*, which together constitute a multi-volume, though still incomplete, political and social history of the nation. Incorporating freely from these, as from my other historical books and biographies, I have spent a decade writing, repeatedly rewriting and revising, a shorter, simplified, yet complete and comprehensive *History of Britain and the British People*. Two successful cancer operations in my 78th year by a brilliant surgeon have added a bonus of additional time for this self-imposed task of re-teaching our history to those deprived of it.

In this I am following the steps of my old friend and master, G. M. Trevelyan, who in 1926 published his widely-read political *History of England* and, sixteen years later, a still more popular sequel, *English Social History 1340–1900*. Instead, however, of treating its political and social aspects in two separate volumes as he did, I have blended them; though, having to cover so vast a span of time in it, my publishers and I have abandoned our earlier plan of launching the whole *History* initially in a single volume.

Instead, it is being issued serially in three volumes of normal readable size.

It is, above all, for the young that I have written it in gratitude for the long working years granted me and in memory of the comrades of my youth who gave their lives for England in battle; and as an attempt, however inadequate, to repay the incalculable debt I owe my country for all she has taught and given me,

> 'Her sights and sounds; dreams happy as her day;
> And laughter, learnt of friends; and gentleness
> In hearts at peace, under an English heaven.'

For it is not intended solely for the educated minority who read scholarly history and for whom I have been writing it for more than half a century, but for the younger generations of a new classless society which has grown up in almost total ignorance of their country's history. Because of this I have refrained from cluttering the text with learned references and footnotes, or adding to its length with appendices, glossaries and other customary evidences of scholarship. Those who require proofs of its authenticity will find them at the end of the volume in a short list of the chief documented works, including my own, on which it is based.

For though in the *History*'s preparation, as in that of my larger and earlier volumes from which it is drawn, I was faced, like all historians, by the necessity defined in John Evelyn's sentence that 'it is not to be imagined what labour an historian (that would be exact) is condemned to; he must read all, good and bad, and remove a world of rubbish before he can lay the foundations', in the final form offered the reader I have relied solely on clarity and simplicity of writing to make the narrative, wherever possible, what Sir Philip Sidney called 'a tale to hold children from play and old men from the chimney corner'. And I have told the story, not as seen from our own age in retrospect, but as it seemed to those living at the time. For history is a record of the order in which events happen, that is of cause and effect. Everything which occurs in the world is a direct consequence of something which has occurred before. A historian's first duty is to be an exact, though balanced, recorder of what actually happened. He must first re-create, and then interpret, the past; he cannot do the second until he has done the first. The key to the writing and teaching of history is to make the past seem as real as it was to those experiencing it.

*   *   *

Set in a Silver Sea, the first of my three volumes, covers all but the most recent five hundred of our ten thousand years of history. It ends with the building of the last great English medieval churches at the close of the fifteenth century when voyages of dis-covery by Genoese and Portuguese navigators to the Americas and golden East were opening new vistas of opportunity to the Euro-pean nations of the Atlantic seaboard. It shows how the founda-tions of our nation were laid and how its people, descendants of Britain's many invaders, were blended, under the impact and teaching of Christianity, into the kingdoms of England and Scot-land and the principality of Wales. It traces the creation and evolu-tion of the laws, institutions, moral beliefs and attitudes which, instinctively governing us from the past, still form the basis of our continuing nationhood.

Like all our history it begins with the Atlantic flood which, ten thousand years ago, by creating what today are the Straits of Dover, cut Britain off from the European mainland and made it an island. Almost completely covered then by dense forest, it was gradually colonised in the course of thousands of years by a suc-cession of, at first minute, groups of sea-borne invaders.

All of them were seafarers who, to reach Britain, had to navigate stormy tidal waters, and who all, though constantly fighting one another, somehow survived, the earlier sheltering from the more powerful and better armed late-comers in the hilly and rainy west and north or in pockets of inaccessible fenland or forest. A mix-ture of many races, in later centuries – after the growth of a strong national polity had made armed invasion of the island no longer practicable – Flemings, Dutch, Huguenots, Jews, Poles, Asiatics, Africans continued the agelong process of infiltration and racial amalgamation. All ultimately intermarried to produce a nation of many strains, which may account for the paradox that a people famed for stolid, patient, practical common-sense – a nation, as Napoleon said, of 'shopkeepers' – has produced more adventurers, explorers and poets than any other known to history.

The most important of all Britain's invaders were those who came armed only with a cross and the faith and courage that cross gave. From western Europe, where, during the dark centuries of barbaric invasion after Rome's fall, Benedictine monks and Roman bishops had kept alive the message and teaching of the obscure Nazarene who, six centuries earlier, had founded the Christian faith from the cross, and from missionary cells in Celtic Ireland and the western Scottish isles, a succession of heroic evangelists, taking their lives in their hands, converted a savage tribal people and their rulers to Christ's gentle creed of love and sacrifice, and to the revolutionary belief, inherent in Christianity, that every individual was a potential soul of equal value in the eyes of God. With those among whom they went, purseless and on foot, they left an image of the Good Shepherd giving his life for his sheep which was to run like a silver thread through the national tradition.

For the most formative part of Britain's long history was that in which the national consciousness of its rival and quarrelling peoples grew out of the Christian faith. History suggests that the normal political state of human society, as it evolved from the family and tribe, was either anarchy or despotism; either the kind of existence in which there is 'continual fear and danger of violent death', or an authority brutally imposed on the weak by the strong. Now out of Christ's teaching arose a higher option for mankind: the creation of law and order and personal freedom through the exercise of Christian love. The central tenet of Christ's teaching was that, through such love, Christians could create a heaven, not only beyond the grave, but in this world as well. The rock on which the Church on earth rested was that love and trust between Christians were capable of creating islands of mutual endeavour and happiness which, Christ taught, could mirror that greater and timeless happiness to be found through faith in the Heaven to come. 'The Kingdom of Heaven,' He said, 'is within you.'

On this belief our civilization was built. Such cumulative works of faith and love made islands of light in the great ocean of barbaric hatred, cruelty and darkness which had swept across western Europe with the disintegration of imperial Rome, itself a cruel and conquering tyranny. Christian civilization in Britain grew out of barbarism because those who preached Christ's gospel of love to its savage tribesmen established centres of example where it could be put into practice and be seen to operate. It was because where monks and missionaries made their settlements they lived and worked together in constructive amity that they were able to achieve advances in agriculture, in the arts of living and, above all, in social and political organisation impossible in societies torn by perpetual strife, fear and mutual destruction. Everything educative and enduring in medieval Britain was the legacy of the Christian Church and its creed of creative love.

For it was Christianity which taught barbarians to base their social relationships on something wider than tribe or kindred. In its quiet monasteries the Church revived the forgotten classical arts of writing and keeping records. It trained men who could show tribal rulers the means of governing peacefully and justly. It gave them clerics or 'clerks' to reduce their chaotic affairs to order, draft laws and reckon accounts and taxes. For the way of life the Church preached called for a law-abiding world – one in which men made and kept promises instead of perpetually resorting to force. 'The King's Peace' was a better basis for Christian relationships than violence and anarchy.

*　　　　*　　　　*

Among the many technical and scientific discoveries of our age, greater even than those of material power – for it may help to save us from the latter's consequences – has been the rediscovery by a succession of great twentieth-century British medievalists of the living reality of the Middle Ages. In a famous passage in his *Tudor History of England*, writing of the dawn of new horizons for western man opened by the maritime discoveries of the fifteenth century, the Victorian historian, J. A. Froude, contrasted the mental and imaginative gap between his nineteenth-century contemporaries and their medieval ancestors:

xviii

'The paths trodden by the footsteps of ages were broken up; old things were passing away, and the faith and the life of ten centuries were dissolving like a dream. Chivalry was dying; the abbey and the castle were soon to crumble into ruins; and all the forms, desires, beliefs, convictions of the old world were passing away, never to return. . . . And now it is all gone – like an insubstantial pageant faded; and between us and the old English there lies a gulf of mystery which the prose of the historian will never adequately bridge. They cannot come to us, and our imagination can but feebly penetrate to them. Only among the aisles of the cathedral, only as we gaze upon their silent figures sleeping on their tombs, some faint conceptions float before us of what these men were when they were alive; and perhaps in the sound of church bells, that peculiar creation of the medieval age, which falls upon the ear like the echo of a vanished world.'

Since Froude wrote historians have dispersed the mists and broken down the mental barriers which concealed from nineteenth-century minds the contribution of our medieval forbears to the institutions and, above all, beliefs and attitudes which still inform and govern our polity. What matters most in history is the continuity in the soul of man. For it is there that the values are formed which prevent the material chronicles of earth from remaining a mere tale

> 'Told by an idiot, full of sound and fury,
> Signifying nothing.'

For all their remoteness from us, what we call the Middle Ages have power to strike a chord in minds not entirely obsessed by the material and ephemeral. Most of the beliefs which men then held have long been abandoned or forgotten. Yet some remain, a towering testimony to the strength and permanence of the greatest of all their beliefs, their intense and abiding sense of the grandeur and immutability of God. To this day the vast cathedrals made with their puny tools and child's machinery tower above the cities of modern Britain; there is nothing in twentieth-century Salisbury which compares with the tower and spire that Richard of Farleigh built in the time of the Black Death or with the choir and nave his predecessors raised a century earlier. That is why, named *Set in a*

Silver Sea after the silvery-grey waters immediately surrounding their remote northern isle, my first volume depicts on its cover a stormy and rocky coast-line and, rising out of the heart of the distant and shadowy land beyond, the soaring spire of Salisbury cathedral – symbol of their Christian faith.

*   *   *

After the Norman conquest England acquired, under its new French-speaking rulers, the framework in which a national civilization could develop. About the same time, or a little earlier, Britain's barren northern and Caledonian moorlands became the kingdom of Scotland. During the next three hundred years, building on their realm's Christian peace, a dynasty of strong Norman and Angevin kings implanted in English minds the habit of feeling and acting together in national matters. Making the hereditary leaders of the country's formerly separatist provinces a responsible part of central royal government, they established a common law for the whole country and made respect for law a continuing English characteristic. In those germinating centuries between 1066 and the dethronement of Richard II in 1399 the essentials of our national society took permanent shape – the Church, Monarchy, the Common Law, the beginnings of Parliament and of that libertarian system which our forbears called Counsel and Consent and which was fashioned, evolved and fought for long before the later seventeenth-century constitutional struggles between Crown and Parliament, so much more familiar to Victorian and Edwardian historians and readers.

With its combination of political and social history, *Set in a Silver Sea* ends politically on the threshold of the fifteenth century with the dethronement of Richard II who tried, so disastrously for himself, to rule without counsel and consent. Socially it continues in four further chapters on how people lived – 'The Medieval Village', 'Travellers, Towns and Traders', 'Gothic Glory', and 'Twilight of Holy Church' – until the penultimate decade of the century when a Welsh and Tudor prince of Lancastrian descent assumed the throne left vacant by the death in battle of England's last Plantagenet king. Coming only a few years before the discovery of America and the sea-route to the Orient, and on the eve of the Reformation, it marked the first step in a free and voluntary union with England of the two indomitable little neighbour nations which had long fought against her and, by their challenge, helped to make her, just as England's had been the challenge which had helped to make them. A century later the process was to be completed by the union of all three under a Scottish crown in the proud name of Great Britain.

*   *   *

Their union is the subject of my second volume, *Freedom's Own Island*, to be published in the early autumn of next year and followed a year later by my third and final volume, *The Search For Justice*. *Freedom's Own Island*, or *The British Ocean Expansion*, describes how a small and hitherto insular people, uniting under a common crown and reformed religion based on the reading of the translated Bible, traded, colonised and spread their love and practice of freedom across every ocean in the course of what, in his noble *English Reformation*, Professor A. G. Dickens calls 'those three great centuries during which Britain placed her stamp upon world history'. Beginning with Chaucer's mirroring in his *Canterbury Tales* the emergence of the English individual from the anonymity of the feudal and ecclesiastical past, and including the islanders' every decisive victory from the defeat of the Armada to Trafalgar and from Agincourt to Waterloo, it comprises the English and Scottish Reformations, the age of Elizabeth, the Stuarts' quarrel with Parliament and the Civil War, the Restoration, the Revolution of 1688, the Hanoverian Settlement, the loss of the American colonies, and the great achievements in commerce, invention, science, literature, art and architecture of the English and Scottish eighteenth century.

Yet the main theme of *Freedom's Own Island* remains the maritime and colonial expansion of a united British people, transforming what, at the start of Elizabeth's reign, had been a small divided North Sea island on the outer fringe of European Christendom into the greatest global empire the world had known. Lying off the western shores of the Eastern Hemisphere and athwart the sea channels between northern Europe and the Atlantic, Britain's geographical potential for strategy and commerce were unique. It is epitomised by Drake's three minute ships – after their crews' apocalyptic experience on the barren gallow-haunted shores of what today is southernmost Argentine – battling their way through the Magellan Straits into the forbidden Pacific, one to sink with all hands in its terrifying storms, one to return to England defeated, her mission unaccomplished, and the third, re-christened the *Golden Hind*, to circumnavigate the globe and bring home inconceivable treasure and glory. And the title and theme of my third volume, carrying our national story from the triumphant aftermath in 1815 of Nelson's victories at sea and Wellington's on land, to the present day, is of that recurrent search for justice which has periodically haunted the English, and British, mind. For the opportunities for almost boundless wealth offered by the freedom of the world's trading oceans ensured by the long nineteenth-century Pax Britannica, and eagerly seized upon by those with the initiative and enterprise to exploit the dazzling mechanical inventions of the Industrial Revolution, brought about alternating contrasts and conflicts between the unprecedented prosperity of its Victorian and Edwardian beneficiaries and the social exploitation, degradation and impoverishment of its less fortunate participants or victims, making two Englands where before there had been – or seemed to be – only one. Twice in the present century re-made one by an aggressor's threat to human freedom and to Britain's very existence, the conflict at her heart still remains to be resolved, as perhaps only a fuller understanding by her people of their own past can enable them to do.

*   *   *

Every generation needs its popular history written in a way it can understand. The great classic historians of the eighteenth and nine-teenth centuries wrote the history of England for their time. J. R. Green wrote it for our great grandfathers', and G. M. Trevel-yan for our fathers'. Trying to write it for mine, I have presented it in a new and different form. For my *History* contains fewer purely political events and Acts of Parliament, but dwells longer on certain deeds and words which have stirred the hearts of the English and British and awoken their imagination. For history, as a modern poet has written,

'is a pattern
of timeless moments.'

Paulinus and Aidan preaching to the Northumbrians; the Saxon thanes dying to the last man at Maldon and the house-carls in the stricken ring at Senlac; Becket towering above his murderers in the darkened cathedral, and the jingling Canterbury pilgrims riding through the Kentish fields 'the holy blissful martyr for to seek'; Robin Hood in the greenwood and the 'grey goose feather' falling like hail at Crécy and Agincourt; the staplers with their wool-packs, and the church towers among the limestone wolds and dales: such were the stuff out of which England's early banner in time was woven. So, in the age of British global expansion, were the circumnavigatory voyages of Drake, Anson and Cook, the missionary journeys of Wesley and the humanitarian crusades of Howard and Wilberforce; and, in the nineteenth century, the fight for social justice of a Shaftesbury and Florence Nightingale, a General Booth and a Keir Hardie.

I have written for both young and old, for those who know a little of the British past and for those who know scarcely anything at all. My aim has been to set down in a small compass all the essential things a child or adult should know who wants to understand our history. And to do so in a book which can be read at school or by the fireside, on a journey or in bed, and leave the reader with a clearer picture of how our institutions, beliefs and ideals came to be what they are.

The most important element in our history has been the continuity of the Christian tradition. Through it Britain developed a polity in which the sanctity of the individual counted for more than that of central authority, and in which power, instead of being concentrated in a few hands, was distributed in those of many. The value set by her people on the freedom of the individual, on justice and fair play, on mercy and tenderness towards the weak, their dislike of lawless violence and their capacity to tolerate, forget and forgive, have been, for all their many past mistakes and faults, and still are, very real factors in their own and mankind's evolution. 'By this sacredness of individuals,' wrote Emerson, 'the English have in seven hundred years evolved the principles of freedom.' From Philip Sidney passing the cup to the dying soldier to Captain Oates walking into the blizzard to save his friends, from Richard Coeur-de-Lion forgiving the archer who shot him to the men of the Forty-third standing motionless on the deck of the sinking *Birkenhead* while the women and children were lowered in the boats, the common denominator of the nation's idealism has remained the same. It was expressed in the fourteenth-century *Piers Plowman*, in the seventeenth-century *A Pilgrim's Progress* and in the nineteenth-century *A Christmas Carol*. Langland, Bunyan and Dickens all spoke with the same voice. Whenever Britain has been false to that voice she has been false to herself. Her people, Disraeli said, have not committed fewer blunders than others but, being free to criticise their rulers according to individual conscience, have shown themselves more sensible of their errors. In the end, history shows, it has usually been they themselves who have made amends for their injuries to others and reformed the abuses they have perpetrated. 'We must choose our friends for the future,' declared General Smuts in 1940: 'I choose the people under whom we suffered forty to fifty years ago, but who, when we were at their mercy, treated us as a Christian people.'

1984   Arthur Bryant

HOW THEY BEGAN

CHAPTER ONE

Silent Vanished Races

'Grey recumbent tombs of the dead in desert places,
Standing stones on the vacant wine-red moor,
Hills of sheep, and the howes of the silent vanished races,
And winds austere and pure.'

R. L. Stevenson

THE STORY OF BRITAIN – of an island alchemy which has changed
human history – began ten thousand years ago when the Atlantic
broke through an isthmus joining an outlying peninsula to the
world's largest land space. To that flood of salt water which created
the Dover strait and the British isle has been due the destiny of
England, the kingdom which grew up in the island's largest and
most fertile region, and of the two smaller rival nations, Scotland
and Wales, which, occupying its more mountainous and remote
parts, ultimately merged with it while retaining their own strong
national identities and characteristics. The history of an adjacent
island, Ireland, though geographically part of the British Isles and
long politically – and still partially – associated with the United
Kingdom, has followed a different course.

The rocks which form the geological bones of Britain belong,
not to the European mainland, but to a vanished continent em-
bracing North America and the Atlantic and, submerged under the
ocean, called by archaeologists Atlantis. The British island's
western mountains were once the eastern peaks of the poets'
drowned land of Lyonnesse. For 'Britannia' was first formed
millions of years ago in the Atlantic bed. It arose, as the song has it,
'at Heaven's command from out the azure main'.

I

Few, if any, of Britain's early inhabitants can have been living here when it was cut off from Europe. At that time it was almost completely covered by dense forest, mostly of gloomy conifers grown up since the last Ice Age but, as a result of the milder oceanic winters since the island's separation from the continent, gradually giving place in the south to the green of deciduous oak, elm, ash, hazel, lime and alder. Had we been able to look down on the island we should have seen that the forests, like the jungles of the East today, were swarming with game: wild boar and oxen, elk and deer and, in the hills, wolves, lynx and bears, eagles and ravens. And, if we had looked closely, here and there, sleeping like beasts on the earthen floor of caves and in huts and wind-breaks made of sods and branches, we might have caught an occasional glimpse of a family group of upright, two-legged creatures, with half-naked, skin-clad bodies, living on roots, berries, eggs and shell-fish and by trapping and slaying wild animals with flint-tipped spears and harpoons. Such men, like the beasts, lived for the hour, their one end today's meal, their unsleeping instinct survival, each generation repeating the pattern of that before. There was no progress, for there was no change.

Yet change was on the way: change of immense significance. It was not those who inhabited Britain before it became an island — aborigines sleeping like beasts in caves and pits among the rocks of the Cheddar Gorge or Gower peninsula — who were to set the course of its history. It was adventurers from distant and more civilized lands who, refusing to be daunted by the waves and tides of the encircling seas, had learnt how to navigate them and, putting out across a stormy ocean, to seek new homes in a rain-swept northern island. For if we had turned from the spectacle of a dark forest-clad Britain — glimpsed through Atlantic rain-cloud and mist — and looked southwards and eastwards beyond the Alps and into the Mediterranean sunlight, we should have seen, in bright islands and peninsulas at the eastern end of that inland ocean, human communities living very different lives from those of the sparse animal-like families dotted about the downs and rocks of misty Britain. And far beyond, in the green Nile valley, in Mesopotamia and on the Persian uplands and, still further away, in India and China, men grouped, not merely in families, but in tribes, cities and even nations. For here, in the sunshine, man had made the greatest step in his history. He had mastered the arts of digging, tilling and planting the soil – of sowing in winter and reaping in summer. Assured of tomorrow's food, he had made a home to hand down to his children and had begun to think beyond the span of his own brief life, to make laws for societies outlasting individuals, and to raise memorials to the dead and altars to the gods whom he imagined controlled his existence. He had learnt, too, to write and keep records. History had begun.

For the real ancestors of the British people were invaders: seamen and colonists, pioneer bearers of new beliefs and techniques. The earliest of all were traders in tin and copper from the Mediterranean, adventuring into the Atlantic through the Pillars of Hercules – today the Straits of Gibraltar. Others were tribal families moving up the eastern coasts of Spain and those of south-western France, in search of fresh soil and hunting grounds. Some of these, striking across the Soundings, made landfalls in Cornwall, Pembrokeshire, Anglesey, Ireland and the islands to the west of Scotland. Others, crossing Europe by a more northerly route, entered Britain across the Dover strait. Such pioneers brought with them a knowledge of agriculture; of grain growing and domestic animals, of the hoe, spade and grinding-stone; of weaving clothes and fashioning pots of clay. They brought, too, another art: that of making boats and navigating.

The settlements of these Iberian and Mediterranean colonisers – little, dark men grouped around Britain's western seas – were at first few and far between. Their primitive mattocks and hoes allowed them to break only the lightest soils: those on the hilltops out of reach of the all-pervading forest, on the drier gravel-terraces above the rivers, and on rocky shores and islands along the coast. Yet during the first five hundred years of their occupation – a period as long as that which divides us from the Wars of the Roses – the appearance of the country had already begun to change. Settlements of beehive-shaped huts, covered with branches and surrounded by little fields, hewn or burnt out of the forests, appeared on higher ground; earthwork entrenchments were dug

3

along the chalk and limestone hills to protect the seasonal round-up
of flocks and cattle; tangled downland bushes and scrub were nibbled away by generations of sheep, goats and swine. And in chalk
galleries beneath the ground – like those of Grimes' Graves at
Brandon – men quarried with antler-picks for flint to grind into
axes and spear-heads. The foundations of settled life, tillage and
pasturage were being laid.

Great stones or 'dolmens' and mysterious hollow mounds and
barrows with tunnelled chambers appeared, too, on the western
coasts and on the high, inhabited uplands: tribal tombs, where the
spirits of the dead were believed to await, like seeds, a day of
resurrection and rebirth. For these primitive farmers, having
raised themselves above animal existence and learnt to contem-
plate past and future, were much concerned with the mystery of
life and death. Like the river valley folk of the East, they worshipped
the dead and the powers of fertility which recreated life in each
generation and spring. To propitiate them and secure their help
for the tribe, their priests or magic men offered up human and
animal sacrifices in sacred places. And when their leaders died,
hopeful of rebirth, they were buried with their belongings around
them.

*   *   *

The first invaders were followed by others. There was nothing to
stop them but the waves and tides. Some continued to come from
the south in search of Ireland's gold and of the tin and copper
which the wandering smiths of that land and Cornwall were
learning to smelt into a hard durable alloy called bronze. Others
came from the east across the shallow straits and North Sea. Among
them were men of a fairer, stronger race, moving from eastern
Europe through dense forests and the plains of the Low Countries.
These Beaker Folk, as archaeologists call them from their buried
drinking-vessels, were nomads from the steppes of western Asia
who had learnt a new technique of living – breeding and pasturing
flocks which they drove from one grazing-ground to another. They
had mastered, too, another technique, that of war, which they
waged with bows and arrows and sharp axes, first of polished stone

and later of bronze. These lordly shepherds had some affinity with the nomadic warrior peoples who overran the ancient city civilizations of the Middle East: the Semitic tribes who founded Babylon, and the shepherd kings who ruled Egypt in the days of Joseph and his brethren. Toughened by their wandering and possessing stronger weapons through their bronze-smiths' skill in metalwork, they were able to impose their will on their lighter-armed, smaller predecessors. They did not annihilate them – for there was still plenty of room for all, even in a little island covered by forest and marsh. But they made them work for them. And they bred from their womenfolk. After a time intermarriage brought a blending of the types; in their burial grounds the bones of the races are mingled.

These newcomers were also concerned with the causes of life and with what happened after death. But, like their fellow pastoralists in the East, they worshipped, not the patient cultivator's earth-mother, but the sun which, as they watched their flocks on the heights, they conceived to be the source of life. At the axis of their radiating sheep-tracks along the bare chalk-downs of the south-west, they and their slaves laboriously dragged and erected huge stones in mysterious clusters, where they sacrificed men and beasts to their flaming god. The stone circles at Avebury and Stonehenge are among the greatest monuments of early man; they seem to have enshrined the religious beliefs and ritual both of the new Beaker and the old Iberian folk.

The men who brought these vast rocks – some, like the blue Pembrokeshire stones of Stonehenge, from hundreds of miles away – and placed them in elaborate patterns based on the movements of the sun and stars must have learnt much, including the practice of subordination to authority. They created something which has lasted for more than thirty centuries and may still stand on the Wiltshire uplands when we and our works are forgotten.

For more than a thousand years the men of the Bronze Age dominated southern Britain. The earthen ditch in the chalk or oolite, the lonely dewpond on the height, the hill-turf nibbled close and enriched by countless generations of sheep are their legacy. Theirs was a society built on the flocks which gave them food and raiment. Their priests tended the sun-temples, their craftsmen made vessels and weapons of bronze from the tin and copper mines of the south-west, their princes wore splendid helmets and rings and bracelets of gold brought by Irish smiths from Wicklow streams. Their traders, travelling the green hill-roads – Icknield Way, Whiteway, Ridgeway – which linked their priestly capital on Salisbury Plain with the uplands of the east and south-west, carried from earthwork fort to fort the bronze weapons, tools and ornaments that were their wealth. Others, more daring, trafficked tin and copper across the Channel or with Carthaginian merchants from North Africa. Irish gold objects of this period have been found as far away as Denmark and the Mediterranean and Aegean cities, where this remote, half-fabulous country at the world's end was known as the Tin Islands.

*   *   *

The Bronze Age men had their hour, giving place in the fullness of time to others. New races were on the march, moving westwards from the great heartland of the human family on the Asian plains. It is doubtful if at any time during the two thousand years which followed the first Neolithic colonisation of Britain such infiltration ever ceased. There was no central government and, save in a few settled places along the coast, no one to oppose a landing. The numbers involved in each invasion must have been very small, for boats were few and minute.

Most of the invaders brought to the island something new, in husbandry, craftsmanship or ways of living. The most important of all was a language which had originated in western Asia and spread, with the movements of the nomadic peoples who spoke it, into India, Persia, the Aegean, Italy and most parts of western Europe. From the basic sounds of this so-called Aryan speech – 'outlines . . . drawn only in sound, in the air, as elusive almost as the call of birds'[1] – are derived certain words, used with variations by successive invaders, which still constitute the foundation of our language and are to be found, in not dissimilar forms, in other countries colonised by tribes of Aryan stock. Among these are

[1] Jacquetta Hawkes, *A Land*, p. 174.

father, mother, daughter, sister, brother, son and *widow*, the first ten numerals, and some of the more important parts of the body, like *knee, foot* and *tooth*. So are *night, wind* and *star*, and the names of domestic animals, *cow, ox, steer* – with their plurality *herd – hound, goat, sow* and *goose, ewe* and *wether* and their product, *wool*. The words *wheel, axle* and *yoke* show the nomadic character of these Aryan ancestors; our modern *wain* or *wagon* is derived from another of their basic sounds. Other words, whose derivations are not to be found in the speech of the Asiatic descendants of the race but are known to its European descendants – *beech, elm* and *hazel, throstle, finch* and *starling* – must have been added in the centuries when the latter were dwelling, in the course of their westward trek, among the forests of central Europe. Similar words were added, too, before the western branch split into Greek, Latin, Celt and Teuton, revealing the substitution of agriculture for nomadic life – *corn* and *ear, furrow, bean* and *meal*.

It was between 1000 BC and 500 BC when an Aryan-speaking race, the Celts or Gaels, first appeared in Britain. They were a tall, blue-eyed, flame-haired folk who had crossed Europe from the east and settled in the country which is now called France and which took their name of Gaul. For as long a time as that which divides us from the Crusades, Celts were moving into Britain and Ireland, first in small bands and families and later in tribal armies, until they had become the dominant racial strain in both islands. The earlier peoples survived, but were mostly driven into the western moors and hills. They figure in Celtic legends as the faeries or little people – the Tylwyth teg – elusive, mysterious and dangerous, who sometimes stole their neighbours' children or provided a bride, dark, shy and inscrutable, for some giant, clumsy, good-humoured Celtic farmer. In such tales a recurrent feature is their dread of iron – the metal whose use the Celtic smiths introduced from the steppes and which, forged into swords and chariots, gave the latter's warriors their long ascendancy. Smelted in charcoal furnaces in the demon-haunted and till now uninhabited lowland forests, it was made also into rotary-lathes to make wheels, and into ploughs which, drawn by oxen, could break virgin soil too stiff for the hand hoes and small wooden ploughs of the past. This brought

7

about a gradual increase in population which, it is estimated, rose during the Celtic occupation to around a quarter of a million – less than a two-hundredth part of its present size. These iron-users were probably the first of Britain's invaders to create permanent fields and villages, mostly on the greensands and light clays of the south-east and south-west. At their zenith they may have occupied a sixth of the country. The rest of it, including the thick forest clays of the Midlands, remained uninhabited.

The island still had no unity; it had not even a name. To visualise it we must think of it as divided into loosely defined and warring tribal areas, rather like South Africa in the days of the Zulu and Kaffir wars. In the south-east were the latest comers, the warlike Belgae, whose territory stretched as far west as Salisbury Plain and the Dorset coast, with their fine blacksmiths and iron chariots and plough-coulters. Their name survives only on the far side of the Channel in the country from which they came, though one of their tribes, the Cantii, gave theirs to Kent and Canterbury. Another tribe, whose name has endured on the continent, were the Parisii – a warlike people from the Seine and Marne valleys who, landing in the Humber, conquered the plain between what is now Yorkshire and Lincolnshire. Others, like the Brigantes of the Pennine dales and the Iceni of Norfolk, dispersed by later invasions, have left little memorial of their sojourn. But in the south-west, where Celtic and pre-Celtic stock has always been predominant, the Dumnonii and the Durotriges have transmitted their names to the Devonians and men of Dorset. And for no very clear reason one group of invaders – the Prythons or Brythons – later gave their name to the whole island.

The hereditary chieftains of these tribes seem to have had a love of beautiful things. They employed craftsmen whose graceful designs surpassed anything yet seen in the barbaric West. When they died their treasures were buried with them – bronze armour and helmets, embossed shields decorated with vivid enamels, like the one found in the Thames at Battersea, golden torques, brace-lets and brooches with which to fasten their tartan plaids; amber cups and hand-mirrors engraved with exquisite circular designs, like the Birdlip mirror in the Gloucester Museum. Vanity was a

8

characteristic of the Celts: a Greek traveller of the time describes them as smearing their fair hair with chalk wash to make it still brighter and then drawing it tightly back from the foreheads till they looked like hobgoblins. 'Their nobles let their moustaches grow so long that they hide their mouths and, when they eat, get entangled in their food. . . . They use amazing colours, brightly dyed shirts with flowing patterns, and trousers called breeches. . . . Their appearance is amazing, with voices deep sounding and very harsh.' They were boastful, threatening and braggart, he added, but their intellects were keen, and they were quick to acquire knowledge. 'When they have killed their foes, they cut off their heads. . . . They nail them up on their walls as trophies and preserve those of their chief enemies in boxes.'

These head-hunting tribesmen cannot have been comfortable neighbours. At Salmonsby in Gloucestershire they were still eating their womenfolk about two thousand years ago. Their religion reeked of blood, and travellers from the civilized South, whose own ideas about sacrifice were far from squeamish, brought back horrifying tales of ritual massacres in dark sacred groves by their magicians or druids. And they were incorrigible fighters. They crowned Britain's hilltops, not with burial-barrows and sun-temples, but with vast earthwork castles with concentric ditches and ramparts, like Mai Dun or Maiden Castle in Dorset, Chanctonbury Ring in Sussex, Almondbury in Yorkshire and the great Dun of Downpatrick in Ireland. In the ancient Celtic ballads of Ireland, Wales and the Scottish Highlands – the parts of Britain least affected by later invasions – pride of battle takes precedence over every other emotion. For centuries these fierce, passionate, braggart, though sometimes touchingly noble, tribesmen constantly raided one another's lands for heads, slaves and cattle, but observed the rules and rites of their savage code of honour. The wars of the early Greeks, fought in the Aegean sunlight and sung by Homer, were matched by wars fought under the misty skies and dripping hills of western Britain by men of the same remote ancestry. In Celtic Ireland, as well as in Wales and the Scottish Highlands, this 'heroic' age continued long after it had ceased in Greece and the British lowlands. The flashing swords and flails of the Fianna, and

9

Finn Mac Cool and Gull Mac Morna setting targe to targe, were
the counterparts of 'godlike Achilles and his squire Automedon
and Alkimas in battle upgrown'. And the story of how Grainne,
daughter of King Cormac, eloped with Diarmuid, echoes the tale
of Helen of Troy.

*   *   *

By now a conqueror of a different kind was approaching Britain.
With their breast-plated, helmeted, disciplined infantry and their
fleets of triple-banked oar-propelled warships, the Romans were
the greatest conquerors the world had known. They were a people
of high courage and patriotism with an instinctive feeling for order,
led by aristocrats of a strong practical bent. Just over two thousand
years ago, having overrun Italy and most of the countries fringing
the western Mediterranean, they crossed the Alps and invaded
Gaul. In three years their great general, Julius Caesar, conquering
by dividing, subdued the warlike Celtic tribes of that land and
carried the Roman rule to the Channel. Behind his legions came
the metalled military roads, the stone-walled cities, the laws and
administration which the Romans took with them wherever they
went.

   Though Caesar made two brief punitive and exploratory expeditions from Gaul to Britain, for nearly another century it
remained outside the great union of races welded together by
Roman discipline and good sense – a misty, unexplored forest land
of squabbling tribesmen on the world's fringe. But in AD 43 the
interference with trade caused by tribal war provoked the Roman
imperial authorities into a full-scale invasion, followed by annexa-
tion. Thereafter for three and a half centuries the southern half of
Britain, comprising virtually the whole of what today is England,
was a Roman province. It was Rome's policy to tame the native
tribal chieftains by making them citizens; the city was the instrument by which, having conquered barbarians, she shaped them to
her ends. They were encouraged to transform the old tribal camps
and cattle-kraals into towns on the universal Roman model; to vie
with one another in raising temples, colonnades, pillars and arches,
and to build themselves houses and gardens where, garbed like

Roman patricians, they could live out their lives in luxury under the eyes of authority. Their sons were educated in Roman schools and taught Latin, and their tribal warriors conscripted into the legions or auxiliary regiments and turned into Roman soldiers.

Behind the legions rose the cities on which Roman civilization depended: rustic miniatures of Rome, even in this remote frontier land, with neat chess-board-pattern streets, forums and temples, porticoed town-halls and amphitheatres, public baths, aqueducts and drains. The capital of the Catuvellauni became *Verulamium*, or, in modern English, St Albans; that of the Atrebates of the Thames valley *Calleva Atrebatum* or Silchester; that of the Iceni *Venta Icenorum* or Caistor-next-Norwich; that of the Dumnonii *Isca Dumnoniorum* or Exeter. Even the wild Silures of Wales built *Venta Silures* or Caerwent and boasted of the little garrison-town of Caerleon with its golden roofs and towers. In these minute but elegant tribal capitals traders built shops, and tribesmen brought their crops and cattle to market and assembled at sacred seasons to sacrifice to their local gods. Yet though Rome, true to her universal policy, encouraged the worship of the older native deities, she subordinated it, as she had done that of her own gods, to that of the all-embracing State. For its head, the distant Emperor, sacrifice and tribute were asked of all. It was to express and enforce that authority that the cities arose. More even than markets and dwelling places, they were temples to Caesar and the imperial bureaucracy.

At the height of the Roman occupation there were more than fifty cities in southern Britain. Most of them were very small by continental standards, with between two and five thousand inhabitants. The largest, Londinium, the hub of the country's road and trading system, may have had four or five times as many.[1] Though all these cities later perished, at Bath or Aquae Sulis, the fashionable watering-place in the southern Cotswolds, the old Roman bath and its tutelary god can still be seen, much as they were when the rich provincials of eighteen centuries ago flocked there for health and amusement. Beyond the tribal capitals and

[1] It covered about 350 acres along the north bank of the Thames. The site of its basilica or town hall is now occupied by Leadenhall Market.

close to the untamed northern and western moors lay the garrison cities of York, Chester, Uriconium and Caerleon, and in their rear Lincoln, Colchester and Gloucester – the *coloniae* where soldiers' families were settled on retirement with land and houses to breed more soldiers. There were also the Channel ports of Richborough, Portchester and Chichester, and naval Dover with its lighthouse or *pharos*, guarding the island's communications with the Mediterranean empire of which it was the farthest province.

Linking the towns and camps ran straight Roman roads, paved and cambered on stone causeways, with milestones marking the distances to the imperial capital on the Tiber. Along them passed, not only the marching legionaries who were the guardians of all this order and prosperity, but the native corn, minerals, slaves and hunting-dogs which were exchanged for jewels, statues, wine and oil in jars, perfumes, marbles, mosaics, glass and pottery from the continent. Britain in those years was called the granary of the north. Though the oak forests of the Midland clays still remained untouched and uninhabited, her population, as a result of agricultural improvements, seems to have risen to more than half a million. The chief grain exporters were the Celtic-Roman landowners, living in villas or country houses on sheltered sunny slopes in the southern half of the island. Here, amid mosaics and tessellated pavements, glazed windows, baths and central heating, statues and terraces, they aped the life of the Mediterranean and tried to ignore the northern mists and forests around them. Drawing their culture from a wider civilization, these aristocrats, with their stately Roman manners and Latin speech, introduced into Britain the poultry and geese of her farmyards, the pheasants of her woods, the pears, cherries, figs and mulberries that, planted in their gardens, survived when their gardens and civilization were no more. They worked their great farms with slave labour which they housed in barracks at their gates.

But there was a flaw in the Roman political system. Everything was centralised in the State's officials, yet the succession to the supreme office of all was uncertain. Again and again the Emperor's death was followed by a scramble for power. Sometimes he was assassinated by rivals or his own Praetorian guards, who became the arbiters of the Empire. The Roman world worshipped a ruler who was the guarantor of its peace, and that ruler turned out, as often as not, a parade-ground bully or a crude political intriguer who stopped at nothing to achieve his ambition.

By treating its possessors as divine, Rome deified despotic power. Those in authority were not responsible to the moral feelings and wishes of those they governed; their sway, while it lasted, was uncontrolled. An all-pervading bureaucracy, increasingly wasteful and petty-minded, represented omnipotence at every level. The cost of that immense army of officials plunged society into ever-deeper debt and taxation and, a millstone round the neck of production and trade, destroyed all private independence and sense of initiative. Little by little it reduced the population of every city in the Empire to a mob.

Rome had grown out of greatness of individual character. It became a community in which individual character counted for nothing compared with an abstraction which proved, in the hour of testing, capable of nothing. By sacrificing the individual to the State, the rulers of the Roman world undermined the real virtues which sustained it. They turned active and self-respecting citizens into inert and selfish ones. They discouraged the capitalist from thrift and foresight, the trader from enterprise, the craftsman from his hereditary skill, the husbandman from pride in the soil, the mother from maternity, and the soldier from courage and self-sacrifice. They made the moral shell which protected society so soft that it could protect it no longer. A creeping inertia paralysed everyone and everything. Even before the barbarians broke in, the elegant cities had begun to crumble, trade to die, for want of purchasers, learning, art and even bureaucratic efficiency to disappear for lack of men of ability. The middle class was exterminated. Civilization slowly gave place to barbarism at the Empire's heart.

By the end of the fourth century after Christ, the Roman Empire was disintegrating, both from internal dissension and inertia and from the attacks of barbaric tribes from outside. Already it had broken into two, one half governed from a Greek city on the Bosphorus named Constantinople, the other – itself split between the rival garrisons of Italy, Gaul, Spain and Britain – nominally subject to Rome. On the last night of AD 406, a vast horde of Teutons from the German forests poured across the frozen Rhine into Gaul. Soon every city north of the Alps was in flames. The last legions in Britain were recalled to defend Italy. In 410 a Visigoth host sacked the imperial city of Rome itself.

CHAPTER TWO

The Coming of the English

'Behind the feet of the Legions and before the Normans'
   ire,
Rudely but greatly begat they the bones of state and of
   shire;
Rudely but deeply they laboured, and their labour stands
   till now,
If we trace on our ancient headlands the twist of their
   eight-ox plough.'

Kipling

FIFTEEN HUNDRED YEARS AGO, with the collapse of the Roman
Western Empire, the British people were cut off from the civilization to which they had belonged for nearly four centuries. Their
appeals for help were unanswered and they were left to defend
themselves. At first, freed from the restrictions of an over-cen-
tralised bureaucracy, they seem to have organised themselves
under local generals or tribal princes, particularly in the north-
west, where the old Celtic organisation had survived and resistance
to the Picts had kept men hardy and self-reliant. The province's
only land-frontier was short, and the northern barbarians of
Caledonia beyond it, though fierce, were few in number, with no
new races on the march behind them. For perhaps fifty years
British-Roman civilization, though fast disintegrating, seems to
have survived.

Yet the threat of barbarism came not only from the land. The
fishermen and whalers of the desolate marshes along the eastern
shores of the North Sea – the 'Saxons' or men of the long knives,

as the British called them – had also felt the pressure of Asiatic hordes moving westward through the forests behind them. Even before Rome fell, spurred on by hunger and hope of loot, they had taken to their boats to prey on the rich Roman island beyond the sunset. From Frisia and the mouths of the Rhine, Ems and Weser, from Schleswig and Angle in what is now Holstein and Denmark, they poured up the estuaries and rivers of southern Britain to plunder and slay. The island became a magnet for the boldest of all the barbarians – the men of the sea. On the continent the cities which had been the glory of Roman civilization escaped complete destruction, for the barbarian chieftains, fancying themselves heirs of the emperors before whom they had so long trembled, made them their own. But in Britain the invaders came from remote shores and mud-flats where the fame of Rome had scarcely penetrated. They despised, not only the effete, luxurious owners of the wealth they seized, but the wealth itself. They took the land, the crops and flocks, the slaves and treasures of gold and silver, but destroyed or shunned the cities – the *chesters*, as they called them – leaving only their charred, lonely, ghost-haunted ruins. For they were countrymen who hated towns and regarded their refinements as vices.

*   *   *

During this confused and savage age, which only the most exquisite scholarship has been able to rescue from oblivion, the island, with its dense forests and undrained valleys, was inhabited by three separate peoples. There were the Teuton invaders, with their boar-crested helmets, woollen cloaks and long ash-shafted spears, moving up the rivers in their shallow war boats or tramping the disused Roman roads – rechristened now with Saxon names like Watling Street and Fosse Way – in search of plunder and land. Behind them came their sturdy womenfolk and children, brought across stormy seas in open boats from the Saxon and Angle settlements in Europe. Opposed to them, fighting also in small divided bands and driven ever farther into the west – into what today are Devon, Cornwall, Wales, the Lake District and the south-western corner of Scotland, then called Strathclyde – were the descendants of the British or Celtic-Roman provincials. But though their petty tyrants or princes, forever squabbling with one another, might still wear Roman armour and flowing togas – or plaids, as they later became called – and boast high-sounding Latin names, the few towns left had become little more than squatters' settlements, bereft of trade and the arts of civilized living, and their inhabitants almost as savage as the barbarians who had driven them from their former homes. And, left behind by the receding British tide in squalid, remote villages as the victors' slaves, were the primitive, pre-Celtic peasants who continued to live much as before. They survived in the impenetrable scrub of the Chiltern hills, on the Pennine and northern moors, in the marshy islands of the Fens – now reverting to inland sea with the decay of the Roman dykes – and on the ancient chalk uplands of the south-west. They were not exterminated but surrounded and absorbed. And their womenfolk, and those of the Celts, bore children to the conquerors.

Nor, for all the bloody battles and massacres of that terrible time, did the British tribes of the west perish. They merely ceased to be civilized and Roman, and became pastoral and Welsh. Like their remote ancestors of the Age of Bronze, they reverted to the hills and sheep. For a time, rendered desperate by suffering and schooled by hardship, they fought back so fiercely that the Saxon advance was halted. And they were sustained, like many others in that calamitous age of falling civilization, by a faith called Christianity which had spread across the Empire during its decline and which, hailing from the East, taught men that happiness could be achieved only by sacrifice. Under two successive leaders with Roman names, Ambrosius Aurelianus and Arturius or 'King' Arthur – heroes of whom little is known save the legends handed down by unlettered folk and later enshrined by poets – they won a series of battles culminating in the victory of Arthur and his cavalry or Knights at Mount Badon which ensured the survival in Britain of the Celtic tribes and Christian faith. The Celtic names of streams, rivers and hills, which, outlasting the Teuton flood, mark our maps, and the scattered farms and hamlets of the West Country are, as much as the Arthurian tales, a memorial to this heroic king of legend and the breathing-space he gained for his people. For fifty more years the invaders were confined to the eastern half of the island, the two races – speaking different tongues and holding different beliefs – facing one another in an uneasy, bitter truce across an uncertain frontier.

But in the middle of the sixth century the Saxons and Angles, first in the south and then in the north, resumed their advance. By the end of it the Britons of the south-west, driven into the Devonian-Cornish peninsula, were cut off from their Celtic kinsfolk of the little, quarrelling principalities of Wales – Gwent, Dyfor, Powys, Gwynedd. In the north an Angle or English kingdom called Northumbria, stretching from coast to coast across the Pennine moors, soon afterwards separated the Welsh from their fellow Celts of the Cumbrian mountains and Strathclyde. For in 603 the Northumbrian king defeated the Britons of Strathclyde and their northern Christian neighbours, the Scots of Dalriada or Argyll-shire, in a great battle in Liddesdale. 'From that day,' a Saxon boasted, 'no king of the Scots dared to meet the English nation in battle.' From the North Sea to the Severn and Dee, from the Channel to the Forth, the conquest of Britain was complete. Except for the rocky, rainswept west and far north, it was Britain no longer. It had become England.

*   *   *

What manner of people were these Anglo-Saxons? They were great seamen, fighters and colonisers. Coming from desolate coasts and windswept mud-flats, gale and storm were in their blood. 'The blast of the tempest,' sang one of their poets, 'aids our oars, the bellowing of the heaven, the howling of the thunder hurt us not; the hurricane is our servant and drives us where we wish to go.' They crossed the seas in undecked, mastless, clinker-built boats – 'foam-cresters' – seventy or eighty feet long, with a paddle in the stern for steering and fourteen or sixteen oars a side. If they were without mercy to their foes, they looked for none at the hands of a Nature very different from that of the sunny Mediterranean of Roman civilization. They viewed even shipwreck as a form of practice. Theirs was a world in which there was no place for the weak or craven. One thinks of them, in those days before they found a permanent home, as wild geese, tense on their solitary flight over the waste of waters as they followed the whale, the herring and the seal.

They loved fighting. Their poetry, chanted in the mead-halls of their chieftains as they sat feasting at the long benches, is full of the clash of 'the hammered blades', 'the serried bucklers', 'the shields of linden wood', of 'arrows sleeting like hail'. They loved the symbols of death and carnage: the raven who followed the host with his beak dripping blood, the hungry hawks hovering over the battlefield, the funeral pyre hung with shields and helmets – 'the beacon of the man mighty in battle' – round which the companions of the fallen sang the joys of war and the warrior's virtues.

Yet they had another side. Though to the defeated Britons, to whose homes they had brought fire and sword, they seemed only cruel, boorish savages, they were great farmers: by far the best the island had known. Their first settlements were on the lighter soils, but presently, with their iron axes and deep four- or eight-ox ploughs, they embarked on the titanic task of clearing the forests and heavier clay soils of the eastern Midlands: rich land that Neolithic and Bronze Age men, Celts and Romans alike had left untouched. For barbarians though they were, they were more patient, industrious and methodical than any of the peoples they had conquered. And, on the lowest and working social level, they had more genius for co-operation. They worked together, just as they had rowed and fought together. They shared the same ploughs, helped to cultivate one another's land and followed common rules of tillage and forestry. In this way they were able to make far steadier progress against the cold, stubborn clay and oaken wilderness around them than any of their predecessors. In their homesteads or *tuns* of thatched, tent-shaped huts, sited by streams in the forest clearings, and in their closely-knit communities whose names – Barkings of Barking, Hastings of Hastings, Gellingas of Ealing – still mark our maps, these sturdy colonists, with their fine smiths, carpenters and wrights, cleared virgin ground to support growing numbers of their folk. In doing so they created in the course of time the English countryside, turning marshy valley bottoms into water-meadows, terracing fields on the slopes and

eating ever farther into the forests. As each village became established, the younger and bolder spirits, for whom the cleared land
was insufficient, 'swarmed off' to found, still deeper in the woods,
new settlements which they distinguished from the old by the
addition of prefixes like Upper and Lower, East, West, South and
North, and suffixes like Bottom and End, Bere and Den – pig-
pasture – Ley and Hurst.

For these people loved the soil and the tending of it and its
beasts. They loved it as much as their fathers had loved fighting
and the sea. They left their memorial, not like the Romans in stone
or the Bronze Age men in burial-grounds, but in the imperishable
shape of the earth they tilled; it is writ large across our shires, with
their villages, meadows, farms and ploughlands. And in the work
of their artists that has come down to us, in their carvings in wood
and stone of leaves, trees and animals, we can see their deep feeling
for nature. 'His coat,' runs the old song, 'is of Saxon green', and
it is as a green-clad folk in a green land that we must think of them,
swinging their axes and driving their ploughs through mysterious
forest and dark earth to make the land we love.

Their main settlements were at first near the coast – the East
Saxons of what became Essex, their big-nosed Jutish neighbours
across the Thames in Kent and the Isle of Wight; the flaxen-
haired, blue-eyed, heavy-limbed South Saxons of Sussex; the
West Saxons who, coming from the Wash or up the Thames, settled
on Salisbury Plain or, in smaller numbers, landed near Southampton Water and followed the Avon to the Plain; the Angles of East
Anglia – the North-folk and South-folk – and their kinsmen who,
pushing up the Midland rivers, established the tribal communities
which by the beginning of the seventh century had merged to form
the kingdom of Mercia. Farther north other Angles, over-running
and inter-marrying with the British tribes of Deira and Bernicia
between Humber and Forth, founded the still greater kingdom of
Northumbria in what today is northern England and south-eastern
Scotland. All brought from their diverse starting-points in Europe
different customs and ways of life. And all were separated from
one another by trackless expanses of oak forest, thorn, scrub and
swamp, like the dense Epping and Chiltern woods which hemmed

in London from the north, the eighty-mile wide Andredsweald between the North and South Downs, Selwood in the west, the Midland forests of Bernwood, Arden and Wyre, Cannock Chase, Sherwood and Hatfield.

The population of these pioneer communities in the backwoods was at first very small. In the whole of Mercia – an area today comprising a dozen crowded counties – a century and a half after the first invasion there were only twelve thousand households. Their form of government, though aristocratic, was far simpler and freer than that of Rome. There were no officials, no central administration, and every village community kept its own peace and justice. No one could write or keep records, and the only checks on a man's conduct were the customary vengeance of his kin and neighbours, or of his lord or the more distant king for breaches of their simple laws.

The pioneer farmer, or *ceorl* as he was called, was the core both of the local community and of the petty kingdom or 'kindred' to which he belonged. He was a freeman, responsible only to his neighbours and to his fighting leader – chief, king or lord: a man, to use the old English phrase, 'moot-worthy, fold-worthy and fyrd-worthy', worthy, that is, of a place in the justice-court, the sheep-fold and the tribal fyrd or militia which turned out at the king's summons in time of war. He was wont to speak his mind out freely in the court of the village or tun, for among this simple people the man who spoke truth fearlessly was an honoured as the man who fought bravely. Though ready to enslave others, the English were great lovers of their own freedom. Their homes, rude and rough though they were, were their castles.

The tribal king was chosen for life by the kinsfolk and chief warriors from the descendants of the hero who had led the war-band or folk during the invasion. He lived in a little earthwork-palisaded fortress called a *burgh* with his thanes or *gesiths* – war-companions – and their servants and slaves. Such kings, some of them ruling kingdoms smaller than a modern county, were little richer than their subjects. They might wear a few ornaments and jewels in their rough, home-spun clothes and own gold or silver-mounted cups, armour of chain-mail and finely made swords, daggers and shields, like those found in the seventh-century royal ship buried in the sands of Sutton Hoo in East Anglia. Yet a king's or lord's hall was merely a gabled log-barn, with stag-horns and rude arms on its unplastered walls, a sunk open hearth in the centre of a rush-strewn earthen floor, and a hole in the roof to let out the smoke. Here on great occasions he and his companions would gorge themselves on meat and hot spiced ale and mead – a fermented spirit of honey and herbs – and, while the harp passed from hand to hand and the minstrels sang their sagas, shout with drunken joy at the remembrance of their forefathers' heroic deeds and battles.

For the gods of these simple forest folk – seamen and warriors turned farmers – were the spirits of Battle, Storm and Nature common to all the Nordic peoples. They honoured only the brave and warlike. It was because of this that, despite their love of independence, they gave such loyalty to their kings and lords, heirs of the warriors who had led them to conquest and who, perhaps, boasted descent from Woden, god of victory and plunder, or Thunor, god of the mountain-thunder, deities whose names, like those of Tiw and Freya, spirits of war and fertility, survive in the days of our week.[1] The greater the king's prowess, the larger his following of thanes and companions. They felt for him as dogs for their hunting masters: 'Happy days,' sang one, 'when I laid head and hands on my lord's knee.' From him they received the meat, bread and salt, the ale and mead on which they feasted in the winter, the bracelets and buckles of gold and silver, the gems and embroidery with which they loved to adorn their shaggy persons, the crested helmets, ringed mail and runed swords, said to be made by Wayland the smith-giant, which they used in battle.

Such men, though they might slaughter man, woman and child in anger or to placate their cruel gods, were not without rough virtues. They were brave, loyal and true to their kin and leaders; there was no shame in their eyes like that of the man who turned his back in fight or betrayed lord or comrade. Those who had eaten a man's salt must die by his side. 'Never shall the steadfast

[1] Also in the names of towns and villages like Wednesbury (Woden's burgh or borough) and Tewesley (Tiw's lea).

"Hand mirrors engraved with exquisite circular designs."

Celtic Mirror, 1st century A.D., found at Desborough, Northamptonshire.

Overleaf:
"The Province's only land frontier against the northern barbarians of Caledonia."

The Emperor Hadrian's seventy-three mile Wall from the mouth of the Tyne
to the Solway, running over hill and dale with watch towers every mile.
2nd century A.D.

"Masons, working high above column and clerestory, fashioned whole legions of tiny figures on the bosses."

Peasant with toothache. Stone capital from the south transept of Wells Cathedral c. 1200–1210.

men round Stourmere,' cried the Essex thane as his *eorl* fell, 'reproach me that I journey lordless home.'

In this lay the nobility of these far-off ancestors of ours. There was no weak comfort in their harsh creed. They believed that the end of all was death: that no triumph or happiness, however great, could last. 'Now,' sang their bards, 'is the flower of thy strength lasting awhile, yet soon sickness or the sword, fire or flood, the arrow's flight or blinding age shall take away thy might.' They saw in the mystery of life a riddle beyond man's explaining. 'Where,' they asked, 'is the steed? Where the rider? Where the giver of treasure? The bulwarks are dismantled, the banqueting-hall in ruins, the lords lie bereft of joy, and all their proud chivalry is fallen by the wall!' It was not in man's power to control his lot; his virtue lay in his capacity for suffering and endurance. Even the gods, feasting in their paradise of Waelhaell or Valhalla, must fall in the end to the hateful hags, Hel and Weird – the Fates to whose inexorable decree all things bowed. There was no escape, no mercy or tenderness on icy earth or under storm-riven sky.

In the eyes of this brave people there was only one rule: to accept without flinching whatever the Fates had in store. The craven whined; the valiant kept his grief locked in his heart. The worse fortune treated him, the truer he must be to creed and comrade; the craven and traitor could gain only shame by their baseness. It was a rough, masculine creed, without much subtlety or refinement. It judged men, not by what they said or thought, but by their deeds. Yet it bred a sense of duty and responsibility without which no nation can be great or endure. It taught the rank and file to be loyal, and their leaders to sacrifice themselves for the led. 'I have bought with my death a hoard of treasures,' cried Beowulf after his fight with the dragon. 'I give thanks that before my dying day I have won it for my people.' So long afterwards on the battlefield of Maldon the outnumbered English fought on without hope of victory:

'Thought shall be the harder, heart the keener,
Mood shall be the more as our might lessens.'

In the hour of adversity and danger they closed their ranks and were true to one another.

CHAPTER THREE

The Faith

'I saw them march from Dover, long ago,
With a silver cross before them, singing low,
Monks of Rome from their home where the blue sea
   breaks in foam,
Augustine with his feet of snow.'

J. E. Flecker

MORE THAN TWO HUNDRED YEARS after the last Roman legions left Britain, and soon after the completion of the English conquest, a tall dark stranger stood before the king and chieftains of Northumbria. His name was Paulinus and, like the men who had once governed Britain, he was a Roman. Yet he bore no arms and stood there at the mercy of the rough warriors around him.

He had come to Northumbria – the wild northern kingdom which stretched from the Forth to the Humber – with a Kentish royal bride for its king. Thirty years earlier, in 597, the Jutish ruler of Kent, the most civilized of the barbarous English tribal kingdoms, had invited to his capital a band of Roman monks to minister to his queen, a Christian princess from Gaul. It proved the most important of all the invasions of England and the most peaceful. Marching across the downs from Dover under their leader Augustine, with banners and a silver cross, they had been received by King Ethelbert sitting at his tent door lest they should cast spells on him. He listened to what they had to say, gave them a ruined Roman church in his capital, Canterbury, and resolved to embrace their creed. After he was baptised thousands of his thanes and warriors had followed his example.

The Northumbrians were no friends to Christianity – the mysterious eastern religion which, officially adopted by the Roman Empire in the days of its decline, had survived the latter's collapse on the continent and, though rooted out of southern Britain by the Saxons, had lingered on in the mountains and islands of the Celtic west. Fourteen years before, they had slaughtered hundreds of its priests after a great victory over the Britons of North Wales. The very word *church*, that they used for its houses of worship, was associated in their minds with plunder. They listened, therefore, to the eloquent Italian with suspicion. Yet what he told caused them to do so in silence. For it was a tale of heroism and devotion. Its purport was that behind the forces of Fate was a God who had made men in his own image and, loving them, had given them freedom to choose between good and evil. He had made them, not helpless actors, but partners in the drama of creation. And because men had misused that freedom and God still loved them, He had sent His son as leader and saviour to show them, by revealing His noble nature, how to live and, by sharing their lot and dying on the cross, how to overcome sin and death.

Paulinus's tale cannot have seemed wholly strange to his hearers. He had spoken of a leader who had been brave and true, who offered his followers a freeman's choice between good and evil and a hero's reward for those who were faithful. But in two respects his message was revolutionary. For the virtues Jesus had shown were not merely those the English honoured, but others they had never regarded as virtues at all. Love not hate, gentleness not force, mercy not vengeance had been the armour of this heroic captain. The Northumbrians' own valour in battle was small compared to the cold courage of facing death with only these meek virtues. And, as proof of it, here was this solitary stranger standing unarmed in their midst.

Most startling of all, Paulinus's message offered the English hope beyond the grave. Here was the reply to a problem deep in the human heart which their priests had never answered. When he ended, an old counsellor spoke. 'The life of man, O king,' he said, 'is like a sparrow's flight through a bright hall when one sits at meat in winter with the fire alight on the hearth, and the icy

25

rain-storm without. The sparrow flies in at one door and stays for a moment in the light and heat, and then, flying out of the other, vanishes into the wintry darkness. So stays for a moment the life of man, but what it is before and what after, we know not. If this new teaching can tell us, let us follow it!'

As the Northumbrians crowded round the man who brought them these tidings, their own high priest was the first to cast his spear at the idols their fathers had worshipped. Afterwards they were baptised in thousands, pressing into the Yorkshire streams to receive from Paulinus's hands the cross of water which enrolled a man as Christ's follower and offered him deliverance from the grave. For Christianity had been presented to them as a correction, rather than a denial, of their own heathen beliefs. They were used to thinking of gods as controlling their fate, though gods of terror. They were now told there was one God – of justice, peace and love. They were used to offering sacrifices to appease the wrath of Heaven; they were told of a new and higher form of sacrifice, self-sacrifice. They believed in magic, and learnt of a heavenly king who was born in a manger, gave his life for man on the 'healer's tree', and rose from the grave to sit at God's right hand. They were wont to celebrate the seed sown in winter darkness and the renewal of life in the spring; they were given a midwinter feast to celebrate Christ's birth and a spring one for his resurrection. Their fertility festival to Eastra, a Teuton goddess, purged of its grossness became Easter; their Yuletide junketings around the December log-fires the Christ Mass or Christmas.

Such a conversion was necessarily incomplete. It made heathens Christian, yet it also made Christianity a little heathen. And it suffered from the disadvantage – the reverse of its bloodless character – that it was a conversion from the top. It rested too much on the Germanic principle of lordship. It depended on the changing policies of a court rather than on the hearts of a people.

Yet it was not only from Rome that the faith was brought to England. Two centuries earlier, when the Saxons had first overrun the lowlands, the Roman-Celts among the mountains and moors of Strathclyde, Wales and Cornwall had fallen back on the one creed of a dissolving civilization that gave them courage and hope to endure. And though, in their harsh life of struggle and poverty, they grew almost as barbarous and illiterate and quite as fierce as their foes, the light of Christ's teaching still shone through the war-clouds which overhung their rugged lands. Chapels of wood and wattle with beehive vaulting, and monasteries with tiny enclosed grass lawns or *llans*, appeared in Welsh valleys, and granite wheelhead crosses flowered beside the Atlantic among the Cornish rocks. All round the western seas, from Brittany to the Isle of Man and Clyde, the names of Celtic saints are still commemorated where once, in tiny cells and oratories, they lived their lives of faith and self-denial – Ninian who converted the Picts of Galloway; Dyfrig, Illtyd, Govan, Teilo, Padern and David, the apostles of Wales; Samson of Dol who crossed the seas from stony Caldey to preach to the Bretons; Morwenna, Cleder, Endellion and a score of others who made the name of Christ loved by the lonely fishermen and herdsmen of Cornwall.

The distinguishing trait of these early evangelists was their selflessness in the love of God and their sublime faith that there was nothing they could not dare in their master's name. St Patrick's mission to the heathen Irish in the fifth century is one of the great stories of mankind. By converting them he made Ireland, in the dark centuries after Rome's fall, a Christian haven in a world of storm. The most famous of his disciples was the evangelist Columba, who founded a monastery church on the island of Iona off the coast of Dalriada. Up and down the northern moors, where even the Roman legionaries had never penetrated, Columba's monks made their way, preaching, healing and winning men's hearts. One of them, St Aidan, became the Celtic apostle of northern England, planting the Christian ideal among the Northumbrian tribesmen. The contribution of these Celtic evangelists to England's conversion lay not in doctrine but in example. It was this that won the simple English to Christ. For if the preachers' arguments were sometimes a travesty of their master's, their lives were touchingly like His. Like Him they took no thought for the morrow, of what they should eat or wear; they put their faith in His spirit and, giving themselves to His selfless gospel, lived it. With those among whom they went, purseless and on foot, they left an image of the Good Shepherd giving His life for His sheep which was to run like a silver thread through the English tradition.

So it came about that during the seventh century England became a Christian land. From Canterbury Roman monks carried their missions into Wessex – the kingdom of the West Saxons – making Christians of the warrior farmers who had driven the Britons beyond Exe and Severn. From Northumbria the disciples of Aidan took their message of faith and goodness to the peoples of Mercia. Though they only partly comprehended Christianity's revolutionary creed of love, humility and self-sacrifice, it came to them as a wonderful revelation. It took the darkness out of their sad, fatalistic beliefs and offered them hope and purpose.

In the century which followed the national genius flowered for the first time. During it the earliest English churches were built, like Brixworth in Northamptonshire and Escombe-by-the-Wear, and the tall, beautiful sculptured Celtic crosses, with their runic inscriptions and Gospel figures of men and beasts, before which the Angles of the north worshipped in the open air. It was the age in which the first English books and manuscripts, with their exquisitely interlaced illuminations of birds and dogs, were copied and painted by monks in their cells; in which the stately Wilfred taught Northumbrian choirs to sing double chants, and Aldhelm, a prince of the West Saxons – the reputed builder of the little cruciform church at Bradford-on-Avon, who became abbot of Malmesbury and first bishop of Sherborne – used to stand on Malmesbury bridge singing the songs of his native land until he had gathered a crowd of listeners, and then preach to them the gospel story and the wonders of God's universe. In that dawn of childlike faith when Cuthbert, the shepherd bishop of Lindisfarne, tramped his wide diocese, the moorland peasants came running to him to confess their sins and beg his intercession. The inspiration of this gentle barefoot saint can still be seen in the beautiful Lindisfarne Gospel in the British Museum, written on Holy Island 'for God and St Cuthbert', and in the great cathedral shrine which long afterwards rose on the rocks above the river at Durham to house his bones.

Perhaps the most wonderful of all the achievements of the time was that of the Venerable Bede, the greatest scholar in Christendom. From his monastery cell at Jarrow he poured out a never-ceasing stream of books: history, theology, poetry, grammar and natural science. To him England owes the practice of dating years from the birth of Christ and the first prose written in Latin by an Englishman. His vision of Hell – 'where there is no voice but of weeping, no face but of the tormentors' – expresses the very soul of the dark ages he helped to illumine. The most famous of his works was the *Ecclesiastical History of the English Nation* – the story of the conversion. Lucid, just, immensely learned, it is a monument to his age, his faith and his country. That life of scholarship and labour, with the tireless hand writing amid the intervals of prayer and teaching, sometimes so frozen that it could hardly grip the pen, is one of the proud memories of England. He left his countrymen the earliest version of the Gospel in their own tongue and a tradition, rare in that age, of gentleness, love of truth and scrupulous fairness.

*   *   *

After the first enthusiasm roused by the barefoot Celtic missionaries, the spread of Christianity among the pagan peasant masses was very gradual. For centuries, in England as on the continent, it remained mainly a religion of the upper classes, drawing its monks, saints and bishops from the well-born. Even for them it was often only a superior kind of magic: a means of buying, by prayers, incantations and pious benefactions, protection from misfortune or foes and, still more important, from the ancient equaliser, death. It was the promise of eternal life which drew most men to Christ's creed. The hope of everlasting heaven and the fear of its dreadful opposite, the eternal Nordic hell, proved a rival to the hope of plunder and the lust for pleasure and power.

Yet, despite the slowness of Christianity's humanising work and the immense obstacles it had to overcome, its survival in such a rude and bloody age is one of the miracles of history. Into a world inherently unequal, where the strong and fortunate ruled without pity, it introduced the conception of the ultimate worthlessness of earthly distinctions in the light of the far more dreadful distinction between Heaven and Hell. By its doctrine that every man had a soul to save during his time on earth, and its insistence that the winning of salvation was no easier for king or lord than for beggar or slave, it gave some meaning to the life of common men. It offered those with no prospect – the poor toiling in the fields, the weak and sick, the slaves and prisoners – the hope of a spiritual and eternal kingdom open to all. For the first time men were made to feel, however dimly, that it was wrong to maltreat those who were in their power but who, in Christ's universal family, were their brothers.

To women, too, Christianity brought a slow but perceptible improvement of status. For the Church taught that, if their bodies were weaker than men's, their souls were of equal importance, and recognised their moral stature by the responsibilities with which it entrusted them. It stressed the sanctity of marriage and the home. It also offered a career, as leaders of religious society, to women who, renouncing the joys of family life, dedicated themselves to Christ's universal family. In these early centuries queens and princesses took vows of chastity and poverty and embraced the conventual life. It was a woman, St Hilda – a Northumbrian princess and head of the great abbey of Streoneshalh[1] – who trained many of the earliest English bishops and set the first Christian poet in England – the poor herdsman Caedmon – to sing the wonders of creation.

Christianity, too, taught men to base their social relationships on something wider than tribe or kindred. It brought the warlike tribes and nations of England into the same communion as other western European peoples and into closer contact with one another. At the time of the conversion there were seven English kingdoms – Northumbria, Mercia, Kent, Wessex, East Anglia, Essex and Sussex. Their princes were almost constantly at war, with their own kinsmen for their crowns and with their neighbours for new territories. There was no sense of nationhood; a man thought of himself as a Kentish man or a Northumbrian, not as an Englishman. Without communications or regular administration no king's authority could reach far. Even that of the strongest died with him.

But with the coming of Christianity, kings were presented with

[1] After the Scandinavian invasions re-named Whitby.

30

the possibility of an instrument of governance more potent in the long run than any army. In its quiet monasteries the Church began to teach men the forgotten arts of writing and keeping records. At Jarrow and Wearmouth, Melrose and Whitby in the north, at Glastonbury, Malmesbury and Pershore in the west, at Canterbury and Minster in the south, it trained men who could show barbarian rulers a means of governing justly. It gave them clerics or clerks who could reduce their chaotic affairs to order, draft laws and reckon accounts and taxes.

For the way of life the Church preached called for a law-abiding world; one in which men made and kept promises instead of perpetually resorting to force. 'The King's Peace' was a better basis for Christian relationships than violence and anarchy. So long as the rulers of society were faithful Christians the Church supported their authority. It bade men, while rendering unto God the things that were God's, to render unto Caesar the things that were Caesar's. It transformed the military institution of Teutonic kingship into a sacred office. In place of the traditional raising of the chosen leader on the warrior's shield by the armed host, the Church crowned him with a sacred diadem and anointed him with holy oil, praying that God would give him the armour of justice to preserve peace and do righteousness. In return, the king – sanctified as the Lord's anointed – guarded the Church's property, made gifts of land and treasure to its monasteries and conferred high office on its clerics, the only men in his realm who could read or write. At least that was the ideal which the Christian Church set before tribal kings and rulers in an age slowly starting to emerge from anarchy and barbarism.

CHAPTER FOUR

Alfred and the Danes

'So long as I have lived I have striven to live
worthily. I desire to leave men who come after me
a remembrance of good works.'

King Alfred

IF ONE COULD HAVE LOOKED DOWN on Europe in the confused and
barbaric centuries following the conversion of England, one would
have seen a continent in whose western half, from the Mediterranean to Scotland, Christianity had become the nominal faith of
its princes and lords. This vast tract of land was divided into many
little principalities, whose uncertain frontiers changed constantly
with the wars and family quarrels of their rulers. Yet one institution transcended tribal frontiers. In a landscape of peasants' huts
and rude wooden hunting-lodges, the monasteries of the Church
were everywhere the largest buildings to be seen. And winding
past squalid villages and little wooden castles, through forests,
fords and mountain passes, ran the grassy tracks, trodden by
horse-hooves and the feet of monks and pilgrims, which led to
Rome, the see of the Pope or 'Holy Father' – the spiritual head of
western Christendom.

Only in the remote Celtic islands of Ireland and western Scotland, and in the south-east, beyond the Balkan mountains, where
the Greek emperors still maintained the ancient pomp of the
Caesars and the Byzantine Patriarch ignored the Pope's claim to
be Christ's vice-regent on earth, were there Christian communities
which refused to acknowledge the spiritual supremacy of Rome.
Yet Christendom was only a world within a world. Europe itself

was half heathen. Its eastern plains and forests and mountainous northern peninsulas were still peopled by savages who had never heard of Christ. And all along the southern and eastern shores of the Mediterranean – the earliest cradle of the faith – the patriarchates of Jerusalem, Antioch and Alexandria had been overrun by Moslem tribesmen from the Arabian deserts. At the very time that England was being converted to Christianity the whole Arab world had been set ablaze by a new fanatic religion. The creed of Islam, or 'surrender', and its devotees, the Moslems, or 'self-surrenderers', united the Near East, long subject to the Greek and Roman West, in a holy war against Christians. A sea, long given over to peaceful trade, had become a pirate-haunted frontier between Christendom and Islam, swept by Arab fleets. Constantinople only escaped capture through its superb strategic position. In the East, emulating Alexander a thousand years before, Moslem armies had passed the Oxus and reached the frontiers of India. And early in the eighth century, while Bede was still working in his cell at Jarrow, the Moors had crossed from Africa into Spain and planted the Crescent on the Pyrenees. Thence they had poured through the passes into Gaul and the land of the Franks.

In that dreadful hour it had seemed as though western Christendom was broken. Then in 732 the Franks under Charles Martel – mayor of the palace and chief minister to their titular king – saved the West at Poitiers. Having secured its southern frontier this great soldier, with his tall Frankish swordsmen, turned eastwards against the heathens of central Europe. It was with his help that St Boniface of Crediton – a Wessex thane's son who became the first archbishop of Mainz – converted the German Saxons and advanced Christendom's outposts to the Elbe. Later this English evangelist, with the Pope's blessing, anointed Charles's son, Pepin, king of the Franks in place of the last Merovingian monarch.

Pepin's son, Charlemagne, like all the men of his age, was haunted by memories of the imperial Roman unity of the past. Though four centuries had elapsed since the western Empire had fallen, every attempt to revive civilization led men back to Rome. Though he could scarcely read and was framed by nature for the saddle and battlefield, Charlemagne had a passionate admiration

33

for learning. This blond, barbarian giant, who slept with a slate under his pillow and made an English scholar, Alcuin of York, his chief counsellor and head of his palace school, conceived the tremendous ambition of reuniting the West in a restored Roman imperium. He tried, though in vain, to reconquer Spain from the Moors; the heroic death of his general, Roland, in the Roncesvalles pass inspired Frankish poetry for centuries. And he sought, with greater success, to embody in his empire all his fellow Teutons beyond the Ems and Weser. For thirty years he warred against them, repeatedly defeating them and striving to break their stubborn savagery by enforced mass baptisms.

Yet more than to the eastern forests from which his forebears had come, Charlemagne's spirit was drawn to the Roman south. He saw himself as the head of Christendom and its guardian. Like his father, Pepin, he led a Frankish army across the Alps against the Lombard conquerors of north Italy. And on Christmas Day 800, as he knelt at mass in St Peter's, Rome, his ally, the Pope, crowned him with traditional imperial rites as Emperor of the Romans. To dreamers it appeared as if the hand of time had been set back and the Roman Empire restored. And it was now, it seemed, a *Holy* Roman Empire.

In Britain, too, attempts were made to revive the Roman past. Under the inspiration of Christianity, the Anglo-Saxon kings were groping towards some wider union of society than the tribal gathering and pioneer settlement. Ine, king of the West Saxons – a contemporary of Charles Martel – published a code of written law for his people and made a pilgrimage to Rome. Half a century later Offa, king of Mercia, established an over-lordship over the whole island south of the Humber and assumed the Roman title of *Rex Anglorum*, King of the English. He encouraged trade with the continent, made a commercial treaty with Charlemagne – with whom he corresponded on friendly terms – and minted gold coins, some of which, bearing his name, circulated as far as the Moslem caliphate of Baghdad. And at home he built an earthen dyke, to keep out Welsh raiders, which, running from Dee to Wye, still marks the border between England proper and Wales and Monmouthshire.

Yet neither Charlemagne's vast empire stretching from the Ebro to the Carpathians, nor Offa's smaller English kingdom endured. Barbarian kings, however lofty their aspirations, could not govern large areas. They lacked roads and bridges, trained servants, regular administration and justice. They could not give their peoples the security from which patriotism and the habit of subordinating self to the public interest spring. They thought of their dominions as family possessions which they were free to treat as they pleased. Even when they ruled, like Charlemagne, with a sense of vocation, they could not transmit it to their sons who, by tribal custom, had the right to divide their patrimony. Charlemagne's empire quickly dissolved after his death. Under his grandchildren and their heirs it was broken up into ever smaller kingdoms.

Nor were the methods by which the rulers of that age sought to widen their realms calculated to preserve them. Their Christianity, though strongly felt, was only skin-deep. Enraged by the resistance of the Saxon tribesmen, Charlemagne massacred his prisoners by the thousands; Offa, founder and patron of monasteries, put out the eyes of a Kentish rival. Such actions created, not love and loyalty, but bitter hatred. When the strong hand of their perpetrators was removed, civil war and vengeance overtook the realms they had created. On Offa's death in 796 his English empire fell to pieces. So did the kingdom of Northumbria, whose rulers had tried to unite the northern half of the island by similar means. In less than a century five of its kings were murdered or slain in battle, five more deposed and four forced to abdicate.

The recurring problem of what historians call the Dark Ages – the long blood-stained centuries after the fall of Rome – was that of preventing society from disintegrating because its stronger members could not be subjected to any law but their own passions. What was lacking was a profession of dedicated kingship, pursued by hereditary princes with the power to preserve peace, social continuity and order.

*   *   *

It was in England that such a king appeared and at a time of universal disaster. For two hundred years Europe had been threatened from the south by crusading Moslems. Now a new and more dreadful threat arose in the north. It came from the fiords of Norway and the Jutland flats where the Scandinavian peoples – Norwegians and Danes – were on the move. The soil they tilled could no longer sustain their rising population, nor a pastoral life satisfy their more turbulent members. These were vigorous, picturesque, flamboyant rascals, younger sons of petty *fiord-jarls* for whom there was no place at home, with long flaxen hair, bright burnished spears and two-handed battle-axes. They delighted in silver-bound swords and jewels, golden bracelets and scarlet cloaks with brilliant borders. And, like all their race, they had a passionate love of independence. Around them they gathered bands of bloodthirsty followers, who feasted and drank in their halls in winter, sallying forth each spring 'to play the game of Freyr'. Berserks and wolfcoats they called themselves; wherever they went, they boasted, the ravens followed.

Accustomed to using the sea as a highway – the only communication between their scattered settlements – they were now offered a wonderful prize. Every spring the young pirate seamen of Norway and Denmark – Vikings as they were called from the *viks* or creeks they haunted – set out in fleets of long, narrow, open-decked war-boats, with carved dragon-heads, raven banners and bright striped sails. The very word sail in English derives from their *seil*. Following the mountainous island fringe of the Atlantic southwards from Norway, they plundered in turn the Shetlands, Orkneys, Sutherland and the Hebrides. In 802 – two years after Charlemagne's coronation in Rome – they sacked the Scottish monastery of Iona. Then they fell on Ireland.

*   *   *

During the three centuries since Patrick's mission the Irish had achieved great things. Their monasteries and monastic schools were among the best and most learned in Europe, their illuminated manuscripts, like the lovely Book of Kells – still preserved at Trinity College, Dublin – the flower of western art. In the monk,

John Scotus, they produced the first philosopher of the age, while their wandering scholars and poets fashioned verses more subtle than any to be found in that barbarous time. But politically they had changed little. Their titular High King still reigned with his fellow kings over their five sovereign and equal provinces, while a host of tribal chieftains kept their petty state and raided one another for cattle and hostages. Of unity, or capacity to combine against an external foe, there was none.

Thus the raiders' impact was calamitous. No one could make any effective resistance to them. With their shallow-draft boats they swept up the estuaries and rivers, sacking every monastery, farm and building, and carrying off the younger men and women as slaves. Soon they took to wintering on the coast, making permanent forts on island and promontory. The round-towers, whose ruins can still be seen, were built as shelters from their ravages. Ireland's 'golden age' of art and learning faded into the Atlantic mists at the whip of a few thousand arrogant Norsemen who knew how to combine and to use the sea as a highway.

The Vikings now turned their dreadful attentions to England. The ancestors of the English had also harried Britain from the sea. Now their successors bore down from the same savage shores to plunder the wealth they had created. The island's coasts ceased to be a quiet retreat for saints and scholars and became what it was four centuries before, a place of terror. In 835, 'heathen men' landed in the Isle of Sheppey at the mouth of the Thames. Thereafter, every spring, their dragon-prowed boats, glittering with spears and axes, crept up the east-coast rivers. Then securing themselves on some marsh-encircled island, they seized the horses of the neighbouring countryside and rode out to plunder and slay. If the bewildered farmers combined against them, they formed a ring and, with their massed battle-axes swinging over the 'linden wall' of shields, hacked a way back to their ships. Wherever they went they deliberately spread terror. At Peterborough a single Viking killed eighty-four monks with his own hand; another cut the ribs off an English prince, drew out his lungs and threw salt into his wounds. Breaking open tombs and coffins and stoning obdurate Christians, 'these pagans marched forwards into

Cambridgeshire' with wagons full of plunder, and 'with a violent inundation, brake into the kingdom of the East Angles'. When everyone for whom no ransom was forthcoming had been massacred, they moved on to the next district. Those who paid them enough to go away they left alone till another year, when they returned for more.

'From the fury of the Norsemen,' prayed the peasants in their churches, 'good Lord, deliver us!' So systematic were the ravages of these fearful pirates that, from the Humber to the Solent, hardly a vestige remained of a Saxon church within a day's ride of the coast. By the middle of the ninth century the island seemed their own. In 851, three hundred and fifty of their ships anchored in the Thames. That autumn, after their crews had burnt London and Canterbury, they encamped in Thanet. Thenceforward their armies wintered regularly in England. In two decades they systematically destroyed the Christian kingdoms of Northumbria, East Anglia and Mercia. The final collapse came after 865, when the sons of Ragnar Lothbrok – greatest of Vikings – landed on the east coast. The ancient realm of Northumbria, with its famous monasteries and beautiful crosses, crumbled to dust. So did the library of York which had trained the great European scholar, Alcuin, and the Fenland abbeys – Crowland, Peterborough and Ely. In 869 Edmund, last of the East Anglian kings, after defeat and capture, was barbarously slain for refusing to renounce his faith. When three years later the ruler of Mercia fled to the continent, only one English kingdom remained.

*   *   *

Since the beginning of the century Wessex – once a dependency of Offa's Mercia – had been growing in importance. Absorbing both the small English states of the south-east and the Ibero-Celts of Devon, its rustic princes, ruling a people half Saxon, half Celtic, had carried their golden dragon banner to the Dover strait and the Atlantic. But by 870, half encircled by sea, and with all England north of the Thames in the Norseman's grip, Wessex seemed doomed. In that year the Danes entered it in force and, encamping in an impregnable position between Thames and Kennet near the site of modern Reading, started to ravage it as they had done its sister kingdoms of the north and east. Everywhere in Europe the Christian cause was failing. In the Mediterranean Moslem pirates, after conquering Sicily, had devastated the whole of southern Italy and plundered the suburbs of Rome.

At that moment the Danes encountered, in a young prince or *atheling* of the House of Wessex, one of the great men of all time. Alfred, youngest son of King Ethelwulf, was born at Wantage in 849, three hundred years after the Saxons first settled in Wessex. As a child he had been taken by his father on a pilgrimage to Rome. The journey across Europe, the sight of the great city with its noble ruins of the world of learning and order, had stirred his imagination so that all his life he longed to restore learning and order to his fellow men. He had even tried to teach himself to read from one of the beautiful illuminated Latin books which the monks copied by hand and, so the story goes, loved it so much – a strange love in a little Saxon prince – that his mother gave it to him. Then, when still a boy, he had had to lay aside learning to be a soldier and fight beside his brothers and their fellow English kings against the Norsemen, who every year were advancing deeper into England.

Unlike many other princes of the time, though he won the love of the rough warriors around him, Alfred refused to take any part in the dynastic quarrels which divided his imperilled country. His one thought was not of himself but of serving her. Instead of seeking the crown, he loyally supported each of his three brothers who wore it in turn. At the time the Danish host invaded Wessex, he was acting as second-in-command to the last of them.

It was due to the presence of mind of this young man of twenty-one that the sole remaining English army was not surprised and destroyed early in 871 on the Berkshire hills at Ashdown. While his brother, the king, was at his prayers, Alfred acted with lightning decision and led his rustic levies, 'like a wild boar', against the advancing Danes. 'All day long the opposing ranks met in conflict, with great shouting from all men, one side bent on evil, the other fighting for life, their loved ones and native land.' By nightfall thousands of corpses lay round the stunted thorn tree in the centre of the battle-field. Among them were a Danish king and five earls

39

or *jarls*. The remainder of their host fled across the downs to Reading.

Yet Alfred's struggle against the invaders had only begun. Ashdown was one of eight battles fought in that dreadful year. A few weeks later fresh Danish armies poured into Wessex, whose own levies, composed of farmers with homes and fields to tend, began to dissolve. It was this, almost as much as command of the sea, which gave the Danes their advantage. That spring, when his brother died, Alfred was hastily elected to a falling throne, and left, with a few personal retainers, to defend the last Christian kingdom in England. Hopelessly outnumbered, he managed to hold out till the winter. Then, by paying a ransom or *danegeld*, he was able to secure a brief respite for his unhappy people.

He used it well. During the next few years the Danes were so busy partitioning Northumbria and Mercia and setting up states of their own in what today are Yorkshire, Lincolnshire, Nottinghamshire, Derbyshire, Leicestershire and East Anglia, that they had little time to spare for harrying Wessex. Alfred worked incessantly, reorganising the peasant levies of his half-ruined kingdom and laying the first foundations of an English fleet. When everyone else was in despair and Christians all round the coasts of Europe were meekly submitting to the terrible sea-heathens, this modest, gentle, scholarly man refused to give in. He saw the weakness of the Viking leaders – their greed and savage rivalry – and knew that if he could win time and sustain the courage of his people, he would beat them in the end.

In the spring of 876 the expected blow fell. The Great Army, as it was called, broke up its camp at Cambridge and marched at high speed across Wessex, ravaging the countryside as it went. Reaching the south coast at Wareham, where it stockaded itself between the Frome and Trent, it seized the approaches to the wide anchorage of Poole harbour. Here Danish fleet-armies from France, Wales and Ireland joined it. For, seeing in Alfred the one man in western Europe who could withstand them, the Norsemen were resolved to crush him once and for all.

He met the challenge boldly. Assembling his levies, he encamped before Wareham and blockaded the invaders. The latter's

control of the sea enabled them to receive supplies and reinforcements and to raid the coasts in his rear. But after a time, as he
anticipated, they grew weary of their confinement. Uninterrupted
summer plundering was essential to the very existence of a Danish
army; it could not maintain itself or its morale without. Its leaders
therefore asked for a truce and, on payment of a *danegeld*, agreed
to quit Alfred's realm. Yet scarcely had they sworn to do so than
they treacherously attacked his outposts and broke out on their
horses to the west where, with the help of a fleet, they seized Exeter
and proceeded to lay waste Devon. But the stubborn English king
followed them, drove them back to their entrenchments and once
more resumed his blockade. Then a great storm off the Purbeck
cliffs came to his aid and destroyed more than a hundred of their
ships and thousands of men who were on their way to relieve Exeter.
Before winter fell the besieged offered hostages, made their peace
and withdrew to Gloucester across the Mercian border.

But the Danes were not used to defeat. They still believed they
could destroy Alfred as they had destroyed his fellow English
kings. At midwinter 877–8, a few days after the Christmas feast,
their army under King Guthrum again broke into Wessex. Once
more they stockaded themselves in an impregnable position – at
Chippenham in Wiltshire – and began to plunder the countryside.
Simultaneously a Viking fleet swept down on the Devon coast.
This time the attack was so unexpected and its ravages so widespread that the morale of Wessex at last gave way, as that of
Northumbria and Mercia had done. There was a sudden panic and
many of its chief men fled to France. Alfred himself with a handful
of followers was forced to take refuge in the lake isle of Athelney,
where he lay for a time, 'in great sorrow and unrest amid the woods
and marshes of the land of Somerset'.[1]

Yet Alfred was no despairer. Quietly and with unconquerable
courage he set himself to repair the broken breaches of his kingdom.

---

[1] He loved to tell stories of his adventures there, among them – according to
later legend – the tale of the burnt cakes in the cowherd's cottage. More than
eight hundred years later, in 1693, a gold and enamelled jewel bearing his name,
Aelfred Mec Heht Gewyrcan – 'Alfred ordered me to be made' – was found on a
farm at Athelney, and is now in possession of the University of Oxford.

While he hid among the Parrett marshes his messengers, travelling the ancient hill-roads of Wessex, carried his orders to his countrymen to rally. Shortly before Easter the men of Devon made a sudden sally against the tormentors, routed them and slew their leader. Then, following a plan prepared by the king, contingents from all the western shires, marching through forest and along the grass hill-tracks, began to converge on a secret rendezvous – a lonely landmark and meeting place of ways called Egbert's Stone, on the downs overlooking the vale of Knoyle east of the forest of Selwood. Here, to their unspeakable joy, Alfred joined them.

Without a day's delay the army set out north towards the enemy's camp. On the second day, after halting for the night near Warminster, they encountered the Danish host, hastily assembling in their path on the rolling chalk downs above Bratton and Ethandun, today Edington. Attacking in a single column of packed shields, after many hours' hard fighting they broke its ranks and drove it in confusion towards Chippenham. In the hour of his victory – perhaps the most important ever won on English soil – Alfred showed one of the rarest attributes of a commander. Exhausted though he and his men were, he pursued his foe relentlessly all the way to their camp fourteen miles off, slaying them in thousands and capturing vast quantities of cattle and stores. He then closely besieged it, preventing every attempt to revictual it. After a fortnight, 'terrified by hunger and cold and fear', the Danes laid down their arms.

In victory Alfred's full grandeur became apparent. Undiscouraged by their past treachery, he took pity on his enemies. He fed them and offered them peace. Having shown heroism in adversity, in triumph he practised the greatest of Christian virtues. He made his cruel foes, who had learnt to respect his valour, realise his nobility. The Danish king at his invitation accepted baptism – the first of his race to do so. 'King Alfred,' wrote his friend and scribe, Bishop Asser, 'stood godfather to him and raised him from the holy font.'

Like his victories, Alfred's peace-making at Wedmore marked a turning-point in English history. It made it possible for Danes and Englishmen – the injurers and injured – to live together in a single island, and opened the way to the former's conversion and civilization. The English king had the wisdom to realise that the sword, though powerful to defend, could settle nothing permanently, and that only a conquest of the heart could endure. And though he and his people had suffered terribly from the invaders, he was too magnanimous to seek revenge and too wise to suppose he could expel them altogether. Christianity and the legacy of Roman order might transform Danes as it had transformed Saxons. No greater act of statesmanship was ever performed by an English king.

Nor was Alfred, in his far-sighted magnanimity, under any illusion. He knew that, though he might make friends with the invaders who had already homes in the east and north of England, other Danish armies would again attack her from the sea. This patient, courageous man refused to rest on his laurels. While he offered friendship to the defeated, he prepared for new attacks from their kinsmen. He used the peace he had won to give his kingdom a fighting force capable of withstanding the worst that could befall her. Once more, seeing that the only certain safety was to defeat the invaders before they could land, he began to build ships. Though he could not hope in his lifetime to defeat a massed Danish fleet – for the pirates' mastery of the northern seas had been unchallenged for generations – the war-galleys he laid down, some twice the size of the largest Viking vessel, made small-scale raiding of the Wessex coast too costly to be profitable.

Even more effective was the English king's re-organisation of his army. To overcome the fatal tendency of a militia of peasants to disperse to their farms after a few weeks' campaigning, he divided the national *fyrd*, as it was called, into two halves, each taking it in turn to serve in wartime until relieved by the other. And to stiffen its amateur ranks, he fostered the growth of a fighting aristocracy by encouraging larger freeholders to assume military rank and responsibility. To every churl with five or more hides of land he offered the right of thaneship and its privileges in return for regular military service with helm, mail-shirt, sword and horse. This semi-professional *corps d'élite*, which in wartime was kept permanently embodied, he also divided into sections, every member in peacetime having to serve for a month in arms for every two at home. This gave him a regular mounted field-force capable of opposing assailants who, living by war, had not, like English fyrdmen, to be for ever thinking about their neglected farms and homes.

The most momentous of Alfred's military reforms was his creation of the fortified burgh or town. The Danish armies had supported themselves by seizing carefully-chosen strategic bases which they provisioned from the surrounding countryside and made impregnable with earthworks and stockades. This had made it impossible for the English either to bring them to action or to maintain themselves in their vicinity. Alfred's answer was to forestall them by turning similar sites into permanently garrisoned English strongholds capable of keeping invaders at bay until his field-army could destroy them. This device of his original yet practical mind not only gave Wessex a shield which, copied later by other European rulers, enabled western Christendom to survive the Viking attacks, but laid the foundations of urban life in England. Our oldest towns arose as sentinels to guard the countryside against the Norsemen.

The strength of these burghs lay, not in imposing fortifications, which Alfred's ill-educated and much-plundered subjects had neither the wealth nor skill to make, but in the valour of their defenders. To people them, he used the pick of his kingdom's manhood. Every district had to support its burgh, and every local thane to build a house in it and either live there in person or maintain a fighting man to defend it. In this way the veterans of Alfred's wars became the burghers of England's earliest towns. Some of these, like Rochester, Exeter and Chichester, and his capital, Winchester, were built on the sites, and partly from the stones, of Roman cities; others, like Oxford and Shaftesbury, were new creations. The most important of all was London – formerly inside the Mercian border – which he won and took over, after it had been destroyed by a Danish raiding party, and re-populated with English veterans. It proved an acquisition of immense strategic and political significance. During the last two decades of his reign, overcoming the national prejudice against urban life, Alfred founded some twenty-

44

five towns, or about half the number the Romans had raised during their three and a half centuries of occupation.

When, towards the end of the reign, the Viking Grand Army again attacked southern England, it was completely frustrated by this ingenious system. After four years' spasmodic and profitless raiding it was driven ignominiously from the land. Only one town in Wessex – the little port of Appledore in Kent – was taken by it, and this had never been an established burgh. Exeter, Rochester and Chichester all successfully withstood sieges, and the invaders were repeatedly brought to battle and defeated by the field-army. The heart of the country was scarcely touched. The English king had both saved his kingdom and given new hope to Christendom.

*   *   *

Yet Alfred's true greatness lay not in war but peace. He wanted to leave behind a kingdom not only secure from foes but rich in the arts of civilization. Around him lay, after two generations of warfare, a ruined country – its farms wasted, its monasteries and schools burnt, its people reduced to ignorance and squalor. Its nobility and even its clergy were almost completely illiterate. At the start of the reign there was hardly a clerk in Wessex who could understand the Latin of the services he repeated. Alone in that ravaged land in his passion for education – the fruit of his early journey to Rome – Alfred set himself to teach his people. Nearly half his revenue was devoted to educational ends: to the training of artificers, to the support of the foreign scholars and craftsmen he brought over as teachers from every country in Christendom; to the restoration of ruined monasteries and convents and the foundation of new ones at Athelney and Shaftesbury; to the great school he established for teaching the sons of thanes and freemen to read and write and which in the course of the next generation created something unique in western Europe: a literate lay nobility. 'All the sons of freemen,' he instructed his bishops, 'who have the means to undertake it should be set to learning English letters, and such as are fit for a more advanced education and are intended for high office should be taught Latin also.' Even their astonished fathers were made to take lessons. 'It was a strange sight,' Alfred's biographer and disciple, Bishop Asser, recorded, 'to see the ealdormen, who were almost all illiterate from infancy, and the reeves and other officials learning how to read, preferring this unaccustomed and laborious discipline to losing the exercise of their power.' 'God Almighty be thanked,' Alfred wrote before his death, 'we have now teachers in office!'

It was characteristic of this modest conscientious man that he taught himself before trying to teach others. He worked with his craftsmen, helping to design houses and even inventing a candle clock and a reading-lantern. And he repaired the defects of his neglected childhood and war-riven youth by making himself a master of Latin – the language in which the knowledge of the civilized past was preserved. Even while he was still fighting the Danes he had learned works read aloud to him at every spare moment until he could read them freely for himself. Then, in the intervals of reconstructing and administering a broken realm, he set to work to translate the books which alone could impart to his people the wisdom he wanted them to share. He made no pretence to being a scholar nor thought of himself as a clever man; he sought only to expound the learning of others. But he personally undertook the task – as heroic as any of his feats in battle – of translating into the rough vernacular of his country the most useful works of Christian and classical knowledge. By doing so – for no one had essayed it before – he became the father of English prose.

Among the books Alfred translated were Bede's *Ecclesiastical History*, St Augustine's *Soliloquies*, Boethius's *Consolations of Philosophy*, Gregory's *Pastoral Care*, and Orosius's *History of the World*. Into the latter he inserted chapters of his own, bringing its geographical knowledge up to date and embodying in popular form the information he loved to collect from travellers. Longfellow's poem about 'Alfred the lover of truth' taking down from the lips of the old Norse sea-captain, Othere, the account of his voyage round the North Cape, is based on one of these insertions. For the warrior who showed Christendom how to defeat the Vikings had an ungrudging admiration for their exploits as seamen and explorers. And his reverence for the past made him recognise their kinship. One of his works was a collection of the ancient heroic songs and poems of the north which were the common legacy of Dane and Englishman – a collection that unhappily perished in the dark and troubled age in which this brave man lit so many candles. The same feeling for the past made him initiate the first history of the English people in their own tongue. For the *Anglo-Saxon Chronicle* – that record compiled by monks of the chief events in England since its occupation by the English tribes – was probably Alfred's conception. It continued to be kept for more than two centuries after his death and is by far the most valuable of sources for the early history of England. No other nation in western Europe possesses any record of the time to compare with it.

Underlying all Alfred's work was the depth of his Christian faith. 'Wisdom,' he wrote, 'is of such a kind that no man of this world can conceive of her as she really is, but each strives according to the measure of his wit to understand her if he may, for wisdom is of God.' In the preface to the collection of laws which he published, he reminded his subjects that, while Christ had come into the world to fulfil the Law, He had bade men be merciful and gentle and do unto others as they would be done by. It was this deeply sincere attempt to model both his life and reign on his Master's that made Alfred's achievement so unforgettable. He not only saved a Christian State by his exertions – and its people by his example – but made it worth saving. His legacy to his country and the world was his conception of what a Christian on the throne could be. Long after his death he was remembered by Englishmen as 'England's darling'.

Because of this, his work – and kingdom – endured. He left no bitterness to be avenged after his death. Having saved Wessex, and with it the English nation, he made no attempt to conquer others. He did not, like Charlemagne, massacre his prisoners, or extend his rule of terror like the Greek emperor who sent fifteen thousand blinded Bulgars back to their heathen land to prove the might of civilization. He did as he would be done by. He defeated enemies, not made them. The suzerainty he won outside his own borders was not imposed by the sword, but by character and example. 'All the English people,' Bishop Asser wrote, 'submitted to Alfred except those who were under the power of the Danes.' The destruction of the other kingdoms had left the king of Wessex the natural leader and protector of all Englishmen. He married his eldest daughter to the patriot ealdorman who led the resistance in western Mercia after its king had fled, and granted him several of his new burghs, including London. Such generosity to less fortunate neighbours made Alfred arbiter of all western England as far as the Dee. Even the Welsh, who had warred incessantly against his race, acknowledged his gentle, unenforced supremacy. So, though their kinsfolk returned for a time to plague his realm, did the Danes he had defeated and who had made their homes in eastern England. Eight years after Ethandun they made a treaty with him by which the frontier between the two races was fixed on the line of the Lea and upper Ouse and thence along Watling Street. Under it, arrangements were made for peaceful commercial intercourse between the two nations.

'I suppose,' Alfred wrote in one of his books, comparing seekers after wisdom with royal messengers, 'they would come by very many roads. Some would come from afar and have a road very long, very bad and very difficult; some would have a very long, very direct and very good road; some would have a very short and yet hard and strait and foul one; some would have a short and smooth and good one; and yet they all would come to one and the same Lord.' He himself had had a very long and hard one, in a hard and barren time. He died soon after his fiftieth year – probably in 899 – worn out by his life of struggle and danger. But he left to those who came after him a free land recovering from its wounds, and an ideal of kingship that was not of vain-glory but Christian service. He had created two things which were to survive disaster and conquest – a kingdom to which all Englishmen instinctively felt they belonged and a native literature to enshrine their culture and tradition. More than any other man he was the first maker of England.

CHAPTER FIVE

The Bones of Shire
and State

'See you our stilly woods of oak
And the dread ditch beside?
O that was where the Saxons broke
On the day that Harold died.'

Kipling

DURING THE CENTURY which followed Alfred's defeat of the Danes, the process of rebuilding Christian society after the attacks of the Norsemen went on faster in England than in any other country. A great king had taught his people to defend their island home and had endowed it with a realm which was not for ever being partitioned among its princes. His descendants, the fair-haired athelings, of the House of Wessex, produced in little more than half a century three other great rulers – Alfred's son, Edward the Elder; his grandson, Athelstan; and his great-grandson Edgar, the first acknowledged king of all England. It was at Edgar's coronation in Bath Abbey in 973 that the earliest form of the service still used at the crowning of England's kings was read by its author, the mystic saint and musician, Archbishop Dunstan. Behind the solemn rites – the royal prostration and oath, the archbishop's consecration and anointing, the anthem, 'Zadok the Priest', linking the kings of the Angles and Saxons with those of the ancient Hebrews, the investiture with sword, sceptre and rod of justice, the shout of recognition by the assembled lords – lay the idea that an anointed king and his people were a partnership under God.

49

After that sacramental act, loyalty to the Crown became a Christian obligation. The ideal of patriotism first began to take vague shape in men's minds, superseding the older conception of tribal kingship.

It was this which helped to give England in the tenth century institutions stronger than those of any western land. Her system of taxation, of currency and coinage, of local government, of the issue of laws and charters were all in advance of those prevailing in the half-anarchical kingdoms and dukedoms of the former Frankish Empire. As a result, though a country of little account at the known world's edge, her wealth increased rapidly. It was part of her king's policy to establish in every shire at least one town with a market-place and mint where contracts could be witnessed and reliable money coined. By the beginning of the eleventh century there were more than seventy towns in the country. A dozen – Winchester, the royal capital, York, Norwich and Lincoln, Gloucester, Chester, Canterbury, Thetford, Worcester, Oxford, Ipswich and Hereford – had perhaps three or four thousand inhabitants, and one, the self-governing port of London, four or five times as many. Though most of them were ramparted, and a few walled, their real security and the source of their wealth was the King's Peace and the confidence it inspired. The countryside was famous for beef, bacon and wheaten cakes, for ale, mead and perry, and for plentiful butter and cheese; a writer recorded that, while Italians cooked with oil, the English cooked with butter. Almost every village possessed a water-mill, and in the rich eastern counties of Norfolk and Lincoln often more than one. The Danish town of Derby had fourteen. The rivers swarmed with fish, and many places had eel-traps; the little Fenland town of Wisbech paid the abbot of Ely an annual rent of fourteen thousand eels. Chester sent its earldorman a thousand salmon a year, and Petersham in Surrey a thousand lampreys.

The heart of England's culture was no longer Northumbria – now a wasted and depopulated province – but Wessex. Here, too, as in the northern kingdom which had welcomed Aidan and bred Cuthbert, Celtic blood and tradition mingled with Saxon. Even its early kings had borne names which were not Teuton, like

Cerdic, Cynric, Ceawlin, and Celtic place-names were intertwined mysteriously in its western shires with English: Axe and Exe, avon for river, coombe for valley. The greatest Wessex figure of the age was Archbishop Dunstan who, like his earlier countryman, St Aldhelm, had been partly nursed in the tradition of Celtic Christianity. At Glastonbury, where as abbot his earliest work was done, legend went back far beyond the English conquest to the tiny wattle church which Joseph of Arimathaea was supposed to have built among the water-meadows for the conversion of Roman Britain. Dunstan was a mystic, feeling his way to wisdom through visions and trances; he wrestled with fiends and monsters and heard mysterious, heavenly voices.

Wessex was becoming a settled land of villages, farms and fields whose names still figure on our maps. Its main outlines – church and parish boundary, mill, ford and footpath – were already what they were to remain for a thousand years. 'See you our little mill,' wrote a twentieth-century poet,

> 'that clacks
> So busy by the brook?
> She has ground her corn and paid her tax
> Ever since Domesday Book.'

He might have added, earlier. Puttock's End, Cow Common, Crab's Green, Woolard's Ash, Doodle Oak – names of Essex fields and hamlets in the reign of Elizabeth II – were given them when the athelings of Wessex sat on the English throne. So were the boundaries of shire and hundred, and the customs – themselves far older than their new Christian forms – with which men celebrated the changes of the year. Such were Plough Monday, when the village lads, with ribbons and cracking whips, resumed work after the twelve days of Christmas; May Day when they marched to the woods to gather greenery and danced round the May pole; Whitsun when the Morris dancers leapt through the villages with bells, hobby-horses and waving scarves; Lammas when the first bread was blessed; and Harvest Home when the Corn Dolly – effigy of a heathen goddess – was borne to the barns with reapers singing and piping behind. At Christmas the houses were decked with evergreen and the Yule candles lit.

51

With its fine craftsmen and the rule of its strong kings, England was beginning once more to accumulate treasures, to become a land worth plundering as she was before the Danes attacked her. Ivories and jewelled crucifixes, golden and silver candelabra, onyx vases and elaborate wood-carvings, superbly embroidered vestments, stoles and altar cloths adorned the churches and the halls and hunting-lodges of the great. As they sat, in mantles of brightly coloured silks fastened with golden collars and garnet-inlaid brooches, listening to song, harp and minstrelsy, the princes and ealdormen of Wessex were served from polished drinking-horns chased with silver and wooden goblets with gold. The century of Athelstan and Edgar saw a new flowering of Anglo-Saxon art. Archbishop Dunstan himself, Edgar's chief counsellor, was a craftsman and loved to fashion jewellery and cast church-bells. He loved, too, to work in the scriptoria, as he had done as a young monk; in his day the illuminators of the monastic renaissance, with their gorgeous colouring and boldly flowing margins, reached new heights of achievement. So did the sculptors of the Winchester school who carved the angel at Bradford-on-Avon, the Virgin and Child at Englesham, and the wonderful Harrowing of Hell in Bristol cathedral. The richer parish churches helped to house such treasures: small barnlike buildings, with primitive rounded arches, high walls and narrow windows and bell-towers crowned with weather-cocks – an English invention. A few survive, like the log church at Greenstead in Essex, flint and rubble Braemore in the Avon valley, with its Anglo-Saxon text which no living parishioner can read, stone Barnack and broad-towered Earl's Barton in Northamptonshire.

In the depopulated north a simpler polity prevailed. Here Christian missionaries from Viking-harried Ireland were busy turning the Scandinavian settlements along the coasts and dales into Christian parishes. The wheel-head crosses that marked their open-air sites of worship show the transitional nature of the conversion: the carved Odin cross at Kirk Andrea in the Isle of Man with ravens croaking on a heathen god's shoulder, while on the other side Christ looks down in majesty; the Gosforth cross in Cumberland where the resurrected Saviour – Baldur the Beautiful of northern legend reborn – tramples the dragons and demons of Hell: Surt the fire-god, Fenris the wolf and Loki the serpent. The word 'cross', derived from the Latin crux, was introduced by these Irish evangelists, gradually taking the place of the Anglo-Saxon 'rood'. It first appeared in northern names like Crosby and Crossthwaite. Other Scandinavian words were being woven into the map of northern England; *gate* a street and *thwaite* a clearing, *fell* a hill and *thorpe* a settlement, *foss* a waterfall and *by* a village. Similar Norse names – Swansea, Caldey, Fishguard, Gresholm, Haverford – appeared on the coasts of Anglesey, Pembrokeshire, Gower and Glamorgan.

Like their kinsfolk in the old Danelaw and East Anglia these northern dalesmen – pirates' brood though they were – had a great respect for law so long as they themselves made it. The very word entered England through their speech. So did the divisions or ridings into which they split the southern part of Northumbria, the juries of twelve leading men employed in the administration of their towns and wapentakes, and their habit of majority decision. For it was a rule among these independent-minded men that, save in a boat or on the battlefield, they were all equal.

*   *   *

Yet all this polity and wealth depended in the last resort on the ability of English kings to keep the good order which Alfred had won. Not all the princes of the House of Wessex were great men or able to ride the tides of anarchy in an age still threatened by Viking invasions. Edgar's eldest son, a boy, was murdered at the instigation of his step-mother; the half-brother who succeeded him in 978 was a spoilt, petulant weakling. Under his inconstant impulses, and those of his brutal favourites, England's new-found unity dissolved. The long reign of Aethelred the Redeless – the unready or lacking in counsel – proved one of the most disastrous in English history. Incapable of running straight, his double dealing set the great ealdormen, who ruled the provinces, by the ears, even before he reached manhood.

Once more, scenting weakness as vultures carrion, the Vikings returned. The European mainland was no longer the easy prey it had been; under the challenge of repeated invasion its divided peoples had learnt to defend themselves. Barred out of Europe, the Norsemen fell on England. For a generation they feasted on the carcass of a rich and now leaderless land. Its monasteries again fell into decay, its farms were plundered, the peasants taxed into starvation or sold as slaves. The worst humiliation came in 1012 when invaders pounced on Canterbury and carried off the primate, Alphege, and most of the monks and nuns. When the brave archbishop refused to appeal for a ransom, he was pelted to death with ox-bones by a pack of drunken pirates.

After Aethelred's ignominious flight to the continent in 1013, his son, Edmund 'Ironside', put up a fight worthy of Alfred himself against the Danish invaders, who were now led by the young king of Denmark, Canute. For nearly three years these two great soldiers fought each other among the forests and marshes of southern England. In the end, after five astonishing victories by the English loyalist forces – at Penselwood on the Somerset-Dorset border, at Sherston in Wiltshire, on the western road to London, at Brentford, and at Otford in Kent – Edmund was defeated by Canute at Ashingdon in Essex through the treachery of one of his ealdormen. Though on his father's death earlier that year he had been elected king by the men of London, he died a few months later at Oxford, leaving his Danish rival master of more than half England.

In that midwinter of disaster the great council of the realm, or *Witan*, met and made its terms with the conqueror. Preferring strength on the throne to weakness, and unity to division, it elected as king, not one of Edmund's infant sons, but the young victorious Dane, Canute. It proved a wise choice. For though Canute was almost as ruthless as his father, he ended the long Norse scourge. At a meeting of the Witan at Oxford he swore to govern his realm by the laws of King Edgar. Henceforward he made no distinction between his new countrymen and his old. He followed Alfred.

For if Canute had conquered England, in a wider sense England conquered him. English missionaries, following Boniface's great tradition, had long been at work in Scandinavia; though born a pagan, Canute had been baptised. With his acceptance of a Christian crown the ravaging of Christendom from the north ceased. While in many things still a heathen, revengeful and hard, he became a devout churchman, enforcing tithes, endowing monasteries, and even making a pilgrimage to Rome where he laid English tribute on the altar of St Peter. He rebuilt the shrine at Bury St Edmunds to the king his countrymen had martyred a century and a half before, and made amends to the murdered Alphege by the honours he paid his tomb at Canterbury.

Had this great, harsh man lived longer, the course of European history might have been different. Being king both of England and Denmark, he tried to make the North Sea an Anglo-Danish lake and England the head of a Nordic confederation stretching from Ireland to the Baltic. After his conquest of Norway he became virtual emperor of the North. But fate was against him. The story of his courtiers telling him he could stay the advancing tide at Lambeth may not have been true but, like many legends, it enshrined a truth. He was not more powerful than death. He died at forty in 1035, his work incomplete and most of his mighty projects still a dream. He was buried at Winchester among the English kings, while his half-barbaric sons divided his Scandinavian empire between them.

They did not even found a dynasty. Seven years later, when the last of them died 'as he stood at his drink at Lambeth', the Witan, in 1042, chose as successor the forty-year-old Edward, son of Aethelred the Unready by his second wife, Emma of Normandy. He was a soft, devout, peace-loving man, with a clerk's long tapering fingers, a rosy face and flaxen hair which turned with age to a beautiful silver. Though exile in his mother's country had made him more French than English, his subjects were much impressed by his piety. He was more like an abbot to them than a king, and they called him the Confessor. His greatest interest was the building of a monastery among the river marshes at Thorney, a mile or two to the west of London. Here, that he might watch his abbey rising – the West Minster, at it was called – he made himself a hall on a site which was one day to become the heart of an empire.

Yet Edward exposed his subjects to almost as many dangers as his father had done. He was so devout that he refused to give his wife a child and his realm an heir. Absorbed in works of piety, he left its affairs to the great ealdormen and his Norman favourites. He made immense grants of land to a Sussex thane named Godwin, whom Canute had created earl of the West Saxons, and who induced Edward to marry his sister and to confer on his spoilt, quarrelling sons the earldoms of East Anglia, Gloucester, Hereford, Oxford, Northampton, Huntingdon and northern Northumbria.

Godwin was not the only subject able to defy the Crown. Equally masters in their provincial strongholds were his rivals, Leofric of Mercia – husband of the legendary Lady Godiva, foundress of Coventry abbey – and the giant Dane, Siward of York, who met his death like a Norse warrior standing fully accoutred with breast-plate, helmet and gilded battle-axe. The power of such magnates was not wholly Edward's fault. It was a result of the cumulative alienation of the royal estates, caused by the difficulty of raising revenue to pay for public services, which had been going on for generations and which deprived the monarchy of its chief and almost only source of income. Appointed in the days of Athelstan to lead the *fyrd* and enforce the royal law in a single shire, the ealdorman by the eleventh century, with his accumulation of shires and hereditary claim to office, had grown beyond the control of any ordinary ruler. His was the disintegrating force of power without responsibility. He was neither a chieftain bound by tribal ties nor a consecrated king with obligations to his people.

When on 5 January 1066, a few days after the consecration of his abbey church at Westminster, the gentle Confessor died, the Witan, meeting in the Godwin stronghold of London, elected the dead Godwin's son and heir, Harold Godwinson, Earl of Wessex, to the throne. In doing so, it ignored three other claimants. One was a son of Edmund Ironside; another Harold Hardrada, king of Norway. The third was the dead king's great-nephew, William, Duke of Normandy, to whom Harold, when shipwrecked there some years earlier, had done homage and sworn to assist his claim to the English throne.

HOW THEY EVOLVED

CHAPTER SIX

Norman Discipline

'There shall be one people – it shall serve one Lord –
    (Neither Priest nor Baron shall escape!)
It shall have one speech and law, soul and strength and
    sword. England's being hammered, hammered,
    hammered into shape!'

———

' "My son," said the Norman Baron, "I am dying, and
    you will be heir
To all the broad acres in England that William gave me
    for my share. . . .

'The Saxon is not like us Normans. His manners are not
    so polite,
But he never means anything serious till he talks about
    justice and right.
When he stands like an ox in the furrow with his sullen
    set eyes on your own,
And grumbles, "This isn't fair dealing," my son, leave the
    Saxon alone. . . .'

Kipling

THE DIFFICULTY FACING RULERS in the Dark Ages was to make any system of government work except naked force. In tribal times a king could only impose his will when the horde was assembled for battle. When Clovis, conqueror of Gaul and the first king of the Franks, wished to preserve a chalice looted from Soissons cathedral, his sole resource was to split open the head of the warrior who voiced the customary right of veto. The attempt even of a great ruler like Charlemagne to recreate an international empire based on Roman law had been shattered not only by the Norse raids but by the difficulty of keeping united large areas inhabited by primitive peoples. Without a trained bureaucracy the Roman system of raising revenue could not work; a Frankish king could only levy taxes by farming them out to local magnates.

Feudalism – the protection of the locality from predatory strangers by its stronger members – seemed the only answer until either the old imperialism could be recreated or a national order take its place. The local knight in his castle, with his horse, lance, shield, and chain and leather armour, proved the answer to the invading hordes of Norsemen, Magyars and Moslems from which the West had suffered so long. His elaborate smith-made protection, his mobility and striking-power and his life-long dedication to arms made him despise mere numbers.

Yet, while he helped to save Europe, the feudal knight added to the problem of its government. If he was invulnerable to his country's foes, he was equally so to its rulers and could become a scourge to everyone within reach of his strong arm. He lived for war and by it. His neighbours had to seek his protection or be ruined. The sole restraint on his power was that of the feudal superior from whom he received his lands. The knight's obligation to his overlord was the counterpart of the loyalty to the crown which Alfred had tried to create in England. He did homage to him for his fief, swore *fidelitas* or fealty to him and gave him in war the precise measure of military service – neither more nor less – laid down in the terms of his enfeoffment.

It was the Church which took the lead in trying to discipline feudalism and harness it to constructive ends. It, too, had suffered from the anarchy caused by the invaders. Simony – the sale of sacred benefices – had become widespread; bishops paid kings and feudal lords at their consecration and recouped themselves from those they ordained, while patrons of livings exacted tribute from parish priests who in turn charged their parishioners for the Church's offices. But in the eleventh century, when Edward the Confessor was governing – or rather failing to govern – England, a succession of great Popes or Bishops of Rome set themselves to reform the Church. Their aim was to rescue the Holy See from its dependence on local princes, to end the commerce in sacred benefices by enforcing canonical election, and to make the parish clergy a sacred caste apart by insisting on celibacy and continence. And in re-establishing law and order in ecclesiastical matters, they tried, also, to end the ravages of private feudal war. They set aside days and seasons for a 'truce of God', when war was forbidden on penalty of expulsion from the Church's communion. They sought, too, by an appeal to conscience, to present knightly power as a trust and to make knight errantry a Christian pursuit; to turn the aggressive, acquisitive Frankish freebooter, armed *cap-à-pie*, into a Christian champion, driving back the heathen, defending Holy Church and punishing iniquity. In chivalry, as it became called, the Church offered the military class a code of honour. It devised an elaborate ceremony at which the young knight, before being invested with arms, knelt all night in solitary prayer before the altar, and, like the king at his crowning, took the sacrament, swearing to use the power entrusted to him in righteousness and the defence of the helpless. And, for the sake of society, it invested the oath of fealty with mystery and sanctity. It was an offence against God, the Church taught, for a vassal to be false to his liege-lord.

In one State, in particular – the little warlike duchy of Normandy – the Church succeeded in establishing a working and mutually profitable partnership with the knightly class. A hundred years earlier, when Alfred's successors were creating a united England, a Viking pirate had secured from the ruler of West Francia or France – the most westerly fragment of Charlemagne's disintegrated empire – a grant of conquered lands at the mouth of the Seine. Here, in what became named after them Normandy, intermarrying with the French and adopting their faith and language, a community of Norsemen established a dukedom whose disciplined chivalry of armoured knights evolved a technique of fighting from the saddle and stirrup which made them the arbiters of western Europe. They rode their horses through the waves of battle as their pirate forebears had sailed their ships. They loved fighting with lance and horse so much that, when they were not at war, they were for ever challenging one another in mimic tourneys or tournaments.

They were masters, too, of law and rhetoric. They knew how to govern, just as they knew how to win battles, because they were quite clear what they wanted. Ruthless, almost entirely without sentiment and, though passionate, self-possessed and cool, they had the simplicity of genius. With their round bullet-heads, blue eyes and long aquiline noses, they looked like intelligent birds of prey. Above all, they had energy. They were as restless as they were greedy and calculating. Like their Norse forebears they would go to the world's end for plunder. In the middle of the eleventh century, four hundred of them seized the south of Italy from the Byzantine Greeks. Then they went on to conquer the rich island of Sicily from the Saracens, the lords of the Mediterranean.

They had a genius for absorbing other civilizations. So thoroughly did they absorb that of the Frankish-Gaulish folk among whom they settled that, within a century of their occupation of Normandy, scarcely a word of their old Norse tongue was in use. They became a Romance or Latin-speaking race and, having conquered a Christian land, fervent champions of the Church and the newly reformed papacy. Nowhere was the monastic reforming movement so enthusiastically supported by the laity, so many monasteries built and such learned and pious clerks appointed to well-endowed benefices. It was as though the Norman knights, the most acquisitive in Europe, were trying to offset their martial outrages by the orthodoxy of their ecclesiastical establishments and, while storming their way into their neighbours' lands, to buy an entry to Heaven. They became the greatest church-builders since the days of Charlemagne and even since those of imperial Rome, whose giant buildings they tried to copy. They were not delicate craftsmen like the English; their chief resource was to build immensely thick walls, and several of their grander achievements fell down. But they had infinite ambition and a sense of space and grandeur.

Their buildings expressed their religion. Their patron-saint, standing above their churches with uplifted sword and outstretched wings, was the warrior archangel Michael, guardian of Heaven; their conception of God, a feudal overlord ready to reward those like themselves who kept the letter of His law. With the spirit they troubled themselves little; they were a practical folk who liked clear definitions. They built, not for comfort like the timber-loving Saxons, but in stone to endure. Their serried arches, marching like armies through space, the vast walls and pillars supporting them, the rude, demon-haunted figures gazing down from the capitals, symbolised the crude magnificence and vigour of their half-barbaric minds. With their grim massiveness and twin-towers rising into the sky like swords, such churches seemed designed, as Henry Adams wrote, to force Heaven: 'all of them look as though they had fought at Hastings or stormed Jerusalem.'

After the collapse of Canute's empire in 1042, the Normans had turned their gaze on England. Its wealth, so much superior to that of Normandy, seemed a standing invitation. They viewed its easy-going provincials with a contempt they hardly tried to conceal: the words *pride* and *proud* first entered the English language to describe the arrogance of the Normans to whom the Confessor granted estates and bishoprics. As he had so conveniently re-frained from giving his kingdom an heir, his great-nephew, William, Duke of Normandy, formed the idea of claiming it for himself. He even succeeded in persuading his saintly uncle to promise it him – though it was not by English law his to promise.

The English at that time were the most civilized people in western Europe. Their achievement in vernacular scholarship, poetry and literature was unique; their craftsmanship – in sculpture, embroidery, goldsmith's and coiner's work – most skilful and sensitive. They had evolved a union of Church and State for national ends which had no parallel outside the Byzantine Empire; their bishops and ealdormen sat side by side in the Witan and the provincial and shire courts. But to the radically minded Normans, England was a land without discipline; where the enthusiasm of saints and scholars had become lost in a sluggish stream of petty provincial interests; where married canons lived on hereditary endowments, and the very archbishop of Canterbury was a simoniac and uncanonically appointed; and where boorish nobles, sunk in swinish drunkenness and gluttony, sold sacred benefices while bucolic warriors, too conservative to change, still fought on foot and with battle-axes. She had lost touch with the new world growing up beyond the Channel: with the international Church, with its reforming Popes and disciplined monasteries, with the new ideals of chivalry, and the mailed knights, battle-trained horses, tall moated castles which were now becoming the dominant features of the European landscape. She was living on the memories of the past, static, conservative, unimaginative. She had barred her mind to change; it remained to be seen if she could bar her gates.

*   *   *

The man who now set himself to conquer England was one of the great men of history. His mother was the unmarried daughter of a Falaise tanner; his great-great-grandfather had been a pirate. Left fatherless as a child, his boyhood had been spent amid the turmoil caused by the violence of his father's feudal barons. The ruin they unloosed had made an indelible impression on him. Far-sighted, patient, prudent, self-controlled, bold but thorough in all he did, and ruthless towards those who stood in his way, Duke William made his little duchy, with its disciplined chivalry of armoured knights and ruddy-faced men-at-arms from the Normandy apple orchards, the most formidable force in Europe. Compelled to wage war in turn against his barons, his jealous neighbours in Maine, Anjou and Brittany, and his feudal overlord, the titular King of France, he defeated them all. He never lost sight of his aims, never over-reached himself, and steadily increased his domains. When in his fortieth year he began to gather ships for the invasion of England, landless knights from every Frankish province flocked to his banners.

All that summer of 1066 two armadas were preparing to invade England, one on the Norman coast, the other in the Norwegian fiords and islands to the north of Scotland where Harold Hardrada, the barbarian King of Norway, was hoping to re-incorporate the British island in a Scandinavian empire. But though Harold Godwinson, concentrating against the nearer of the two, waited all summer in the south, by the autumn his peasant levies began to slip away to their homes and harvests. Only the house-carles of

64

the royal bodyguard remained until, in September, news came that the King of Norway had landed at Ouse, near York.

Harold at once set out on the long march up the straight, grass-grown highroad which the Romans had built a thousand years before. Four years earlier the lightning speed of his marches had broken the power of the Welsh. Now he was resolved that the Viking king who had come to seize his kingdom should meet the same end, promising him six feet of English earth or, as he was tall, seven. On 25 September, after covering thirty miles since dawn, he fell on the Viking host at Stamford Bridge. All afternoon the clangour of axe and sword continued. By dusk Hardrada had fallen, and King Harold – 'a little man sitting proudly in his stir-rups' – had made good his boast that his foe should win nothing in England but a grave.

Two days later, William, who had been waiting for a favouring wind, sailed from the Somme. On 28 September he landed at Pevensey Bay. The news, galloped through the Midland forests, took two days to reach York where Harold was celebrating his victory. Without a moment's hesitation he and his battered house-carles set out again for the south. In six days they covered the one hundred and ninety miles to London. Waiting there a few days for the *fyrd* of the southern shires to join them, they marched on 12 October for Hastings. Uncertain of his kingdom's loyalty and fear-ful lest his jealous earls should play him false, Harold had to turn out the southern wasps' nest quickly, like the northern, or perish.

The battle which was to decide his fate and England's took place on 14 October at Senlac where the Hastings track emerged from the Sussex oak-forest. The English king, who had meant to attack, was forced to remain on the defensive, as only half his troops had arrived. His house-carles, with their double-handed battle-axes, were probably the finest infantry in Europe, but the rest of his army was a rabble of peasant levies, armed with spears, clubs and pitchforks, and no match for Duke William's armoured knights. Fighting continued all day, but by the evening only the house-carles were left holding the ridge against the Norman horse-men. They were so closely packed that the slain had scarcely room to fall. It was almost dark when a band of knights closed in on

Harold who had been wounded in the eye by an arrow and, as he bent bleeding over his shield, hacked him to pieces. 'In the English ranks,' wrote a Norman chronicler, 'the only movement was the dropping of the dead. They were ever ready with their steel, those sons of the old Saxon race, the most dauntless of men.' By nightfall all lay dead round their fallen king and his banner of the Fighting Man.

*   *   *

The kingdom Alfred had made thus became a colony of a foreign dynastic empire – that of the Dukes of Normandy, whose language and culture were French and who had little understanding of English ways. With a few thousand knights and men-at-arms William the Conqueror subjected a nation of more than a million and a half. Duke of Normandy, he now also became King of the English. At first, like Canute, he tried to govern them with the help of the native lords and prelates who accepted his conquest. Many of his earliest officials were English and some of his first writs and charters were issued in their tongue – the last for three hundred years. But he was faced by two inescapable difficulties. One was the need to reward the followers with whom he had won and without whom he could not maintain his throne; the other the obstinacy of the English and their hatred of foreigners, particularly the French.

He began by confiscating only the lands of those who had fought against him at Hastings and whom, in keeping with his claim to be the Confessor's heir, he treated as traitors. But the discontent aroused by the arrogance of his acquisitive barons and their rough knights forced him to carry the process of confiscation further. A widespread rising three years after the Conquest he suppressed with terrifying ruthlessness. During the next generation, seizing on every act of disobedience or rebellion, he transferred the ownership of almost every large estate from English hands to Norman. At the end of his twenty years' reign there were only two major English landowners left and one English bishop. Almost every Englishman held his land at the will of some Norman.

In this way William substituted for the old loose aristocratic direction of the State a new and far more efficient one. He resumed the royal rights over the nation's land which his Anglo-Saxon predecessors had improvidently 'booked' away. He kept a fifth for himself and his family, and a quarter for the Church. Of the remainder he redistributed all but an insignificant fraction among his hundred and seventy chief Norman and French followers on strictly defined conditions of military service. Nearly half went to ten men. Having learnt from his harsh life that no State or throne was safe unless organised for instant war, he attached to every grant of land an inescapable martial obligation. In return for their fiefs or 'honours', as they were called, his tenants-in-chief, including bishops and abbots, had to swear to support the Crown with a fixed number of mounted and armoured knights, to pay specified dues at stated times and to attend the royal courts and councils. To meet these commitments they in turn had to farm out their lands on similar terms to professional knights or fighting-men, whom they 'enfeoffed' as their vassals.

Thus every substantial holding of land, whoever its immediate occupier, was made to furnish and maintain an armoured, mounted and battle-trained knight ready to take the field at any moment. As well as giving protection to its peasant cultivators, who had to perform the same manual services for its new owner as its old, it became a knight's fief or fee, itself part of some greater fief. If its feudal holder failed to perform his military services, it reverted to the overlord to whom he had sworn allegiance for it. It could neither be broken up nor sold without the latter's consent, and on its holder's death his heir, after paying a fine and doing homage, had to render the same services.

To a large extent this system had already been established in France and other parts of western Europe. Yet William's was unique – a mark of his creative genius – in its identification of the protection of the fief with that of the realm. It was the absence of this that had so troubled his own early life in Normandy and broken up the old English kingdom. In the Conqueror's new England the holder of every substantial military fief had to do homage for it, not only to his overlord, but to the Crown.

For after William had crushed two rebellions in which disloyal

Norman tenants-in-chief had called out their vassals against him, and at a time when a new rising and a Danish invasion were threatened, he held, at the Christmas feast and council at Gloucester in 1085, 'very deep speech with his wise men'. Next year he summoned a meeting at Salisbury, not only of his tenants-in-chief, but of all principal land-holders in the country. And by making them swear to obey him even against their own overlords, he made them directly responsible to the Crown as in no other State in Europe. By this simple device, he turned feudalism, without weakening its military efficiency, into an instrument of royal power. He became not only, like the King of France, the nominal lord paramount of the realm, but the actual one. He was able to do so because, having conquered England and its land, he started with a clean slate.

Nor did William make his nobles rulers of provinces like their English predecessors or their counterparts in France. Whether by accident or design, he scattered their estates about the country. This not only made it harder for them to rebel, but forced them to think in national as well as regional terms. Abroad the feudal count, like the old Anglo-Saxon earl, thought only of his county or province; in England, like the King himself, he had to think of the country as a whole. Henry de Ferrers, rewarded with 114 manors in Derbyshire, was given 96 in thirteen other counties. A still greater tenant-in-chief, Robert de Mortain, held his 793 manors in twenty different shires. The only exceptions were on the Welsh and Scottish borders, where the local magnates needed vast powers to keep the tribesmen of the Celtic west and north at bay. The prince bishop of Durham, and the earls of Chester, Shrewsbury, and Hereford, ruled what later were called counties palatine. Yet even these were small compared with the independent provinces of France, and the King appointed to them only men he could trust. He watched them very closely. Within half a century of the Conquest only two of these compact, semi-independent jurisdictions remained.

Within these limits – a framework of discipline in which every baron enjoyed his just feudal rights, but no more – William scrupulously respected the 'liberties' of his nobles. They were the instrument by which he ruled. Fewer than two hundred French-speaking barons – closely inter-related and accustomed to working together – and five or six thousand knights became the principal land-holders of England. Having both a duty and incentive to protect the Conquest, they guaranteed its permanence. They formed a new ruling caste; a colonising warrior aristocracy which possessed not only privilege but creative energy. The names they brought from their Norman homes are writ on our maps and across our history – Montgomery and Mandeville, Warenne and Giffard, Baldwin and Mortimer, Mowbray and Beaumont, Neville and Lacy, Bohum and Courcy, Beauchamp and Percy.

Beneath this military superstructure the Conqueror had the sense to leave England much as it was. He kept the Witanagemot which became the Great Council of his tenants-in-chief, lay and ecclesiastical. He kept the elaborate secretarial and financial machinery which the English kings had devised for raising gelds and land-taxes, and for sending out enquiries and orders to their officers in the shires. He kept the old divisions of shire and hundred; the shire-courts where, under the royal sheriff's eye, the freemen interpreted the customary law of the locality, and the hundred-courts where representatives of the villages – priest, reeve and leading peasants – settled their disputes and answered for breaches of the peace. He left unchanged the free communities of the Dane-law and the ancient tenures by which the Kentish cultivators were protected in their holdings. He left, too, with the Norman manor superimposed on it for military and taxing purposes, the midland English village, with its strip-divided fields, its hereditary rights of cattle-pasture and pig-pannage, its communal system of cultivation and wide variety of tenures. He left the Londoners the rights they had always enjoyed under their elected portreeve and burgesses. And he kept the old Anglo-Saxon shire *fyrd* or militia – an invaluable counterpoise to the Norman feudal array.

Wherever an English institution could serve his end, William improved on it. Having got rid of the independent provincial earls who under Aethelred and the Confessor had acquired the un-English right to own and rule land without relation to the service to the Crown for which it had been granted, he used in their place

69

the sheriffs or royal officials with whom his predecessors had vainly tried to check the earls' powers. The Norman sheriff administered the royal estates in the shire, presided at its court, collected the taxes and led the shire militia in time of war or rebellion. This linked the Crown with the forces, so strong in medieval society, of local patriotism and self-interest and made for national unity. So did the system – possibly brought from France, but adapted also from Anglo-Saxon and Danish practice – by which sworn juries or panels of neighbours were made judges of local questions of fact. William used these repeatedly to discover the rights of the Crown against his powerful Norman followers and the taxable value of their estates.

*   *   *

For most Englishmen all this was a terribly painful process. 'Cold heart and bloody hand,' wrote a Norse poet, 'now rule the English land.' William was guilty, in his own dying words, of 'the barbarous murder of many thousands, both young and old, of that fine race of people'.[1] To many the Conquest brought bitter tragedy; the families of those who died in battle, the peasants on the line of march, the thanes whose lands were seized to provide fiefs for William's foreign barons and knights. All who made the least resistance were ruthlessly stripped of their estates in pursuit of the royal policy. Most of the old English nobles and thanes who survived Hastings and the later rebellions in the west, north and midlands became mere farmers; at Marsh Gibbon in Buckinghamshire – the Conqueror's great tax-survey records – Aethelric, the farmer, 'now holds it of William, the son of Ansculf, in heaviness and misery'.[2] Some fled to Scotland, where they strengthened the Saxon elements of that wild land, or took service in the Varangian bodyguard of the Greek emperor at Constantinople. A few brave

---

[1] 'I have persecuted its native inhabitants beyond all reason. Whether gentle or simple, I have cruelly oppressed them; many I unjustly disinherited; innumerable multitudes, especially in the county of York, perished through me by famine or the sword.' Ordericus Vitalis, The Ecclesiastical History cit. *English Historical Documents*, 1, p. 286.

[2] '*Graviter et miserabiliter*' – one of the few human touches in that grim, invaluable record.

men, preferring liberty to life, took to the marshes and forests as outlaws, like Hereward the Wake, a small Lincolnshire land-owner who held out in the Fens till 1071. 'Most,' as William Fuller wrote six centuries later, 'betook themselves to patience which taught many a noble hand to work, foot to travel, tongue to entreat.'

Humbler folk were left in possession of their holdings; Norman and English alike would have starved otherwise. Yet many of them were subjected to the tyranny of the special courts which the Conqueror set up in the forests, still covering more than a quarter of the land, to preserve the red and fallow deer for his hunting. 'He loved the tall stags like a father,' we are told. To guard them, his forest officers put out the eyes of any man found killing hart or hind, and mutilated poor peasants caught in the woods with dogs or arrows. In these sacred precincts even the lopping of a bough was punished. Rich and poor alike murmured at the King's forest laws, but 'he was so sturdy that he recked nought of them'.

William was hard and ruthless: 'so stark a man', an English monk called him. After the second rising of the northern counties in 1070, when five hundred Norman knights were massacred at Durham, he so harried the countryside that along the road from York to Durham not a house remained standing. Even the northern capital and its famous minster were burnt. It took the north generations to recover. Seventeen years later the royal commissioners, surveying the tax capacity of Yorkshire, entered against place after place the grim word, 'Waste'.

Above all, the Conqueror was a merciless taxer. His first act after his coronation was to 'lay on a geld exceeding stiff'. Close-fisted and grasping – a monk complained that, while the Saxon kings gave their courtiers four meals a day, he gave his only one – he had compiled after 1085, mainly that he might tax his realm more closely, a record of all feudal holdings directly or indirectly liable to the Crown. 'So narrowly did he cause the survey to be made,' wrote an English chronicler 'that there was not one single hide nor rood of land, nor – it is shameful to tell, but he thought it no shame to do – was there an ox, cow or swine that was not set down in the writ.' Using commissioners to hold local enquiries or inquests in every shire and hundred, he had recorded, with meticulous efficiency[1], the ownership and taxable value of every manor or village under lordship, both at the Conquest and at the time of the survey. This included the number of its ploughlands or hides[2], of the freemen, villeins, cottars and slaves living on it, of its mills, fish-ponds, and plough-teams, the extent of its woodland, meadow and pasture – everything, in short, that was capable of being taxed. Originally drawn up on long parchment rolls stored in the Treasury at Winchester, the survey was copied into two volumes christened by the English 'Domesday' because there was no appeal against it. It was the most remarkable administrative document of the age; there is nothing like it in the contemporary annals of any other country. It enabled the King to know the landed wealth of his entire realm; 'how it was peopled and with what sort of men', what their rights were, and how much they were worth.

The taxation William imposed fell directly on the rich but, as the rich could pass it on, even more severely on the poor. The peasants' burdens, the labour and boon-services demanded of them by their lords, became heavier. The English thane, who had taken part of the village produce as his due and occasionally summoned its reluctant young men from the plough to serve in the ealdorman's levies, was supplanted by a Norman or Frenchman. There was a new face – and a new tongue spoken – at the manor house. It is never pleasant to have to pay taxes and rent. It is worse to have to pay them to a foreigner. And these foreigners were great sticklers for their rights. They left no one in any doubt that they were the masters of the country and regarded the natives as a conquered race. In those harsh years when Norman knight and English churl were learning uneasily to live together, many an English back must have smarted from the lash of a French man-at-arms. So must many a sullen English heart.

Behind the Norman knight's bailiff, with his bullying ways and grasping demands, was the castle which his master built to house his retainers and overawe the neighbourhood. Everywhere, on

[1] He employed a second body of commissioners to check the findings of the first. F. M. Stenton, *Anglo-Saxon England*, p. 609.

[2] Usually reckoned at about 120 acres, though its size varied in different parts of the country.

strategic hill and vantage point, the castles rose – little islands of foreign power in a subjected countryside: the high, circular, moated mound, raised by English labour and crowned by a wooden, and often later stone, keep or tower; the outer bailey with its earth-work enclosure and barracks, whence knights and men-at-arms rode forth to police and terrorise the countryside; the moat with its drawbridge. Even proud London was overawed by its Tower, begun in wood immediately after the Conquest and in stone a generation later. [1] The heavily armoured Norman retainers – *cnihtas* or knights, as the English called them – who garrisoned these strong-points, had the whip-hand of the countryside. A poor man, if he was to live and till the soil in peace, had to make what terms he could with them. Otherwise he might find his house burnt over his head, his wife and children driven into the woods, and himself thrown into a stinking dungeon.

*   *   *

Yet the Norman Conquest brought compensations to the underdog. William conquered more than the English. He used the heritage of Alfred to curb his own turbulent nobility. He brought feudalism under royal control. The stark King fastened his English version of the feudal system, with all his Norman thoroughness, on the free-booter barons and knights who had so long kept western Europe in an uproar with their selfish civil wars. It was this which completed the work that Alfred had begun. It made England a disciplined land, disciplined not only at the base but at the summit. A man could cross her, it was said, with his bosom full of gold.

By making England one, William saved her, too, from future conquests. He closed the door on the northern barbarians who had ravaged her for three centuries and who now withdrew into the Scandinavian mists. Twice during his reign the Danes were invited by rebellious subjects to land on the east coast, and twice were driven out with no profit to themselves and disastrous consequences to their sympathisers. Though, with Norsemen settled round her

[1] The White Tower, with its fifteen-feet thick walls, is the only surviving part built by the Conqueror. The words *castle* and *tower* both entered the English language at this time.

northern and western shores, Scotland still looked for another generation to the barbarian North, England ceased to be a frontier land between the Viking world and the reviving civilization of western Europe. Henceforth her lot lay with the lands which inherited the memories and traditions of Rome. Having under Canute been part of a Scandinavian empire spanning the North Sea, she became part of a Norman-French empire spanning the Channel.

Her military forces were now far more formidable than they had been even in the days of Athelstan. In open country the Norman knights on their war-horses were the masters of every field. Six years after his conquest of England, William invaded the lowlands of Scotland, whose king, Malcolm Canmore, had married the atheling's sister, Margaret. His mounted armour quickly reached the Tay, where he forced Malcolm to do homage and surrender his eldest son as a hostage. A later punitive force, following a Scottish raid into England, advanced as far as Falkirk and built a fortress on the Tyne called Newcastle to guard northern England.

The Welsh cattle-raiders learnt the same lesson. From the great border 'Marcher' earldoms of Hereford, Chester and Shrewsbury the Norman barons went out to seize strategic positions in every lowland valley, driving the natives into the hills. The kingdom of Gwent became Norman; so did Chepstow and Monmouth, Gower and Cardigan, Radnor and Brecknock, Montgomeryshire and the Vale of Clwyd. In all of them stone castles rose to dominate the countryside. Even in the far west beyond the mountains, the Marcher lords planted their power in the Pembrokeshire plain. Early in the twelfth century they settled it with English and Flemish farmers, so that it became known as 'little England'.

*   *   *

In a society so warlike and predatory, kingship called for rare qualities. An eleventh-century king had to appoint and dismiss his own officers, preside over councils and law courts, raise and lead armies and, if his realm was not to relapse into anarchy after his death, choose his successor and secure for him the loyalty of his lords. He had to hear and determine lawsuits, give judgments in person, and constantly travel the country both to preserve order and feed his court. An Anglo-Norman king had not only to do so in England but in Normandy, Brittany and Maine. Wherever he went, he was followed by throngs of suitors, seeking favours and redress of grievances. Even the poor English villeins used to surround William on his progresses, holding up their wooden ploughs to draw attention to their woes.

Above all, the King had to overawe the rough, half-barbaric warriors who surrounded him and on whom his power depended. When he wore his crown in public at the great annual Easter, Ascension and Christmas Feasts at Winchester, Westminster and Gloucester – ceremonies attended by the entire baronage – the peace of the realm turned on the majesty with which he spoke and moved. In days before even the greatest could read and write, formal pageantry – coloured, gilded robe, heraldic device on banner, shield and tent, splendid trappings for horse and throne, glittering arms and armour – were the medium through which the might of the State was expressed. So was the King's presence.

It was England's fortune that during the first centuries after the Conquest so many of her rulers possessed kingly qualities. William himself had tremendous presence. 'He was of moderate height,' wrote the historian, William of Malmesbury, 'immense corpulence, going rather bald in front; of such strength of arm . . . that no one could bend the bow which he drew when his horse was at full gallop. His dignity was of the highest, whether sitting or standing, despite the deformity of a protruding stomach.' It was because his able, tough, short-set, second son, William, had character too that the Conqueror on his deathbed in 1087 sent his English crown, sword and sceptre to him instead of to his weak, good-natured, eldest son, Robert of Normandy. 'Rufus', or the Red King, as he was called from his flaming hair, was a bad man – reckless, vicious, illiterate, cruel and blasphemous. But his English subjects, shocked though they were by his life, remembered with gratitude 'the good peace he kept in the land'. 'He was very strong and fierce to his country,' wrote one of them, 'and to all his neighbours and very terrible.' He feared, it was said, God little, and man not at all. When the Norman barons, who turned his eldest brother's duchy into an inferno, raised trouble in England, they got short shrift. He had his cousin, who was one of them, whipped in every church in Salisbury and hanged. And when he needed help against his stronger subjects, he did not hesitate to arm his weaker: his 'brave and honourable English', as he called them.

After William II's death in 1100 from a mysterious arrow in the New Forest, it was the English who enabled his successor, the Conqueror's youngest son, Henry, to wrest Normandy from his brother, Duke Robert. At the battle of Tinchebrai, forty years after Hastings, English infantry, fighting side by side with Anglo-Norman knights, overthrew the baronage of the duchy and annexed it to the English crown. They were trained by the King himself, who showed them how to repel cavalry. Though he was as grasping as his father, the English, whose despised tongue he learnt to speak, made a hero of Henry who, unlike his brothers, had been born in their land. His title to the throne being doubtful, he proclaimed his adherence to English law, swore in his coronation oath to maintain justice and mercy, and promised to 'abolish all the evil practices with which the realm was unjustly oppressed'. He claimed that he had been called to the throne in the old electoral way, 'by the common counsel of the barons of the realm'. Soon after his accession he married a daughter of the Scots king, who through her English mother was descended from Edmund Ironside and Alfred. In later years he loved a Welsh princess, Nest, wife of one of his Marcher barons, who helped him – ruler of a realm speaking three different languages – to understand not only his English subjects but his British.

Henry I, 'the Lion of Justice' as he was called, deserved his people's confidence. 'There was great awe of him,' testified the Anglo-Saxon chronicler; 'no man durst misdo against another in his time; he made peace for man and beast.' For thirty-five years this squat, avaricious, smooth-spoken man gave the English that political stability which those who have known anarchy value most. He was a tremendous worker, a man of business who could read Latin, understood the importance of administration, and introduced into government regular habits and routine. His father had given England a taxing system more accurate and honest than any in Europe; building on his foundations, Henry gave it a permanent officialdom. He made it out of the domestic officers of his household – the treasurer; the chamberlain who looked after the bedchamber; the constable of the knights and the marshal of the stables; the steward who presided in the hall where scores of ushers kept order with rods; the reverend Chancellor with his seal and writing-office – an innovation of the Confessor's – where writs were prepared for the sheriffs.

Henry, a particularly parsimonious man, kept these functionaries in the strictest economy. Their wages and 'liveries' of bread, wine and candles were meticulously laid down in the royal accounts. The Chancellor, the most highly paid of all – for he had to maintain a large staff of clerks – received five shillings daily, three loaves, one of the best quality and two less good, two measures of wine, a wax candle and forty candle-ends. He was also allowed two meals a day at the King's table. A humble official like the man who looked after the cloths in the pantry, only got three halfpence a day and his food; the ewerer had an extra penny a day when the King went on a journey – for drying his clothes – and threepence whenever he had a bath. The state baths before the three great feasts of the year, however, had to be provided free.

The greatest of all the royal servants, the Justiciar, who kept order when the King sat in judgment and deputised in his absence, became, in the person of Roger of Salisbury, a poor Norman priest whom Henry made a bishop[1], head of the national administration. He and his fellow officers formed a kind of inner standing court of the Great Council known as the *Curia Regis*, to which both judicial appeals and affairs of State were referred. With their staffs of trained clerks and chambers where suitors could wait on them, they were the first fathers of our civil service. In the great stone hall of Westminster, which Rufus raised over the marble bench where the English kings had done justice in the open air, public business continued even when the Court was travelling. Here twice a year,

[1] Chosen by Henry, it is said, because of the time-saving speed with which he read the offices in chapel.

under the chairmanship of King or Justiciar, officials called barons of the Exchequer sat at a table with counters and a chequered cloth, carefully checking with the sheriffs the taxes, rents, fines and debts due to the Crown. Every penny had to be accounted for. There was nothing else like it at the time in western Europe.

This capacity for organisation, for creating institutions which continued irrespective of great persons, made a deep impression on Henry's subjects. They admired the unhurried regularity and dignity with which he did business: his daily reception before the midday meal of all who came for justice, the sober recreation after it, the carefully planned arrangements for State progresses through his dominions. His influence was felt in every county, where the sheriffs were kept perpetually busy, receiving writs, making records and collecting the revenue under the eyes of the royal officers at Westminster.

*   *   *

After Henry's death in 1135 from a surfeit of hunting and lampreys, Englishmen again had an experience of life under a weak king. His only legitimate son having been drowned crossing the Channel, Henry had nominated as successor his daughter, the Empress Matilda, widow of the German emperor and wife of the Count of Anjou, Geoffrey Plantagenet – so called from the sprig of broom he wore in his helmet. But the Council, deeming a woman unfit to rule and exercising the old English right of election from the royal house, offered the crown instead to his nephew, Stephen of Blois, son of the Conqueror's daughter. This good-natured monarch lacked the qualities for kingship. 'A mild man, soft and good, and did not justice,' an English chronicler wrote of him. He 'began many things, but never finished them'. Though he reigned for nineteen years – 'nineteen long winters', the chronicler called them – he left little behind save a chapel at Westminster bearing his name and an abiding memory of the anarchy unloosed by his weakness. Taking advantage of his indecision, the Welsh descended from their mountains to sack farms on the Dee and Wye, and a savage horde from Scotland marched into England, massacring the inhabitants and driving off the women and girls as slaves, roped naked

78

together. It was only halted by the resolution of the aged archbishop of York – Thurstan, friend of St Bernard and founder of Fountains – who called out the *fyrd* of Yorkshire. Fighting under the banners of the north-country saints and led by a handful of Norman nobles – one of them named Bruce and another Balliol – the Yorkshiremen routed the invaders at the Battle of the Standard near Northallerton.

In 1139 Matilda, too, invaded the country from Anjou. For eight years England was racked by civil war, while local barons, playing their own selfish game, threw in their lot, first with one side, then the other. It was hard indeed for them to avoid doing so with two sovereigns claiming their allegiance. Freed from the control of the officials of the *Curia Regis*, the worst of them built castles from which they plundered their neighbours and indulged in all the licence – so familiar in Europe, but now almost forgotten in southern England – of private war. Some, like King Stephen himself, brought murderous foreign mercenaries into the country who turned royal fortresses of which they were custodians into private strongholds. In the Isle of Ely – the district that suffered most – the terrible Geoffrey de Mandeville – earl of Essex, made life a hell with his savage foreign soldiers. 'They put men in prison for their gold and silver, they hung them up by the feet and smoked them with foul smoke . . . They put knotted strings round their heads and writhed them till they went into the brain. They put them into dungeons crawling with adders and snakes. Men said that Christ and his saints slept.' The fields were untilled, the crops destroyed, the cattle driven away. On the continent such doings were normal. In England, after seventy years of strong rule and royal justice, they were not. The result was to create a universal longing among Englishmen and even among Norman knights and barons for the strong monarchical rule their fathers had enjoyed.

In the end the disorder was resolved by a compromise. It was agreed that Stephen should reign till his death and be succeeded by Matilda's twenty-year-old son, Henry Plantagenet, Count of Anjou. His father – the most powerful of all the independent vassals of the French king – had left Henry ruler, not only of Anjou, Maine and Touraine, but of Normandy, which he had conquered in Matilda's name. Six months after his accession the young count

79

doubled his dominions by marrying the gay divorced runaway queen of Louis of France, Eleanor of Aquitaine. Twelve years his senior and the greatest heiress in Europe, she brought him the fiefs of Gascony, Guienne, Poitou, Saintonge, Limousin, La Marche and Auvergne, and control of more than half France.

In the spring of 1153, Henry came to England to rally his mother's supporters. In a whirlwind campaign he transformed the military situation. That November at Winchester, amid tumultuous rejoicing, he was accepted by Stephen as his 'son' and heir. When, in 1154, on the King's death, he was crowned and invested at Westminster with the regalia of England – golden crown and sceptre, silver-gilt rod and spurs, embroidered sandals and mantle of white silk – every bell in London rang for joy.

CHAPTER SEVEN

The Lawyer King

'The King is under no man,
but he is under God and the Law'

Bracton

AT TWENTY-ONE Henry II was the richest prince in Europe. He was ruler not only of England and his native Anjou, but of Maine, Touraine and Normandy. His marriage with Eleanor of Aquitaine – the divorced wife of the French King and the greatest heiress of the age – had made him master of south-western France. He was well-read, eloquent, courteous, a lover of learned conversation and a good linguist.

Yet he was as at home in the field as at court, indifferent to hardships and never happier than when jesting with rude soldiers round a camp fire. His short, homely cloak and frugal meals were a by-word; when he cut his finger he sewed it up with his own needle. He bore the press of suitors that surrounded a medieval king with cheerful good-humour; even when vexed by importunity, he let the crowd bear him from place to place while he listened patiently to every man's case. With his round head and eager, freckled face, his sandy, close-cropped hair contrasting with the effeminate locks of the nobles and troubadours of his wife's glittering court, his squat, sturdy frame and long boxer's arms, he looked rather like a good-natured lion; affable, modest and open to all.

Beneath these winning attributes lay a steely will, determination to achieve his ends and tireless industry. 'In night-watches and labours,' wrote one of his secretaries, 'he was unremitting.'

He never forgot a face or a lesson. He was as businesslike and methodical as his grandfather. And like him he was adamant in reducing his affairs to order. Those who opposed him were met with unrelenting, unscrupulous resolution. Beneath his urbane manner ran the diabolical temper of the Angevins; there were times when he tore off his clothes in rage and gnawed the straw from his mattresses. 'From the devil we come,' boasted one of his sons, 'and to the devil we shall go!' Yet in Henry, as in them all, ferocity and subtlety were deceptively mingled. And in him, both were subjected to a strong commonsense and prudence.

The greatest master of diplomacy of the age, he liked to settle accounts without bloodshed. Swift to strike, unrelenting in pursuit, he was in victory unusually merciful and magnanimous. He preferred mutilation as a punishment to death and a fine to either. For an avaricious man he was even moderate in fining. And, though he gave his heart to none save his undeserving sons, he was seldom cruel or vindictive. He made enemies, as all who reform with passion must; his vitality drove both his wife and children to rebellion.

Yet those who worked with Henry loved him. The praises of his judges and Exchequer officials were founded on more than flattery. For his devotion to their common task – the creation of order in his kingdom's affairs – was the consuming passion of his life.

At the core of his being lay a daemonic energy. He was always moving, always active, and so restless that even in chapel he chattered and scribbled incessantly. He rose before cock-crow, and only sat down to ride or eat. Slaving like his grandfather far into the night over public business, he shared the passion of all the Conqueror's line for the chase; on his journeys he hunted and hawked along every stream. He never brooked or wasted a minute's delay.

As soon as he ascended the throne this restless genius began, with furious energy, to restore his kingdom. He sent away the foreign mercenaries, dismantled the unlicensed castles, and demanded back the filched Crown lands. When the earls his mother and Stephen had created ignored his writs, he marched against them, scaring the Midland magnate, Peverel of the Peak, into a monastery, and making the great Marcher lord, Hugh de Mortimer, yield up his castles of Bridgnorth, Cleobury and Wigmore. Having restored order in England, he turned against the Welsh princes and Scottish king. He chased the former back to their mountains, and made the latter restore the shires of Northumberland, Westmorland and Cumberland taken during the troubles of Stephen's reign, and do homage at Chester. After which, in the autumn of 1158, this tireless man set out for France to apply, from the Vexin to Toulouse, the same treatment to his own and his wife's continental vassals.

Yet Henry was too shrewd to suppose that much could be won by war. Dominion had come to him so early that conquest made little appeal. What he wanted was to consolidate his possessions and make them a reality instead of, as with other medieval empires, a shadow. He was a realist. The campaigns he fought were either to repress rebellion or secure his frontiers. His reduction of Brittany was to safeguard the long, narrow corridor of his French provinces; his chastening of the Welsh and Scots to save the English Marches from raiding and rapine.

Most of all, he sought to make his rule endure. It is this that constitutes his claim to greatness. The supreme object of his crowded, stormy life was to create institutions which could preserve his inheritance after his death from the disintegrating forces threatening it. The chief of these was the power that had made it; military feudalism. In the hands of a ruler like the Conqueror or Henry I, feudalism gave strength and security to a nation. Under a weak one, like Stephen, its dynamic of self-interest could tear the State to pieces. It was not enough, Henry saw, to discipline it during his lifetime. He had to leave the means of doing so to his successors.

Yet feudalism was an inherent part of society. It could only be destroyed by destroying society itself. In England it was the mainstay of the foreign monarchy. Every earl, baron and knight, as well as being a leader and organiser of the local community, was a trained fighting man, dedicated to arms from boyhood and ready for instant war. He had to be able to leap fully armed into the saddle without touching the stirrups, to wield lance, sword and shield, to wear all day without tiring the heavy armour of his caste. This grew ever more elaborate, and the knight's advantage in battle correspondingly greater. By now even his face was completely covered by a ponderous visor, which let down like a castle portcullis and which, after being dented in action, had to be hammered off his head at the nearest smithy.

The members of this warlike caste, who viewed everyone else with contempt, had two interests: fighting and landed property. They thought of them as synonymous, for each sustained the other. They fought for land, not only under their liege-lords on the battlefield, but in the feudal courts of law, where the sole process for determining ownership was trial-by-battle. If a man was not fit to fight for land, the knightly class felt, he was not fit to own it. His only resource was to hire or enfeoff a young knight or champion to fight for him.

The knight's goal – the end of all his prowess – was the fief. The price of a fief was feudal loyalty. And the chief point of honour with most of the hard-bitten men who lived by knighthood was fidelity to the overlord who had enfeoffed them. Every great lord kept his court of armed vassals – 'all his barons and men French and English', as one charter put it – his courtiers and officials, marshal and constable, treasurer, seneschal and chamberlain, dapifer, dispenser and butler. The principal seat of his honour, like Castle Acre in Norfolk with its hundred knights' fees or Pleschey in Essex, was a capital in miniature. At Bridgnorth, Robert de Bellême housed a thousand knights and retainers in the castle; the palatine earls of Chester dispensed open hospitality all the year round, with feasting, sport and minstrelsy. The great feudal lord sat enthroned in his court like a king, with his tenants-in-chief below him, his 'barons' on one side and abbots on the other, ready, like the peers of the realm, to give him aid and counsel, witness his charters and adjudicate disputes.

In France, where his feudatories could evoke against him his own overlord – the French king – Henry was never really able to discipline such magnates. He was one himself. But in England his grandfather and the Conqueror had already curbed their power.

They were still what the Norman kings had made them, part of the realm. For all their retainers, imposing armour and battle-horses, they shrank from war against their acknowledged sovereign. Perhaps it was because they knew that the English people, who ploughed their fields and served as infantry in the *fyrd*, were on his side; perhaps there was something unsympathetic to lawlessness and blood-letting in the very air of the island. Even the tournament – that substitute for private war, in which fully-armed knights jousted, often to the death, for horses, armour and ransoms – was regarded with disfavour in this peaceful realm. Compared with the glittering bloody pastime it had become in chivalric France, it was so tame an affair that many young Anglo-Norman knights took service under some continental duke or count who could show them proper sport. Only in a few places did the English civil war degenerate into the ferocious, town-sacking, village-burning slaughter habitual abroad. When Stephen was barred out of his castle of Newbury by his own marshal, instead of hanging the latter's little son, who had been left with him as a hostage, or catapulting him as he was urged to do into the defiant fortress, he had merely paraded him under a tree in view of the battlements and then carried him back to his camp. He had refused even to gouge his eyes out. A few days later he was seen outside his tent playing conkers with the boy.

It was this gentler strain in English feudalism which enabled Henry to disarm his barons so quickly. So long as he respected their just rights and avoided violence, he knew they were unlikely to combine against him. Having got rid of their mercenaries and unlicensed castles, he subjected them, like his grandfather, to fiscal discipline. He recalled to their old work of punishing infringements of royal rights the Exchequer officials whom the latter had trained. At their head he placed his Treasurer, Nigel of Ely – nephew of the great Roger of Salisbury, gratefully remembered as 'that man of prudence, far-sighted in counsel, eloquent in discourse and, by the grace of God, remarkably qualified to deal with great affairs'.

The methods of these watchdogs were described in the *Dialogue of the Exchequer*, written by Nigel's son, Richard FitzNeal.

Its guiding principle – still enshrined in Treasury practice – was 'devotion to the King's interests with a single mind, due regard being paid to equity'. In its pages we can watch the presiding Justiciar, with the Treasurer, Chancellor and barons of the Exchequer, sitting on the covered benches round the black-and-white squared table, as each sheriff presented his accounts, and the official calculator, as in some gigantic chess-match, moved the piles of coins or counters that represented money. We see the humbler officials of the Lower Exchequer – silverer, melter, ushers, chamberlains and tellers – receiving and weighing the cash, and sometimes assaying or 'blanching' it in the furnace, while the tally-cutter notches and splits the wooden tallys which serve for receipts. And we can still read the Latin entries on the sheep-skin pipe-rolls on which were recorded the state of the sheriff's annual account with the Exchequer, the debts due to the Crown, the farms and rents of the royal estates and woods, the legal fines, the escheats of those whose fiefs had become vacant, and the year's feudal reliefs and tallages. Among the latter was a war-tax on knights' fees called scutage or shield-money, initiated earlier to meet the case of ecclesiastical tenants unable to serve in the field and which Henry adapted to give lay tenants, too, an alternative to accompanying him on his foreign campaigns.

For the field in which Henry mastered his barons was not that of arms but law. At the time of his accession there were at least four different systems of jurisdiction in England. There were the great franchises of the baronial honours, and the village manorial courts, both the private property of their lords. There were the old Anglo-Saxon public courts of shire and hundred, presided over by the sheriff – nominally a royal officer, but in practice a local magnate who farmed their profits and taxes of the county and who, during Stephen's lax rule, had often encroached on the Crown's rights and, in some cases, even tried to make his office hereditary. And there was the King himself, who not only sat in his *Curia Regis* as supreme feudal overlord but, as successor of the athelings, was the traditional fount of national justice.

Henry first sought control of the shire and hundred courts. He revived his grandfather's practice of sending out Exchequer barons on circuit to sit beside the sheriffs and enforce his fiscal rights. Before long he had made these progresses annual events. And since there was then little distinction between the profits of jurisdiction and jurisdiction itself, he empowered his officers, not only to look into revenue matters but to hear and try local pleas of the Crown. To these he added offences which had hitherto been dealt with by the sheriffs. By two assizes or royal councils – one held at the Wiltshire hunting palace of Clarendon in 1166 and the other ten years later at Northampton – trials of murder, robbery, larceny, rape, forgery, arson and harbouring criminals were reserved to the justices *in eyre*. The criminal jurisdiction of the Crown – formerly confined to *lèse majesté* and breaches of the King's Peace on the royal domains and highways – was made nation-wide, and the sheriffs' chief judicial powers transferred to officers under the sovereign's eye.

These Henry chose carefully for their loyalty and impartiality and, as he and they gained experience, for knowledge of the law. At first he had to rely on bishops, Exchequer officials and minor barons temporarily executing judicial commissions. But by experiment he gradually created a body of trained judges whose business it was 'to do justice habitually'. Some were clerics, others laymen, but all were drawn from the lesser Anglo-Norman families whom he used as a counterpoise to the great feudal magnates. They were assigned to six, and later four, regular circuits of counties, round which, escorted by sheriffs and javelin men, they rode on annual progresses. Others, sitting on the royal bench in Westminster Hall, formed a permanent judicial tribunal of the *Curia Regis*, which later grew into the courts of King's Bench and Common Pleas. One of its members, Ranulf de Glanvill – or, possibly, his clerk, Hubert Walter, who succeeded him as Justiciar – wrote the nation's first legal classic, a Latin treatise on the laws and customs of England and the procedure of the royal courts.

It was through such procedure that Henry traversed the power of the feudal jurisdictions. One of the commonest sources of disorder during the civil wars of Stephen's reign had been the baronial habit of forcibly seizing land on some trumped-up excuse. The victim had two alternatives: to counter-attack with like force, if he could command it, or to appeal to his overlord's court to the only process recognised there, trial-by-battle. In this, whether fought by the principals or by professional champions, victory almost invariably went to the strongest and richest, the largest purses securing the longest lance.

By adapting the old English principle – enshrined in the coronation oath – that it was the King's duty to see that justice was done and that every freeman had a right of appeal to him, Henry and his judges devised writs or royal commands restoring possession to any freeman forcibly dispossessed of his land. They offered these for sale to all, Norman and English alike, whose tenures were free from servile services: to all, that is 'free to go with their land where they would'. A writ of summons called *praecipe* directed the sheriff to order the overlord of any land seized to restore it immediately or answer for his failure in the royal court. Another called *novel disseisin* commanded him to reinstate any dispossessed freeholder pending trial and summon 'twelve free and lawful men of the neighbourhood' to 'recognise' and declare, under oath before the King's judges, to whom its possession had belonged. A later writ called *mort d'ancestor* similarly protected the peaceful possession of a freeholder's heir against all claimants not able to prove a superior right in the royal courts.

These possessory writs, as they were called, had three effects. They protected a man's right to possession as distinct from his legal ownership – a matter which might otherwise be disputed for ever. They made everyone with a claim to a freehold plead it, not in the court of the feudal overlord, who was powerless against a royal writ, but in the King's. And, through the procedure laid down for investigating such claims, they substituted for the barbarous custom of proof-by-battle a sworn inquest or 'recognition' by 'twelve free and lawful men of the neighbourhood', summoned by the sheriff to 'recognise' with whom the disputed possession lay.

These 'recognitors' or jurymen were not the doomsmen of the old formalistic English law, swearing in support of a neighbour's oath. Nor were they necessarily witnesses to acts that had happened under their eyes. They were men of substance assembled to answer questions of common knowledge put to them under oath by the King's judges. The Conqueror had used such inquisitions for fiscal purposes. His great-grandson used them for judicial. It is immaterial whether they derived, as some think, from a long-disused device of Charlemagne's from that of the twelve thanes of the Anglo–Danish wapentake swearing to accuse no innocent man and conceal no guilty one. What matters is that, imposed by the royal prerogative, they were at once accepted in a country where presentment and judgment by a man's neighbours had been part of popular law from time immemorial. Through the ingenuity and good sense of this strong, subtle-minded and original ruler, the corporate conscience of a group of neighbours, acquainted with the persons and facts involved and sworn to speak the truth, was substituted for the unpredictable arbitrament of battle. It seemed a more sensible way of ascertaining God's will, in other words the truth. And it was certainly a better way – and this may have appealed even more strongly to Henry – of keeping the peace.

The same procedure was extended to actions to determine legal ownership. By a process called the grand assize a freeholder whose title was challenged could decline trial-by-battle in his overlord's court and, opting for a trial in the King's, put himself 'upon the testimony of the country'. In this, twelve knights of the shire declared in the presence of the royal judges which of the litigating parties had the better right. Once determined, such recognition by grand assize was final. 'So effectively does this procedure,' wrote Glanvill, 'preserve the lives and the civil condition of men that every man may now legally retain possession of his freehold and at the same time avoid the doubtful event of the duel.'

Through these writs – 'infinitely diversified for different causes' – Henry achieved a major and peaceful revolution. He did so under the guise of restoring 'the good old laws'. Appealing to native English tradition, he used the prerogative to bring the whole system of freehold tenure under national law. By making the smaller landowner's right to his property dependent on the royal instead of the feudal courts, he struck at the root of the great lord's power over his military tenants. And he dealt a death-blow to trial-by-battle and private war. He did not abolish the feudal courts and their processes; like the lesser, and very active, private manorial courts they survived for centuries. He merely drove them out of such business as imperilled the unity and safety of the State by offering their clients cheaper, surer and quicker justice in the royal courts. His writs attracted to the latter an ever-growing volume of litigation and revenue. 'The convincing proof of our King's strength and justice,' wrote a grateful subject, 'is that whoever has a just cause wants to have it tried before him.'

Henry's enemies – the great and strong – complained that he wore out their patience with his perpetual assizes and cunning legal formulas: his 'mousetraps', as one of them called them. His justification, in Richard Fitzneal's words, was that 'he spared the poor both labour and expense'. Selfish, crafty, unscrupulous, the great lawyer-king wielded the sword of justice 'for the punishment of evil-doers and the maintenance of peace and quiet for honest men'. His judges made his remedies available in every corner of the realm. With the precedents they enshrined in their judgments, they little by little created a common law for all England. Even that of the shire and hundred courts had varied from district to district; Kent, Wessex, Mercia, the Danelaw, London and the Celtic West had all had their separate customs and practices. Henry's judges established the same system for north, south, east and west, for town and country, for Norman and Englishman. They nationalised, as it were, the law.

In doing so they drew from the principles which Italian jurists had recently rediscovered in the great legal codes left behind six centuries before by the Byzantine Emperor Justinian. But, while the continental lawyers who studied Roman jurisprudence in the new universities of Bologna and Paris had little chance of applying it except in the church courts, law in England, thanks to Henry's triumph over the feudal jurisdictions, was no academic study confined to learned doctors and pursued only in palace courts, but a practical, day-to-day business affecting the whole nation. However much they might admire the logical maxims of imperial Rome, Henry's judges had to administer the kind of law to which ordinary Englishmen were accustomed. In their judgments, based on the decisions of their predecessors, they embodied from popular and local custom whatever seemed compatible with a common national system.

The growth of such case-law, as it was called, was a two-way process. It was not merely imposed from above but grew from below. It was, above all, a collaboration between professional judges stating the law and laymen, drawn from different classes of society, deciding questions of fact. The classic example, pregnant with far-reaching consequences for the future of England and the ocean nations which sprang from her, was the use in criminal jurisdiction of the old Anglo-Saxon principle of enlisting local worthies to sift local accusations. The assize of Clarendon directed the itinerant judges to enquire of twelve 'lawful' men from every hundred, and four from every township, whether any of their neighbours were reputed to have committed felony. Only those so presented were to be put upon their trial. So resolved was Henry to stamp out the violence unloosed by civil war and such the weight he attached to the verdicts of these local worthies that, even when those they accused were proved innocent by the customary 'judgement of God' or trial by water, they were banished the realm.

This principle of allowing representatives of the neighbourhood to decide questions of fact in criminal law was applied to the trials not only of Englishmen but of Normans. So was the rule – unknown to ancient Rome – that every case should be tried in public, as in the presence of the Anglo-Saxon tribe. The secret tribunal, that instrument of imperial tyranny, was never allowed a lodgment in English Common Law.

When, long afterwards, the kings of other lands brought the feudal jurisdictions under their control, the authoritarian maxims of Roman civil and canon law, deeply rooted in the minds of continental royal lawyers, often became instruments of despotism. In England, where law was founded on popular custom and the open participation of the ordinary man in its processes, it proved a bulwark of public and private liberties.

Henry's achievement was far in advance of his age. No other ruler could offer his people such a system of national justice. By the end of his reign there was no major offence against the public peace which could not bring the offender within range of a royal writ. Even the killing and maiming of villains and cottars were punished by his courts. Within five years of his death an ordinance of his greatest disciple, Hubert Walter, the Justiciar, created in every county officials called coroners to hold inquests on all sudden and suspicious deaths.

All this prepared the way for the rule of law which was to become the dominant trait in England's life. Henceforward, whoever gave law to her was to have a machinery by which it could be enforced – against the strong as well as the weak. The professional judges Henry trained, the regular courts in which they sat, the writs they devised to meet popular needs, and the judgments they left behind to guide their successors, helped to ensure that justice should be done even in the royal absence or in the reign of a weak or unjust sovereign. By making the Common Law the permanent embodiment of a righteous King sitting in judgment, the great Angevin established the English habit of obedience to law which was to prove the strongest of all the forces making for the nation's peaceful continuity and progress.

CHAPTER EIGHT

Bell, Book and Candle

'There is no power but of God;
the powers that be are ordained of God.'

St Paul

IN TRYING TO SUBJECT every part of the nation's life to the law the
great Plantagenet fell foul of the one power which in that age no
prince could safely challenge – the Church with its hold on
Christian hearts and imaginations. By doing so he suffered a
defeat which impressed his contemporaries more than all his
legal triumphs.

For even the proudest kings – born to the purple and gold,
riding in glittering armour to the sound of trumpets, feasting and
hunting and giving law – were members of Christ's universal
Church. '*Non nobis, Domine!*' they heard their priests chant, 'Not
unto us, O Lord, but unto Thee the power and the glory!' Behind
their crowns and sceptres lay the memory of the 'mocking reed and
crown of thorns'. They acknowledged a faith which proclaimed
that whoever exalted himself should be humbled, bade the rich
give to the poor and men be brothers to one another. When sickness
came and death threatened – and death was never far from the
filthy disease-haunted towns and villages of the Middle Ages –
even the strongest trembled. It was at such times that princes,
barons and rich merchants made gifts to the Church – to endow
abbeys, schools and hospitals, to teach the young and nurse the
sick, to pay monks and priests to offer prayers for their souls and
intercede for them. So when the Conqueror lay dying, remembering the rivers of blood he had shed, he 'hastened to make provision

93

for the future welfare of himself and others, ordering all his treasures to be distributed among the churches, the poor and the ministers of God'. Even his vicious, braggart son, Rufus, who 'kept down God's Church' and blasphemed against every hallowed belief, became a craven when death threatened, crying for the saintly monk Anselm whom he had so long refused to install as archbishop in order that he might retain for himself the revenues of Canterbury. For without the Church's intercession, it was believed, there was no escape from the powers of evil and the eternal torments over which they presided. The greatest ruler and poorest peasant thought the air was full of fiends, that the Devil lay in wait to cast men into hell-fire, that the sole hope of salvation lay in the prayers and services of those ordained of God. Into the hands of their supreme head, the Pope or Bishop of Rome, had been given, it was supposed, the keys of Heaven and Hell.

The God in whom half-heathen medieval man believed was an intensely personal God, forever appearing in acts of nature, visions and apparitions, plagues and cures, storms, fires and miracles. And not only God, but the whole hierarchy of Heaven, angels and saints, apostles and martyrs, lay on the frontiers of the visible, tangible world, ready at any moment to reveal themselves. So did the Devil and his fiends, witches and ministers of evil. A flight of crows could seem a swarm of demons come to fetch the soul of a usurer, the howling of the wind the cries of some wicked lord borne through the middle air to Hell. When Henry I granted the abbey of Peterborough to a simoniac – a notorious purchaser of Church preferments – the country folk throughout the Fens believed they heard horns blowing in the night and saw hunters, 'black and big and loathsome', riding in the woods with satanic hounds. At a time when men knew little of the laws of nature or the world outside their village homes, they accepted such tales with no more question than their twentieth-century descendants the latest scientific marvels.

Behind all this superstition lay a conception shared by rich and poor alike, educated and ignorant. It was that the universe, from its greatest to its minutest part, was governed by divine law. Everything that happened in the world – that had happened, was happening, or was going to happen – was part of the same majestic rule, only partly intelligible to man's puny intellect. All that lay within his power was either, at the instigation of the Devil, to neglect or oppose that law or, with Christ's grace and the guidance and intercession of His Holy Church, to further it. The Church existed to explain it, to help man obey it and, through Christ's love and sacrifice, to obtain forgiveness for him when he broke it.

And the Church existed for everyone. Alone in a world of in-equalities it opened its doors to all. It was not merely for certain families or tribes, for kings and landowners, for the successful or learned. It was for fools and failures, for the weak and sick, for women and children, for prisoners and paupers, for saints and sinners. Two things bound the whole of Christendom: belief in Christ and membership of His Church.

It was this universal quality which made its appeal so over-whelming. It gave purpose and significance to every life. The priest praying for souls, the king doing justice, the knight fighting the infidel and invader, the peasant working in the fields, the woman rearing children, the artist and craftsman glorifying creation, all were members of one body and in God's eyes equally important. And it was the Church which united the members of this great family, dead, living and unborn, interceded for their sins and helped them to everlasting bliss. Within the wide limits of human frailty – for which the Church made full allowance – medieval man relied on its guidance at every point. There was a place in its creed and ritual for everyone and everything.

Everywhere, in a still half-barbaric and primitive western Europe, man was confronted by the majesty of the Church. He could not read a book that churchmen had not written and copied by hand; unless he was himself a churchman trained by church-men, he almost certainly could not read at all. When most people lived in huts little bigger or cleaner than pigsties, the Church's buildings towered above the landscape, and blazed within with colours, jewels and vestments. For the Church did not teach only by its prayers and sermons. Through stone and wooden panel, altar-piece and reredos, painting, glass and embroidery, it depicted the Nativity or the Adoration of the Shepherds, St Michael leading the heavenly host or St George slaying the dragon, the Lamb of God or the flowering Tree of Jesse. In a thousand forms it illuminated the lives of saints and apostles, martyrs and prophets; the clash between Virtue and Evil, Truth drawing the tongue of Falsehood or Sobriety dosing Drunkenness over the door of the Chapter House at Salisbury, the devils carting the souls of the damned to Hell in rustic wheelbarrows whose colours still blaze down from the great fifteenth century window of Fairford church in Gloucestershire. So too the lovely and dramatic ritual of its services helped to shape the imagination of every man, rich and poor, in Christendom. On Good Friday, the crucifix was taken from the altar and hidden in a curtained wall called the Easter sepulchre, from which on Easter morning it was borne in triumphant procession before the rejoicing congregation. The poorest peasant took part, as actor and audience, in the never-ceasing pageantry, drama and music with which, in even the remotest village, the Church invested the changing year. His holidays or 'holy days', were its feasts; his daily work was performed against the familiar background of religious intercession and rejoicing, prayer and ceremony.

Everything medieval man did was blessed or cursed, approved or disapproved, explained and solemnised by the Church. He was baptised by it, married by it, buried by it. He went into battle calling on its saints to aid his arms; he sought a cure for all his ills at its martyrs' shrines or in its holy waters and wells; he made his oaths on its sacred relics. Its superstitions, often touchingly beautiful, were part of his daily life. He prayed before the painted images of its saints and angels for help, comfort and forgiveness. The bells rang, and the familiar gargoyles grinned from the village church tower to guard him from demon or storm; he brought his corn to be blessed at its altars and, repeating its hallowed Latin incantations, danced round his apple trees to make them fruitful. The very oxen of the fields, he believed, knelt in the byres on Christmas night in remembrance of the manger birth.

The Church not only controlled men's minds and imaginations. It enjoyed immense wealth. It commanded in every country a host, not of warriors, but of men and women vowed to its service. They ranged from scarlet-robed cardinals and mitred archbishops to humble parish clerks, bell-ringers and church-sweepers – members of the Minor Orders as they were called; from judges, lawyers and physicians to the poor ragged students who begged and sang their way along the roads of Europe to hear the Church's famous doctors lecture on theology and canon law in its cathedral schools and universities. In its heyday in the twelfth and thirteenth centuries, it has been reckoned, one out of every thirty adult males in western Europe was a cleric of some kind.

The flower of this vast army were the 'regulars', the monks and nuns who had forsworn the world and embraced that of God, living in disciplined communities under rules or orders stricter than those of any other existing society, military or civil. In hundreds of monasteries and convents in every land these dedicated men and women followed a life of routine whose end was Christ's worship and the service of His Church. They rose from their pallets in the dormitories an hour or two after midnight to troop down cold corridors to celebrate Matins and Lauds in chapel; assembled in the chapter-house for admonition or punishment and to discuss the business of the day; dined in silence in the refectory, where the officers and their guests sat in state on the dais and the monks at long tables below, as in an Oxford college today, while one of the brethren read aloud a Latin homily; laboured in the monastic fields, gardens and workshops, or copied and illuminated books in the scriptorium, whose desks looked through unglazed arches on to the grass garth of the cloisters; taught the novices and prescribed to the sick until the hour of Vespers recalled them once more to their devotions. From the first moment of the day to the last when Compline was sung before they withdrew at dusk to their dormitories, their lives were ordered by the chapel bell – a sound familiar in every corner of Christendom.

It would be hard to exaggerate the part played by the monastic houses in forming the character of English and European institutions. They were the centres and creators of civilization, and the principal meeting places of learned men. Our schools, universities and charitable foundations have all grown out of their rules and ordered life. The names of their officers still survive in our collegiate bodies: the precentor in charge of the music, services and books, the chamberlain of the clothing and bedding, the sacristan of the church fabric and sacred vessels, the cellarer of the provisioning and the bursar of the finances, the infirmarer of the hospital, the almoner of the charities. In that simple rustic world there was nothing to compare with these establishments; their chapter-houses, dormitories and guest-houses; their libraries, workshops, kitchens, butteries, bakehouses, breweries, laundries and dairies; their granges, barns, fish-ponds, orchards, vineyards and gardens, their water-pipes, drains and filter-tanks. Far in advance of the richest layman they possessed even lavatories with long stone or marble washing-troughs, brass water-cocks and towels. And in their infirmaries, where the monks were periodically bled, bath-houses were provided for bathing the sick and aged and, before the great Christian feasts, the entire chapter.

During the eleventh and twelfth centuries, the wealth of the greater monasteries grew with every generation. In the magnificent services held at their shrines – the chief events of the medieval year – offerings were showered on them by multitudes of deeply moved Christians. Most visitors left donations with the houses which sheltered them; every rich man wished to win prestige on earth and a friend in Heaven by some gift or legacy to the saint or martyr commemorated by the local shrine; blessed Alban or Edmund, Peter or Paul, or the tender, merciful Virgin. In men's minds the monasteries were personally identified with these divine person-ages. Their jewelled shrines and crosses, golden and silver vessels and candlesticks, silken and embroidered altar-cloths, chasubles and dalmatics, their rare books bound in gold, and the hallowed relics brought from afar by visiting kings and princes were the glory of neighbourhood and kingdom. Their wealth was im-mense. An abbey like St Albans or Bury St Edmunds might have estates in a dozen counties. Its officers were constantly travelling to collect its rents and dues. Every fortnight Ramsey drew, from the village whose turn had come to supply its kitchens, twelve quarters of flour for the monks' and guests' bread, two thousand loaves for its servants, ten fat pigs, fourteen lambs, one hundred and twenty hens, two thousand eggs, and vast quantities of malt, honey, lard, cheese, butter, beans and horse-fodder.

The abbot of a major monastic house was a prince of the Church, ruler of a famous society, and lord and administrator of a vast property. He sat in the Great Council of the realm, and presided over the feudal court of the abbey's barons, knights and freeholders. He played a leading part in the political, economic and social life of the neighbourhood, and acted as a judge in a wide range of secular affairs. And, like the monastery itself, he had to provide hospitality for a constant succession of travellers, including the King himself. In days when there were no hotels, newspapers or posts, the monasteries, with their international organisation, were the chief means of communicating news, learning, crafts and discoveries. They provided the schools, hospitals and libraries of the age. Most of the larger abbeys maintained a succession of historiographers who compiled elaborate, if somewhat inaccurate, chronicles of their times; William of Malmesbury, Florence of Worcester, Eadmer and Gervase of Canterbury, and the two thirteenth-century chroniclers of St Albans, Roger of Wendover and Matthew Paris, are among the fathers of English history. And from their cloisters the Christian kings, who were slowly creating England and the other infant States of Europe, drew officers trained in regular habits of routine, business and accountancy and, still more important, in ideals of public service. The monastic officers were called 'obedientiaries'; they commanded because they obeyed. Nowhere else could those who had to keep order over large areas find men so fit for their business. For the Church offered a far wider choice of trained servants than the feudal families whose sons were usually taught only to hunt and fight. Through its hierarchy unaccounted men could rise to the proudest posts in Christendom: could become bishops and abbots, justiciars, chancellors and royal ministers. So the great statesman, Suger, who, as minister to two kings, laid the foundations of French monarchial power in the second quarter of the twelfth century, began his career as an acolyte, serving the altar of the monastery for which his father had worked as a serf. His contemporary Adrian IV – the only Englishman ever to become Pope – had begged his boyhood's bread at the gates of St Albans abbey.

The Norman conquest had coincided with a monastic revival

throughout western Europe. During the next half-century, not only were the older Benedictine houses in southern England revitalised by the French and Italian abbots whom the Conqueror imported from the Cluniac foundations on the continent and the monastic schools of Normandy but, for the first time since the Danish invasions, monasteries had reappeared after a lapse of two hundred years in the ravaged lands beyond the Humber. In the second decade of William's reign a Norman prior and two English monks from the abbeys of Winchcombe and Evesham set out on foot for the north, with a donkey laden with sacred books and vestments, to restore the tradition of Aidan and Bede in ravaged Northumbria. Two great abbeys, St Mary's at York and St Cuthbert's at Durham, sprang from this act of faith.

But the real revival of monastic life in the north had occurred in the reign of Henry I with the coming of the Cistercians. The splendour, wealth and magnificent ritual of the Benedictine houses, even after the Cluniac reforms, left the more austere spirits of the age unsatisfied, and a movement began in France to restore the simplicity and poverty of early monastic rule.

In 1128 the first Cistercian house in England had been founded at Waverley in Surrey. But it was among the desolate Yorkshire hills and the remote valleys of the Welsh Marshes that the Order made its chief settlements. It was part of its Rule that its monks should live far from the haunts of men, in silence and austerity, and support themselves by their own labour. Even their rough homespun woollen tunics and cowls were undyed, giving them their name of white monks in contrast to the black monks of the older Rule. Their simplicity of life and love of solitude and country pursuits made a deep appeal to the English. By the end of Stephen's reign, there were twenty Cistercian monasteries in Yorkshire alone, and forty in the kingdom. Fountains, founded in 1132 on waste ground in Skeldale by a dozen pioneers from St Mary's, York, grew from a few huts under an elm tree into the great abbey of St Mary's. Rievaulx, Jervaux, Byland and Kirkstall, Tintern, Valle Crucis, Neath, Abbey Dore and Margam, raised in the twelfth and rebuilt in the thirteenth and fourteenth centuries, were among the grandest achievements of the Middle Ages. Bare now of ornament, sculpture and painting, their grave, simple outlines have still the power, even in ruin, to stir the heart. Equally impressive were the woods the monks planted round their homes, and the sheep-runs the lay brethern or *conversi* – drawn from the peasant class – made on the bleak northern and western hills. They were the most enlightened landlords and finest farmers of the age, sowing alternate corn and grass leys and transforming scrubby wilderness with flocks that grazed by day on the uplands and folded at night on the barley ploughlands. Theirs was an instinctive genius for blending the works of God and man; in the Great Coxwell barn in Berkshire we can still see the reverence and skill with which they turned nature to human ends while enriching and beautifying it. *Laborare est orare* was their founder's motto: to work is to pray. They built roads and bridges, drained marshes and planted trees, quarried stone, wrought in wood and metal, laid out gardens and vineyards, and bred fine horses, cattle and sheep. To them England owed the noble Lion breed whose golden hoof raised the Cotswold towns and villages. They made her wool as famous as their brother monks of Cîteaux made the vineyards of the stony Côte d'Or. And if the great names of Chambertin and Clos de Vougeot still recall for lovers of wine the skill of the French Cistercians, their brethren in England are commemorated by the homely cheese which the monks of Jervaux made from ewe's milk in lonely Wensleydale.

Nothing gives a clearer idea of the might of the medieval Church than to stand in one of the cathedrals, still towering above the roofs of modern towns, which were first raised as monastic churches. They express the universal sense of the all-importance of religion and the soaring imagination and practical genius of men who had mastered the lost Roman art of vaulting great spaces in stone. Most of them were originally built on the site of smaller Saxon churches by English masons in the massive Norman style under the prelates whom the Conqueror imported from Normandy, and rebuilt in a still more ambitious style under their successors in the later twelfth and early thirteenth centuries. Canterbury, whose choir the Conqueror's Archbishop Lanfranc started to build with Caen stone in 1072; Rochester begun seven years later; Gloucester in 1080; Ely with its magnificent nave in

1083; Worcester in 1084; and the incomparable Durham in 1093, with its ribbed vaulting – the earliest of its kind in Europe – and its still surviving Norman nave and choir; Norwich, Winchester, Coventry, Carlisle and Chester – were all originally made for monks. So were the abbey churches of St Albans – built partly from Roman tiles and stones – Gloucester, Westminster, Peterborough, Chester, Malmesbury, Tewkesbury, Pershore, Sherborne, Romsey and Bury St Edmunds, whose nave, over three hundred feet long, surpassed that of our largest cathedral today.

These vast edifices were miracles of construction. So were the non-monastic cathedrals served by secular canons, which the Normans raised in London, York, Old Sarum, Lichfield, Lincoln and Winchester; for the last a whole royal wood was felled. They were built without any but the most elementary mechanism for moving and lifting large weights, by men whose wealth consisted almost entirely of crops, flocks and herds and whose sole means of transport were wheeled carts drawn by oxen. Their architecture expressed the unity of existence in which their builders so profoundly and passionately believed: the ordered vaulting; the pillars rising out of the earth like trees; the stone walls and arches carved with flowers and leaves, animals and men; the light of heaven flooding in through windows, at first plain but later painted, like the ceilings, in brilliant colours; the arches soaring into the sky, and the whole made one by the idea, implicit in every image and symbol, of God over all and judging all, and Christ and his Mother, the Virgin, pitying and loving all.

*   *   *

It was no wonder that an institution which evoked such devotion and love should possess power. In a still half barbaric world of shifting, warring feudal states the Church alone had unity and permanence. The election in 1073 to St Peter's apostolic throne, under the title of Gregory VII, of a Tuscan peasant of genius named Hildebrand, had marked the beginning of an age of intensive ecclesiastical reform. During it a succession of great Popes sought to carry the austere standards of the Cluniac monasteries into the still half primitive organisation of the diocese and rural parish. It was the aim of Hildebrand and his successors to bring under their direct control the entire international army of those who wore the tonsure – the symbolic shaving of the crown which set the servants of the Church apart from the rest of mankind. A system of canon law, derived from early Christian and Roman practice, was to provide the machinery – meticulous, bureaucratic, authoritative – for enforcing papal control over all clerics, ordained or not. And a hierarchy of graded courts, administered by ecclesiastical lawyers and stretching upwards to the papal Curia in Rome, was to offer immunity from the jurisdiction of secular courts of law to every churchman, however humble, who, by his ability to mumble a Latin text from the Bible, could claim 'benefit of clergy' and so escape subjection to the criminal and civil law of the land. If any servant of the Church – even a poor church-sweeper or wandering ragamuffin student – committed a murder, rape or burglary, the Church claimed the exclusive right to try and to punish him.

Such a claim seemed incompatible with the social order and discipline which more enlightened European rulers like Henry II were trying to impose on their subjects after the anarchy and lawless violence of the Dark Ages. At a time when, through the pious benefactions of past conquerors and rulers, the Church owned something like a quarter of the taxable wealth of every realm in Christendom, the Pope's denial of secular sovereigns' right to control and tax such wealth struck at the very root of government. Having piously endowed Christian sees and abbeys with land, kings and princes not unnaturally claimed the right to tax their ecclesiastical beneficiaries, not as the heirs of Christ's apostles as the Church claimed they were, but as feudal tenants-in-chief. In return for conferring on them the insignia of their holy office – the episcopal staff and ring – and the broad feudal domains bequeathed for its support, they demanded homage and fealty. Yet to the Gregorian reformers, in their zeal for the Church's independence and doctrinal purity, this seemed a blasphemous infringement of spiritual rights. To them the staff and ring symbolised no earthly lordship but the sacred charge Christ had laid on his apostles. That they should be conferred by a layman – even a crowned and consecrated one – was sacrilege. Nor, they contended, should a layman be allowed to choose, let alone consecrate, those who were to exercise such sacred functions. It might be tolerable in a god-fearing king like William the Conqueror who filled sees and abbeys with reformers and loyal churchmen. It was intolerable when the crown was worn by a blasphemous wretch like his son, Rufus, who appointed evil-living favourites to bishoprics.

Against the dream of the vanished Roman Empire which Charlemagne had tried to recreate and in which a Frankish Emperor had been crowned by a Pope as the secular head of western Christendom – one which still lingered on in the shadowy *imperium* of the German or 'Holy Roman' emperors – Gregory VII sought to substitute one of an ecclesiastical empire transcending all frontiers. And because of the simple piety and faith which its early monks and priests had by example and precept taught Christians everywhere, the Church possessed a weapon which, in a deeply superstitious age, no secular ruler could easily withstand.

During the reign of William the Conqueror in England, by using the dread curse with bell, book and candle which excommunicated a man from the Christian communion, the Pope had made the German Emperor an outcast to his own feudatories and subjects. Deriving his authority as Emperor, not from tribal or national ties like other rulers, but solely from his title as Charlemagne's successor and the bearer of the temporal sword of Christendom, his excommunication and deposition by the Holy See destroyed the grounds of his subjects' allegiance. In the winter of 1077 the first prince in Europe stood barefoot in the snow outside the castle of Canossa to implore the Pope's forgiveness for daring to claim feudal rights over his own clergy. It was the only way he could keep his throne.

In England attempts to make the Church independent of the State had proved less effective. It was not that the Church was less respected, but that the Crown, under rulers like William I and the first two Henrys, was more so. For this reason the lay investiture contest between the English Church and Crown had not ended in a Canossa. It had ended in a working compromise. In 1106 that shrewd monarch, Henry I, recognising that the public was behind the Church's demand for independence in purely ecclesiastical affairs, had granted it the monopoly of investing its bishops with the sacred episcopal staff and rod, He also agreed that their cathedral chapters should elect them. But their right to do so was made dependent on his leave to elect, and his own right to nominate, a candidate himself and to veto any other candidate. And before consecration his nominee had to do homage to the Crown for the stewardship of the episcopal lands and castles conferred on him by royal writ. In this eminently practical way the English King retained control of his kingdom's wealth and political power, while acknowledging the Church's right to confer spiritual authority. This sensible compromise was later adopted in other lands, even, after the Concordat of Worms in 1122, in Germany.

Yet at Canossa the Church had tasted blood. Throughout the twelfth century the initiative lay with the canon lawyers who, seeking to organise the Church as a completely self-governing institution, tried to free it from all secular control. Even in England during Stephen's weak rule it had established the right of clerical appeal to Rome and the freedom of papal legates to exercise independent powers within the realm, together with the exemption of clerics from the processes of ordinary criminal law and the Church's exclusive right to try and punish its own. And, as canon law forbade the use of mutilation or death, and the worst that could befall a clerical malefactor, even a murderer, was a fine or brotherly scourging, Henry II, seeking to restore order after the civil wars of Stephen's reign and establish a common law for all Englishmen, was confronted by ecclesiastical privileges incompatible with his object. For the Church's punishments for its erring members were far too light to maintain order in a violent and unpoliced age. During the first few years of Henry's reign more than a hundred murderers escaped death by pleading clerical immunity. And to Henry II's orderly and autocratic mind it seemed intolerable that episcopal tenants-in-chief should have the right to appeal over his head to a foreign court.

CHAPTER NINE

The Holy Blissful Martyr

'From every shire's end
Of Engeland to Canterbury they wend
The holy blissful martyr for to seek.'

Chaucer

IN HIS ATTEMPT to bring the excessive legal powers of the Church into line with the royal and national law that it was his life's work to establish, Henry II proceeded with great caution. As in his attack on the powers of the feudal magnates, he merely claimed that he was restoring ancient customs which had been infringed during the civil war of Stephen's reign. And, as with the baronial franchises, he relied on subtly disguised and harmless-looking legal devices to bring the ecclesiastical courts under his control before anyone could realise what was happening. In this he was assisted by a brilliant ecclesiastical lawyer whom he had made his Chancellor and who, while serving in that capacity, showed as small respect as himself for clerical claims which conflicted with the needs of royal revenue and justice. Seven years after his accession, the death of the Archbishop of Canterbury presented Henry with what seemed a wonderful opportunity. In the summer of 1162, brushing aside all opposition, he induced the monastery-chapter of Canterbury to elect to the vacant see his gorgeous counsellor, favourite and boon-companion, Thomas Becket – one who, though a cleric, was not even ordained a priest until the day before his consecration as head of the English Church.

In doing so, however, the King made a grave miscalculation. For Becket, who received his sacred office with reluctance, had no sooner accepted it than, at the age of forty-five, he completely changed his way of life. The most resplendently arrayed and attended man in England, who had taken the field at the head of seven hundred of his own knights and worn the long-embroidered sleeves of a baron, now donned the black robes of a Canterbury monk, attended midnight masses, and daily – and with his habitual ostentation – entertained and washed the feet of the filthiest beggars in Canterbury. A shameless pluralist who had collected benefices and prebendal stalls to support his magnificent entertainments, he insisted on resigning the Chancellorship regardless of the entreaties of his sovereign, who had seen in the union of the primacy and the royal chancery a solution to all his problems.

For, with the thoroughness with which he did everything, Becket refused to serve two masters. Having been the most loyal of royal lieutenants, he now transferred his allegiance to a more powerful and divine master. Instead of applying his vast legal and business experience to subject ecclesiastical encroachments to Exchequer scrutiny, he used them to extend the rights and revenues of his see. He revived long-dormant claims, demanded the restoration of estates alienated by his predecessors, and insisted on receiving homage from knights holding church-lands. When a fellow tenant-in-chief usurped an advowson he summarily excommunicated him, thus depriving the Crown of his services, for no one could have dealings with an excommunicated man. Nor would he yield an inch to the King's demands about criminous clerks. He seemed to go out of his way deliberately to enrage his former friend and benefactor.

Thus the King's attempt to bring the Church under the Law was frustrated by the very man who had been his chief assistant and who, as the repository of his secret plans, was ideally situated to defeat them. His love for his brilliant lieutenant turned to bitter hatred. With all his resolution and cunning he set himself to remedy his mistake. At all costs he had to get Becket out of the key position in which he had so injudiciously placed him.

*   *   *

The two men – the one with the strongest throne in Europe, the other representing the international Church – seemed well matched. They had been the complement of one another and now became the antithesis. Each had the same imperious, overbearing will, each was thorough, persistent and electric with restless energy, each had behind him a career of unbroken triumph. And each knew, or thought he knew, his opponent by heart.

Yet within a year the King had completely outmanoeuvred the tall, gaunt, dark archbishop. For, with all his boldness and courage, Becket lacked the virtues in which Henry, the Achilles-heel of his temper apart, was so strong. He had none of his capacity for patient statesmanship and *finesse* in handling political situations. He was a perfectionist rather than a man of the world. During his seven years as Chancellor he had shown himself a tireless organiser and worker, with a wonderful quickness and versatility. He possessed dazzling address and charm; could be all things to all men and, though revealing his heart to none, win from subordinates affection and even devotion. But while he appealed to the multitude by his dramatic genius and emotional power, his equals could not depend on him. He was far too much of an egoist to be a good colleague. He lacked constancy and stability: was a man of extremes who lived on his nerves. He seemed capable of every attitude except moderation.

The King, who had been so well served and delighted by his Chancellor's genius, understood his weaknesses perfectly: his vanity and hypersensitiveness, his inability not to overstate and dramatise his case, his pathological desire – the result of a lonely childhood – to win applause and justify himself. And in their triangular relations with the English bishops and the Pope, both of whose support was essential to Becket's position, he played the brilliant, excitable archbishop like a fish. First he joined issue with him over what was by far the weakest point in the Church's position – the trial of crimous clerks, to which a notorious murder and an equally notorious acquittal had just drawn everyone's attention. It was an issue on which the Church itself was divided and about which doubts were felt even by the Pope. In October 1163 at a Council at Westminster Henry outlined his proposals for dealing with this pressing scandal. He did not challenge the

Church's right to try its members, but demanded only that clerics found guilty by ecclesiastical courts of major crimes should be degraded and handed over to his officers for punishment. Those who could not be restrained from such outrages by the thought of their sacred orders, he pointed out, could scarcely be wronged by the loss of them.

In January 1164 the King called a Council at his hunting-lodge at Clarendon near Salisbury. Here he placed before it sixteen carefully prepared written clauses, known to history as the Constitutions of Clarendon, and demanded from the archbishop, in the presence of the barons and his fellow bishops, a solemn declaration of agreement. Most of them set out, not unfairly, the relationship which had existed between Church and State in the time of Henry I. Others traversed what had become during the anarchy of Stephen's reign the accepted practice of the Church. And they laid down a procedure for dealing with criminous clerks: preliminary investigation before a lay judge, trial in the ecclesiastical courts in the presence of a royal observer and, where guilt was proved, degradation and delivery to the King's officers for sentence and punishment.

The most contentious provisions were that no regal tenant-in-chief should be excommunicated, no cleric leave the realm and no appeal be made to Rome without the King's leave. This was tantamount to making the King supreme ecclesiastical judge in the realm – a principle which, however much it might conform with ancient English practice as Henry contended, ran diametrically counter to the existing canon law of the reformed Roman Church. It struck at the latter's fundamental claim to international ecclesiastical sovereignty and made the Crown, as in Anglo-Saxon times, the constitutional link between the Pope and the English clergy.

Though it was one thing for the King to try to restore the ancient unwritten and peculiarly English relations between Church and State in a tacit agreement with his own bishops, it was another to reduce these to writing and demand from churchmen a public avowal of principles which violated the displinary canons of their Order. And though the emotional Becket continued to play his cards badly,[1] the Pope, while anxious to reach an agreement with Henry, could not publicly repudiate the principles for which Hildebrand and his predecessors had fought. His refusal to underwrite the Constitutions of Clarendon was laid at Becket's door by the angry King who now resolved to ruin and destroy him. Sentencing him for contempt of his royal Court to the loss of all his own and his see's moveable goods, and calling on him to account for the vast sums which had passed through his hands as Chancellor, he summoned him in October 1164 before the Council to receive judgment.

Yet by making him desperate, Henry drove his adversary back on something greater than either himself or the Church. He forced him on to the rock of the inner spirit. Though ill and afraid, the archbishop resolved to compromise no more and to take his stand, not merely on the Church's tenets, but on the cross of suffering and sacrifice it enshrined. By doing so he became the champion of thousands to whom the rights and wrongs of the constitutional principles under dispute meant nothing.

And for the lonely, spectacular role he now chose Becket was superbly equipped. His towering height, his pale, sensitive face, the aquiline nose and restless penetrating eyes, the white feminine hands and quick eager movements made him look what he aspired to be, a saint and martyr. And the very theatricality and emotionalism, which so annoyed high-born men of the world, appealed to the heart of common folk, who only saw him from afar and knew nothing of his weaknesses. Here was a man who even in that age of pageantry and outward symbols made his meaning ten times clearer than anyone else, speaking to them across the immense barriers of power, rank and wealth. Almost alone among the rulers of the time he laid himself out to please the masses – the peasants and craftsmen of a conquered England who were without the rights and liberties of their Norman feudal lords.

Through the King's vindictiveness Becket had reached solid ground. From that moment, despite all the odds against him, he never quitted it. At the Council meeting at Northampton, wearing

[1] A detailed story of Becket's duel with the King is in Chapters 8 and 9 of the author's *Makers of the Realm.*

his archbishop's cope and pallium and bearing his own cross, he faced all day the insistence of armed barons that he should yield to the King's demands and resign. 'This is a fearful day,' murmured one of his followers as angry baron after baron came in with summons and threat. 'Ay,' replied the archbishop, 'but the Day of Judgment will be more fearful!'

As the bishops – even those most opposed to Becket – dared not, in face of his prohibition, join in judgment against him, the King demanded it from his earls and barons alone. But when the magnates made their way to the archbishop's chamber to inform him of the sentence, he rose and refused to hear them. 'You are come to judge me,' he cried. 'It is not your right . . . It is no sentence; I have not been heard. You cannot judge me. I am your spiritual father; you are lords of the Household, lay powers, secular personages. I will not hear your judgment! Under protection of the Apostolic See I depart hence.' Then, rising to his full height and bearing his cross, he swept into the darkening hall and towards the door, while knights and royal servants, rising from the straw-strewn floor and benches where they had dined, shouted, 'Traitor!' 'Perjurer!' Outside in the wet streets the people thronged round him to beg his blessing, so that he could hardly control his horse.

For the next six years, deprived of the revenues of his see, and his office declared forfeit, Becket remained in exile. From the position he had taken up – that ultimate appeals affecting the Church must lie to the Pope and not the King, and that no lay court had the right to lay hands on an anointed priest – nothing could move him. Against the royal forfeiture of his see he retaliated by surrendering it to the Pope, who restored it to him, thus immeasurably strengthening his position. From time to time he emerged from the French monasteries, into which he had retired to a life of the sternest austerity, to hurl anathemas and excommunications at any of his fellow English prelates who dared to compromise with the King.

Henry was equally unappeasable. But he could not govern England without the Church. And in an international age, himself an international ruler, he could not cut the English Church off from the universal Church, and make himself its ruler instead of the Pope. In the end, using the King of France as a mediator, he agreed to restore the archbishop's forfeited estates and end his banishment.

Yet, although the two disputants met in the French king's presence and were apparently reconciled, their quarrel was only patched up, not appeased. And in agreeing to return to England the primate knew the risk he was running from a passionate and injured autocrat of unpredictable moods. But his own safety was the last thing with which he was now concerned. His only thought was a spiritual victory. Nor did he return unarmed. Before setting out, he secured from the Pope letters of suspension and excommunication against his fellow metropolitan of York and two of his own suffragan bishops for their recent part in crowning Henry's heir without his participation. Just as he was about to embark, he learnt that they were on their way to join the King in Normandy to consecrate royal nominees to five vacant English bishoprics. Faced with the prospect of a packed and hostile episcopal bench, Becket at once used the discretionary powers with which the Pope had armed him and launched his sentences of excommunication and suspension against them.

Then, on 1 December 1170, having shown that he was prepared to abate not one tittle of the Church's authority, and avoiding the royal officials who, infuriated by his latest act of war, were waiting at Dover to seize him, he landed at his own cathedral's port of Sandwich. All the way to Canterbury the roads were lined with praying and rejoicing multitudes; it was like a triumphal procession. In the city he was welcomed with trumpets, psalms and organs. As he took his throne in the cathedral his face was transfigured with happiness. 'My lord,' one of his monks whispered to him, 'it matters not now when you depart from the world. Christ has conquered! Christ is now king!'

When Henry in Normandy learnt what had happened he flew into an ungovernable rage. 'What idle and coward knaves have I nourished as vassals,' he shouted, 'that faithless to their oaths, they suffer their lord to be mocked by a low-born priest!' Four of his knights took the King at his word and, without informing anyone of their intention, set out for England. There they made their way to Saltwood Castle in Kent, the home of Becket's bitterest enemy, Sir Ranulf de Broc, the man who during his absence had farmed his see's revenues.

On 29 December the four knights, with a rabble of de Broc's followers, arrived at Canterbury where the archbishop was sitting after dinner in his chamber. Ostentatiously refusing his servants' offer of food, they strode up to his chamber and sat down on the rushes before him, watching him in grim silence. When after a time he addressed them they broke into curses, telling him that they had something to say to him by the King's command and asking if he would have it said in public. Then they told him that, unless he absolved the excommunicated bishops, he must immediately leave the realm. To which the archbishop replied that they should cease from brawling and that, as his trust was in Heaven, no sea should ever again come between him and his church. 'I have not come back to flee again,' he said; 'here shall he who wants me find me.'

They found him that night in the cathedral. The knights were completely covered in armour save for their eyes, and their swords were naked. They all began shouting together, 'Where is Thomas Becket, traitor to the King and realm?' As the clamour increased, Becket, descending the steps from the choir, called out, 'Lo! here I am, no traitor to the King, but a priest. What do you seek from me? I am ready to suffer in His name who redeemed me by His blood.' Whereupon the armed men came shouting and clattering through the darkness to where he stood beside a pillar in the transept. As they closed in on him, apparently intending to carry him off, they again called on him to absolve the excommunicated bishops. Rising above them in his great height, he answered: 'There has been no satisfaction made, and I will *not* absolve them!' 'Then you shall die this instant,' cried one of the knights, 'and receive your deserts.' 'I am ready to die for my Lord; may the Church through my blood obtain peace and liberty!' As he resisted their efforts to drag him away, the knights, fearing a rescue, began to strike furiously at him with their swords. A blow cut off his scalp, while another severed his cross-bearer's arm. Two more blows brought him to his knees, and a fourth scattered his brains on the pavement. Then the murderers burst out of the cathedral to plunder his lodgings and make their escape before the city could be roused.

*   *   *

When that night in the desecrated cathedral the monks bent over the body of the proud, fastidious archbishop and stripped off his bloodstained Cistercian's habit to replace it by his pontifical vestments, they found to their amazement a covering of filthy sackcloth and a horsehair shirt, long-worn and alive with lice. Beneath it they saw the festering weals of repeated self-scourging. Then, through their grief and fears, they rejoiced exceedingly. For they knew that he had been a true monk and a saint of God.

By death the archbishop had triumphed. As the news became known, a thrill of horror ran through Christendom. The King, against whom Becket had contended, collapsed in an agony of lamentation. Exchanging his robes for sackcloth he shut himself in his chamber, where for three days he refused all food, groaning and crying exceedingly, and from time to time falling into a stupor. When he at last calmed down, he threw himself and his realm on the Pope's mercy. If it was not to disintegrate, it was the only thing he could do.

But it was not the great alone who were shaken. The common people left their rulers in no doubt as to their attitude. Within a few hours of the murder, rumours of miracles began to spread outwards from Canterbury. Four times, it was said, the candles round the bloodstained pall had been lit by invisible hands. A monk in the abbey had seen the archbishop in a vision going towards the high altar in episcopal robes; his deep, beautiful voice had joined in the singing of the introit. A blind woman who touched her eyes with a handkerchief dipped in his blood had regained her sight; 'the blind see, the deaf hear, the dumb speak', wrote John of Salisbury, 'the lame walk, the devils are cast out!' Meanwhile the de Brocs, who had threatened to move the body, were besieged in their castle by a furious crowd.

It was easy for twelfth-century kings and lords to ignore the rights of the individual poor. But they could not ignore popular beliefs. Because the common people everywhere were convinced that Becket was a saint, the Pope, who had so often tried to restrain him during his life, was forced within two years of his death to canonise him. His shrine at Canterbury, blazing with jewels and surrounded by the discarded crutches of those he had cured, became the most famous place of pilgrimage in England. For a time the cult of St Thomas almost rivalled that of the Virgin Mary. Churches were dedicated to him and memorials erected in lands as remote as Scandinavia and Iceland.

In his own country, whose fame he had blazoned through Christendom, Becket's name became better known and more honoured than any other of his age. Before the Reformation there can have been few English churches which did not have a retable, wall-painting, window or other treasure depicting some scene in his troubled life. Even today, despite the wholesale destruction by sixteenth- and seventeenth-century iconoclasts, many survive, like the boss in the roof of the Norwich cloisters with its demons standing over the Canterbury murderers, or the panel at Elham in Kent in which the saint defies the royal anger at Northampton. By a strange paradox – for it had been to strengthen the realm that Henry had fought against him – Becket lived on, not merely as a martyr, but as a national hero to a submerged and conquered people. A Norman born in England who had stood up to her foreign rulers and died at their hands, he became, in a modern writer's words, 'one of the people of England as well as one of the saints of God'.

In a constitutional historian's sense the martyrdom achieved comparatively little. It saved for English clerics the right of appeal to Rome in purely clerical matters. It established the immunity of criminous clerks from lay justice. And it brought the English Church, beyond doubt or cavil, into line with the universal practice of the Roman Catholic Church and the canon law, even though that practice conferred on churchmen a greater independence than had been customary in the Anglo-Saxon and early Anglo-Norman state. As a result power in England, as elsewhere in western Europe, continued to be regarded, not as a force to be operated by a single

untrammelled will, but as a balance in which rulers were subjected to the check of organised Christian conscience expressed
through the Church. When four centuries later the rulers of
England repudiated the authority of Rome, the habit of thought
remained – a potent check to tyranny.

In everyday administrative practice, after the first shock of the
murder had passed, it was the commonsense views of Henry which
prevailed rather than the extreme and unrealist claims of the dead
archbishop. Of the sixteen Constitutions of Clarendon only those
governing the freedom of appeals to Rome and the trial of criminous
clerks were abandoned. Subject to certain formalities the Crown
continued to control the election of bishops and abbots, and to
deny to English prelates the right to excommunicate their fellow
tenants-in-chief without royal permission.

Yet Becket's martyrdom created an emotional content which
for centuries remained of immense significance in English life and
helped to form the enduring values of England. The Canterbury
martyr created the *Canterbury Tales* and all the generations of
pilgrims riding or tramping through the Kentish countryside 'the
holy blissful martyr for to seek'. It was not the worldly ends for
which Becket had fought that mattered after his death. It was the
spiritual means with which he had fought for them. That a man in
high place who had notoriously loved, and to excess, the wealth
and fine things of the world and enjoyed them in dazzling splendour, should voluntarily renounce them and live in exile and
poverty, should mortify his body and at the end return to his
native land to brave and suffer a violent death for the sake of an
ideal, was to reveal the power of Christ and enhance the spiritual
dignity of man. It is not easy for one who has lived fine to subdue the
flesh, to face unarmed the naked swords of brutal warriors, to place
himself in the power of insulting foes. Whoever voluntarily chooses
these things is, whatever his failings, a great man. In this sense
Becket was great – 'great,' as one of his followers put it, 'in truth
always and in all places, great in the palace, great at the altar; great
both at Court and in the Church; great, when going forth on his
pilgrimage, great when returning, and singularly great at his
journey's end.' Historians, who condemn him for contending

against administrative measures which were in themselves reasonable, sometimes forget this. But his contemporaries, who witnessed his martyrdom or those who heard of it from their fathers and went on pilgrimage to kneel on the steps where he died or touch with trembling fingers the bloodstained hem of his garments, saw it very clearly. For all the world's coarse obsessions and stupidity and blindness, the saints and martyrs have the last word. It is their triumphs over the frailty of the body which causes men to believe in God.

*   *   *

It was a measure of Henry II's greatness that he and his work for England survived the flood of horror and indignation which overwhelmed him when the news of Becket's death became known. His continental dominions were placed under interdict, and for a time it seemed that, with all Christendom against him, he would be excommunicated and his throne declared forfeit. But, his anger against Becket turned to repentance, the great lawyer King's patience and statesmanship reasserted themselves. He let time do what time alone could do.

Leaving the cauldron to simmer, he vanished from his troubled realm and went on crusade. It was characteristic of him that it was one which served his ends as well as those of the Church in whose name it was undertaken. Sixteen years before he had persuaded an English Pope – Adrian IV – to entrust him with a mission: to conquer for the Roman Church the heretical, slave-raiding island of Ireland which St Patrick had converted to Christianity seven centuries before but which, since the Viking invasions, while remaining nominally Christian, had relapsed into its primitive Celtic division and savagery.

Among the Church's many claims to dominion was one to the sovereignty of all islands. It was in pursuance of this pious, if sweeping, aspiration that Henry now embarked with a papal bull authorising him to subdue and rule the island 'for the enlargement of the Church's borders, the restraint of vice, the correction of morals and planting of virtue, the increase of the Christian religion and whatever may tend to God's glory and the well-being

117

of that land'. A few years earlier one of Ireland's ever-warring petty kings – Dermot of Leinster – had sought aid at the English court against his subjects and fellow kings. Unable at the time to help him, in return for his homage Henry had furnished him with letters authorising any of his own feudatories to do so. Such aid Dermot had found among the warlike Norman adventurers or 'Marchers' whose ancestors had conquered and settled south Wales. Among them was the ruined earl of Pembroke, Richard de Clare who, in an attempt to repair his fortunes, promised King Dermot help in return for his daughter's hand. In the late summer of 1170 this great soldier and adventurer, commonly known as Strongbow, with a force of 1200 men stormed, first the Danish port of Waterford, and then Dublin. Six months later, on the death of his father-in-law, he claimed the kingdom of Leinster.

The news caused Henry to act. He could not afford to let his vassals set up an independent feudal power in an island so near England. During the summer after Becket's murder, while Europe waited for the curse of Heaven to fall on him, he assembled a fleet of little ships in Milford Haven. In October he sailed for Ireland with five hundred knights and several thousand archers and men-at-arms.

Against this disciplined force the unarmoured foot-horde of Ireland, armed with stones and javelins, was as impotent as the ancient Britons against the Romans. The kingdoms of Leinster and Meath fell without a blow. That winter Henry spent in a palace of wattle outside Dublin built by his new subjexts. Here he accepted homage from both the Norman–Welsh adventurers who had preceded him and from the native Irish kings and princes. And here, too, he received the submission of the Irish bishops, who swore to conform to the canon law and practices of the Catholic Church, and to acknowledge him and his heirs as kings of Ireland.

Thus, in the winter following Becket's murder and as an indirect consequence of it, the foundations of English government in Ireland were laid. It was an alien one but better than none at all. Politically the island was much what it had been a thousand years before – a disunity of warring Celtic tribes. Ecclesiastically, it had scarcely progressed beyond the primitive organisation set up by the first evangelists, with colonies of missionary priests living in beehive wattle huts round monastery churches whose abbots wielded episcopal powers. The austerity, scholarship and enthusiasm of three centuries earlier had vanished; most of the monks were married.

By setting up an orderly government at Dublin Henry did what neither the Roman emperors nor the native princes of Ireland had done. Around the east-coast ports which the Vikings had founded, his English 'Pale' became a civilized province, with royal castles and castellans, regularly enforced laws, a Justiciar and justices, and a settled agriculture. To stimulate trade with England and the continent the monopoly of the Scandinavian pirates and slavers was ended, and a colony of Bristol merchants established in Dublin with the same liberties as in their native town. And to provide hereditary warriors, administrators and prelates to maintain order, organise manorial estates and build castle and cathedrals, Irish land was confiscated and granted on the usual feudal terms to members of the ruling Anglo–Norman caste.

It was a realm, however, with little depth and with fluctuating frontiers beyond which, among the bogs and mountains of the west, the kings and clans of Connaught and Munster, admitting only a nominal allegiance, maintained their ancient, savage independence. The work Henry had begun, and which only such a man could perform, was never to be completed. In the spring of 1172, growing daily more anxious for news of England and the continent, he sailed from Wexford, never to return. A few days of his usual rapid travelling carried him from St David's to Portsmouth and thence to Normandy, where the Pope's legates were impatiently awaiting him.

There, at Avranches, the peccant but penitent crusader made his formal submission to the mighty Church, swearing on the Gospels to accept whatever penance the legates might impose. He agreed to allow appeals to Rome, to restore the possessions of Canterbury as they were before his breach with the martyred Archbishop, and to compensate all who had suffered in the latter's cause. Then he turned against the formidable coalition of enemies who were seeking to seize and partition his dominions. They included the kings of France and Scotland and his own wife and sons, the eldest of whom – 'the young King' as he was called – he had had crowned during his fatal duel with Becket to ensure the future allegiance of his subjects.

Yet though the wolf-pack rounded on the old wolf, he met his enemies with his usual resolution and energy. With the speed which made him so formidable a soldier he out-manoeuvred the slow feudal chivalry of France. While he was chasing King Louis back to his own dominions and reducing Norman and Breton castles, rebellion broke out in England. Its higher feudal nobility, long uneasy at encroachments on their jurisdiction, had been particularly alarmed by a purge of sheriffs in the year of Becket's death and their replacement by Exchequer officials. Encouraged by the rebellion of the young King, to whom at Henry's request they had sworn allegiance, the bolder of them took up arms. The earl of Leicester, head of the great Anglo-Norman family of Beaumont, landed in Suffolk with an army of Flemish mercenaries, while Hugh Bigod, the old earl of Norfolk – a veteran of the civil wars of Stephen's reign – tried from his castle of Framlingham to rouse the eastern counties. Simultaneously William the Lion, King of the Scots, laid siege to Carlisle and, with an army of Lothian knights and naked savages from Galloway, swept across Northumberland.

Yet though Henry himself was forced to remain in France, his island realm withstood the shock. Led by the Justiciar, the official nobility of service which he and his grandfather had created out of the lesser baronage proved as strong as the rebellious feudatories. The 'new men' – the de Lacys, Bohuns, Glanvills, de Veres, Trussabuts, Vernons, Balliols and Bruces – counterbalanced the mighty Beaumonts, Mowbrays, Bigods, de Masseys and Tancarvilles. Even the Welsh princes stood by their allegiance. And the English people, who had no love for French-speaking earls, and even less for plundering foreign mercenaries, supported the royal government vigorously. When an army of Fleming weavers landed at Walton, they were met near Bury St Edmunds by 'the host of England' – the *fyrd* or militia of the eastern counties under the Constable, Humphrey de Bohun – and were cut to pieces by Suffolk peasants with forks and flails.

For, having made his peace with the international Church and purged his crime and sacrilege, Henry had by now done so with the common and Christian people of England. After recovering his continental dominions, in the summer of 1174 he returned, a penitent, to the scene of Becket's murder. From Harbledown, a mile out of Canterbury – the village of 'Bob-up-and-down' of Chaucer's *Canterbury Tales* – he made his way on bare feet through the cobbled streets to the cathedral. Here, before a vast crowd, he prostrated himself before the archbishop's tomb while the monks, at his entreaty, scourged him. At dawn, after kneeling all night before the shrine and showering endowments on it, he rode in haste to London.

Here wonderful news reached him. At midnight on 17 July 1174 a travel-stained messenger from the Sheriff of Lancashire arrived at the royal palace of Westminster with a demand for immediate admission. Asked what brought him, he replied that his master, Ranulf de Glanvill, held the King of Scots in chains in his castle of Richmond. Four days before, on the morning after Henry had knelt all night at Becket's shrine, a handful of English knights under Glanvill and the Sheriff of Yorkshire had made a raid from Newcastle into the heart of the Scottish army then ravaging Northumberland. Riding through thick mist, they had surprised the Scottish king outside Alnwick castle. Despite the odds against them they had resolved then and there to carry him off. Such courage met its reward. A day later, his feet tied beneath his horse's belly, William the Lion was carried into Richmond castle and the drawbridge raised behind him. As the news spread, the bells of all the English churches began to peal.

After that miraculous deliverance everything came Henry's way. The Scottish host, deprived of the leader who was the focus both of its own and of Scotland's precarious unity, dissolved into its component parts and, fighting furiously among itself, vanished into the northern mists. The rebel English magnates, despairing of help, surrendered their castles to the King's officials and his loyal English *fyrdmen*. It was the last time that the higher Norman nobility dared to challenge the joint forces of Crown and Law. Henceforward, the greater feudal magnates, like the lesser, accepted the ancient Anglo-Saxon conception of Alfred and Athelstan that power in England could only be exercised within the framework of royal supremacy and law.

CHAPTER TEN

Magna Carta

'To none will we sell, to none will
we deny or delay right or justice.'

Magna Carta

'And still when mob or monarch lays
Too rude a hand on English ways,
The whisper wakes, the shudder plays
   Across the reeds of Runnymede.
And Thames that knows the mood of kings
And crowds and priests and suchlike things
Rolls deep and dreadful as he brings
   The warning down from Runnymede.'

Kipling

BY THE BEGINNING of the thirteenth century a remarkable thing had begun to happen. The people of England – conquered a hundred and fifty years earlier by a foreign aristocracy who had seized their land and despised their language – were becoming increasingly conscious of their unity and nationhood. And though their new kings and lords still spoke French and boasted French descent, even they had begun to think of themselves as English and of their country as England. Within a generation of the Conquest an Italian Archbishop of Canterbury was writing of 'we English' and 'our island'.

For there seemed to be something in the land which naturalised foreigners and, adapting their ways, absorbed them. It was due largely to its being cut off from Europe by sea, so that its diverse inhabitants gradually came to think of themselves, not merely as barons or knights, churchmen, merchants or peasants, but as members of a distinct community that was both part of western Christendom and yet apart from it. Before Frenchmen had come to regard themselves as Frenchmen, Germans as Germans or Italians as Italians, Englishmen, including the Normans settled in England, were thinking of themselves as Englishmen. This sense of separateness was aided by their kings' insistence on the unity of the realm and on a common system of law. And it was stimulated by the difficulty the conquerors – a few thousand warriors speaking a foreign tongue – experienced in ruling so stubborn a race. A hundred years after Hastings there were still Englishmen who persisted in going unshaved as a protest against the Conquest. Living in this misty land of rain and deep clay forests among an alien population, the Norman knights could only exploit their conquest by meeting the natives half, and more than half, way. They needed English men and women to plough their fields, tend their homes, nurse their children and help them in battle. And the English did so – on terms: that their conquerors left them English and became in the end English themselves.

Since their numbers were so small, the conquerors soon became bilingual. They continued to think and converse among themselves in French, but spoke English with their subordinates. They learnt it from their nurses and servants, reeves and ploughmen, and, after the conquest was complete, from their men-at-arms. Abbot Samson of Bury – head of the richest monastery in the land – preached to the common people in the dialect of Norfolk where he had been born and bred. And by the end of the twelfth century even Normans were coming to take a pride in the history and traditions of the island they had won and to treasure the legends of its saints and heroes. The monkish historians, Henry of Huntingdon and William of Malmesbury, collected the ballads and tales of Britain, and Gerald de Barry, a Marcher's son, loved to boast of his Welsh ancestry and the beauties and antiquities of his Pembrokeshire home. It was a Norman – Geoffrey of Monmouth, bishop of St Asaph – who wrote the romantic tale of King Arthur and his British court and made it almost as favourite a theme with the French-speaking ruling-class as the exploits of Charlemagne and the Song of Roland. It helped to make Britain's inhabitants –

Normans, Welsh and English alike, and even southern Scots – believe they had a common history.

French and English place-names were blended on the map – English place and Norman owner grown English – Norton Fitz-warren, Pillerton Hersey, Sturminster Marshal, Berry Pomeroy. And the marriage of Church and State, spiritual and secular, was consummated, too, in this land where everything ultimately merged and became part of something else: Abbots Bromley and Temple Guiting, Toller Monachorum and Salford Priors, White-ladies Aston and Whitechurch Canonicorum. The great bishop, Richard le Poore, who built Salisbury cathedral, left his heart to be buried in the little Dorset village of Tarrant Crawford.

From all this sprang a new force with which kings and barons and even the Church had to reckon: that of national opinion. Its chief repositories were the men who were growing up between the greater feudal barons and the inarticulate peasant mass of the nation. It was an upper middle class composed mainly of descend-ants of the Norman knights who had been enfeoffed as owners – or rather feudal holders – of the soil, and whose fiefs, though origin-ally granted for life, had become, like other property, hereditary. As their military functions fell into abeyance, they became, instead of professional soldiers, landed gentlemen with administrative responsibilities. They served on the new juries of the grand assize and in the 'oversight' of the royal forests, performed the customary duties of suit-of-court in the shire and hundred courts, and gave testimony on oath in the periodical inquests of kings and sheriffs. They intermingled increasingly with the wealthier Anglo-Saxon freemen and landholders and with the Anglo-Norman traders of London and the new towns. Many of our oldest families – Berkeleys and Nevilles, Lumleys, Leghs and Clavells – sprang from this twelfth-century knighthood rising into gentility. It found its natural leaders in the officials and judges whom the Norman and Angevin kings set up as a counterpoise to the higher feudal aristoc-racy and ennobled with grants of land. It was employed by the Crown for an ever-growing host of local administrative and legal tasks. It provided laymen of trust and character with the time for public service, and ecclesiastics with sufficient personal status to make the Church in England rather more independent of foreign control than elsewhere.

The Norman and Angevin kings' establishment of common law and central administration helped to train this new upper or upper-middle class. So did the ancient Anglo-Saxon institutions of local government. The shire and hundred courts, the juries impanelled to pronounce on questions of fact, the larger towns buying rights of self-government from their overlords, all gave men opportunities of learning to act in co-operation, of administering corporate affairs and finance, and of reaching practical decisions after ordered discussion. As the nation grew in wealth and civilization, more and more public business was left to local men of worth, rich enough to take communal responsibility under the Crown yet not strong enough, like the greater feudal lords, to act without it.

*   *   *

The closing years of Henry II's long and germinative reign were embittered by the rebellion of his restless, turbulent sons. The eldest having died before him, he was succeeded on his death in 1189 by the thirty-two year old Richard 'Coeur-de-Lion'. A giant, golden-haired warrior, his one ambition was to join the Third Crusade to recover the Christian kingdom of Jerusalem, the news of whose capture by the Moslem Saracens in the year before his accession had shocked western Europe. This chivalrous romantic young knight, poet and musician, was so eager to raise an army that he was ready to sell anything, even London, to do so.

Though he turned his back on his kingdom and sailed away into the Orient, he proved a magnificent leader. Despite the fiery temper which made enemies of all his fellow sovereigns, he was the hero of the crusade and put new heart into the dispirited, plague-ridden army besieging Acre. The zeal with which, stricken with fever, he pressed home the attack, led to the city's early fall. Two months later, by his great victory at Arsuf, he re-opened the road to Jaffa and Jerusalem. And though the final prize eluded him, and he was forced to return with his work incomplete, he made a treaty with the Saracens which for another half-century secured the beleaguered Christian kingdoms of the Levant and the pilgrims' road to the Holy Places. He made the name of the northern land over which he ruled more honoured than it had ever been before. Even Saladin praised him. And, though hated by crafty and intriguing princes, he was loved by simple fighting men for his lion heart, his constancy to his word and his frank open nature and generosity. His shield of golden lions and scarlet crusader's cross became part of the heritage of England.

Though during Richard's ten years' reign he was almost continuously out of the country, the judges and officials his father had trained continued to enforce justice and order in his absence. But the real test for them and Henry's rule of law came after the succession in 1199 of the latter's youngest son, John. This erratic and moody tyrant, who inherited much of his father's genius but none of his creative capacity, used the legal and administrative machinery he had inherited to subject the landed classes to intolerable and arbitrary taxation. He levied scutage after scutage – the composition which tenants-in-chief and the military vassals had to pay in lieu of the service in the field by which they held their lands – not only after his campaigns but before them, so getting their money whether he incurred the expenses of a war or not. While his father in thirty-five years had levied only eight scutages and his crusading brother two, John in fifteen years imposed eleven, several for service on campaigns which never took place. Hitherto the extent of such service and of composition for it had been limited by feudal custom. John varied it at his pleasure. The rate at which it was assessed was almost double that of his brother's day.

As well as scutage and the customary feudal aids from his tenants-in-chief, John imposed levies on the capital value of all personal and moveable goods – an impost originally instituted for Richard's crusade to recover Jerusalem – and at least seven general tallages on the manors and boroughs of the royal demesne. Some of these, like Worcester, Northampton and Oxford, had to pay three or four times as much as they had paid before. When his tenants' estates, through death or other cause, fell into his custody John stripped them by special tallages of almost their entire realisable capital. He seized men's children as hostages and trafficked the wardships of minors and the marriages of heiresses to the basest agents. He made mercenary captains sheriffs and simultaneously allowed them to hold judicial office, so enabling them to blackmail property-owners with vexatious writs and false accusations. Summonses were issued in order to extract fines for non-attendance, writs were withheld or sold at exorbitant rates, crushing penalties imposed without regard to the nature of the offence or means of the accused, justice delayed or even denied altogether. The elaborate fiscal and legal system of the two Henrys and the great Justiciars was turned into a merciless machine for extortion.

In the light of his son's use of it, Henry II's achievement had presented England with a terrible dilemma. The great Angevin had convinced the nation and even its feudal magnates that, after the disorders of Stephen's reign, security and prosperity for all depended on the supremacy of the Crown. He had created a legal and financial machinery for making that supremacy effective, and a self-renewing school of trained administrators to operate it. But when his son proved a diabolical maniac, who used the royal power to make life intolerable for his subjects and alienated everyone in turn, those whom Henry had made the agents of that power were, little by little, driven into making a choice. They had either to destroy it, and with it the order and unity on which the prosperity of the realm depended, or subject the wearer of the crown himself to it. The first course might have been easy; the second was superlatively hard. It is the supreme measure of Henry II's achievement in educating his greater subjects that the best of them chose the second, and carried their reluctant fellows with them.

Yet the very cunning and ability of his son also impelled men to that wiser choice. Had John been a weakling as well as an impossible king, the monarchical power which had become the expression of England's unity could scarcely have survived the storms raised by his misdeeds. Yet for all his periodic lethargy, when driven into a corner he fought back with a fury that made even the most reckless or arrogant opponent chary of going to extremes. It was no child's play to dash from his hands the sceptre and rod he misused. The alternative of restraining and controlling him – and with him the royal power – was thus kept open.

It was an alternative, too, to which Englishmen now instinctively turned. It was of the Crown that they thought when they used the word England, for without it there would have been no England. Ever since the days of Alfred the monarchy had been implanting in the English the habit of acting together. The great alien princes who had grasped in their strong hands the athelings' sceptre – Canute the Dane, William and Henry the Normans, Henry II the Angevin – had all strengthened it. It had become natural even to Anglo-Norman barons to act with and through the Crown. They still tried to do so when its wearer of the hour became their oppressor and enemy.

Only the barons, with their armour, horses, castles and men-at-arms, had the means to withstand such a tyrant. Even for them it involved intense danger. But they had been driven to desperation. Some were reactionaries who sought to restore the untrammelled rights of provincial feudalism. Others were selfish bullies who wished to free themselves from royal control in order to oppress their weaker neighbours. Most, however, were members of the new aristocracy of office which Henry II had used to discipline the older nobility and fashion the administrative machine which had now been turned into an instrument of irresponsible tyranny. They were strongest in the north, where authority had always been left to the man on the spot and where local magnates were used to defending themselves against Scottish raiders. It was these northerners who, goaded beyond endurance, in the summer of 1213 refused a royal demand for scutage. In this they were acting beyond their rights, for it was part of the feudal law that an overlord could tax his tenants-in-chief to support his wars. But they maintained that such a right could be denied if it was not used justly and within the limits set by custom.

Others felt that their first duty was to the Crown, irrespective of its wearer. The King's majesty had become more important to them than the King himself. The tenure of their lands, their dignities and honours, the functioning of their local institutions and the administration of justice and order were all inextricably bound up with it. The nation was drifting into war, not only between its best elements and its worst, but between the best themselves. Men were appealing from the King to the King's law and taking their stand; in the name of the just laws of the King's father, against the King's government. The perils inherent in the situation were intense.

To resolve it called not only for loyalty and selflessness, but for the most subtle, comprehending statesmanship. And in its primate, Stephen Langton, England found what it needed. Langton was a scholar trained in the close logic of the medieval Church, with a vision which embraced all Christendom. His temper was essentially moderate, conciliatory and unassuming. He had the kind of good sense and quiet, rather whimsical, humour that takes the hysteria out of strained situations. He was always seeking to achieve what men of goodwill, after calmly hearing and debating all the arguments, considered both just and expedient. His aim was reasonableness even more than reason. In this he was most English. So was he in his respect for established custom and dislike of extremes.

It was not Langton's wish to see the Crown overthrown, the law ignored, the realm divided, the barons petty sovereigns as in the days of Stephen. For two years – amongst the most crucial in English history – he struggled, not only with his treacherous and tyrannical sovereign, but with the factious interests and violent passions of those who were trying to use the resentment the latter had aroused to destroy the peace and the unity of the realm. He repeatedly urged them not to carry things to extremes, while reminding the King of his coronation oath and the solemn compacts of his predecessors to govern justly. All that was needed to restore justice and peace to England, he claimed, was to renew such compacts. 'A charter of Henry I has been found,' he told the barons, 'by means of which, if you desire, you may regain your lost liberty.' And he tried unceasingly to induce them to base their demands on its terms.

Langton's wisdom and moderation failed to save England from the civil war he feared – one in which John, after ravaging his own country, met his death in October 1216 after a disastrous march through the flooded Nene. But before war broke out, on 15 June 1215 in a Thames-side meadow called Runnymede, the armed barons, with the archbishop's aid, forced the reluctant monarch to set his seal to a document which became a blue-print for England's future constitutional development. Ostensibly a restatement of ancient law and custom, it promised that the King should not without 'general counsel', that is without the consent of the Great Council, demand any scutage or aid from his tenants-in-chief other than the three regular aids long recognised by feudal custom; that the heirs of earls and barons should be admitted to their inheritances on payment of the customary reliefs; that the estates of heirs-in-ward should not be wasted during their infancy, nor widows robbed of their dowries or forced against their will to marry royal nominees. It laid down that no free man should be imprisoned or dispossessed save by process of law and the just judgments of his equals; that he should not be taxed or fined unreasonably or to his ruin; that his means of livelihood, including the merchant's stock, the craftsman's tools and the peasant's wainage, should be free from amercement; that London and the chartered boroughs should enjoy their ancient liberties; that merchants should come and go safely in time of war; and that the foreign mercenaries should be dismissed. It provided for the regular administration of the judicial system; ordered that the Common Pleas should be held at Westminster and not follow a perambulating court; that none should be made justices, bailiffs or constables who did not know the law of the land; that sheriffs should not sit in judgment in their own shires; that two justices with four knights of the shire should hold assizes in every county every quarter; that royal writs should not be sold at exorbitant prices or withheld from those entitled to them. 'To none,' the King was made to swear, 'will we sell, to none will we deny or delay right or justice.'

In all this the Charter, consisting of more than sixty clauses, was a recital of the wrongs suffered by subjects under a tyrannical King. And, as men of property – and, above all, landed property – were the only subjects with rights enforceable in the King's own courts, it confined itself in the main to setting out particulars of the redress granted them. It was a charter of 'liberties', and to the medieval mind a liberty was a right to the enjoyment of a specific property. It was a freedom to do something with one's own without interference by the King or any other man.

Called Magna Carta because of its length, the Charter was not, therefore, a declaration of general principles, let alone of human rights. Medieval men thought of these only in connection with religion. The Charter enunciated no theories; it was nothing if not specific and practical. Yet, though its chief beneficiaries were tenants-in-chief of the Crown, it was a national as well as feudal document. It made no distinction between Norman and English and guaranteed the liberties of small property-owners as well as large. Thirty-two of its sixty-one clauses dealt with the relations of the King and his subjects and not merely his tenants-in-chief. 'We grant,' it declared, 'to all the freemen of our realm, from us and our heirs forever, all the undermentioned liberties to have and to hold for them as our heirs from us and our heirs.' And it established two precedents of immense significance for the future. One was that when an English king broke the feudal compact and gave his vassals the right – universally recognised by feudal law – to renounce their allegiance, it was not necessary to dissolve the bonds of political society and disintegrate the realm. Magna Carta was a substitute for deposition: a legal expedient to enforce customary law which left the King on the throne and the sword of civil war undrawn. Government in England, though exercised by the King, was to be rooted in justice and based on law, or it was not to be accepted as government at all. Magna Carta was the first great political act in the history of the nation-state – itself an institution of which the English had been the pioneers.

The barons' unity in the face of John's injustice, and their decision to act within the law, had created a new phenomenon: a corporate estate of the realm to prevent the unjust exercise of power by the realm's ruler. The taxpayers had combined to control the tax-imposer. Magna Carta was the product not of a rebellion, as it seemed at the time to the King and his more bitter opponents, but of a revolution carried out by process of law. By the provisions for summoning the Great Council before any new aid or scutage could be granted, it made a representative assembly of feudal tenants a preliminary to taxing those tenants. This was something wholly new. And in establishing the principle that the King must conform to the law which he administered, it created a constitutional device for compelling him to do so. In addition to provisions for regulating the summons of lords to the Council – archbishops, earls, bishops and greater barons by individual writ, and lesser barons by collective summons through the sheriffs – the Charter contained a clause by which twenty-five representative barons, chosen by their Order, were to become its guardians. They were to 'observe, keep and cause to be observed, with all their might' the liberties it guaranteed. Should any of them be infringed, and just redress be refused, these twenty-five lords – almost all of whom had served, or were the sons of men who had served, as royal officials – were empowered to take up arms against the King to enforce the Charter. The indignant John was made to admit his subjects' right to restrain the wearer of the Crown whenever he infringed their liberties. 'These barons,' he had to announce on behalf of himself and his heirs, 'with all the commons of the land shall distrain and annoy us by every means in their power; that is, by seizing our castles, lands and possessions, and every other mode, till the wrong shall be repaired to their satisfaction, saving our person, our queen and our children. And when it shall be repaired, they shall obey us as before.'

By this device, though a clumsy and primitive one, the men who had wrung Magna Carta from the King sought to ensure its permanence. It was dictated by fear and the just belief of the barons that the moment their force was dispersed John would try to destroy both them and their settlement. Its dangers were clearly foreseen by Langton who tried, though in vain, to introduce a mediating body between the King and the barons' council. 'They have given me,' declared the furious monarch, 'twenty-five over-kings!' Yet the pattern of constitutional thought thus set out was to be reproduced in a thousand forms in the history of the English – and British – nation. It is still enshrined, after seven centuries, in the words of the national anthem:

> 'May he defend our laws
> And ever give us cause
> To sing with heart and voice,
> God save the King!'

It was a prayer that the best of those who stood by the King's shoulder at Runnymede had tried to answer.

*   *   *

However great the implications of Magna Carta for the future of the country and the world, few of England's then inhabitants can have been affected by, or even aware of, the barons' struggle with the Crown. But in the years immediately preceding John's surrender at Runnymede, the foundation by an Italian, Francis of Assisi, and a Castilian Spaniard named Dominic, of two new religious Orders was to have a profound effect on contemporary English life. Designed to carry Christ's creed and teaching from the cloister and sanctuary, and from the rich and privileged to the poorest and least accounted, unlike the regulars of the monastic houses, both Dominicans and Franciscans abjured the possesion of all property or land. Open to both clerics and laymen, bound by vows of poverty and chastity, and calling themselves brothers or friars – after the French *frères* and Latin *fratres* – they shunned the static, conventual life of the older monastic Orders, taking the world as their parish and the street and market-place as their cloister.

The two Orders, meeting a universal need, spread rapidly, founding missions in every western land. The black-robed Dominicans – the more scholastically inclined of the two Orders – first came to England in 1221, five years after the death of King John and the succession of his child son, Henry III, being welcomed at Canterbury by Stephen Langton himself. But it was the Franciscans who aroused the real enthusiasm of the English. Following the example of their founder, a rich clothier's son who had abandoned a life of wealth and luxury to preach to the lepers and outcasts of the trading towns of northern Italy, the first Franciscans – a band of nine, three of them Englishmen – landed at Dover in 1224, just under a decade after Magna Carta and when the first stones were being laid of Salisbury Cathedral. Penniless, barefoot and bare-headed, in coarse grey gowns and girdles of rope, they made their way to Canterbury and thence to London and Oxford, begging their bread along the highways and preaching

"An instinctive genius for blending the works of God and man. We can still see the reverence and skill with which they turned native to human ends while enriching and beautifying it."

One of the "great barns of stone and timber." Great Coxwell, Berkshire. 13th century.

"The Marchers, resolved to prevent further raids from the north, had been building strong castles like the mighty Caerphilly, which Gilbert de Clare, the red earl of Gloucester, raised near Cardiff in Henry III reign."

Caerphilly Castle, 13th century.

to the poorest of the poor. Followed by hundreds of others, both native and foreign, they took for their diocese the lazar-house door, the stews and the stinking hovels along the stagnant ditches outside the town walls; for their pulpit the dung-hill and garbage-pit, the pot-house and brothel. They made their habitation in strongholds of poverty, vice and misery whose very names – the Greyfriars in Stinking Lane, Sheer Hog and Scalding Lane – testify to their lives of dedication.

The all-embracing charity, cheerfulness and courtesy – virtues prescribed by their founder – and the heroic example of these evangelists made a profound impression on the native English. They revived memories of Aidan and the Celtic saints and mission-aries of Anglo-Saxon days. Despite the haunts of wretchedness in which they lived and worked, they were so merry that they were known as God's jesters. They seemed to take a special joy in serving outcasts and sinners. They washed the feet of the unclean and kissed their sores. To the rich monks of the conventional houses, they seemed only vulgar sensationalists and interlopers, 'utterly shameless and forgetful of their profession and Order'. To the neglected masses of the city slums, they seemed like heavenly messengers. Their sermons, racy, eloquent, charged with fervent emotion and illustrated by lively, colloquial tales that the simplest could understand, went straight to the hearts of uneducated men and women whose knowledge of the Christian story had been hitherto derived from services conducted in a tongue intelligible only to the learned.

The coming of the friars gave an immense stimulus to works of charity. Till now these had tended to be somewhat spasmodic, like the annual distribution of flour – still made after eight centuries – to the Hampshire villagers of Tichborne. London's two greatest hospitals – St Bartholomew's, first founded by Rufus's courtier, Rahere, in the Smithfield marshes, and the even older St Thomas's in Southwark for sick and needy travellers – had been established by Augustinian canons in the twelfth century. Such 'spitals, as they were called, were very small: St Thomas's, rebuilt after the fire of 1207, had rush beds for forty patients, and a staff of four canons, three nursing sisters and a warden. Following the example of their founder, the Franciscans made a cult of lazar-houses, often establishing their friaries beside them and making their novices undergo a period of training in them. By reminding men that Christ was poor and lived among the poor, they started to deflect Christian alms and legacies from the over-endowed monasteries to institutions which relieved want, sickness and suffering. They introduced into the vernacular speech words of faith like mercy, pity, patience, comfort, conscience and salvation. They were enthusiastic practitioners of medicine – a science recently revived by contact with the Moorish and Jewish scholars of southern Spain[1] – and administered it free to the poor among whom they worked. It was a ministration desperately needed, for the slums of medieval cities, situated mostly by the swampy side of streams outside the walls, were dreadful haunts of disease and wretchedness.

Above all the friars, both Dominicans and Franciscans, were teachers, and played a leading part in the universities which had grown during the previous century out of the cathedral schools. Their eloquence made them the natural leaders of the young students, as penniless and ragged as themselves, who, living in crowded garrets and taverns, flocked to the lectures of the learned doctors of theology, law and grammar in their hired rooms or schools and endeavoured to earn from the chancellor or bishop's representative the Church's licence to teach. These turbulent communities, for all their poverty, were intensely alive – gay, ardent and speculative. Though little accounted by the rich and powerful, it was with them, rather than with the sedentary and devotional monks of the Benedictine and Cistercian houses, that the future of European learning now lay. The friars, in touch with common humanity, had the perception to see this and, through their work in the universities, to mould that future. The famous Dominican house in the Jacobin convent at Paris was for the next half-century the inspiration of Europe's greatest university. It gave her the two most eminent schoolmen of the age: Albert the Great, the Swabian Regent Master, who made the works of Aristotle, rediscovered by Arab commentators, the basis of western scholasticism; and Thomas of Aquinas, 'the big dumb oxe of Sicily' who,

[1] Arabic symbols are still used today by doctors for prescriptions.

136

seeing natural law as 'the mind and will of God', sought to harmon-
ise Christian faith with reason. His vision of the universe was one
in which everything was ordered and balanced by the will of God;
'they are called wise,' he wrote, 'who put things in their right
order.' His elaborate exposition, through the argumentative
method of question and answer, antetype and antithesis, sought
to carry men's minds, by a series of stages, to the comprehension
of Heaven itself. In the disputations in which they maintained
their theses against all comers, these Dominican schoolmen tried
to prove God by logic – a heroic feat of mind that in the end, by its
failure, proved almost as dangerous to faith as to intellectual
freedom.

In no land in Europe was the impact of the friars' teaching
greater than in England. It gave a new and European importance
to the schools of Oxford – founded in a small stone building in the
churchyard of St Mary's after Henry II, during his dispute with
Becket, had recalled the English scholars from Paris. Both Dominicans and Franciscans established missions there, and at the new
East Anglian university which had arisen at Cambridge, on the
site of a 'little waste chester', following a murderous affray in 1208
between town and gown at Oxford. For a time, too, there were
nascent universities at Stamford, Northampton and Reading. The
exposure to vice and possible heresy of the indisciplined youths
who herded together in such places was a challenge to the mendi-
cant friars. The school which the Franciscans built in their friary
at Oxford formed the model for the University's earliest halls and
colleges. William of Durham's charitable foundation for theological
students which grew into University College, Sir John de Balliol's
slightly later one that became Balliol, and Merton, founded between 1264 and 1274 by one of Henry III's chancellors 'for the
perpetual sustenance of twenty scholars living in the schools', were
all inspired by the discipline and communal industry of the friars'
house. The lectures and disputations held there drew such crowds
that the secular masters were left, we are told, at their desks 'like
sparrows alone upon the housetops'. All this, two centuries after
the Norman Conquest, tended in a hundred different ways to make
the indigenous English majority, particularly in the towns, more
politically conscious.

One of the earliest triumphs of the Franciscans in the universities was to persuade the Master of the Oxford Schools, the great Robert Grosseteste, to become their Lector. Until his election in 1235 as bishop of Lincoln – the diocese in which the university lay – he was the inspirer of a group of young Franciscan scholars, whose experimental approach to the problems of the universe constituted the first serious challenge to the authoritarian ecclesiastical cosmology of the Middle Ages. A Suffolk farmer's son, Grosseteste was a mathematician and physicist, as well as a theologian and grammarian, and was famous for experiments with lenses. His methods, unlike those of most medieval philosophers, were experimental and inductive. The greatest of his pupils, Roger Bacon – 'the marvellous doctor' – a Franciscan from Ilchester in Somerset, carried his practice even further, making an investigation of natural science which brought him at times into conflict with the Church authorities for unorthodoxy and even suspected heresy. His mind, reinforced by his study of Arabic scientific writers, was forever voyaging into the unknown, dreaming of boats without oars, self-propelled carts, and bridges which hung suspended over space. His *Opus Magnus*, written and secretly published at the request of the Pope, is the greatest scientific work of the thirteenth century and possibly of the entire Middle Ages.

CHAPTER ELEVEN

Counsel,
Consent and Parliament

'Let us not be divided from the common
counsel, for . . . if we are divided, we shall
all perish.'

Robert Grosseteste

'The laws of England . . . since they have been
approved by the consent of those who use them,
and have been confirmed by the oath of kings . . .
cannot be changed or destroyed without the
common consent of all those by whose counsel
and consent they were promulgated.'

Bracton

SEVERAL TIMES DURING the fifty-six years' reign of John's son – who
succeeded to the throne in 1216 at the age of nine – the Charter was
re-confirmed. Henry III was a good, weak, obstinate, unreliable
man who got himself and the country into grave financial difficulties
through an ambitious foreign policy which he was incapable of
implementing. In 1255, forty years after Magna Carta, at the
Easter feast at Oxford, he appealed to the assembled magnates –
the country's chief taxpayers with whom he had been quarrelling[1] –
to rescue him and the administration from his almost bottomless
debts. The barons' leaders took counsel of one another and at the
end of April came to the Council armed. They left their swords at

[1] For a fuller account of Henry III's reign, see the author's *Makers of the
Realm*, pp. 311–358.

the door – a custom still enshrined in the ritual of Parliament – but made the King and his eldest son, the young Lord Edward, swear to abide by their advice. It was agreed that a Committee of twenty-four, half chosen by the barons and half by Henry, should draft proposals for a plan of reform to redress the nation's grievances and restore the ancient co-operation between Crown and magnates.

That summer, at a meeting at Oxford of the Great Council, the reforming committee's provisions were announced. They were accepted by the King, who saw in them his only hope of obtaining the aid he needed. They were of a most drastic kind. An *ad hoc* Council of Fifteen was to 'have the power of advising the King in good faith concerning the government of the kingdom . . . in order to amend and redress everything that they shall consider in need of amendment or redress'. If its members failed to agree or were not all present, a decision of the majority was to bind all – a principle of great future significance. It was to have authority over the Justiciar, Treasurer and Chancellor – who was to seal nothing by the King's will alone without the Council's knowledge – to reform the royal household, to place the castles in the hands of native-born custodians, and to appoint sheriffs annually from men of the counties they administered.

Of these measures the most important was that which regulated the meetings of the Great Council of the realm, or Parliament as it was now beginning to be called – the enduring embodiment of the ancient English custom that a King should take counsel of his chief men and have 'deep speech' with them. Parliament was a French word for such deep speech, for talking things over. Magna Carta had indicated the means by which the magnates, earls, barons, bishops and greater abbots were to be summoned to meetings of this body. It was now enacted that Parliament should meet regularly three times a year, at Michaelmas, Candlemas and in June. 'To these three Parliaments,' it was declared, 'the chosen councillors of the King shall come, even if they are not summoned, in order to examine the state of the kingdom and consider its common needs and those of the King.' And to them were to come twelve representatives of the general 'community' – that is, the general body of barons. Their approval of whatever the Council decided was thereafter to bind the community.

The reforming Fifteen acted quickly. While Parliament received and investigated hundreds of judicial petitions, it began with furious energy to reform the kingdom's internal wrongs, appointing four representative knights in every shire to draw up for the consideration of the royal judges lists of grievances and unjust administrative practices. For, with all their limitations, the barons had learnt the lesson Langton had taught them at the beginning of the century. Their attitude was now not only feudal but national; their business, as they saw it, not only to defend their interests, but to champion those of the community as a whole. 'We wish,' their spokesman had declared in the Council as far back as 1234, 'to keep in mind the common welfare of the realm and not to burden the poor.' They had made provision in their periodic meetings for relieving poor suitors from a ruinous attendance on the royal courts by permitting them to plead by attorney, and had sought to protect merchants from royal purveyors, and widows and minors from grasping overlords. Now, at a time of widespread hardship and discontent, when a succession of bad harvests, with famine and pestilence, had brought many to the verge of ruin, they proclaimed their intention of investigating the complaints of the lesser freeholders, even the poorest and most obscure.

Yet in doing so, their movement lost its unity. The zeal of the more ardent reformers outran the disinterestedness of the more conservative. The barons had been united in their resolve to check the King's extravagant foreign adventures, to rid the government of aliens and to take their rightful place in the control of the realm. But when it was proposed that, having reformed the abuses of the royal administration, the Council of Fifteen should investigate those of the baronial courts – in other words, the grievances of their own tenants – many barons, led by the great Marcher earl of Gloucester, Richard de Clare, felt that it was time to call a halt.

Yet, as much as the magnates, the lesser landowners of the shires had been politically awakened by the growing efficiency and extortionate power of the royal officials. They, too, had had to unite to control them or lose their self-respect. And the very use the barons were making of them and the part they already played in the kingdom's administration rendered them a force to be reckoned with. They had been called upon in the past year to elect four of their members in every shire to ensure that the sheriff observed the law and to report his misdemeanours to the Justiciar. They had now been given the duty of electing in the county courts four men from the shire from whom the Exchequer was to choose the sheriff of the year. And they were accustomed, in a humble and attendant capacity, to send representatives or knights of the shire to the King's courts at Westminster, and had occasionally been sum-moned to meetings of the Great Council or Parliament to answer questions on oath on local matters of taxation or justice.

Had King, barons and prelates – the privileged ruling Orders of the realm – been united, these rustic knights, or bachelors as they were called, would have counted for little. But in the revolu-tionary situation which now existed they were able to make their voice heard. They did so – in no uncertain fashion – for the first time in English history in the autumn of 1259, when at the royal feast of St Edward held at Westminster before the meeting of Parliament they addressed a corporate protest to the Lord Edward, the King's son and heir. In this document, known as the 'protest of the Community of Bachelors of England', they complained that, while 'the lord King had performed and fulfilled all and singular that the barons had ordained . . . the barons themselves had done nothing of what they had promised for the good of the realm; but only for their own good and to the harm of the King elsewhere'.

The twenty-year-old prince – the future Edward I, whose ardent, noble head as a youth can be seen carved in stone above a capital in the north transept of Westminster Abbey – responded to this tactfully phrased appeal with characteristic frankness. Though devoted to his father, he was in his directness his complete opposite. He had sworn, he declared, a solemn oath at Oxford and, though he had made it reluctantly, 'he was not on this account less prepared to stand by it and to expose himself to death for the community of England and for the advantage of the State'. He therefore in-formed the barons that unless they fulfilled their oath he would support the 'community' of bachelors and help to enforce it.

As a result, further reforms entitled the Provisions of Westminster – the complement of the earlier Provisions of Oxford – were enacted in Parliament. These laid down among other things that no one except the King and his ministers should levy distraints outside his fief, that no one without a royal writ should compel his free tenants to respond in his court to any matter concerning their free tenements, that none but the King should hear appeals of false judgments, and that no charter of exemption from assize or jury service should exempt a man, however great, from the obligation to testify on oath in the royal courts if his doing so was essential to justice.

The reforms for which the Council of Fifteen had been set up were now complete. A wilful, vain monarch had been taught the lesson that England could only be ruled with the assent of her leading men. And, unlike his father, he had learnt it without bloodshed. Moderate and informed opinion, therefore, began to veer towards the Crown, feeling that the nation should return to the form of government to which it was used.

*   *   *

Yet England had a further lesson to learn and a harsher. Her sovereign's obstinacy had awoken feelings which could not be easily resolved. There was a strange ferment in the air: of vague, vehement talk of justice and treason, not to the King but to the community; of friars preaching apocalyptic sermons in streets and on village greens; of cities arming their men and watching their gates; of war in the Marches where the Prince of Gwynedd, Llywelyn ap Gruffydd, enraged by the encroachments of English officials, was making a new nation of the Welsh and burning the lands and castles of the Marchers.

All this might have come to nothing in that politically immature age but for one circumstance. That circumstance was a great man. Simon de Montfort had come to England from France thirty years earlier to claim the earldom of Leicester and marry the King's sister. He had little liking for the English and never really understood them. But he was obsessed with the belief that power should

143

be exercised as a sacred trust and that it was a Christian noble's duty to enforce justice. It was this conviction, and his dynamic capacity to communicate it to others, which won him the devotion of all whose hopes of a juster society had been quickened by the baronial reforms. He appealed to the discontented, to the hothead young lords and bachelors, to the men outside the Constitution, to the merchants and apprentices of the eastern towns, particularly of London and the Cinque Ports, to the preaching friars who went among the poor, to the ragged scholars and simple craftsmen and artisans who wanted to see God's kingdom made on earth. The son of the crusader who had crushed the Albigensians and won Provence for the French Crown, he invested every policy he championed with a passionate religious earnestness. He was a man, it was said, who watched more often than he slept; 'Sir Simon the Righteous' they called him. The Provisions of Oxford, which he had helped to frame, had become in his eyes divine commandments. 'He stood firm like an immoveable pillar,' wrote a monkish admirer, 'and neither threats, promises, gifts nor flattery could avail to move him . . . to betray the oath which he had taken to reform the kingdom.'

The trouble was that Simon did not attach the same meaning to that oath as either the King, who had subscribed to it, or the ordinary conservative-minded Englishman of his day. He maintained that the Council of Fifteen set up at Oxford was no mere temporary expedient to reform abuses and re-establish government by assent, but a permanent executive Council to rule in the King's name. Yet the throne had always been the medium through which Englishmen had been governed, and it was hard for them to conceive of any other, and still harder to devise a substitute for it. To contrain an English king to rule with the assent of his magnates was one thing, to exercise his functions for him another. De Montfort, in the name of reform, was advocating a form of government wholly foreign to English tradition.

Without this provocative challenge Henry, an ageing man who had learnt his lesson, would almost certainly have acquiesced in the baronial reforms. They had been demanded by the entire nation. But this oligarch, with his haughty claims to subject him to a council of nobles and summon Parliament in his absence, aroused all his obstinacy and petulance and his most treacherous, dangerous mood. And the jealousy and alarm which the proud unbending Frenchman awoke in his associates, and in moderate and conservative men generally, created a party for the King which had not before existed. For Simon's violence and intransigence sooner or later alienated everyone who tried to work with him as an equal. He was incapable of sharing power: he could only give orders and be obeyed. Compromise – the breath of self-government – was alien to him. He wished to establish the rule of righteousness on earth and viewed everyone who opposed him as an agent of unrighteousness.

That winter a final attempt was made to avert disaster by an appeal to the arbitration of the King's brother-in-law, the saintly Louis IX of France. But when his award in Henry's favour was published at Amiens early in 1264, de Montfort refused to accept it. 'Though all should forsake me,' he declared, 'I will stand firm . . . in the just cause to which my faith is pledged.' On 14 May of that year, to the amazement of everyone, his army defeated the royal array on the Lewes downs in Sussex. It was a triumph of youth over numbers, of the towns over the country, of the green-clad archers of the weald – prototypes of the yeoman infantry of England's future – over the glittering but old-fashioned feudal chivalry of the Court. Both Henry and his son were taken prisoners, and de Montfort became virtual dictator.

For a year he ruled England in the King's name, with the help of a nominated council of oligarchs. He proved no more capable than Henry of simultaneously founding the rule of justice on earth and pleasing everyone. His dilemma was that his only legal claim to authority in a land inherently monarchial was either the captive King, in whose name he governed and who could not be permanently constrained by force, or a conception wholly repugnant to a nation which liked law without a sovereign as little as a sovereign without law. Yet, though his triumph at Lewes was ephemeral and the civil war itself unnecessary – since the King had already accepted the principle of government with baronial counsel – the representative conception of Parliament was enlarged through de

Montfort's need to obtain wider support for his rule. In January 1265, he summoned to a Parliament not only the greater barons and prelates by separate writ and two knights elected in the shire court of every county, but two burgesses from each of the larger towns to represent the urban freemen and taxpayers. This was revolutionary, for at law no burgess had any right to refuse consent to a tallage demanded by the Crown. Only a few years earlier such a claim had caused Henry III to imprison some rash London citizens who made it. By this step de Montfort unconsciously placed what, in a precedent-loving nation, was to prove a barrier across an avenue of taxation which might, as commercial wealth grew, have made the Crown independent of a Parliament of land-owners.

The rule of the great champion of oligarchy lasted little more than a year. His difficulties and critics multiplied; the one made the other. In the spring of 1265 he fell out with his chief supporter, the young Marcher earl of Gloucester. At the end of May, Prince Edward – whose political stature had been growing fast – escaped from his captors at Hereford and, joining the Marcher lords with whom he had been secretly negotiating, routed and destroyed de Montfort at Evesham.

Yet, though the royal party had triumphed, there was no going back on the principle for which so many had striven: that the government of England, though primarily and fundamentally monarchial, should be with the counsel and consent of the realm expressed through frequent meetings of its chief men in Parliament. The real victor in the war was the Lord Edward, who was a man of his word and understood England. Unlike his father he was a prince of dominant personality who wished to rule a strong and united people and instinctively saw that the only way to do so was through frequent counsel with their leading representatives. It was this knowledge, learnt from the tragic experience of his father's reign, which made him, when his time came, one of the greatest of English kings. And seeing how bitter and stubborn was the resistance of de Montfort's defeated followers, when the first feelings of triumph and bitterness were over, he took a leading part in their reconciliation. In the 'Dictum of Kenilworth' in 1266, he offered the right to the 'disinherited' to buy back their estates at a judicially assessed rate. A year later he was the moving spirit in the great Statute of Marlborough, by which, while subordinating once more and for all time the baronial franchises to the royal, the King in Parliament formally confirmed the Provisions of Oxford and Westminster and made them part of the mainstream of English law.

Nor did de Montfort's influence end with his death. In a sense it became stronger when his over-powerful personality had been removed. Thousands of simple Englishmen sympathised with the disinherited; it was this that had made Edward offer them reconciliation. During this time there seems to have first arisen the popular legend of Robin Hood and merry men, lurking in the greenwood to war against the rich and proud and seize their wealth to help the poor. Sung as ballads and passed from mouth to mouth in hedgerow and ale-house, such tales constituted a new ideal of chivalry: a chivalry so far unknown in feudal Europe, for it glorified the lowly against the great. Simon's own memory was venerated by the poor as that of a saint and martyr. His ideal of the rights of the 'universitas' or 'commonalty', of an imaginary community of the whole realm to which even village craftsmen and petty traders and peasants could appeal in the name of justice, struck deep roots in the English heart.

*　　　　*　　　　*

It was Edward I's supreme achievement – more even than his legal reforms – that he took the nation into a kind of partnership and, by regularly consulting its representatives and seeking their consent, laid the foundations of the greatest of all English institutions: a royal Parliament in which King and subject could meet to treat, co-operate and, if necessary, dispute over matters of common concern. When his father died in 1272 Edward was out of England on a crusade to free the Holy Land. But as soon as he returned, after appointing commissioners to make an exhaustive inquest and report on the grievances of the subject, he called his first Parliament. To it he summoned the magnates, lay and ecclesiastical – the earls and barons, archbishops, bishops and abbots who were his tenants-in-chief – and, through the sheriffs, four elected and representative knights, 'discreet in law', from the shire-court of every county, and four merchants or burgesses from the *burgemote* or borough court of every important town. They were to come without arms and under the King's peace and protection and to be immune from the ordinary processes of law while the court of Parliament was in session. 'And because elections ought to be free,' ran the writ to the sheriffs, 'the King commandeth upon great forfeiture that no man by force of arms nor by malice nor menacing shall disturb or hinder any to make free election.'

For, having learnt through his inquest what was wrong with his realm, Edward had resolved on great changes. For these he needed his subjects' witness and approval. In the Middle Ages there were laws which were seen, not as something that could be changed at will, but as sacred and immutable. However unquestioned a King's right to act, ordain and give judgment, the ancient law of the kingdom was a public inheritance which it was his duty to preserve and enforce. His ordinances might have the force of law but only while he himself could impose them. After his death, if they were contrary to custom, they could be ignored or forgotten. Even in England, where the power of the locality had been far more strictly subordinated to the State than on the continent, the King's word was law only in his lifetime.

If society was to progress, some authority, associated with the Crown yet more enduring than the King's life, was needed to register the nation's acceptance of major changes in the law. In an age of isolated and intensely localised communities the tendency of custom to ossify was a mountain in the path of a reforming King. '*Nolumus leges Angliae mutare*' – 'we do not wish the laws of England to be changed' – Henry III's barons had replied at the Council of Merton to Bishop Grosseteste of Lincoln's plea for a more humane attitude towards children born out of wedlock. Edward could not overcome this traditional inertia merely by devising ingenious legal writs and directives to his judges as his great-grandfather, Henry II, had done. But with his strong practical sense he saw that a royal ordinance or judgment could be given a sanction more than ordinarily binding by having it publicly witnessed and approved in a session of Parliament or the *magnum consilium* – that supreme national Council or court of royal officials and judges, feudal tenants-in-chief, prelates and magnates to which his father in times of need had had resource for 'colloquy and treating' and to which in his later years both he and Edward, as his deputy, had increasingly referred the vast mass of petitions and appeals to the Crown from those unable to obtain justice from the ordinary courts. In the Statute of Marlborough of 1267 Edward himself, in his father's name, had legalised the baronial reforms of the past decade by a solemn public act of the Crown, issued in Parliament under the great seal and enrolled in writing as a permanent national record. By this means he had given to the royal decisions which resolved the controversies of the civil war an enduring validity which, despite his unchallenged right to declare law by ordinance, they could have had in no other way. Henceforward such statutes, as they became called, were cited in pleadings in the royal courts. Like Magna Carta they became part of the continuing life of the nation.

When after their slow, laborious and reluctantly undertaken journeys, the magnates and the representatives of the local communities met the King and his Council at Westminster, they were presented with a document drafted by the royal judges in French – the speech of their knightly class – and read to them by the Chancellor, Robert Burnell. Its object was to define, clarify and, where found necessary, reform the law. 'Because,' ran its preamble, 'our lord the King hath great desire to redress the state of the realm in such things as require amendment for the common profit of holy Church and the realm, and because the state of holy Church hath been evil kept and the people otherwise entreated as they ought to be, and the peace less kept and the laws less used and offenders less punished than they ought to be, the King hath ordained by his Council and the assent of the archbishops, bishops, earls, barons and all the commonalty of the realm the acts under written.'

The fifty-one clauses of this royal enactment of 1275 covered a vast field. They set forth, in easy, almost conversational, speech, a legal remedy for most of the worst abuses the King's commissioners had noted in their winter's visitation. The ideal of securing, by a specific remedy, the just rights of every man according to his status, ran through the whole enactment. Drafted by practising judges, it reflected the preference, always marked in English law, for concrete remedies over abstract principles.

Copies of the Act – the 'new provisions and statutes . . . ordained for the good of the realm and relief of the people', and known as the first Statute of Westminster – were sent, like Magna Carta, to the sheriffs. It was proclaimed in the courts of every county, hundred, city, borough and market-town, and all judges, sheriffs and bailiffs were ordered to enforce it. It was the first of a long succession of parliamentary statutes enacted by Edward in Council in the presence of the assembled magnates and representatives of the nation. Such statutes both changed and became part of the common and customary law. They derived their authority, not from verbally transmitted custom, but from a written document issued under royal seal and preserved in the rolls or records of Parliament which, before the end of his reign, Edward ordered to be kept at Westminster. Copied by pleaders into handbooks which became part of every practising lawyer's equipment, they were cited in the courts and accepted as evidence of law by the judges.

The Parliament which Edward held at Westminster in the spring of 1275 was not only summoned to endorse his proposals for reforming legal procedure. It was called to approve a new kind of tax. With changes in the landed and economic structure of the country; most of the older feudal sources of revenue were drying up and, to support the growing charges of State, the King needed new and extraordinary aids. Sixty years earlier the Great Charter had forbidden the levying of additional aids on land save by consent of the assembled magnates – a thing always hard to obtain. In its search for new revenue the Crown had been forced to turn increasingly to the taxation of moveable or personal wealth, which had not the same sanctity as land in the eyes of the ruling class. Its chief possessors in a taxable form were the merchants of the chartered towns and the flock-masters and wool-exporters who, during the past century, had been creating a new form of national wealth out of the downland sheep.

Legally the King was not obliged to consult merchants before taxing their goods. From time immemorial feudal lords had tallaged the towns and markets of their demesnes; it was for this that they had founded them. But times had changed, and merchants were no longer the helpless, half-emancipated villeins they had been before the crusades had introduced the feudal nobility of Europe to the luxuries of the East. Ever since they had been driven into the rebel ranks by his father's insistence on his right to tax them at will, Edward had wooed the traders of the capital and south-eastern ports, seeing with his realist's eye the power that came from control of cash and credit. He saw that a freely-negotiated agreement under which the merchant community assumed corporate responsibility for its own taxes was likely to prove more valuable to the Crown and, in the elementary administrative conditions of the time, provide a more readily accessible revenue than any forced imposition.

It was this which had caused him to follow de Montfort's revolutionary precedent and to summon to his first Parliament the proctors or representatives of all the cities, boroughs and 'towns of merchants'. He did not call upon them to take part in the discussions about his new land-laws – matters far above them – but to grant him a share of the increased trading profits which his strong rule and wise foreign policy were helping to create. In return for a standing duty of half a mark, or 6s. 8d., on every sack of wool exported and 13s. 4d. on every last of leather, he offered to surrender the royal prerogative of imposing direct taxation on merchandise. This gesture was as far-reaching as it was imaginative and generous. The 'Great and Ancient Custom', as it became called, 'granted at the instance of the merchants' and approved by the magnates, was the beginning of the Crown's permanent customs revenue. Henceforth it took its place, with the older 'tonnage' on wine imports, beside the feudal aids and dues, the rents of the royal estates – now much reduced by the grants of earlier sovereigns – the sheriffs' 'farms' of the shires and the proceeds of justice.

Later that year, in a second Parliament summoned to Westminster at Michaelmas and attended by knights of the shire as well as by the feudal and ecclesiastical magnates, the King obtained an 'aid' of a fifteenth on all other lay moveables. The idea of representation, of the right of those present to bind the absent, and of the majority to outvote the minority – a conception which the friars in their provincial assemblies had first introduced into England – was beginning to take shape under Edward's guidance. In his writs to the sheriffs he insisted that elected knights and burgesses should have full power of attorney to bind their fellows to 'whatever should be ordained by common counsel'. Needing his subjects' co-operation, he pursued every means of obtaining it.

*   *   *

After Henry II no king ever did so much to make England law-cônscious and law-abiding as his great-grandson, Edward I. He took his legal responsibilities very seriously. As a boy he had studied law under his tutor, Hugh Giffard, one of his father's justices. The hero of his youth had been his uncle, the great French king, St Louis, who had loved to sit under the oak at Vincennes dispensing justice to his subjects. His ideal and that of his age was of a delicately poised balance between conflicting claims, one in which every man's right to his own could be ascertained, weighed and enforced. For to the medieval mind, haunted by the memory of dark centuries of barbarism, justice was the highest earthly good, a mirror of the heavenly state in an imperfect world. It had nothing to do with equality, a conception then unknown. Its purpose was expressed by a phrase in a legal treatise called *The Mirror of Justices* written, it is believed, by a London fishmonger who had held the office of city chamberlain: that 'folk should keep themselves from sin and live in quiet and receive right according to fixed usage and holy judgments'. The goal was a society in which every man was offered the peaceful means of enjoying his particular rights. Law was the mechanism provided by the Crown for ensuring him that opportunity.

Edward's sense of justice was of a narrower, less altruistic nature than that of St Louis. He was resolved to do justice to all, but he did not except himself. Lordship to him was the first prerequisite of a Christian society – a right to be exercised justly and firmly and, wherever possible, extended. His duty to God and his people, he conceived, was to hold fast to his royal prerogative. He was always appealing to his coronation oath against suggestions that he should part with any of his rights, real or imagined; he held them, he said, in trust for his people. While endorsing the dictum of his subject, Andrew Horn, that 'law requires that one should use judgment, not force', he saw it as a contest, like the older trial-by-battle, in which a man was justified in using every technical nicety. He observed the full rigour of the game. Of its hard, intricate rules he showed himself as much a master as of war, seizing every advantage and never yielding a point without the clearest necessity. The courts were his, established to ensure not only that justice was done but that the kingdom was firmly ruled. Though after one or two early attempts he refrained from insisting that his judges should act as his advocates in disputes with the subject, he kept special pleaders or serjeants to 'sue for the King', like William of Gisleham and Gilbert of Thornton, the earliest-known King's Serjeant. They and his attorney, Richard de Bretteville – forerunner of our attorney-general – were kept incessantly busy. 'O Lord,' wrote a clerk at the foot of a membrane recording that officer's many activities, 'have pity on Bretteville!'

Yet Edward abided by his own rules. He used them to further his kingly ends but respected them. His favourite motto was 'Keep troth'. And though he was a strict upholder of his legal rights, his judges were not afraid to take their stand on his law rather than on his will. It was this growing acceptance of law by King and subject that made justice a more realisable commodity in England than in any other land. To offer relief to the subject and strict and impartial justice to all in their degree, to ensure that under the Crown both the obligations and rights of a feudal society were observed, to unify and strengthen the realm, these were Edward's objects, tirelessly pursued. His instruments were the prerogative, the Common Law and royal courts of justice which had grown out of it and the periodic assemblies or Parliaments of magnates, prelates, shire-knights and burgesses that he had taken to summoning whenever he needed common counsel and consent in support of his measures. His three great Statutes of Westminster of 1275, 1285 and 1290 were the crowning heights of his achievement. Each was a comprehensive code framed to amend, clarify and supplement the law and enable him to control the many-sided life of a passionate, turbulent yet conservative people, rooted in ancient ways and divided by regional loyalties, rights and customs.

The summer of 1285 saw the most intensive piece of law-making in medieval history. Drafted by the Chancellor and judges, it bore the impress of the King's authoritative, unifying mind. In accordance with his favourite adage that 'that which touches all should be approved by all', it was submitted to the magnates and representatives of the counties and boroughs at his Whitsun and Michaelmas Parliaments. Like all his reforms of the law, it dealt with things in a severely practical way. It made great changes, yet never for the sake of change, only for clarification and greater working efficiency. Its object was to make the law operate justly and expeditiously.

First place, in that hierarchical age, was given to the grievances of the larger landowners. At a time when revenue from land was almost the sole source of wealth for everyone except a few merchant speculators, its owner had to make provision during his lifetime, not only for his heir, but for his other children and his widow after his death. To prevent them from being left penniless he had to carve out of the family inheritance subsidiary estates to support them and their children and children's children. Yet if his own heirs were not to suffer, he had to ensure that such offshoots from his hereditary estate should revert to it after they had fulfilled the purpose for which they were intended. In his gift to a son when he came of age or a daughter on her marriage, a donor would stipulate that the land should return to him or his heirs if the donee's issue failed within so many generations.

Such settlements were immensely complicated by the rules of feudal enfeoffment. And during the thirteenth century the Common Law lawyers, with their fine and subtle definitions, had adopted the view that, if land had been given 'to X and to the heirs of his body', this must mean to X and his heirs absolutely as soon as an heir of his body was born. By availing himself of this interpretation an unscrupulous person – the husband, say, of a daughter to whom a conditional estate had been given – could dispose of the property as though it was his own fee simple and not a mere life-interest. In this way both the issue of the marriage could be deprived of the gift intended for them, and the donor's estate of the reversion.

Naturally donors and their heirs, unversed in legal subtleties, regarded such alienation as a species of fraud. It particularly outraged the magnates who, as tenants-in-chief of the Crown, had still to find out of their truncated fiefs the feudal services and aids due for the whole. Their plea that the King should redress the wrong that the operation of his own law had made possible was now met in the second Statute of Westminster. This did not seek to establish a perpetually enduring entail – a thing the Common Law regarded as unreasonable and unattainable. Its aim, as stated in the preamble, was to ensure that where a gift had been made on certain conditions to provide what were called estates of curtsey, dower or frank marriage, the rights of both beneficiaries and reversioners should be respected and that 'the will of the donor expressed in the charter of gift should be observed'.

Named after its opening words, *De Donis Conditionalibus* established what was to be the basic principle of English land law for seven centuries. Not only did it protect the reversion to the donor's heirs but, by forbidding alienation by the donee and so safeguarding the rights of his issue, it gave recognition to a new kind of heritable estate, inalienable as long as there was issue-in-tail of the original donee. Within practicable limits it ensured the primogenitary principle in the descent of both the parent estate and its offshoot. Owing to a flaw in one of its clauses, a generation later a loophole was found in the statute which enabled not the donee but his son to alienate the land and so disinherit his issue. But a great judge of Edward II's reign, Chief Justice Bereford, who had known what was in the mind of Edward I and his chief justice, Hengham, when they framed *De Donis*, insisted in a famous judgment on looking to the spirit instead of the letter of the statute and restored the entail in the grandson's favour, so establishing a precedent which was followed by the courts. And though, a century later, lawyers had found other ways of enabling tenants-in-tail to bar the entail, by that time it had become established that the principle of English landed inheritance, in families of modest wealth as well as large, should be primogeniture and not, as was the case in other western kingdoms, partition. Instead of being divided among younger sons, landed property in England was to be transmitted dynastically.

The effect of this on the nation's future can scarcely be exaggerated. It did not render the alienation of entailed estates impossible – for the ingenuity of lawyers proved inexhaustible – but it made it very difficult. At a time when the rigid feudalism of the past was giving place to more elastic forms of tenure, a new land-owning class was encouraged by the Common Law to adopt the feudal military device for preserving landed property intact by transmission through the eldest son. Read aloud in Westminster Hall on 28 June 1285, the second Statute of Westminster subordinated the promptings of personal affection to the long-term interests of the realm. It helped to create landed families whose estates and traditions, preserved from generation to generation, formed a school for training men for public service and the capacity to rule. The heads of such families looked after and enhanced their estates, making England in time to come the wealthiest farming country in the world, while relays of energetic and ambitious younger sons, educated for wealth but not endowed with it, went out from homes rich in transmitted standards of living and behaviour to make their fortunes and serve the State. *De Donis* helped to prevent the landed gentry from becoming, as on the continent, an exclusive caste divorced from responsibility. It made for an elastic as opposed to a rigid system of government, for enterprise and adventure instead of stagnation.

It was from this new landowning class, standing between the greater feudal magnates and the mass of the nation, that Edward created a new local judiciary. In every shire a number of trusted knights and landowners were appointed to act, in an unpaid capacity, as conservators or keepers of the peace. This was an extension of the Plantagenet system of dividing and broadening the exercise of provincial authority, formerly centred in the hands of the sheriff. For, in days of feudal delegation and inadequate communication, it had been found that too much power in a sheriff's hands ended in his becoming an irremoveable and even hereditary official, as ready to defy the Crown as those he was appointed to control. It had, therefore, been the policy of every king since Henry II to entrust every new power of the Crown, not to the sheriffs, but to other officers – to county coroners, justices of assize, commissioners of array and taxes, knights of the shire, and now conservators or, as they became in the next century, justices of the peace. In the reign of Edward's grandson, Edward III, these were to be given power to try felonies and misdemeanours and, in their courts of quarter sessions, to take over much of the criminal jurisdiction hitherto performed by the shire-courts. Working within the traditional unit of local government, with all its binding ties of neighbourhood and regional sentiment, they were subject, not to some provincial satrap whose interest it was to defy the Crown, but to the King's courts and officers at Westminster by whom they were appointed and in whose hands lay the power to dismiss them. The source of their authority was the King, the terms under which they exercised it the Common Law, the link between them and the government the royal judges on their periodic visitations of inquest and gaol-delivery. This interplay of central authority and local representation, of the rule of law and popularly delegated self-government, is the key to much of England's history.

*   *   *

In the century between Henry II's death and Edward I's reign, the legal institutions he had created had continued to grow. It was an age of fertile judicial invention, when a little group of royal justices – sitting on the bench of Common Pleas at Westminster, travelling the country on *eyre* or attending the sovereign's person in the court of King's Bench – were devising and offering the subject an ever-growing number of writs and building up by their judgments a body of law that made England the justest land in Europe. Among them were some very great men – Martin Pattishall, whose tireless industry on assize wore out all his fellow judges; William Raleigh of Devonshire, who became bishop of Norwich and Winchester; and his still more famous pupil, Henry de Bracton – another west-country man who held the rectorships of Coombe-in-Teignhead and Bideford and who lies buried in Exeter cathedral, of which he was chancellor. His text book on litigation, *The Laws and Customs of England*, citing more than five hundred decisions collected from the plea rolls of the royal courts, was the most germinating legal work of the age.

Though case-law was not yet binding on the courts, it was fast becoming so, for the professional judges were the sole interpreters of the 'custom of the King's court' which became through them the Common Law of England. Its strength lay in its popularity with all classes of free Englishmen. It was in the thirteenth century that the words judgment and plea, inquest, assize and heir, acquit and fine first became part of English speech. Even the poorest freeman felt that he could get justice from the royal courts and at a cheaper rate than that offered under any other system of law. For it was a point of honour with the King's judges that, while the sale of writs formed an important source of revenue, a poor litigant should be able to obtain an essential writ for nothing.

In their work of enforcing the law the King's ministers had been faced by a decision – made in 1215 at an international Church Council at Rome – that the clergy should no longer take part in the practice of ascertaining legal guilt by the time-honoured ordeal of fire or water. This sign of growing reliance on human reason, which the Church, through its educational institutions, was slowly if unconsciously creating, robbed the primitive 'judgment by God' of its religious sanction. It presented courts of law throughout Christendom with the problem of finding some alternative method of reaching verdicts when there was a clash of evidence. In southern lands, where there were plenty of clerks trained by the law-schools of Ravenna and Bologna in the rediscovered principles of classical jurisprudence, resort was had to Roman rules of evidence. In England, far removed from the fount of classical learning, a simpler native substitute was found. In 1281, the King's Council issued to itinerant justices a direction that, sooner than keep persons charged with felonies indefinitely in gaol, they should use their discretion. They were to experiment and make use of their experience in ascertaining and estimating local opinion. Just as Henry II's judges had accepted, as proof of a man's right to his lands, a sworn

oath from an assize or jury of his neighbours, so his great-grandson's judges met the Lateran Council's repudiation of trial-by-
God by summoning similar, though humbler, juries to resolve the
guilt of those accused of felony. Juries of presentment, drawn
partly from the knightly class and partly from representatives of
the villages, were already presenting suspected criminals to the
King's justices. The latter now adopted the idea of using the small
freeholders or sokemen assembled by the sheriffs for this purpose
to resolve, with a simple yes or no, whether those presented were
actually guilty of the crimes of which they had been accused. They
took counsel, as the saying was, of the neighbourhood.

Thus for the supposed verdict of God through the elements
was gradually substituted the conception – a curiously English one
– of a verdict through the inspiration of a dozen decent honest
freemen, equipped with local knowledge and sworn under a solemn
religious oath to speak the truth in open court. *Vox populi* – not of
an anonymous mob but of a group of 'worthy and lawful' men who
knew their neighbourhood – was to be accepted as the voice of
God. The accused could take his choice of submitting to such a
verdict, of putting himself, as it was called, upon the country, or of
remaining in gaol. It was a rough and ready way of getting at the
truth, but one whose roots lay deep in English history. And in the
course of their everyday practice – though it was a process which
took centuries to complete – the trained judges of the Crown
contrived methods of making evidence available to such petty
juries that eventually proved more realistic than all the elaborate
rules of Roman Law. The judges expounded and interpreted the
law, and the jurymen, who began their long career as corporate
witnesses to the opinion of the locality, became in the end judges of
fact and assessors of evidence.

*   *   *

The English chain of law was a partnership between Crown and
people: between, that is, the hall of justice at Westminster and the
local courts, officers and jurymen of the shire, hundred and vill,
and the delegated jurisdictions and franchises of the feudal landowners. These last remained as numerous as ever but now derived

their strength not, as in other feudal States, from their separateness but from their participation in the royal machinery of government. The sword and rod of equity with which the King did justice were the earls and barons of the realm, the sheriffs and knights of the shire, the constables of the hundred and vill. And they in their turn depended on the royal authority for the peace, order and growing prosperity of their society.

Behind the royal courts lay 'the community of the realm'. It consisted not only of barons and prelates but of the lesser landowners of the shire, of the petty freeholders of the villages and the burgesses of the free towns. The first, increasingly styled knights of the shire, performed a multitude of duties. They served as sheriffs, escheators and coroners, and as justices on special commissions of gaol-delivery to relieve the overworked royal judges; they sat in judgment in the shire court at its monthly meetings in the county-town, and attended the two great annual assemblies when the lord, knights and freeholders of the shire gathered to meet the justices on *eyre*. They served on the committees which scrutinised the presentments of the hundreds and villages, and carried the record of the shire court to Westminster when summoned there by the King's judges. They acted as jurymen on the grand assize, assessed, as elected representatives of their fellow knights of the shire, any taxes due from each hundred, and investigated and reported on local abuses and grievances. They were constantly being called on for their views in questions put to them on oath by the King's judges and Council. So were the humbler freeholders and sokemen who also, as elected representatives of their neighbours, assessed the village taxes. Even outside the privileged ranks of 'free men', the community of the unfree was represented by the six *villani* or villein-farmers who presented, with the parish priest and reeve, the local malefactors and answered for the village's offences and omissions before the terrible all-enquiring *eyre*.

Co-operation between central officials, paid and trained for their specialist functions, and unpaid and part-time amateurs representing the interests, property and good sense of the local community, was the means by which the Plantagenet kings both ordered and unified their realm. With the growing complexity of legal procedure, the royal justices had become something more than temporary deputies delegated from baronial or episcopal bench to try particular cases in their sovereign's place. They were now permanent royal officials. They still performed a multitude of services, hearing assizes, delivering county gaols on *eyre*, acting as commissioners of array, supervising the collection of subsidies and sitting on the royal Council. Some were in clerical orders like John le Breton or Britton, the bishop of Hereford who is believed to have written a condensation of Bracton's treatise on the laws of England; the much-used Martin of Littleburn; and the Norfolk-born Ralph de Hengham, canon of St Paul's and archdeacon of Worcester, who began his legal career as a clerk to one of Henry III's judges and rose to be Chief Justice both of the Common Pleas and the King's Bench, leaving behind two important tracts on procedure and pleadings. Others were laymen, county knights and local notables or legal specialists who had practised as lawyers in the courts before they became judges. Of the fifteen members of the King's Bench appointed during Edward I's reign seven were clerics and eight laymen, including both the chief justices of his latter years.

Below them were the attorneys, who represented clients, prosecuting their writs and entering their pleas by proxy, and the skilled narrators, pleaders and serjeants-at-law – successors of the professional champions of trial-by-battle – who composed the pleas and narrated and argued the pleadings, so saving suitors from the verbal slips which could so easily unsuit the untrained. For the rules of an action-at-law before the King's judges were most strictly enforced; the very language, a kind of bastard French interlaced with Latin and designed to ensure the utmost precision of meaning, was almost impossible for a layman to understand. Any freeholder who had been dispossessed or kept out of his land could buy from the Chancery clerks a writ addressed to the sheriff of his county directing him to summon the dispossessor to answer the plantiff in an action-at-law. The number of such writs had been steadily increasing in order to cover all conceivable causes of action over freehold-land. Yet, unless the exact one appropriate to the wrong complained of was chosen, the action was bound to fail. The forms of pleading and procedure of the particular remedy sought had to be meticulously observed by both plantiff and defendant, even to the minutest details of wording.

The earliest forms of action, in civil as opposed to criminal law, were all concerned with the ownership or possession of land – the wealth on which the military and political organisation of a feudal State depended. In England, alone among the medieval kingdoms of Christendom, it became established principle that no man need answer for his freehold without a royal writ and that no suit touching the ownership or possession of land could be commenced without one. During the thirteenth century the number of such writs and actions available – *right, praecipe, novel disseisin, mort d'ancestor, aiel, besaiel, cosinage* – steadily increased in order to cover all conceivable disputes over land between freemen. Later they were extended, though with great caution, to cover cases affecting the ownership or possession not only of 'real' property as land was called, but of 'moveable' or 'personal' property. Such was the writ of *replevin* for wrongful distraint of cattle; of *trespass*, ordering the sheriff to compel the defendant to answer a complaint that, 'with force and arms' and against the King's peace, he had carried off the plaintiff's goods or done him some other injury; of *detinue* for wrongful detention of some specific chattel like a plough or horse; and of *debt* to compel the defendant to repay a fixed sum of money of which he was alleged to have 'deforced' the plaintiff; of *account* to make a bailiff, agent or, later, a partner submit an account of moneys received; *covenant* to enforce rights under seal such as leases; and *assumpsit* for certain breaches of general undertakings not under seal; of *case* which was eventually extended by legal fictions to cover all sorts of wrongs for which no redress existed earlier, including slander and libel. But the bounds of each form of action and the remedy provided by it were most narrowly prescribed and only gradually widened, if at all, to cover new wrongs. For many civil injuries, particularly of a contractual kind, no remedy was as yet available in the royal courts, though in some cases it might be so in the mercantile courts of the boroughs, where the international 'law merchant' was adjudicated, or in the ecclesiastical courts administering canon law.

The Exchequer enforced the king's fiscal rights, the King's Bench tried pleas of the Crown and heard appeals from other courts, the Common Pleas sat permanently in Westminster Hall to adjudicate, with the help of local juries from the shires, disputes between the owners of freehold-land. Below them, though also subject to the King's overriding writ, were local courts of an older kind, administering the customary law of the neighbourhood. The most important of these was the shire-court, presided over by the sheriff, which met once a month in the south and every six weeks in the wilder north. Held in some spot hallowed by immemorial usage and dating back to days when the shire had been almost an independent province, it was attended, not only by litigants, but by all, either in person or deputy who, holding freehold-land in the county, owed it suit. For it was the basis of Anglo-Saxon and Danish law – long adopted by England's French-speaking kings and lords – that all freemen should by 'witness of the shire' share responsibility for the administration of justice in the county where their lands lay.

At this great concourse of neighbours and men of substance, held either in the open air or, more often now, in a fine new hall of plea, like the one Edmund of Cornwall built for his duchy at Lost-withiel, royal ordinances and statutes were proclaimed, officers and bailiffs were sworn in, inquests were held into dispute rights, and presentments made on matters relating to pleas of the Crown for trial by the itinerant justices. The suitors of the court also elected those required by the King to 'bear the record of the shire' in the courts at Westminster or in Parliament, and the coroners whose business it was to keep a record, independently of the sheriff, of all crimes and incidents affecting the Crown's rights and to hold in-quests on sudden deaths, shipwrecks and discoveries of treasure trove. Sentence of outlawry was passed, too, in the shire-court on anyone who had failed on four successive occasions to answer a summons to a criminal charge. Though its work was being in-creasingly superseded by the King's courts, it still had cognizance of cases in which the accused elected to be tried by the older methods of compurgation. Sometimes, too, when neither party wanted a jury, a plea of land would remain in the county court to be resolved by two professional champions contending all day with minute horn-tipped pickaxes until one or other yielded as 'craven'.

Below the sheriffs' court was the hundred court, held once every three weeks by a bailiff to whom the sheriff or the owner of the hundred jurisdiction had sublet its profits, but who, as a royal officer, was responsible to the sheriff or, in a few special cases, directly to the Crown. It was usually held in the open air, the suitors of the court – freehold tenants of certain parcels of land – sitting on benches round a table occupied by the bailiff and his clerk. Its business was of a petty kind – claims for services arising out of land, detention of chattels and small debts, complaints about the maiming of beasts, and personal assaults and brawls not amounting to felony. The most common plea was trespass – an elastic offence which it was often easier to bring home to a neighbour in the hundred court than to compass in the rigid limits of a Chancery writ. It is doubtful, for instance, if Robert Kite could have obtained redress at Westminster from Stephen Winter whom he sued in the court of Milton hundred for coming into his garden, breaking down his hedges and carrying off his roses 'against the peace', or John Malkin from Maud-atte-Hythe and her son for beating his pig and egging on their dogs till they bit off its tail. There were other pleas, like verbal contracts and slander, for which the royal courts offered as yet no remedy, but under which rustic litigants could sue one another in those of the hundred.

Twice a year, at Easter and Michaelmas, the sheriff visited every hundred in the shire to hold a tourn or criminal court. Everyone who held freehold-land in the hundred except the greater magnates had to attend or be fined for absence. In the tourn or 'law-hundred', peasants of villein blood as well as freemen played a part. For by Anglo-Saxon law every layman without land that could be forfeited for felony had to belong to a tithing – a group of neighbours responsible for one another's good conduct. Before the sheriff's annual view of *frankpledge*, as it was called, the bailiff checked the tithing lists of every village in his hundred, crossing out the names of those who had died since the last view and swearing in any lad who had reached the age of twelve and so become, in the eyes of the law, a responsible citizen. With his hand on the

Bible the boy had to promise to keep the peace and be neither a thief nor a helper of thieves. 'I will be a lawful man,' he swore, 'and bear loyalty to our lord the King and his heirs, and I will be justiciable to my chief tithing man, so help me God and the saints.' Then he and every other villager paid his tithing-penny, which constituted, with the various court fees and assized rents, the profits of the hundred jurisdiction.

At the sheriff's tourn every village or township was represented by its reeve and four men who answered for any omission in its public duty and for such offences as ploughing up the King's high-way or executing a thief caught red-handed without first securing the official witness of a royal bailiff or coroner. They were respon-sible, too, for the township's payment of fines imposed on it for breaches of the regulations for baking of bread and brewing of ale. They had to report to twelve freeholders called the jury of present-ment all crimes that had been committed within the township. The tourn dealt, also, with nuisances like washing clothes in wells and polluting drinking-water. More serious offences were presented by the jury to the royal justices for trial on their next visit to the shire. When this happened the humble representatives of the village found themselves answering questions put to them under oath by the King's chief legal officers.

* * *

If, thanks to her strong line of kings, the law and its subtle complex processes had taken the place of the sword, it was employed, by Crown and subject alike, with the ruthlessness of the battlefield. And it was often grossly abused. In a medieval state without a police force and only a minute administrative service, corruption and maladministration of justice were inevitable. Twice in his reign Edward I was forced to take drastic action against his own officers for abuses of the law. Sheriffs and their servants took bribes, were extortionate, refused writs or sold them at exorbitant prices, and imprisoned men under legal pretences to make them pay for their release. Judges and their clerks let it be known that success in their courts would never attend a suitor who did not fee

165

them. In 1289, on his return to England after three years' absence in his French dominions, Edward I found no less than seven hundred officials guilty of malpractices. Only two of the eight judges of the King's Bench and Common Pleas escaped disgrace, while five justices of *eyre* were found guilty and dismissed.

The most important result of these judicial scandals was a reorganisation of the legal profession. The task was entrusted to the new Chief Justice of the Common Pleas, John de Metyngham – one of the two members of the original bench to escape the purge. In 1292 he and his fellow judges were commissioned to choose from every county a number of the more promising students of law to be officially attached to the courts either as attorneys or as apprentices to the serjeants or *servientes ad legem* who pleaded before the King's judges. They were to enjoy a monopoly and their numbers, fixed at first at a hundred and forty, were to be left to the judges to add to as required. In other words, the profession was to regulate its own recruitment, education and rules of practice.

It was the beginning of a new form of learned education, one outside the Church and independent of it. A century after Henry II had been forced to concede immunity for clerics from lay justice, his great-grandson, Edward I, established secular training for the Common Law as an alternative to the study of civil law which, like every other form of learning, the Church in its universities reserved exclusively for its own members. It was an education based on the practice of the courts, necessitating great precision of thought and speech. It was taught, not by theorists in lecture rooms and libraries, but in crowded courts of law where, under the eye of the King's judges, quick and trained professional wits were pitted against one another, as the masters of forensic science, thinking and arguing on their feet, sought to fit the conflicting facts of their clients' disputes into the sharply defined framework of Common Law writs and procedures.

These tyros or apprentices assisted and devilled for their seniors as they do today, attended their consultations and listened to the thrust and parry of their contests from enclosures called 'cribs' built at the sides of the courts. In the year in which the King entrusted their education to his judges there appeared the first of

"Where dynamics and pure poetry blend and become indistinguishable."
The nave of Wells Cathedral. 13th century.

"The graceful multi-shafted central pillar which bore the vaulted roof."
Chapter House, Salisbury c. 1268–1280.

the Year Books – manuscript notes of cases, pleadings and forensic argument made for young advocates to help them master the intricacies of the law. Written in the legal French of the courts, they set out in staccato jottings the arguments and altercations, exceptions and answers of the great serjeants who dominated the courts at the end of the thirteenth and beginning of the fourteenth century – Lowther, Heyham, Howard, Hertpool, Huntingdon, Spigornel – and the interruptions and often caustic comments of the judges. 'Leave off your noise and deliver yourself from his account,' Chief Justice Hengham interrupts an over-persistent pleader. 'Get to your business,' his successor, Bereford, enjoins. 'You plead one point, they about another, so that neither of you strikes the other.' And when learned counsel tried to gain the day by arguing, 'We have seen damages awarded in similar circumstances,' Bereford replied, 'You will never see them so long as I am here.' 'Where have you seen a guardian vouch on a writ of *dower*?' asked another judge and, when the incautious serjeant answers, 'Sir, in Trinity term last past, and of that I vouch the record,' there came the crushing rejoinder, 'If you find it, I will give you my hat!'

The interest of these early Year Books – and no other nation has anything like them – is the greater because, in those formative years, judges were helping by their judgments and the precedents they created to shape the future course of the law. Some of them, like Hengham, had even drafted it in the King's Council chamber; 'do not gloss the statute,' he remarked on one occasion, 'we know it better than you, for we made it.' For all their insistence on the rigid rules of pleading and procedure, such judges were very conscious of the immense discretionary power to do justice and equity delegated to them by their royal master. 'You wicked rascal,' Saunton, J. interrupted a dishonest attorney who had prayed for a *postea* in defiance of the rules of just dealing, 'you shall not have it! But because you, to delay the woman from her dower, have vouched and not sued a writ to summon your warrantor, this court awards that you go to prison.'[1]

The apprentice pleaders did not only learn together in the courts. They lived together in inns or hospices presided over by

[1] Selden Society XXII, Year Book Series IV, p. 195.

their senior members. In the leafy suburb of Holborn and in the Thames-side meadows between Westminster Hall and London's western walls there sprang up, during the years of expanding litigation which followed Edward I's legislative reforms, a whole colony of such bachelor establishments. Keeping an inn seems to have become a highly profitable source of revenue for leaders of the legal profession, for some of them kept several; a Chancery clerk named John de Tamworth had, in the reign of Edward's grandson, no fewer than four in the neighbourhood of Fetter Lane. Similar inns were kept for the clerks of Chancery. Nearly all were rented from ecclesiastical corporations or dignitaries – Templars, Hospitallers, Black Friars, the priory of St Bartholomew, the convent of Clerkenwell, the abbey of Missenden, the bishop of Ely – who owned most of the land immediately to the west of London. Though never formally incorporated like the Church's residential colleges and halls at Oxford and Cambridge, they helped to create *esprit de corps* and standards of professional conduct among those studying and practising the law.

After Edward I had placed the education of the legal profession under his judges and divorced it from the Church, its wealth and influence grew very rapidly. In an acquisitive and evolving society in which litigation had taken the place of private war, the brethren of the coif – the white silken hood worn by the King's serjeants-at-law and the judges who were chosen from their ranks – constituted a new aristocracy. 'Law,' wrote the poet Langland in the reign of Edward's grandson, 'is grown lord!' By then the judges in their scarlet robes trimmed with white budge or lambskin and the serjeants in their long part-coloured gowns of blue, green and brown, cut almost as great a figure in the realm as the magnates and prelates.

CHAPTER TWELVE

Wild Wales

'Bold immortal country whose hilltops have stood
Stronghold for the high gods when on earth they go,
Terror for fat burghers in far plains below.'

Robert Graves

'Their Lord they shall praise,
Their language they shall keep,
Their land they shall lose
Except wild Wales.'

Taliesin's Prophesy

WHILE USING ROYAL PARLIAMENTS to make and establish new laws for England – some of which, like his land laws, were to last for centuries – Edward I longed to give law and lordship to the whole of Britain, including the barbarous and mountainous west and far north. For the claim of his remote ancestors to a suzerainty over all the princes of Britain appealed to him deeply. It was one to which he attached far more importance than any of his immediate predecessors. For, half Frenchman though he was, he had never shared his father's and grandfather's dream of regaining their Norman and Angevin continental patrimony. The only empire he coveted outside Gascony – the inheritance of his great grandmother, Eleanor of Aquitaine – was that of the British Isles. Nursed in the new courtly fashion of regarding the legendary King Arthur and his knights as the champions of Britain and its vanished Roman *imperium*, he saw himself as their heir.

This, however, was not at all how the real descendants of Arthur's warriors saw him. To the Celts of western Britain Edward was merely a king of the Saxons who had slaughtered and dispossessed their forbears. He was the overlord, too, of the armoured horsemen from France who, while giving the Saxons discipline and leadership, had raised so many outposts of England in the valleys of central and southern Wales. To the fierce tribesmen beyond the Severn the stone castles of the Normans seemed as alien as the Roman legionary camps of a thousand years before.

Divided by tribal and dynastic feuds, the southern and central valleys of Wales had been colonised soon after the Conquest by Norman adventurers who had brought them under the overlordship, though not the direct rule, of the kings of England. From the upper reaches of the Severn in Powys to the ancient princedoms of Deheubarth and Morgannwy along the Bristol Channel, the great Marcher lords – Clares and Mortimers, Bohuns and Fitzalans, Braoses, Chaworths and Giffards – ruled by the sword, the King's licence and their own wits. With their castles and mounted knights they dominated the lowlands, leaving the bare uplands of sheep and heather to the migrant Celtic tribes.

For their penetration was only valley deep. Around them the ancient life of mountain Cambria, half warlike, half pastoral, continued as it had done for a thousand years. Its people lived by raiding and keeping cattle and sheep. In the summer they fed them on the hill-pastures or *hafod*, in the winter on the lowlands or *hendre*. So wild was that sparsely populated countryside that two pilgrimages to St David's were regarded by pious Englishmen as the equal in peril and hardship of one to Jerusalem. Its few minute towns huddled for safety round the Marchers' castles; its very churches, crowning tactical vantage-points, resembled forts. Its petty 'kings' or *brenins* spent their summers in forays on one another and the Saxon, and their winters listening to their bards and harpers nostalgically commemorating the glories of old. With their golden torques and white horses, their bands of young warriors and proud memories of ancient victory, they deemed it 'ignoble to die in bed and an honour to fall on the field of battle'. Every spring the clansmen set out along the cloud-hidden tracks above the valleys to burst in a torrent on some rival tribe or distant English farm. It had been so as long as men could remember.

So long as the Marchers left them to follow this immemorial life the Welsh, preoccupied with tribal and family feuds, made no attempt to combine against them. Only when England was weakly ruled or divided was any concerted effort made to drive the Anglo-Norman lords from the country. For outside their castle walls the latter seldom had the last word against the tribesmen of the hills. Plunder and arson could always be met by plunder and arson and, as their farms offered tempting booty, their presence was accepted philosophically. In their turn the Marchers entered into the life of Wales. They married the native chieftains' daughters and took sides in their tribal affrays. The inconveniences of cattle-raiding and seasonal war were offset for them by the freedom they enjoyed, unknown in judge-ridden England, of living under their own, not the King's law. Theirs was an independence which existed no-where else in Edward's dominion. No writ ran in their liberties and no appeal lay from their courts. They raised private armies to harry their neighbours' lands and guard their own, as in the far days before a Plantagenet king had made feudalism a political strait-jacket for their warlike class.

In the same way the Cistercian monks and their monasteries became naturalised and part of the life of Wales. Their solitude and austerity recalled to a primitive hill people the lives of their own early evangelists. Despite their Latin affiliations and the splendid churches with which the Marchers and the Welsh princes endowed them, the Cistercian houses in Wales were far more Celtic than Roman, conforming to a traditional pattern in which personal piety and local loyalty counted for more than dogma and the regimenta-tion of an international order. What little Llantwit and Llancarfan had been in the centuries of Rome's eclipse, Margam and Tintern, Abbey Dore and Strata Florida, Aberconway and Valle Crucis became in the new age of Rome's ecclesiastical grandeur. Yet though they formed centres of native learning and culture, they also helped to link Wales to the wider world of Christendom and to render possible her peaceful co-existence with her more orderly neighbour.

Had it not been for one circumstance the absorption of Wales into the Anglo-Norman kingdom might have come about in the end with as little violence as that of Celtic Cornwall. In 1237, with the death of its last hereditary earl, there had lapsed to the Crown the greatest of all the Marcher lordships – the palatine earldom of Chester, whose historic function it was to guard the Cheshire and Shropshire plains from the raiders of the Snowdon hills. Though still remaining a separate legal entity, its administration passed into the hands of royal officials whose orderly minds, schooled in the discipline of the Exchequer and Common Law, abhorred such time-hallowed Cymric customs as cattle-raiding and the blood-feud. And confronting them across a no-man's-land of little wooded hills and uncertain lordships lay the principality of Gwynedd, the last of the old independent 'kingdoms' of Wales and the one place where, guarded by the precipices of Snowdonia, there existed a Welsh royal court, a body of Welsh law administered by native judges and a focus for a sentiment which was not only tribal but national.

A century earlier, after the civil wars of Stephen and Matilda, another semi-independent Welsh principality had flourished on the southern shores of Cardigan Bay under Rhys ap Gruffyd, a prince of the ancient house of Tewdwr or Tudor. Having seized Cardigan castle from the Marcher, Roger de Clare, he had kept it by a shrewd mixture of resistance and subservience to Henry II, whose supremacy he acknowledged and whose vice-regent he claimed to be. In 1176, at his Christmas feast, he had held the first recorded *eisteddfod*, at which entrants from every part of Wales contested for the bardic crowns of music and poetry.

After his death Rhys's dominion had disintegrated, and the primacy among the native chieftains had passed to the heirs of his northern ally, Owen, Prince of Gwynedd. The latter's grandson, Llywelyn ap Ioworth – Llywelyn the Great, as the bards called him – took advantage of King John's difficulties to seize Marcher territory on the upper Dee and Severn and later, by siding with his fellow tenants-in-chief in England, to win concessions from the Crown. Three of the clauses of Magna Carta had been inserted at his instance. At one time he even captured Shrewsbury and, controlling two-thirds of Wales, aroused a surge of national pride in his countrymen. Yet, conscious of their incorrigible separatism, he made no attempt to flaunt his power and, dividing his conquests among the lesser chieftains, chose to reign over his fellow Welshmen's hearts rather than their lands. Recognising the strength of a reunited England, he did homage for Gwynedd to the young king, Henry III, and lived in peace for the rest of his days.[1]

It was this Prince's grandson, Llywelyn ap Gruffydd, who was now, after many vicissitudes, lord of Gwynedd. He, too, had taken advantage of England's troubles under Henry III to impose his suzerainty on the Welsh chieftains of Powys, to seize the Mortimer stronghold of Builth on the upper Wye, and to overrun with his fierce spearmen the Cantrefs of Perfeddwlad, as the Crown fiefs in the disputed coastal borderland between Chester and Gwynedd were called. But by allying himself too closely with de Montfort he had united the royal Earl of Chester, Prince Edward, with the other Marcher lords. After they had overthrown de Montfort they compelled him to make his peace with King Henry who, in return for homage and military service, acknowledged Llywelyn's lordship of Gwynedd and his self-chosen title of Prince or *pendragon* of Wales. Since then the English power had again been rising, and the Marchers, resolved to prevent further raids from the north, had been building new and stronger castles, like the mighty Caerphilly which Gilbert de Clare, the red earl of Gloucester, raised near Cardiff in the closing years of Henry III's reign.

The Prince of Gwynedd and Edward I were thus old rivals. Llywelyn, whose father had been killed trying to escape from the Tower, had tasted triumph over the English when Edward was a raw untried youth. He resented his supremacy and thought of himself as the overlord of all the native chieftains of Wales, whose allegiance he was always trying to deflect to himself. Even more fiercely he resented any legal control from Westminster, Chester or Shrewsbury, not only over, his own rocky acres in Snowdonia and Anglesey – where for geographical

---

[1] He died in 1240 at Aberconway abbey. The village of Beddgelert is said to commemorate the name and grave of a favourite dog who saved his infant son from a wolf.

reasons there had never been any – but over the disputed border-lands in the Marches.

Edward had no wish to deprive Llywelyn of what was lawfully his. But he was a feudal king, brought up in the strict tradition of feudal rights and obligations. He thought of the Prince of Gwynedd as the Welsh equivalent of an Anglo-Norman earl. By ancient prescription and a solemn treaty made after the barons' wars, Llywelyn owed him homage and fealty. And by the English con-ception of feudalism all lordship under the Crown involved sub-jection to the Common Law except where a clearly defined liberty had been granted. What stuck in Edward's gullet was the Welsh prince's claim, not merely to a feudal liberty like those of his forbears and the Marchers, but to a completely self-governing lordship like the Scottish kingdom which, under the kings of England's nominal suzerainty, had been independent from time immemorial.

For Llywelyn sought to be ruler, not only of Gwynedd, but of Wales. Nursed in bardic lore and deeply conscious of his country-men's right to nationhood, he voiced his claim in a letter to Edward in 1273, after the royal authorities had refused to allow him to build an unlicensed castle on land of his own in the Marches near Montgomery. 'We are sure,' he wrote, 'that the writ was not issued with your knowledge . . . For you know well that the rights of our principality are entirely separate from the rights of your kingdom . . . and that we and our ancestors had the power within our bound-aries to build castles and forts and create markets without pro-hibition by anyone.'

This was the inevitable reaction of a Welsh chieftain to any scheme of centralised control: one bound to arouse the challenge of a reforming king with a passion for legal definition. Both un-consciously wanted something new – Llywelyn the sovereignty of an independent Welsh nation, Edward the legal administration of the country on the closely-knit pattern of England. It was natural that, alarmed by the castles which the Marchers were building against his power, Llywelyn should wish to see not only Gwynedd, but his new fiefs in the Marches, guarded by castles of his own. Yet it was by now a principle of English law that a vassal's right to erect a military fortress could only be granted by royal licence.

Shortly after Edward's coronation, which Llywelyn failed to attend, a new dispute arose. The latter's brother, David, suspected of a plot to dethrone him, fled to England. Instead of handing him back to Llywelyn for punishment, the King's officers, contending that the matter must first be investigated by law, allowed him refuge at Shrewsbury. To Llywelyn this seemed proof that his brother's treachery was being condoned by Edward so that he might plot his death from English soil. Not until he was returned to him, he declared, would he do homage to an overlord who so criminally wronged his own vassal.

According to his lights, the King behaved with considerable restraint. Alone of his tenants-in-chief, Llywelyn had failed to do homage on his accession. By feudal law the price of such contumacy was forfeiture of the fief. After waiting for nearly a year, and after the prince had ignored a further summons to Westminster, Edward invited him to meet him at Chester under safe conduct. To this and the royal journey to the Dee, Llywelyn's only response was to summon a parliament of his own vassals to endorse his refusal. Before he would meet the King, he announced, the latter must surrender as hostages his eldest son, his Chancellor Burnell, and the Marcher earl of Gloucester.

Even this demand did not exhaust Edward's patience. He did not wish to incur the cost of a Welsh campaign or to be deflected from his work of reform in England. Yet he was determined to have his relationship with Llywelyn clarified. Three times he summoned him to do homage: at Westminster in November 1275, at Winchester in the New Year of 1276, and again at Westminster that Easter. It was characteristic of his habit of crossing the t's of his legal claims that the proposed meeting-places were no longer on the Welsh border but in the heart of his own realm.

This made Llywelyn still more indignant. Again he refused, save on conditions to which no overlord could agree. He appealed to the Pope for justice, declaring that the King was harbouring traitors and, as though to underline the breach between them, sent to France for the daughter of Simon de Montfort, with whom ten years earlier, when they were in arms against the English Crown, he had made a treaty of marriage. This was a double offence against feudal law, for not only was Eleanor de Montfort the daughter of a traitor but, as a member of the royal house, she could not marry without the King's consent. By chance the ship bringing her to Wales was intercepted in the Bristol Channel and she was taken prisoner. Henceforward her release became an added condition of Llywelyn's homage.

At the Easter Parliament of 1276 the prelates asked if they might make a last appeal to the stubborn Welshman. A trained canonist was sent as envoy, and the summer passed in fruitless negotiation. When a new Parliament met in November neither its members nor Edward were in a mood for parleying. They agreed that Llywelyn's contumacy must be punished and that the King should 'go upon him as a rebel and disturber of his peace'. The Marches were ordered to be put into a state of war and the feudal host summoned to meet at Worcester at midsummer 1277. A warning was also sent to Llywelyn by the Archbishop of Canterbury – metropolitan of the see in which Wales lay – that unless he submitted he would be excommunicated.

Llywelyn treated the excommunication like the King's summonses. The English had never conquered Gwynedd, neither before nor after their subjection to the Normans, and it was natural for its brave, half barbaric chieftains to regard it as unconquerable. Its ruler was taking no very apparent risk in defying his overlord. He was prince of the mountains and mountain tribes and despised the English host. His forbears had repelled it under Henry II and John and, more lately, under the young Edward himself. He had only to withdraw into the trackless hills to ambush the heavily cumbered invaders in some forest defile or, lying concealed amid mists and precipices, starve them and their horses into retreat. Inspired by the prophesies of the legendary Merlin, he even dreamt of driving them out of Britain altogether and ruling, like his Roman ancestors, over the whole island. For the triumphs won by himself and his grandfather during England's baronial wars suggested to his enthusiastic, mercurial mind that what a few thousand Norman knights had done the Cymri under his leadership might do again.

Though they could never refrain from quarrelling with one another the Welsh tribesmen were magnificent fighters. War was their occupation, and training for it their education. Under their laws six weeks of every summer were spent in marauding expeditions and their entire youth was ready for instant service at their chieftains' call. Unlike the English, they were not pinned down by husbandry and harvest; they were used to living hard and travelling light. Able to subsist on the whey of their mountain goats and the cheese of their herds, they needed no commissariat. Some of them, in the hills of the south, had evolved a new and terrifying weapon: the longbow of Gwent, 'made of wild elm, unpolished, rude and uncouth', whose arrows, fired faster than a crossbow's, could pierce the mailed shirt, breeches and saddle of an armoured knight and pin him to his horse's side. Their sudden, swift-footed charge with javelin, sword and war-horn down glen or hillside could break the nerve of all but the hardiest and, though quickly discouraged if withstood, their recovery after defeat had again and again turned the tables on their victors. With their bare, sinewy legs, their squat bodies wrapped in scarlet plaids, their capacity to live out of doors in the depth of winter, they seemed as impervious to weather as the rocks among which they lay in ambush. Their trackless terrain and climate of mist, snow and driving rain made any prolonged campaign against them profitless. Punitive expedition after expedition of English knights had advanced up their mountain valleys only to withdraw, famished, horseless and empty-handed, after a few months in that starve-acre land.

'Grevouse est le guerre et dure à l'endurer
Quand ailleurs est l'été, en Galles est hiver,'

wrote a disgusted Anglo-Norman poet.

Yet Llywelyn had forgotten that times had changed. Under its new ruler England was no longer divided as in the days of de Montfort. Its whole administrative effort was now directed to bringing Gwynedd to heel. Nor was Edward the raw youth who had fought against the Welsh twenty years before. He was a commander of international fame who had led the armies of Christendom and rivalled the fame of his great-uncle Coeur-de-Lion. He was no amateur like his dilettante father.

His preparations for the coming campaign left nothing to chance. During the winter and spring of 1277, while the Marchers took the offensive against Llywelyn's supporters in Powysland and Cardiganshire, Edward was gathering not only the largest English army since the Conquest, but the best-equipped. Agents were sent to France to buy up the huge war-horses that would be needed as remounts for the cavalry of his household guard and, with the help of the feudal levy, nearly a thousand heavily armoured horsemen were assembled in support of the Marchers along the Welsh borderland. But most of the troops Edward raised were infantry. They came from Cheshire, Lancashire and Derbyshire, from Rutland, Shropshire and Worcestershire, from Radnor and Brecon. Some were conscripted by commissioners of array from the *fyrd* or *posse comitatus*, others were veterans who had fought under Edward in the Barons' War or on crusade. In all, over fifteen thousand foot soldiers were brought together, more than half of them Welsh. To these the King added a small force of professional crossbowmen, mostly Gascons, and a contingent of archers from Macclesfield Forest.

It was not an experienced army, for it was twelve years since Evesham, and few young Englishmen outside the March had taken part in a campaign. But their commander was the greatest military organiser of the age, and he knew what was necessary for a campaign in a barren land. He had set himself to do what no one had yet succeeded in doing – not merely to drive the Welsh into the mountains, which was comparatively easy, but to hold them there and wear them down till they yielded. Hitherto it had always been the invaders of Snowdonia who had starved and given up the struggle. This time, by organising a massive commissariat and transport train, Edward meant to see that the defenders did so.

Early in July 1277 the King took command of the host at Worcester. Attended by the hereditary Constable, the Marshal and Llywelyn's brother, Prince David, he marched up the Severn and Dee to Cheshire where, to invoke a blessing on his campaign, he laid the foundation stone of a new Cistercian abbey at Vale Royal.[1]

[1] The largest Cistercian church in England, larger even than Fountains. Scarcely a stone now remains.

His plan was to advance by stages along the coast from Chester to Flint, Rhuddlan and the mouth of the Conway, driving clearings through the forests – a bowshot's width – along which his knights and their war-horses and baggage could move in safety. At each point at which the army halted to consolidate before tackling the next stage, he planned to build a castle on or near the coast. For this he employed – impressing where necessary and paying the customary rates of wages – thousands of craftsmen and labourers, drawn from every county of western England, woodmen and carpenters, masons, carters, charcoal-burners, quarrymen, blacksmiths, lime-burners, hodmen, guarding them as they worked by relays of archers.

But the King's trump-card was sea-power. With a fleet to protect his flank and bring up supplies as he moved along the coast, he meant to drive a wedge, not into the high mountains, where the odds would be all in favour of the defenders, but between Gwynedd and the rich isle of Anglesey, the granary on whose crops Llywelyn depended to maintain his tribesmen and their flocks during the winter. Under the terms of their feudal service, the Cinque Ports of Kent and Sussex had to furnish the Crown in time of war with ships and seamen at their own expense for fifteen days. By taking their crews into his pay Edward had secured a weapon which offset all his adversary's geographical advantages.

The advance from Chester began in the middle of July. The King was everywhere, supervising the transport and organising the relays of soldiers and workmen as they drove steadily forward through the densely wooded hills. By the 26th he was at Flint, where a century before his great-grandfather, Henry II, had been ambushed in an attempt to conquer Gwynedd. Three weeks later he moved forward to Rhuddlan, establishing his headquarters there on 20th August. By the 29th he had reached the mouth of the Conway.

The moment had now come for which he had been preparing. Using his fleet to ferry an expeditionary force to Anglesey, he over-ran the island just as the harvest was being got in and robbed Llywelyn of his winter's supplies. By doing so he also threatened a further landing in the rear of the prince's impregnable position on the west bank of the Conway at Penmaenmawr. In two months Edward had completely out-manoeuvred the Welsh.

Llywelyn saw he was checkmated. He did not wait for the end, but surrendered and threw himself on Edward's mercy. By the treaty of Conway on 9 November 1277, he restored the Four Cantrefs of Perfeddwlad, accepted the old frontier of Gwynedd on the Conway and abandoned all claims to suzerainty in the Marches. He also agreed to give hostages for his behaviour, to pay an indemnity for the war and a rent for Anglesey. Next day he swore fealty to the King in his new castle at Rhuddlan.

Edward had won what he sought – the recognition of his lordship and law. He at once remitted the indemnity and rent, and within a year released the hostages. At the Christmas feast at Westminster, where Llywelyn again did homage, he gave him the kiss of peace. Ten months later, satisfied by his peaceful conduct, he permitted his marriage to Eleanor de Montfort and himself presided over their wedding feast.

*   *   *

Yet the Welsh volcano was only slumbering. On the eve of Palm Sunday 1282, without the slightest warning, Edward's former ally, David, fell by night on Hawarden castle, massacred the garrison and carried off the royal Justiciar who had hanged one of his men for an offence unpunishable by Welsh law. Forgetting earlier wrongs at his brother's hands, Llywelyn threw in his lot with him. Everywhere the Welsh rose, laying siege to the hated new castles of Flint and Rhuddlan, storming Llanbadarn – the modern Aberystwyth – and carrying fire and sword to the walls of Chester and through the lands of the Marchers to the Bristol Channel. Everywhere, in that spring of Celtic fury and vengeance, the King's fortresses, except the very strongest, went up in flames.

The rising took Edward completely by surprise. He had showered favours on David, forgiven and befriended Llywelyn, and thought he had done with the barren hills of Wales and its petty princes for ever. The cause of their anger was the English King's denial of Llywelyn's contention that disputes about his lands outside the principality should be governed by the code of of the famous tenth-century Welsh legislator, Hywel Dda or the Good. Yet for more than a hundred years English as well as Welsh law had operated in the Marches. The greatest of all the Cymric chieftains of central Wales – Llywelyn's rebellious vassal, Gruffyd ap Gwenwynwyn, lord of Pool – flatly refused to have his dispute with the Prince of Gwynedd tried by Welsh law, claiming that he should be judged as an English baron. He was prepared, he said, to answer any man according to the Common Law, but in no way according to Welsh Law.

This was too hard a poser for the justices of the March, and the matter was referred to the King. He laid it, as was now his custom with all baronial pleas, before his Council at the next meeting of Parliament. Here it was held that justice could only be done according to the law that Parliament itself administered. The supreme royal court could not give judgment by rules it regarded as unjust, barbarous or unchristian. The Crown, the indignant Welsh Prince was informed, must 'according to God and justice do what the prelates and magnates of the realm shall advise'. Instead of having the matter decided out of hand and by a Welsh judge interpreting a highly elastic local law, Llywelyn was forced to apply for a writ like an English baron and endure the long formalities and delays attendant on a parliamentary suit. The matter was still undecided when, in the spring of 1282, he threw in his lot with his brother.

It was not only Llywelyn and David who felt the irons of subordination to English law. The men of the Four Cantrefs bitterly resented being placed by the Treaty under the jurisdiction of the Justiciar of Chester and the Cheshire shiremoot. It was not like that of the Princes of Gwynedd, or even of their earlier Anglo-Norman rulers, the palatine earls – swift, rough and ready and framed for a warlike society. A nomadic people, who for centuries had viewed cattle-stealing as a branch of agriculture, and war against one another and the Saxon as the poetry of life, did not take kindly to the Common Law. Its slow and elaborate processes seemed to them only tricks for evading justice, its pursuit of truth by the laborious interchange of pieces of parchment an affront to hot-blooded men in search of their rights. They could only respect judgment given instantly and on the spot.

181

Edward had declared that he would uphold Welsh law and custom in the Four Cantrefs so far as they were not barbarous or at variance with reason and the Ten Commandments. Yet this was just how they seemed to any Englishman trained in the royal courts. The officials of the County Palatine who took over the administration of the conquered borderland had nothing but contempt for Welsh law. To them the code of Hywel Dda seemed as archaic and savage as the laws of their remote Anglo-Saxon forbears. How, they asked, could they be expected to administer a legal system which treated civil war as a legitimate activity, that regarded a judge as a private arbitrator hired by a criminal's kinsmen to compound with his avengers, that punished the murder of a bard with a fine of a hundred-and-twenty-six cows? And how could they keep order in a violent land without a death penalty?

It was hard for the English, with their comparatively law-abiding and stable society, not to regard the Welsh robbers and plunderers as savages. To them, as to the sheriff of Shropshire who offered a shilling for every scalp taken during a Welsh raid on Strattondale, they were wolves' heads outside the law. Unlike the Marchers, with their half Welsh ancestry and love of fighting, the farmers of the Cheshire plain could not appreciate the virtues of a people who burnt homes instead of making them and preferred robbery and idleness to honest husbandry.

This assumption that everything Welsh was beneath contempt aroused deep resentment. During the years immediately after Edward's victory, everyone in the Four Cantrefs who had a suit in the Palatine courts became a passionate nationalist. Every departure from ancient custom, every legal and administrative innovation was seen as an affront. Though far more efficient than any rulers Wales had known, and convinced that they were bringing civilization and justice to a backward people, the bureaucrats of the County Palatine imposed a strait-jacket on the life of an ancient community.

Under the rule of the great athelings and the Norman and Angevin kings the English had mastered political lessons far in advance of the Welsh or even of their most civilized continental neighbours. They had learnt to keep the King's Peace, to pay taxes, to abide by a single law, to take personal part in an administrative and legal hierarchy which stretched from the parish and manorial court to the Council of the realm in Parliament. But their system was far too centralised and complex to be intelligible to a primitive, pastoral race. Everything had to be referred to distant authority or remote precedent. And the rules they imported to the Celtic borderland were too often applied in a narrow, pedantic spirit. When Llywelyn, in full cry after a stag, accidentally crossed the frontier-stream between Gwynedd and the Marches, 'the King's officers came to the huntsmen and immediately called out with horns and cries almost the whole countryside', seizing the hounds and imprisoning the riders.

Nor were the administrators England sent to govern the borderland always honest. The theory of thirteenth-century law was one thing, its practice another. King Edward's judges and bailiffs enforced law and order and did justice as they were trained to do, but they also feathered their own nests. Many subordinate officials took bribes and falsely accused the innocent. In the light of their conduct high-sounding talk about the moral superiority of English law struck the Welsh as nauseating.

Above all, the new rulers of the Four Cantrefs were English, not Welsh. The Welsh did not like Englishmen; they had been accustomed from time immemorial, not to nationhood, but to governing themselves. Most of them preferred to be ruled by an unjust fellow countryman than by an upright foreigner – a thing no Englishman could understand. As the Marchers had always recognised but as the administrators of the borderland had still to learn, only a Welshman could understand Welshmen.

For though Wales had never been a kingdom, and only a handful of her people yet thought of her as a nation, the Welsh loved their country. They loved its land, its traditions, its speech, its faith. 'I am persuaded,' an old Welshman had told Henry II a century before, 'that no other race than this and no other tongue than of Wales, happen what may, will answer in the great day of judgment for this little corner of earth.' Since then, under the two Llywelyns, a growing number of Welshmen, including for a time the inhabitants of the Four Cantrefs, had learnt what it was to live as members, not merely of a Welsh tribe, but of a Welsh State.

With its impenetrable mountain barrier to the east and its rich island-granary of Anglesey, Gwynedd had become something more than a group of loosely-knit tribes. In its prince's wooden hall or *neuydd*, where native bards sang the glories of Wales in the presence of a ruler who claimed the allegiance of all Welshmen, the institutions of a modern national kingdom were beginning to take shape.

It was this that made Llywelyn regard the denial of Welsh law in the Marches as a monstrous injustice and affront. Because as lord of Gwynedd he enjoyed his own law under the titular sovereignty of the imperial Crown, he felt that the law should be equally valid in every part of the land of which he called himself prince. With indignation he brooded over the slights that he and his people suffered. 'Each province,' he wrote to Edward, 'under the *imperium* of the King of England has its own customs and laws according to the mode and use of their respective parts where they are situated, such as the Gascons in Gascony, the Scots in Scotland, the Irish in Ireland and the English in England. I, therefore, seek, being a Prince, that I likewise shall have my Welsh law and proceed according to that law. By common right we ought to have our Welsh law and custom, as the other nations in the King's empire have – and in our own language.'

But, though in Gwynedd no one denied him that right, Llywelyn forgot that, whatever he might call himself, he was not the ruler of Wales as the Scots king was of Scotland and Edward of Gascony. Wales was not, and had never been, like Gwynedd, a single state. Yet though on false ground legally, in a wider, poetic sense Llywelyn was right. Because her people were aware of their separateness, even though politically divided, Wales was already one in spirit. Her bards sang of her now as *Cymru* – the land of all the Cymri – and of Llywelyn as 'the great chieftain of fair Wales'. Those who heard them shared his belief that to be punished by English judges in accordance with English-made law was for Welshmen a kind of servitude. 'All Christians,' wrote one of them, 'have laws and customs in their own lands. The Jews among the English have laws. We and our ancestors in our lands had immutable laws and customs until after the last war the English took them from us.' It was this conviction which made the rising of 1382 such a passionate affair.

It made it, too, a cruel one. The Welsh tribesmen did not spare the English in their path. And in those early weeks of the rising they travelled far. Ruthin castle was captured, the earl of Gloucester ambushed in the hills near Llandeilo Fawr, the valleys as far south as Builth and Cardigan harried. Many perished in cold blood, churches and farms were sacked, atrocious acts done. And these were exaggerated in the telling.

This time the English as well as their King were thoroughly aroused. They were resolved to be done with the Welsh, their raids and broken truces, and to subject them to government.

The strategic problem was the same as in 1277. But it was harder to solve because Llywelyn's successes in the south-west had widened the area of fighting. During July the King worked his way along the coast from Chester to his besieged castles at Flint and Rhuddlan, both of which had held out since the spring against David's attacks. Meanwhile he sent the earl of Surrey to clear his left flank in the vale of Clwyd and to drive David from the Four Cantrefs. His aim was, by encircling Snowdon from the south, to force Llywelyn to abandon his conquests in central and south-western Wales in order to save his principality.

Once again sea-power proved decisive. With forty ships from London and the Cinque Ports, Edward was able to turn the enemy's northern flank. As his army advanced slowly through the wooded defiles to the Conway, a seaborne force under a former seneschal of Gascony, Luke de Tany, landed in Anglesey to knock, in the King's words, the feathers out of Llywelyn's tail. It took a month's fighting to clear the island, for this time the Welsh were expecting the blow. But by the middle of October de Tany had almost completed a bridge of boats across the Menai Strait to enable him, at the decisive moment, to take the Welsh position at Penmaenmawr in the rear. Ruthin and Denbigh had already fallen in the south, and in the centre Edward had reached the Conway.

Faced by this triple threat to Snowdonia, Llywelyn abandoned his southern offensive and hurried back to defend his base. Then, just as an English victory seemed certain, de Tany's impatience precipitated disaster. On 6 November, in disobedience to his orders and without waiting for the concerted attack which had been planned, his lieutenant crossed the Menai Strait at low tide, expecting to surprise the Welsh. Instead he was ambushed near Bangor and overwhelmed, losing his life and his entire force as it tried to escape across the rising waters.

It seemed as though Gwynedd had been saved. Llywelyn was jubilant and, leaving his brother in command in the north, set off on a punitive raid against England's Welsh allies in the Marches. But Edward was never more dangerous than when fortune turned against him. Withdrawing to Rhuddlan he resolved to continue the campaign through the winter. And six weeks after the disaster at Bangor, dramatic news arrived from the headwaters of the Wye. About to plunder the lands of the dead Marcher baron, Roger Mortimer, Llwyelyn had been surprised by Mortimer's sons at Orewin bridge and killed.

With his death the soul went out of the rising. David, who claimed his principality, had been too long in the English camp to take his place in his fellow Welshmen's hearts. For half a year he fought on in the northern mountains while the remorseless ring of Edward's men and the Marchers closed round him. In June 1283, a fugitive in the barren hills round Cader Idris, he was betrayed by his own countrymen and handed over to Edward who refused even to see him. Condemned to a traitor's death by a Parliament called at Shrewsbury to try him, he was dragged to the gallows by horses, disembowelled and quartered and his head set beside his brother's over the Tower.

The rebellion – for it was as such that every Englishman regarded it – ended the last hope of a self-governing Welsh state within the island *imperium*. But, having grown up in the March and absorbed its warlike traditions, Edward had more under-standing of the Welsh than his English subjects. He remained in Wales with his court of King's Bench for nearly eighteen months after his victory and threw himself, with his usual passionate mastery of detail, into the settlement of the country. He did not merge the principality with England but preserved its separate existence under the Crown and royal law. In his Statute of Wales, issued from Rhuddlan castle in March 1284, he divided Gwynedd into three counties on the English model – Caernarvon, Anglesey and Merioneth – and appointed a Justiciar of Snowdon, with a treasury and capital at Caernarvon. At the same time he made a fourth county, Flintshire, out of part of the Four Centrefs, placing it under the Justiciar of Chester. Two other counties, Carmarthenshire and Cardiganshire, already created out of Llywelyn's former fiefs in the Marches, were provided with the usual English administrative hierarchy of sheriffs, bailiffs and coroners.

The settlement would not have been Edward's without the hard cement of a uniform system of law. It was for this that the war had been fought. Welsh and Anglo-Norman law were now made one. A body of law, half English, half Welsh, and current throughout the six shires, took the place of the old law of Gwynedd and of the many contending laws around its borders. The Welsh were allowed to keep their system of inheritance by which all a man's sons shared his property equally but, in deference to the orthodox Christian view of marriage, the illegitimate were excluded. Civil law remained Welsh, criminal law was anglicised.

For the rest Edward left Wales much as he found it. He left to the Marchers, who had helped him with the war, their feudal jurisdictions and martial lordships. He left the people of the former principality and the Cantrefs as much of their customary law as was compatible with peace and order and of the standards of morality and justice prevailing in Latin Christendom. He left them – the most precious thing of all – their language and, with a few exceptions, their Welsh officers and chieftains to fill the English legal and administrative posts which he imposed on them for their better ordering. He left them, in other words, not a Welsh State, which under provocation he had taken from them, but the wherewithal of Welsh nationhood.

The bards, the repositories of Cymric culture and learning who had shared Llywelyn's dream, bitterly lamented his death. And many Welshmen, who hated all government, including some who had fought on Edward's side, felt the iron of the new law enter into their souls. Twice in the decade after the conquest of the north the Welsh rose, once in 1287 – when Edward was in Gascony –

and again in 1294. Yet such risings could achieve little in the face of the castles which Edward raised after the conquest to hold down the north. Four great fortresses were built – Conway and Caernarvon on strategic promontories on the northern coast, and Criccieth and Harlech on the hills dominating the western coastal corridor round the shores of Cardigan bay. A fifth followed at Beaumaris in Anglesey to control the Menai Strait. Together with the Tower of London and the earl of Gloucester's Caerphilly – both newly rebuilt – they formed the greatest expression of the medieval military engineer's art raised in Britain before that art was superseded.

Edward was very proud of his new principality. For he was not merely King of the English; he was a prince of Christian chivalry. And Celtic Wales, at least in legend, was the most romantic of all the lands of chivalry; the fabled home of Arthur and his Round Table knights, of Gawain and Perceval and Galahad. Four weeks after the proclamation of the Statute of Wales, Queen Eleanor gave birth at Caernarvon to a son who, on his elder brother's unexpected death a few months later, became heir to the English throne. The King, who christened him with his own name, gave the boy a Welsh nurse and attendants and, sixteen years later, the title of Prince of Wales. By such means he hoped to win the Welsh people's hearts as well as their land.

CHAPTER THIRTEEN

Scotland the Brave

'The awful thistle . . . keep it
with a bush of spears.'

Dunbar

'Scots, wha hae wi' Wallace bled,
Scots, wham Bruce has aften led;
Welcome to your gory bed
Or to victorie . . .
Liberty's in every blow!
Let us do or die!'

Burns

IN THE SUMMER OF 1284, to celebrate his conquest of Wales, Edward, King of England and Ireland, Duke of Aquitaine and rightful heir, as he believed, to the vanished Roman *imperium* or empire of Britain, held a 'round table' tournament at Nevin, the furthest point of his dominion. At it, all the most famous knights in Christendom jousted in his honour. With the last of the Welsh princes gone, there was now no one to challenge his claim to be the representative of the fabled paladins of British antiquity, Arthur and Brutus of Troy. A decade earlier, on his return from the Holy Land, he and his Queen had laid the bones of Arthur and Queen Guinevere – miraculously just rediscovered – before the high altar at Glastonbury. Now, with equal solemnity, he transferred to his royal peculiar of Westminster Abbey the supposed iron crown of King Arthur and the bones of the Emperor

Constantine's British father, together with a fragment of the true cross – the 'rood of St Neot' – which had been found among the vanquished Prince of Gwynedd's relics of the Christian and Roman past.

Wales was not the only part of the British *imperium* to which Edward wished to bring order and law. Four years after his victory over the Welsh princes, when returning from a council meeting at Edinburgh and a stormy March crossing of the Forth, King Alexander III of Scotland, galloping through the night to rejoin his young French bride at Kinghorn, had ridden over a cliff. His death at forty-four, following that of his last surviving child, the Queen of Norway, left her infant daughter sole heir to the Scottish throne.

Alexander's rule and that of his father, Alexander II, had given the Scottish lowlands three quarters of a century of freedom from the perpetual border wars with England which had raged in the days of Henry II and William the Lion of Scotland. Descended from Pictish chieftains and the Irish pirate 'kings' who had given their Scots name to the unconquered peninsula of mountain and moor which the Romans had called Caledonia, a dynasty of able princes, with the help of an Anglo-Norman baronage to which they were kin, had created, in this wild mist-soaked land, the embryo of a feudal kingdom and, with it, a unity it had never known before. In the last fifty years they had forced even the Viking conquerors of Sutherland and the Western Isles to acknowledge their sovereignty. Their rule had brought about an almost complete cessation of the agelong Scottish raids on the farms and monasteries of northern England. For their policy was to be friends with their powerful Plantagenet kinsmen and titular suzerains and, under cover of their benevolent neutrality, to impose some sort of order on the turbulent highlands and islands of the north and west.

With Alexander's death, the prospect of a return to the anarchy of the past appalled the more reasonable Scottish leaders who had sworn to accept the Maid as his heir. In their dilemma they turned to Edward. For by now it had become natural to Scottish nobles and prelates with English estates and affinities to look for support to the more civilized neighbour kingdom. Soon after Alexander's death two friars arrived in London with a message from the

Guardians of Scotland to suggest the possibility of a marriage between their child-queen and the infant son and heir of the English King.

In July 1290, a treaty was sealed at Brigham near Durham by commissioners from both countries. It provided that the rights of neither should be diminished by the proposed marriage and that, if the young couple left no issue to make the union of the two crowns permanent, Scotland should revert to the nearest heirs of its ancient throne, 'free and intact of any subjection to the King of England'. No Parliament was to be held outside Scotland on any matter that concerned it, and no taxes should be exacted from its people except to meet the common expenses of the Crown. It was agreed, too, that until the pair could marry and take the oaths to preserve the customs of the realm, Edward should hold the Scottish royal castles to ensure peace and order.

At the end of the month Edward left Westminster for his usual summer progress to the Midland shrines, while hearing suits and petitions and hunting the great forests of Whittlebury, Rockingham and Sherwood. Here, later that autumn, a rumour reached him that, after a stormy voyage from Norway, the Maid had died in the Orkneys and, what was even more ominous, that the Bruces and other Scottish nobles with rival claims to the throne, were gathering arms and forces. Soon still more dire news reached him. His Queen, Eleanor of Castile, had been taken suddenly ill at Harbey in Nottinghamshire. On 20 November she died in his arms.[1] 'My harp is turned to mourning,' he wrote, 'in life I loved her dearly, nor can I cease to love her in death.' She had been his inseparable companion for thirty-six years. For the rest of his life nothing ever went wholly right for him.

[1] She had saved his life by her devoted nursing when he was struck down by an assassin's poisoned dagger at Acre during the crusade. Daughter of the Castilian king who won Cordoba, Seville and Cadiz for the Cross, her memory is preserved by her noble effigy in Westminster Abbey, her favourite residence, Leeds Castle in Kent – the loveliest of all medieval castles – and the Crosses which her stricken husband raised wherever on its journey to Westminster her bier rested. The last of these, the *chere reine* – or Charing Cross – gave its name to the London thoroughfare where Dr Johnson maintained that the full tide of human existence was best encountered.

Death had not only taken from Edward his queen. It had robbed him of a great opportunity. Yet it was not in his nature to despair. The Scottish leaders' request for arbitration revived his hopes. Though he could no longer achieve a single law for Britain by marrying his heir to Scotland's queen, he might still do so as *bretwalda* of the island empire over which he believed King Arthur had ruled and over which his predecessors had claimed suzerainty.

He therefore accepted the regents' invitation. From Amesbury Abbey, where he went after Christmas to visit his dying mother, he asked for extracts from the monastic chronicles to prove his right to Scotland's overlordship. Her last two kings, both of whom had married English princesses, had done homage for their English estates. In accepting such limited fealty Edward had expressly reserved the right to call for a wider. And there had been occasions when it had been rendered. Both William the Lion and Alexander II had paid tribute, the first, after his capture, doing homage to Henry II for his Scottish fief and crown – a vassalage subsequently renounced by Richard Coeur-de-Lion in return for money to finance his crusade. And before the union of the Scottish kingdoms two centuries earlier, homage of a kind had occasionally been rendered to England's Anglo-Saxon rulers by the princes of northern Britain, even though the circumstances were shrouded in the mists of war and antiquity.

Armed with these records of hereditary right, which he had marshalled with his usual thoroughness, Edward summoned the claimants to the vacant throne to meet him at Norham in Northumberland. At the beginning of May 1291, accompanied by judges, monastic chroniclers and a papal notary, he met the representatives of Scotland, announcing through his new chief justice, Roger Brabazon, that out of pity for their plight he had come, 'as the superior and lord paramount of the kingdom of Scotland', to do his lieges justice. Yet he could only do so, Brabazon explained, under the terms of feudal law. Before the King's court could adjudicate, the vacant fief must be surrendered and his right as overlord acknowledged. After which the judge read out the evidences collected by the English chroniclers, reciting all instances of Scottish homage up to the reign of Henry II and ignoring everything that had happened since.

At this point some of the Scots representatives asked if they might consult those who had sent them. In one reply, presented on behalf of 'the community of the good people of Scotland', they argued that, while they did not doubt the king's sincerity, they knew of no right to his overlordship and could not bind their future sovereign to it. Edward thereupon offered them three weeks for consideration. As the only alternative to his adjudication was civil war, in the end none of the competitors refused what he asked. At the beginning of June they all swore to submit to his judgment and abide by his decision.

Having secured his point, in accordance with feudal practice Edward demanded the surrender of the Scottish royal castles while the claims were determined. He reappointed the regents, added an Englishman to their number and proclaimed his peace, promising to govern Scotland according to its ancient laws and customs. Then, pending examination of the claims, he set out on a tour of the country. During July he visited Edinburgh, Stirling, Dunfermline, St Andrews and Perth, installing constables in twenty-three castles and exacting as many oaths of fealty as possible.

The preliminary hearing took place at Berwick at the beginning of September 1291. The full judicial resources of both kingdoms had been mobilised. There were twenty-four English judges or auditors and eight Scottish assessors to advise them on Scottish law. As Edward prided himself on the good justice he offered, the utmost legal nicety was observed. Each of the competitors, who included the King of Norway and the Count of Holland, appeared before him in person or by attorney, and traced his descent from the ancestor from whom he claimed. Those with the strongest claim were the heads of the three Anglo-Scottish baronial families of Balliol, Bruce and Comyn.

By the autumn of 1292, 'the prodigious labours of Brabazon' and his fellow judges were completed. On 17 November he awarded the throne to John Balliol.[1] Two days later Edward ordered his constables to deliver the Scottish castles to him. The magnates did homage to their new king, and the latter did homage

---

[1] His father, a northern English as well as Scottish magnate, had founded an Oxford college for poor students from the north which still bears his name.

to Edward as supreme sovereign lord. The unsuccessful runner-up or 'Competitor' – old Robert Bruce, who had fought by Edward's side at Evesham – avoided acknowledging his rival's claim by relinquishing his rights to his son, the earl of Carrick who, with the same object, made over his Scottish estates to his own son, Robert Bruce, then an eight-year old minor.

Balliol was installed at Scone on St Andrew's Day 1292 on the Stone of Destiny, brought there, it was believed, by the ancient 'kings' of Scots from their native Ireland. He was a quiet unassertive man, little fitted to serve as a buffer between a turbulent native nobility and a suzerain as zealous for formal law and order as Edward. Trouble began almost immediately.

Almost before Balliol had been crowned, one of his subjects, a Berwick merchant, appealed to the English courts against a decision of the Scottish Justiciars. Edward, whose pride it was never to refuse any man justice, ordered the record to be brought before the King's Bench at Newcastle where he was keeping the Christmas feast. When Balliol reminded him of his undertaking at Brigham that no Scottish subject should be made to plead in any court outside Scotland, Edward replied that he was not bound by a marriage-treaty which had not been carried out.

It was a major political blunder. Edward was one of the greatest definers of law ever to wear a crown. He had received Balliol's homage both as an English baron and as King of Scotland and, as his liege-lord, had pledged himself under the feudal compact to safeguard his rights in both. He had sworn to respect the laws and institutions of Scotland, as he had done to respect those of Gascony, Wales, Ireland and all his other dominions. But as a sovereign lord he was also bound to offer justice, according to the highest standards, to all his subjects alike. If any of them could not obtain it in the court of his immediate lord – even though that lord was a king – he was entitled to appeal to the supreme overlord and seek it in his court. It was the same right which Henry II had given to his English subjects when he had offered them writs entitling them to apply to the royal courts for justice unobtainable in those of their feudal lords. Nor could the King's courts do justice by rules less enlightened than those they habitually administered or by any which conflicted with the principles of natural law.

The same claim to override the primitive codes of a backward people in the name of justice had shipwrecked Edward's plans for a peaceful union with Wales. Once Balliol had renounced his kingdom's rights to the conditions secured at Brigham, he was lost. During the next two years he was repeatedly called to answer appeals in his overlord's court at Westminster as though Scotland were an English barony. Torn between the growing resentment of his turbulent subjects and his English liege-lord's legalistic and feudal demands, he was between the devil and the deep sea. In the end, taking advantage of a similar dispute between Edward and the French king, to whom the latter owed homage for his French dominions, he asserted Scotland's independence by concluding a military alliance with France.

By doing so he precipitated an English invasion of Scotland. In 1296 Edward crossed the Tweed and stormed Berwick, putting its garrison to the sword. A month later John de Warenne, earl of Surrey, routed the Scottish army at Spottsmuir. On July 2nd, Balliol acknowledged himself in mercy. A week later he abdicated in the hall of Brechin castle. Sending him to England under escort Edward continued his northern march. By the end of the month he was on the Moray Firth. No ruler of England had penetrated so far since the Romans.

On the way back he took the Stone of Destiny from Scone abbey – the ancient crowning place of the Scottish kings – and sent it, with Scotland's royal regalia and archives, to Westminster. Then he held a parliament at Berwick. Here, receiving the homage of two thousand Scottish landowners – the entire 'franchise' of the land – he restored their estates in return for sealed submissions, copies of which were sent to Westminster on thirty-five parchment skins known as the Scottish Ragman roll. Scotland itself he treated as non-existent or rather as though it had become a part of England, leaving it to be governed by an English earl, treasurer and Justiciar. 'Now,' wrote a ballad-monger, 'are the two waters come into one and one realm made of two kingdoms. . . . There is no longer any king except King Edward . . . Arthur himself never had it so fully.'

Yet though Scotland's noble, landowning and military classes had submitted to him, within a year Edward was faced by a new kind of unrest in the remoter parts of Scotland. It came from the smaller gentry, farmers and peasants who had hitherto had no share in the government of their wild land. Like the earlier discontent in Wales it had arisen through the tactlessness and corruption of English officials who, contrary to Edward's ideals but in accordance with the general practice of the age, had seized the opportunity to feather their own nests.

The risings, though small affairs, had occurred in widely separated areas, in Galloway and Clydesdale, Ross, Moray and Aberdeenshire. At Lanark the English sheriff and garrison had been overwhelmed and massacred in a sudden night broil by a gang led by a young man of gigantic stature named William le Walyes or Wallace – son of a local knight from Elderslie, a few miles from the little city of Glasgow. Rendered desperate by his bloody exploit and heartened by the enthusiasm it aroused, Wallace had then led his band of fellow outlaws across Scotland and, suddenly descending from the hills, all but captured the royal Justiciar, William de Ormseby, as he was holding his court at Scone.

A new phenomenon, at first unperceived, had appeared in the world to confront the centralising encroachments of great organisers and legalists like Edward. It arose out of the regional loyalties of ordinary men and women and the instinct for personal liberty and dignity which the spread of Christian teaching had implanted in them. It was to become known as patriotism. Five years before, when Edward and his judges had been laboriously selecting the right king for the kingless Scots, the peasants of three remote forest cantons in Alpine Swabia – one of the feudal dukedoms of Germany – had made a league with the neighbouring burghers of Lucerne to resist the unifying attempts of the Emperor Rudolph of Hapsburg to subordinate them to what they regarded as an alien and oppressive vassalage. It was the beginning of the Swiss Confederation which, helped by the wild mountain terrain in which these sturdy hillfolk lived, was to defy every assault of their Hapsburg and Austrian dukes. By his disregard for the feelings of Scottish graziers and crofters, Edward had unconsciously aroused a similar resistance in northern Britain.

*   *   *

What sort of a country was this 'Scotsland' whose humble folk had so unexpectedly defied their English overlord? With a few fertile plains and valleys along its eastern and south-western coasts, it was a narrow, rocky peninsula, tapering away into a remote, misty and inaccessible *ultima Thule* of mountain, lake and island. Across it, cutting off its inhabitants from one another yet forming a series of formidable barriers to any invader from the south, ran a succession of barren mountain ranges and stormy inlets or firths of the sea. Such livelihood as its stony soil afforded could be won only by constant battle with the elements – snow, gale and flood – an existence rendered the more precarious by the lawlessness of its inhabitants. Cattle- and sheep-stealing was the most profitable activity in wide areas – one which united chieftain and laird with their clansmen and tenantry in continual forays and feuds. In such a society human life was held cheap; courage, hardihood and loyalty to the local leader in war honoured above all other virtues.

Partly English or Angle in the south-east and an inter-mixture of Romanised Briton and piratical Irish settler in the wet, wooded south-west, Scotland beyond the Highland line in the sparsely populated mountains and mists of the Gaelic north and west – the old Pictland – afforded its half-million people the same barbaric and pastoral life as their ancestors a thousand years before. Shepherds, graziers, crofters, fishermen, they were as accustomed to violence as to wind and rain and, like the Spartans, were nourished in proud poverty from childhood. They lived in huts of turves and mud, usually of only a single room, with a pile of dung – their chief wealth – on the floor.

Scotland's only contacts with the outer world were her Church, the dual allegiance of her Anglo-Norman lords for their English lands, and a trickle of trade across the North Sea with England, Flanders and northern Europe through the little eastern ports of Berwick, Leith, Kinghorn, Crail, Arbroath, Montrose and Aberdeen. Of these links with European civilization the Church was the greatest. Though Christianity had originally come to Scotland from Ireland and Iona, until the end of the twelfth century the

Scottish Church had been a part, though only a loosely bound and fiercely disputed one, of the province of York and, as such, nominally subordinate to the northern English metropolitan. But after its quarrel with Henry II the papacy had taken the Church in Scotland under its direct control and, though no Scottish archbishop had been appointed, its eleven bishops under the primacy of St Andrews had for the past century acknowledged no spiritual superior but the Pope. This had ensured that though, as the champion of civilization and opponent of war, the Church had at first welcomed a union with England through the marriage of the two crowns, its leaders were foremost in rejecting Edward's claim to suppress the nation's separate identity by force.

Since the country was at least a hundred years behind England in civilization, Scottish Christianity was more monastic than episcopal, particularly in the south-east. Here in the first half of the twelfth century David I, inspired by his mother, Queen Margaret, had established a chain of priories and monasteries – Augustinian at St Andrews, Lochleven, Holyrood, Jedburgh and Cambuskenneth, Cistercian at Melrose, Newbattle, Kinloss and Dundrennan. Superseding the hermit communities of the primitive past, they had begun to perform for Lowland Scotland something of the cultural and artistic service that the great Cluniac houses had done for England in the days of St Dunstan and the Anglo-Saxon kings.

In that civilizing mission David himself – greatest of Scotland's royal line – had played a major part. Open to all from the highest to the lowest, a Scottish Alfred from whom, through his mother, he was descended, he had created a small hard core of civilization on either shore of the Forth, which his successors, William the Lion and the two Alexanders, had consolidated and enlarged. It was this Edward had undermined by his attempt to enforce English law and obedience. By doing so he had broken such civilization as Scotland possessed. As a result he found himself confronted by what lay beneath – the stark, savage, native turbulence of a people to whom feuding, violence and vengeance were second nature. Such was the detestation that he and his 'southron' officers and soldiers aroused that, wherever the English penetrated, the Scottish people, for the first time in their history, seemed almost united.

From this rude, tough, resourceful community were drawn the followers of Wallace and his fellow hedge-knights, Andrew de Moray and Sir John Graham – 'the guid Graeme' of the legends. Armed with home-made spears and axes, they wore animal skins and hessian cloaks and carried their rations of oatmeal and dried lentils on their backs or ponies' saddles. Even by the standards of that hardy age they were almost incredibly mobile, traversing vast distances of lonely moor, mountain and forest to waylay and fall on their foes. They were animated by a passionate hatred of the English; Wallace himself, it was said, as a matter of principle slew every 'southron' who started an argument with him. According to the Scottish bard, Blind Harry, when the guerilla chief captured a batch of 'English knaves' he made them drag his loot to his forest lair where he hanged them on trees. Like all partisan warfare in primitive lands, his campaign was waged with merciless ferocity and intimidation. What was most disturbing to the authorities was that it became impossible to collect taxes. 'Not a penny can be raised,' the Treasurer of Scotland, Hugh de Cressingham, reported to his royal master from Roxburgh, 'until my lord the earl of Warenne shall enter in your land and compel the people by force and sentence of law.' For old Surrey, the Warden of the North, resting on his laurels of Spottsmuir, had gone home for the winter to his English estates, leaving Cressingham – a fat cleric of the ledgers – in charge.

However, an army under Surrey, hastily recalled to his charge, was hurrying up the east coast to restore order. With his ragged horde, Wallace was by now besieging Dundee castle. He had no siege-train and could only hope to starve it out. Hearing of Surrey's advance, he broke off the siege and, joining his fellow rebel, Moray, took up a position on the southernmost spur of the Ochils, barring the road from Stirling to the north. Sooner than allow the invaders to penetrate to the liberated lands beyond the Forth, he decided to give battle about a mile from the point where the Stirling road crossed the river, here deep and tidal.

It was a bold decision. The royal forces were far better trained, armed and disciplined. They were particularly strong in mailed cavalry – the dominant arm in war and one in which the Scots, a rabble of low-born, unaccounted men, were almost totally deficient. But Wallace had gained an extraordinary ascendancy over his men and possessed a born soldier's eye for ground. The earl of Surrey was old and infirm, and Cressingham – an Exchequer official of gross girth who had made himself universally hated by his meanness and greed – was notoriously impatient and arrogant. Against the advice of more experienced soldiers, Surrey reluctantly yielded to the importunity of the Treasurer who, in his obsession with financial considerations, viewed every day's delay as a waste of money. On 11 September, in face of a strongly-posted enemy, they committed the army to an advance across a narrow wooden bridge scarcely wide enough for two horsemen and with no room to deploy on the far side.

This was just what Wallace wanted. He had already rejected overtures for an armistice from the Steward of Scotland and the earl of Lennox who, trying to hunt with the hounds and run with the hare, had been offering their services as mediators. 'Tell your people,' he said, 'that we have not come here to gain peace but for battle to avenge and deliver our country. Let them come up when they like and they will find us ready to meet them to their beards.' He ordered his men not to move from their position among the rocks until he blew his horn. He waited till as many of the enemy had crossed as he felt certain he could destroy. Then he gave the signal.

The Scots' charge threw the English armour into confusion while it was trying to deploy in a swampy, congested meadow. A phalanx of Wallace's spearmen reached the bridge, cutting off those who had crossed from their comrades on the other bank. For the next hour Surrey was forced to watch the massacre of his cavalry, with an unfordable river behind them and the only bridge held by the Scots who hacked them to pieces with gusto. Cressingham was slain, and his skin afterwards cut into strips by the victors. Then panic set in, and the rest of the English army fled, not resting till it reached Berwick.

Stirling Bridge restored the independence of Scotland. The Steward and the earl of Lennox threw in their lot with the insurgents, Dundee and Stirling surrendered and by the end of September only the castles of Edinburgh, Dunbar, Roxburgh and Berwick remained in English hands. Wallace himself occupied Berwick town, putting to the sword the few English merchants who had been foolhardy enough to remain.

His triumph, however, was shortlived. In 1298, set on avenging his lieutenant's defeat, Edward invaded Scotland with a huge force of mounted knights and archers, and on 28 July at Falkirk destroyed the flower of the ragged Scots' army, which had rashly defied him in the open field. Yet for a further seven years Wallace continued to hold out in the wilderness, thereby pointing a way to his country's future. For this brave man and his foot kerns had proved that on ground of their own choosing they could defy the proudest chivalry and survive in a war of endurance without giving battle at all. Had he not tried to repeat his earlier success in the field, he might have remained at the head of an undefeated army, while his adversary could have accomplished little in that wild and hungry land save a succession of fruitless marches.

As it was, still fighting, Wallace survived till the summer of 1305. Early that August he was betrayed near Glasgow. Brought south he was paraded through the London streets and tried in Westminster Hall, charged with treason, murder and robbery. Sentenced to be hanged, drawn and quartered, he was dragged for four miles on a hurdle to the Tower and thence to the gallows at Smithfield, where 'he was hung in a noose and afterwards let down half living, his privates cut off and his bowels torn out and burnt'. His severed head was stuck up on London Bridge and his quarters sent to the chief cities of the north – Perth, Berwick, Stirling and Newcastle.

Something went with them, to take root, in Andrew Lang's words

'like a wild flower
All over his dear country.'

Abandoned by the lords and prelates of Scotland and by almost all the members of his knightly class, Wallace's memory lived on in the legends and ballads of the common folk he had led. In the fifteenth century the bard, Blind Harry, enshrined in the vernacular the ineradicable belief of peasant Scotland in his achievement:

> 'Scotland he freed and brocht it off thirlage
> And now in Heaven he has his heritage.'

It was this which, after a summer evening's walk to the Leglen wood in 1793, inspired the greatest of all Scottish peasants to write a song on his hero 'equal to his merits'. Burns's 'Scots wha hae' is still sung wherever Scotsmen honour their native land or men decide to stand or fall for freedom.

*   *   *

With Wallace out of the way Edward issued his ordinance for the administration of Scotland. It was to be ruled, under a royal lieutenant, by an English Chancellor and Chamberlain assisted by an advisory council of eight prelates and fourteen magnates, including the former runner-up claimant, young Robert Bruce, and two Comyns. Judges, coroners and sheriffs were to be appointed on the English model and, though the civil law of Scotland was retained, customary laws, like those of the Celtic Highlands, 'plainly against God and reason' were abolished. Pleased at having set Scotland, as he believed, on the road to civilization and order, the English King graciously suspended the sentences on the remaining exiles.

Yet six months after Wallace's execution terrible news arrived from the north. On 11 February 1306, in a quarrel in the Grey-friars church at Dumfries, Robert Bruce – the thrice pardoned earl of Carrick – had slain his fellow councillor and rival for the forfeit throne, John Comyn the Red – head of the house of Bade-noch. Having committed murder and sacrilege, broken the King's Peace and involved himself in a blood feud with the most powerful family in Scotland, he had then imprisoned the royal judges who were holding an assize in the town and appealed to the cause of national independence, not in the dethroned Balliol's name, but in his own. Hurrying north, he had sought the aid of old Bishop Wishart of Glasgow, who heroically gave him absolution, produced from its hiding-place the royal standard of Scotland and accompanied him to the crowning-place of the Scottish kings at Scone. Here on Palm Sunday, with a golden circlet made by a local smith and in the presence of Wishart and Bishop Lamberton of St Andrews and a hundred disaffected lords and knights, mostly from the Celtic north and west, he was crowned Robert I of Scotland by the countess of Buchan, wife of Comyn's closest kinsman and sister to the young earl of Fife with whom the hereditary right of crowning lay.

When the news of the rebellion reached Edward he was in Hampshire, travelling from hunting-lodge to hunting-lodge and seeking, in the milder air of the southern counties, relief for his failing health. He at once ordered the mobilisation of the northern levies and summoned a Parliament to Westminster. Bruce and all concerned in the death of Comyn were to be castrated and disembowelled and those who aided him hanged.

Once more in the spring of 1307, the English King assembled a vast army, vowing that he would not rest till 'the Lord had given him victory over the crowned traitor and perjured nation'. As soon as the magnates and knights of the shire and burgesses assembled in Parliament had voted him taxes for the campaign, too ill to ride he set out by litter on his northward journey. Already his vanguard had crossed the Forth. On 20 June Bruce was surprised at Methven and all but taken, only saving himself, like Wallace after Falkirk, by vanishing into the heather; as his wife had remarked at their coronation, he and she were but King and Queen of the May. Many who had rallied to him in the first flush of enthusiasm were by now on their way to England in fetters.

For Bruce, throughout that summer of 1306, disaster followed disaster. In August he was defeated at Dalry by a Scottish force under John of Argyll, lord of Lorne. Two of his brothers were hanged, drawn and quartered; his Queen – perhaps to her relief, for she was more than half English – was taken, while his sister Mary and the countess of Buchan were imprisoned in cages in the castles of Roxburgh and Berwick. And the familiar train of desertions, so characteristic till now of Scotland's wars of independence, began again.

'Bruce durst not to the plainys ga
And all the commons went him fra:
That for their lives were full fain
To pass to the English peace again.'

In October Edward established himself for the winter at Lanercost priory, a few miles east of Carlisle. Most of the insurgents had
by now been caught and hanged and their lands given to Englishmen; Bruce himself had disappeared into the glens and islands of
the far west. No record of his movements during the next few
months exists, but according to one account he spent some time in
the little island of Rathlin off the Irish coast where, sheltering from
his terrible adversary, he is said to have taken heart through watching the efforts of a persistent spider. In February 1307, evading
Edward's searching ships, he reappeared in Arran and in the middle
of the month landed on the Ayrshire coast where he tried to surprise the English garrison of Turnberry castle and captured the
governor's plate. Then he vanished once more into the hills and
heather.

A month later his lieutenant, young James Douglas – a Dum-
friesshire knight whose father had died in the Tower – surprised
Castle Douglas while the garrison was at Mass, slew every man and,
leaving their bodies and stores to roast in the blazing keep, disappeared again into the moors. The 'Douglas larder', as it was
called, caused a tremendous sensation. The tall, dark, sallow
young knight, with his lisp, courteous ways and daring imagination,
possessed just the qualities to mystify and terrify the English and
inspire his followers. 'The maist coward,' it was said, 'stouter he
made than a leopard.' In him Bruce possessed what Wallace had
never had: a lieutenant as bold as himself and loyal to the Scottish
cause as the heather.

Edward was eagerly waiting for news of Bruce's capture as he
had waited for Wallace's. In April the English armies closed round
him in the lonely glen of Loch Trool among the Galloway hills.
Yet just when he seemed in the net, Bruce broke the ring of his
pursuers by a sudden charge and again vanished. A month later,
on 10 May, he encountered the viceroy, Pembroke, 'in a fair even
field' at Loudon in the valley of the Ayrshire Avon and defeated

him. Three days later he fell on another searching party under the earl of Gloucester and drove them into Ayr castle. Scotland in arms was once more a reality.

Edward was now sinking fast. But, resolved to put himself at the head of his troops and capture the hated will o' the wisp, he left Carlisle on 3 July, mounting his horse for the first time in a year. The agony proved insupportable. For three days he struggled on, reaching Burgh-on-Sands six miles from his starting point on the 6th. Here on 7 July 1307, within sight of the Scottish border, he died in the arms of his attendants. His last command was that his son should carry his bones at the head of his armies till every Scot had surrendered.

*   *   *

Had Edward lived another year Bruce could not have survived. By Comyn's murder he had aligned against himself England, the papacy and half Scotland, and had alienated not only those of his fellow nobles who were loyal to Edward, but those who had been loyal to Balliol. Now, in place of the greatest soldier of his age, command of the forces of vengeance had passed to an overgrown, self-indulgent youth of twenty-three. For the first time since the Conquest a king sat on the English throne with no feeling for arms.

The first thing Edward II did on his accession was to recall his foreign favourite and foster brother, Piers Gaveston, a handsome but insolent Gascon knight and, by loading him with honours, precipitate a five years' struggle with his English baronage. The second was to abandon the campaign, for he had no love for war and its hardships. Disregarding his father's request that his bones should be borne at the head of his army, he made a brief perfunctory march into south-western Scotland. At the beginning of September he returned to London where, to the unspeakable fury of his nobles, he invested Gaveston with the royal earldom of Cornwall.

The new King's abandonment of the campaign gave Bruce a breathing-space to settle accounts with his Scottish enemies. Leaving Douglas in the Galloway hills, he turned north to harry the lands of the earl of Buchan, head of the house of Comyn. The valleys were swarming with English troops and the principal strongholds were in their hands, while half the Scottish nobles, adherents either of Balliol or the English King, were bitterly opposed to Bruce's claim. But the lesser gentry and common people, smarting under the invaders' injuries, turned instinctively to this God-sent champion whom they saw as Wallace's successor. And though surrounded by enemies and with a price on his head, Bruce himself was already thinking in terms of hunting his hunters.

For weak and divided though she had long been, with all but two or three of her great families in the pay of England, Scotland was now to enjoy real leadership. Bruce had all the traits which the world has learnt to associate with Scottish character, magnified to the point of genius: dogged courage, persistence, unshakeable loyalty to friend and unrelenting enmity to foe, tenderness to women, genial ironic humour, logical uncompromising ruthlessness in pursuit of his purpose. This king in the heather, this mountain-fox with the mist in his beard – 'King Robbe in the mures', as the English contemptuously called him – was one of the great national leaders of all time. Never commanding more than a few thousand men and at first only a few hundred, he evaded every attempt at capture. Whenever his foes thought they had beaten him he reappeared and, in the end, inflicted on them one of the decisive defeats of history.

He and James Douglas, who was waging the same will o' the wisp campaign against the English in the south-west, followed the rules taught by Wallace and improved on them. By mounting their men on moorland ponies they gave them an astonishing mobility. They trained them to disperse after a fight in small companies, to join again and fall on the foe whenever he was momentarily at a disadvantage before vanishing once more into the hills. 'Better,' said the good Sir James, 'to hear the lark sing than the mouse cheep.' And his leader, who knew that certain death awaited him in captivity, shared the same philosophy. Yet when the hour of opportunity came, no man could be swifter or bolder. Nor, in adversity, more wily.

When 1308 began, Bruce was lord of little more than Moray,

with Buchan still in superior force to the east, a hostile Ross to north and west, his enemies of Lorne and the Isles between him and Douglas in the south-west. The English were still in control of every major fortress in Scotland. That February, after bringing home his twelve-year-old bride, the princess Isabella, from France, King Edward II was crowned with every circumstance of pomp at Westminster, Gaveston – 'his brother Peter' – at his side 'so decked out that he more resembled the God Mars than an ordinary mortal'. Scarcely were the celebrations over when Bruce struck at Buchan, routing him at Inverurie. Then, seizing Aberdeen and Forfar, he harried the lands of Buchan, teaching by fire and sword the partisan's unchanging lesson that, in the hour of revolution, no man, however peaceable, can adhere to the powers-that-be with safety. Neither Comyn nor England, Scotsmen discovered that summer, could give protection against Bruce's vengeance. A stark, primitive people, who honoured resolution and hardihood and had no love for the English and little for their own predatory nobles, observed the fact with relish. Bruce's 'harrying of Buchan' became a national legend, establishing his claim to the throne in every Scottish heart.

While the young English King and his lords remained at loggerheads, the run of Scottish successes continued. Bruce's brother, Edward, won a spectacular victory on the Cree; by the summer he and Douglas were in control of the entire south-west except the fortresses of Dumfries, Dalswinton, Caerlaverock and Lochmaben. In August King Robert defeated the men of Lorne and Argyll in the Pass of Brander. In October he received the submission of Ross in the far north. Even in the border country south of Edinburgh, guerilla bands threatened the English convoys as they made their way through moor and forest to revictual the royal castles.

By the end of the year Bruce was *de facto* ruler of almost all Scotland north of the Tay. In 1309 he liberated the major part of Fife and that March held his first parliament in St Andrews. Three of the Scottish earls – Ross, Sutherland and Lennox – now supported him, while the earldoms of Menteith and Caithness, held by infants, were represented in his parliament. After three years of continuous peril and struggle he was a real king at last, enthroned in the hearts of a people resolved to fight to the death for their freedom. 'His mishaps, flights and dangers, hardships, weariness, hunger and thirst, watchings and fastings, nakedness and cold, snares and banishments,' wrote one of them, recalling those years, 'the seizing, imprisonment, slaughter and downfall of his near ones, and – even more – dear ones . . . no one now living, I think, recollects or is equal to rehearsing.' They formed his royal title-deeds.

Meanwhile the English were at sixes and sevens. Edward's childish irresponsibility and dependence on Gaveston infuriated his feudal nobility. For four years they had tried by first one device, then another, to constrain him and his favourite until in 1312, after civil war had broken out, the latter met a brutal death at their hands. Even before he did so Bruce, in the summer of 1311, freed from the threat of an English invasion, had taken the offensive and crossed the Solway to raid the farms of upper Tynedale. A month later he returned and, wasting Coquetdale and Redesdale, penetrated as far as Durham. Scotland, after six years of war, was starving behind him; northern England, he intended, should taste the same medicine. Despairing of help, the men of Northumberland offered him a ransom for their homes and crops. When he recrossed the border it was with £2000 of English money paid for a truce till February.

Next year King Robert, as Bruce had now become to almost every Scotsman, again crossed the border and harried Tynedale, penetrating to the walls of Durham and sacking Hartlepool. Northern England was in a panic, and the Border counties paid £1000 for a truce till spring. With a long trail of hostages and the loot of five towns, Bruce returned to his ravaged poverty-stricken land well content.

During the early months of 1313, under cover of his truce with the northern counties, he struck at the royal garrisons in Scotland. On 8 January, after a seven weeks' siege, he led his men neck-deep through the icy waters of the moat to capture Perth in a midnight escalade. A month later his brother Edward took Dumfries and the Bruce castle of Lochmaben. And at the end of the summer a farmer named Binnock, who was in the habit of supplying the garrison of Linlithgow with hay, blocked the main gate with a wagon, enabling armed men concealed in it to rush the portcullis and capture the fortress.

At this point, Edward Bruce, who lacked his brother's Fabian sense of strategy, brought the long-drawn-out war to a crisis. He made a truce with the governor of Stirling, Sir Thomas Mowbray, by which the latter agreed to surrender the castle if it was not relieved by midsummer. This put both kings in a dilemma. Edward could not ignore the challenge without ignominy, while Robert could only allow Stirling to be relieved at the expense of laying northern Scotland once more open to invasion and jeopardising the successes of the past six years.

During the opening months of 1314 the summons went out to all English fighting men. The greatest army England had ever sent forth was to march to the castle's relief before the day agreed for its surrender. But while Edward was mobilising England's might to crush once and for all 'Robert de Brus who calls himself King of Scotland', the latter was wresting from him his last bases in the north. On the night of Shrove Tuesday Douglas captured the chief fortress of the marches, Roxburgh, while the garrison was keeping the feast in the great hall. A month later Bruce's nephew, Thomas Randolph, to whom he had given the earldom of Moray, secured an even greater prize. Scaling Edinburgh castle from the ravine which today divides the new city from the old, while a frontal attack engaged the garrison, Randolph and his men, wearing darkened armour, reached the ramparts by a track down which one of them in his youth had been wont to visit his lady-love.

Having dismantled the captured castles Bruce withdrew into the Torwood, close to the Roman road to Stirling up which the English would have to march. Here, training his men for the battle which was now inevitable, he awaited the supreme test of his own and his country's life. He had to pit the fighting forces of a nation of less than half a million, desperately impoverished by twenty years of invasion and civil war, against those of a kingdom with more than eight times its population and resources.

For it was an immense array which assembled at Wark on 10

June 1314. There were probably between two thousand and three thousand knights and nearly twenty thousand archers and spearmen. On the 17th they set out, advancing up Lauderdale to Edinburgh and the Forth, while their supplies followed by sea to Leith. This time there was no indecision. The English King meant to make a speedy end of Scotland's defiance. By the evening of 22 June – two days before Stirling had to be relieved – he reached Falkirk, having covered nearly a hundred miles in six days.

That night Bruce's scouts brought news of the invading host – 'so great that it was ferly'. The whole glittering panoply of a rich nation's chivalry was displayed in the summer twilight as the armoured horses and men passed in endless procession through the streets of Falkirk:

> 'Banners right fairly flaming
> And pencels to the wind waving.'

So impressive was the sight that Bruce forbade those who had seen it to speak of it to their comrades. His own force numbered little more than a quarter of the English: some five thousand infantry, mostly spearmen equipped with twelve-foot spears, padded coats, steel helmets and mail gloves, together with a few archers from Ettrick forest and about five hundred lightly armed horse. Another two thousand auxiliaries, 'small folk' from the neighbouring farms and boroughs, roused by the magnitude of the country's peril, had recently joined him. Save for these, his men were all veterans who had been drilling for many weeks for the battle they would have to fight. And they were defending all they held dear.

Soon after midday on Saturday 23 June, hot and weary from its twenty-mile march from Falkirk, the English army reached the little Bannock burn that, crossing the Roman road to Stirling, serpentined north-eastwards through pools to the Forth. The beleaguered castle, clearly visible on its height, was now only three miles away. The Scots were posted on rising wooded ground barring the road, their front protected by rows of carefully dug pits or *pottis* concealed by turf and branches, with steel calthrops for maiming horses strewn between them. The governor of Stirling had ridden out to warn the King of these. He also pointed out that,

as he was within three leagues of the castle, it was already technically 'relieved' and that there was therefore no need for haste.

But, inexperienced in Scottish warfare and believing Bruce's
hopelessly outnumbered army to be at their mercy, Edward and
the younger English lords would not wait for victory. Despite the
long morning's march they decided to attack at once. Throughout
the hot afternoon haze the armoured knights under the Constable
and earl of Gloucester pressed forward across the burn on their
great war-horses without waiting for the rest of the army to deploy.

The Scots were not expecting this move which, after so long a
march and so late in the day, seemed contrary to every prudent
rule of war. Bruce himself was in front of his outposts, recon-
noitring the English positions. At the top of the rise, near the
Borestone on the Stirling road, Sir Humphrey Bohun, the earl of
Hereford's nephew, suddenly encountered him. Seeing the crown
over his helmet and a chance of immortal glory, he put his horse
into a gallop and bore down. But Bruce, mounted on a small grey
palfrey, was too quick for him. Rising in the stirrups as the English
knight thundered past, he cracked open his skull with his battle-
axe. Then he galloped back to join his waiting men in the wood.

Here the English cavalry, confronted by the pits and calthrops,
were soon in difficulties. The earl of Gloucester himself was
thrown and unmounted, and, after some ineffective skirmishing,
the exhausted knights and their heavily laden horses fell back in
confusion without having penetrated the Scottish position at any
point. Meanwhile a smaller contingent of six or seven hundred
horse under the lords Clifford and de Beaumont had been feeling
its way northwards towards Stirling round the Scots' retracted
flank where, immediately below the escarpment, a narrow corridor
of firm ground lay unguarded between Bruce's left and the carse
that stretched between the Bannock burn and the Forth. Lacking
the strength both to hold the road through the wood and bar this
alternative approach to the castle, Bruce had deliberately left it
open, hoping that, if Edward's troops were to advance along it
without first dislodging him, he might, by descending on them
while they were still strung out, force them into the carse where
their armour would be helpless and unable to manoeuvre.

Confident of being able to drive Bruce from the wood, King Edward had ordered Clifford to take up position between Stirling and the Scots' rear, ready to cut off their retreat and destroy them. Instead of obeying their orders and continuing their march, the English wheeled left and engaged the schiltrons who at once halted, closed and confronted them with the usual impenetrable hedgehogs of spears. Though the riders flung their maces and battle-axes into the Scottish ranks in the hope of breaking them, nothing would make the horses face those steady, glittering circles of steel. In the end the attackers dispersed, some taking refuge in Stirling castle and the remainder galloping back to the English host beyond the Bannock burn, spreading dismay.

A council of war was now held. As no hope remained of driving the Scots from the wood that day, the more prudent urged a halt. But Edward, anxious to obtain water for his horses, fell into the very trap Bruce had baited. Intending next day to attack from the east the position that he had failed to carry from the south, he ordered his entire army to move down into the valley of the Bannock burn and the boggy carse beyond. Here, its morale badly shaken, it passed the night, as one present described it, 'in a deep, wet, evil marsh'. The lights of the Scottish camp-fires could be seen shining through the trees a mile away on the higher ground to the west. Bruce had his enemy at last where he wished him.

Sunday, 24 June, Midsummer Day 1314, was the feast of St John the Baptist. At the first light the Scottish priests, moving from schiltron to schiltron, celebrated mass at the head of each division. Afterwards the men knelt in prayer while the abbot of Inchaffray, armed with sacred relics, blessed them. Meanwhile the trumpets were sounding in the English camp along the burn, and thousands of knights, assisted by their pages, were buckling on their armour and mounting their huge barded horses after their comfortless night among the pools and peat.

But before the ranks could be marshalled the Scots were seen to be on the move. To the amazement of the invaders, instead of awaiting their attack on the higher ground or withdrawing into the forest westwards, the schiltrons were descending the slope towards them in three huge 'battles' of massed spears. Like the great commander he was, rather than wait for the English blow, Bruce had chosen to anticipate it. Using his schiltrons as a slowly moving wall of steel, he sought to compress the vast, unprepared mass of invaders into a steadily diminishing space with the marshes of the carse and the reaches of the Forth behind them. As he brought his right forward and swung his steady footmen north-wards along the course of the burn, without the English realising it, he was driving them into the one place where he could destroy them.

Hitherto, in their nine years of trying to bring him to book, the leaders of England's chivalry had encountered only the cautious side of Bruce – the Fabian general who had repeatedly survived by vanishing into his native mists, leaving them to starve amid barren mountain and flood. Now, like their subordinate garrison commanders who had long experienced his sudden lion pounces on lonely moor and midnight escalade, they discovered his other side. For, once he had chosen his moment, no man could be bolder. His chief danger were the English and Welsh archers who, so long as his schiltrons kept their ranks, alone possessed the power to break them. He had only five hundred horse, but knew that the time had come to use them. Most of the enemy's archers were still in the rear of the dense, confused English armour as it struggled to hold back the advancing spears, and their arrows were falling impartially on friend and foe alike. Seeing that they were unpro-tected by pikesmen, Bruce ordered the Marischal to move his horsemen round their flank and charge.

The move was a brilliant success. In a few minutes the archers had been cut to pieces and the English were without one of their two principal weapons. The other, their armour, unable to deploy and with its horses getting more and more out of control, was by now unusable. Unable either to break or stop the contracting ring of Scottish spears, it was gradually pushed back in confusion into an ever-smaller area of firm ground. Now, King Robert saw, was the moment to throw in his reserve, hidden in the wood to the west of the Stirling highway. Calling on Angus Og, MacDonald of the Isles, in the words still borne on the Clanranald coat-of-arms, 'My hope is constant in thee', he launched the islemen against the receding English flank where, a mile or more to the east of St Ninian's chapel, the Bannock burn narrowed into a small precipitous gorge. Into this the English cavalry were driven as the Scottish officers repeatedly called out, 'Press! Press!', and the pikesmen, keeping their steady ranks, raised the shout of, 'On them! On them! They fail! They fail!'

As the mêlée of falling knights and terror-stricken horses continued in the narrowing space left by the Scottish spears, a further force was seen to be entering the battle. Emerging from the wood on the hill beyond St Ninian's chapel, 'the small folk' and camp followers of Bruce's army moved into the fight to take their share of whatever slaying and plundering there might be. They had made themselves banners of blankets slung on saplings, and the sight filled the by now demoralised invaders with despair.

By this time panic had set in; it was Stirling Brig over again. The English were far from home in a wild hostile land, and their line of retreat was cut by relentless enemies and the bogs of the carse. The only way open was northwards across the narrowing plain to Stirling. The first thought of those immediately about him was to save the King. The tall Plantagenet, his horse stabbed under him, helped to clear a way with his battle-axe, while his entourage hustled him through the milling mob towards the north. But when he reached the walls of Stirling Castle he was reminded by the governor that any stay there would be fatal, since he was obliged to surrender it by the terms of the truce. There was nothing for it but to make a wide detour to the west round the rear of the Scottish army. With five hundred followers the King set out into the ununknown, vowing to endow a college of Carmelite friars if he reached England in safety. Riding day and night with Douglas in pursuit, he reached Dunbar castle where he took boat to Berwick.

Other were less fortunate. The Constable, flying towards Carlisle with the earl of Angus and other Balliol supporters, was handed over to his pursuers by the governor of Bothwell castle. Those taken on the field included the Keeper of the Privy Seal, which itself fell into Scottish hands. In all some five hundred men of high rank were made prisoner. Thousands more, including seven hundred knights and many of England's greatest lords, perished in the carse or in the waters of the Forth or were slaughtered by the country folk. Of the magnates who had accompanied the King to Scotland, only Pembroke – flying on foot with a handful of Welsh archers – reached England.

Had Bruce commanded a substantial force of cavalry, it is unlikely that any of the invaders would have got away at all. His booty included the royal wardrobe, a vast haul of jewels and ecclesiastical vestments – brought to celebrate an English victory – and over £200,000 in bullion, worth many millions in modern money. The whole of the royal siege-train and military chest remained in his hands. He treated his prisoners with magnanimity and courtesy like the great gentleman he was. Sir Marmaduke de Twenge, the English hero of the rout of Stirling Brig who, after a night hidden in a bush, surrendered to him personally next day, was sent home without ransom. For nearly a year after the Battle of the Pools, as the English called it, a stream of agents visited Scotland under safe conduct to negotiate the exchange of prisoners.

*   *   *

After Hastings, Bannockburn was the greatest military disaster in English history. It ended any real hope of reconquering Scotland by arms. For a generation the Scots had suffered invasion. Now, under Douglas and Randolph, they took the offensive. Having expelled the English from every corner of their land save Berwick, they swept across the border. And as the government at Westminster was neither prepared to recognise their independence nor able to oppose them, the people of northern England had to make what terms they could. Cumberland and Durham paid ransom for a truce, and Tynedale did homage to the Scottish King. Such was the terror which Bruce's lieutenant, Douglas, inspired that for generations to come North Country mothers rocked their babies to the refrain,

> 'Hush thee, hush thee, do not fret thee,
> The Black Douglas shall not get thee.'

It was not until 1328, fourteen years after Bannockburn, that the English could be brought to recognise the independence of

Scotland. After a generation of war Bruce had accomplished his work and freed his country. He died a year later, on 7 June 1329, at his favourite hunting palace of Cardross on the Clyde.

CHAPTER FOURTEEN

The Grey Goose Feather

'No warring guns were then in use:
    They dreamt of no such thing;
Our Englishmen in fight did use
    The gallant grey-goose wing.

And with the gallant grey-goose wing
    They shew'd to them such play
That made their horses kick and fling
    And down their riders lay.'

Old Ballad

'There are periods at which the history of its wars
is the true history of the people, for they are the
discipline of the national experience.'

Bishop Stubbs

IN 1327, THIRTEEN YEARS after Bannockburn, Bruce's defeated adversary, Edward II, preceded him to the grave. Undeterred by the tragic fate of Gaveston and the failure of his earlier attempt to govern England without 'counsel and consent', Edward had once more tried – for a time with success – to rule through an all-powerful and upstart favourite. This time it had cost him his own life as well as that of the favourite – Hugh Despenser, an intensely ambitious Marcher[1] who, with his equally avaricious father, led Edward, 'like a cat after a straw'. In 1326, following a spontaneous rising

---

[1] The Despensers were not, by Marcher standards, of the first hereditary rank, being descended from the household 'dispensers' of the former Palatine earls of Chester.

and an invasion by his estranged French Queen, Isabella, and her exiled lover, Roger Mortimer – the Despensers' fellow Marcher and bitterest enemy – he was forced to abdicate in favour of his fifteen-year-old son, Edward III. Deposed by an improvised Parliament on the grounds that, through evil advice and refusal to 'hear good counsel', he had 'stripped his realm' of Scotland and his hereditary lands in France and Ireland, the hapless King was incarcerated by the triumphant Mortimer in one vile dungeon after another until, mocked by brutal jailers as a madman in a crown of plaited straw, he suffered an unspeakable death at their hands in Berkeley Castle.

But in overthrowing the Despensers and ridding themselves of an irresponsible sovereign, the English had merely exchanged the rule of one ruthless Marcher lord for another. From this dilemma they were rescued by the courage of the young King, who in 1330, eluding the vigilance of Mortimer's guards, admitted, through a secret passage under the moat of Nottingham Castle, an armed band of his friends at whose head he surprised the hated dictator disrobing in Queen Isabella's apartments. Sent in fetters to the Tower and tried for treason by his fellow peers of Parliament, Mortimer was sentenced, like the Despensers before him, to an ignominious death and, drawn to the common gallows at Smithfield, hanged, disembowelled and quartered.

At eighteen Edward III thus became King in fact as well as in name. Like his grandfather, he meant to rule. Having seen since childhood the fatal consequences of a break between a sovereign and the lords through whom, in an age when a journey from London to York took a week, so much of the administration of a feudal kingdom had to be conducted, he knew there could be no ruling England without the counsel and consent of its nobles. After the struggles of the past generation what was needed was a compromise – a reconciliation between royal authority and the 'liberties' of the magnates. It was the supreme merit of this firm, conciliatory, yet shrewd young King to realise it.

Generous, impulsive, profuse in display, a laggard neither in love nor war, with a boyish charm which won the hearts of warriors and fair women, Edward III was the *beau idéal* of chivalry and of the elaborate code of knightly conduct and manners known as courtesy. To the young English lords, his contemporaries, he seemed a reincarnation of their legendary hero, King Arthur. It was thus that he saw himself – the crowned leader of a brotherhood of Christian knights. Inspired by the long rambling tales of the Arthurian legends, his ambition was to build a Round Tower in Windsor Castle to house a round table at which he and his knights could feast as equals 'in fair fellowship' after their jousts and tournaments.

It was not only with his hereditary magnates that, taught by his father's failure, Edward III achieved a working accord. Resolved to regain the dominions which his father had lost to his feudal overlord, the King of France, and having to go to war to do so, he set himself to woo the non-hereditary and elected representatives of the lesser taxpayers who, throughout his reign, he called to almost every meeting of Parliament. Summoned not by individual name like the lords and prelates, but by general writs addressed to the sheriffs, the seventy-four representative knights of the shire and the two hundred or so burgesses of the chartered towns at first behaved as very humble partners in the *universitas* of the realm. As late as 1348 they declined to advise the King on his conduct of the war as being 'too ignorant and simple to counsel on such important matters'. Yet entrusted, in the traditional words of the royal summons, 'with full and sufficient power for themselves and their respective communities to do and to consent to those things which in our Parliament shall be ordained', so stubbornly did they exercise their right to withhold consent to any new form of taxation which they had not approved – not only direct taxes on moveables but even custom duties in the royal demesnes – that, with a wartime Government's need for additional sources of revenue, they little by little became an indispensable part of the national machinery of 'counsel and consent'. The Crown's demands for money caused the representatives of two very different social groups, the landowning warrior knights of the shires and the trading burgesses of the towns, to draw together for consultations on finance. In doing so they unwittingly created a single assembly representing the communities of both shire and borough. Thus unique among the rigidly divided class 'estates' which made up the parliaments of European kingdoms, by the end of Edward III's fifty years' reign they had grown into a permanent body, which in the next century became known as the House of Commons. Sitting separately from the Lords in their own chamber – at one time the Painted Chamber of the Palace of Westminster, at another the chapter house of the Abbey – in the course of the fifty or so Parliaments of the reign, they developed a procedure of their own, distinct from the parliamentary procedure of earlier days designed for the convenience of King and Council. This was largely due to the lawyers who, chosen by local communities to represent them because of their professional expertise, brought to the work of an evolving institution their habits of mental precision and insistence on procedure and precedent.

The members of the Commons thus acquired a corporate sense. Their first elected spokesman or Speaker appeared by the end of the reign. Though with their superior social status the knights of the shire led the debates, they constituted, with the burgesses, a single estate – the commonalty or *populus* of the realm as distinct from the Lords, and not, as in continental parliaments, two separate estates of knights and burgesses. They represented, not classes or callings, but localities and, by acting together for the 'common good', made the needs and views of those localities known to the Crown. Their influence and prestige were the greater because, even when, as sometimes happened, they were cadets of baronial families, the knights sat with the burgesses as commoners. More perhaps than any other factor this created a sense of national identity and common interest. It made it easy for Lords and Commons to act together, and hard for any monarch to encroach on the community's liberties by setting class against class. Without this, the tendency to absolutism inherent in the growing power of national monarchy might have become too strong to resist, as it did in almost every other European kingdom between the fourteenth and seventeenth centuries.

*　　　*　　　*

By observing the forms of parliamentary consultation and utilising the representative taxing assembly which his grandfather had created out of the Great Council of the realm, Edward III was able to put into the field a professional army better equipped and supported than anything possessed by feudal France with its far greater population and wealth. And in doing so, when the time came, he was able to resort to a novel weapon which, in the hands of his humbler subjects, was to prove a more deadly and accurate instrument of war than anything yet seen on Europe's battlefields. For by Edward I's Statute of Winchester, embodying the old Anglo-Saxon rule under which every free man between the ages of fifteen and sixty was expected to turn out in the shire levy with his personal arms to defend the realm and maintain the peace, the English countryman was trained to arms, unlike his counterpart in the feudal kingdoms of the continent, where fighting was the preserve of heavily armoured mounted nobles and knights and hired professional mercenaries.

The long-bow had first appeared in England at the end of the thirteenth century among the yeoman of Macclesfield and Sherwood forests, who had learnt its use from the Welsh hillmen during the wars of Edward I. Originally in its native Wales made of rough unpolished wild elm, in England it was usually of yew. Drawn not by strength of arm but of the whole frame, it seemed a weapon designed for the Anglo-Saxon Englishman's fine physique. The arrows it fired, a cloth-yard long, were plumed with the feathers of the geese which fed on the village greens:

> 'Their arrows finely pared, for timber and for feather,
> With birch and brazil pierc'd to fly in any weather,
> And, shot they with the round, the square or forkèd pile,
> The loose gave such a twang, it might be heard a mile.'

By the time of Edward III's accession, after more than half a century of campaigning against the Welsh and Scots, the long-bow had become the popular English weapon *par excellence*. Archery competitions on feast days and holidays were a favourite recreation of the rustic commonalty, and later in the reign, under pressure of war, practice at the butts after Sunday service was enjoined by law. In the popular ballads of Robin Hood – the legendary North Country outlaw who lived with his merry men in the greenwood and robbed the rich but spared the poor – Robin was depicted as an unfailing marksman. 'Bend all your bows,' he bade his men,

> 'and, with the grey goose-wing,
> Such sport now show as you would do
> In the presence of the King.'

Thrice, we are told, at the sheriff's archery competition at Nottingham,

> 'Robin shot about
> And always sliced the wand.'

And when in the ballads he and his followers switched their aim from the butts to the sheriff's men who had tried to apprehend him at the moment of his triumph, the latter had to run for their lives under a hail of arrows.

It was the Scots who first encountered the power of this formidable new national weapon. Nineteen years after Robert Bruce's victory over England's chivalry at Bannockburn, a Scottish army was attempting to relieve Berwick, then besieged by the young English King. When, on 19 July 1333, it came within sight of the town, it found the English barring its path on the northern slopes of Halidon Hill. They were drawn up in a long thin line from which projected four triangular salients formed by archers, one on either flank and two in the centre. The three gradually narrowing funnels formed by these salients were closed at the summit of the hill by three brigades of dismounted armoured knights and men-at-arms, with banners and pennons fluttering above the sheen of their swords and lances. Behind them was a reserve brigade to deal with any attempt to drive in the archers on the wings, while in the rear, encircled by baggage-wagons, were laagers packed with horses awaiting a summons from their riders in the battle-line and guarded by the pages who looked after their masters' steeds and armour.

The trap thus set for the Scots proved as deadly as the Bannockburn bogs and the pits which Bruce had dug on the road to Stirling a generation before. For in the hands of English archers the longbow of Gwent had come of age, and Edward and his lords had found a way to turn it into a tactical arm of startling mobility and killing-power. One of them, the crusader Henry of Grosmont – son

of the King's cousin, the earl of Lancaster – had fought at Bannockburn, and it may have been this brilliant, imaginative commander
who first saw how the long-bow could be used to revolutionise the
art of war. What seems certain is that during those waiting weeks
while the English army was blockading Berwick, the archers, whom
Edward's commissioners of array had gathered from the northern
and midland counties and forests, were trained to manoeuvre and
exercise their art under orders, just as Bruce's pikesmen before
Bannockburn had been trained to fight the battle he had foreseen.
Brigaded with knights and men-at-arms from their native shires
and disciplined by veterans who had learnt war the hard way on
the Welsh and Scottish hills, they were taught to operate, not
merely as individual marksmen, but in massed phalanxes from
which, at the word of command, rhythmic volleys of arrows,
travelling at incredible speed, could be directed first at one part of
an attacking force, then at another, until every living thing in the
target area had been killed or maimed. In their metal helmets and
padded deerskin jackets, these light, active men could manoeuvre
in extended order, enfilade a column from flank or even rear and,
combining fire-power and movement, at a bugle call or other signal,
re-form, under cover of their comrades' volleys, in massed ranks
in which, so long as their ammunition lasted, they were virtually
unassailable.

As the Scottish pikesmen moved forward in dense schiltrons
across the marshy ground at the foot of the hill, they suddenly came
into range of the archers. Though hundreds fell as the showers of
steel-tipped arrows struck home, they pressed stubbornly on.
Lowering their heads against the blinding hail and closing their
ranks they instinctively edged away from the salients of archers on
either side and started to climb. Packed together till they were
almost suffocated, riven and tormented by the massed volleys from
the close formations into which the archers withdrew at every
attempt to attack them, they stumbled up the slope towards the
waiting line of English armour and the one place on the battlefield
where no arrows were falling. When, breathless from the ascent,
the survivors reached that hedge of levelled lances, the knights and
men-at-arms started to hack at them with their swords and battle-

axes, forcing them down the slope where they came once more into
that enfilading hail. The Regent of Scotland was mortally wounded,
and six of his earls left dead on the field. Altogether seventy Scots
lords and five hundred knights and squires fell, and almost the
entire infantry. The defenders lost one knight, one man-at-arms
and twelve archers.

*   *   *

Four years after Halidon Hill – whose result was little noticed at
the time outside the British Isles – England became involved in a
long inconclusive war with France, caused by the refusal of King
Philip Valois to restore to Edward his father's forfeited fiefs in
Ponthieu, Guienne and the Agenais. During the past half-century
France had become by far the most powerful state in western
Christendom, with a population of over twelve millions, or four
times that of England. She was the military, cultural, artistic and
even religious leader of western Christendom; the papacy itself
had been transferred from Rome to a French enclave on the Rhône
where, in their palace at Avignon, a succession of French Popes
wielded the authority of their Italian predecessors. While England
had been engaged in her long costly attempt to conquer Scotland,
Philip the Fair of France, seeking to extend her outer frontiers to
the Pyrenees, Rhine and North Sea, had brought under his direct
rule Champagne, Brie, Franche-Comté, the Lyonnais, Navarre
and part of Lorraine. When he died in the year of Bannockburn, of
the great outlying provinces of royal France only Flanders,
Brittany and Gascony – the rump of the early Plantagenets' vast
duchy of Aquitaine – remained independent fiefs.

To recover his lost feudal territories from his powerful continental neighbour, Edward at first relied on an alliance with the
rulers of four small states in the borderland between Germany and
France's northern frontiers: Brabant, whose reigning duke was his
cousin, and Hainault, Gelderland and Juliers, with all of whom he
was allied by his happy marriage to the Count of Hainault's
daughter, Philippa. But though, with the forces they put into the
field – heavily subsidised through taxes voted by English Parliaments – Edward and his knights 'rode against the tyrant of the

French with banners displayed', ravaging frontier villages and crops in revenge for the burning of English south-coast towns by Norman and Breton privateers, King Philip refused to give battle. Secure behind the fortifications of his northern cities, he merely watched these costly proceedings from the walls of Amiens, ignoring the English King's taunts and challenges. And presently the Hainaulters, Brabanters and Germans tired of the campaign and insisted on returning home for the winter, leaving Edward heavily in debt. 'Our allies,' he wrote in disgust to his son, 'would no longer abide.'

But during the winter of 1339–40 he had an unexpected stroke of fortune. Driven desperate by an embargo on the export of English wool to Flanders, under a rich Ghent merchant, James van Artevelde – a patriot rabble-rouser of the type which had recently risen to power in the Italian city-states – the unemployed workers of the Flemish cloth manufacturing towns rose against their pro-French count and drove him from the country. To save themselves from France's vengeance they then appealed to Edward for help, imploring him to assume the crown of France and so become their suzerain and protector.

It had been the defeat of the French chivalry at Courtrai in 1302 by the burghers and weavers of Bruges and Ghent – the despised 'blue nails' of the clothiers' factories, emulating Wallace at Stirling Bridge and fighting on foot with pikes – which close on half a century earlier had enabled Edward I to recover his Gascon dominions. Regardless of his debts his grandson now promised them arms, the removal of the English wool-staple from Antwerp to Bruges and a subsidy of £140,000. And to legalise their repudi-ation of homage and protect them from an interdict for their breach of feudal faith, he laid formal claim to the throne of his Capet ancestors. On 24 January 1340 he entered Bruges and was acclaimed by the burghers as king and overlord. Two weeks later, in a proclamation to 'the prelates, peers, dukes, counts, barons, gentle and simple dwelling in the realm of France', he announced that Philip of Valois 'had intruded himself by force' onto his throne while he had been 'of tender years', and that he was now resolved to regain it and 'with unshakeable purpose do justice to all men'.

Henceforward he and his heirs quartered the fleur-de-lys of France before the leopards of England, bearing them in the semi-position on royal seal and surcoat.

Having secured his alliance Edward hurried home to obtain the wherewithal to finance it. So desperate were his straits that he was forced to leave his Queen and children and the earls of Derby and Salisbury at Antwerp as a pledge for his debts. His expenditure had by now almost drained England of specie. Yet his popularity was still sufficient to rouse the country. Though in the autumn, after being told by the Council that unless they helped him he would have to surrender himself to his foreign creditors, the Commons had asked for time to consult those they represented, they now joined with the magnates in giving him a ninth of every sheaf, fleece and lamb for two years, a ninth from the royal boroughs and a fifteenth from the rest of the community.

Yet they made their grant dependent on his answer to four petitions, one of which, by finally ending the Crown's right to tallage merchandise at will even in the royal demesnes, was a major step on the road to parliamentary control of taxation. In return for allowing Edward to collect the hated *maltote* for another fourteen months they received a promise that it should never be levied again 'except by common consent of the prelates, earls, barons and other lords and commons of the realm'.

Having obtained supplies for a new campaign, Edward prepared to return to the continent where the French were burning the towns and villages of Hainault and threatening Flanders. In his absence a fleet of nearly two hundred French, Genoese and Spanish ships had arrived off Sluys at the mouth of the Zwim to bar his passage and blockade the Flemings. Throughout the past year the position at sea and the raids on England's southern ports had been causing increasing anxiety; in the autumn of 1339 several of the King's own ships had been seized in the North Sea. In its debates, Parliament had stressed the country's maritime weakness and 'how the sea should be guarded against enemies so that they . . . should not enter the kingdom to destroy it'.

As it seemed that the King would have to fight his way back to Flanders, every ship that could be requisitioned was assembled at

Orwell and packed with archers and men-at-arms. Apart from a few royal cogs and galleys specially built for fighting – kept normally at Winchelsea and Portsmouth and administered from the Tower by an officer called the clerk of the King's ships – the fleet consisted of one-masted, single-decked merchant and fishing boats, most of them of under a hundred tons. Impressed by the sheriffs of the maritime countries, they had been adapted for battle by the addition of fighting-tops to the masts and timber superstructures at bow and stern called 'forecastles' and 'aftercastles', from which archers and slingers could shower arrows and stones on the enemy's crews and rigging and from which boarding parties could take off. In honour of the King these were brightly painted and adorned with golden lions. The two largest vessels were the flagship, the cog *Thomas*, and a 240-ton ship called the *Michel*, contributed by the Cinque Port of Rye.

Yet England was only in the second rank in naval force. Her fleet was far inferior to the armada lying off the Flemish coast. To cautious minds it seemed insanity for the King to attempt to break through it to Sluys by ramming and boarding its taller and more heavily manned ships – then the only known method of fighting at sea. Appalled by the shortage of money and reports that the French and Spaniards intended to capture his royal master, the Chancellor, Archbishop Stratford, begged him to abandon the voyage. Both admirals backed the archbishop's request. When the King refused, to his indignation Stratford resigned the seal. 'I will cross in spite of you,' Edward said, 'and those who are afraid where no fear is, may stay at home.'

The fleet sailed on Thursday 22 June 1340, reaching the mouth of the Zwin next day. 'About the hour of noon,' Edward wrote to his son, 'we arrived upon the coast of Flanders before Blankenberghe where we had a sight of the enemy who were all crowded together in the port of Sluys. And seeing that the tide did not serve us to close with them, we lay to all that night. On Saturday, St John's Day, soon after the hour of noon at high tide, in the name of God and confident in our just quarrel, we entered the port upon our enemies who had assembled their ships in very strong array.' There were so many of them, an eye-witness wrote, that 'their masts seemed like a great wood'.

Both sides fought as if on land. The English went in to attack, with wind, sun and tide behind them, in three columns, the King leading the centre in the cog *Thomas*, and each ship manned alternately with men-at-arms and archers. The French and Spanish ships were chained together in four lines across the estuary like the walls of a castle. Built for the Atlantic with high seaboards, they towered above their adversaries, their decks crowded with knights armed with lances and the rigging with stone-throwers and crossbowmen.

It was the English archers who decided the day. As they came into range, they loosed such a storm of arrows that the enemies' decks were strewn with dead before the boarding-parties reached them. So deadly was the marksmanship that many threw themselves into the water. Thousands were killed or drowned; only the Genoese, who had refused to anchor, managed to escape to sea. By morning two-thirds of the allied fleet had been taken or destroyed.

His victory at Sluys sent Edward's prestige soaring. Hitherto he had seemed to his fellow princes only a king of the tournament field and the Scottish moors; now he had proved himself in a major European battle. Though its consequences had still to be realised, he had broken the command of the Channel by the Bay of Biscay seamen. What mattered to him most was the opportunity offered by his victory for an invasion of France. On 18 July he entered van Artevelde's capital, Ghent, as a conquering hero. His Queen was there to greet him with a new-born son, who was to go down to history as John of Ghent or Gaunt.

Together the two men – English King and Flemish clothier – drew up plans for freeing the cities of Artois from the Valois. At the end of July they crossed the French frontier. While Robert of Artois, the exiled claimant to the fief, attacked St Omer, Edward and the German and Netherland princes laid siege to Tournai. But quarrels soon broke out between the allies. When, with the brusque impatience of the self-made, van Artevelde reproached the duke of Brabant for failing to storm the walls, the duke, furious at such low-born insolence, threatened to march his army away. It took all Edward's tact to restrain him. Meanwhile, instead of advancing to the relief of the town, Philip once more refused battle. When Edward challenged him to single combat, Philip merely reminded him of his broken homage.

The final blow to Edward's hopes came when money to pay his allies ran out just as Tournai seemed on the point of surrendering. At that moment the Abbess of Fontenelle – his mother-in-law and a dowager countess of Hainault – appeared in the allied lines with the Church's proposals for a truce. As there was no hope of any more English money, everyone except Edward welcomed her mission with enthusiasm. Such was her immense prestige, the respect felt for the Pope's wishes and the longing of the Netherland princes to return home before the winter, that in his penniless condition Edward was unable to stand out against them. By the truce of Esplechin the combatants agreed to withdraw for a year to their own boundaries, leaving everything as it was before the war, everything, that is, except the English King's and taxpayers' money which had gone beyond recall.

Furious, Edward laid the blame for everything that had happened on the ministers in England who had failed to send him the additional money for want of which the campaign had collapsed. Two summers before, when he first sailed for Brabant, he had issued from Walton in Suffolk a series of administrative ordinances which virtually placed the great permanent offices of state, the Exchequer and Chancery, under the control of the household officers of the Wardrobe and Chamber who accompanied him abroad. The great seal itself had been entrusted to his Keeper of the Privy Seal, William Kilsby. Kilsby was an ambitious and not over-scrupulous cleric who had pleased his master by his ingenuity in raising money. He was on bad terms with the Chancellor, John Stratford – mentor of Edward's early years as King – who since 1333 had also been Archbishop of Canterbury. This dislike was reciprocated by Stratford – the son of a Stratford-on-Avon burgess – who, with his brother, the bishop of Chichester, and his nephew, the bishop of London, formed a powerful family group within the Church and administration. When the archbishop resigned the Chancellorship before Sluys he had been succeeded by his brother and, after the King's return to Flanders, they had been left virtually in charge of England.

There were thus two governments, one at home representing the traditional elements, lay and ecclesiastical, through which the country was normally governed, and the other – in Flanders – composed of courtier-soldiers and the officers of the royal household. But in Edward's eyes the sole function of the first was to keep him supplied with money. Owing to the difficulty of obtaining payment from the overburdened taxpayer and the disappointing results of the wool subsidy, this had now become almost impossible. The growing arrears in the remittances from England and the 'anguish and peril in which the King, Queen and magnates of the host lay for lack of money', made the correspondence between the two branches of government increasingly acrimonious.

By the end of November, getting nothing but excuses in reply to his demands and reproaches, lacking the wherewithal to pay his troops and household, and dunned beyond endurance by his creditors, Edward decided to return, unannounced, to Westminster. Stealing away from Ghent with only eight followers – including Kilsby – he took boat at Sluys and, after a stormy three days' voyage, landed on the night of St Andrew's Day just before cockcrow at the Tower watergate. His temper was not improved by finding the governor absent. He at once ordered his arrest and began a furious investigation into the miscarriages of his ministers. Among those whom he summarily dismissed were the Chancellor, the bishop of Chichester, the Treasurer, the bishop of Coventry, the Chief Justices of the King's Bench and Common Pleas and several other judges, as well as a number of Chancery and Exchequer officials. He also arrested the financiers, William de la Pole and John Pulteney, who had failed to sell the wool he had requisitioned at a sufficiently high price. But his chief anger was reserved for Archbishop Stratford. Accusing him of having counselled him to 'cross the sea without provision of money and horses' and of then withholding supplies, in order to bring about his ruin, he was only with difficulty and, after being reminded of the penalties that would follow such an outrage, prevented from forcibly shipping him and his fellow bishops to Flanders as a pledge for his debts.

As it was, he laid charges against the primate of treason and conversion of public moneys and summoned him to answer at the

Exchequer. In place of the dismissed ministers he appointed a lay Treasurer, Sir Robert Parving, and a lay Chancellor – the first in English history – Sir Robert Bourchier. Both had served as knights of the shire, had held judicial appointments and could be trusted to do his will. Never again, he declared, would he employ anyone as chief minister whom he could not hang if guilty of felony.

Believing, or affecting to believe, that his life was in danger, Stratford took shelter with the monks of Christ Church, Canterbury. On the anniversary of Becket's death he preached a sermon in the cathedral on his martyred predecessor. And on New Year's Day 1341 he addressed a long letter to the King. 'You have had victory of your enemies of Scotland and France,' he told him, 'and at this day are held the most noble prince of Christendom. Consider well your great undertaking and the strong adversary you have, and the great peril of your land . . . Take it not ill, sire, that we send you so largely the truth, for we are moved to do this by the great affection which we have towards you, the safety of your honour and of your land, and, because it belongeth to us, for that we are, all unworthy though we be, primate of all England and your spiritual adviser.'

For while he protested his affection for his royal master, which seems to have been genuine, the archbishop did not shirk from telling him home truths. Though a worldling and a conciliator, he was also a man of courage who in the past had stood up to both Edward II and Queen Isabella and, at the risk of his life, defied the dictator, Mortimer. The veiled menace in his letter was unmistakable. 'Very gentle lord,' he wrote,

> 'may it please you to know that the most sovereign thing which holds kings and princes in due and fitting estate is good counsel. And let it not displease you to remember it in your time, for, by the evil counsel which our lord your father had, he caused to be taken, against the law of the land and the great Charter, the peers and other people of the land and put some to shameful death and of others he caused their goods to be seized . . . And what happened to him for that cause, sire, you know well.'

The archbishop was resolved not to let the underlying constitutional issues be obscured by the royal accusations against his honesty or by his dispute with the household 'intimates' who had poisoned the King's mind. Having been an Oxford doctor of law, a Chancery clerk and dean of the Court of Arches, he knew how to put the issue in its clearest and most compelling form. As in the crisis of 1297 and the days of the Despensers, the principle at stake was whether a King of England, good or bad, could govern without resort to established law and to those who could speak for the nation. 'By evil counsel,' he told the King, 'you begin to seize divers clerks, peers and other folk of the land. You make suit, quite unfitting and against the law of the land, which you are bound by the oath taken at your coronation to keep and maintain, and contrary to the great Charter.' The only place for judging such charges as Edward had brought against his chief subjects was Parliament – the national assembly in which an English King could look into the hearts and minds of his people. 'For the salvation of your enterprise,' he urged, 'be willing to take to you the great and the wise of your land . . . Be willing, sire, if it please you, therefore, to cause them . . . to assemble in a fitting place where we and others may securely come.' The Archbishop had been accused by his master; he was entitled to be judged by his peers in Parliament.

It was a tremendous claim, going to the root of the problem men had been trying to solve since the days of Magna Carta; of how to allow a King the overriding executive power on which the peace and safety of the realm depended and at the same time safeguard the rights and liberties of the subject. And though the angry King denounced Stratford as 'a wily serpent and cunning fox' and, with Kilsby's help, published a venomous attack on him, it soon became clear that the archbishop had judged the issue rightly. Once again, as in 1297 and 1327, magnates, knights of the shire and Londoners came together under the archbishop's lead to protest at a royal attempt to rule by personal will instead of by established law. Stratford's demand to be tried by his peers was a shrewd stroke, for it was a right which every magnate in the land wished to secure for himself.

So it came about that the national crisis set in motion by the King was resolved, as Stratford had proposed, in 'a full Parliament'.

Edward's need for supplies to meet his debts and maintain the Scottish war forced him to yield, and at the end of April the magnates and commons met at Westminster. When Kilsby tried to bar the primate from the House of Lords, John de Warenne, earl of Surrey, doyen of the independent magnates, and his nephew, the earl of Arundel, protested that those who by their rank should be foremost in Parliament were being excluded while others who had no right there were being admitted. 'Lord King,' Warenne is reported to have said, after the manner of his famous grandfather of *quo warranto* fame, 'how goes this Parliament? Things were not wont to be thus. They are all now turned upside down.' And though Stratford never received the trial *in pleno parliamento* which he had been demanding, since the King dropped his charges and, later, even had them annulled as contrary to truth and reason, the principle for which he had contended was triumphantly vindicated. It was Edward who, needing the support of his people, had had to submit to the judgment of Parliament. Seeing that, if he was to have their support in his wars, he must conciliate them, he yielded with grace and good sense.

Before the session ended in May, in reply to petitions from both Lords and Commons the royal assent was given to an Act which not only conceded the right of peers to trial by their fellow magnates in Parliament before suffering imprisonment or forfeiture, but made all ministers and officials of the Crown liable to answer to the same high court for breaches of Magna Carta and the statutes. The Commons also obtained a promise that parliamentary commissioners should audit the moneys voted for the war and that the Lords should share in the appointment of Ministers. Though the magnates later allowed the King to withdraw this last radical concession as unworkable and incompatible with the custom and law of the realm and the royal prerogative, Edward made no further attempt to govern without consultation with the nation's traditional leaders and his customary constitutional advisers.

*   *   *

So far, except for his victory at Sluys, the King's war to recover his French fiefs had been a costly fiasco. Nor, since France came to

233

Scotland's rescue, had his campaign to reduce the Scots to vassalage fared any better. While Parliament was discussing the royal charges against the archbishop, Douglas's son, the knight of Liddesdale, captured Edinburgh castle by the old ruse of blocking the drawbridge with a supply-wagon. A few weeks later Bruce's son, King David, now eighteen, returned from France. At the end of 1341 the truce expired, and Edward took the field against him, spending Christmas at Melrose abbey and afterwards 'riding' through Ettrick forest in what the chronicler described as 'a very ill season'. His foray into that war-wrecked, starving land achieved nothing. By February 1342 the Scots were once more over the border, raiding Northumberland where they 'brent much corn and houses'. And at Easter, Alexander Ramsay of Dalhousie captured Roxburgh, the last English stronghold in Scotland.

Yet that year, with the death of the duke of Brittany, a new opportunity opened for England. When his younger brother, John de Montfort, visited Windsor to obtain the earldom of Richmond to which, under English law, he was heir, he secured from Edward a promise of support for his claim to Brittany against the late duke's son-in-law, Charles of Blois, who was backed by the French King and French-speaking aristocracy against the Celtic-speaking peasantry and townsfolk who favoured de Montfort. The crippling of France's naval strength at Sluys had made the maintenance of an English base in Brittany possible and, in the spring of 1342, after a French army had overrun the duchy and captured de Montfort, a small expedition was despatched to rescue his countess who was besieged at Hennebont. Arriving just in time, its commander, Sir Walter Manny, took the offensive. Later in the summer he was joined by a larger force under the Constable, William Bohun, earl of Northampton. With him came Edward's French protégé, Robert of Artois, and his cousin, Henry of Derby – heir to the royal earldom of Lancaster and the most famous English fighting man of his day.

In Brittany the English had no longer to wait on their allies as in Flanders. They were free to fight when they chose. If the enemy outnumbered them they could apply the tactics which had proved successful at Halidon Hill – a well-chosen defensive position, the men-at-arms dismounted in the centre, the horses and baggage wagons in laager in the rear, the archers on either flank behind projecting hedges of stakes, to enfilade the attacking cavalry. Landing near Brest and forcing Charles of Blois to abandon the blockade of that town, Northampton laid siege to Morlaix. Here against a French relieving army seven or eight times as large as his own he won, on 30 September 1342, the first English victory on the continent since the days of Coeur-de-Lion. Fighting with their backs to a wood, his troops were at one time surrounded but, with their incomparable archery, shot their way out and put the French to flight. Morlaix fell almost immediately, while a hundred miles away, by a use of amphibious power, Robert of Artois captured Vannes, the second city of Brittany. A few weeks later this brave French exile, with his handful of Englishmen, was overwhelmed by superior force and died of his wounds.

By this time Edward himself was in Brittany. Having waited for several weeks at Sandwich for the return of Northampton's transports, which were held up by adverse winds, he had marched his troops to Portsmouth and seized enough ships to take them to Brest. Though it was now the end of October he at once took the field. Sweeping across the peninsula in two columns, one under his personal command, he recaptured Vannes and laid siege to Rennes, while a small flying force reached the walls of Nantes on the Loire.

With southern Brittany lost, King Philip was compelled to intervene. Gathering an army at Angers far larger than Edward's sea-borne expedition, he marched to the relief of Nantes and Rennes. The long-awaited test between the rival Kings seemed imminent when two cardinals arrived from papal Avignon to negotiate an armistice. As both armies were now running short of supplies, their mission proved successful. By the three-years' truce of Morbihan it was agreed that both sides should keep what they had won. De Montfort's supporters retained the southern and western parts of the country and those of Charles of Blois the northern and eastern. The truce was also extended to the chief participants' clients, Scotland and Flanders.

Though the war had now gone on for six years Edward had still made no impression on France, while Scotland was almost as free as in the days of Bruce. He had neither recovered his lost lands in Guienne nor unified Britain. Yet his dream of doing so and of winning immortal fame by arms remained. It may have been during his long and stormy voyage home, in which he narrowly escaped shipwreck on the Spanish coast, that he finalised the idea of founding an Order of Christian chivalry to perpetuate the ideals of his hero, King Arthur, and give expression to his desire for knightly glory. Nine months after his return, in January 1344, he held a tournament at Windsor 'for the recreation and solace of men of war who delight in arms'. During it he and nineteen of his bravest knights jousted for three days against all comers.

When Edward of Windsor set his heart on a project no trouble or expense was too great. Within a few weeks workmen were covering the bridges of the castle with sand for the passage of stone and timber to build a round tower crowning the Norman motte. On 16 February letters patent were issued to William of Ramsey, the King's master-mason – designer of the new octagonal lantern at Ely – and the royal carpenter, William of Hurley, empowering them to choose as many masons and carpenters from 'the cities, towns and other places in England' as they might need. Over seven hundred workmen were engaged at wages ranging from 4s. a week for master-masons to 2d. a day for labourers. And within the castle a huge circular table was made to accommodate the companions of the new knightly brotherhood at an annual Whitsuntide feast.

Yet Fate had more in store for England's King than to preside at tournaments. Before the year ended, contending with the same Celtic separatism in Brittany as Edward in Scotland, Philip seized de Montfort's chief supporters and put them to death. Escaping to England, de Montfort did homage to Edward as King of France and appealed to him to avenge the broken truce and recover his duchy. The challenge was accepted. While the Constable, Northampton, returned to Brittany with de Montfort, Edward himself, using his new-found freedom of movement at sea, prepared a triple attack on France from north, west and south. Despatching his cousin Henry of Grosmont, earl of Derby as lieutenant of Aquitaine to rally the loyal forces in Gascony, he sailed in July 1345 for Flanders with the fifteen-year-old Prince of Wales to take counsel with van Artevelde.

Once again the allies on whose aid he had counted failed him. After conferring with Edward on board his flagship at Sluys for a joint invasion of Artois, van Artevelde on his return to Ghent was murdered by a mob of discontented weavers. Though, bound to England by their need for its wool, the Flemish burghers eventually remained loyal to their alliance, Edward was forced to return home with his plans for attacking France from the north still-born.

But at this juncture events in south-western France took a spectacular turn. Landing at Bayonne in June 1345 and marching to Bordeaux, with five hundred men-at-arms and two thousand archers, Derby had been received with immense enthusiasm by the Gascons, who after six years of resisting the French had developed an almost passionate loyalty to their absent English duke. A soldier in the tradition of William the Marshal, simple, pious and courteous, [1] Henry of Derby had fought in every English campaign since Bannockburn and had been a crusader in Cyprus, Prussia and Granada. He was now forty-six – an age at which most men were then considered past fighting. But he had lost none of the fire and speed of youth. Assembling his little force at Libourne he suddenly struck eastwards at Bergerac, fifty miles up the Dordogne, where the French had withdrawn after his landing. Keeping the ramparts under continuous attack by his archers, he stormed the town at the end of August. Then, having regained most of the Agenais, he turned north against Périgord, where he established an outpost at Auberoche, only nine miles from the capital, Périgueux, before returning to Bordeaux with his prisoners and booty.

Derby's six weeks' campaign made an immense impression on southern France. So did his courteous treatment of his prisoners and the civil population. It aroused, too, the French military authorities to action. Early in October they laid siege to Auberoche with seven thousand men. Receiving an urgent appeal from its garrison, Derby at once gathered four hundred men-at-arms and

---

[1] At a time when literacy was only beginning to reach the aristocratic laity Henry was remarkable for writing two works of devotion, in one of which, *Mercy Gramercy*, he set down all the sins he could recall having committed and all the mercies he had received, asking God's forgiveness for the first and giving thanks for the second.

eight hundred archers and, ordering his second-in-command, the earl of Pembroke, to follow, marched at high speed to the relief of the town. Hiding his men in a wood, he waited twenty-four hours for Pembroke, then decided to attack without him rather than fail the garrison. Having made sure that every man knew what to do, he fell on the besiegers as they were cooking their evening meal, his archers spraying them with arrows and his men-at-arms charging out of the wood with shouts of 'A Derby! A Derby!' In the confused fighting which followed, the enemy's superiority in numbers was beginning to tell when the garrison threw themselves on the besieger's rear. By nightfall the French commander and all his lieutenants were prisoners, including eight viscounts and the flower of the Languedoc nobility. 'There were many a proper feat of arms done,' wrote Froissart, 'many taken and rescued again . . . If the night had not come on, there had but few escaped. No English man-at-arms but had two or three prisoners.'

Striking once more, Derby turned south to take La Réole in the Garonne valley, thirty miles above Bordeaux. Without a proper siege-train he succeeded after ten weeks, not only in capturing the town – for years a standing threat to the capital – but in bluffing the garrison into the belief that the walls had been undermined, whereas his miners had found them so strongly built as to be impregnable. In this way he made himself master of the strongest fortress on the Garonne.

With Aiguillon, thirty miles up the river, already taken by Lord Stafford, the entire Agenais had been cleared. In four months two provinces and fifty towns and castles had been regained by a few thousand archers and men-at-arms. Derby, who that autumn inherited his father's earldom of Lancaster, had proved that France was no longer invulnerable. For the first time since John's loss of Normandy a French King had been forced to take England's military threats seriously. By the spring of 1346 the whole chivalry of southern France was mobilised at Toulouse under Philip's eldest son, the duke of Normandy, to recover his lost province.

*   *   *

Meanwhile, fired by the success of his soldiers and resolved to share in their glory, Edward himself was preparing to strike. His brilliant cousin had given him the chance for which he had been waiting nine years. While that April the Dauphin laid siege to Aiguillon, and Derby, with only a fraction of his force, watched from La Réole for a chance to relieve the tiny garrison, Edward started to assemble on the Hampshire coast the largest army that had ever sailed from England. He raised it, not by the feudal levy of the past nor even by over-much reliance on the commissions of array which Edward I had adapted to conscript the shire militia for war, but by offering those willing to fight high wages and still more tempting prospects of ransom and plunder.

He was able to do so because he had learnt from experience the value of the representative taxing assembly which his grandfather had created out of the Great Council of the realm. By observing the forms of parliamentary consultation, and ruling with the advice of the great officers of Church and state in whom the taxpayers' representatives reposed their trust, he could now obtain the where-withal to raise a professional army far superior in quality to anything feudal France could put into the field. Developed during the past half-century in the course of many a bitter tussle between Crown and taxpayer, a system of taxation by consent gave to the English King financial resources unknown to his Valois rival, though the latter ruled a kingdom far richer and more populous.

Having the nation's financial resources behind him, Edward was able to make a royal campaign a national one. He raised his army by indentures made with local leaders with a vocation for war, under which they recruited, at agreed rates of pay, the precise numbers and types of fighting men required. Each indenture speci-fied the number to be raised, the time for which they were to serve and the contribution to be made by the Exchequer. The contin-gents thus raised were known as 'retinues'. An earl, who was paid eight shillings a day for his services, would contract to raise, say sixty men-at-arms, of whom ten should be knights and a hundred and twenty bowmen, all equipped and with horses, for three months to a year 'at the accustomed wages of war', together with pages called *valets aux armes* who served as apprentices to the knights, cleaned their armour and looked after their horses when dis-mounted.

The rates of pay were high. At a time when in some places land let for as little as fourpence an acre a year, a mounted archer received sixpence a day if he provided his own horse – or threepence otherwise. Even the Welsh spearmen, the lowest grade of professional fighting men, were paid twopence. The wage of a mounted man-at-arms was a shilling a day, of a knight-bachelor twice as much, of a banneret four shillings a day. Bannerets were knights of proved valour and experience who, distinguished by a rectangular banner, arrayed and directed contingents in the field, commanded castles and acted as staff officers to the commanders-in-chief. Such were Sir John Chandos and Sir Robert Knollys, the Cheshire yeoman who rose to be one of the most famous captains of the age and, through ransom and plunder, one of the richest.

Knights carried a triangular pennon and led the men-at-arms or armoured troopers who, like them, usually provided their own horses and horse-armour. They were armed with a long sword and either a lance or battle-mace, with a dagger for in-fighting. The mail-armour of the past was now giving way to plate-armour; a knight in the 1340s wore a short surcoat marked with his armorial bearings and a baldric or sword-belt over a metal breast-plate, plate-guards for his arms and legs, and on his head a heavy helm crowned with his crest and closed, when in action, with a vizor. There is a picture of one in the Luttrell psalter, bidding farewell to his lady before a tournament, his charger magnificently decked in heraldic trappings.

The archers who, as a result of their spectacular successes, had by now become the largest part of every English army, wore either light steel breast-plates or padded hauberks of boiled leather, rough frieze cloaks and steel caps, not unlike the splinter helmets of modern infantrymen. In addition to their bows and sheaves of goose-quill arrows, they carried short swords, knives and steel-tipped stakes for building protective hedges against cavalry.[1]

[1] There is a contemporary picture of one, the yeoman, in *The Canterbury Tales* of Geoffrey Chaucer, who had served in youth as a page in one of Edward III's military expeditions to France.

> 'And he was clad in coat and hood of green,
> A sheef of peacock arrows bright and keen
> Under his belt he bare full thriftily.
> Well could he dress his tackle yeomanly;
> His arrows droppèd not with feathers low,
> And in his hand he bare a mighty bow.'

Though they fought in separate contingents or phalanxes, for purposes of recruitment and discipline they served under the lords or knights who paid them, the army's disciplinary unit being a 'lance'[1] – a professional team, rather like the crew of a modern aircraft, consisting of a knight or man-at-arms, two archers, a swordsman or *courtillier*, and a pair of pages armed with daggers.

The army was also accompanied by auxiliaries: Welsh spearmen and light unarmoured horsemen called *hobelars* – often drawn from Ireland – for reconnaissance and terrorising the country; miners from Durham and the Forest of Dean for siege-operations, smiths, armourers and pavilioners, carpenters for making bridges, *cementarii* for building fortifications, and wagoners for the baggage-train. The King himself was accompanied by a bodyguard of personal knights and archers and a band of minstrels – a dozen trumpeters, a clarioner, fiddler, pipers, a wait or two, a nakerer, a citole and a man playing a shawm. For their services to morale these musicians ranked as archers.[2]

Running through this English army and transcending differences of rank and class was a new-found pride in common nationhood. Two-thirds of those who served in it were yeomen armed with a weapon which, as Morlaix and Auberoche had proved, could match, and more than match, the proud feudal cavalry which had lorded it in Europe for three centuries. Leading them were the representatives of all the great feudal houses – Bohun and Beauchamp, Warenne and Arundel, Mortimer, Despenser, Ufford, Hastings, de Vere – whose ambitions and jealousies in the last generation had all but wrecked the realm, but who, won over by their young King's generosity and magnanimity, were now united behind him and ready to follow him anywhere. Among them were his father's one-time jailers, the lords Berkeley and Maltravers, and the sixteen-year-old grandson of Roger Mortimer, to whom he had restored the fallen traitor's castle of Radnor and other lands.

Such was the force, prepared with all the King's tireless drive and attention to military detail, which with its bright pavilions and

[1] From this our modern rank of lance-corporal derives.

[2] A naker was a kettledrum; a citole a plucked-string instrument, the ancestor of the guitar; and a shawm a wind one, ancestor of the oboe.

banners, encamped that May and June on Southsea common, waiting for a wind to carry it to the continent. Some imagined that its destination was Brittany. Others thought that the King would sail to Flanders where that June the men of Ghent, Bruges and Ypres had agreed to invade Artois and to whose aid he had recently sent six hundred archers. But most supposed the royal host was bound for Gasgony where the earl of Pembroke and Sir Walter Manny were still holding out in Aiguillon against the Dauphin's vast army while Lancaster, with a few thousand archers and men-at-arms at Le Réole, barred the road to Bordeaux.

Yet Edward intended none of these things. When, at long last, on 11 July 1346, the south-westerly winds changed and the great armada of seven hundred vessels sailed from St Helens, sealed orders opened at sea revealed that its destination was the Cotentin peninsula of Normandy, the rich duchy once owned by Edward's Norman ancestors and lost by King John. By ravaging it and threatening Paris he could draw the Dauphin's army from Aiguillon and, linking hands with the Flemings in Artois, strike at France from three sides.

By the secrecy with which he had cloaked his plans, the King had kept the French guessing. Having to guard eight hundred miles of coastline from the Garonne to the Scheldt their fleet was strong nowhere; Edward's, concentrated in one place, was able to put the army ashore on 12 July at St Vaast near La Hogue almost without opposition. Once ashore he wasted no time. On the 18th, after knighting the Prince of Wales and some of his young companions, he began his march on Rouen. Crossing the marshes at the south-eastern foot of the Cotentin peninsula, he reached St Lo on the 22nd. By keeping abreast with the army's left flank the fleet provided a moveable base, while the troops lived on the countryside, avenging the raids of Norman seamen on the English south-coast towns by burning their harbours and ships. The Welsh spearmen and Irish *hobelars* particularly distinguished themselves in this atrocious business – the usual accompaniment of fourteenth-century warfare – though after a few days, the King, as claimant to the French throne, issued an order threatening death to any soldier who should 'set on fire towns or manors, rob churches or holy places, do harm to the aged, the children or women of his realm'.

Edward's new French subjects, however, showed no enthusiasm for their would-be sovereign. The peasants fled in terror from his march and, when on 25 July he summoned Caen, the bishop of Bayeux tore up the summons and imprisoned his messenger. Yet, though a formidable town – larger, a chronicler wrote, than any English city save London – the invaders carried it in a day after the archers had out-shot the crossbowmen defending the Orne crossings, and the fleet, sailing up the river from Ouistreham, had joined in the fight. They took a rich haul of prisoners and a copy of a treaty made eight years before by King Philip with the Norman authorities for an invasion of England, which Edward sent home to be read in Parliament.

On the last day of July the march to the Seine was resumed. On 2 August the army reached Lisieux. But on the same day the French King entered Rouen forty miles ahead, interposing his force between the English and their Flemish allies who, two hundred miles to the north, were just setting out from Ypres. As soon as news had reached him of Edward's landing King Philip had raised the oriflamme at St Denis and, summoning the Dauphin from Aiguillon to join him, had hurried to the Norman capital, gathering troops as he marched. The Seine here was three hundred yards wide and, with the city held in force, the English could not hope to cross.

Instead, on reaching the river at Elboeuf, twelve miles above Rouen, they turned upstream to seek a narrower crossing. By doing so they abandoned their communications with England but threatened Paris. For the next six days the rival armies marched south-westwards along opposite sides of the Seine. Everywhere the English found the bridges demolished or strongly held. But on the 13th, when they were only a dozen miles from the capital, Edward allowed the French to outmarch him and, by a sudden feint, turned back to Poissy, where the bridge, only partially destroyed, was lightly guarded. Crossing by a single sixty-foot beam only a foot wide, Northampton the Constable got a detachment to the far side. For the next two days, while skirmishing parties set fire to St Cloud and other villages under the western walls of Paris to deceive the enemy, the carpenters worked feverishly to repair the bridge. Meanwhile, though by now in far superior strength, King Philip remained in a frenzy of indecision, marching first to one side of his capital and then the other, uncertain whether the English were about to assault it or to move south to relieve Aiguillon.

On 15 August the carpenters finished their work, and during that night and next morning the army and its baggage train crossed the Seine. In the next five days it marched seventy miles due north, hoping to cross the Somme between Amiens and Abbeville and join hands with the Flemings who were besieging Béthune, fifty miles beyond that river. But though he had been temporarily out-witted, when he found that his foe had crossed the Seine, King Philip acted with equal speed. Realising at last Edward's relative weakness, he covered the seventy-three miles from Paris to Amiens in three days, ordering the feudal levies of the north to join him there. With him were the flower of France's chivalry, together with King John of Bohemia and his son, Charles of Moravia – titular King of the Romans.

The position of the English was now grave in the extreme. Between them and their Flemish allies in Artois lay the marshy valley of the Somme, with the French King at Amiens only a day's march away and every bridge over the river in his hands. All contact had been lost with the fleet, whose seamen, with their usual indiscipline, had returned to England in the wake of the ships that had taken home the sick and the spoils of Caen. The army's food supplies were almost exhausted and in the closing stages of their march the troops had been living on unripe fruit. After covering nearly three hundred miles their boots were worn out and the horses dying for lack of forage.

Edward had been far too bold. Yet he showed no sign of his anxiety. On 23 August he started westwards in the hope of finding a crossing above Abbeville but, as the estuary here widened to two miles, the prospect was unpromising. Scarcely had he set out when news arrived that Philip had left Amiens and was moving up the south bank after him, and had almost reached the village where the English had spent the previous night.

Cut off in a strange land and without maps – a military commodity then unknown – the King ordered the prisoners to be brought before him and offered a huge reward for anyone who would reveal a crossing place. A native told him of a submerged causeway across the estuary at Blanchetaque, midway between Abbeville and the sea, where at low tide a man could cross waist-deep. Without hesitation Edward decided to take the risk.

Before dawn on the 24th the English advance-guard reached the ford. The far bank was held by a French force of more than three thousand men. As soon as the tide was low enough for a man to stand without being swept away, the troops started to cross, led by Hugh Despenser, whose father had been hanged on a fifty-foot gallows by Edward's mother.[1] Carrying their bows above their heads to keep them dry, the archers struggled through a mile and a half of water, while the knights followed on horseback. A few hundred yards from the northern bank they came within range of the enemy's cross-bowmen but continued to advance till they were within killing distance. Then, standing ten abreast on the causeway and shooting over one another's heads, they loosed their usual devastating hail. When their arrows were exhausted they stepped into the deeper water on either side and let the mounted armour splash past them into the shallows where, after a brief skirmish, it put the French cavalry to flight. Meanwhile on the south bank Edward's rearguard had been holding off the advance echelons of Philip's host until the baggage-wagons, with their precious load of arrows, had passed through the water now starting to rise. Save for a few stragglers caught by the tide the whole army passed over in safety. Barred by the rising flood, the enemy could only watch in amazement.

That night the English encamped in the forest of Crécy in Edward's confiscated hereditary fief of Ponthieu. Though his troops were still short of rations, their morale was high, for in a deeply religious age the passage of the river had seemed a miracle.

---

[1] He lies in his armour of alabaster, his hands crossed in prayer and a lion at his feet, in the Despenser tomb in Tewkesbury Abbey, whose glorious vaulting posterity owes to his and his wife's munificence. He died in the first Black Death three years after Crécy.

Rather than resume his march to his allies in the north, the King therefore decided to stand and give battle. The odds against him were enormous, but with so cautious an adversary the opportunity might never recur.

All day on Friday the 25th, while the French were crossing the Somme, Edward searched for a defensive position. He found one on a low ridge facing south-west, between the villages of Crécy and Wadicourt. Behind lay forest into which his woodland-trained archers could withdraw in case of need.

On the morning of 26 August 1346, having attended mass, Edward marched his army to its position. He had now about thirteen thousand men, more than two-thirds of them archers, with, at the outside, some three thousand armoured knights and men-at-arms. These he deployed in three divisions or 'battles', two of them a little way down the forward slope of the ridge, which was about a mile long, and the third under his personal command in reserve. He himself took station in a windmill in the centre, with an extensive view of the valley which the French would have to cross. The right-hand division was under the earls of Warwick and Oxford, with the sixteen-year-old Prince of Wales in titular command, and the other under the Constable. As usual, the knights and men-at-arms were dismounted in single line, their horses being taken by the pages to the wagon-leaguer in the rear.

Forming four projecting salients on both flanks of each of the forward divisions were the archers, along whose lines, before they withdrew to the leaguer, the baggage-wagons unloaded a supply of arrows. To protect themselves from cavalry, they hammered in iron-pointed stakes and dug pot-holes as the Scots had taught their predecessors to do. Such a formation, like that at Halidon Hill, was calculated to force the attackers into two narrowing gulleys at the top of which they would have to contend with the armour while raked by arrows from the flanks.

When the troops were all posted, the King rode along the ranks on a small palfrey, carrying a white wand and wearing a crimson surcoat of golden leopards. To each contingent he spoke a few words. Beside him was Sir Guy de Brian, bearing the dragon banner of Wessex – the standard under which the English had

"Leaves and flowers carved on the capitals; Like Galatea they possess all the qualities of life except movement, though made of stone."

Southwell Minster, c. 1290–1295.

Overleaf:
"Save for its spire and upper tower, added a century later, the only medieval cathedral in England which is all of a piece."

Salisbury Cathedral 1220–1268, and c. 1280–1330.

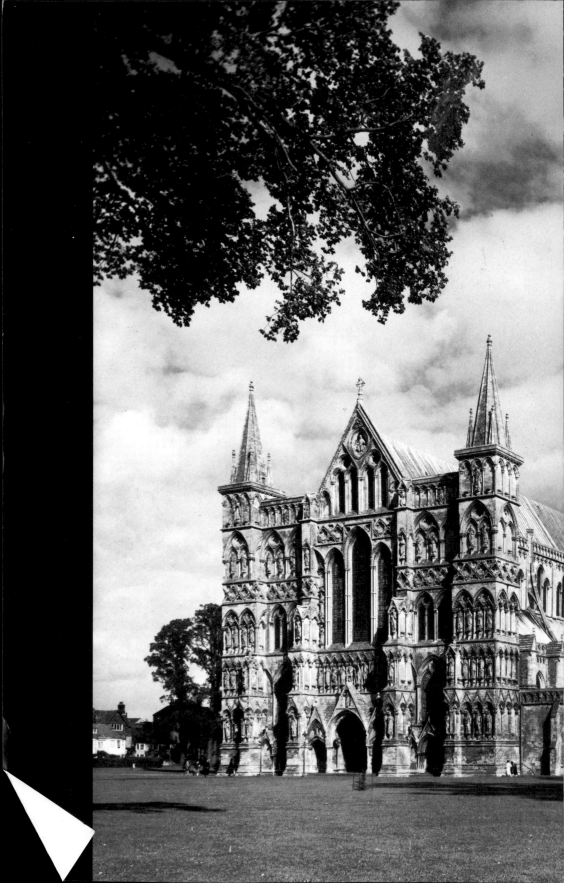

"Cathedrals still towering above the roofs of modern towns."
Lincoln Cathedral, West front. Early 14th century.

fought at Hastings. It was a symbol of the national character Edward had given his army. 'Next to God,' it was said of him, 'he reposed his confidence in the valour of his subjects.' Norman, Angevin, Saxon and Celt, his men all thought of themselves as Englishmen.

After the King's inspection the army dispersed for the midday meal which the cooks had been preparing in the baggage-leaguer, the men-at-arms leaving their helmets to mark their stations and the archers their bows and arrows. It had been arranged that the trumpets should recall them at the first sign of the enemy, who were now believed to be moving up from Abbeville. During the afternoon there was a heavy shower, which brought the archers scurrying back to their lines to guard their bowstrings, each man unstringing his and placing it in a coil under his helmet. Afterwards the sun came out and the men sat down in their lines with their weapons in front of them. There was still no sign of the French, and it was felt that there would be no battle that day.

But a little before four o'clock the trumpets sounded and everyone stood to arms. Coming out of the woods three miles to the south-east along the track still known as *le chemin d'armée* was the French vanguard. For a whole hour the English watched as Philip's immense host moved into view, 'the fresh shining armour, the banners waving in the wind, the companies in good order, riding a soft pace'. According to the lowest estimate that has come down from the fourteenth century, they were forty thousand strong, of whom more than twelve thousand were mounted knights and men-at-arms. They rode in eight successive divisions, so that there seemed no end. The advance-guard was commanded by the blind King John of Bohemia – a romantic figure and world-famous warrior – who was accompanied by the French King's brother, the count of Alençon, and the count of Flanders whom Edward's allies, the burghers of Ghent, had driven from his country.

The King – 'Philip Valois, tyrant of the French', as the English chroniclers called him – followed with the rearguard, together with the German King of the Romans, Charles of Moravia, and the exiled King of Majorca. There were nearly a score of ruling counts, French, German, Luxemburg and Spanish. It was not so much a national army as the embodiment of the international chivalry which for three centuries had dominated the battlefields of the continent, commanded by the greatest monarch in Christendom. Above him waved the oriflamme – the sacred banner flown when no quarter was to be given to France's enemies. For there had been disputes on the previous night about the allocation and ransom of the prisoners, and to prevent quarrelling the King had given orders to slay them all.

In addition to this array of chivalry there marched among the vanguard six or seven thousand Genoese crossbowmen, the best trained troops on the continent and the only professionals in the host. The rest of the army was composed of peasant levies – the 'communes' as they were called – low-spirited serfs considered incapable of standing up to gentlemen, but useful to follow in the wake of their mounted superiors and help crush the foe by sheer weight of numbers. In the French army infantry were despised; it was knights – 'the crested helmets' – who alone counted.

Goliath was pitted against David, but David had a sling. David, too, had discipline, which Goliath lacked. When the French vanguard reached the valley in front of the English position the sun was already starting to sink, and Philip's advisers urged him to halt for the night and deploy for battle in the morning. To this – the only sane course – the King, who had not expected to find the English barring his path, agreed. But his vassals had other views. Seeing the English with their banners on the ridge, the young knights, arrogant and inexperienced, pressed forward, impatiently confident that they were at their mercy. Before even a blow had been struck the French army was out of control and committed to an attack undeployed.

The vanguard, therefore, came straight on, halting only to let the Genoese bowmen open the attack. With trumpets and clarions sounding they started to climb the ridge. The setting sun was in their eyes, and it was hard to focus their target, waiting motionless and ready.

At this point, wrote Froissart, 'when the Genoese began to approach, they made a great leap and cry to abash the Englishmen. But they stood still and stirred not for all that. Then the Genoese again the second time made another leap and a fell cry and stept forward a little, and the English removed not one foot. Thirdly again they leapt and cried and went forward till they came within shot; then they shot fiercely with their crossbows. Then the English archers stept forth one pace and let fly their arrows so wholly together and so thick that it seemed snow.' Firing four or five times faster than the crossbowmen, they shot them out of the field.

As the Genoese broke, the French knights, with a cry of 'Ride down the rascals', charged through their ranks, trampling down the wounded and dying. They rode in a dense, glittering line of solid armour, waving plumes and levelled lances. Everyone expected them to crush the thin, defending line of the Prince of Wales's division before them. But they never reached it. For once again the English archers stepped forward.

As their arrows, aimed at the chargers, struck home, the stately advance dissolved into disorderly heaps and clusters of dead and wounded horses and of dismounted knights weighed down by their armour. Those who went forward on foot, or succeeded in driving their terrified beasts through the hail of arrows, came up against a solid line of English men-at-arms, as steady as the archers who continued shooting down each new batch of attackers as they struggled up the hill through the fading light.

The fight had now become general, with the second French wave assailing the Constable's division. But everywhere the result was the same: the mounted knights struggling to reach and break the line of defenders' armour and the archers continuing to massacre their horses. There was no one to give the attackers orders or co-ordinate the attack. For five hours, though darkness had fallen, the mêlée continued, wave after wave of knights entering the fight only to meet the same fate. At one moment it looked as if the Prince of Wales's slender force would be overwhelmed, and Godfrey de Harcourt hurried across to the nearest unit of the Constable's division to beg its commander to make a flanking attack to relieve the pressure. But when a similar appeal reached the King, he only remarked. 'Let the boy win his spurs', for he knew that the moment to throw in his reserves had not yet come.

When the messenger returned he found the Prince and his commanders leaning quietly on their swords, taking breath as, amid mounds of French corpses, they waited for the next attack.

Soon after midnight, after fifteen or sixteen assaults had failed, the French army began to dissolve. The dead were now piled in walls before the English lines. Among them was the blind King of Bohemia, the reins of his bridle tied to those of the knights with whom he had charged. Two archbishops, the royal count of Alençon, the duke of Lorraine and the counts of Blois and Flanders had all fallen. King Philip himself, his horse shot under him, was led from the field as Edward II had been from Bannockburn. There was no pursuit, for the English King, who had never once lost his grip on the battle, had forbidden his men to break rank.

As the French melted away into the darkness and no more attacks came, the exhausted victors lay down, supperless and waterless, to sleep where they had fought. When, on the misty morrow, they counted the dead, they found the bodies of more than fifteen hundred knights and ten thousand common soldiers. The French army had ceased to exist. Edward himself, with his son, attended the burial of John of Bohemia – a paladin after his own heart who had long predicted that he would die in battle against the bravest knights in the world. His helm-plume of ostrich feathers has ever since graced the arms of the Princes of Wales.

A new phenomenon had appeared in the western world: the military power of England. 'The might of the realm,' wrote the astonished Froissart, 'most standeth upon archers which are not rich men.' The English had shown that on their own ground they could conquer against any odds and almost without cost. Their losses at Crécy were fantastically low; the official figure was forty dead, only three of them men-at-arms.

Edward was now free if he chose, to lay waste the Île-de-France and attack Paris. But he would not be able to reduce the city itself, as he was without catapults and a seige-train. The alternatives were to strike south to join his victorious cousin in Guienne, or resume his interrupted progress towards his Flemish allies. Fifty miles north of Montreuil, where he marched his army after Crécy, lay the port of Calais. Commanding the Dover strait, the haunt of pirates who preyed on the vital trade between London and Flanders, it was the nearest continental harbour to England. If it could be turned into an English settlement the islanders would possess a permanent door into France.

The *annus mirabilis* of 1346 ended with one more victory. Earlier Philip had invoked the Franco-Scottish alliance and called on King David of Scotland to invade England. In the belief that Edward had drained the country of troops, the young Scots King crossed the border. After burning Lanercost abbey he struck eastwards across the moors into the Durham plain. Here, on 17 October, just outside the cathedral city at what became known as Neville's Cross, he encountered an English army under Archbishop de la Zouche of York, the warden of the Marches Lord Percy, and Lord Neville of Raby. Once more the English archers proved irresistible, annihilating every schiltron in turn, as with stubborn courage, the Scots pikesmen in packed ranks faced that hail of driven steel and goose-quill. By nightfall, both King David, wounded in the face by an arrow, and the famous Black Rood of Scotland, were in the victors' hands. Her Constable, the Marshal and two earls were among the dead, and three other earls taken prisoner. Only the Steward escaped.

*   *   *

The next year Edward spent systematically besieging Calais, raising his expeditionary force to more than thirty thousand men and requisitioning more than half the country's ships and fifteen thousand seamen. At the beginning of August 1347, after he had beaten off a last desperate attempt by the French King to relieve it, the city surrendered from starvation. It was then that the famous incident of the Calais burghers occurred, Queen Philippa kneeling before her victorious lord to obtain their pardon as they stood in front of him, bareheaded and barefooted with halters round their necks. Thereafter Edward made Calais what it was to remain for the next two centuries, an English town. He sent those of its inhabitants likely to oppose his rule to the nearest French territory and offered English traders incentives to settle in their stead. He left the town its old franchise, under which magistrates were elected by the leading householders, promised to respect its customs and appointed an English governor. He also transferred the staple there, making it the sole port for the export of wool, tin, lead and cloth to northern Europe. With both sides of the Straits of Dover in his hands he could now claim with some justice to be lord of the narrow seas. On his new gold coin, the noble, issued four years after his victory at Sluys, he appears standing in a ship crowned with sword in hand.

In October 1347, he returned to England. For two dazzling years victory had crowned her every effort: a few thousand of her sons, most of them humble countrymen armed with a weapon which they alone could use with effect, had again and again overcome almost inconceivable odds and laid the chivalry of the first kingdom in Christendom in the dust. Two months after his return from Calais, Edward ordered for himself and the knights of his new Round Table twelve garters of royal blue embroidered with the cross of St George. They wore their insignia for the first time at a tournament at Eltham in January 1348 when nine of the original founders jousted before the King, among them the young Prince of Wales – known from his armour as the Black Prince – and the liberator of Gascony, now earl of Lancaster, who, in three brilliant campaigns against impossible odds, had recovered for the Crown four great provinces, overrun half Poitou, including its capital Poitiers, and carried the English power almost to the gates of Toulouse.

CHAPTER FIFTEEN

War's Nemesis

'There is full many a man that crieth "War,
war", that wot full little what war amounteth.
War at his beginning hath so great an entering
and so large that every wight may enter when him
liketh and lightly find war. But, certes, what end
that shall thereof befall, it is not light to know.'

Chaucer

WHILE THE ENGLISH, after their miraculous victory at Crécy and their spectacular conquests in southern France, were besieging Calais, another army two thousand miles away had been blockading a small Genoese grain port in the Crimea where a band of traders, operating at the end of the seven-thousand-mile caravan route from China, had taken refuge from the Tartar horsemen of the Steppes. Suddenly the besiegers had been struck down by a pestilence which, spreading everywhere through Tartary and known as 'the death', had begun, it was believed, in the putrefaction of unburied multitudes in the wars and earthquakes of China and Central Asia. Before they raised the siege the Tartars are said to have catapulted infected corpses into the town.

What is certain is that the disease was carried into Europe at the end of 1347 or beginning of 1348 by Genoese ships trading with the Black Sea. No one knew its exact cause or even its nature, but it is now known to have been bubonic plague – a flea-borne epidemic of the black rat which had invaded Europe from Asia at the time of the crusades and with which the wooden trading-ships of the day were heavily infested. By the time vessels that had called in the Crimea reached the Bosphorus and Mediterranean the plague was raging among their crews, and every port at which they touched became infected. It struck so suddenly that at first no one had time to escape. The symptoms were a gangrenous inflammation of the lungs, vomiting and spitting blood, vilely infected breath and the appearance, on the second day, of hard black buboes in the arm-pits and groin which were almost always the heralds of death. Few who caught the disease in its first onslaught outlived the third day.

By the end of January 1348 the plague was raging in all the great ports of southern Europe, including Venice, Genoa, Marseilles and Barcelona. In the Mediterranean, ships were found drifting with every member of the crew dead. One after another, despite frantic attempts to isolate themselves, the Italian cities went down before the pestilence. In the spring, having made Venice and Genoa cities of the dead, the plague reached Florence. In the introduction to his *Decameron*, Boccaccio left a first-hand picture of its horrors: the helplessness of the doctors, the stench of the sick, the cautious shutting themselves up in their houses until the infection crept in and the reckless drinking in taverns day and night, the multitude of corpses lying uncovered before every church and the pits into which the dead were packed in layers. The poor perished in the streets or among the crops, the swine rooting in the deserted streets dropped dead as they nosed the bundles of rags stripped from the plague-stricken, and swarms of oxen, sheep and goats – 'and even dogs, those most faithful friends to men' – wandered untended through the fields. The dying were abandoned, the dead were dragged out of the houses and stacked by the roadside, the houses of those who had fled were left open to all, 'the reverend authority of the laws, divine and human, being almost wholly ruined and dissolved'.

All that summer of 1348 the Black Death was drawing nearer to England. In the spring it reached Gascony where it struck down King Edward's youngest daughter, the Princess Jean, who was on her way to Spain to marry the heir of Castile. Soon afterwards it broke out in Paris where vast multitudes died, including the Queens of France and Navarre. By July, creeping north through

Poitou and Brittany and round the coasts, it was in Normandy, where 'it came to such a pass that no one could be found even to carry the corpses to the tomb. People said that the end of the world had come.' All the while clouds and continuous rain poured down on England and, towards the end of the month as men watched the ports, Archbishop de la Zouche of York wrote to his deputy ordering processions and litanies to be held in all parish churches twice a week 'for the stay of pestilence and infection'.

Yet life in England that summer seems to have gone on very much as usual. In days when news travelled only by word of mouth and was carried from village to village along the grass roadways by friars and pedlars, the people of an isolated northern island can have heard little of the fate that had befallen their fellow Christians beyond the Channel. Absorbed in their local affairs, they were more concerned about the weather, the ruin of their crops and the murrain which had broken out among the sheep and cattle. Even the King, who must have been aware of the danger, seemed obsessed with his magnificent building projects for housing the college of his new Order of the Garter. On 6 August, he issued orders for the conversion of St Edward the Confessor's chapel, Windsor, into one 'of befitting splendour' and for the provision of accommodation for the additional canons and twenty-four 'helpless and indigent knights'.

It may have been on that very day that, despite every precaution by the port authorities, the plague crossed the Channel. Some time early that August it broke out in the little Dorset coast town of Melcombe Regis, now Weymouth, 'depriving it almost of inhabitants'. Within a few weeks it reached Bristol, probably by sea, turning it into a mortuary. It treated England as it had treated western Europe, and the English reacted in the same way. At Bristol 'the living were scarce able to bury the dead', and 'the men of Gloucester would not suffer the Bristol men to have access to them'. But no constable's guard could stop the swift-running rats from infecting one another, or their parasites from deserting their putrescent bodies for living men and women. Nor had anyone any idea what caused the mortality: the pallor, the sudden shivering and retching, the dreaded scarlet botches and black boils – 'God's tokens' – the delirium and unbearable agony which came without warning and carried off its victims in a few hours.

During that autumn the plague struck down southern shire after shire. Dorset and its adjoining counties suffered terribly; Poole was so depopulated that it did not recover for more than a century – a hundred years ago a projecting strip of land known as the Baiter was still pointed out as the burial-place of its victims. In some villages, like Bishopstone in Wiltshire, scarcely a soul survived, and when life was renewed after the plague the site was left deserted. The crops rotted in the fields, the church bells were silent, and everywhere corpses were flung, blackened and stinking, into hastily dug pits.

The plague reached London at the beginning of November – 'about the feast of All Hallows'. It took the great financier, Sir Thomas Pulteney – four times mayor and builder of the parish church of Little All Hallows, Thames Street – the Princess Joan of Kent's uncle, Lord Wake of Liddel, four wardens of the Goldsmiths' Company, and the abbot and twenty-six monks of Westminster. The courts of King's Bench and Common Pleas came to a standstill; a Parliament summoned for January was prorogued indefinitely. All though the winter the pestilence raged in the rat-haunted streets and alleys until, having carried off nearly half the population, 'by the intervention of the grace of the Holy Spirit on Whit-Sunday it ceased'. 'The cemeteries,' a chronicler wrote, 'were not big enough and fields had to be set aside for the burying of the dead . . . Men and women bore their own offspring on their shoulders to the church and cast them into the common pit, from which there proceeded so great a stench that hardly anyone dared to cross.' A croft near Smithfield given by the bishop of London for the burial of the dead became known as Pardon Church yard; another just outside the north wall of the city bought by the defender of Aiguillon, Sir Walter Manny, was endowed with a Carthusian cell which was to become the site of the Charterhouse and the great London school which still bears its name.

Owing to the speed with which the plague slew, the worst was over in the south before it struck the midlands and north. By the spring of 1349 it had reached Norfolk. Before the summer ended it had crossed the Humber. In the West Riding the incumbents of nearly half its parishes died; in the East Riding almost as many. The great Cistercian abbey of Meaux in Holderness lost its abbot and all but ten of forty-two monks and seven lay brethren; Fountains was so reduced that one of the twin fireplaces in the calefactorium, where the quarterly bleedings took place, was permanently bricked up. Scotland, protected by a hundred miles of moorland, escaped until the end of the year. At first the Scots ascribed the affliction of their neighbours to English wickedness, swearing 'by the foul death of England' and congratulating themselves on their own immunity. But when they gathered in Selkirk forest to harry the border, 'their joy turned to mourning as the sword of the wrath of God . . . scourged them in fury and suddenness, smiting them not less than the English with abscesses and pustules'. Next year it was the turn of the Welsh mountain valleys, and 'at last, as if sailing thither, the plague reached Ireland, striking down great numbers of the English dwelling there' and wrecking the precarious framework of the manorial system of the Pale. 'It scarcely touched the pure Irish who dwelt in the mountains and upland areas until 1357, when it unexpectedly destroyed them far and wide in terrible fashion.'

Though the Black Death visited every part of England its incidence was uneven. Some villages like Tilgarsley in Oxfordshire and Middle Carlton and Ambion in Leicestershire – site of the future battle of Bosworth Field – were so depopulated that they were never re-occupied. At St Albans the abbot, prior, sub-prior and forty-six monks died; at Christ Church, Canterbury, only four. Those who suffered most were the poor in their over-crowded hovels, and the parish and regular clergy. The nobility, living in comparatively clean and spacious conditions, escaped lightly. Isolating themselves in some retired country place and keeping a strict guard against strangers, they let the pestilence pass them by. A few caught the infection; three Archbishops of Canterbury died in that terrible year, one of them, John Stratford, at the end of August 1348, possibly from natural causes, but the other two of plague. The rest of the episcopal bench, immured in their country manor-houses, escaped, though Gynwell of Lincoln, true to his diocese's great tradition, toured his eight counties throughout the epidemic as usual. Of the parish clergy at least forty per cent died, most of them probably at their posts. The episcopal registers – better preserved and more complete in England than in any other country – suggest that, including monks and friars, nearly half the personnel of the Church was taken.

Of the general public it is impossible to estimate with any certainty the proportion who died; the verdict of modern scholarship is that the first outbreak probably carried off about one in three of the population. What is certain is that, once established in the soil, the plague remained endemic. Dormant for perhaps a dozen years it would suddenly flare up, first in one city, then in another, at least once in a generation. For three hundred years – a period of time as great as that which divides us from the last outbreak in Charles II's reign – the red cross on the stricken door, the cart piled with corpses on its way to the plague-pit, the cry of 'Bring out your dead!' formed a recurrent part of the background of English life. During the three centuries since the Norman Conquest the population of England had probably doubled. The generation born in the middle of Edward III's reign saw it halved.

For anyone who has not experienced it, it is hard to realize the impact of a cataclysm carrying off one in every three, perhaps one in every two, of a civilized community. Its immediate effect, and of the shock and terror that accompanied it, was chaos. In the dirt and squalor of medieval life men were used to epidemic disease, but this was no ordinary epidemic. While it continued, all activity was suspended. The harvest could not be gathered, taxes or rents collected, markets held or justice done. Everywhere there were vacant holdings and uncultivated farms, and for a time it was almost impossible to sell anything.

For most people, it was its impact on labour which constituted the chief post-plague problem. 'So great was the deficiency of workmen of all kinds,' wrote one, 'that more than a third of the land remained uncultivated.' At an inquest on the estate of a Wiltshire landowner who died in June 1349, a jury found three hundred acres of pasture valueless because all the tenants were dead. At another manor near Salisbury only three tenants remained, all the rest having been carried off by the pestilence.

Yet, though even after six years, the Vice-Sheriff of Cumberland complained that the greater part of the manor lands of the royal castle of Carlisle were still lying waste and uncultivated 'by reason of the mortal pestilence lately raging in these parts', the remarkable thing is how quickly the country recovered from its ordeal. Despite a mortality rate higher than that expected today from nuclear war, England showed an astonishing resilience. In the work of the greatest English poet of the age there is only one reference, and that an oblique one, to the Black Death which three times swept across the England of his youth and early manhood. But men were far more used than now to the contemplation of death, and Chaucer grew up as a page in the royal court which largely escaped the fate overwhelming the rest of the community. Even as early as St George's Day 1349, while the plague was still raging in London, the first service of the Order of the Garter was held at Windsor, every knight in plumes and garter-blue robes taking his place in his stall; the great two-handed sword which the King carried on that day still hangs behind the altar of St George's Chapel.

*   *   *

Though both France and England had been denuded of a third of their people, the war had not ceased. While the Black Death was alive, the truce made in 1347 had been extended by mutual consent to the summer of 1350. But that spring, word reached King Edward at Windsor of a French plot to surprise and recapture Calais. A Lombard knight deputising for the governor, who had died of the plague, was bribed to admit a French raiding party into the castle by night. But the plot was betrayed, and it was the raiders who were surprised. For, having secretly crossed the Channel in disguise with a band of picked companions, Edward and the Prince of Wales fell on the intruders as they were being admitted to the castle and took them all captive. Afterwards the royal victor feasted his prisoners and, signalling out a knight who had long resisted him in single combat, crowned him with a chaplet of pearls and set him at liberty.

In August of the same year the King and the Black Prince took part in a more important action, this time at sea. A Castilian fleet, bringing merino wool to Flanders, had taken advantage of the depopulation of the Cinque Ports to plunder English merchantmen in the Channel. To intercept it on its return voyage, a squadron of fifty small vessels and pinnaces was assembled at Sandwich and manned by the flower of England's chivalry. Among them were nearly all the original Knights of the Garter; even the King's ten-year-old son, John of Gaunt, was there. Sailing from Sandwich they sighted the Spanish fleet off Dungeness on the afternoon of 29 August and at once went in to attack. Like Sluys, the battle was a triumph for the English archers who, outshooting the Spaniards' crossbowmen and catapultmen, made their decks a shambles before the knights and men-at-arms swarmed up their sides to complete the slaughter. Though both the King's and the Prince's ships were sunk, the day ended in the capture of seventeen galleons and the flight of the remainder, while crowds cheered the victors from the Winchelsea cliffs. That night the Queen, who had spent the day praying in Battle abbey, was joined by Edward and his sons at Pevensey castle, 'where the lords and ladies passed the night in great revel, speaking of war and love'.

The victory helped to restore England's sea communications with her depleted garrisons in Gascony. For the plague had left the country dangerously short of military man-power. There were not enough seamen to man her ships, or archers and men-at-arms to guard her gains in Guienne and Brittany. A small country suffers more from attrition than a large, and the disproportion between the populations of France and England now mattered far more. With hers reduced to between two and three millions, England was forced to fill her foreign garrisons with Gascons, Bretons, Flemings, Irish and Germans.

In August 1350, a week before Edward's naval victory off Winchelsea, having taken to himself a bride of eighteen Philip of Valois died at the age of fifty-eight. He was succeeded by his son, John II – *le Bon* or 'good fellow'. A devotee, unlike his father, of chivalry and martial glory, he refused to renew the truce. The war, therefore, continued in a rather desultory fashion while both countries recovered from the Black Death. In the south the French gradually built up a large army which, at the beginning of 1353, invaded Saintonge. Henry of Lancaster, crusading in the Baltic with the Teutonic knights, was no longer available to defend his sovereign's southern dominion. But the governor of Calais, Sir John Beauchamp – Lord Warwick's brother – was sent to save the threatened province. Reaching the beleaguered capital, Saintes, just in time, he won with his archers on 7 April another astonishing victory against odds. Two marshals of France were among the captives, the victors making a fortune in ransoms. Afterwards, hurrying back to his post at Calais, Beauchamp defeated the French at Ardres.

In Brittany, with Charles of Blois a prisoner and the de Montfort claimant a minor, the attempt of the English to rule the country in their protégé's name was growing increasingly unpopular. For the Bretons had not only to pay for their garrisons but were plundered by them into the bargain. English prestige had suffered a serious blow in 1351 in a chivalric encounter called 'the battle of the Thirty', when thirty Franco-Breton knights defeated thirty Anglo-Breton, Gascon and German ones, killing nine of them. But in 1352, when a French army under Marshal de Nesle invaded the duchy and, after regaining Rennes, advanced towards Brest, it was intercepted on 14 August at Mauron by Sir William Bentley. Bentley, who had succeeded Sir Thomas Dagworth as Keeper of Brittany after the latter's death in an ambush, had been vainly trying to obtain reinforcements from England. But, though he had only a minute force, he drew it up in one of those strong defensive positions on which the English relied, with the men-at-arms dismounted in line and the archers in wedges on the flanks. There were not enough men even to form a reserve. The French attacked at four o'clock on a hot summer's afternoon; those waiting on the ridge long afterwards remembered the droning of the bees in the heather. Though the initial assault forced back the archers on the English right, their comrades on the left wrought the usual execution on the French horses, subsequently attacking their riders with their swords as they struggled to rise. Meanwhile the men-at-arms, falling back up the hill to a belt of trees, put up so staunch a fight that the enemy was halted there too. When Bentley, dangerously wounded, was carried from the field crying, 'Fight on! fight on!'

his lieutenant, Sir Robert Knollys, took command and completed the enemy's rout. Marshal de Nesle was among the dead and more than six hundred knights and nobles were killed or taken prisoner, among them forty-five knights of the Order of the Star – the new Order of chivalry which King John had founded in rivalry of the Order of the Garter.

Mauron left the English masters of Brittany. It brought the little handful who fought there immense wealth. When, two centuries later, Shakespeare wrote of another Plantagenet victory against odds, 'the fewer men the greater share of honour', he might have substituted the word 'ransom' for honour. For the English army in France was raised on the same principle as that of a joint-stock company. The incentive to do or die was the knowledge that the survivors would share the fruits of victory – the booty of every city stormed and, for any man who took a prisoner, two-thirds of the ransom money, the rest being reserved for his commander, who in turn paid a third of his gains to the Crown. That, the use of the longbow and an iron discipline were the secret of the English success. How stern was that discipline was seen after the victory at Mauron when Knollys had thirty archers executed for retreating.

Probably at no time after the Black Death had the English more than ten thousand men in France. Their garrisons were only kept up to strength by recruiting from every western nation. But from earl to archer they were adventurers, with the plunder of the richest country in Europe as the prize for which they staked their lives. Chivalric honour in the higher ranks, loyalty to captain and comrade, even a kind of dawning and arrogant patriotism among the humbler English-speaking men-at-arms and archers, were elements in their courage. But the strongest of all was the gambling spirit and passion for gain which made them ready for any risk.

*　　　　　*　　　　　*

Though the war brought fortunes to England's fighting men, it was proving a growing strain on the taxpayer. When, having negotiated a year's truce with the war-weary French, the King in 1354 through his Lord Chamberlain asked the assembled Lords and Commons in Parliament whether they desired a permanent peace, they answered with one voice, 'Oeil! oeil!' – forerunner of the 'Aye, aye' with which the House of Commons still signifies its assent. Struggling with the dislocation of her economy by the plague, the country was having to contend not only against France – but also Scotland, with whom, on and off, she had been at war for half a century. That poor, insecure, war-ridden land, her King a captive and her treacherous nobles at constant loggerheads, was still determined not to acknowledge England's overlordship and to fight to the last man to resist it. When, two years before, having secured a provisional recognition of homage from his captive, King David, Edward sent him home on parole, a Scottish parliament unanimously rejected such terms and allowed him to return to captivity.

Edward was no more successful in persuading the French King to abandon claim to his homage than in inducing the Scots to acknowledge his right to theirs. For when in the winter of 1354, through the mediation of a new Pope, he opened peace negotiations with France, his plenipotentiaries on arriving at Avignon found the French, for all their defeats, unwilling to surrender their sovereign's overall right of suzerainty over even the smallest particle of conquered soil. Edward proposed that, in return for renouncing his claim to the French throne, King John should release him from the obligations of homage for Guienne, Ponthieu and the towns he had taken in Brittany and Normandy. He also secretly instructed his ambassadors that he would be prepared to abandon his Norman claims in return for the over-lordship of Flanders. His terms were contemptuously rejected. Despite twenty years of war neither monarch was prepared to abandon his fundamental aim – the English King to full sovereignty over his dominions beyond the Channel, the French to lordship over all France.

The war, therefore, continued. Once more, as ten years before, Edward planned a triple attack, from Gascony, from Calais and, under his personal command, from Normandy, whose largest land-owner, Charles of Navarre, had offered to throw in his lot with him. The disgruntled son-in-law of the French King and a descendant, like Edward himself, of the old Capet line, Charles proposed that they should march on Paris together with the idea of partitioning the Valois inheritance between them. In September 1355, as a preliminary to the combined operations planned for the following summer, the Prince of Wales accordingly sailed for Bordeaux with a force of 3500 men, including a strong contingent of Cheshire and Derbyshire archers. He was received with immense enthusiasm just as Lancaster had been ten years before. His mission was to win back the territories and towns which the count d'Armagnac had recovered in south-western Guienne.

The Black Prince had been brought up in the same school of war as Lancaster and Dagworth. He was now twenty-five and at the height of his powers. His recipe for dealing with superior force was to strike with the utmost audacity and speed. By carrying the war into the rich province of Languedoc and wasting it from end to end, he meant to force d'Armagnac to dance to his tune. Though by the conventions of chivalric war the season for campaigning was over, the Prince set out from Bordeaux on 5 October on a *grande chevauchée* with a mounted Anglo-Gascon force of 5000 men. For a hundred miles he marched south, crossing into French territory on the 11th. Then he turned east towards Toulouse, traversing the country through which Wellington's armies were to march three and a half centuries later. It was lovely weather and the cavalcade presented a brilliant spectacle, each of its captains, as Froissart described Sir John Chandos, riding 'with his banner before him and his company about him, with his coat of arms on him, great and large, beaten with his arms'. Strict discipline was observed, and while buildings, stores and crops were burnt as part of the plan of campaign, churches, monasteries and civilian lives were spared. Yet scarcely a day passed in that luxuriant countryside without some wealthy merchant or local landowner being brought in by the English patrols. Everyone down to the humblest archer was in high spirits, for there was ransom and plunder for all.

The army was equipped with portable pontoons for bridging the broad rivers of southern France, but not with siege-engines for reducing fortified cities. Toulouse was therefore by-passed, while d'Armagnac, not daring to give battle, watched from its walls the smoke of burning villages. Five more days of marching brought the English to Carcassonne, where they fired the lower town. On 8 November they reached Narbonne, only ten miles from the Mediterranean. All southern France was in panic; the Pope at Avignon a hundred miles away barricaded himself in his palace and sent an embassy to the Prince to plead for peace.

By this time two French armies were in the field. The count of Bourbon was advancing south from Limoges to bar the passage of the Garonne while, under the pressure of an angry public opinion, d'Armagnac had at last ventured out from Toulouse. On 10 November therefore, the Prince began his homeward march, intending to fight d'Armagnac before Bourbon's army could join him. But though both were in superior numbers, neither French commander dared give battle, for the memory of Crécy still haunted them. Even when they had joined forces they left the raiders alone.

On 2 December the Prince returned to La Réole, laden with booty, after covering nearly seven hundred miles in nine weeks. Meanwhile his father had been conducting a similar *chevauchée* in northern France. Having waited all the summer for word from Charles of Navarre, who had now composed his quarrel with the French King, he crossed to Calais at the end of October. But nothing would induce King John to leave the shelter of Amiens, and Edward's march through Artois in November rain and mud proved a very different matter from his son's campaign in Languedoc. As winter fell on the Flemish plain he was forced by lack of forage to return to Calais.

Here he was greeted by news that the Scottish Regent, William Douglas, had broken the truce and, with the help of a small French expeditionary force, had laid siege to Berwick castle, capturing the town. As both the warden of the March and the bishop of Durham had withdrawn their troops from the border in order to join him at Calais, Edward was forced to return to England and hurry north. Having secured supplies from Parliament and obtained from his captive, King David, a recognition of his suzerainty, he prepared to teach the Scottish nobles a lesson. In January 1356, in the depth of the winter, he crossed the border to take 'seisin,' as he put it, 'of his kingdom'.

With the twin banners of both nations borne before him, Edward reduced to ashes every village and farm along the road to Edinburgh, driving out the inhabitants onto the wintry moors. Yet the 'burnt Candlemas', as it was long called in Scotland, produced nothing except a greater hatred of England. Like Bruce, the Regent Douglas cleared the country of everything edible and vanished into the hills and forests. Campaigning in such a land was an unrewarding business after the rich plains of France, and no one's heart was in it. Storms held up the supply-ships, and by March there was nothing left but to withdraw or starve. The Scots, still evading combat, hung on the flanks of the retreating army and murdered the sick and stragglers, while the English set fire to the beautiful friars' church at Haddington – the 'lantern of Lothian'. Everyone was the loser.

Having safeguarded his northern border, Edward resumed his plans for conquering France. At that moment, back from the crusade in Lithuania where he had taken part in the Battle of Tramassene,[1] Henry of Lancaster was about to sail from Southampton for Brittany whose young duke, now sixteen, was eager to take possession of the duchy. With 500 men-at-arms and 800 mounted archers whom he was taking to reinforce the English garrisons, Lancaster was now deflected to Normandy with orders to relieve three rebel cities – Evreux, Pont Audemer and Breteuil – which the French royal forces were besieging.

Landing at La Hogue on 18 June 1356, the old warrior was joined by a small Norman force and by Robert Knollys of Mauron fame with 300 English men-at-arms and 500 archers. Lancaster, who had been rewarded for his services with a dukedom, was now fifty, but he acted as boldly as ever. With 2500 mounted men he set out on 22 June to relieve the insurgent cities, all of them more than a hundred and thirty miles away and threatened by an army

---

[1] Like the knight commemorated in *The Canterbury Tales*:
       'In fifteen mortal battles had he been
       And foughten for our faith at Tramassene.'
Chaucer, whose first patron was the duke's daughter, wrote *The Canterbury Tales* about the time that his own sister-in-law married Lancaster's widowed son-in-law, John of Gaunt, and may have had Lancaster in his mind when he described his 'very parfit gentil knight'.

which King John has assembled at Dreux to overawe them. Covering sixteen miles on the first day and thirty on the second, he reached Lisieux on 28 June. Next day, after a twenty-three-mile march, he relieved Pont Audemer, surprising and capturing the besiegers' siege-train. Having revictualled the town and strengthened the garrison with some English men-at-arms and archers, he set out again on 2 July and, by the morning of the 4th, after covering a further fifty miles and storming the castle of Conches, had relieved Breteuil.

As Evreux had by now fallen, the duke completed his mission by striking on the same day at Verneuil, the second city of Normandy. Using the siege equipment taken at Pont Audemer, he carried the walls that night, all but one tower which held out till the 6th. Then, on 7 July, with much booty and many prisoners, he set out for home. For with John's huge army only a dozen miles away he was in grave danger. With 2000 fighting men heavily encumbered with booty and prisoners, even Lancaster could not hope to defeat an army of 20,000. That night, in silence, the wily old duke vanished, leaving only a minute rearguard to deceive the French as they deployed next morning for battle. By nightfall he was thirty-five miles away at Argentan. On the 9th he covered a further fifty-two miles and by the 10th was across the Vire and safely back in the Cotentin, having marched three hundred and thirty miles in fifteen days. At his base camp he found that Robert Knollys, with a handful of men-at-arms, had routed a force of local militia men who had tried to ambush him, slaying them all except three rich landowners whom he had kept for ransom.

Leaving the French King to resume the siege of the revictualled insurgent Norman cities, Lancaster now marched south into Maine; while, three hundred miles away at Bergerac, the Prince of Wales set off north towards him. Between them the two English commanders hoped to pinch off a quarter of the French kingdom and, joining hands on the Loire, regain the Angevin inheritance which their ancestor, King John, had lost a century and a half before.

Since his *grande chevauchée* the Black Prince had taken some fifty towns and castles on the northern and eastern borders of

Guienne regained by the French during the years when the English garrisons had been depleted by the Black Death. By the middle of the summer of 1356, having established the English rule as far north as Périgueux, he was ready to strike. On 4 August, while Lancaster was laying siege to Domfront preparatory to marching on Angers, he crossed the Dordogne with 6000 men. Advancing at the rate of about ten miles a day, he passed the old Aquitaine border into France at the end of the month and began to ravage the towns and villages of Touraine.

After covering three hundred and twenty miles in just over a month, the Prince reached the Loire at Amboise in the first week of September, hoping to make contact with Lancaster. Finding all the bridges held or down, he turned downstream towards Tours, before which he encamped for several days while his foraging parties reduced the neighbouring castles. The weather had turned wet and the river was in flood. Meanwhile the French King, making a hasty composition with his Norman rebels, hurried south to oppose the intruders. From Chartres he started during the second week of September to send advance parties across the Loire.

On 10 September, when John was about to march on Blois, the Black Prince gave orders to retreat. His supplies were running short and there was no sign of Lancaster. Without a bridgehead a crossing of the river was out of the question, and his little force was far from home and laden with plunder. During the next four days both armies raced south on parallel courses, the French gathering reinforcements and trying to cut off the English from their base. Yet even now the Prince had not abandoned hope of a junction with Lancaster. On 15 September, disregarding the risk, he halted for two days at Chatellerault on the Vienne, waiting for tidings from the north, while the French King continued to march ahead of him towards Poitiers which he reached on the 17th.

That evening there was a skirmish between the Prince's scouts and King John's rearguard on the Chauvigny-Poitiers road, the English capturing two French counts and the steward of the household. But they were short not only of food but water, and their two days' wait for Lancaster – who, though he had now taken Domfront, was held up before Rennes – had placed them in deadly peril.

They put, however, a bold front on it and on the 18th – a Sunday – took up a defensive position on a ridge near Nouaillé, just above the little hamlet of Maupertius, eight miles from Poitiers.

To the French it seemed certain that the English had tempted fate once too often. All that day two cardinals, sent by the Pope to negotiate a truce, passed backwards and forwards between the armies with surrender terms. The English position was so desperate that the Prince of Wales offered to give up his spoil and prisoners and even, according to one account, not to serve in France for seven years. But the French, who by now outnumbered his little force by something like five to one and were daily growing stronger, refused to let him off so lightly. Nothing but his unconditional surrender and that of a hundred of his best knights would content them.

That night the English commanders held a council of war. Sooner than accept such terms they decided to await the French in the defensive position they had chosen and give battle, and then, if the enemy failed to attack, to slip away by night and make a run for it. The Black Prince had taken the precaution of sending his baggage and plunder across the Nouaillé bridge over the Miosson, and a day's delay would give them a sporting chance to get away. When, therefore, at dawn on 19 September the cardinals arrived in the English camp with the French King's final uncompromising terms, they were told that the sword must decide.

The truce ended at 7.30 a.m. on Monday morning, 19 September 1357. The English held a low ridge facing north-west, crossed by two roads, both from Poitiers, in an undulating, well-wooded countryside of small vine-clad hills. Before them lay a valley with a marsh protecting their left. Along the ridge ran a thick hedge behind which the Prince drew up his dismounted knights and men-at-arms, with Salisbury's division on the right and Warwick's on the left. The archers were posted as at Crécy among vineyards on the flank of each division and protected from cavalry by stakes. A small reserve of mounted knights remained out of sight behind the ridge. On the extreme right, to avoid being enveloped, the Prince had constructed a strong-point of wagons and trenches.

As the horses had to be watered in the valley, several hours elapsed before the whole army was in position – a circumstance which caused French observers to suppose that the English had already started to retreat. When everyone was assembled, the Black Prince rode along the lines, addressing his troops. His words have been handed down by the chroniclers. To the knights and men-at-arms, he said, 'Though we be but a small company, let us not be abashed. If it fortune that the day be ours, we shall be the most honoured of all the world.' To the archers he declared,

> 'You have made it plain that you are worthy sons and kinsmen of those for whom, under the leadership of my father and ancestors, the Kings of England, no labour was too great, no place invincible, no mountain inaccessible, no tower impregnable, no host too formidable . . . If victory shall see us alive we shall always continue in firm friendship together, being of one heart and mind. If envious fortune should decree, which God forbid, that in this present labour we must follow the final path of all flesh, your names will not be sullied with infamy, and I and my comrades will drink the same cup with you.'

It was not till nearly midday that the French vanguard appeared. It came on in two divisions, led by the Constable and two Marshals of France, each following one of the roads from Poitiers. The left-hand column had some initial success, forcing its way through a gap in the hedge, until it was driven back by a counter-attack by the earl of Salisbury. Before it reached the summit the right-hand column was shot to pieces by the archers who, moving down with superb battle-discipline into the swampy ground on the attackers' flank, directed such fierce volleys at the horses' hind-quarters that almost every rider was thrown to the ground and the Marshal in command captured. On both flanks the survivors fell back in confusion. So perfect was the English discipline that not a man moved in pursuit.

The larger part of the French host was now approaching, marching in three successive columns commanded by the Dauphin, the young Duke of Orléans and the King himself. Each division as it appeared seemed as large as the entire English army. At the suggestion of a veteran of the Scottish wars, William Douglas, who was serving in the French host, the knights and men-at-arms had left their horses at Poitiers. But the long march and the weight of their armour had caused them to straggle and, by the time they neared the battlefield, there was a wide gap between the columns.

The Dauphin's division attacked first. Despite the fire of the archers, who were by now running short of arrows, it reached the hedge. But the French knights, who on Douglas's advice had cut down their twenty-foot lances to six foot, were unaccustomed to fighting without their horses and soon began to tire. In the end they, too, fell back in confusion.

At this point, just as the English were beginning to think the battle was over, the last and largest of the French columns, led by King John, appeared on the ridge on the other side of the valley. The effect on the tired defenders of this great host, glittering with steel and banners, was shattering. Almost everyone except their commander gave himself up for lost. The waverers started to leave the field, leading off the wounded, and the rest prepared to sell their lives dearly.

But as the French moved up the hill, the Black Prince showed himself the great commander he was. Instead of waiting to be over-whelmed he decided to attack along the whole front. Ordering the battle-horses to be brought from the rear, he made his exhausted knights and men-at-arms mount and, with a cry of 'Banner, advance in the name of God and St George!' launched them in open line against the foe, himself leading. Simultaneously he sent a small detachment of cavalry which he had kept in reserve round the enemy's left flank under the Gascon, Captal de Buch, one of the founder Knights of the Garter.

The archers, throwing aside their bows, had now joined in the mêlée, striking at the French with their short swords. Suddenly, at the crisis of the fight, Captal's armour charged into the French rear. The result was devastating. Beset on both sides and fight-ing on uneven ground against mounted men, the French broke and fled, pursued by the English knights, hacking and slaughter-ing all the way to the walls of Poitiers. 'Fortune turned her giddy wheel, and the Prince of Wales penetrated the ranks of the enemy and, like a lion with noble wrath, spared the lowly and put down the mighty and took the King of France prisoner. With him were one the latter's sons, an archbishop, thirteen counts, five viscounts, twenty-one barons and nearly two thousand knights. So much potential ransom had never been taken at one time before. Another two thousand five hundred knights and men-at-arms were found dead on the field before the English lines, including two dukes. The oriflamme itself – the most sacred emblem of France – was barely saved.

That night the victor waited at supper on the French King in his tent, serving him on bended knee and saying that 'he was not sufficient to sit at table with so great a prince'. With exquisite courtesy he consoled him with praise of his gallantry. Once during the feast the Prince was called out by those collecting the dead and wounded to say that they had brought in Sir James Audley, one of the heroes of the day, who had been found wounded on the field. The chivalrous prince conferred on him an annuity of five hundred marks and when he learnt that Audley, a Knight of the Garter, had made it over to the four Cheshire squires who had fought so bravely by his side – Dutton of Dutton, Delves of Doddington, Fulleshurst of Barthomley and Hawkstone of Wrinehill – he doubled his award.

*   *   *

When news of Poitiers and the French King's capture reached England anxiety turned to rejoicing. The Black Prince's victory had transcended even that of Crécy. And England was raised to a new pinnacle of glory. Foreigners noted 'the proud mien of Englishmen everywhere'. Having found what seemed an infallible way of winning against almost any odds, they saw before them an endless vista of ransoms, loot and profit. The land of France was their oyster, and the longbow had opened it.

For the wealth won was prodigious. The price put on the King of France was 300,000 crowns. 'I am so great a lord,' the Prince told his officers after Poitiers, 'as to make you all rich.' Even the humblest returned with the sale of battle-horses, swords, jewels, robes and furs. There was hardly a woman in England, it was said, without some ornament, goblet or piece of fine linen brought home by the conquerors. Those fortunate enough to capture some great magnate became themselves lords. Sir Thomas Dagworth was offered £4,900 – an enormous fortune in the money of the time – for the ransom of Charles of Blois. The north country squire who had taken King David prisoner at Neville's Cross received an annuity of £500 – equivalent to an income perhaps of £100,000 today – with the rank of a banneret.

The pageantry which accompanied the bringing home of the French King in the summer of 1357 outshone even that of the year following the capture of Calais, when the Order of the Garter had been founded. Attending him on a small black palfrey, the Prince paraded his prisoner through the London streets on a white charger while bells clanged, fountains spouted wine and thousands of liveried guildsmen marched behind mounted wardens and aldermen through streets hung with tapestry. When the procession reached Westminster Hall, King Edward rose from his throne to embrace his fellow sovereign. Lodged in the duke of Lancaster's new palace of the Savoy, rebuilt from the spoils of Guienne, the fallen monarch took part, with the captive King of Scots, in a succession of feasts and tournaments – the most splendid, it was said, held in England since the legendary days of Arthur. The poor man was under no illusion as to their purport.

For though the Scots were able to ransom their King by selling on his behalf their entire wool export, France was in no condition to meet England's demands. Not only were large parts of Normandy and the north in rebellion against the government of the eighteen-year-old Dauphin, but hordes of professional soldiers, ignoring the two years' truce after Poitiers, refused to return home and, taking service with anyone who would hire them, continued to live at large on the country. One such mercenary band or 'Free Company', led by the Cheshire knight, Robert Knollys, descended on the rich countryside south of Paris and made itself master of forty castles. The charred gables that marked its progress were known as 'Knollys's mitres'. Another band under a Welshman, John Griffith, ravaged the Loire valley, while a Gascon, nicknamed 'the Archdeacon', plundered Provence, making even the Pope pay blackmail.

With all this misery, and her King and so many nobles in

captivity, France dissolved into civil war and anarchy. While the Dauphin and his government were struggling against a bourgeois revolution in Paris, the starving peasantry of the Île-de-France and Picardy rose and avenged themselves on their feudal rulers with massacre, torture and rape. Under the circumstances, all attempts to ransom the King and conclude a peace with England broke down. The only terms Edward would consider were the surrender of all French rights over the whole of the lands he had conquered. And though, in return for the abandonment of his claim to the French throne, King John was now ready to agree to even this, Edward's subjects in Parliament, intoxicated by his victories, insisted on demanding the cession of Poitou, Anjou, Maine, Touraine and Normandy. This was more than any French government would concede, however desperate its plight.

Edward prepared, therefore, to give his enemies a further taste of what he could do. 'He said plainly that his intention was to pass over into the realm of France and not to return again until he had made an end of his war or else a sufficient peace to his great honour and profit.' To bring matters to an issue he proposed to march on Rheims and have himself crowned in its cathedral as King of France. Once more he collected a great army. Not only Englishmen, but Flemings, Hainaulters, Brabançons, Germans and even Frenchmen flocked to his standards to share in the spoils of victory. Eleven hundred ships were assembled at Sandwich and unprecedented quantities of food and stores. There were more than six thousand wagons and carts, mobile workshops for armourers and smiths, handmills and field-ovens, even portable leather coracles from the Severn for supplying the army with fish during Lent from the French rivers, and thirty falconers and sixty couple of greyhounds for the King's sport. For contrary to every rule of medieval war, Edward meant to invade in the autumn and cam‐paign through the winter.

At the beginning of October 1359, the advance guard under Lancaster landed at Calais. The King followed at the end of the month. Never before, it was said, 'departed out of England such an army nor so well ordered'. Nearly all the great figures of English chivalry were present – the King's sons, Edward of Woodstock,

John of Gaunt, Lionel of Clarence and Edmund of Langley; the earls of Warwick, Suffolk, Hereford, Northampton, Stafford, Salisbury, March and Oxford; the lords Despenser, Percy, Neville, Mowbray, Grey, Fitzwalter, Hastings, Burghersh, Cobham and the Garter Knights, John Chandos and James Audley. Early in November they set forth, marching out of Calais 'with all their company and carriages in the best order that ever any army issued out of any town; it was a joy', wrote Froissart, 'to behold them.'

It rained all the way. They rode through Artois and past the city of Arras and over the chalky Somme uplands – one day to be the battlefield of another and greater English army. 'The country,' wrote Froissart, 'had been long poor and sore wasted and it was a drear season in the realm of France . . . Day and night it rained without cease so that wine that year was little worth.' Nor, though strict march-discipline was enforced and the army was kept in constant readiness for action, did any enemy appear. The Dauphin had learnt from his father's folly, and his orders were that no one was to challenge the English in open field. When, after four weeks' marching, the latter arrived, wet and dispirited, at the gates of Rheims, they found them barred. Nor, despite repeated summonses, would the archbishop and citizens open.

The English could still destroy any army France could put into the field. But they could not reduce a strongly fortified city except by surprise or starvation, and Rheims was prepared for a long siege. For nearly two months in bitter weather they occupied the surrounding heights while patrolling parties scoured the country-side as far as the walls of Paris, trying to provoke a relieving force to battle. But none came.

In the middle of January, unable to maintain his troops on the frozen Champagne plain any longer, Edward abandoned all idea of being crowned in Rheims and marched south into Burgundy, hoping to find early grazing for his horses. But the winter of 1360 proved the longest of the century. After capturing the wine-town of Tonnerre he remained in the Burgundian uplands for most of Lent, hawking and keeping the fast while he waited in vain for the grass to grow. Finally, having extracted an indemnity of 200,000 florins and a three years' truce from the young duke of Burgundy, he struck north again for Paris, still hoping for the weather to turn and for a chance to force the issue. On the way he learnt that a Norman raiding party had sacked and burnt the royal port of Winchelsea, raping some unfortunate ladies who had taken shelter in St Thomas's church and killing several hundred townsmen before being driven off by the local milita. In his fury, while he halted at Corbeil for Holy Week, the indignant King set fire to every village in sight of the French capital.

But though after Easter he paraded his army in battle array under its walls, the garrison never stirred. The Dauphin was wiser than his years. After waiting for four days, while the heralds issued challenge after challenge, Edward was again forced to retreat. For, with April as cold as March, there was still nothing for his horses to eat and, thanks to the Free Companies, very little for his men. His only resort was to seek the milder country to the south-west and re-provision the army in the Loire valley or Brittany until he was able to resume the siege of Paris in the autumn. Nor, even now, had winter done with him. For on the first day of the retreat, 13 April, long remembered as Black Monday – 'a foul dark day of mist and of hail, so bitter cold that sitting on horseback many died' – an icy storm swept over the army, causing hundreds of vehicles to be abandoned. A fortnight later, when it was moving down to the Loire, a thunderstorm, with hailstones as big as pigeons' eggs, struck it as it traversed the stony heaths beyond Chartres. Helpless in their armour, more knights were said to have been killed that day by lightning than fell in the English ranks at Crécy and Poitiers. It was this storm, according to one chronicler, which caused the English King to 'turn toward the church of our Lady at Chartres and devoutly vow to the Virgin that he would accept terms of peace'.

Even in retreat Edward continued to try to tempt the French to battle. 'Certain knights in the following of the Duke of Lancaster,' wrote Gray of Heton, 'disguising themselves as brigands or pillaging soldiers without lances, rode in pretended disarray in order to give the enemy spirit and courage to tackle them. Some . . . overdid the counterfeit to such an extent . . . that they came to grief and were taken.' It was in such a foray earlier in the year that a young squire named Geoffrey Chaucer, in the service of Prince Lionel of Clarence, had been captured, subsequently having to be ransomed for £16, together with other officers of the Household.

But if Edward had failed to be crowned at Rheims or to tempt the Dauphin to another Crécy, the French on their side could no longer endure the war. Almost anything seemed better than its indefinite continuance, for, so long as the English remained, the country could not rid itself of the Free Companies and the misery and anarchy they caused. Even before Edward had landed in France, Knollys had offered him the services of his Great Company and had been taken back into favour, and all over the land he and his like were continuing their enormities.

At the end of April, therefore, plenipotentiaries arrived at the Black Prince's headquarters at Chartres. This time they were ready to concede the principle for which Edward had contended for a quarter of a century – the complete independence of his French dominions. And thanks to their experiences of that winter and Lancaster's moderating influence, the English were at last ready to be reasonable. 'My liege,' the wise old warrior is reported to have said, 'this war you are waging may be wonderful to all men; it is not so favourable to yourself! If you persist, it will last you a lifetime, and it seems to be doubtful that you will gain your desires. You are wasting your time.'

Negotiations were opened on 1 May 1360 at the village of Brétigny. A week later, 'eight days into the sweet month of May,' as Chandos's herald put it, 'when the birds were no more in dismay', the terms of a provisional treaty were announced. Under these, Edward renounced his claim to the French throne and to the overlordship of Normandy, Anjou, Maine, Touraine, Brittany and Flanders. He also promised to restore any castles and cities held in these provinces. In return he was to receive the unconditional cession, free from the French King's suzerainty, of Calais, Ponthieu and the whole of Aquitaine – nearly a quarter of France. It was to include the Limousin, Agenais, Angoumois, Poitou, Périgord, Quercy and Rouergue and the cities of Limoges, Poitiers, Angoulême, Cahors, Tarbes and La Rochelle, the headquarters of the European salt trade. France also agreed to pay the full 300,000 gold crowns for her King's ransom in six instalments, the first of which was to secure his release on royal hostages being given for the remainder. She was to renounce the Scottish alliance, and England the Flemish. The question of the Breton succession was to be left to discussion. Provision was also made for the subjects of both kingdoms to study once more at each other's universities.

*   *   *

On the morning of 29 May 1360 Edward and the Black Prince returned to Westminster, after galloping through the night from Rye. It was a day of pealing bells, Te Deums and rejoicings. Edward himself announced the good news to his royal prisoner; 'You and I,' he declared, 'are now, thank God, of one accord.' Five weeks later, after three and a half years' imprisonment, King John took leave of him at Eltham palace. But on his arrival at Calais, the poor man was detained for a further three months owing to delays in carrying out the treaty's preliminary terms. Even when on 25 October the two Kings formally ratified it, kneeling together before the altar of St Nicholas church and swearing perpetual friendship, the transfer of territories was still not complete, the people of La Rochelle proving particularly reluctant to change their allegiance. In consequence both Edward's renunciation of the French throne and the French King's of his claim to allegiance were omitted from the treaty and left to letters of ratification to be exchanged later. From this much trouble was to follow, though none seems to have been anticipated, at least by the English. Three of the French King's sons accompanied Edward back to England as hostages, but were subsequently released on parole in return for a promise of 200,000 more crowns.

For Edward felt he could afford to be generous. In his fiftieth year he had obtained all he wanted of France – military glory transcending even his romantic dreams and full dominion over territories far larger than those he had inherited. He was regarded, by foreigners and subjects alike, as the most victorious, chivalrous and magnificent monarch in Christendom – an Arthur, it seemed, reincarnated. Under her 'clement King', too, England had enjoyed a longer period of internal tranquillity than at any time in her history. 'The bringer of peace to his people,' was how Edward's epitaph in the abbey was to describe him, and it was thus that his subjects saw him during his life. There had been times when the greatest threat to an English sovereign's authority and his kingdom's peace had come from his own sons; the first Plantagenet had been harried to the grave by them. Edward's were devoted to him. It was an essential part of his policy of national conciliation to marry them to the heiresses of the greater feudal families. Of his four surviving younger sons, the eldest, Lionel of Antwerp, had been betrothed to the only child of the earl of Ulster, William de Burgh, who also represented on the distaff side the great Marcher house of Clare. Shortly after the Treaty of Brétigny the young prince was sent to govern Ireland with the dual object of securing the profits of his wife's vast but largely illusory inheritance and of restoring order to that turbulent country which, since its invasion by the Bruces after Bannockburn, had been in a state of more than usual anarchy. His younger brother, John of Gaunt, had made a still more splendid marriage with his cousin Blanche, daughter and co-heiress of Henry of Lancaster. On the latter's death in 1361 and of his other co-heiress shortly afterwards, he acquired the whole of the vast Lancastrian inheritance, including the earldoms of Lancaster, Derby, Lincoln and Leicester. A year later, to mark his own fiftieth birthday, Edward created him Duke of Lancaster.

'Clement and benign, familiar and gentle to all men', Edward was not, however, an iron man like his grandfather. His supreme object was to please and excel and, being able, courageous and immensely energetic and possessed of wonderful charm, he was at first completely successful. But as difficulties grew he became more and more apt to follow the line of least resistance; to promise, and when promise became impossible of fulfilment, to evade and equivocate. At this time, either through a wish to gain a tactical point or through some unaccountable negligence, he made a fatal blunder. In February 1361, with four sons and the French royal hostages by his side, he had opened the Parliament which ratified the treaty of Brétigny, first marching in procession to the abbey, where Simon of Islip, Archbishop of Canterbury, celebrated High Mass in honour of the Holy Trinity. Yet the one essential condition of the treaty for which England had fought for nearly a quarter of a century was allowed to go unratified, ostensibly on account of French delays in making the promised ransom payments and in handing over certain of the towns and territories agreed under the treaty. The final date fixed for the exchange of mutual renunciations of sovereignty had been 1 November 1361. Yet when, two days before, the French envoys arrived in England they were told that the King was not prepared to abandon his title to the French crown until every detail of the treaty had been complied with. The envoys, therefore, refused to make a unilateral surrender of their master's suzerainty over Aquitaine.

As a result, by far the most important gain of the peace was lost, and the question of ultimate sovereignty was left unsolved to bedevil future Anglo-French relations. Without it, neither the transfers of territory nor the huge ransom instalments were of any permanent use to England, even though, when delays occurred in the time-table for the latter and one of the French royal hostages – temporarily given leave to visit his wife at Boulogne – broke his parole and failed to return, King John most honourably surrendered himself again to his former captors. Returning to England at the beginning of 1364, perhaps not without relief at exchanging his own war-harried and poverty-stricken realm for the luxury and chivalric splendour of the English court, he died there that spring at the age of forty-five.

The French were given another and better excuse for renouncing the terms of the treaty of Brétigny, should they ever wish to do so. For though the disbandment and withdrawal of the Free Companies had been one of its main conditions and when, in Froissart's words, 'their captains departed in courteous manner out of those fortresses they held . . . and gave leave to their men of war to depart', the latter 'thought that to return into their own country was not to them profitable'. After which they continued to behave as they had always done and as though no peace had been made. 'They wasted all the country without any cause and robbed without sparing all that ever they could get and violated and defiled women, old and young without pity, and slew men, women and children without mercy.'

For the English army of which the French had been so anxious to be rid was neither a feudal array bound by social obligations nor a national militia defending its own soil. It was a collection of private war-bands raised by indenture by adventurous nobles and knights for the pursuit of profit. And when, replete with their gains, the larger share-holders withdrew, the smaller took over. Though many of these 'great pillagers' were not English, but Germans, Brabanters, Flemings, Hainaulters, Gascons and even Frenchmen, they had all served England's King, and the blame for their evil doings was laid at his door. One of them, an archer named John Hawkwood – the son of an Essex tanner – after ravaging southern France, led his gang of desperadoes to Avignon 'to see,' as they put it, 'the Pope and cardinals'. Later he transferred himself to Italy where for thirty years he lived by placing his trained and disciplined band – the 'White Company' as it was called – at the disposal of first one warring city or republic, then another. After making an enormous fortune and marrying a natural daughter of Bernabo Visconti, tyrant of Milan, he died in 1394, in the service of Florence, whose grateful government gave him a funeral in the duomo and commissioned as his memorial a magnificent equestrian fresco by Paolo Uccello.[1]

Two years after the end of the war with England the 'brigands' were still strong enough to destroy a French army under a royal duke at Brignais near Lyons. But the accession in 1364 of the twenty-five-year-old Dauphin as Charles V proved the turn of the tide for France. A few weeks later a rough Breton knight with a genius for war, Bertrand du Guesclin, won a victory at Cocherel in Normandy over the forces of the traitor, Charles of Navarre, and an English freelance captain, John Jewel. It was the first decisive French victory for a generation and ended the Norman rebellion. In Brittany, where civil war had again broken out, Sir John Chandos with a few hundred English volunteers again showed that autumn at Auray the unbreakable ascendancy of his countrymen in pitched battle, defeating and killing Charles of Blois and taking du Guesclin

[1] With Robert Knollys and Hugh Calveley he was one of the founders of the English hospital at Rome and, through a daughter who married John Shelley, MP for Rye, an ancestor of the poet.

prisoner. But the new French King turned the defeat to his advantage by recognising the rival claimant, de Montfort, as duke in return for his homage. In doing so he regained Brittany for France and brought the war in that country to an end and, with it, any further pretext for English intervention.

Charles V had none of his father's love of knight-errantry. After his early experience at Poitiers he never took part in another battle. He was a delicate young man, matured by misfortune, with a sharp nose, quizzical look and, under his scholarly appearance, a will of iron. Devout, learned and immensely shrewd, he was a brilliant judge of men; it was he who raised the younger son of a Breton hedge-squire to the command of France's armies. He loved the company of scholars and artists and strove to make his court and Paris once more the centre and arbiter of western civilization, identifying his throne with a stately ceremonial that recalled, in a more luxurious age, his hero and great-great-grandfather, St Louis. Yet, though operating from the library and counting-house rather than the saddle, he proved the most successful director of war of his age, attaining his ends with a minimum expense of life and treasure. Knowing precisely what he wanted, he pursued it with cunning, patience and inflexible resolution. In his sixteen years on the throne he raised France from the depths of defeat and poverty to renewed wealth and grandeur.

Above all, he sought to identify himself with the needs and hopes of the French people. His supreme object was to unite all Frenchmen under a single throne and law. Where the feudal nobility, with their arrogance and selfish separatism, had left France wide open to her enemies, this young King set himself to show that, from the highest to the lowest, safety for life and property could only be won by rallying round the Crown. Little by little he gained his ends, letting Edward leave unratified the renunciation of his claim to the French throne and, with it, his right to untrammelled overlordship over Aquitaine; and, while there was peace with England, driving or bribing out of the country, first one, then another of the plundering Free Companies. All the while, as he restored order and prosperity to France's long tormented countryside, he built up her financial resources and reorganised her armies. The price he had to pay was a heavy one: the *gabelle* or salt monopoly, which he made permanent, and his system of farming the taxes, which led to grave social abuses and oppression. Yet the poor who felt them most saw in him their protector against the English and the lawless soldiery who had so long preyed on them and, when he died at the age of thirty-eight, it was said that the lilies were engraved on every peasant's heart.

*   *   *

Though the return of the plague in 1361 had fallen with equal severity on France, striking down no less than eight cardinals in the court of Avignon, it was again the smaller of the two countries which suffered most from its attrition. Yet the area which England with her reduced man-power had to control had been trebled by her conquests. In 1363, faced by the difficulty of finding archers for its foreign garrisons, the government issued a proclamation deploring the nation's degeneracy and enjoining archery practice on saints' days and holidays for all able-bodied men. About this time, too, Edward tried once more to forestall any renewal of a joint attack from France and Scotland by using the latter's poverty and internal anarchy to coax her King and nobles into a union with England. He made generous, if calculated, concessions to her merchants and pilgrims, reopened English universities to Scottish students – for Scotland still had none of her own – and in the autumn of 1363 offered to remit the remaining instalments of King David's ransom and restore Berwick, Roxburgh and Jedburgh and the Stone of Scone in return for the Scots' acknowledging him, or one of his sons, as David's heir should the latter die without children. The Scottish King, who had learnt to love the fleshpots of the Plantagenet court, was ready to agree, as was also, for a time, his chief opponent, the earl of Douglas, who hoped to recover his English estates. But when the treaty was presented to the Scottish Parliament in the spring of 1364, its members proved worthier of the great Bruce and James Douglas than their degenerate successors. Notwithstanding 'the dark and drublie days' through which their country was passing, they declared themselves 'in no way willing to assent' and rejected the terms as 'insufferable'. A few years later, the issue, as Scotsmen saw it, was put by John Barbour, archdeacon of Aberdeen, in the prologue to his epic, *The Brus*, which he wrote round the story of Scotland's liberator.

> 'Ah, freedom is a noble thing! . . .
> Freedom all solace to man gives,
> He lives at ease that freely lives!
> A noble heart may have none ease
> Nor ellés naught that may him please
> If freedom fail.'

Edward's hopes, therefore, came to nothing, and Scotland, poverty-stricken, proud and racked by constant civil war, remained the independent nation that Bruce and Wallace had made her and, as a result, a standing threat to England's back door. Meanwhile, beyond the Channel, the latter continued to maintain her vast military empire, the new outlying districts of which, in contra-distinction to a still loyal Gascony, were growing every year more hostile to her arrogant and predatory dominion. In the past the English Kings – descendants of the ancient princes of Anjou and Aquitaine – had behaved as Frenchmen and governed their French provinces through the local nobility and bureaucracy. But with their victories over the Valois kings and the growing identification of England's French-speaking lords with her Anglo-Saxon yeomanry – a union cemented on the battlefield – England's rulers were becoming increasingly insular. Pride in their common Englishry and, with it, contempt for foreigners, were beginning to transcend the unity of class, speech and ideology which had so long identified their French-descended rulers with their ancestral lands across the Channel. In October 1362, the Chief Justice of the King's Bench opened the proceedings of Parliament for the first time in English – a precedent followed at the opening of the next Parliament by the Chancellor. In the same year it was enacted that all pleadings should be in the vernacular on the ground that French was 'too little known in the realm' and that 'people who impleaded or were impeached in the courts knew not what was said for or against them by their serjeants or pleaders'. And though lack of precision in the English language – for so long the despised speech of 'uplandish men' – made this technically impracticable, and for several more centuries lawyers continued in their pleadings to use French to express the exact concepts demanded by their profession, forensic argument in the King's courts was henceforward conducted in English. The old romance tongue of western chivalry was ceasing to be the speech of the ruling class; a generation later Chaucer's high-born prioress spoke French, not after the French of Paris 'which was to her unknowe', but 'after the school of Stratford-atte-Bowe'.

*　　　　*　　　　*

In 1363 the English heir-apparent was sent to govern Aquitaine as a sovereign and independent prince, subject only to his father's overlordship. Here he maintained a splendid court where, in Chandos' herald's words, 'abode all nobleness, all joy and jollity, largesse, gentleness and honour'. Yet, however much the Gascons might admire their new Duke as a model of knightly chivalry and the first warrior of his age, they loved neither the taxation he imposed to maintain his extravagant court nor the horde of English lords and officials he took with him to administer the duchy. Still less did the peoples of the new provinces which had been added to England's French dominion. The new High Seneschal of Aquitaine was a Cheshire knight, Sir Thomas Felton; the Seneschal of Poitou his cousin, Sir William of the same name; of Saintonge Sir Baldwin Treville; of Quercy Sir Thomas Walkfare; of Limousin Lord Ros; of the Agenais Sir Richard Baskerville. Even the chivalry, good sense and moderation of the High Constable of Aquitaine, the universally loved Sir John Chandos, did not remove the sense of shame felt by the proud Gascon nobles that foreigners should hold the highest offices of their ancient dukedom.

The sense of outraged nationality and longing for revenge aroused in Gallic peasants and merchants by a generation of invasion and rapine by English bowmen had spread from France proper into the south-west and had even begun to show itself beyond the Garonne. This growing anti-English, pro-Valois feeling of a countryside which had hitherto preferred the remote rule of its French-speaking English duke to that of Paris was brought to a head by the romantic extravagance and belligerency of the Black Prince. In 1366 the kingdom of Castile became the scene of one of those periodic civil wars that reflect the inability to compromise, impassioned partisanship and fanatic valour of the Spanish temperament. Its King, Don Pedro 'the Cruel', was challenged by his bastard half-brother, Don Erico of Trastamara. Repudiated by a large part of his people, excommunicated by the Pope and opposed, though without open intervention, by the French King who, seeing an opportunity for getting rid of the Free Companies, set off as many of them as possible under Bertrand du Guesclin to help the Bastard, whom he saw as a future ally against England, Pedro was driven from his capital. Taking refuge at Corunna he appealed to the Black Prince for help.

This challenge to his chivalry, as well as to the principle of legitimacy, was more than the Prince could resist. He saw himself as the knight-errant of Christendom leading a righteous war. Obtaining his father's unofficial consent and a promise of help from his younger brother, John of Gaunt, Duke of Lancaster, he assembled an army at Dax and, in the winter of 1366–7, prepared to cross the Pyrenees. Joined by the latter with a thousand archers from the forests of Cheshire and the north, the Prince turned his back on his restless duchy, his debts and the watchful French King beyond his borders, and in February 1367 crossed the Roncesvalles pass, driving his heavily accoutred men, horses and wagons through the wintry gorges of Navarre to the Castilian border.

This chivalric expedition into Spain, ten years after Poitiers and conducted in extremes of winter cold and scorching heat on Castilian mountain and plain, proved the hero Prince's undoing and, ultimately, that of English rule in France. Despite his brilliant victory at Nájera on 3 April 1367, when the flower of the feudal nobility of yet another European kingdom went down under a hail of English steel and goosequill, the Black Prince's last crusade of chivalry ended in disillusionment and disaster. After it, the victors waited all summer under a burning sun for the gold which was to have been paid by King Pedro for their aid, while dysentery, contracted from stagnant pools, continued to diminish their numbers. When in the autumn the Prince sadly led the survivors back across the Pyrenees, they were only a shadow of the splendid host which had crossed them at the beginning of the year. Not one in five, it was said, ever saw England again. All that their leader had to show for his victory was a handful of jewels wrung from Don Pedro in place of the million crowns he had been promised.

At thirty-seven, his giant frame emaciated by dysentery, the Black Prince returned to Bordeaux. His troops were unpaid and his duchy restless under taxation. So troublesome were the survivors of the Free Companies whom he was now forced to quarter on his subjects that, when he summoned the estates of the duchy to meet at the little hill-town of St Emilion, the deputies of Rouergue were forced to turn back by the 'companions' ravaging the Dordogne valley. At the beginning of 1368, disregarding the advice of Chandos, the Prince got the estates to impose a five years' *fouage* or tax on every hearth in the duchy to meet his war debts. It was bitterly opposed by two of the leading magnates of Guienne. When the Prince 'insisted that, right or wrong, his vassals should do his bidding', they refused to allow the tax to be levied in their domains and appealed, first to the King of England, and then, without waiting for an answer, to the King of France.

It was the opportunity for which Charles had been waiting. Yet he proceeded with his usual caution. Privately promising the apellants that he would investigate their case but pledging himself to nothing, he played for time and with the Pope's aid secured the release of the last hostages from the unsuspecting and now ageing Edward in return, it was said, for papal approval of the appointment of the English King's favourite minister, William of Wykeham, to the see of Winchester. Continuing the pretence of non-intervention in Spain, he sent back the now ransomed du Guesclin to restore the Bastard and, through an alliance with Castile, Aragon and Navarre, to circle England's southern dominion with enemies. By getting a French Pope to refuse a dispensation on the grounds of consanguinity, he had already thwarted Edward's hope of marrying his son, Edmund of Langley, to the heiress of Flanders. Now, when English policy had suffered a further set-back through the death in Italy of Prince Lionel of Clarence after his wedding to the niece of Bernabo Visconti of Milan, he brought off a still greater coup by inducing the count of Flanders to give his daughter to his own brother, Philip the Bold of Burgundy, thus bringing Flanders once more into the orbit of royal France. All the while he observed the letter while violating the spirit of the treaty of Brétigny.

By the end of 1368 he was ready. He had already allowed the Gascon appellants to lay their case before the *parlement* of Paris, making a secret pact with them that if it came to war they would stand together. Knowing that hundreds more of the Black Prince's subjects were eager to appeal to him, he now announced that his judges had found that, as Edward had failed to ratify the renunciation of his claim to the French throne, his own father's surrender of the overlordship of Aquitaine had never become effective – and that province was, therefore, still part of France. As its overlord he was entitled, and morally bound, to pronounce judgment on the appeals.

In January 1369 Charles formally summoned the Black Prince as a peer of France to appear in person at Paris. The Prince was taken completely by surprise. When he realised that all that he and his father had fought for had been in vain he swore a mighty oath. 'We shall willingly,' he said, 'attend on the appointed day at Paris since the King of France sends for us. But it will be with helmet on head and with sixty thousand men at our back.'

What the victor of Poitiers threatened and what he could perform, however, were now different things. It was not he who took the offensive, but his discontented vassals and the French King. All round the eight-hundred-mile perimeter of Aquitaine, bands of fighting men poured in to help their compatriots, while the clergy everywhere took the lead in preaching rebellion. Within a few weeks more than nine hundred castles and towns had repudiated allegiance to the English; most of Armagnac, Limousin, Rodez, Quercy and the Agenais was lost without a fight.

Yet Charles still proceeded with caution. In March 1369 his troops helped the Castilians to a decisive victory over Don Pedro, who was taken prisoner and killed. With the Bastard back on the throne, Castile and her fleet, as well as Aragon and Navarre, were now aligned against England. At last, in May 1369, Charles took the decisive step, first declaring the Black Prince contumacious for failing to appear before the *parlement* of Paris, and then informing the English King that, as he had failed to observe the letter of the treaties, his French lands were forfeit. Simultaneously he seized Pontheiu.

Furious, Edward III appealed to Parliament for money and resumed the title, discarded nine years before, of King of France. At this moment the Black Death broke out in England for the third time. Among those who died that summer were the bishops of Norwich, Hereford and Exeter, the earls of Suffolk and Warwick and the young Duchess of Lancaster – the lady Blanche,[1] wife of John of Gaunt. Not till the autumn was it possible to collect even a small force for France, when, to forestall an invasion of the Isle of Wight, Gaunt crossed to Calais with 600 men-at-arms and 1500 bowmen. By striking at Artois and Picardy he was just in time to stop the embarkation of an army in Normandy under the French King's brother. But though he marched to the gates of Harfleur, burning and ravaging, he was unable to tempt the French to battle. For Charles had resolved to give no chance to the English archers to repeat their holocausts of a generation before. By November, unable to supply his troops any longer, John of Gaunt returned to England, to find that he had lost not only his wife but his mother, Queen Philippa having died that month at Windsor.

If 1369 was a disastrous year for England, it saved Scotland. Without enough men to defend both the northern Marches and Aquitaine, a plague-riven England agreed to a fourteen-year truce. But for this, famine, baronial and tribal war and the crushing taxation to pay for her King's ransom would have forced the northern kingdom to accept Edward's terms and acknowledge him as David's successor. As it was, though England still held Berwick, Roxburgh and Annandale, the Scots, freed from danger from the south, were able to put down a rebellion of the Lord of the Isles which had threatened to disintegrate their country. When eighteen months later, in February 1371, King David died, the son of Robert Bruce's daughter, Robert the Steward, succeeded under the

---

[1] 'Who died fair and young, at about the age of twenty-two years. Gay and glad she was, fresh and sportive, sweet, simple and humble semblance, the fair lady whom men called Blanche.' *Froissart*. Daughter of the great warrior Henry of Lancaster, she was the heroine of Chaucer's earliest major poem.

terms of the settlement of half a century before. Without their in-
volvement in a losing war with France the English would never
have recognised him.

The campaign in Guienne fared no better in 1370 than in 1369.
The English could not contend indefinitely against a nation several
times their size. Though they still did not realise it, the door of
opportunity, once wide open, was now bolted against them. They
could no longer finance the war from plunder, which, as they
burnt, ravaged and wasted, brought in diminishing returns. In vain
they called in their Free Companies – Hugh Calveley from Spain
and the 'terrible Robert' Knollys from Burgundy – and enrolled
them to defend the duchy; unpaid and forced to live on the countryside, the companions only made the situation worse, arousing the
hatred of every peasant and burgher. In vain they made *chevauchées*
in the old familiar style to provoke the French to battle. In the
summer of 1370, with fifteen hundred men-at-arms and four
thousand bowmen, Knollys marched from Calais to Troyes and
thence, passing under the walls of Paris, to Brittany. But the only
result was a further growth of French national consciousness, while
the young English lords, humiliated by their lack of success,
grumbled furiously at having to serve under such a low-born
commander; 'the old brigand', they called him.

The French King's strategy was admirably adapted to his
means. It was to avoid pitched battles at all costs, use his superiority
in numbers and the growing French sympathies of the Black
Prince's vassals to liberate first one district, then another, and, by
strengthening the defences of every castle in French hands, to make
it impossible for the English to recover their lost gains. Gone were
the days when a few daring Englishmen could surprise and escalade
supposedly impregnable but weakly guarded strongholds; once
Charles's engineers had put the defences of any fortress or town in
order, nothing but a major army with a siege-train could reduce it.
And this was something far beyond the capacity of the English.

Early in 1370 Sir John Chandos – the most loved figure on
either side – fell in a skirmish near Poitiers. 'Courteous and benign,
amiable, liberal, preux, sage and true in all causes,' Froissart wrote
of him, 'nor was there ever knight better beloved nor praised of

every creature.' His death caused the defection of thousands of Gascons who, as long as he was Constable, adhered to the English cause. With his passing, the Black Prince lost his wisest counsellor and the last hope of an accommodation with the French King.

That summer, Moissac, Agen and even Aiguillon, which twenty years before had defied a French army for months, fell after sieges of only a few days. The count of Armagnac was now less than fifty miles from Bordeaux. At the end of August came the crowning humiliation when the city of Limoges was surrendered to the duke of Berri by its bishop after the townsmen had risen and overpowered the small English garrison under Sir Hugh Calveley. Bitterly resentful – for the bishop had been one of his closest friends – the Black Prince roused himself from his sick bed at Angoulême and, borne in a litter in the midst of his army, marched on the city. Breaching its walls by mining, he stormed it by night. The vengeance taken by his unbridled troops shocked even that unsqueamish age and marred his reputation for chivalry. It did the English cause untold harm.

A month later the French King raised Bertrand du Guesclin to the great office of Constable of France and commander of all her armies. This short, squat, coarse-featured veteran, with his long experience of mercenary war, was exactly the lieutenant Charles needed for his Fabian strategy of wearing down the invaders. In the days of the arrogant feudal nobility that had perished at Crécy and Poitiers, such a promotion would have been unthinkable. Now after a generation of civil war and anarchy it seemed inevitablé, for the Breton knight had become the hero of France. But the chief credit for the collapse of the hitherto invincible English belonged to the unmartial, unspectacular sovereign who had seen so clearly, and so cunningly pursued, the means by which they could be defeated.

In November 1370, two months after the sack of Limoges and only three years after his victory at Nájera, the Black Prince, a sick, frustrated man, handed over his command and the lieutenancy of Aquitaine to his brother, John of Gaunt. In January 1371 he sailed for England where he found his father, once the hero of Europe, sunk in a doting dependence on his mistress, Alice Perrers, a former lady-in-waiting of the dead Queen. Withdrawing to Berkhamsted castle and taking no further part in public life, he watched from a bed of sickness the continuing decline of England's fortunes.

His departure made no difference to the course of the war. John of Gaunt, an ambitious, hustling and habitually unlucky man, was no more able to stem the French advance than his brother. In the late summer of 1371, after six months' campaigning, he too relinquished his command and handed over the governance of what remained of England's dominion to the Gascon veteran of Poitiers, Captal de Buch. A few weeks later he married the eldest daughter and co-heiress of the dead Don Pedro and thereafter became increasingly preoccupied with a claim to the Castilian throne.

Yet, though he now called himself a king, the only dowry his wife brought him were 'castles in Spain'. French aid had by now firmly seated the Bastard on that country's throne and aligned him permanently against England. Henceforward Castile's ocean-going fleet became a major factor in the war. In their obsession with military glory the English had omitted to remain strong at sea, and the command which Edward had won at Sluys and which had enabled his armies to ravage France at will had slipped from his hands. Ever since the first Black Death he had overstrained the country's maritime resources by impressing ships and seamen and neglecting to pay for them. He still held both sides of the Dover strait and called himself lord of the seas, but in the Atlantic waters between England and Gascony the great galliasses of Castile were a growing menace to his communications. In the autumn of 1371 Guy de Brian – the standard bearer at Crécy and a founder Knight of the Garter – won an action against French privateers near Roscoff off the coast of Brittany. But on 22 June 1372, a much larger English fleet attempting to relieve La Rochelle under the new Lieutenant of Aquitaine, the earl of Pembroke, was routed by the combined fleets of Castile and France, and with most of his crews, made prisoner. A final attempt by Edward III and the Black Prince to take a new army to Gascony in person failed in a terrible autumn storm which sent thousands to the bottom after six weeks of buffeting at the mouth of the Channel. It was the old King's last appearance in the war.

With La Rochelle in French hands and the Castilian and French navies in control of the Bay of Biscay, the English cause was lost. The Gascon wine trade was ruined and the age-long link between England and the Garonne all but broken. In the summer of 1373 John of Gaunt made an attempt to do by land what could no longer be done by sea, setting out from Calais on 4 August with an army of 15,000 men and crossing eastern France in a *grande chevauchée* which ended at Christmas at Bordeaux after a wintry march across the Auvergne. This feat of endurance, in which vast numbers of horses perished, was regarded as 'most honourable to the English' and probably saved Bordeaux. But as the French avoided battle, it achieved nothing else.

With the fall of La Réole at the beginning of 1374 all that remained of England's overseas empire was Calais and a thin coastal strip between Bordeaux and Bayonne – smaller now even than at Edward's accession. Having awoken the French people to nationhood, her King and princes could no longer retain the willing allegiance of Frenchmen. But the English still could not see this; after so many victories their defeats seemed to them only explicable as a judgment for their rulers' failings. They looked with horror at the spectacle of their King – once the model of Christian chivalry – decking his concubine with the jewels of his dead Queen and enthroning her in the tournament lists as Lady of the Sun. They learnt with pity of the plight of the great warrior, his son, bedridden in his castle at Berkhamsted. And they laid the blame on the King's ministers and, when they were able, through their representatives in Parliament, hounded them from office.

Two years later the victor of Poitiers, England's darling hero – 'the chief flower of chivalry of all the world', as Froissart called him – was laid to rest at Canterbury close to the shrine of St Thomas. His effigy, clad in gilt metal armour, still rests there on its tomb of Purbeck marble, his helmet open, his hands folded in prayer, his dog at his feet and, above the canopy, his crested helm, sur-coat and shield, gauntlet and sword. When a year later, on 21 June 1377, his royal father, the victor of Crécy, a dotard with long white beard, deserted by his servants and plundered by his very mistress, followed him to the grave, nothing remained of England's conquests in France but Calais, Brest and a precarious dwindling strip of Gascon coast, while a French army was poised to invade and occupy the Isle of Wight. Before he could be laid in his tomb all the principal English Channel ports – Fowey, Plymouth, Melcombe Regis, Poole, Hastings, Rye – and even Gravesend – had been sacked and burnt by French and Spanish raiders, the mouth of London river was being hastily guarded by booms and chains, and the prior of Lewes, at the head of the posse of East Sussex, called out to resist invasion, had been carried off into captivity.

CHAPTER SIXTEEN

Peasants in Revolt

The Hurling Time

'Englishmen suffer indeed for a season, but in the end they repay so cruelly that it may stand as a great warning . . . There is no people under the sun so perilous in the matter of its common folk as they are in England.'

Froissart

WITH THE ISLE OF WIGHT OVERRUN by a French army and Castilian and French fleets riding the Channel, the reign of the ten-year-old Richard II began in national defeat and humiliation. The Council of Regency which governed in his name had to face the affronted patriotism and resentment of the nation's representatives in Parliament. For there was a general belief that the sums voted for the war had been embezzled or, at best, wasted. The man whom everyone blamed for England's misfortunes, probably unfairly, was Edward III's fourth son, John of Gaunt, Duke of Lancaster, whose military lack of success had been in such sorry contrast to the victories of his brother, the Black Prince, and his father-in-law, the great warrior Henry Grosmont, Duke of Lancaster. Gaunt's pride, arrogance and autocratic ways and his vast wealth, the inheritance of his dead wife and her sister and co-heiress – whom he was even popularly suspected of having murdered to secure the whole of his father-in-law's huge patrimony – made him the most hated man in the kingdom. Laying claim to a foreign throne through his second marriage to a Spanish princess while living in open adultery with his children's governess – the great love of his life and ancestress of the future British royal line – he seemed to be calling down heaven's wrath on the realm.

Nor was it only the discontent of the politically enfranchised classes that the King's government had to face. There was widespread unrest, too, among the toiling peasant masses outside the constitution. For the most enduring consequence of the Black Death had been a general shortage of labour caused by the death in its first three outbreaks of half the country's population. One result had been a spectacular rise in wages, which the Council and successive Parliaments of landowners had tried vainly to halt by punitive ordinances and legislation. These Statutes of Labourers, as they were called, aroused bitter class feeling.

Yet for a century before the Black Death the position of the English peasant had been slowly improving, whether he was a well-to-do yardlander farming two or three hundred acres or a landless cottar earning his daily bread by wages. Compared with the wretched peasantry of the continent, he was not too badly off except when the harvest failed. For the bowmen of Crécy had not been drawn from an oppressed populace. It was a commonplace to contrast the lot of the English husbandman with that of the French serf, wrapped in sacking and living on apples and bitter rye-bread.

Yet somewhere near half the English peasantry were not legally free, but tied by inheritance to the soil they cultivated. Described as villeins and subject to the discipline of the lord's manorial court or leet – on whose juries and inquests they served – they could not claim a free man's rights under the Common Law, let alone representation in Parliament. Like the feudalism of which it was part, the servile manorial system of the open field villages of central and southern England had long been in decline and was gradually giving way to an economy based on paid labour and rented farms. But it was still the basis of life for nearly a million men and women who were bound by birth to the soil and compelled to perform unpaid menial services for its lord. They could only gain release by a formal grant of manumission or by flight from their homes and fields to some neighbouring chartered borough where servile status had been abolished, and residence for a year and a day gave a man his freedom.

The extent of the services the villein had to perform for his lord varied with the size of his holding and the custom of the manor. But wherever the open-field system operated, as it did in most parts of the country except the pastoral north and west and in Kent, the peasant was confronted by uncertain demands on his time and by galling restrictions on his economic freedom of action. Among these were the obligation to grind his corn, bake his bread and brew his ale at the lord's mill, oven and brewery – 'suit of mill' and 'oven', as they were called – which not only enriched the lord, but offered opportunities for every kind of chicanery and imposition by those to whom the latter leased his rights. An equally resented monopoly was the lord's dovecot and 'free warren', from which hordes of pigeons and rabbits descended on the peasant's crops, while, if he retaliated by trapping such pests, he faced a heavy fine in the manorial court. If he wished to sell a beast, to reside outside the manor, to marry his son or daughter, even if the latter became pregnant – for this depreciated her value – he was fined. And on his death his widow or heir was forced to pay a heriot – the value of the best beast and chattel – and an entry-fine equivalent to a year's rent as the price of taking over the family holding.

All this had come to be intensely resented. Villeinage was seen by the bondsman as an economic imposition and a degrading distinction. It was no longer taken for granted, and every opportunity was seized to escape or evade its burdens. Those who resented them most were the richer villagers who occupied the traditional yardlands – holdings of thirty acres or more in the arable fields, with corresponding rights in the manorial meadowland, waste and woodland. A yardlander had to perform for his holding, in person or by proxy, not only a full half-day's labour on the lord's land for three or four days a week throughout the year but additional services called 'love-boons' – given, in theory, out of love for his feudal protector – at the very seasons, haymaking and harvest, harrowing and sowing times, when he needed all the labour he could command to wrest a living from his own villein soil.

Those who could afford it, therefore, seized every opportunity to commute as many of such services as possible for money payments. In the expanding agricultural economy of the thirteenth and early fourteenth centuries many peasants had been able to free themselves from the more onerous burdens, for progressive land-owners found it paid to hire labour rather than depend on the un-willing services of disgruntled serfs. The halving of the national labour-force by the Black Death halted this gradual emancipation. Labour had suddenly become the most precious commodity in the kingdom. A landowner who had made no composition with or con-cessions to his serfs found himself able to cultivate his depopulated estates far more cheaply than one who had commuted his villeins' services for a cash payment. Bound by agreements to let their serfs enjoy their holdings at rents which now bore no relation to what they themselves had to pay for hired labour, and desperate for lack of workers, many lords, therefore, tried to enforce rights which had lapsed or to stretch those that remained.

If the Black Death made lords more conscious of the value of compulsory services, it made every serf more eager to evade them. Shaking off their ancestral shackles, bondsmen fled from their homes and took service for wages with distant employers who asked no questions. It was the poorer members of the village community with no land to lose who were best able to seize such opportunities – the young and those with no possessions but their tools and skill as husbandmen or craftsmen. The attempts of Parliament and of local justices to keep down wages by branding, imprisonment and the stocks drove them to make common cause with their richer neighbours, who were confronted by demands from their lords for services which they regarded as unjust and oppressive.

It was against the lord's officers and agents that the peasant's indignation was, in particular, directed. From the receivers and bailiffs who wrung from him the services and rents on which the landowner lived, from the steward who presided at his manorial court and the lawyers who made extreme claims on the lord's behalf, he received little mercy. Times were bad, money hard to come by for a luxurious ruling class in need of the income it could no longer obtain from victories abroad. The business of its agents was to exact the uttermost service and payment obtainable. In the process they often took – and even more often were suspected of taking – more than was due or than the lord himself received.

Some of the hardest task-masters were the monasteries who, hit by the economic recession and the plague, had never enjoyed, like the secular lords, the opportunity of making good their losses by the plunder and ransoms of war. Intensely conservative and, like all corporations, impersonal in business relationships, they had the justification that their exactions were for the service of God. More easily than most they were able to prove rights to long-lapsed services by the charters which every religious house pre-served and added to by cultivating the friendship of the great and sometimes, if their critics are to be believed, improved by a little pious and skilled forgery. Nor, conscious of the sanctity of their claims, were they always very tactful with those whose labour they exploited; the abbot of Burton told his tenants that they owned nothing but their bellies.

Of all who enforced the lord's rights the lawyer was the most hated. To the peasant the purpose of the law seemed to be to keep him down and enforce the servile status which deprived him of liberty and opportunity. In the thirty years following the first post-Black Death statute against what Council and Parliament called 'the malice of labourers', nearly nine thousand cases of wage en-forcement were tried by the courts and, in nearly all, judgment was given in the employer's favour. The peasant's indignation at those who put such restraints on him was increased by the spectacle of expanding freedom in the chartered towns which had sprung up in every part of England and to which so many of the younger villagers had fled to better their conditions. Some of these, who had survived the harsh conditions and competition of the medieval town, had themselves grown rich and famous.

*   *   *

Because of this, as well as for other reasons, there was a captious, bitter, disillusioned spirit abroad. The strain and cost of the war, with its latter disasters and humiliations and the successive visita-tions of Black Death had all tended to shake men's faith in society. The pestilence which had driven weak natures to a hectic pursuit of pleasure, elevating the self-indulgence of the moment above duty and morality, had left only half the labour formerly available to do the nation's work and supply the luxuries of the rich. For a generation the burden of war debts and taxes had fallen with what seemed insupportable severity on the survivors. The result was a widespread sense of frustration, of loss of familiar standards, of resentment between employer and employed, landowner and husbandman, government and taxpayer. Everyone tended to blame someone else for his sufferings.

Deep down the malaise of England after the Black Death was spiritual. It was the sickness of soul of a people who felt that justice was being outraged. The old static feudalism, in which every man knew and accepted his place, was disintegrating; the more fluid society that was replacing it was on the make and given to lavish and ostentatious luxury. The reign of Edward III had witnessed a steady rise in the standards of comfort, not only of the aristocracy but of new classes – financiers, merchants, woolmasters, franklins, master-craftsmen, millers, even farmers. Hearths with chimneys had taken the place in rich men's houses of sooty open fires; Flemish glass had appeared in traceried windows; dovecots, fishponds and nut-alleys were laid out in parks and gardens; manorhouses and fine merchants' dwellings, with private bedrooms and plastered walls, were rising in place of the old gloomy fortresses where men and beasts had slept together on filthy, rush-strewn floors in draughty halls, full of smoke and stink. Yet such signs of progress struck moralists like the poet William Langland as symptoms of a diseased society; of a selfish decline from the virtues of austerer days:

> 'Ailing is the hall each day in the week
> Where the lord nor the lady liketh not to sit.
> Now hath each rich man a rule to eaten by himself
> In a privy parlour, for poor men's sake,
> Or in a chamber with a chimney, and leave the chief hall
> That was made for meals and men to eaten in.'

All this was the result of an advance in civilization, arts and sciences. Exchange of goods and merchandise had thrown the career open to the talents. In every city a race of men had arisen who pursued money-making as an end in itself, who bought and sold not primarily to supply the consumer with goods but to increase their stock of money and use it for making more. Usury, forestalling, regrating, making a corner in commodities, and artificially lowering market-prices in order to buy and raising them in order to sell – all the practices which the Church had taught were unchristian and unneighbourly – were pursued as a profession by men who made fortunes by doing so and put ordinary folk out of countenance by extravagant living and the grandeur of their ways. Merchants, whose grandfathers or even fathers had been simple craftsmen or serfs, were addressed by their fellow townsmen as worshipful or sire, wore scarlet robes and costly furs as masters and liverymen of monopolistic merchant companies founded originally to protect and foster honest craftsmanship, but since grown into exclusive chartered societies of wealthy entrepreneurs – Mercers, Drapers and Goldsmiths, Grocers, Fishmongers and Vintners, Skinners, Salters, Leathersellers and Ironmongers – famed for their lavish hospitality and elaborate ritual and pageantry. Instead of mixing socially with their employees they hobnobbed with lords and even princes; Sir Henry Pickard, Master of the Vintners Company, on one day in 1364 entertained four kings to dinner in the livery hall.[1] The bitterest hatred of the 'good' Parliament was reserved for another vintner, Richard Lyons, whose memorial brass, as recorded by Stow, depicted him with a 'little beard forked, a gown girt down to his feet of branched damask wrought with the likeness of flowers, a large purse on his right side hanging in a belt from his left shoulder'. With his patron, Lord Latimer, the Treasurer, he was accused of 'buying up all the merchandise that came into England and setting prices at their own pleasure, whereby they made such a scarcity of things saleable that the common sort of people could scarcely live'.

Not all great merchants were crooks; even Lyons was probably maligned. By their own standards most of them were worthy, if self-important, men whose bond could be trusted by their fellows; they could hardly have continued to succeed otherwise. Yet there was a widespread feeling that vintners diluted wine, that woolmongers cheated wool-growers, that grocers and corn-merchants

[1] Of France, Scotland, Denmark and Cyprus – the first two being then prisoners in England.

301

sold false measure, that those who lent money to the Crown cheated the taxpayer, and that if a man had grown rich by trade he must be a rogue. And some of those who had made money out of the French wars were vulgar upstarts with extravagant standards of display and notorious for jobbery and corruption. 'Soapmongers and their sons for silver,' wrote the indignant Langland, 'are made knights.' 'Covetise hath dominion over all things,' complained his fellow poet, Gower; 'there is no city or good town where Trick does not rob to enrich himself. Trick at Bordeaux, Trick at Seville, Trick at Paris buys and sells; Trick has his ships and servants, and of the noblest riches, Trick has ten times more than other folk.'

Running through society, including the Church, was this sense of division, strife and covetousness. 'Avarice,' a preacher said, 'makes men fight one another like dogs over a bone.' By its side went 'the foul sin of pride'. Both the old ruling class and the new vied in the extravagance of their clothes, feasts and entertainments; 'in such manner they spent and wasted their riches with abuses and ludicrous wantonness that the common voice of the people ex-claimed'. The age was marked by absurd fashions in clothes; peaked and curled shoes with toes so long that their wearers were sometimes forced to walk upstairs backwards or hand their shoes to their pages to carry; ladies' fantastic and towering head-dresses; the mincing gait, long hair and trailing sleeves of the young courtiers who often squandered as much on their pampered bodies as would have fed and clothed a whole village. Contrasted with 'the gay robes, the soft sheets, the small shirtes' of the rich was the peasant, with his garment of hodden grey, living on cold cabbage, bacon and penny ale; his wattle-and-log hut full of holes; the poor Norfolk deerstalker whose feet were so putrified by the dungeons of Norwich castle that he could not walk at his trial, and his eight fellow-prisoners who died in Northampton gaol from hunger, thirst and want. 'I have no penny,' declared Langland's Piers Plowman,

> 'pullets for to buy
> Neither geese nor gris but two green cheeses,
> A few curds and cream and a cake of oats,
> And two loaves of beans and bran to bake for my bairns.'

To him it seemed a denial of Christianity that the honest poor should be defrauded. His heart was stirred and his indignation roused for 'prisoners in pits' and poor folk in cottages 'charged with children and chief lord's rent', and country women 'rising with rue in winter nights to rock the cradle',

'To card and to comb to clout and to wash; . . .
Many the children and nought but a man's hands
to clothe and feed them and few pennies taken.'

Out of the air of fourteenth-century England, with all its glaring inequalities, arose a popular conviction – so strangely contrasted with the assumptions of the warrior and prelate class – that 'the peasant maintained the state of the world' and was receiving less than justice. It was put in its highest form by Langland, the underlying theme of whose poem on the divine mercy and forgiveness of God was that Christ's sacrifice demanded from men in return just living and just dealing – honest work and loving kindness:

'For we are all Christ's creatures and of his coffers rich
And brethren of one blood as well beggars as earls; . . .
Therefore love we as true brethren and each man laugh on
    the other,
And of that each man can spare give aid when it is needed,
And every man help the other, for go hence we all shall.'

He himself examined his conscience on this issue, comparing his idle life as a chantry clerk with that of the peasant folk among whom he had grown up. 'Can you,' Reason asked him,

'cock up haycocks and pitch them in the cart?
Or can you handle a scythe or make a heap of sheaves?
Or keep my corn in my croft from pickers and stealers?
Can you shape a shoe, cut clothes or take care of cattle?
Can you hedge or harrow or herd the hogs or geese?
Or any kind of craft the community needs?'

Langland's poem voiced the recurring English reaction to the contrast between ill-used wealth and undeserved destitution, with its characteristic resolve, not to destroy society, but to redress the balance. Though it never seems to have attained the dignity of an illuminated manuscript – the *imprimatur* of fashionable esteem in that intensely aristocratic age – for a work written before printing by a man without rank or fortune it had an astonishing success. Some sixty copies have survived and, since it circulated among the poor and lowly, many more must have perished. Overlooked by the rich like *A Pilgrim's Progress* of a later age, its readers and copyists were probably parish priests – for it is hardly likely to have appealed much to friars – and it may have been through them and their sermons that the name of its humble peasant hero and his identification with the crucified Christ became so widely known. At the end of the fourteenth and the beginning of the fifteenth century there appeared on the nave walls of parish churches in southern England a number of paintings, crude and almost certainly executed by local hands, of Christ naked, lacerated and bleeding, with a carpenter's tools – mallet, hammer, knife, axe, pincers, horn and wheel – haloed round his head. This figure of 'Christ of the Trades' is to be found in churches as far apart as Pembrokeshire and Suffolk. Many more probably disappeared during the Reformation; among the best preserved are those at Ampney St Mary in the Cotswolds – not far from the hillside on which Langland saw silhouetted the tower of Truth – at Hessett in Suffolk and at Stedham in Sussex. In the first, the labouring Christ faces a painting of the hero of knightly chivalry, St George slaying the dragon; in the last, of the Virgin sheltering the congregation under her cloak.

*   *   *

There was a wide gap between the patient, Christ-like craftsman and peasant of the wall-paintings of Langland's dream, and the angry labourer refusing service for his lord, cursing landlords, monks and lawyers and fingering his bow. It was not hard to inflame uneducated men with a sense of injury, and it was not the selfless side of human nature that was inflamed. The poet himself was well aware of it. 'Then,' he wrote,

> 'would Wastour not work but wandren about . . .
> Labourers, that have no land to live on but their hands,
> Deigned not to dine today on yesterday's cabbage.
> No penny ale may please them nor no piece of bacon,
> But if it be fresh flesh or fish fried or baked.'

He depicted the runagate villein, demanding ever higher wages, who, when refused,

'would wail the time that ever he was workman born;
Then curseth he the King and all his Council with him
That lay down such laws and labourers to grieve.'

Parliament was being flouted and the Statute of Labourers made a dead letter by surly villeins standing idle in the fields or tramping in angry companies to the nearest town to sell their labour to those who would pay highest for it. Phrases like 'Stand together!' 'Make a good end of what hath been begun!' passed from shire to shire, and wandering agitators preached incendiary sermons on village greens. 'Things will never go well in England,' proclaimed the defrocked hedge-priest and demagogue, John Ball, 'so long as goods be not in common and so long as there be villeins and gentlemen. By what right are they whom we call lords greater than we?' 'We are formed,' he declared, 'in Christ's likeness and they treat us like beasts.'

It was an age of war and violence; war always breeds violence. Resentment amongst the labouring classes against their oppressors was not confined to England. In the middle of the century the Roman mob had risen under the demagogue Cola di Rienzi; a decade later occurred the terrifying *jacquerie* in northern France. Wherever men were brought together in large numbers to serve masters who catered for the luxuries of the rich, the spirit of rebellion was present. In 1378 the oppressed wool-carders of Florence revolted against the merchant oligarchs of the city, stormed the palazzo of the Commune and installed one of their members as Gonfalonier of Justice. A year later the weavers of Ghent and Bruges and the Flemish cloth towns had risen and, under a second van Artevelde, son of Edward III's old ally, were still defying their count and the French King.

In England, unrest had so far mainly taken the form of mass withdrawals of labour-services, particularly in places where the lord was an impersonal ecclesiastical corporation. In 1378, after the jurymen of Harmsworth, Middlesex – the property of a Norman abbey – had defied the lord's steward by returning a false verdict in favour of their fellow villeins who had absented themselves from the previous year's haymaking, the villagers deliberately opened the river sluices to flood the hay. There were mob rescues of fugitive bondsmen as they were being haled back to their 'villein nests', and armed assemblies by night to poach the lord's woods and slay his game. The labour laws, too, help to explain the passion and vehemence of some of these sudden explosions of rustic wrath, often on seemingly trivial pretexts. Englishmen were not prepared to suffer the indignity of being branded on the forehead with an 'F' for 'falsehood' because they took day-hire or demanded more than the inadequate statutory wage allowed by Parliament. As far back as the year before Poitiers, when feeling against this form of class legislation was running particularly high, the peasants from the villages round Oxford joined the townsmen in a murderous attack on the university – later known as St Scholastica's Day – distinguishing themselves by their savagery and furious cries of 'Havak, havoc, smygt faste, gyf good knock!'

During the opening years of Richard's reign such riots had grown ominously in number. They were fomented by the egalitarian sermons of friars and wandering priests like John Ball, who for the past twenty years had been tramping the country preaching, in defiance of the ecclesiastical authorities, against the rich 'possessioners' of Church and State. In the words of the chronicler Walsingham, he preached 'those things which he knew would be pleasing to the common people, speaking evil both of ecclesiastical and temporal lords, and won the good will of the common people rather than merit in the sight of God. For he taught that tithes ought not to be paid unless he who gave them was richer than the parson who received them. He also taught that tithes and oblations should be withheld if the parishioner was known to be a better man than the priest.' Forbidden to preach in church, he continued to do so in streets, villages and fields until he got himself excommunicated. Nothing, however, stopped him and, though he several times suffered imprisonment, as soon as he got out he started again. He also took to circulating inflammatory letters full of dark riddles and rhymes calling on the virtuous poor to prepare for the day when they could fall on their oppressors. 'John Ball, St Mary's priest,' ran one, 'greeteth well all manner of men and biddeth them in the name of the Trinity, Father, Son and Holy Ghost, stand manlike together in truth, and help truth, and truth shall help you.'

*　　　　*　　　　*

On top of this strained situation came the demand for a new and crushing tax. Like all medieval peoples the English tended to regard taxes as a form of robbery and injustice. The evolution of their polity had turned largely on their rulers' recognition that the consent of the taxed to new imposts could only be won by allowing them a share in their imposition. When, Magna Carta having placed limitations on the feudal taxation of land, imposts had been levied on personal wealth and merchandise – moveables, as they were called – the same rule had been adopted.

Superseding the feudal lord's right to tallage at will, the principle that the subject should be party to the fiscal burdens imposed on him had been applied at every stage of the tax-structure. Whenever Parliament agreed that a fifth, tenth or fifteenth should be levied on moveables, justices had been sent into every county to assess the local proportion payable with representative knights from every hundred who, in turn, met the representatives of every vill, where a jury of inquest swore to the number, quantity and value of taxable goods in the township. Shortly before Crécy, as a result of an agreement between Exchequer officials and representatives of the localities, a fixed proportion of the subsidy rate voted by Parliament had been allocated to every county, hundred and township. During Edward III's reign, which lasted fifty years, vast sums were raised by this method for the war with France, which, after the victorious 1340s and 1350s, ceased to finance itself and forced Government and Parliament to seek ever new ways of raising money.

In 1371 the latter adopted the novel device of a tax on every parish in England at a standard rate. Six years later a still more revolutionary innovation was adopted by Edward's last Parliament. This was a poll-tax of fourpence a head on the entire lay adult population except beggers. This 'tallage of groats', as it was called, mulcting the poorest at the same rate as the richest, proved intensely unpopular and very hard to collect. But it appealed to a Parliament of landowners and employers, since for the first time it imposed a direct fiscal burden on the peasant and unpropertied wage-earner.

Three years after Richard II's accession, faced by the Government's now desperate need, a new Parliament, meeting at Northampton in the autumn of 1380, imposed the tax for a third time, trebling the rate per head. For a poor rustic householder with a large family who might have to defray as well the tax of several aged or female relatives, this was a crushing burden. Reflecting the belief of the rich that the labour-shortage caused by the Black Death had placed 'the wealth of the kingdom in the hands of artisans and labourers', it not only showed astonishing ignorance of the circumstances of 'common folk whose occupations standeth in grobbying about the earth'; it ignored the principle for which Parliament had long contended: that there should be no taxation without representation and consent. For the peasantry and town-artisans, on whom the tax bore so hardly, were completely unrepresented in a Parliament of magnates, prelates, landowners, merchants and lawyers.

The consequence of the shilling poll-tax was a wholesale falsification by the villages of southern England of their tax-returns. When these reached the commissioners appointed to collect the money, it seemed as though the population had shrunk by a third since the poll-tax of two years before. The amount brought in fell far below what was expected, and the Government was furious. On 16 March 1381 the Council found that the local collectors had been guilty of gross negligence and favouritism, and appointed a new commission to scrutinize the lists and enforce payment from evaders.

The decision was received with universal execration. It was spoken of as a corrupt job engineered for the private profit of the head of the commission of revision, John Legge, a serjeant-at-law, and of the Treasurer, Sir Robert Hales – 'Hob the robber', as he was called. When news of a further descent of tax assessors reached the villages, the ignorant supposed that a new tax was to be levied on top of that already paid. Everywhere in the populous counties of the south-east, rustic opinion was at boiling point against tax-collectors, escheators, jurymen, lawyers and royal officials in general and against the Chancellor and Treasurer in particular, and, illogically enough, for he was no longer actively engaged in government but absent on a mission in Scotland, the young King's hated uncle, John of Gaunt.

No one in authority treated the dissatisfaction of the peasantry very seriously. But when at the end of May the new poll-tax commissioner for Essex, Thomas Bampton, appeared at Brentwood with two serjeants-at-arms to open enquiries into the returns for the hundred of Barstaple, he was met by the representatives of the defaulting townships with a sullen refusal to pay. They possessed, they said, their receipt for the subsidy and would not pay a penny more. But it was the fishermen and fowlers of the Thames estuary – the men of the sea and salt-water creeks – who provided the spark which fired the revolution of working-class England. Summoning to their aid their neighbours from Corringham and Stanford-le-Hope, the men of Fobbing-by-Tilbury met Bampton's threats of arrest with open violence, and with sticks and stones drove him and his men out of the town.

*   *   *

This was more than the Government could ignore. On Sunday 2 June, the Chief Justice of the Common Pleas, Sir Robert Belknap, descended on Brentford with a commission of trailbaston and an escort of pikesmen. His business was to punish the rioters and hang the ringleaders. He found the place in a ferment. For by now the rebellious fishermen had prevailed on the entire neighbourhood to rise. Armed with staves, pitchforks and bows, a mob surrounded the judge, seized and burnt his papers and made him swear on his knees never to hold another commission. They then murdered his three clerks and three local tax-assessors or jurymen whose names they had made him reveal. Sticking their heads on poles they bore them in triumph round the villages of south-east Essex, while the terrified Belknap fled back to London.

On the same day trouble began on the other side of the Thames.

At Erith in Kent a band of rioters broke into the monastery of Lesnes and made the abbot swear to support them. The ringleaders then crossed the river to take counsel of the men of Essex. During the next few days rebellion spread northwards across the county as rioters carried their messages from parish to parish. Everywhere government agents were attacked, their houses plundered and their records and papers thrown into courtyard or street and burnt. The admiral of the Essex coast, Edmund de la Mare of Peldon, and the sheriff, John Sewall of Coggeshall, had their homes sacked, the former's papers being carried on a pitchfork at the head of the triumphant fishermen. At every manor visited, a bonfire was made of all charters and manorial rolls.

It was as though the whole system of law and government, built up over centuries, was being repudiated by the common people. Yet though damage to property was widespread, there was comparatively little loss of life, most of the local lords managing to escape. The chief escheator of the county was murdered, as well as a number of Flemish merchants in Colchester, where the mob rose at the approach of the peasantry. Had the Treasurer been at his home at Temple Cressing instead of in London, he would certainly have been torn to pieces; as it was, his 'very beautiful and delectable manor', as a chronicler described it, was burnt to the ground after the populace had eaten the fine fare and broached 'the three tuns of good wine' which he had laid in for an impending meeting of the chapter-general of the Order of St John of Jerusalem, of which he was Master.

Meanwhile trouble was growing in Kent. On the day after the assault on the Chief Justice at Brentwood, two serjeants-at-arms acting for Sir Simon Burley, the King's tutor, arrested a respected burgess of Gravesend on the ground that he was a runaway serf. When the townsfolk declined to pay £300 for his manumission – at least £15,000 in today's purchasing-power – the poor man was sent to the dungeons of Rochester castle. Two days later, on Wednesday 5 June, heartened by the arrival of a hundred insurgents from Essex, the people of all the towns and villages on the south bank of the river between Erith and Gravesend rose in rebellion. They were careful, however, to stress in a proclamation listing the crimes of their young sovereign's ministers that, though there were 'more kings than one in the land', they wished for none but Richard. Patriotically they added that, 'none dwelling within twelve miles of the sea should go with them but should keep the coast of the sea from enemies'.

Next day, 6 June 1381, decided the fate of Kent. At one end of the county the men of Gravesend and Dartford marched on Rochester. At the other end a commission of trailbaston, directed against tax-evaders and accompanied by the hated John Legge, was prevented from entering Canterbury. Rochester castle, though strong enough to withstand a siege for weeks, was surrendered by its Constable that afternoon after several ineffective attempts to storm it. Probably it was under-garrisoned but, like almost everyone else, the defenders were bemused by the fury and turbulence of the mob. For the rustic population of England to behave in such a way seemed something outside nature: it was as though the animals had rebelled.

Certainly the Government seemed unable to grasp the situation. Like the local authorities it remained inert throughout that critical first week of June, helplessly watching the course of events. The Chancellor, its head, was the gentle primate, Simon Thebaud of Sudbury – son of a Suffolk trader whose family had grown rich supplying the local gentry with luxury goods and developing the new rural cloth industry. He was utterly without martial instinct or experience. The King's uncles were far away; John of Gaunt was in Edinburgh negotiating a truce with the Scots, Thomas of Woodstock was in the Welsh Marches, and Edmund of Cambridge had just sailed for Portugal. On news of the outbreak a messenger had been sent to Plymouth to countermand the expedition but arrived too late. Owing to the needs of the English garrisons in France and Brittany, the country was almost denuded of troops except on the remote Scottish and Welsh borders. In the capital and the crucial south-east there were only a few hundred men-at-arms and archers guarding the King, and a small force which the old *condottiere*, Sir Robert Knollys, had started to collect in his London house to reinforce Brittany. Nothing was done to call out the country gentry and their retainers who, in the insurgent counties to the east and north of London, were paralysed with fear.

But if the Government was without an active head, the insurgents had found one. On Friday 7 May, the men of Kent marched up the Medway valley from Rochester to Maidstone, where they were welcomed by the populace who rose and plundered the richer inhabitants, murdering one of them. Here they chose as their captain one Wat Tyler. Little is known of his past, but according to Froissart he had seen service in the French wars and, it subsequently transpired, like many old soldiers, had since been earning a livelihood by highway robbery. He was clearly a mob orator of genius, for he immediately reduced to discipline the motley throng of excited peasants and artisans. And he quickly showed himself a man of action and military talent.

On the day he assumed command Tyler issued a proclamation setting out the insurgents' aims. They would admit, he said, no allegiance except to "King Richard and the true commons' – in other words, themselves – and have no king named John, a reference to the duke of Lancaster. No tax should be levied 'save the fifteenths which their fathers and forbears knew and accepted', and everyone should hold himself in readiness to march, when called upon, to remove the traitors around the King and root out and destroy the lawyers and officials who had corrupted the realm.

The rebels had not only found a military leader. They acquired a spiritual one. Among the prisoners released from Maidstone gaol was John Ball. Only a few weeks before, the long-suffering archbishop had clapped him in again, describing how he had 'slunk back to our diocese like the fox that evaded the hunter, and feared not to preach and argue both in the churches and churchyards and in markets and other profane places, there beguiling the ears of the laity by his invective and putting about such scandals concerning our person and those of other prelates and clergy and – what is worse – using concerning the Holy Father himself language such as shamed the ears of good Christians.' The irrepressible preacher now found himself free again and with a ready-made congregation of twenty thousand ragged enthusiasts after his own heart. According to Froissart who, though often an unreliable witness, visited England soon after the rising and was clearly fascinated by the whole affair, he addressed them in these terms:

'My good friends, matters cannot go well in England until all things be held in common; when there shall be neither vassals nor lords; when the lords shall be no more masters than ourselves. How ill they behave to us! For what reason do they thus hold us in bondage? Are we not all descended from the same parents, Adam and Eve? And what can they show, or what reason can they give, why they should be more masters than ourselves? They are clothed in velvet and rich stuffs, ornamented with ermine and other furs, while we are forced to wear poor clothing. They have wines, spices and fine bread, while we have only rye and the refuse of the straw; and when we drink, it must be water. They have handsome seats and manors, while we must brave the wind and rain in our labours in the field; and it is by our labours that they have wherewith to support their pomp. We are called slaves and, if we do not perform our service we are beaten, and we have no sovereign to whom we can complain or would be willing to hear us. Let us go to the King and remonstrate with him. He is young and from him we may obtain a favourable answer, and, if not, we must ourselves seek to amend our conditions.'

At the same time the preacher sent out to the villages of Kent and Essex more of his inflammatory missives:

'John Ball
Greeteth you all,
And doth you to understand
He hath rung your bell.'

Another, written under a pseudonym and addressed to the men of Essex, was subsequently found in the pocket of a rioter condemned to be hanged:

'John Schep, sometime Saint Mary's priest of York, and now of Colchester, greets well John Nameless and John the Miller and John Carter and bids them that they beware of guile in the town, and stand together in God's name, and bids Piers Plowman go to his work and chastise well Hob the Robber. And take with you John Trueman and all his fellows and more, and look sharp you to your own head and no more.

'John the Miller hath ground small, small, small.
The King's Son of Heaven shall pay for all.'

Tyler and Ball – brigand and hedgerow preacher – were the leaders 'the true commons' needed. While Ball addressed himself to his sympathizers, Tyler acted. Sending emissaries to urge the surrounding villages to rise and join him at Maidstone, he set out with several thousand followers for Canterbury. By midday on 10 June he had reached the city, where he was greeted with enthusiasm by the inhabitants, all those, that is, who had nothing to lose. On enquiring whether there were any traitors in the town, he was directed to the houses of the local notables, three of whom he had executed on the spot. Then, having burnt the judicial and financial records of the shire, beaten up the sheriff and sacked the castle, letting out the prisoners from the gaols, he and his followers poured, a vast tumultuous multitude, into the cathedral during Mass. Here with one voice they cried out to the monks to elect a new Arch-bishop of Canterbury in place of Sudbury whom they declared to be a traitor and 'about to be beheaded for his iniquity'. They also extracted an oath of fealty to the King and true commons from the Mayor and corporation and – for the summer pilgrimage season was at its height – recruited their ranks by a number of pilgrims. At the same time they dispatched agitators to the towns and villages of east Kent.

Early on Tuesday 11 June, having spent less than twenty-four hours in Canterbury and set the eastern weald and coast from Sand-wich to Appledore aflame, Tyler set off again. Reinforcements poured in as he marched. By nightfall he was back in Maidstone, having covered eighty miles in two days. Then, pausing only for the night, he marched with his entire host before dawn on the 12th for the capital, sending messengers into Sussex and the western counties to summon the commons to join him and 'close London round about'. Simultaneously on the other side of the Thames the Essex insurgents, who by now had won complete control of the county, began a parallel march under the captaincy of Thomas Farringdon, an aggrieved Londoner.

While the two hosts converged on the capital, terror reigned on either side of their march as village mobs smoked out royal and manorial officials, lawyers and unpopular landlords, breaking into their houses and burning every record they could find. They would have, they declared, 'no bondsmen in England'. Many of the gentry took to the woods, among them the poet John Gower, who afterwards recalled in his long Latin epic, *Vox Clamantis*, the pangs of hunger he suffered while living on acorns and trembling for his life in wet coppices. Others, less fearful or unpopular, made timely contributions to the 'cause' and took the oath of fidelity to the 'King and true commons'. A few, but only a few, were murdered, while others, being persons of distinction who had not done anything to make themselves unpopular, were carried off as hostages to grace Wat Tyler's entourage, including Sir Thomas Cobham and Sir Thomas Tryvet, a hero of the wars.

Meanwhile the authorities had at last resolved to act. On either the Tuesday or Wednesday Tyler's men, pouring towards the capital, were met by messengers from the King at Windsor to ask why they were raising rebellion and what they sought. Their answer was that they were coming to deliver him from traitors. They also presented a petition asking for the heads of the Duke of Lancaster and fourteen other notables, including the Chancellor, Treasurer and every leading member of the Government. On receipt of this the King and his advisers left hastily for London and the Tower to form a focus of resistance round which the forces of order could rally. The King's mother and her ladies, who had been on a summer pilgrimage to the Kentish shrines, also set out for the same place of refuge. On the way they encountered the rebel vanguard. Yet, though greatly frightened, they were subjected to nothing worse than a little ribald jesting and were allowed to continue their journey to the capital. Here the Mayor, William Walworth, after escorting his sovereign to the Tower, was busy putting the city into a state of defence.

That evening the Kentish host encamped on the Blackheath heights, looking down across the Thames to the distant city. On the opposite bank, the Essex men took up their station in the Mile End fields outside the suburb of Whitechapel and about a mile to the east of the walls and the Aldgate. Some of the less exhausted Kentish rebels continued as far as Southwark where, welcomed by the local mob, they burnt a bawdy house rented by some Flemish women from Mayor Walworth and let out the prisoners from the Marshalsea and King's Bench. Finding the drawbridge in the centre of London Bridge raised against them, they went on to Lambeth where they sacked the Archbishop's palace and the house of John Imworth, warden of the Marshalsea.

It was not only the proletariat of Southwark who sympathised with the insurgents. There were thousands of journeymen, apprentices and labourers inside the city walls who did so too. On the Mayor's orders the gates had been closed and entrusted to the aldermen and watch of the adjacent wards. But there were bitter rivalries among the city's rulers. The victualling interests were at daggers drawn with the older merchants, drapers and mercers who, employing labour on a large scale, favoured a policy of free trade and low-priced food in order to keep down wages and feed their journeymen and apprentices cheaply – a matter of vital importance to them since the labour shortage caused by the Black Death. Both were monopolists but, to overthrow their rivals, the victuallers had formed an alliance with the discontented city proletariat – wage-earners and small craftsmen – who regarded their employers and the capitalists who controlled the market for their handiwork in much the same light as the villeins regarded their lords. Among three aldermen whom the Mayor despatched to urge the insurgents to keep the peace was a certain John Horne, a fishmonger who, separating himself from his companions, sought a private interview with Tyler and secretly promised his support. When he returned to London he not only assured the Mayor that the marchers were honest patriots who would do the city no harm but, under cover of darkness, smuggled three agitators across the river to stir up the mob.

Earlier that evening an emissary from the rebel camp had travelled by boat from Greenwich to London to seek an interview with the King and Council. This was the Constable of Rochester castle, Sir John Newton, who for the past week had been a prisoner of the insurgents. Brought into the presence and given leave to speak, he explained that, though his captors would do the King no harm, they were determined to meet him face to face to communicate certain matters of which he had no charge to speak. Since they held his children as hostages and would slay them if he failed to return, he begged for an answer that would appease them and show that he had delivered his message.

To this after some hesitation the Council agreed. Next morning at prime the King and his lords embarked in five barges for Greenwich. Here, on the shore below Blackheath, the Kentish men, after a hungry and sleepless night, were assembled in battle array under two great banners of St George. While they waited, Mass was celebrated, it being Corpus Christi day, and afterwards John Ball preached, taking as his text the old popular rhyme:

> 'When Adam delved and Eve span
> Who was then the gentleman?'

According to the St Albans chronicler, 'he strove to prove that from the beginning all men were created equal by nature, and that servitude had been introduced by the unjust oppression of wicked men against God's will, for, if it had pleased Him to create serfs, surely in the beginning of the world He would have decreed who was to be a serf and who a lord . . . Wherefore they should be prudent men, and, with the love of a good husbandman tilling his fields and uprooting and destroying the tares which choke the grain, they should hasten to do the following things. First, they should kill the great lords of the kingdom; second, they should slay lawyers, judges and jurors; finally they should root out all those whom they knew to be likely to be harmful to the commonwealth in future. Thus they would obtain peace and security, for, when the great ones had been removed, there would be equal liberty and nobility and dignity and power for all.' 'When he had preached this and much other madness,' wrote the disgusted chronicler, 'the commons held him in such high favour that they acclaimed him the future Archbishop and Chancellor of the realm.'

Whether it was this sermon or the presence of the Archbishop in the royal barge or the fact that the Kentishmen had not breakfasted, they greeted the King's arrival with such a tumult of shouting that he was unable to make himself heard. 'Sirs,' he kept calling across the water as the rowers rested on their oars just out of reach of the frantic multitude, 'what do you want? Tell me now that I have come to talk to you.' But as the crowd steadily grew more

317

threatening, fearing lest some of the bowmen might start to shoot, the earl of Salisbury – by far the most experienced soldier present – ordered the boats to put out into midstream and return to the Tower.

At that both the Kentish host and the Essex men, who had been watching from the other shore, set up a great shout of 'Treason' and, with their banners and pennants, moved off towards London. Access to the city's markets and provision shops had by now become essential if they were not to have to disperse through hunger – a fact on which the authorities were counting. Within the city, processions of clergy were marching through the streets praying for peace, while the crowds of sympathisers with the insurgents were gathering in the poorer lanes and alleys. For, though the city gates were still barred against them, the agitators whom Horne had slipped into the city had not been idle. As Wat Tyler's men neared the southern approaches to the bridge they were again met by this liberal-minded fishmonger waving a royal standard which he had procured by a trick from the town clerk. And as, headed by this emblem of loyalty and respectability, they surged on to the bridge, the drawbridge in the midst of its shops and houses was lowered to them by the alderman of the Billingsgate ward. About the same time another alderman of the opposition faction let in the Essex men through the Aldgate.

Once the head of the rebel columns was in possession of the southern and eastern entrances the whole multitude poured in to the city, while the apprentices and journeymen and the labouring poor of the slums flocked into the streets to greet them. For a time the newcomers were too busy eating, drinking and gaping at the city sights to do much harm. But presently, refreshed by several huge barrels of ale which some rash philanthropists had broached in the streets, and incited by the apprentices who had old scores to pay off against John of Gaunt, they set up a cry of 'To the Savoy! To the Savoy!' The Duke might be in Edinburgh, but the superb palace he had furnished from the plunder of France – and, as many supposed, of England – stood a mile outside the western walls where the fields and gardens sloped down to the riverside from the Strand that linked London to Westminster. Thither the men of

Kent, with thousands of excited apprentices – a great company with torches – made their way in an angry tumult, breaking into the Fleet prison on the way and letting out the criminals while the Duke's servants fled as the shouting came nearer.

No time was wasted. In the general desire for justice or revenge even plundering was forbidden. Everything in the great house, was hurled out of the windows – tapestry, sheets, coverlets, beds – and hacked or torn to pieces. Then the building was set on fire and burnt to the ground. At the height of the fire there was an explosion caused by three barrels of gunpowder, which were thrown into the flames in the belief that they contained specie. Some of the rioters afterwards continued towards Westminster where they destroyed the house of the under-sheriff of Middlesex and let the prisoners out of the gaol. Others, on their way back to the city, broke into the laywers' home in the Temple, tore the tiles off the roof and took all the books, rolls and remembrances from the students' cupboards to make a bonfire. They also fired some shops and houses which had recently been built in Fleet Street, declaring that never again should any house deface the beauty of that favourite country walk of the Londoners. Those who had gone on to Westminster returned by way of Holborn, setting light to the houses of several 'traitors' pointed out to them by their London comrades and breaking open Newgate still further to enlarge their company. Meanwhile the men of Essex descended on the priory of St John's, Clerkenwell, the headquarters of the Knights Hospitallers just outside the city's northern wall. Here they burnt the priory and hospital and murdered seven Flemings who had taken sanctuary in the church.

That night, while the insurgents camped round the royal fortress in the open spaces of Tower Hill and St Catherine's wharf and while their leaders drew up lists of persons to be liquidated, the King and Council debated long and anxiously what was to be done. Since the morning their position had changed dramatically for the worse; instead of waiting behind London's walls while the rebels starved outside, they themselves were hemmed in the Tower, and the city it was supposed to dominate was in possession of a fanatic, uncontrollable mob. From a garret in one of the turrets into which he climbed, the boy King could see twenty or thirty fires burning in different parts of the town. Beyond, the whole of the home counties to south and east were in revolt, while, unknown as yet to the beleaguered Council, the revolutionary ferment had spread that afternoon into Hertfordshire and Suffolk, where burgesses and bondsmen had risen together against the monks of England's two most famous abbeys, St Albans and Bury.

The key to the situation lay, however, in the capital. If the mob who had taken possession of it could be defeated, the flames of revolt might be put out elsewhere. But, with London lost and the court imprisoned inside it, there was nothing round which the forces of order could rally. Mayor Walworth, a bluff and vigorous man, urged an immediate sally against the insurgents while they were sleeping off the effects of their evening's debauch. There were six hundred armed men-at-arms and archers in the Tower and a hundred or so more in Sir Robert Knollys's house and garden; with a bold front they would probably be joined by all the law-abiding in London. Only a small minority of the insurgents wore armour; if the loyal forces struck at once, thousands might be slain as they slept. But the earl of Salisbury, who had fought at Crécy and Poitiers, thought otherwise. Once fighting began in the narrow streets and lanes, the rebels' immense superiority in numbers would tell and total disaster might ensue. 'If we should begin a thing which we cannot achieve,' he said, 'we should never recover and we and our heirs would be disinherited and England would become a desert.' Instead, he offered the Ulysses-like counsel that an attempt should be made to induce the rebels to disperse by fair words and promises, which could afterwards be repudiated as obtained under duress.

An earlier attempt that evening to persuade them to do so by putting up the King to address them from the ramparts and offer a free pardon to all who should go home had been shouted down in derision. Some more signal mark of royal trust was needed if the populace were to be appeased. It was, therefore, proposed that the King should offer to confer with the rebels in the Mile End fields and to ride out there next morning through their midst with such of his lords as were not expressly marked down for execution. While under cover of this bold move the crowds were drawn away

from the Tower, the Archbishop and Treasurer and John of
Gaunt's son and heir, young Henry Bolingbroke, earl of Derby,
could be smuggled out to safety by water.

The plan depended on the King's readiness to take the risk.
But, though he appeared a little pensive, the boy was ready and
even eager. He was now fourteen, and it was something to find that
at last all the great lords and counsellors around him looked to him
for leadership. As soon as it was light a proclamation was made from
the walls and soon afterwards, surrounded by an immense multitude of excited country folk, the royal cortège set out along the
Brentwood road for Mile End. But many of the Londoners stayed
behind to watch the Tower, for the rebels' leaders were not so easily
fooled. When the boat by which their intended victims attempted
to escape appeared, it was forced to put back as soon as it emerged
from the water-gate.

Nor did the royal ride to Mile End prove easy or pleasant. At
one moment the Essex leader, Thomas Farringdon, a highly
excitable man, seized the King's bridle, demanding to be avenged
on that false traitor Prior Hales, the Treasurer, who he said had
deprived him of his property by fraud. So threatening was the
crowd that the King's half-brothers, the earl of Kent and Sir John
Holland, finding themselves at the edge of the throng, seized the
opportunity to gallop away and escape into the open country to the
north. When, however, the royal party arrived in the Mile End
fields, the simple country folk who were waiting there knelt before
the King crying, 'Welcome, our lord King Richard, if it pleases
you we will have no other King but you.' It was like the scene in the
ballads when the sovereign whom Robin Hood and his men had
captured revealed his identity and promised to restore to every
honest man his own.

It must have seemed to many present that such a golden time
had come when their young King – the son of England's dead hero,
the Black Prince – announced that he would grant all their demands.
He promised the abolition of serfdom, of villein services and
seigneurial market monopolies, and that all holders of land in
villeinage should henceforth become free tenants at the modest
rent of fourpence an acre a year. Nor did he only promise them all

321

free pardons and an amnesty if they would return quietly to their villages, but offered to give a royal banner to the men of every county and place them under his special protection and patronage. His words, as Froissart put it, 'appeased well the common people, such as were simple and good plain men'. They rather took the wind, however, out of their leaders' sails. The latter, therefore, returned to the charge. 'The commons,' Tyler told the King, 'will that you suffer them to take and deal with all the traitors who have sinned against you and the law.' To which young Richard replied that all should have due punishment as could be proved by process of law to be traitors.

This, however, was scarcely what Tyler and his fellow-leaders wanted. While the King, surrounded by the better disposed of his humbler subjects, was helping to set them on their way to their distant villages, the two captains of the Commons of Kent and Essex hurried back with a band of picked followers to the Tower where a large crowd was still waiting outside the gates, clamouring for the Archbishop's and Treasurer's blood. Pushing through them they succeeded in bluffing their way into the fortress itself, either through the treachery of the guards or, more probably, because, with the King and his lords expected back at any moment, the portcullis was up and no one knew what to do. Fraternising with the soldiers, shaking their hands and stroking their beards, the crowd pressed after their leaders into the royal apartments, shouting for the traitors' blood. In their search the King's bed was hacked to pieces and the Princess of Wales subjected to such rude treatment that she was borne off in a dead faint by her pages and put into a boat on the river. John Legge, the serjeant-at-law who had drawn up the poll-tax commission, and three of his clerks, the Duke of Lancaster's physician, a Franciscan friar named Appleton, and several others were found. The Duke's son, Henry Bolingbroke – who eighteen years later was to become King – was more fortunate, being saved by the resource of one of his father's retainers. The Archbishop and Treasurer were taken in the chapel where, expecting death, the former had just received the confession of the latter and administered the last rites. Dragged by the mob into the courtyard and across the cobbles to Tower Hill, they were summarily beheaded across a log of wood. It was the third time in the country's history that an Archbishop of Canterbury had been assaulted at the altar and brutally done to death.

After that, all pretence of moderation and order vanished. While the primate's head, stuck on a pike and crowned with his mitre, was being borne round the city before being set over the gateway to London Bridge – the traditional place for traitors – and the King, shunning the desecrated Tower, made his way with his escort to the royal Wardrobe at Baynard's Castle near St Paul's where his mother had taken refuge, the riff-raff of the capital and the peasants' army ran riot in the streets, forcing passers-by to cry, 'With King Richard and the true commons' and putting everyone to death who refused. By nightfall 'there was hardly a street in the city in which there were not bodies lying of those who had been slain'. The chief victims were the Flemish merchants who were hunted through the streets and killed wherever found; more than a hundred and fifty are said to have perished, including thirty-five who had taken shelter in St Martin-in-the-Vintry and who were dragged from the altar and beheaded outside on a single block. Every disorderly person who had old grudges to pay off or property he coveted seized his opportunity; Alderman Horne, with a mob at his heels, paraded the streets bidding anyone who wanted justice against a neighbour to apply to him. Tyler himself hunted down and cut off the head of the great monopolist, Richard Lyons, whose servant he was at one time said to have been, while his lieutenant, Jack Straw, led a gang to burn the home of the murdered Treasurer, Sir Robert Hales, at Highbury. Far away in Suffolk at about the same hour the head of Sir John Cavendish, Chief Justice of the King's Bench, was being carried on a pike through the rejoicing streets of Bury St Edmunds, while his friend and neighbour, the prior of the great abbey, who had been hunted all day on the Mildenhall heaths, cowered before his captors awaiting the trial that was to lead to his death next morning. Later, on the Saturday, when his head, too, was borne back on a pike to Bury, the crowd carried the heads of the two friends round the town together, making them converse and kiss one another.

Dawn on Saturday 15 June saw the nadir of the once proud

kingdom whose princes a quarter of a century before had led the French King captive through the streets of London. From Lincolnshire, Leicester and Northampton to the coasts of Kent and Sussex its richest and most populous counties were aflame, while, as the news spread of London's capture and the King and Council's humiliation, other shires as far as Cornwall and Yorkshire crackled with rumours of impending rebellion. The greatest officers of state – the Primate and Chancellor, Treasurer, and Chief Justice – had all been brutally done to death, and everywhere magnates and gentry were flying to the woods or, isolated and helpless in their homes, awaiting the sound of mobs and the light of torches. In London riot, plunder, arson and murder had continued all night and, though thousands of law-abiding peasants had returned to their homes on receiving the King's promise, thousands more, including their leaders and all the more violent and criminal elements, were in control both of the capital and what remained of the Government.

The King spent the night at the Wardrobe in Baynard's Castle, comforting his mother. His surrender at Mile End seemed to have achieved nothing, and though thirty royal clerks had been employed all the previous afternoon copying out pardons and charters, the hard core of the insurgents remained both unsatisfied and seemingly unsatiable. Yet, since there was no other way of loosening their stranglehold, Richard resolved, regardless of the risks involved, to try again. Accordingly on the morning of Saturday the 15th he proposed a further meeting with the Commons and their leaders. This time the rendezvous was to be the cattle market at Smithfield, just outside the city's northwestern walls close to the church of St Bartholomew the Great and the smoking ruins of the priory of St John's, Clerkenwell.

Before proceeding there the King rode to Westminster Abbey to pray at the shrine of his ancestor, St Edward the Confessor. Murder and sacrilege had been there that morning before him, a mob having broken into the sanctuary, tearing from the pillars of the shrine to which he had clung in terror the marshal of the Marshalsea – a man hated by the populace as being 'without pity as a torturer'. The monks of Westminster and the canons of

St Stephen's met Richard at the abbey gates, barefooted and carrying their cross. For a while all knelt before the desecrated shrine
while the young King confessed to the abbey's anchorite and
received absolution, afterwards repairing to the little oratory in the
royal closet of St Stephen's chapel to pray before a golden image of
the Virgin which had been a treasured possession of his family since
the days of Henry III and was believed to have special protective
powers. It is possible that it is this deeply moving incident in the
King's life rather than his coronation four years earlier that is
depicted in the Wilton Diptych – the young Plantagenet, robed
and crowned, kneeling before the figures of St Edward, King
Edmund the Martyr and St John the Baptist, whose hand rests on
the boy's shoulder and all three of whom seem to be gazing fixedly
and sternly as at some threatening force, while a winged galaxy of
guardian angels, wearing Richard's badge of the white hart, gather
round the Virgin and her child beneath the banner of St George. [1]

The King and his retainers, about two hundred strong, now
mounted and rode on to Smithfield. Because of their peril they
wore armour under their robes. They were joined at St Bartholomew's church by Mayor Walworth and a small party, while on the
opposite side of the market-place the entire insurgent army
awaited in battle order. It must by now have been about five
o'clock in the afternoon and the weather very hot.

Tyler now felt himself to be master of the kingdom. He was at
the head of a host which outnumbered by many times the little
royal band, and all day news had been coming in from every quarter
of new risings. On the previous evening he had boasted to the rebel
delegates from St Albans that he would shave the beards – by which
he meant slice off the heads – of all who opposed him, including
their abbot, and that in a few days there would be no laws in

[1] In discussing the date and occasion of this lovely painting neither Dr
Evans in her volume of the *Oxford History of English Art* nor Margaret Rickert
in her *Painting in Britain in the Middle Ages* seems to have considered this
possibility, both inclining to attribute its occasion either to Richard's coronation at the age of eleven or his re-coronation in St Stephen's chapel after his
assumption of power in 1389 at the age of twenty three. Yet, whenever painted,
the King depicted is neither a child nor a full-grown man, but unmistakably a
boy in his teens.

England save those which proceeded from his mouth. 'He came to the King,' wrote the Anonimalle chronicler, 'in a haughty fashion, mounted on a little horse so that he could be seen by the commons and carrying in his hand a dagger which he had taken from another man. When he had dismounted he half bent his knee and took the King by the hand and shook his arm forcibly and roughly, saying to him, "Brother, be of good comfort and joyful, for you shall have within the next fortnight 40,000 more of the Commons than you have now and we shall be good companions."

'When the King asked Tyler, "Why will you not go back to your own country?" the insurgent chief replied with a great oath that neither he nor his fellows would depart until they had their charter and such points . . . in their charter as they chose to demand . . . The King asked him what were the points that he wanted . . . He asked that there should be no law except the law of Winchester, and that no lord should have any lordship . . . and that the only lordship should be that of the King. That the goods of Holy Church should not remain in the hands of the religious nor of the parsons and vicars and other churchmen; but those who were in possession should have their sustenance from the endowments, and the remainder of their goods should be divided amongst their parishioners; and no bishop should remain in England save one. And that all the lands and tenements now held by them should be confiscated and shared amongst the commons, saving to them a reasonable substance. And he demanded that there should be no more bondsmen in England, no serfdom nor villeinage, but that all should be free and of one condition. And to this the King gave an easy answer, and said that he should have all that could fairly be granted saving to himself the regality of the Crown. And then he commanded him to go back to his home without further delay. And all this time that the King was speaking, no lord nor any other of his Council dared . . . to give any answer to the Commons except the King himself.

'After that Tyler, in the King's presence, called for a flagon of water to rinse his mouth because he was in such a heat, and when it was brought he rinsed his mouth in a very rude and disgusting fashion before the King; and then he made them bring him a flagon of ale of which he drank a great deal, and in the King's presence mounted his horse. At this time a yeoman of Kent, who was among the King's retinue, asked to see the said Wat, the leader of the commons; and when Wat was pointed out to him, he said openly that he was the greatest thief and robber in all Kent. Wat heard these words and commanded him to come out to him, shaking his head at him in sign of malice; but the yeoman refused to go to him for fear of the mob. At last the lords made him go out to Wat to see what he would do in the King's presence; and, when Wat saw him, he ordered one of his followers, who was riding on a horse carrying his banner displayed, to dismount and cut off the yeoman's head. But the yeoman answered that he had done nothing worthy of death, for what he had said was true and he would not deny it . . . For these words Wat would have run him through with his dagger and killed him in the King's presence, and because of this, the Mayor of London, William Walworth, reasoned with Wat for his violent behaviour and contempt done in the King's presence and arrested him. And because he arrested him, Wat struck the Mayor with his dagger in the stomach with great anger; but as God would have it, the Mayor was wearing armour and took no harm. But like a hardy and vigorous man he drew his cutlass and struck back at Wat and gave him a deep cut on the neck and then a great cut on the head. And in this scuffle a yeoman of the King's household drew his sword and ran Wat two or three times through the body, mortally wounding him. And Wat spurred his horse, crying to the commons to avenge him, and the horse carried him some four score paces, and there he fell to the ground half dead. And when the commons saw him fall and did not know for certain how it was, they began to bend their bows to shoot.'[1]

It was thirty-five years since Crécy and Neville's Cross and a quarter of a century since Poitiers, and even the youngest who had shared in these masterpieces of the bowman's art were now, by the standards of the fourteenth century, old men. Even Nájera was fourteen years away, and few of the English archers who had wrought that Pyrrhic victory can ever have returned to England. Yet there must have been at least several hundred in the insurgent host who

[1] *The Anonimalle Chronicle* (ed. V. H. Galbraith).

had served in the French and Breton wars and many thousands more who had learnt to use the long-bow at the butts after church on Sundays and were armed with the terrifying weapon – the most formidable in the world – which the Plantagenet kings had given the yeomanry of England. It seemed, as hundreds of bows were drawn in the rebel ranks, that it was going to cost the last of them his life and throne.

At that moment Richard clapped spurs into his horse and rode straight across the square towards the massed insurgents. 'Sirs,' he cried as he reined in before them, 'will you shoot your King? I am your captain. I will be your leader. Let him who loves me follow me!' The effect was electric; the expected flight of arrows never came. Instead, as the young King slowly wheeled his horse northwards towards the open country, the peasants in ordered companies followed him like the children after the piper of Hamelin.

As they did so, the Mayor galloped back into the city to rouse the loyalists and call them to rescue their sovereign. His chief adversary – Alderman Sibley who had lowered the river drawbridge two days before – arrived just before him, spreading the rumour that the whole royal party had been killed. But Walworth's appearance gave him the lie and, sickened by the plunder, murder and arson of the last forty-eight hours, the shopkeepers and wealthier citizens flocked with their arms into the streets as the sole hope of saving their homes and possessions. Mustered by the aldermen and officers of their wards and led by old Sir Robert Knollys with his archers and men-at-arms, they hurried in thousands out of the Aldersgate in pursuit of the imperilled King and his rabble following. They found them in the Clerkenwell cornfields with the boy, still unharmed, sitting on his horse in their midst, arguing with the insurgents, now leaderless and confused in the absence of Tyler who had been borne dying into St Bartholomew's hospital. While they were so occupied, Knollys quietly deployed his men, outflanking and surrounding the multitude, while a band of heavily armoured knights pushed through the crowd to the King's side.

The threat to the Crown and capital was over. The insurgents made no resistance; it was the end of a long hot day and they must

328

have been parched and exhausted. Encircled by armed men and appeased by the King's promises, even the extremists had no more fight in them and were ready to return home. He refused to listen to the proposal of some of his rescuers that, as his former captors were now at his mercy, he should order them to be massacred; 'three-fourths of them,' he is said to have replied, 'have been brought here by force and threats; I will not let the innocent suffer with the guilty.' Knollys, who was himself of yeoman birth, strongly counselled the course of mercy and helped to organise the march of the Kentish men through London to their homes.

The whole multitude now dispersed. When Richard returned to the Wardrobe amid the rejoicings of the Londoners whose Mayor he had just knighted in the Clerkenwell fields, he said to his anxious mother 'Rejoice and praise God, for today I have recovered my heritage that was lost and the realm of England also.'

*　　　　*　　　　*

Had the King fallen at Mile End or Smithfield there would have been no authority but that of the rebellious peasantry left from Yorkshire to Kent and from Suffolk to Devon. When he and Walworth so unexpectedly, and at the eleventh hour, turned the tables on Tyler, the revolution was on the point of complete success. For on the very afternoon that Richard, preparing for death, confessed and received absolution in the desecrated abbey, the fires of rebellion, fanned by the news of the previous day's massacre in the Tower and the insurgents' triumph, spread to St Albans, Cambridge and Ipswich and into Bedfordshire, the Fens and Norfolk. At St Albans, led by a local tradesman called William Grindcobbe – a brave man with a burning love of freedom – the townsfolk invaded the abbey, seized its charters and burnt them in the market-place, ripping up the confiscated millstones – symbols of the abbey's monopolistic privileges – with which the abbot had paved his chamber, while the countryfolk drained the fish-ponds and trampled down the fences enclosing the monastic woods and pastures. At Cambridge, as during that Saturday village after village rose in the Fenland, the bell of Great St Mary's brought out the mob in a riotous crusade against the university and the adjacent priory of Barnwell. Corpus Christi College, the chief owner of house-property in the town, was gutted, and the university charters, archives and library were burnt next day in the Market Square while an old woman shouted, as she flung parchment after parchment into the flames, 'Away with the learning of the clerks! Away with it!' During the weekend other risings occurred in hundreds of villages in East Anglia, the Fenland and east Midlands. In all of them justices of the peace, tax commissioners, lawyers and unpopular landlords, particularly monastic ones, were attacked, their houses sacked or burnt and their charters and court-rolls destroyed.

The most formidable of all the risings outside the capital occurred in Norfolk, the richest and most populous as well as most independent-minded county in England. In west Norfolk, where it broke out during the weekend of the King's triumph and lasted for ten days, it was without a leader and apparently quite purposeless, the one common denominator being robbery under threats of violence. Many of the victims were persons in humble circumstances, farmers, priests and village tradesmen; in only two of the 153 villages in which felonies were committed did they take the form of attacks on landlords. But in the eastern half of the county, where a leader of Tyler's calibre appeared, rebellion took a political course, though a different one from that of the home counties. Its aim, natural in so remote an area, was not the reform and control of the Government, but the setting up of an independent East Anglia. But though for a week its leader, a dyer named Geoffrey Litster, kept regal state in Norwich, with the King and Council in possession of the capital the revolution collapsed as suddenly as it had begun. By the end of June all resistance was over.

Except for the summary execution of a few ring-leaders like Tyler's lieutenant, Jack Straw, and John Starling – the Essex rioter who had decapitated Archbishop Sudbury and who was taken still carrying the sword that had done the deed – the insurgents were tried and punished by the normal processes of law. Though a large number of persons were charged with treason or crimes of violence, only about a hundred and fifty suffered the death penalty, nearly all of them after being found guilty by a local jury. Most of the ring-leaders perished, including John Ball, who was found hiding at Coventry, and John Wraw, another priest who had led the Suffolk insurgents and who tried to save his life by turning King's evidence. The noblest of all – the leader of the St Albans townsmen against the tyranny of the great abbey that held them in bondage – died with sublime courage, protesting the righteousness of his cause. 'If I die for the liberty we have won,' he said, 'I shall think myself happy to end my life as a martyr for such a cause.'

Before the end of the summer the King put a stop to further arrests and executions, and in December a general amnesty was declared. The peasants' revolt and its repression were over. Only the smouldering ashes of anger and resentment remained; that and fear of its recurrence. But for two circumstances the King would have perished with his ministers. One was his courage, the other the deep-seated loyalty to the throne which transcended the sense of injustice and desire for revenge of the peasant multitude. Fierce as were the passions aroused during 'the hurling time', as it was called, and cruel and atrocious some of the deeds done during it, the majority of those who had marched under the banner of 'King Richard and the true commons' sincerely believed that they were restoring the realm to justice and honest government and rescuing their young sovereign from traitors and extortioners. Unlike their leaders they did not seek to destroy either him or his kingdom and, even at the height of the rebellion, provided for the defence of the country. And, though they released the criminals from the jails and allowed the more savage of their companions to wreak their will on those whom they regarded as oppressors, they made no attempt to massacre their social superiors as in the French Jacquerie of a generation before. When, in their wretchedness after their feudal rulers' defeat in war, the French peasants had risen, they had loosed their vengeance on the entire ruling class, murdering, raping, torturing and mutilating every man, woman and child within their reach. In the contemporary accounts of the English peasants' revolt no instance is recorded of violence to a woman, though for three days the capital and for several weeks the richest parts of England lay at their mercy.

Yet they and their leaders had come very near to overthrowing

331

the government of the country, far nearer than the rebellious peasants of France, Flanders and Italy had ever come. They had done so because their cause was based, not on mere desperation or unthinking anger, but on certain elementary principles of justice on which, when they could free their minds from class prejudice, all Englishmen were agreed. And though they seemed to have been defeated and reduced once more to bondage, they had, in fact, as time was to show, achieved their object. When, a week after the Smithfield meeting, a delegation of peasants waited on the King at Waltham to ask for a ratification of the charters, he replied that his pledges, having been extorted by force, counted for nothing. 'Villeins you are still,' he told them, 'and villeins ye shall remain!' He was wrong. For the present the lords might enforce their rights: they could not do so permanently. The magic of their old invincibility was gone. Given arms by the Statute of Winchester and taught to use them on the battlefields of France, the peasants had tested them on the Crown itself and knew their strength. They would no longer brook servitude.

As an economic means of cultivating the soil for profit, villeinage was doomed. With such surly and mutinous labour and no police to enforce it, it proved impossible to make it pay. Faced by the growing competition of the towns the lord had to make concessions to keep his villeins on the land. And as the population began to rise again after the first annihilating waves of Black Death, the process of commuting services for money payments was resumed and paid labour increasingly took the place of servile. In other places, lords found their demesnes so hard to work that, to maintain their incomes, they were forced to let them to the wealthier and more industrious peasants. Within half a century of the revolt, even in the open-field villages of the Midlands tenant-farming with hired labour had become the norm, and hereditary servile status had ceased to have any practical significance. It was only a question of time, before the Common Law, with its bias in favour of freedom, transformed villein tenure into legally enforceable copyhold. The propertyless bondsman became the copyholder enjoying, by virtue of his copy from the manorial rolls, virtually the same protection from the King's courts and the same right to enjoy or dispose of his hereditary holding as a freeholder.

CHAPTER SEVENTEEN

Dethronement
of an Anointed King

'Such crimson tempest should bedrench
The fresh green lap of fair King Richard's land.'

Shakespeare

'The greatest theme of history still is,
and perhaps always will be, the unending
story of men's efforts to reconcile order
and liberty, the two essential ingredients
of a truly great civilization.'

B. Wilkinson

IN THE SPRING OF 1384, three years after the Peasants' Revolt, the seventeen-year-old King of England, Richard II, presided at Salisbury over a Parliament of his chief subjects and representatives of his lesser ones. As had become customary at the start of such gatherings, petitions from the subject were considered by the assembled Lords and Commons before, in their respective estates, they voted the Crown whatever additional taxes and subsidies it needed to supplement its hereditary revenues. During the debates the earl of Arundel, who was also earl of Surrey, complained in the strongest terms of the misgovernment of the realm. He was supported by the King's youngest uncle, Thomas of Woodstock, earl of Buckingham, and by Thomas Beauchamp, earl of Warwick, after Arundel the richest man in the kingdom not of royal blood.

The young King was furious. Rising from his throne, he told Arundel to go to the devil. 'If you charge me with responsibility

333

for bad governance,' he said, 'you lie in your throat.' Since his accession seven years before, the realm had been governed for him by a succession of elder persons – of whom Arundel was one – who had treated him like a child and directed its affairs regardless of the sacred attributes which it was believed God at their crowning invested Christian sovereigns. Son and grandson of the victors of Crécy and Poitiers, namesake of the crusader, Coeur de Lion, and eighth king of the Plantagenet line, Richard II had grown up with an unshakeable belief in the divine right of anointed princes. In that dreadful summer of 1381, with his capital in the hands of an infuriated peasantry and the great lords who ruled in his name panic-stricken and without resource, he had quelled the multitude solely by the magic of his royalty, riding alone in their midst while his guardians and counsellors cowered behind walls and port-cullises. Yet once the rebellion had been suppressed and the peasants dispersed to their homes, instead of allowing him to assume the powers God had granted him for the good of subjects, his guardians and counsellors had continued to keep him in tutelage.

Nor had their stewardship been attended by success. The long dragging and now profitless war with France had continued to go badly. In the year after the Peasants' Revolt the lords of the Council, with Parliament's backing, had authorised the warlike bishop of Norwich, Henry Despenser, to lead an expedition to Flanders in support of the Ghent weavers against their count and his French son-in-law, Philip of Burgundy. Yet before he could arrive, the Flemish pikemen had been routed at Roosebeke by the chivalry of France, and the bishop, after a brief, ignominious campaign, des-pite the valour of the old Cheshire *condottiere*, Sir Hugh Calveley, had been driven from the continent. This disaster to the chief buyers of England's principal product, wool, had temporarily brought her export trade to a standstill and dried up the Crown's most valuable source of additional revenue. Since then, helped by a band of French knights, the Scots had broken the peace imposed by Richard's grandfather and re-negotiated by his uncle, John of Gaunt, and had harried the English borderland. This had provoked two unavailing and costly invasions of Scotland, the first under

334

Lancaster and a second, in the summer of 1385, when the whole feudal host turned out under the nominal command of the young King, only to return after a few weeks to England, its stores exhausted and its leaders quarrelling violently.

For almost a generation, during the dotage of Edward III and the minority of his grandson, England had been without a ruling King. It was not a deprivation a medieval kingdom could afford. Defeat abroad, division in high places and near-anarchy at home had succeeded the great years of Crécy and Poitiers when the whole nation had been united under a strong and, judging by his success, divinely favoured sovereign. Instead of having one royal ruler capable of enforcing justice and maintaining order, a succession of greedy territorial magnates contended for power, each supported by adherents drawn not only from the lesser feudal barons but from the episcopal bench, the knights of the shire and the rival London trading-guilds.

Chief among the contending lords were the King's uncles, the surviving younger brothers of Richard's father, the Black Prince. Of these by far the most powerful was John of Gaunt, Duke of Lancaster, already in his middle forties – a far more advanced age then than now. Heir through his first wife, the Lady Blanche – herself of royal blood – to the four earldoms and vast domains of her father, the great Edwardian soldier, Henry Grosmont of Derby and Lancaster, he was able to raise more armed men from his estates than the King himself. Having enjoyed untrammelled power during his father's declining years, Gaunt for a time had been the most unpopular man in England, suspected by many, including his royal nephew, of designs on the throne. This was unjust for, while still exercising immense influence through his nominees on the Council, since the young King's accession he had deliberately refrained from monopolising office and had directed his ambitions to a claim through his second wife – a Spanish princess – to the throne of Castile. In pursuit of this phantom he had induced the Council to intervene in the affairs of the Iberian peninsula, where a contingent of English volunteers from his northern estates had been assisting Ferdinand of Portugal to preserve the independence of that country against King Juan of Castile – son of the Black Prince's old enemy, the bastard Don Enrico of Trastamara.

Two other of Edward III's seven sons, Edmund of Langley, earl of Cambridge and Thomas of Woodstock, earl of Buckingham, were still alive, while the grandson of their elder brother, Lionel of Clarence – the infant Roger Mortimer, son of the Princess Philippa – stood between all three royal uncles and the succession. All were masters of estates and retinues which constituted a potential challenge to the Crown. For though it had proved successful in uniting a martial nobility for a victorious and, for a time, highly profitable foreign war, Edward III's policy of marrying his sons to the heiresses of the greater feudal earldoms had resulted during his dotage and his grandson's minority in the growth of centrifugal forces beyond the capacity of the throne to contain.

Outside this divided royal family, set apart from the rest of the nation by statute and landed wealth, were the remaining earls and barons. Their right to individual summons by writ to the periodic Parliaments in which the King and his Council met the nation's representatives had, during the past half-century, gradually come to be regarded as automatic, until they by now constituted an hereditary peerage with, at least in their own opinion, an un-challengeable right to share in the royal counsels. For the past fourteen years, during Edward III's dotage and his grandson's minority, this share had grown to be greater than a consecrated King in possession of his full faculties could be expected to allow, and it was inevitable that Richard, as he approached manhood, should mean to challenge it. It was equally inevitable that those who had so long exercised his functions for him should try to retain them.

It was the King's awareness of this reluctance, and the challenge it implied to everything in which he believed, that precipitated a constitutional crisis almost as grave as that which had destroyed his great-grandfather, Edward II, sixty years before. When at the age of fourteen Richard had put his elders to shame and saved the kingdom from anarchy by the courage with which he had con-fronted the peasants at Mile End and Smithfield, it had seemed as though he might assert his regality before his time and show him-self another Edward of Windsor. But he was still too young – and, as the event showed, too neurotic and sensitive – to master the great

336

lords who, as soon as the peasants had been crushed, reasserted their power. Instead of biding his time and giving rein to his resentment only when he had made himself master of the means to do so, he showed his hand too soon and put his constitutional gaolers on their guard.

For Richard had been brought up by his lovely, pleasure-loving mother, who had borne him by her third husband and cousin, the Black Prince, in what by fourteenth-century standards was middle age. Her own father, half-brother to Edward II and, like him, executed by Roger Mortimer, was a son of Edward I by his second wife, Princess Margaret of France, and she herself had been reared in the royal courts of France and of the young Edward III in the highest traditions of hereditary kingshop. Joan was a creature of chivalry, the 'fair Maid of Kent' of courtly legend for whom Arthurian knights had jousted in tournament in the days before Crécy, and her notions of the rights and responsibilities of monarchy derived from a closed society in which a King's word was sacred law. She could not be expected to understand, still less approve, the constitutional changes which had been gradually coming about in England as a result of Edward III's dependence on parliamentary grants for his long war with France and Edward I's creation of representative periodic Parliaments for changing the law. And her spoiled son, born prematurely at Bordeaux just before the Black Prince set out on his ill-omened march into Spain, and left fatherless at the age of nine, had grown up in the firm conviction that lords who opposed him in the Council or parliamentary delegates who criticised his expenditure, his ministers or his friends, were little better than traitors.

Without realising it, young Richard, and the little group of personal favourites and courtiers who surrounded him, were seeking to put back the constitutional clock. They wanted to recover for the monarchy the powers it had exercised at the beginning of the century before confederate lords and even humble shire knights and burgesses had learnt how to use the increasingly frequent meetings of tax-voting Parliaments to call the King's ministers to account. These, by constraining him to give his assent to laws which appeared to encroach on his sacred powers and prerogatives,

337

put into effect Edward I's far-reaching libertarian concept – as yet still in its infancy – of seeking the 'counsel and consent' of the governed for the enactments of the Crown.

Ironically it was thus the very mystique of hereditary kingship which, in the hands of a boy King, had miraculously saved the monarchy in the revolutionary crisis of 1381, in the hands of the same boy grown to manhood was all but to destroy it. For, having seen it effect such magic when his ministers and elders had failed to save the kingdom from otherwise certain destruction, Richard was to spend the rest of his life convinced that he enjoyed a divinely inspired right and capacity to rule. The tall, yellow-haired Plantagenet, with the passionate stammering speech and pale womanly face which flushed when he was crossed, had inherited his warrior grandfather's love of pomp and pageantry and his hero father's passionate temper which, in him, if thwarted, took the form of querulousness. But unlike his grandfather Edward III, who within three years of his accession at sixteen had turned the tables on his usurped father's murderers, Richard was no warrior. Despite his tall stature and splendid Plantagenet looks – 'fair among men as another Absalom' – there was something feminine about him, both in temperament and temper. His tastes were all for the arts of peace – architecture, fine clothes, painting, courtly poetry – instead of the robust pleasures of the chase, tournament and battlefield; his closest friends 'knights of Venus rather than of Bellona'. Quick to resent an injury and seek revenge, he embarked on enterprises with enthusiasm, but quickly tired of them.

His gravest defect was his excitability and imperfect control of his temper; it was this which had caused his outburst in Parliament against his former guardian, Arundel: one account described him as striking him and drawing blood. According to Froissart he aimed a blow, too, at the Archbishop of Canterbury who had rebuked him for 'his insolent life and ill governance'. 'Abrupt and stammering in his speech,' as a contemporary described him, 'prodigal . . . extravagently splendid . . . timid and unsuccessful in foreign war . . . remaining sometimes till morning in drinking and other excesses not to be named', rumour attributed to him the same perverted affections which had sullied the name and ruined the reign of his great-grandfather.

Unlike Edward II, however, Richard was neither abnormal nor starved of natural affection. The political loneliness of his position was mitigated by a happy marriage. In January 1382, when he was just fifteen, he had married the Princess Anne of Luxemburg and Bohemia, a year older than himself. After his mother's death she became the central influence of his life and, by her devotion, introduced into his impulsive, wayward temperament a self-confidence and constancy of purpose that made him, so long as she lived, a far more formidable challenger to his warlike nobles' political pretensions than he could otherwise have been.

Already, though still more than a year short of legal age, he had begun to build a party of his own within the royal Council. At its head was a glittering young noble, a few years older than himself, Robert de Vere, ninth earl of Oxford and hereditary Chamberlain, for whom he had conceived a strong affection, lavishing on him every favour. Its moving spirit was the acting Chamberlain of the Household, Sir Simon Burley, the young King's military tutor and a former servant of his father, the Black Prince. A veteran of Nájera, Burley's fidelity to his old master's son was never in doubt, and his unchanging aim, selflessly if injudiciously pursued, was to increase the royal power and reduce that of the great feudal lords who wished to keep the King in perpetual leading-strings. The brain of the royal party was Michael de la Pole, son of a rich Hull merchant who had helped to finance Edward III's first Flemish campaign. A highly conscientious administrator and a first-rate man of business, he had increasingly identified himself with the royal prerogative against aristocratic pretensions. In the summer of 1385, during the abortive invasion of Scotland, Richard had created him earl of Suffolk, simultaneously, to appease their jealousy, conferring the dukedoms of York and Gloucester on his royal uncles, Edmund of Langley and Thomas of Woodstock.

After fifteen years of unsuccessful war against France it was not hard to raise popular indignation against the Crown. Whoever headed it, the royal administration was perpetually short of money and, as a result, repeatedly compelled to ask the nation's representatives in Parliament for new taxes. And as, in those years of defeat and mismanagement, there never seemed anything to show for its

339

expenditure, accusations of corruption and mis-appropriation of public funds were widely believed – especially by the landowning and commercial classes, who were the chief taxpayers. There was a feeling – by no means always unjustified – that the members of the court were feathering their nests and using their influence with an extravagant and generous young sovereign to obtain grants of royal land and other perquisites which, by whittling away the Crown's revenues, increased still further its demands on the tax-payer. In particular, such resentment fastened on Richard's young favourite, de Vere, on whom in 1385 he conferred the marquisate of Dublin – a title new to England, giving him prece-dence over all the earls.

Despite his share in the government of the country during the past few years Richard Fitzalan, earl of Arundel, was just the man to voice such resentment. He was a magnate of the old school, with the martial accomplishments and temper associated with the vic-tories of an earlier generation of Englishmen. He had served as Admiral of the West and, in the hour of danger after the Chancel-lor's murder in the Peasants' Revolt, had been temporarily en-trusted with the Great Seal. But he was arrogant, rude and tactless – the prototype of the traditional baron who for three centuries had defied the Crown whenever its wearer showed weakness or chal-lenged ancient rights – and the young King had grown to resent and detest him. He was supported by his brother, Thomas Arundel, bishop of Ely – a far more subtle man – by his fellow magnates, the earl of Warwick and, most ominous of all, by Thomas Woodstock, royal Duke of Gloucester. A spoilt, hot-tempered, ambitious magnifico in his early thirties, married to the co-heiress of the great feudal house of Bohun, Edward III's youngest son had grown up too late to share in the chivalric victories of his father's reign and had only known the era of defeats and fruitless marches which had accompanied the decline of English power in France. Because of this, the military glories of the past made an irresistible appeal to him, and he treated with contempt both the unadventu-rous foreign policy of a government forced to cut its martial coat to its fiscal cloth, and the civilized and pacific tastes of his nephew – a contempt not lessened by the fact that, like so many of the warrior-lords who surrounded the throne, he had owed his life, at a time when his own nerve and everyone else's had failed, to the courage with which the young King had ridden out from the beleaguered Tower to calm the murderous anger of the peasantry.

Only the moderating influence and immense power of John of Gaunt had so far prevented an open breach between his arrogant younger brother, with his aristocratic backers in Council and Parliament, and the impulsive, hypersensitive King. As long as Gaunt remained at the centre of affairs and ignored, as he wisely did, his nephew's boyish tantrums and unjust suspicions of himself, no one in either the aristocratic or the royal party was strong enough to upset the uneasy *status quo*. But during the summer of 1385, as the royal minority drew to a close, Lancaster again became heavily involved in the affairs of Spain. That August at Aljubarrota, two hundred English bowmen from the forests of his northern duchy helped a heavily outnumbered Portuguese army to win a decisive victory at the very moment when his rival, Juan of Castile, seemed about to extinguish Portugal's independence. This almost miraculous defeat of France's principal ally, wrought by English archery and reviving, as it did, memories of the Black Prince's victory at Nájera, caused the Council to approve the despatch to the peninsula of a new expedition, financed partly by Parliament and partly from the revenues of the duchy of Lancaster. It was led by Lancaster himself, who sailed in July 1386 for Galicia with seven thousand archers and men-at-arms, taking with him his daughter, Philippa, as a bride for the victor of Aljubarrota, John I of Portugal.

*   *   *

Lancaster could hardly have left England at a more inopportune moment. During that summer and autumn the French were threatening England with invasion and, though it came to nothing, for many months everyone in authority, national or local, had been engaged in preparing to resist it and in raising money to pay for the country's neglected defences. A year earlier the Commons had petitioned that, in order to be able to 'live of his own', the King should make no further gifts for a year and submit his private accounts to a parliamentary commission. They had been met by an angry rejoinder that he would do whatever he pleased with his own and submit his accounts to no one. When, therefore, in October 1386 – with everyone complaining of intolerable taxes raised to pay for the nation's defence, and with constant requisitions and hungry unpaid soldiers billeting themselves on the country, robbing, raping and murdering – the earl of Suffolk as Chancellor asked the community's representatives for the enormous subsidy of four-fifteenths, a storm burst over the heads of him and his fellow ministers. Charging them with extravagance and corruption, the Commons demanded their immediate dismissal and the banishment of the royal favourite, de Vere. Richard's response, from the seclusion of his luxurious Kentish palace at Eltham, was a refusal to discuss such matters with subjects and a contemptuous message that he would not dismiss a single scullion at their command. A few days later, to underline his defiance, he created his favourite, de Vere, duke of Ireland.

As, however, there seemed no other way of getting the four-fifteenths subsidy voted, in the end the King grudgingly agreed to receive a deputation of forty knights of the shire. But with rumours circulating that the courtiers meant to have them waylaid and murdered, Lords and Commons, acting together, sent to Eltham instead the King's uncle, the Duke of Gloucester, and the earl of Arundel's brother. the bishop of Ely, who were too powerful to be intimidated. A stormy scene ensued, in the course of which Gloucester declared that, by an ancient statute, if the King stayed away from Parliament by his own will 'without infirmity or other needful cause but by his own uncontrolled whim', it was lawful for its members to return to their homes without his permission, leaving his financial needs unmet. When an angry Richard, declaring that his subjects were plotting rebellion, spoke of seeking help from his cousin, the King of France – who was still threatening invasion – Gloucester broke into a tirade, denouncing the French King as the mortal foe of the realm and reminding Richard how his grandfather and father had 'worked untiringly all their lives, in sweat and toil, in heat and cold, for the conquest of the realm of France', which was theirs, and his, by hereditary right.

There remained, Gloucester went on, one thing more to say.

'It is allowed by another ancient law and one put into practice not long ago, that if the King by malignant counsel, foolish contumacy or wanton will . . . should be unwilling to be governed and guided by the laws and statutes and laudable ordinances with the wholesome counsel of the lords and magnates of the realm, but rashly in his insane counsels exercises his own peculiar desire, then it is lawful for them, with the common consent of the people of the realm, to pluck down the King from his royal throne and to raise in his stead some near kinsman of the royal house.'

Faced by this stark reminder of his great-grandfather's dethronement, Richard surrendered. He returned to Westminster, met Parliament and let its members do as they willed. 'All the Commons with one accord,' ran the French record in the rolls of Parliament, 'met in a single body and came before the King, prelates and lords in the Parliament chamber, complaining bitterly about Michael de la Pole, earl of Suffolk and Chancellor of England.' Though, in the face of his spirited defence, they were unable to substantiate their charges of treason, Suffolk was replaced as Chancellor by the bishop of Ely and the Treasurer, John Fordham, bishop of Durham, by the bishop of Hereford. In return for a parliamentary subsidy a wholesale purge of household officials followed. While Suffolk suffered a forfeiture of his property and was sent to the Tower, even such minor functionaries as the favourite court poet, Geoffrey Chaucer – controller of the London Wool Customs – lost their posts. And, as in the days of the Lords Ordainers eighty years before, government was vested in a commission of magnates in continual session – fourteen in all, including Gloucester and his brother the Duke of York, the two Arundels and the Archbishops of Canterbury and York, with four other spiritual and four secular peers. Its purpose was to wean the King from unworthy favourites, reform the administration and, by taking the offensive against France, renew the martial glories of the past. It was to have power to correct all defects in the administration, examine and investigate the King's records and documents, enter his palaces and supervise and dismiss his Household officials. It was even given custody of his jewels and seals.

For, as with Edward II, and his favourites, Gaveston and

343

Despenser, it had been through his private Household and Household servants that the King had been able to increase his power. Just as Edward II had used his Privy Seal to by-pass the Great Seal kept by the Chancellor and his clerks, so, now that the Privy Seal had become an instrument of the permanent administration of the realm and its keeper a national rather than a court official, Richard had used a secret private seal called the Signet to give effect to his will without resort to either Great or Privy Seals. Kept by a courtier known as the Secretary, it had enabled him to disregard the restraints imposed by his constitutional advisers.

*　　　　*　　　　*

The first round of the battle between the nineteen-year-old King and the magnates had now gone to the latter. Richard was once again powerless and at their mercy. He felt the humiliation keenly. Yet his minority was nearing its close and, for all their ingrained distrust of him, Gloucester and Arundel had been unable to prevail with the more moderate elements in the Opposition to prolong his tutelage indefinitely. Their authority, sweeping though it was, had only been entrusted to them for a year; after that the powers inherent in the Crown would automatically revert to it unless King and Parliament together could again be induced to limit them. The future thus still remained uncertain.

No one knew this better than the King. He had only to bide his time and by the next autumn the magnates, if they wished to control him, would have all to do again. Yet, being impulsive and impatient, Richard was not prepared to wait. Even before the end of 1386, he had procured the transfer of Suffolk from the Tower to Windsor, remitted his forfeiture and invited him to join his Christmas feast. A few weeks later, repeating the pattern of his great-grandfather's battles with the Ordainers over Gaveston, he set out on a ten months' progress through the midlands and north, leaving the Council of Fourteen in uneasy control at Westminster.

The royal plan, and that of his favourites, was to meet the magnates' challenge, not merely in the sphere of law and constitutional precedent, but in that in which the latters' true power resided, military force. The private armies which Edward III had

344

authorised them to raise for war abroad and which, despite all enactments to the contrary, they still maintained in their pay and livery, enabled them to threaten the peace of the realm and intimidate the throne. Richard, therefore, proposed to meet theirs with a private royal army in his own pay and livery. All through the spring and summer of 1387, while he moved about the midlands, his officers were enlisting men and distributing royal liveries of red and white, with crowns of gold and badges of the white hart – his personal emblem. Their success was greatest in Cheshire and north Wales, where in his capacity as earl of Chester Richard was the principal landowner and where, from the forest of Macclesfield, his father, the Black Prince, had drawn many of his archers. To preside over his forces there he appointed, as Justiciar of Chester and north Wales, his favourite, the hated duke of Ireland.

While the King strengthened his military position he sought also to strengthen his legal one. In August, first at Shrewsbury and then at Nottingham, he put ten loaded questions to the royal judges under an oath of secrecy. The purport of their answers was that the commission given to the magnates in the previous autumn had impugned the prerogative and that those who had counselled and procured it were therefore guilty of treason. He also obtained from them a declaration that Parliament was under an obligation to discuss any business submitted to it by him before it discussed its own, that he could dissolve it at pleasure, and that those who had urged it to consult the records of his great-grandfather's deposition were traitors and should be punished as such.

Armed with the judges' sealed answers Richard was in a position to bring in a true bill of treason against his enemies. But, his secret betrayed, the latter were too quick for him. Threatened by the terrible penalties of treason – hanging, quartering, disembowelling, forfeiture of property and, for their descendents, attainder of blood – the magnates and the Council of Fourteen did not remain idle. Ignoring Richard's summons to Westminster, to which, leaving de Vere at Chester, he had returned at the end of October, Gloucester, Arundel and Warwick met at Harringay Park, a few miles north of London and on 10 November moved on the capital with their private armies.

The King had made a political blunder of the first order. Before he was strong enough, he had declared war *á l'outrance* on his enemies and, to destroy them, had assumed a weapon which struck at the security of every magnate in the land. He and his judges had ignored the statute of 1352 in which, in order to placate his nobles, Edward III had expressly excluded from treason and its penalties the offence of 'accroaching the royal powers'. Not only Gloucester, Warwick and the Arundels were now aligned against him, but almost the entire nobility, threatened as it was by his judges' interpretation of treason. Even the absent John of Gaunt's son, young Henry Bolingbroke, earl of Derby – who, as husband of the co-heiress of the Bohuns, was not normally on friendly terms with his brother-in-law, Gloucester – had now joined the malcontents. Nor had Richard any real support in the country to withstand such a coalition. Except in the western midlands and Wales, and among a small group of royalist merchants in London, there was little sympathy for the court; when de Vere's recruiting officers appeared in East Anglia they were arrested by the local authorities at the orders of the Council of Fourteen. The earl of Arundel was something of a popular hero; in the previous winter, shortly after the Commission had been set up, he had won a spectacular victory off Margate over a French fleet that had been harrying the Thames estuary, subsequently delighting the London mob by releasing on the market at low prices a large quantity of wine captured at sea. And as the Council, which was still the lawfully appointed government of the country, controlled both the Great and Privy Seals, the King's efforts to raise money by the use of his Signet had been only very moderately successful. He had not even sufficient funds to continue to pay his own and de Vere's archers.

Since Richard in his personal capacity had appealed to his courts and lawyers to impugn the authority of the Crown-in-Parliament and the Council set up by it, the magnates now proposed to appeal against his subservient judges and irresponsible advisers in a court of their own. They were the heirs of the great military feudatories who during the past two centuries had called John, Henry III and Edward II to book and at times set limits to the arbitrary power even of such strong monarchs as Edward I and

III. Though trial-by-battle had long been replaced by the assize-at-law, their training and heredity still inclined them to think of justice and the enforcement of rights in ultimate terms of the battlefield, and it was to these they now resorted. Their leader, Gloucester, as Constable of England, was president of the Constable's and Marshal's courts – the supreme chivalric tribunal which settled disputes affecting knightly and martial honour, not by process of Common Law, but by the old Roman Civil Law and, in the last resort, by trial-by-battle. Instead of letting themselves be accused of treason, they meant to strike at the royal minions who were threatening their lives, honour and property, and appeal them of treason under the laws of chivalry in the *Curia Militaris* whose procedure they controlled. Taking up a strategic position at Waltham Cross north of London, where armed sympathisers flocked to them from every part of the country, they confidently awaited their sovereign's surrender and the delivery into their hands of his advisers. The days before Magna Carta seemed to have come again.

Under the circumstances Richard temporised; it was the only thing he could do. He agreed to receive Gloucester and the earls of Arundel and Warwick and let them bring their charges against his ministers and judges. Sitting in the hall of Westminster Palace with the members of the hated Council of Fourteen around him, on 17 November – only two days before their commission expired – he watched the three Lords Appellant, as they now styled themselves, enter the hall in chain mail with an armed throng of followers and abase themselves, almost as though in mockery, three times before him. Then their spokesman, Sir Richard Scrope, declared that there were in the state 'certain traitors, gathered around the King who deserved to be dismissed and punished'. And he named the duke of Ireland, the earl of Suffolk, the Archbishop of York, Chief Justice Tresilian and the London financier, Sir Nicholas Brembre.

The humiliated King accepted the Appeal. He acknowledged the Appellants to be under his protection and designated the Feast of the Purification of the Blessed Virgin – 3 February 1388 – as the date for a meeting of Parliament before whose lords their Appeal was to be judged. But he was still playing for time, and except for

Brembre, who continued bravely championing the royal cause in London and allowed himself to be taken prisoner, the accused had gone to ground – hiding, it was believed, in the cellars of the palace. A few days later it became known that the duke of Ireland was in Cheshire raising an army under the secret seal, and about to march to the King's aid. It was neither in Parliament nor in the courts that the issue between the sovereign and his subjects was to be decided but in the field of battle.

Yet it was where the magnates, not the King, were strongest, and they met the challenge as their forbears had done that of Gaveston and Edward II eighty years before. Spreading their forces in an arc from the Severn to Northampton they barred all roads to London, while the King took refuge in the Tower. When five days before Christmas, after a forced march, de Vere and his motley crowd of Cheshire archers and Welsh and Irish clansmen reached the Thames at Radcot bridge near Eynsham, they found the passage barred by Henry Bolingbroke. While they were hesitating, shaken by the spectacle of so many great lords gathered against them, the Duke of Gloucester came up with a force in their rear and surrounded them. The Constable of Chester and two others who showed fight were killed, but the rest yielded without a struggle. Only de Vere, plunging with his horse into the river, reached the far bank and escaped into the fog, subsequently flying to the continent.

The King was now helpless. There was talk of deposing him, but the two latest and younger Appellants, Derby and Nottingham, were opposed to anything so revolutionary, while the earl of Warwick, whose warlike front concealed a somewhat hesitant character, shrank from such an extreme course. Richard was still an anointed king and, even when, with five hundred armed retainers at their back and a vast threatening concourse of angry Londoners waiting outside, the triumphant Appellants waited on him in his last refuge in the Tower, he received them under a canopy of state, enthroned on a chair draped with cloth of gold while they performed the traditional three-fold prostration at his feet. Yet they left the lonely and friendless youth in no doubt that, if he wished to retain the crown, he must amend his ways, surrender the friends who had so misled him, and submit himself utterly to the governance of his rightful lords and advisers. If he did not, Gloucester warned him, there was a successor of full age and royal blood – by which he apparently meant himself – ready to take his place.

Thereafter the Appellants took possession of the palace of Westminster. There, according to the monkish chronicler, they investigated the number of officials in each office of the Household, finding that there were a hundred in the buttery alone. Similarly in the kitchen and all the other offices they found hordes of unnecessary officials. They deprived Sir Simon Burley of the custody of Dover castle, and Sir John Beauchamp, steward of the Household, of his office. And on the first day of January 1388 they held a council at Westminster causing many to be arrested, among them Sir Nicholas Dagworth, Sir William Elmham, Sir James Berners, Sir John Salisbury and Sir Nicholas Brembre, who were all sent for safe custody to various fortresses. By the time they had finished, Richard had not a friend left in the palace.

On 3 February, Parliament met at Westminster to hear the Appellants' appeal of treason. Like all medieval Parliaments it took its colour from the great lords who dominated it, in this case Gloucester and his fellow Appellants. Seated in the white hall of his palace, with the prelates on his right and the secular lords on his left and the new Chancellor, Archbishop Arundel – himself an Appellant's brother – on the woolsack below, the King faced the expectant throng of knights and burgesses who filled the hall, while the five Appellants, in surcoats of gold and with linked arms, made their formal entry and obeisance. Thereafter, for two hours, a clerk of the Crown read aloud at high speed in French the thirty-nine articles setting out the crimes of the five favourites whom the Appellants accused of treason. Throughout, formal blame was laid, not on the King but on his advisers. At its conclusion the hapless Richard, surrounded by his enemies, asked what sentence ought to be passed for such grave and treasonable offences. Proclamation was then made in the hall, and at the door of the palace, that the accused should come to answer the appeal. As none appeared, the Appellants asked for judgment by default.

Yet they did not have everything quite their own way. For all their readiness to resort to the sword when their rights were impugned, the English were a law-loving people accustomed to observe legal processes, and their lawyers were trained to insist on adherence to their letter. When the King and lords of the Council withdrew to consider the Appellants' demand, the question arose, not whether the crimes appealed were treasonable – which no one now questioned – but whether an appeal of treason in Parliament was valid either in Civil or Common Law. When the point was put to the serjeants of the Common Law and the learned doctors of Civil Law, they unanimously agreed that it was not. Nor was this decision that of men who, like the royal judges at Nottingham in the previous summer, were subservient to the King, for they were all lawyers who enjoyed the trust of the Council of Fourteen. But their first and instinctive responsibility was to the law in which they had been bred, and they were not prepared to gainsay it.

The Appellants, however, had little respect for the law, and possessed the power to shape it to their will. They induced their fellow lords, of whom they were the strongest and richest, to declare that, in a matter affecting the estate of the Crown and safety of the realm, Parliament was not, like lower courts, bound by legal rules of precedent and procedure, and was subject to no other law and custom but its own. Having thus proclaimed the untrammelled legal sovereignty of Parliament, they proceeded to sentence the accused unheard and in their absence, adjudging them guilty of treason because they said they were. As this process of condemnation by Parliament in a treason trial would involve the shedding of blood, the prelates, headed by the Chancellor, in accordance with Canon Law, withdrew from the court, leaving the secular peers and commons to pronounce judgment alone. And so, eight days after Parliament's meeting, the Appellants carried their point, and the steward of the court deputising and speaking for the King, pronounced that de Vere, Suffolk and Tresilian should be drawn alive through the city from the Tower of London to Tyburn, there to be hanged on the gallows, their goods confiscated and their successors not to enjoy them. The Archbishop of York escaped the death penalty by virtue of his sacred office, his punishment being referred to the Pope who subsequently translated him to St Andrews in remote poverty-stricken Scotland. The merchant Brembre – the only commoner in their custody – was sentenced separately by judgment of his fellow commoners and, despite an attempt by the King to save him and his own plea to be allowed as a knight to defend himself by battle, was hanged, drawn, and quartered. About the same time Tresilian was found hiding under the table of an attic in the precincts of Westminster Abbey. Clad in an old russet tunic reaching to his shins and looking, with his stiff, thick beard, like a poor pilgrim, the former Chief Justice was dragged from his hiding place with shouts of 'We have him!', bound to a hurdle and, amid the yells of a revengeful crowd which remembered his part in suppressing the Peasants' Revolt, dragged to the gallows.

But the Appellants and their Parliament had only begun, and their thirst for revenge was not yet sated. They now turned to lesser fry. Sir Simon Burley, who was alleged to have helped Suffolk escape, with three other Chamber knights, the royal serjeant-at-law who had drafted the questions to the judges at Nottingham, and the under-sheriff of Middlesex who had angered the anti-victuallers' faction in the city, all perished at their hands. The King's confessor, the bishop of Chichester, and the remaining Nottingham judges were saved by the prelates and suffered only forfeiture and exile to a remote and savage district of Ireland. Two of the Appellants – Derby and Nottingham – pleaded for Burley, who was ill and old and had to be brought from his cell in the Tower to Westminster Hall leaning on the arms of two friends. But Gloucester was adamant, and neither his knighthood of the Garter nor fame as a veteran of Nájera could save him. The Queen went down on her knees before Gloucester to beg for the old courtier's life but was brutally told to spare her prayers for herself and the King.

On 4 June the 'Merciless Parliament', as it became called, was dissolved after a four months' session in which the Commons had showed themselves as eager for blood as the Lords. Before the closing ceremony in the Abbey, at which oaths of allegiance were taken with Richard swearing to be 'a good King and Lord', it voted

351

the five Appellants the enormous sum of £20,000 – the equivalent of millions today – 'for their great expenses in procuring the salvation of the realm and the destruction of traitors'. It also declared that any who should at any time seek to reverse its judgments should be treated as a traitor and enemy of the realm, adding, with a fine disregard for the sovereignty of future parliaments, that its proceedings and the overriding rights it had claimed for itself were not to be regarded as precedents and that Edward III's merciful Treason Act of 1352, which it had flaunted, was henceforth to be observed.

*   *   *

The Lords Appellant had not only got rid of their enemies and by the most drastic of methods; they had substituted government by an aristocracy for government by a King. And almost at once it was made clear to the country that, even in the sphere which the nobles regarded as peculiarly their own, government by aristocracy alone could not meet England's needs. It was the Scots of the fierce, half-barbaric kingdom beyond the Cheviots who supplied the test. Pitifully poor, almost wholly without native industry and trade – 'things come ready made to them from Flanders,' wrote Froissart, 'and when that fails they have nothing' – and subsisting on the most primitive agriculture, they had been struggling to preserve their independence against their rich and powerful southern neighbour for nearly a hundred years. Broken only by brief, grudging truces and attended since the middle of the century by periodic visitations of plague and famine, the long war had almost completely stripped their rocky, starveacre land of what little wealth it possessed. Even their much-raided, oft-burnt capital had now only about four hundred houses huddled between its castle-crowned rock and the abbey of Holyrood below. Nor was the country welded, like England, by the institutions of a firmly established dynasty. The reigning King, Robert II – son of the great Bruce's daughter by her marriage to the hereditary Steward – was an old tired man of fifty-five when he succeeded to Scotland's precarious throne in 1371, and had now passed the psalmist's span. With a swarm of unruly sons, both legitimate and bastard, to provide for out of a patrimony far smaller than those of the jealous, treacherous, quarrelling nobles who surrounded the Scottish throne, the first of the Stewart line was a figurehead without power or resources.

Yet though the Scots were for ever fighting among themselves, and though the English were quick to exploit their divisions by offering a refuge and plotting-ground to any disaffected Scottish magnate – of whom there was nearly always at least one in England's pay – the Scots' readiness to take up arms against their southern neighbours was instinctive and ineradicable. To harry the valleys of the English March was both a national pastime and a national resource – almost the only way in which a Scotsman could hope to grow rich. It was thus crass negligence on the part of the Appellants, when the existing truce with Scotland expired in June 1388, not to make provision for the defence of the north. Almost at once the Scots began to raid along both sides of the Pennines, and smoking farms and churches and trails of corded prisoners and cattle tramping northwards into slavery were to be seen once more in all the lonely dales between Tyne and Cheviot.

That August the largest Scottish army that had crossed the border since King David's capture at Neville's Cross, forty years before, swept down on Newcastle under James, earl of Douglas – the great-nephew of Bruce's dreaded lieutenant. Though few of his turbulent race had inherited their progenitor's loyalty, and their ambition and treachery had proved a recurrent menace to Scotland's peace and shaky throne, no name was so dreaded in the English Marches. Even the earl of Northumberland shut himself up in his castle at Alnwick, and his fiery son, Harry 'Hotspur' – already at twenty-four one of the most famous knights in Christendom – was forced to withdraw with his brother, Ralph Percy, behind the walls of Newcastle. In the course of a skirmish outside the city gates, Douglas succeeded in capturing Hotspur's personal banner.

Some sort of a challenge for its recovery seems to have passed and, before bearing it off in triumph to his native Dalkeith, Douglas, apparently deliberately, halted his army at Otterburn, thirty miles to the north-west of Newcastle on the Jedburgh road, and laid siege to its little castle. Here on a warm August evening two avenging English columns attempted to surprise the Scottish camp. As so often in medieval warfare, there was a failure in co-ordination, while a third pursuing column from Newcastle under the bishop of Durham never reached the battlefield at all. In a desperately fought moonlit encounter which continued all night Douglas himself was slain, but the Scots were left in possession of the field and both Percies taken prisoner.

The battle, which was attended by exceptionally heavy casual-ties, made a deep impression on both sides of the border. Early in the next century it became the subject of a ballad in which, in ful-filment of an old prophesy, Douglas foretold his end:

> 'Last night I dreamed a dreary dream
> Beyond the Isle o' Skye –
> I saw a dead man win a fight,
> And I think that man was I.'

As he lay dying he bade his lieutenants conceal his fall lest it should rob his men of victory. 'Few of my fathers died in their beds,' he cried. 'Raise my banner! Cry Douglas!'

> 'My wound is deep – I fain would sleep –
> Take thou the vanguard of the three,
> And bury me by the bracken bush,
> That grows on yonder lily lea.'[1]

It was not only in chivalric legend and border ballad that Otter-burn had repercussions. Even more than Barbour's patriotic epic of *The Brus* – finished a few years before at a dark hour of Scotland's fortunes – it re-animated the national spirit of the hard-pressed, divided northern kingdom. For the first time since the great days of Bruce, Scotland's fighting men had won a victory over an English army in equal fight, exorcising the black memories of Halidon Hill and Neville's Cross. And it gravely discredited the Appellants' claim to be able to restore England's martial glories. Even more than the young King whom they had humiliated they had shown

[1] Lines quoted by Walter Scott on his own death-bed and which caused another poet, Philip Sidney – himself to fall in battle – to write, 'I never heard the old song of Percy and Douglas that I found not my heart moved more than with a trumpet.'

themselves incapable of containing the country's enemies. Before the year ended the bishop of Durham was heading an embassy to France to renew a humiliating truce with that kingdom which restored none of England's lost dominions. Meanwhile further Scottish raids kept the border in a state of panic, while a new Parliament, meeting in September in Barnwell priory at Cambridge, was forced to find £3,000 for Hotspur's ransom.

*   *   *

It was not without significance that the same Parliament made an attempt to restrain the abuses of livery and maintenance – the system under which the great lords who had muzzled the young King retained the private armies that were the source of their excessive and lawless power. It was the first sign of a rift in the parliamentary alliance between the Appellants and the shire-knights of the Commons which had broken the King's party. For, though the Commons complained of royals as well as baronial livery, it was the latter which now constituted the real threat to the country's peace and administration of justice, and the King drove a wedge between the two houses by offering to disband his own retainers if his nobles would do the same. In the end a compromise forbade the wearing of all liveries and badges of later origin than the accession of Edward III. It made little difference to the greater magnates whose rights derived – in most cases through the distaff – from the remote feudal past when retinue by tenure, as distinct from the more modern system of indenture, had been part of the military and constitutional structure of the realm.

Though, after the execution, dismissal and banishment of his friends and advisers, Richard had been left on the throne, he still remained as complete a cipher as when he had inherited it at the age of ten. England had a King living in idleness and luxury in his Surrey palace of Sheen – but a King only in name. His dearest friend and his wisest counsellor were in exile, their lives proscribed; his loyalest servants had been hanged. He presided at the Council table, but the realm was still governed by his uncle, Gloucester, and by the earls of Warwick and Arundel, with the latter's brother – now Archbishop of York – as Chancellor. Yet

355

during the winter of 1388–9 the pendulum began imperceptibly to swing towards the King, whose right to rule was inherent in the law and custom of the realm and who, as was traditionally believed, had been ordained to do so by God. For the very exercise of authority made the Appellants unpopular, and men soon started to murmur against them. The nemesis of all medieval government pursued them, just as it had pursued Richard's favourites. For to rule was to take from men, by taxation or otherwise, some part of their liberty and goods, and whoever suffered loss of either automatically became the ruler's critic and enemy. And as veneration for rank and ancient lineage was in the air of the age, it was to the great man out of power or favour – a de Montfort, a Bigod, a Thomas of Gloucester – to whom subjects instinctively turned for redress of their supposed grievances, so long, that is, as he remained out of power. As men wearied of the rule of Gloucester and his fellow Appellants, they pinned their hopes on that other royal uncle, John of Gaunt who, when he had been ruling the country in his dead father's name a decade earlier, had been the most hated man in the kingdom but who now, having been out of England for three years, seemed to embody all the wisdom and virtue which those in authority should possess but failed to possess.

For, having won, if not the throne of Castile, all he could reasonably expect in the Iberian peninsula, the Duke of Lancaster was now contemplating return to his native land. He had married one daughter to the King of Portugal and the other to the King of Castile, from whom, in return for relinquishing his claim to his crown, he had secured a further addition to his enormous fortune. In 1388, in the hope of keeping him abroad for a further spell, Gloucester and the Council had appointed him Lieutenant of Gascony – an honour traditionally conferred on the King's heir. But Bordeaux was far nearer England than Lisbon, and by the spring of 1389 everyone was aware that the country's greatest magnate and landowner was unlikely to leave his own or the kingdom's affairs in the hands of others much longer.

Already his son, Henry Bolingbroke, earl of Derby, had begun to take sides against his fellow Appellants in the Council. And on 3 May, sure of his support, Richard took a dramatic step. Taking his place in the Council, he asked those who were ruling in his name his age. When they replied, as they could not help doing, that he was twenty-two, he pointed out that the law assured to every heir of full legal age whose father was dead the right to manage his own estate and household. 'Then,' he said, 'I am of full age to govern my house and household and also my kingdom.' Why, he asked, should a right allowed to his meanest subject be denied him? Whereupon – for his foes had no answer – with the assent of a majority of the Council, whose members were tiring of Gloucester's and Arundel's pretensions, he announced that he would now dispense with the services of those who had exercised his functions during his infancy and conduct his own affairs. And, as his first reigning act, he requested the Chancellor, Archbishop Arundel, to surrender the Great Seal. Gathering it under a fold of his dress, he left the Council chamber, returning a few minutes later to confer it on the aged bishop of Winchester, William of Wykeham, who had been his grandfather's Chancellor twenty years before. Next day he appointed a new Treasurer and Keeper of the Privy Seal. A few weeks later the court poet, Geoffrey Chaucer, returned to the payroll as Clerk of the King's Works.

Having freed himself from his former masters, Richard made no immediate attempt to avenge the wrongs and insults he had suffered at their hands. He seemed to have learnt to be politic or, at least, circumspect. Nor did he any longer give the impression of wishing to rule his kingdom without that counsel from its hereditary magnates whose birth, under the long-established custom of the realm, best fitted them to act as constitutional advisers to the throne. In the writs issued to the sheriffs informing them of the King's assumption of full regal authority, stress was laid on his wish 'to promote peace and tranquillity everywhere and firmly to observe the laws and customs of the realm and to administer justice and full right to each of our lieges and subjects, by the advice, assent and counsel of the prelates, peers and magnates of our realm'. The enactments of the Merciless Parliament were confirmed and the balance of the vast sums it had voted to reimburse the senior Appellants for the Radcot Bridge campaign were duly paid. Nor was anything done to recall de Vere, Suffolk and Neville, all of whom were left to die in exile.

357

For that autumn, while Gloucester and the earl of Arundel left the country to crusade with the Teutonic Knights against the pagans of Lithuania, King Richard rode out in person along the Plymouth road to the great Benedictine abbey of Reading to greet the returning John of Gaunt, whom he installed as his most honoured counsellor – a position held till his death a decade later. For the next few years the government of England could be seen to be once more both royal and conciliar without any clash between these two seemingly conflicting conceptions.

During them, Richard made no attempt to avenge the wrongs he had suffered from his former political oppressors. Nor did he show signs of seeking to re-impose the personal rule he had sought during his minority. Perhaps it was because joint royal and conciliar administration was the kind of government most politically conscious Englishmen by now wanted, that the next few years of internal peace and prosperity came to seem in retrospect, in the troubled times to follow, almost a golden age.

*   *   *

Passionately though Richard, now in his middle twenties, wished to excel and unable, as ever, to endure opposition to his imperious will, it was in the rule of his court rather than that of the realm that during the first years of the last decade of his reign and the century the young King found for a time fulfilment. He was an artist, not a man of action; in this he resembled his church-building ancestor, Henry III. So long as, with his Queen by his side, he could dictate his court's personnel, ceremony, pageantry and artistic life, he was for the moment content. For the century into which he had been born had seen the birth of a new and elaborate court culture – one in which the monarch dictated the behaviour, life and fashions of those immediately surrounding the throne. In the closely related French-speaking royal families of western Europe, it had been increasingly taking the place of the rough, masculine and martial baronial and knightly culture which had flourished in feudal castle and hall ever since its emergence, three centuries earlier, under the tutelage of the Roman Church, from the barbarism of the Dark Ages. Brought back by returning

"The pillars of the new nave of York were like the trunk and branches of a beech wood."

York Minster, 14th century.

"Henry Yevele, the King's master mason, earlier supervised by the clerk of the works, the poet Geoffrey Chaucer, reconstructed William Rufus's Hall at Westminster, calling in the royal carpenter, Hugh Herland, to span its 240 foot length and 70 foot width with a hammer-beam roof of Sussex oak – the first of the great hammer-beam roofs which, with the Fan Vault and the Perpendicular style, were England's most original architectural achievements."

Westminster Hall, rebuilt 1393–1400.

crusaders from the Aegean and Levant through contact with the luxurious court of the Byzantine emperors at Constantinople – the last unbroken link with the majestic civilization of the Roman past – it had first taken shape on western Europe's Mediterranean littoral at the beginning of the fourteenth century in the Neapolitan court of King Robert of Anjou. Thence, heralding by a hundred years the Renaissance, it had spread northwards through the Italian city states and princedoms to the Visconti and papal courts at Milan and Avignon and the French capital, and even to remote London, where, in the chivalric circles presided over by the youthful Edward III, it had formed the background to the romantic youth of Richard's future mother.

Nowhere did it flourish more elaborately than in the Hradschin palace at Prague, home of the Bohemian king and of his daughter, Richard's future Queen. Elected Holy Roman Emperor as Charles IV in 1347, he had held that high-sounding but hollow title for more than thirty years and, as such, was the subject of one of Gibbon's most ironical passages in which the great historian contrasted the shadow German, and Holy Roman, Emperor's position as an impecunious ruler of a minor central European state with the unreal grandeur and majesty with which he presided over the periodic meetings of the Diet and Imperial court. 'When a hundred German princes bowed before his throne . . . and, at the royal banquet, the hereditary Electors, who in rank and title were equal to kings, performed before them their solemn and domestic service of the palace.'

It may have been on the elaborate, though meaningless, ceremonial of his father-in-law's imperial court that Richard modelled his own. With its ten thousand retainers and gorgeous heraldic clothes embroidered with gold and jewels, it was famed in an age of splendid royal courts. It gave mankind the handkerchief, which Richard himself is said to have invented, and – for, like all the royal courts, it had a strong feminine bias – the side-saddle. An aesthete with a natural love of beautiful things, especially those which enhanced his personal appearance and gave him that preening

359

vanity of carriage which the age called *superbia*,[1] the young King dressed himself and his court in clothes glittering with jewels. One of his state dresses is believed to have been worth more than a thousand pounds, equivalent of a hundred times that sum today. A royal doublet of white satin, whose description has come down to us, was embroidered with golden orange-trees each bearing a hundred silver-gilt oranges, and its sleeves hung with fifteen silver cockles and thirty mussels and whelks in silver gilt. The fashionable wear set by the King for his courtiers was of huge padded shoulders, vast bell-mouthed sleeves trailing along the ground, skin-tight hose and fantastically long curled and pointed shoes.

Richard's palaces, of which he had seven or eight, were full of treasures – Kentish Eltham with its gardens and vineyards; Sheen, where the royal barges were moored by an island in the Thames; King's Langley; Windsor manor five miles south of the Norman Castle and Round Tower which his grandfather had built for the Knights of the Garter; Leeds castle, hereditary seat of the Queen. Most renowned of all was the palace of Westminster, on the re-building of whose hall – originally dating from Rufus's time and still surviving after six centuries as the central glory, though now only in bare stone and timber, of the parliamentary heart of Britain's government – he employed the greatest architect of the age, the stone-mason Henry Yevele who, during his reign, had refashioned Canterbury's glorious nave. With his fellow craftsman, the master carpenter Hugh Herland, he spanned the new West-minster Hall with a wonderful hammer-beam roof, each beam with pendant angels holding vast heraldic shields. In these palace homes the stately King kept his ivories and alabasters, painted and gilded jewelled chaplets, silver-gilt goblets and ewers, and his own and his Queen's exquisitely painted manuscripts with illuminated capitals and miniatures. For, like her, he was a lover and collector, if not reader, of books. And everywhere were wall paintings in gold and vermillion and brilliant primary colours, adorned with roses and fleur-de-lys and Richard's personal emblem of the white

---

[1] In the nave of a Suffolk church there is a wall-painting, dating from the last decade of the fourteenth century, depicting a young man in Richard's favourite attire, holding in one hand a sceptre and in the other a looking-glass.

hart with its fantastic horns, crowned neck and long golden chain, stamped or embroidered on whatever belonged to him or his retainers.

Richard was not only an aesthete. He was a sensualist, though never a gross one, of a sensibility far in advance of his age. His palaces were equipped with stone-paved or tiled bath-houses, baths with bronze hot and cold taps, for he was a lover of hot baths, and with personal latrines for himself, his Queen and his favourites. He was also a gourmet, famed as 'the best and ryallest vyander of all Christian kings', whose master chef produced the first known English manuscript cookery-book, the *Forme of Curry*.[1] Instead of the customary glutton feasts of roasted oxen, vast loins and haunches of mutton, beef and venison loved by the feudal nobility, he affected small delicately blended and highly spiced dishes of contrasted flavours, with much use of pepper, ginger, cinnamon, cardamon, nutmeg, saffron and mace and other far Eastern spices, and a liberal use of fine and rare wines – white Vernage from northern Italy, Greek, Rhenish and Rochelle, cooked with such foods as shelled oysters and hare's flesh, flavoured with honey and sugar of Cyprus.

*　　　　*　　　　*

In the summer of 1394, when he was twenty-seven, Richard lost his Queen, who since his marriage twelve years earlier had been the sheet anchor of his life. Partner in all his artistic projects and the lodestar of his Court, such was his grief at her death that he ordered their favourite palace, Sheen, to be razed to the ground, so unbearable was the memory of all that they had shared there together. When his old enemy, Arundel, failed to attend the procession which bore her body to the Abbey and, next day, with his habitual lack of tact, interrupted the funeral service with a blunt excuse for absence, the bereaved King was so enraged that he seized a baton from an attendant and struck the earl over the head with such violence that his blood spattered the pavement, and the service had to

---

[1] It was printed for the Society of Antiquaries in the reign of George III. Gervase Mathew, *The Court of Richard II*, p. 23.

be postponed until the clergy could free the sacred building from pollution.

Henceforward, as in the old days before the Merciless Parliament, it was politics which once more took precedence in Richard's restless mind. That autumn he resumed a project on which his long exiled and now dead favourite, de Vere, had embarked ten years before, of making Ireland, with its turbulent tribes, a recruiting ground, like the Welsh and Cheshire forest borderland, for a private royal army with which to discipline his stiff-necked and constitutional-minded English baronage and gentry. Gathering a strong force of retainers from Wales, he crossed to Ireland, the first English King since Henry II to do so, landing in October at Waterford and marching to Dublin where at Christmas he kept court in great splendour, graciously receiving the homage of the ever-warring chieftains or petty 'kings' of Leinster, Meath, Thomond and Connaught, and conferring on them English knighthoods.

Having thus widened his potential base for recruiting future retinues for reducing England to his will – though whether this was his only motive in spending the winter in Ireland there is no means of knowing,[1] for this loneliest of English rulers had few, if any, confidants – during the rest of 1395, Richard concentrated on further widening his power-base by wooing the French King's six-year-old daughter, Isabella. For her dowry and a promise of Valois' help against disobedient subjects he paid with a twenty eight years' extension of his earlier three years' truce with France and the even more unpopular return to Brittany of the port of Brest – the last, save Calais, of Edward III's conquests. The fact that he could not hope for an heir from his child bride for at least a decade left the problem of a disputed succession, with his royal uncles and their heirs competing for the throne, wide open for both him and his subjects.

By the summer of 1397, at the end of his thirtieth year, Richard felt ready to strike back at his former enemies. For, despite all appearances to the contrary, he had never forgotten or forgiven those who had humiliated him. That February, in a Parliament

[1] Gervase Mathew in his brilliant study of *The Court of Richard II* attributes to him more consistency of purpose and will than do most historians.

packed by sheriffs appointed from his Household, he put up one of his retainers in the commons to denounce the ever-mounting expenses of his Court, and then got a subservient Lords to declare it a treason, punishable by death, to excite the Commons to criticise the royal person, government or regality. So armed, at midsummer he struck at the former Lords Appellant. Holding them guilty, on grounds, real or invented, of secretly conspiring against him, he invited Gloucester, Arundel and Warwick to a banquet at White-hall. Only Warwick was brave or foolish enough to attend and, greeted with fine words, was arrested at the end of it. On the same night, 10 July, with a contingent of City militia led by the young acting Mayor, Richard Whittington – the famous Dick Whitting-ton of popular legend – the King galloped thirty-five miles through the night to Plessey castle in Essex where he arrested the second of his two intended guests and victims, his royal uncle the duke of Gloucester. Him he packed off without a struggle under guard to Calais where, as was widely believed, he had him secretly done to death. His other intended guest, Arundel, who had taken refuge in Reigate castle, was induced to surrender, and then tried for treason and executed on 21 September, his lands being distributed among Richard's followers, while his brother, the archbishop, was sus-pended from the primacy and banished the realm.

Yet it was *superbia* – vain glory – even more than revenge which still animated the King. The amount he expended in personal magnificence, in jewels, in maintaining his private army and the vast swollen departments of his Court, above all in fantastic liberality to all and sundry, was costing the country as much as his grandfather's wars. In successive years he gave away in pensions in Germany and France and, during the festivities for his second marriage, almost as much as the total normal revenue of the Crown. His benefactions in the closing years of his reign included a grant of £2000 – a hundred times as much in present-day money – to a potentate as remotely distant from himself and his realm as the Byzantine Emperor. At this time he seems to have nursed nebulous hopes of himself becoming German – and Holy Roman – Emperor, like his former father-in-law. He even spoke of himself as one, claiming to be '*entier empereur de son royaume*', whose laws, he claimed, resided solely in his own breast.

The strain of all this on his and the kingdom's finances only drove him the faster down the tyrant's perilous path. Having secured an unprecedented grant of the wool and leather duties for life from a Parliament overawed on the day before its meeting by a massive parade of the Cheshire archers of the royal bodyguard, Richard's next step was to raise forced loans, compelling the rich to lend to the spendthrift Crown. It fell with particular severity on civic and merchant corporations like the city of London. This was followed by a far more unjust and onerous tax – for at least it was intended to repay the forced loans – a widespread system of fines called La Plesaunce. Under it those who had ever forfeited the King's pleasure, or opposed him at any time since his accession, were compelled, in order to escape the terrible penalties for treason, to regain his favour by a heavy fine.

At the beginning of 1399, desperate for money to pay for his extravagances, Richard struck still deeper at the property rights, or liberties as they were called, of his subjects. During the previous year a quarrel had broken out between the two younger Lords Appellant, Henry Bolingbroke of Derby and Thomas Mowbray of Nottingham, who ten years before had refused to allow their merciless elders to proceed to extreme measures against the young King and on whom in his policy of enhancing the majesty of the throne by surrounding it with high-titled satellites – *dukettis* as his subjects called them – he had recently conferred the nominal dukedoms of Hereford and Norfolk. Each accused the other (not, it seems, without grounds) of secretly nursing and confiding to the other treasonable fears of the King's good faith towards him. After their charges against one another had been declared insufficient in evidence by a parliamentary committee, the King ordered that they should be judged in trial-by-combat under the rules of chivalry. In arranging that the proceedings should be accompanied by every attendant of dramatic and resplendent pageantry, Richard was in his element, presiding personally over the lists, which were held near Coventry on 16 September 1398.

Just as the combatants, armed *cap-à-pie*, were about to enter the lists, the King threw down his warder. He then proceeded to decree that both should be exiled, Norfolk for life and Hereford –

the former Bolingbroke – for five years. Subsequently, after they had left the realm, he confiscated their estates. But a far more drastic act of confiscation followed. Six months later, on 3 February 1399, Hereford's father, old John of Gaunt, Duke of Lancaster, died, and with him his four ancient earldoms of Lancaster, Derby, Lincoln and Leicester – by far the richest single inheritance in the kingdom.

With Gaunt's son in exile, Richard immediately seized possession of all his vast estates. By doing so he threatened every property owner and heir in England, outraging the most fundamental of all an Englishman's rights – that of inheritance.

The division between Richard and his subjects was now complete. He had alienated the sympathy of every section of the community. It was his misfortune to embody and feel the pageantry and symbolism of his position acutely without being able to understand and realise the national history and spirit which had created it. We see him, through the mists of time, presiding, during the closing months of his reign over his Parliament, in his royal robes before the painted arras in his hall at Westminster, the crown on his head and the sceptre in his hand; his prelates, earls and barons, seated on stools below him, and the knights and burgesses from 'the cities and good towns of the land' on steps below them. There is a contemporary account of him doing so, sitting resplendent and silent from dinner time until Vespers, 'and whenever he looked at any man, that man had to bow the knee'. For by now he was monarch of all he surveyed or supposed himself to be.

At this point Richard 'the Redeless' – the counsel-less, as the author of *Piers Plowman* called him – embarked on a course of action little removed from insanity and which could only have one end. Taking his crown and treasure with him, on 1 June he sailed again for Ireland with most of the private army he had created to overawe his cowed subjects, intending both to put down a rebellion there and gather increased forces to do so in England. In the meantime he left the realm under the regency of his easy-going royal uncle, the Duke of York.

Almost immediately after his arrival in Ireland, while his army, hastily embarked and ill-provisioned, was half starving in the dense forests of the elusive rebel chieftain, Art MacMurrach, Richard's wronged cousin, Henry Bolingbroke – now, by his father's death, Duke of Lancaster – left Paris, where he had been spending his exile, for Boulogne. Sailing with a small band of adherents for Yorkshire and announcing that he had returned to regain his inheritance, he landed at Ravenspur in the Humber on 4 July. An experienced and resolute soldier, he acted with the utmost speed. Marching through Knaresborough to Pontefract and Doncaster and raising an army from his Yorkshire tenants on the way, he was joined by the northern earls of Northumberland and Westmorland with a following of Percies and Nevilles bent, like himself, on saving their possessions from a tyrant King under whom no one could any longer feel secure. Marching together down the London road, at Leicester they swung westward for the Bristol Channel to intercept the King's expected return from Ireland. Here, at Berkeley castle, also hurrying west to meet him and feeling, in that hour of universal repudiation of a failing monarchy, discretion to be the better part of valour and loyalty, the Regent threw in his lot with them. And on 28 July at Bristol, the city having been surrendered to them by its governor, the triumphant invaders seized and executed Richard's Treasurer, William Scrope, earl of Wiltshire, and his hated henchmen, Sir John Bussy and Sir Henry Green of the royal Household, who had also hurried there from an insurgent London to meet their returning sovereign.

Two days later, when the latter, hurrying homewards, landed at Milford Haven with a handful of retainers, he found that his kingdom had already slipped from his grasp. Hurrying north across the Welsh mountains without an army to seek support from his Cheshire stronghold, he found that the invaders had forestalled him there by a forced march up the Severn to Chester, which they reached on 9 August. By the time, after his weary wanderings through the Welsh hills with half a dozen followers, Richard came to rest at Conway castle, joining there his chief remaining armed adherent, the earl of Salisbury, the triumphant Bolingbroke and a powerful army faced him menacingly from Flint.

Here, fluctuating between self-pitying despair and furious defiance, at one moment declaring that Bolingbroke should die a death that would make a noise as far as Turkey, the doomed and forsaken King was prevailed upon by his accommodating and equivocal Regent, the Duke of York, to leave the safety of Conway for Bolingbroke's camp at Flint on 19 August. Thence, next day, he accompanied the latter to Chester. Though his victorious cousin received him with a sovereign's honours, proclaiming that he sought only the restoration of his forfeited estates, to which the defeated King meekly acceded, neither cousin could now for a moment trust the other. During their journey together to London – in the course of which Richard attempted to escape – the royal state changed imperceptibly from that of a monarch returning to his kingdom to that of a state prisoner charged with treason to the realm. On the day after his arrival at Westminster on 1 September, he was consigned to the Tower.

During the next month, while awaiting in that place of tragic memories the meeting of a Parliament called in his name to dethrone him, the state of the captive King's mind is known to us only through the play written two centuries later by Shakespeare who, with his instinctive understanding of human nature in every situation, put into Richard's mouth the words in which he yielded his crown to the man he had wronged. 'Not all the water in the rough rude sea,' he made him declare before his surrender at Conway,

> 'Can wash the balm from an anointed King;
> The breath of wordly men cannot depose
> The deputy elected by the Lord.'

In those secret hours in the Tower, of which history has no record and subject to what unknown pressures, the King, on the day preceding the formal announcement of his abdication on 1 September, was invested by the poet with the words and feelings in which, abject and in despair, he renounced his kingship.

> 'I give this heavy weight from off my head,
> And this unwieldy sceptre from my hand,
> The pride of kingly sway from out my heart;
> With mine own tears I wash away my balm,
> With mine own hands I give away my crown,
> With mine own tongue deny my sacred state'

A fortnight later a new Parliament met, called by Bolingbroke to succeed the one which had accepted Richard's abdication and declared the throne vacant. Claiming the succession 'by right of descent vindicated by conquest', the royal usurper was crowned Henry IV in the Abbey on 13 October 1399 with the ancient and sacred rites used at the crowning of all England's kings. Within six months of the dethronement, imprisoned in turn at Leeds Castle in Kent and at Pickering, Knaresborough and Pontefract in Yorkshire, his broken predecessor, following an unsuccessful rising of his sympathisers in the New Year, was dead, possibly of starvation at his own hand, more probably, like Edward II before him, at that of his merciless gaolers.

Son and grandson of the two greatest heroes of the age, happily married and surrounded by a brilliant Court, at the zenith of his power and fortune, Richard had used time, a private army and not inconsiderable political skill and cunning to destroy his enemies. His reign had seen a flowering of native art and culture which bade fair to anticipate that of fifteenth-century Burgundy and rival that of contemporary Italy. He had Yevele for his architect, John Siferwas for painter, Chaucer for poet. Yet, when he claimed that the laws existed only in his own breast, he made the same mistake as the abbot who told his serfs that they owned nothing legally but their bellies. Because he failed to see that whoever claims absolute power in England will in the end be repudiated by her people, he lost everything and was dethroned by a Parliament of his own subjects. Like his foolish great-grandfather – and others to come – he discovered too late that the English could only be ruled by those who acknowledged the sanctity of their laws and liberties and, when threatened, their right to defend them.

*   *   *

The century and a quarter which ended with the dethronement of Richard II had seen the first evolution of Parliament, the legislative and land reforms of Edward I – 'the English Justinian' – and that great King's attempts to unify Anglo-Saxon and Celtic Britain under a single law and monarchy, successful, after a heroic resistance, in Wales, but in Scotland defeated in an epic war of independence which ensured, happily for mankind, the continued nationhood of the Scottish people. They had been years fraught for England with alternating achievement and disaster. They witnessed her greatest military defeat, Bannockburn, and her first great continental victory, Crécy. On the morrow of that inconceivable triumph she had been struck down by a calamity comparable to that which would today follow a nuclear war. And after further military successes culminating in an even greater victory, Poitiers, and a peace, never ratified, which recognised her King's claim to a quarter of France, during a further two decades of war she lost almost her entire foreign conquests, learning the lesson, not for the last time, that continental conquest can offer an island people nothing but frustration.

Between the accession of Edward I and the tragic fate of his great-great-grandson, England became what, under changing forms, she was to remain, a parliamentary monarchy. By finding a constitutional means to reconcile strong centralised authority with the liberty of the subject and the right to oppose, criticise and reform government, she had made a political contribution of supreme importance to mankind. The creation of England's unique Parliament, with its triple components of Crown, Lords and Commons, makes these years vital to an understanding of all that was to follow. During it, rights were won by trial and error that became the basis of the laws and institutions by which free men still live. In the early part of that struggle the championship of private liberties and of the right to oppose arbitrary power had rested with the greater lords and churchmen; later, as a result of Edward III's French wars, the knights of the shire and the still humbler burgesses of the chartered towns began to share in the process. Out of that conflict between the expanding power of royal central government and the medieval tradition of feudal and religious liberty was wrought the first great English reconciliation between order and freedom. When, twice in a century, a successful revolution ended in the dethronement of a tyrannical hereditary King and the recognition by Parliament of a usurping but still hereditary successor, the victors had the wisdom to preserve the continuity of strong royal government. This combination of respect for central

369

national authority with insistance on individual rights and liberties was to remain the dominating political motive of English, and later British, history.

HOW THEY LIVED

CHAPTER EIGHTEEN

The Medieval Village

THE FOUNDATION OF England's medieval polity was the labour of some nine thousand scattered agricultural communities. Her government, law, landed wealth, merchandise, architecture and art rested on the native clearing in the wild and Piers Plowman in the 'field full of folk' raising food for all. The owner of the soil, if not the Crown or an ecclesiastical institution, was usually – at least until the latter fourteenth century when English became the language of all classes – a French-speaking lord, resident or absentee, with his manor court or leet to which every villager owed suit. Its pastor was the parish priest with his church, to which everyone repaired for communal worship on Sundays and feastdays and for all the important occasions of life. But its hard core and that of England's economy was the husbandman. In Kent and the Danelaw and the pastoral west and north he was as often as not a freeman, owning the land he tilled and able to sell it. But until the fifteenth century in the south and midlands the majority of cultivators were villeins: men tied to the soil. They went with it and could not leave it without its lord's consent. They were not, legally speaking, slaves, for they could not be bought or sold as individuals but only with the land they cultivated. Nor, so long as they paid the feudal dues and services with which it was charged, could they be deprived of its fruits. At a time when there was more land in England than labour to work it, they were indispensable. They held it by hereditary tenure of 'fork and flail'.

Yet a villein, or serf as he was called, was far from free. If he or his children left the manor they could be brought back to it in chains on proof of villeinage. Their service was 'in the blood'. The only legal escape was by public manumission, by entry into the

373

Church – for which the lord's agreement was necessary – or by residence for a year and a day in a chartered borough. There were many types of villein. They ranged from substantial farmers, employing other men's services and commuting for their own by money payments, to humble cottars and bordars holding only a few acres and supplementing their yield by working three or four days a week on their neighbours' land for wages. The average villein-holding was a yardland or virgate of thirty acres. For this a man had to till the lord's land with his own implements for two or three days a week, personally or by deputy perform cartage or carrying duties, give additional 'boon' services at the spring and autumn sowing, harvest-time, hay-making and sheep-shearing, and render on special days a seasonal tribute of farm-produce, like the Easter eggs which still appear on our children's plates. Thus in a survey of Martham at the end of the thirteenth century Thomas Knight held twelve acres in villeinage, paid 16d. for it and 14d. in special aids. 'He shall do,' it was stated, 'sixteen working days in August and for every day he shall have one repast [viz. bread and fish]. He shall hoe ten days without the lord's food – price of a day $\frac{1}{2}$d. He shall cart to Norwich six cartings or shall give 9d., and he shall have for every carting one loaf and one lagena [or gallon] of ale. Also for ditching 1d. He shall make for malt $3\frac{1}{2}$ seams of barley or shall give 6d. Also he shall flail for twelve days or give 12d. He shall plough if he has his own plough, and for every ploughing he shall have three loaves and nine herrings . . . For carting manure he shall give 2d.' These arrangements, which varied from manor to manor, were supervised by the lord's bailiff and by an elected or nominated representative of the villeins called the reeve who directed the common husbandry. The larger the holding, the greater the services demanded. A poor cottar with four or five acres might owe only a single day's labour a week.

Though, like all holders of land, a villein had to pay tallages and aids to his lord, such as the merchet on his daughter's marriage, he enjoyed the usual hereditary rights of feudal tenure. On payment of a heriot of the best beast on his holding, his heir was entitled to succeed to it. Nor were the 'boons' he proffered to his lord wholly one-way. Attached to his services were certain customary privileges,

like the haymaker's right at Borley in Essex to receive for every
load of hay three quarters of wheat, a pat of butter and a piece of
cheese of the second sort from the lord's dairy, the morning milk
from the cows, salt and oatmeal for a stew, and as much hay as
each man could lift on the point of his scythe. A sower was usually
entitled to a basketful of any seed he sowed, a cowherd to the first
seven days' milk of every cow after calving, a shepherd to twelve
nights' dung from the folds at Christmas and a bowl of whey or
buttermilk during the summer.

What distinguished villein service from the higher feudal
tenures was that it was menial and 'servile'. To the extent of the
time for which his service was due, the serf was at the disposal of
the lord and his bailiff. He was not his own master and, as the great
thirteenth-century lawyer Bracton wrote, legally speaking did not
know in the evening what he should do on the morrow. The stigma
in his status was that he was not, in the old English phrase, 'law-
worthy'. He could not defend his person or property in the royal
courts or claim a freeman's right to be tried by his equals, though
gradually, as the power of the Common Law grew, he received from
it protection of life and limb and of the tools of his labour.

Yet though the courts at Westminster in the latter Middle Ages
were often narrow and inflexible, and though, being tied by inherited serfdom to the soil they cultivated, nearly half the English
people could not yet sue in the royal courts in respect of their
'villein' land, livestock or property – all of which in the law's eyes
belonged to their lords – the Common Law operated imperceptibly
to widen the bounds of justice. For its spirit did not favour serfdom.
However strong the class bias and interest of its officers, it leant
instinctively towards liberty. In this it differed from the Civil Law
of the continental kingdoms which derived from Roman imperial
law and a civilization whose economic basis had been slavery.
The English ideal was the 'free and lawful man' – *liber et legalis
homo* – entitled to equal justice, answerable for the acts of others
only if he had commanded or consented to them, and presumed
by the law to be a rational and responsible being and, as such,
expected to play his part in administering justice by representing
the local community before the King's judges and assisting them

in the determination of fact. Though vast numbers of once free peasants had become tied to the soil during the feudal anarchy of the Dark Ages, and their liberties had been further eroded under their grasping Norman conquerors, even before the Peasants' Revolt of 1381 the genius of the Common Law was granting to the bondsman rights which it regarded as the heritage of all. It treated him as free in his relation to everyone except his lord, protected him against the latter's crimes and gave him the benefit of the doubt in questions affecting feudal status, holding, for instance, that the illegitimate child of parents, one of whom was free, must be free too, contrary to the practice elsewhere. Though it enforced serfdom where serfdom could be proved, it construed every sign of freedom as a proof of freedom.

Yet the rule of the royal courts was comparatively new. They were not the only source of protection from violence and injustice. There were other and older courts to which a man could resort. The manor-court or moot belonged to the lord; its jurisdiction and fines were among the most valuable of feudal rights. It was presided over by his steward and met once a fortnight in his hall or outhouse, or in summer under the village oak tree. But it was open to the whole village, and the assessors or jurymen, who stated the local customs on which its judgments were based and which formed the law of the manor, were the tenants who owed it suit. Those customs were handed down from father to son and recorded on the court rolls. They expressed the common experience and conscience of the neighbourhood. Nor was it easy for even the most powerful lord to ignore the custom of those on whose labour and skill he depended. Like the great Council of tenants-in-chief, who made the despotic King John promise to observe ancient law and govern with the consent of his chief men, the manor-court was the means by which, little by little, the English peasant community, often in the teeth of tyrannical encroachment, preserved and extended its rights.

In such courts, in thousands of villages up and down England, justice was done between man and man; offences against manorial custom were punished, and the services and rights of the villein-tenant enforced and recorded. On its rolls were entered the exact terms under which he held his land. In time, copies of these entries came to be regarded as title to his holding. It gradually became customary to claim possession of land by 'copyhold', a form of tenure which was later recognised, as the villein acquired full legal rights, by the King's judges.

Service in the manor-courts helped to train Englishmen for a free system of society. It taught them to weigh evidence and distinguish between personal feelings and public needs. 'Richard Smith,' ran the entry of a court leet in 1311, 'beat Alice Hannes twice – Mercy, Order, Poor.' The village jury, that is, found him guilty and recommended him to the mercy of the court, which ordered a fine but remitted part of it because he could not afford it. In his everyday task of helping to administer a little corner of the realm of which he was part, the English peasant learnt to blend legal precision with human give-and-take. The village halimote, which dealt with cases of trespass, neglect of manorial duties and offences against the village peace, and which twice a year became a police-court to try crimes short of felony presented by a jury, had its formal pleadings like a royal court. A thirteenth-century book, written to enable stewards and bailiffs to know their business, gives such examples as,

> 'Alice, widow of . . . complaineth of . . . her neighbour, that on such a day his pigs entered her garden and rooted up her beans and cabbages, so that she would not willingly have had that damage for 2s. nor that shame for 12d, and she demandeth that amends be made.'[1]

*   *   *

Keeping the King's Peace in the village and enforcing his law and ordinance was a bucolic officer called the petty constable. Appointed by the high constable of the hundred from a rota of householders, he was usually unpaid and served, nominally at least, for a year. By traditional Anglo-Saxon law every able-bodied man between the ages of fifteen and sixty was obliged to take his share in the policing and defence of his native place, and it was the constable's business to see that he did so. An English village was responsible to the sheriff for public order within its boundaries and could be

[1] F. W. Maitland, *The Court Baron* (Selden Society), p. 75.

collectively fined for crimes committed in it. It had its stocks, ducking-stool – for scolding wives – and pillory. Its priest, reeve and four 'lawful men' represented it at the sheriff's tourn and hundred court, at coroner's inquests and at the assizes where it had to answer for its corporate offences and present those suspected of felony. It had to keep a nightly 'watch and ward' against suspicious travellers and, when the constable raised the 'hue and cry', to chase and apprehend them. 'If any such passing strangers do not allow themselves to be arrested,' ran an ordinance of Henry III, 'then the watch shall raise the hue upon them on all sides and pursue them with the whole township and neighbouring township with hue and cry from township to township until they are taken!'

The petty constable was not only an amateur policeman but a soldier. In time of invasion, riot or rebellion he had to see that every man turned out at the sheriff's summons in the shire *fyrd*. England's Norman and Angevin kings used this rude national militia more than once against their turbulent French-speaking nobles. At first it was confined to free men – for to the continental feudal mind there was something shocking in the idea of a bondsman bearing arms – but it was later extended to all classes, including villeins. Edward I's great defining Statute of Winchester of 1285 placed it on a permanent basis. In every county, hundred and township, muster-rolls were prepared from which, in time of war and emergency, Commissioners of Array selected and impressed men to serve as paid soldiers. Armed with daggers, spears, pikes and longbows, clad in quilted jerkins and iron headpieces, and exercised together once a year in the autumn array of muster, this reserve of amateur soldiers formed a second line of defence on which, in days before she had learnt to command the seas, England was able to draw in all her wars. *Fyrd, posse comitatus*, fencibles, militia, by whatever name it was called, it remained a homespun body, affording from the days of Shakespeare's Falstaff to those of Rowlandson much material for humorists. Of its services to the country perhaps the greatest was that, when royal despotism might otherwise have triumphed, it obviated the need for a standing army.

The Statute of Winchester also defined the subject's duties as a policeman and preserver of the peace. Instead of leaving the village community answerable only for felonies committed within its borders, Edward I made it jointly responsible with its neighbour townships for all felonies committed in the hundred. The unit of policing was made to conform to the needs, not merely of the village, but of the nation. As part of this policy the townships along the royal highways were also ordered, on pain of indictment before the justices on *eyre*, to cut back the brushwood on either side of the road to a distance of two hundred feet to reduce the risk of ambush from brigands and outlaws.

In the last resort such a system of delegated self-government depended on the readiness of the local community to identify itself with the assumptions and requirements of the remote royal authority in whose name the law was enforced. When, in the general breakdown of confidence and economic relationships which followed the Black Death and the failure of the French Wars, the peasants of south-eastern England rose against the attempt of their lay and ecclesiastical lords to impose new taxes and enforce anti-quated feudal dues, the system failed completely to stem a revolutionary flood that all but destroyed the kingdom. There must have been scores of Kent and Essex constables who marched under Wat Tyler and Jack Straw in their assault on the capital of 1381. Yet once the rebellion collapsed and the young King and his ministers had re-established their authority, the village resumed its traditional method of ruling itself under the supervision of the royal officers of the shire and hundred and the manorial courts.

*　　　　*　　　　*

The manorial system of cultivation was communal, though ownership was individual. In the Celtic and pastoral west scattered homesteads and hamlets, small unified holdings and little stone-walled fields were the rule. But in the flat, clay midlands and the south, where corn-growing was the principal activity, the arable land around the village was grouped in two, or, in the better farmed manors, three fields, according as to whether a two- or three-year rotation of crops was followed. These open fields, fenced against the cattle in the summer, were usually several hundred acres in extent. They were divided, without hedges, into narrow, curving strips like elongated Ss, each a furlong or ox-plough-furrow's length. Between the strips were ridges made by the ploughs. As the course of husbandry was the same for all and enforced by the manor court, every villager had so many strips in each field, according to the size of his holding. In some villages the lord's land, called the demesne, and sometimes the parson's glebe land, were enclosed; in others they were scattered about the open fields, where their cultivation, like everyone else's, had to conform to the common rule. The crops were wheat, rye, barley, oats, vetches and peas. They were threshed on barn floors by flails cut from holly or thorn, and winnowed by hand. The wooden ploughs were usually drawn by teams of eight oxen. As few could afford a whole plough-team, they were shared. The normal arrangement was a team to every four yardlands, the hide – approximately 120 acres – being the measure, though it varied widely, of what an eight-ox team could plough in a year.

In addition to the arable there was the meadow lying beside stream or river and tended by the village hayward. Here, too, every peasant had his strip or strips. When the hay had been cut the village cattle were pastured on it and, after the harvest – from Lammas to Candlemas – on the arable stubble, which they helped to dung. They were very small and scraggy, for, under a communal system of grazing, selective breeding was impossible. As there was little winter-feed – root crops were unknown – they were mostly slaughtered and salted at Michaelmas. A few stalled cows and the breeding stock struggled through the winter till the spring.

Beyond the fields and meadow was the waste – forest, moorland, swamp and brackeny common – still covering more than half the country and surrounding the lonely villages like the sea. The lord of the manor might own the soil, but his tenants enjoyed the common use of its rough grasses and herbage for pasture and of its turf and brushwood for fuel. Every holding carried a right or 'stint' to feed so many cattle, horses, geese and swine on the waste, and to take, 'by hook or crook', sticks, fallen timber and loose bracken for litter, sand and clay for building, nuts, berries, rabbits and small birds for the pot. The adjoining woods were full of the villagers' thin, half-wild pigs feeding on beechmast and acorns.

They also abounded in game and, in the wilder parts of the country, with robbers and outlaws, and occasionally wolves.

The life which such a system supported was very simple. There was little scope for initiative or progress, and the pace was that of the least enterprising. The cottages straggling along either side of the unpaved village street and flanked by heaps of manure – the peasant's principal wealth – were mere rectangular-shaped shacks of timber-framing, filled in with wattle, turf and mud and thatched with straw or reeds. They contained usually a single unfloored, hearthless room in which the family slept in verminous squalor with the oxen stalled at the bed's foot, pigs roaming the floor and poultry perched on the beams. The only household goods would be a straw mattress or sack, a few cooking-pots, some home-made tools and, in the homes of the richer villeins, a rude oak chest and perhaps a stool or two. Behind the houses were little closes, growing cab-bage, parsley, onions, leek, garlic, herbs, apples and quinces. Their owners' clothes were of coarse, greasy wool and leather, unwashed and unwashable, made from their own beasts. Their diet was cheese, bacon and, in the summer, milk; bean and vegetable broth; oaten cakes and rough, black wholemeal bread; herrings or other salt-fish, honey from their own hives; and small ale or cider. Its staple was cereal; a thirteenth-century English agricultural writer reckoned the labourer's average allowance of corn at thirty-six bushels a year. Butcher's meat was a rare luxury. In Lent everyone fasted, not only because the Church enjoined it, but because, with the harvest so far away, there was no alternative. 'Fridays and fast-days,' wrote the fourteenth-century poet, William Langland, 'a penny's worth of mussels were a feast for such folks.'

Though by the fourteenth century, especially on the large monastic and baronial estates, the village exported much of what it grew for cash-sales to the towns or to feed and finance some distant lord, it still supplied nearly all its own wants except for salt and iron brought by travelling chapmen. It spun and wove wool for clothes from its own sheep, and linen from its own flax. It made shoes from its own wood or skins. It had a miller – a tenant of the lord and usually the richest man in the place, for every villein had to have his corn ground by him – a smith, a wheelwright and a millwright, a tiler and thatcher, a shoemaker and tanner, a carpenter wainwright and carter. Their callings, and those of the parish agricultural officers survive in our names: Shepherd and Foster, Carter and Baker, Parker, Fowler and Hunter; Wolf and Forester; Smith, Cooper and Carpenter. So do the country places, buildings and beasts among which they spent their skilful, laborious lives: Field, Pitt, and Fox, Lane, Bridge and Ford, Stone and Burn, Church and Hill, Brook and Green, Lamb, Bull and Hogg, Sparrow, Crow and Swan. Other men were called after the masters they served – King, Bishop, Abbot, Dean, Prior, Knight, Squire – or after their own appearance – Black, Brown and White, Short, Round and Long.

*   *   *

Book education for the husbandman there was none. Few could read, nor was there opportunity for doing so. There were no printed books – only the priceless, laboriously-copied, jealously-hoarded manuscripts of the monastery libraries and of the very rich. The peasant's hours of labour were long and, when daylight failed, wax candles were far beyond his reach: his sole illumination was a feeble rushlight dipped in fat. There was no travel for him, unless his cart was requisitioned for some baronial or royal service, for the vast majority of villagers never left home.

Yet he was not a wholly uncultivated man. From his father and the fields he learnt a knowledge of nature's laws. He learnt, too, from his earliest years to look after animals and to take pride in his hereditary work as husbandman or craftsman. Nor did he live by plough or adze alone; he was partaker in a faith and a civilization. If he could not read, he could see and he could hear. The brightly coloured and beautifully fashioned images and paintings that covered the walls and, later, windows of his parish church; the legends and parables of the Christian legend linked him with the culture of Catholic Christendom. Its festivals, which were his days of rejoicing, gave him, it has been reckoned, something like six weeks' holiday in a year. Deeper than the servile divisions of class, the harsh bonds of status, the grinding poverty and squalor of the peasant's lot, the unity and consolation of the Christian faith sustained him and gave his life meaning.

The cold dark winters in the wild northern landscape must often have seemed very lonely and comfortless. It is no wonder that men suffered from superstitious fears and were haunted by ghosts, witches and demons. They must often, too, have been hungry. When the harvest failed, famine followed and, in its train, pestilence, haunting the noisome ditches and insanitary hovels. Yet at the darkest hour of the long northern night, rich and poor, old and young celebrated the beginning of things and the mystery of Christmas. The interminable procession of days in rain-sodden or frozen fields, with bare trees and grey, colourless skies, and the nights of shivering in draughty hovels, were broken by the sweet wintry festival of Christ's birth, with its bright fires, lighted windows and good fare. It came just when it was most needed and broke the winter into two halves, each bearable for the hope of the Christian feast which ended the one and the coming of spring which ended the other. Soon after it the first lambs were born and the earliest snowdrops appeared in fields made rigid by bitter winds. When everything was at its bleakest, a light was lit in darkness.

*   *   *

Every village possessed its priest or parson – the *persona* of the place – serving an ecclesiastical unit known as a parish, administering the Christian sacraments of baptism, confirmation, communion, marriage, penance and extreme unction, and entitled by law to an annual tenth or tithe of the produce of every parishioner. The system dated from pagan times when the lord's priest or magic man who served the former's temple had performed magic rites for his farming neighbours in return for a share in the common fields. The incumbent was usually a peasant's son, living the same rustic life as his flock. Taught, at best, in monastic or cathedral grammar school enough Latin to read the scriptures and declaim the services in a language his parishioners venerated but could not understand, and usually the only literate person in the parish, he lived by cultivating the glebe or 'parson's close' – a holding usually of some fifty or sixty acres in the common fields. He also received dues and offerings from his parishioners for baptisms, weddings, churchings, death-bed visitations and burials. In many of the richer livings the right of presentation or advowson, as it was called, had been given by its patron – a descendant, perhaps, of the church's original donor – to some monastery, college, cathedral or other ecclesiastical foundation which, retaining the bulk of its revenues, paid a deputy to exercise the cure of souls. In other cases the owner of the advowson conferred the living on someone with family claims or on some promising youth marked out for preferment who, by obtaining an episcopal dispensation to reside out of the parish, was allowed to employ a resident vicar or 'perpetual curate' while he completed his education at the Church's universities of Oxford or Cambridge or performed some remunerative ecclesiastical function elsewhere. Usually the absentee rector kept the 'great' tithe on crops, sheep and cattle while allocating to his vicar the farm of the glebe and the 'lesser' tithes on pigs, geese, poultry, eggs, garden-produce, flax, honey and fish.

By the beginning of the fourteenth century nearly a fifth of the country's churches had been appropriated in this way. As only about a third of their income filtered through to the incumbents and, as the holder of a cure was supposed by Canon Law to devote two-thirds of the tithe to the upkeep of the chancel and relief of the parish poor, the latter and the church fabric tended to suffer. Deprived of the 'great' tithes, a vicar was tempted to press his parishioners too strictly for the lesser ones – those which most affected the bondsmen and small-holder – and to spend too much time cultivating his glebe and looking after his live-stock.

Yet there was a compensation. To the average countryman the Church was represented by one of his own class, accustomed from childhood to the same agricultural pursuits and way of life as himself. Though he might not be able to construe the Latin prayers and services he chanted by rote at the altar, he understood the problems of those to whom he ministered. In the market-towns and a few of the richer country parishes the incumbent might be a man of substance like the parson of Trumpington in Chaucer's tale who gave his daughter – he should not, by rights, have had one – a dowry when she married the miller. Usually he was a small free-holder's son or a manumitted villein, for a bondsman could not be admitted to holy orders until he had been freed by his lord.

To a university doctor such a poor rustic priest might seem little better than a 'brute beast' who, immersed in mercenary calcu-lations about crops and beasts, could scarcely expound an article of the faith and was fit only to 'patter up his Matins and Mass'. To his parishioners he was invested with mysterious powers on which rested their hopes and fears of reward or punishment after their hard, brief lives on earth. When, as the sanctus bell sounded, he stood before the altar and officiated at the Mass, bringing about by his priestly office the miraculous transformation of the bread and wine into Christ's body and blood, he seemed a creature of another world. And when death struck and he hastened to the side of the dying, carrying lantern and bell, holy water for sprinkling, oil for anointing and the pyx containing the sacred elements, on him and his power to grant absolution and administer the sacrament of extreme unction depended the lonely, bewildered soul's readiness for its passage to salvation or eternal damnation.

Of what the service of the Church at its best could mean to a country village we have the testimony of Chaucer. For when, in his cavalcade of worldly pilgrims, lay and ecclesiastic, he reached the humble village priest, that cynical, tolerant but scrupulously honest observer of the fourteenth-century scene paused in his amused catalogue of human frailty to draw the portrait of one who came as near to fulfilling the precepts of Christianity as a man can:

> 'This noble example unto his sheep he gave
> That first he wrought and afterwards he taught . . .
> He waited after no pomp or reverence
> Nor made himself no spiced conscience,
> But Christë's lore and his apostles twelve,
> He taught, but first he followed it himself.'

However unsatisfactory many priests may have been, a good priest could make a Christian village.

*   *   *

Every great event of a poor man's life, everything which raised it
above that of the beasts and invested it with beauty or significance,
centred round the parish church. Here every Sunday and on the
more important of the thirty or forty holy days of the year which
were his holidays and the occasion of his feasts and fasts, he listened,
in awe and with bowed head, to the 'blessed mutter of the Mass'
and took part in the ritual dramas and processions which told for
an unlettered people the Gospel story – the lighted candles carried
round the church by the congregation at Candlemas, the distribution and blessing of the ashes on Ash Wednesday, the hanging of
the Lenten veil before the altar, the distribution of branches on
Palm Sunday, the dramatic creeping to the Cross in the darkened
church on Good Friday, the triumphant procession with vestments and banners on Easter Sunday as the Host and Cross were
borne, amid pealing bells and the chanting of the Resurrection
anthem, from the Easter Sepulchre, where they had lain since
Good Friday, to the High Altar. At Pentecost a dove was loosed
from the rafters amid clouds of incense; at the feast of Corpus
Christi the entire community knelt in church and village street
while the Sacrament was borne in procession through their ranks.
At Rogationtide the fields were blessed by the priest, at Lammas
the loaf – first-fruit of the harvest – was presented by him at the
altar, on New Year's Day he led his parishioners round the apple
orchards to bless the fruit of the coming summer.

Except in Lent the village parson seldom preached. Four times
a year he was expected to expound in English the Creed, the Gospel
precepts and Ten Commandments, and expatiate, like Chaucer's
'poor parson of the town', on the seven deadly sins and their
consequences, the seven virtues and the seven sacraments of grace.
For the rest he relied, like every parish priest from Calabria to
Scandinavia, on the dramatic ritual of the Catholic Church; the
rites at the altar, the sonorous Latin prayers and incantations, the
statues, images and pictorial representations of Christ crucified or
risen in majesty, of saints and martyrs and angels, of the Last
Judgment and Harrowing of Hell depicted in brilliant colours and
terrifying detail over the chancel arch, of the stories from Bible and
Apocalypse which covered even the humblest church.

In weaning pagan man from his primitive and bloodstained creeds of terror and human sacrifice, the Church's supreme achievement had been to domesticate and humanise the conception of eternity. Everywhere he was confronted, in church and wayside shrine, with homely and familiar reminders of the Heaven he was enjoined to earn through the virtues of love, faith, compassion, humility, truthfulness, chastity, courtesy – virtues that came so hard and were so much needed by a hot-tempered, ignorant, primitive people. To help them on their way to Paradise and make them shun temptation were the likenesses of men and women who, the Church told them, had struggled and overcome the infirmities of human nature and were now, like the Master whose example they had followed, blessed spirits enthroned in Heaven yet ready to intercede for struggling mortals who called on them for aid. So human were the saints, Christians were taught, that they would help them in their humblest concerns. So St Christopher, who once carred Christ on his shoulders, was the patron and protector of porters; St Bartholomew, who was flayed alive, of tanners; St Apollonia, whose jaw was smashed by his torturers, of those with toothache; St John, who had been plunged into a chaldron of burning oil, of candlemakers. St Giles looked after cripples, St Crispin cobblers, St Katherine little girls, St Eustace and St Hubert huntsmen, St Cecilia the makers of music, St Blaise sufferers from sore throats. And because she had anointed Christ's feet with aromatic oils Mary Magdalene was the protectress of perfumers. If one's oxen were sick one called on St Corneille, if one's pigs on St Anthony, if one's chickens on St Gall. There was even a patron saint, St Osyth, for women who had lost their keys.

Best loved of all who interceded for man was the Virgin. The Gabriel bell rang at evening to call Christians to recite Ave Maria, and the pilgrims flocked to see the replica of her house in the Augustinian priory at Walsingham, believing that the heavenly galaxy, the Milky Way, had been set to guide them there. The events of her life, the Annunciation, Purification, Visitation and Assumption, had taken their place among the great feasts of the Christian year; at the Purification in February, known as Candlemas, everyone walked through the streets carrying candles blessed at the altar in her honour. She was thought of as the embodiment of every womanly virtue; tender, pure and loving and so full of pity that even the most abandoned could hope for forgiveness through her aid.

In no land was Mary more honoured than in England. The number of churches and shrines dedicated to her was past counting; no other name figures so often in the lists of the royal oblations. When William of Wykeham founded his colleges at Winchester and Oxford he placed them under her protection, and at both the bishop still kneels in stone with outstretched hands before her to beg a blessing on his endowments. Nearly every church of importance possessed her image in silver, gold or alabaster given by some benefactor, and along the highroads and pilgrim ways were wayside chapels where travellers could tell their beads and say their prayers to the Queen of Heaven. The names on our parish maps, Ladygrove, Ladysmead, Mary's Well and Maryfield, and the flowers that country folk called after her, marigold and ladysmantle, bear witness after four centuries of Protestantism to the homage paid by our Catholic ancestors to Christ's mother.

It was this union of earth and heaven, matter and spirit, the assumption that the other world and this were in continual contact, which made medieval Christianity such a germinating and educative religion. For the ordinary man his parish church was the centre both of his spiritual and terrestrial life. It was the place where the whole community met. Its nave and aisles were the setting not only for prayer and liturgical processions but for proclamations and business transactions. Its porch was used for coroners' inquests and betrothals and for the payment of legacies; its oaken chest for depositing wills, charters and title-deeds. In the churchyard where the village children played and the dead, carried in the parish coffin, were laid in their shrouds to await the reunion of all Christians on Resurrection day, the parishioners met to beat the parish bounds, fairs were held, and miracle plays or 'mysteries' were enacted by bucolic actors in which rustic exuberance and horse-play mingled, incongruously, with the piety of unquestioning faith.

For medieval Christianity was an intensely human religion. It had place for comedy and farce. In the Palm Sunday procession a

388

boy dressed as an angel standing above the west porch threw down cakes for which the congregation scrambled, while a wooden ass was drawn along behind the choir with a man belabouring it with a whip. Even in the deeply impressive Tenebrae services in Passion week when, one after another, the lights on the altar were darkened, the rustic singers in the loft were sustained during their long ordeal by wine and beer provided by the churchwardens, while the resurrection on Easter morning was hailed by the entire congregation banging on clappers.

All the community's corporate life that was not purely economic centred round the church. When a church was rebuilt or added to – and throughout the fourteenth and fifteenth centuries almost every town and village was refashioning and refurbishing its church – the churchwardens raised the money by arranging archery meetings and door-to-door collections. They appointed a village 'Robin Hood' and 'Little John' to lead the way to the butts after Mass on Sundays and holy days and collect the fees of the competitors, and organised the annual Hocktide collection when the young men and wives and maidens went in turn to one another's houses to rope in those of the other sex and make them pay forfeits for the church's benefit – 'the devocyon of the people on Hoke Tuesday', as the churchwardens of St Edmund's, Salisbury, called it. They held, too, the annual church audit when the parishioners, grouped under their respective trades and callings, came in turn to present their gifts and collections – 'comyth in the yonglings and maidens', 'comyth in the weavers', runs the account of the proceedings in one Somerset parish. It was then that the churchwardens received any bequest left to the parish: the keep of a cow for the poor, a swarm of bees to provide wax for candles and honey, a woman's wedding ring, clothing for making into vestments and coverings.

At a time when most men lived in bare, almost unfurnished mud and wattle huts little bigger than those in which a smallholder today keeps his farrowing sows, the wealth lavished on the church by even the poorest village seems little short of miraculous. As the parish inventories of the fifteenth century show, small and remote churches, with no rich benefactors to endow them, possessed chalices, patens, mazers, censers, candlesticks of silver and silver-gilt, panelled and gilded reredoses and altars, jewelled processional crosses and pyxes for the Host, embroidered vestments and altar-cloths of gold. They were furnished with carved rood screens, misericords and bench-ends, stone and alabaster statues, finely cast and engraved bells, and windows blazing with glass bought from the *verriers* of France and Germany. All was paid for and accumulated from generation to generation by the village community, many of whose members – carpenters, masons, smiths – had helped to fashion this great but, after the Reformation, soon to vanish, heritage of rustic corporate life.

"Hearths with chimneys had taken the place in rich men's houses of sooty open fires, Flemish glass had appeared in traceried windows . . . manor houses and fine merchants' dwellings with private bathrooms and plastered walls were rising in place of the old gloomy fortresses where men and beasts slept together on filthy rush-strewn floors in draughty halls, full of smoke and stink."

"14th century additional wing to Beeleigh Abbey, Maldon, Essex, built as a summer homestead for a luxury loving Abbot. Today the home of Christina Foyle and her husband, Ronald Batty, by whose kindness it is illustrated."

"The flowering of the Perpendicular style, England's supreme contribution to the art of architecture."

The chapel of King's College, Cambridge, begun by Henry VI as the companion foundation of his school at Eton, and completed by Henry VII at the end of the 15th century.

CHAPTER NINETEEN

Travellers, Towns and Traders

BRIDGING THE UNCULTIVATED WILD between England's villages and little towns ran the roads, trodden by growing numbers of men and horses. The metalled highways with which Rome had spanned the country had long become a ghostly network overgrown with grass, their paved surfaces defaced, their causeways broken by quarrying and their course deflected to serve local needs. The medieval road did not run straight from city to city. It meandered round field, park and pale, respecting a thousand local 'liberties' and quirks of history. It was not surfaced for wheeled traffic or swift travelling. It was a grassy trackway for horses, carts, cattle and sheep – a mere way over which travellers had a right to pass. Where it was a national highway subject to the King's Peace, the proprietors along its course were under an obligation to keep it open. No one might raise fences across it or dung-heaps or use it for quarrying stone or gravel. Towns and villages which permitted such encroachments were constantly being fined. In winter, in the clay lowlands, such soft roads became quagmires; in summer a maze of hard-baked hoof-holes and ruts. But so much of the countryside was still waste that it was easy to make a detour across adjoining land. This, however, created a multiplicity of tracks and made it equally easy to lose the way.

During the Dark Ages travel had been so arduous and dangerous that the Church in its prayers grouped travellers with prisoners and captives, sick persons and women labouring with child. The repair of bridges and the provision of hospitality for wayfarers were regarded as matters for Christian charity. Crosses were erected by the wayside in lonely places, lanterns kept burning in church-towers at night, and bells sounded to guide benighted wayfarers.

Rich men left sums to provide rest-houses and *maisons dieu*, and monasteries and incumbents of rectories were enjoined to entertain and relieve travellers.

The lords of the highway, as of everywhere else in that aristocratic age, were the earls, barons and prelates, with their trains of followers, their armour, ceremonial furs and emblazoned mantles and banners, making their way to Council or Parliament or travelling from one estate to another. The greatest of all were the King and his Court. In a single half-year Edward I moved his residence seventy-five times. In days when there no regular posts or means of transmitting news, it was the only way in which a ruler could know and control what was happening in his realm. The grander members of the Court travelled on horseback, the vast army of menials, scullions and poor suitors on foot. Its treasure, plate, pavilions, hangings, beds, cooking-utensils, wine, legal and financial rolls were borne in panniers on pack-horses or in rough, box-like, two-wheeled carts, drawn by oxen, donkeys or dogs, and requisitioned from the countryside. A few great ladies – a queen or some royal invalid – might ride in a litter borne between horses or in a gilded wagon with an arched roof hung with tapestry and suspended on carved, un-sprung beams and huge nailed wheels. But the normal mode of transport was the cavalcade: the long procession of jingling, brightly accoutred, splendidly caparisoned horses, with riders chattering or singing as they wound their way across the fields. To journey in company and make music as one went was the mode of the time. Only the King's messengers, forerunners of the post, travelled alone, and lepers with their bells and clappers, sores and pallid, hooded faces, and adjured felons making their way from sanctuary to the nearest port with bare feet and loose white tunics and carrying wooden crosses as signs of the Church's protection.

The chief interest of the age being religion, there were many clerical travellers. Monastic officers visiting their estates and bishops' commissaries perambulating the diocese, pardoners selling indulgences, summoners with writs for breaches of ecclesiastical law, papal agents collecting money, poor clerks on the way to the universities, and black-gowned Dominican and, even more

392

numerous, grey-gowned Franciscan friars. For every monk on the road there were a dozen friars.

For the mendicants, as they were called, who had first appeared in England in Henry III's reign, had been founded to serve God, not like the monks in the cloister, but in the street and highway. Bound by vows of chastity and poverty, their original mission had been to the very poor. With the spread of civilization and luxury, their mission, though ostensibly the same, had changed. By the fourteenth century they had ceased to be only evangelists to the poor and had become as well confessors to the rich middle class of the merchant towns. Leaving their squalid abodes in the city slums, they had raised great preaching churches – like the famous three-hundred-foot-long Greyfriars church in London – out of the benefactions of merchants who recalled with gratitude the days when they or their forbears had fled from villeinage to the hovels of the nearest town and had been befriended there by the mendicants. They still begged their way wherever they went, but the need to do so had vanished. For more than a century the benefactions and bequests of the rich had flowed into their coffers, and as the confessors of kings, nobles and merchants, their leaders enjoyed vast influence. But they were still to be encountered everywhere, ministering to rich and poor alike, enjoying hospitality wherever they went and employing popular, and even sensational, devices to win converts to their faith and subscribers to their Order. They were particularly popular with the ladies, to whom their gaiety, good humour and here-today, gone-tomorrow approach, and the understanding and ingratiating way with which they heard confessions much endeared them – according to their enemies – far too much.

These were the religious professionals of the road; others were amateurs. Every spring men and women would set out in company, with wallet, staff and scallop shell, broad-brimmed hat and jingling Canterbury bell, to visit some distant or local shrine and return with relics – for the rich a splinter from a saint's staff or a flask of holy water; for ordinary folk, a pewter-badge to be worn on cap or breast as a souvenir. Pilgrimage was one of the penances set by the Church for winning remission of time in purgatory – the place of punishment to which it was believed those not immediately translated to Heaven or Hell were consigned after death until they expiated their sins.

Pilgrimage could be a penance of the most onerous kind, one in which a man left home and family for years, braving immense hardships and perils to visit the Holy Land or Rome or some remote shrine like St James's of Compostella in Spain. But for most people, though seen as a means of acquiring grace, a pilgrimage was an excuse for a holiday, to be taken preferably

> 'When that Aprillë with his showers sweet
> The drought of March hath pierced to the root.'

As soon as the roads dried out after the winter they were thronged with parties making their way to some favourite shrine and beguiling the journey with tales, singing and the playing of bag-pipes. The most popular places of pilgrimage, and there were hundreds, were St Thomas's shrine at Canterbury – the word 'canter' entered the language through it – and Our Lady's statue at Walsingham in Norfolk, 'the most holy name in England' with its famous phial of the Virgin's milk. Both were visited every summer by huge crowds. So were Joseph of Arimathaea's winter-blossoming thorn at Glastonbury, the philtre of Christ's blood at Richard of Cornwall's abbey of Hayles in Gloucestershire, and the Confessor's glittering shrine at Westminster, where the hollows worn by the feet of kneeling pilgrims can still be seen.

The most cautious road-users were those who travelled with merchandise or money, for the woods and thickets were full of thieves. In the early Middle Ages the main roads, especially those to the southern and eastern ports, were much used by foreigners – Flemings and Italians buying Cotswold or Yorkshire wool, Spaniards with steel blades from Toledo, Lombards with silks and spices, Easterlings with furs and tar from the Baltic. But by the end of the thirteenth century much of such trade was beginning to pass to Englishmen. As there were no posts and few facilities for trans-ferring money from one country to another, a merchant had con-stantly to be on the road attending his business. Like the poor man in Chaucer's tale who was deceived by his wife and the young monk, he was always off to Bruges or Bordeaux at break of day.

Humbler traders like pedlars, chapmen and charcoal-sellers went on foot, with their wares on a pack-horse or in a box or sack on their backs. So did a host of poor itinerants, travelling from one village to another: minstrels, buffoons and ballad-singers, some aiming high at the castles and others at gaping rustics on the village greens; bears and bearwards; men with performing monkeys; clowns, jugglers, girls who danced on their hands with swords in their mouths, and herbalists selling panaceas for every disease. There is a picture of one in a thirteenth-century herbal, spreading his wares on his carpet or drugget and haranguing the villagers.

At certain times of the year the roads became crowded with travellers converging on a single spot. Fairs were occasions when a rural neighbourhood did its shopping and caught a glimpse of the outer world. The greatest fair in England was Stourbridge near Cambridge – the property of Barnwell Priory. Here for three weeks every September a town of wooden booths offered for sale everything a rustic community needed. There were streets that sold soap, streets that sold garlic, streets that sold coal. Others vended fish, nails, grindstones, Sussex iron and Worcestershire salt, shovels, brushes and pails, oil and honey, pots and pans, horses and pack-saddles. The centre of the fair was the duddery, where the 'duds' or cloths of East Anglia were displayed. Among those who brought their wares were Spaniards and Moors with Damascus blades and armour, Venetians with gems and velvets, Flemings with linen, Dutchmen with cheeses, Greeks with almonds and spices and Germans or Easterlings with tallow, fur and pitch. A special court of *Pied Poudre* or 'dusty foot' – called by the English 'Pie Powder' – was held to preserve order and enforce the regulations of the fair's owners about weights and measures and the quality of foodstuffs. In the jovial mode of England the fair also provided horse-races, wrestling-matches, tippling, gambling and music booths, rope-dancers and a maypole.

*   *   *

What fairs were temporarily, towns were permanently. During the reigns of the first three Henrys there had been a steady growth in the size and number of towns. The Crown and the great secular and ecclesiastical lords found the sale of free burgess-tenures and the tolls of markets and fairs a valuable supplement to their agricultural revenues. They encouraged commerce by letting the citizens and guild-merchants of favoured towns buy charters of freedom from the tolls and custom-dues which impeded the flow of goods at city gate, port and river crossing. Control of the hours of dealing, of prices, weights and measures, and of the quality of goods sold, was delegated by royal or baronial charter to their corporations and, often, to associations of their traders. These merchant-guilds were empowered to fix wages and prices fair to both buyer and seller, to exclude non-members from trading in the town and to fine and punish for breaches of their rules. They appointed hours, announced by bell, for the opening and closing of markets and levied tolls on goods brought for sale. They also made treaties, interchanging commercial privileges, with the traders of other towns. And in the larger cities, craftsmen and traders associated themselves in livery companies or fraternities, partly commercial and partly religious and social, to regulate the conditions of their trade and afford one another mutual protection.

Like the juries of the villages, these self-governing corporations helped to train Englishmen for political responsibility. They were administered by voluntary officers elected annually, whose duties were borne by the members in turn, and governed by rules reached after mutual and open discussion. Members were punished for selling inferior goods, for sharp or shoddy practice that lowered the name of their craft, for brawling and eavesdropping and breaches of social and professional etiquette. A trader who sold food made from diseased carcasses, who put sand in his bread or water in his wine or otherwise tricked the public, was sentenced by his fellow craftsmen to be drawn through the streets on a hurdle or to sit in penance in the pillory with the offending goods hung round his neck and his crime published on a placard. 'The said John Penrose,' ran the order of one London court, 'shall drink a draught of the same wine which he sold to the common people, and the remainder of such wine shall then be poured on the head of the same John, and he shall forswear the calling of a vintner in the city of London for ever.'

Every English town, with the possible exception of London, had originally grown out of a village. Its institutions had a rustic origin: the borough and ward officers with agricultural names; the moot which had begun as a manorial jurisdiction, and the burgh-mote horn that summoned the burghers to its meetings; the annual perambulation of the bounds when the city fathers, like their village forbears, solemnly beat the young fry over the boundary-stones to make them remember where they stood. The sanitary arrangements of the borough also derived from the village. Such drains as it had, ran down the unpaved or, at best, cobbled roadway. The household refuse and ordure, thrown out of the windows at nightfall, were scavenged by pigs, dogs and kites. Even in London, where the poorer dwellings were totally without privies, there was for long only one public latrine for every ward and a dozen dung-carts for the whole city. The larger the towns grew, the more unwholesome they became, though, after a time their corporations, alarmed at the rising death-rate, began to issue regulations about street-cleansing and water-supply.

Yet, though the towns were dirty, they were also beautiful, with their church towers and spires, their stately gateways and half-timbered houses, and the trees and blossom of their gardens. Their encircling walls were designed more for preventing robberies and controlling suspicious travellers at night than for war. Except on the Welsh and Scottish borders they were seldom the elaborate affairs of the continent, where even the smallest town was heavily fortified. Some of the later boroughs, like Cambridge, never even had walls, but only palisades and ditches crossed by gated bridges. Being in little danger of attack, they were free from the military restrictions that cramped life for European burghers. They did not need governors and garrisons.

For this reason, too, they spread outwards rather than upwards, running to leafy suburbs which, secure in England's immunity from invasion, nestled outside instead of inside the walls. Yet, as no town save London had more than 10,000 inhabitants, and few a third of this number, the fields were never far away. Most of the richer merchants had farms or orchards in the surrounding countryside, as well as gardens, stables and cowstalls round their

houses. English urban economy was as much rural as urban. Even
the city of Norwich, capital of the clothmaking industry of East
Anglia and the third largest town in England, suspended trade
during the harvest and sent its weavers into the fields.

*   *   *

One town in England stood alone. With the royal courts of law
sitting permanently in the King's palace or hall of Westminster,
London had long taken the place of the old Anglo-Saxon capital,
Winchester, as the seat of government. One of Henry II's subjects,
William FitzStephen, wrote an account of it as it was a century
after the Conquest: its clear river bordering it on the south, the
royal castle in the east, the high and massive walls with their seven
double-gates and towers, the thirteen conventual and hundred and
twenty-six parish churches. Most of the houses were still flimsy
single or two-storeyed wooden structures; one winter gale flattened
more than six hundred, and fires often swept away whole wards.
But the richer merchants' and knights' houses were already being
built of stone, and red-brick tiles were gradually replacing thatch.
Two years before Henry's death in 1189 the Londoners began
their first stone bridge; a monument of faith in the country's
stability, which took thirty years to complete and lasted for six
centuries.

FitzStephen described the merchandise which flowed up the
river to the Pool beside the Tower and the little hithes and quays
along the north bank – gold and spices from the East, arms from
Scythia and purple silk from China; the wine and cook-shops
where travellers could buy hot dishes at any hour of the day or
night; the market outside the walls in the meadow called Smithfield, where high-stepping palfreys with gleaming coats were put
through their paces and country folk brought their goods and live-
stock for sale. He drew a picture, the first in our history, of the
Londoners at play; their summer evening walks among the suburban wells – St Clement's, Holywell, Clerkenwell – and the
sparkling streams whose mill-wheels made so cheerful a sound;
the hunts in the great Middlesex and Essex forests after stag, fallow
deer and wild boar; the apprentices and schoolboys playing

398

football in the fields while 'the fathers and wealthy magnates came on horseback to watch the contests and recover their lost youth'; the archery, running, jumping, wrestling, dancing and stone slinging, rowing and skating, with which the youths and maidens regaled themselves on holy days.

By the fourteenth century, the population of London had risen to about 50,000. Though still much smaller than the great continental cities of Paris, Milan and Florence, with its 'square mile' along the Thames between the Tower and Ludgate it was by far the country's largest town – four or five times the size of York, Bristol, Plymouth, Coventry or Norwich and probably ten times that of Gloucester, Newcastle, Salisbury, Exeter or Winchester. Newcomers were all the time being drawn into it by the commerce of its tidal river and the business of the royal Chancery and the courts of law at Westminster two miles to the west. Already the Strand – the highway between the two places – was lined with nobles' and prelates' palaces whose gardens sloped down to the un-embanked Thames. The King himself, unlike his cousin of France, had no palace in his capital – only the Tower on its eastern wall, with its little garrison of knights and men-at-arms, and the Wardrobe or Household clothing store at Baynard's Castle.

For the City was a law to itself. 'Come what may,' ran an old saying, 'the Londoners should have no King but their Mayor.' This functionary, though only a merchant, had taken his place at Runnymede among the great magnates of the realm who imposed Magna Carta. He ruled the capital with the help of two sheriffs, elected annually like himself, and a court of aldermen representing its twenty-five wards. Behind this court's weekly hustings in the Guildhall lay the general body of the corporation – the old folkmoot of the citizens assembled three times a year by bell in the open air outside St Paul's. With the population growing fast, there was a constant tendency on the part of the less privileged to try to gain control of the city's government and oust the older merchant families who monopolised it – a struggle which resulted in frequent faction-fights and rioting. During Edward I's reign the antiquated and unmanageable public assembly was abandoned in favour of an elected Common Council. Through its officers the corporation collected the royal customs on foreign merchandise and levied its own tolls on all goods coming in from the country. It made bye-laws on such matters as building, public order, the use of fountains and precautions against fire. It decided who should have the right to trade in particular districts, where swine should be allowed to wander, when taverns should close and slops and refuse be emptied from the windows. It also fixed the hour of curfew, after which none with swords were allowed in the streets, 'unless some great lord or other substantial person of good reputation'.

London could be a very turbulent city. Behind its bridge and seven portcullised gateways crowded the warlike rabble of appren-tices and journeymen who, when roused, became a terrible raging beast. Any infringement of its rights brought it swarming through the narrow streets like a torrent. Once, when some Hoxton resi-dents enclosed a meadow where the Londoners had long taken their Sunday walks, a turner in a fool's coat ran through the streets crying, 'Shovels and spades!', upon which the whole town turned out to level the hedges and ditches. The German merchants of the Cologne Steelyard in Thames Street and the rich Italians of Galley Quay and Mincing Lane barricaded their houses against their English neighbours like fortresses.

Yet the beauty of medieval London impressed travellers even more than its turbulence. It was bordered on the south by a wide, clear river, teeming with fish and with swans on its waters. Beyond it, save for the disorderly little suburb of Southwark, lay unsullied meadows and the wooded Surrey hills. To the north of the walls cornfields and pastures, diversified with streams and water-mills, stretched to the heights of Hampstead and Highgate. To the east lay the great hunting forests of Epping and Hainault. All round were thriving villages supplying the city's needs – Stepney, Bethnal Green, Islington, Hoxton, Holborn, Marylebone and, farther afield, Bow and Bromley, Hackney, Highbury and Stoke Newing-ton, Kilburn, Paddington and Knightsbridge. Though, save for its immense cathedral on the hill and its famous twenty-arch bridge crowned with houses, London lacked imposing buildings, the towers and spires of its churches and monasteries made a wonder-ful show as they crowded above the walls and river. The sound of their bells was almost continuous. And between the brightly painted wooden houses and red-tiled roofs were countless little gardens or 'herbers' and orchards of waving fruit-trees – mulberry, apple, plum, peach and cherry.

* * *

The country of which London was the capital was still predominantly agricultural: a rich primary producing land, with a population only about a third of that of France and Italy, exporting vast quantities of fine wool and, in good years, grain and dairy produce. It also exported hides, leather goods, dried and salted fish, embroideries, metalware, tin, coal and lead; mostly to the overpopulated Low Countries, to Gascony and the Rhineland in exchange for wine, and to the Baltic for timber and shipbuilding stores. Wool was its main source of wealth. The finest – the short wool of the Ryelands sheep and the long of the Lincolns, Leicesters and golden Lion breed of the Cotswolds – came from the Severn valley and the limestone belt between Somerset and Lincolnshire. Yet almost every part of the country, except the far north and extreme south-west, exported wool of some kind. It was reckoned that on an average thirty thousand sacks or eight million fleeces went abroad every year, mostly to northern Italy and the cloth-manufacturing towns of Flanders, Artois, Brabant and Hainault.

Though for most of the Middle Ages England was primarily a supplier of raw wool to others, cloth was always manufactured on a small scale for home consumption in most of the larger towns. Edward III's marriage in 1330 to a Hainault princess brought a new stimulus to native manufacture. Colonies of Flemish weavers, attracted by the cheap and abundant supplies of the raw material of their trade and the social stability of England, established themselves during his reign at Norwich, York and Cranbrook in Kent. Queen Philippa herself made a practice of visiting one of these settlements in Norwich whenever her husband went on progress in East Anglia.

Export of wool and the increased imports which it paid for of spices, wine, silks, furs, timber, pitch, tar, oil, salt, alum, rice and fruits were a great stimulus to native shipping and shipbuilding.

401

Southampton, Bristol, Plymouth and Falmouth were the chief ports of the west, Lynn, Boston, Newcastle-on-Tyne, Kingston-on-Hull and the Cinque Ports of the east. After London the most important was Southampton, whose deep tidal water, protected by the Isle of Wight from Breton, Gascon and Flemish pirates, rivalled the Thames estuary as the starting-point for the convoys of little sailing-ships, mostly of less than a hundred tons, which carried England's wool to the continent. It was a terminus port, too, for the wine fleets from Bordeaux, Bayonne and La Rochelle, and for the Genoese and Pisan carracks which during the early years of the fourteenth century started to export woolfells from the Solent and Thames to the mills of the Arte della Lana of Florence in return for luxuries from Italy and the Orient. To Southampton came by barge down the Itchen – then navigable as far as Winchester – the wool of the Wiltshire, Berkshire and Gloucestershire downs, while coastwise vessels from Poole, Melcombe Regis, Bridport, Lyme and Exeter brought that of Dorset, Somerset and Devon. Other wool travelled down the Severn and Warwickshire Avon for shipment at Bristol. Carts and packhorses took the canvas-wrapped bales and fells on their journey from the upland pastures to the nearest river.

In days when water provided by far the cheapest form of transport, England's commerce gained from two circumstances. Though her rivers were small compared with those of the continent, the sea was never far away and her coast abounded in estuaries where goods could be shipped either abroad or to her own ports. And at a time when every ruler was trying to fill his coffers by levying tolls on merchandise, England with her strong, unified royal government was the largest free-trading area in Europe. Almost her only internal transportation-tolls were petty portages and viages levied to recoup expenditure where a bridge or road had been provided by private enterprise. Only at the courts of Brabant and Hainault and in the Italian and Flemish cities was the movement of trade as free.

With a coastline longer for her size than that of any western kingdom, England possessed a substantial maritime population living by fishing, coastal trade and voyages to the Baltic, Low Countries, France and Biscay. Though most of her ocean carrying-trade was still in the hands of foreigners and her ships were of much smaller tonnage than those of the Mediterranean trading states – Genoa, Pisa, Venice and Aragon – her seamen, accustomed to the Channel and North Sea tides and storms, were tough, skilful and notorious for their pugnacity. Constantly involved in harbour broils with their Norman, Breton, Flemish and Basque rivals, they fought as often among themselves. Whenever the seamen of the Cinque Ports met the fishermen of Yarmouth, whom they viewed as interlopers, they engaged them in pitched battle 'on lond and strong'. With their seven chartered ports – Winchelsea, Romney, Hythe, Dover, Sandwich, Hastings and Rye, and their outlying 'limbs' – the portmen of the Sussex and Kent lagoons and inlets had long been the aristocrats of the narrow seas, producing their feudal quota of ships for the King in time of war and living in peacetime by a well-tried blend of fishing, piracy and trade with northern France and the Low Countries. But, with the gradual silting up of their harbours and the development of sail, their ascendancy was already beginning to be challenged by the West Country seamen. With the richest fishing grounds in the world at their gates and a Catholic country to feed that lived on fish all Lent and Fridays, coastal Englishmen were learning the business of mastering the watery wastes in which their island was set. Though they seldom yet ventured further than Spain or Norway – Chaucer's shipman knew the coasts from Jutland to Finisterre – the stormy and changeable seas they sailed were well adapted for teaching the finer points of seamanship. A breed apart, transmitting their sea-lore from father to son, they introduced into the make-up of a rustic people an adventurous, carefree strain which was to have far-reaching consequences in the sixteenth century after the discovery of America and the ocean trade-routes round the Cape.

*   *   *

The merchant town, with its life of freedom and opportunity, was little by little transforming the racially divided society that England had become after the Norman conquest into a fluid one in which every social grade shaded imperceptibly into the next. Many of the leading merchant families, especially in London and the larger

403

ports, traced their descent from foreign traders who had settled in England, like the Bocointes and Buckerells who had come from Italy and the Arraxes who took their name from Arras. Far more were enterprising English countrymen, often of villein blood, who had fled from bondage on their paternal acres to seek their fortunes behind the walls of the self-governing chartered boroughs. Many who did so perished of poverty or disease in their overcrowded slums, defeated by the monopolistic restrictions with which the established burgesses protected themselves and their crafts and trades. Others passed, sometimes in less than a generation, from the harsh, unchanging life of the manor to affluence, the dignity of aldermanic or mayoral status, and even office under the Crown – always in England quick to avail itself of the services of men of business and financial experience. Merchants unknown to the hereditary feudal hierarchy, with rustic names like Dunstable, Haverill and Piggsflesh, served as royal chamberlains, butlers and purveyors, loaned money to the Crown or some great magnate, arranged for the transfer of funds from one part of the Plantagenet Empire to another and offered mortgages to supply their social superiors, lay and ecclesiastic, with the ready cash to cater for their increasingly luxurious tastes. In doing so, though many fell by the way, they made fortunes for themselves, investing their gains in land and founding landed and knightly families.

The prolonged conflicts with Scotland and France of the three Edwards provided an enormous stimulus to the development of the merchant class. Though no English trader could at first offer the Crown the credit facilities of the great banking and cloth-manufacturing houses of Florence and Lombardy, by the end of the thirteenth century there were already native financiers rich enough to play a leading part in equipping the royal armies. It was to those who dealt in wool, 'the sovereign merchandise and jewel of this realm of England', as Parliament put it, that the Crown turned. For alone of England's commodities wool could always be converted into cash; Flanders and Italy could never have enough of it. It was with the help of the great Shropshire woolmonger, Laurence of Ludlow, the builder of Stokesay castle – *'mercator notissimus'* as the royal lawyers described him – that Edward I equipped an expedition to Flanders in 1297. When Laurence was drowned in an over-loaded ship taking the wool to Holland, the monastic chroniclers saw in it the hand of God avenging the lowered prices to the home – and ecclesiastical – producer with which the financier and his fellow monopolists passed on their losses.

The bargaining power which the collection and export of wool gave to the rich subject in his dealings with the Crown played a major part in the development of national taxation and of Parliament. There were three ways in which the Government could raise money from the trade. The first was to requisition part of the season's crop and, treating it as a forced loan from its owners, sell it abroad. The second was to borrow from foreign or English capitalists in return for a temporary monopoly of the wool export. The third – the method finally adopted after much trial and error – was to procure from Parliament a tax on exports and set up a customs-staple in some town or towns, either at home or abroad, through which all exported wool had to pass. The right to levy customs had always been a royal prerogative but, in an age of primitive economy, if the Crown wished to raise money quickly it could do so only with the co-operation of those who dealt in the goods it wished to tax. Sometimes, instead of summoning a Parliament and asking for a subsidy from the entire merchant class as represented by the elected burgesses, the King convened an assembly of leading wool-merchants and negotiated with them a levy on exported wool. But as soon as it became realised that the woolmongers invariably passed on the tax by lowering the prices paid to wool-producers, the latter's representatives in Parliament began to demand that the Crown should negotiate with them instead of with those who paid the tax only in name. In doing so they put forward as a *quid pro quo*, however at first humbly and tentatively, demands not only for redress of grievances but for control over the expenditure of the money raised and of the royal officers who administered it.

The means by which the wool tax was collected was the staple. It was first set up in London and thirteen other English ports at the beginning of Edward I's reign to collect the 'ancient or great custom' or half a mark – 6s. 8d. – per sack, granted to him by Parliament. When in 1297 he forcibly borrowed all the available stocks of English wool to finance an expedition to the Low Countries, a foreign staple had had to be set up, first at Dordrecht and later at Antwerp, to weigh and price the commandeered wool and levy the hated *maltote*, as it was called, on that of the merchants. Here, and in the domestic staple towns in England, the royal officials – collectors, controllers, searchers, surveyors, clerks, weighers and crane-keepers – administered both the ancient and great custom and the so-called petty custom which Edward at the end of his reign imposed on foreign exporters. For though freedom in trade increased both the export of wool and the prices paid to the producer, the Crown could no longer subsist without the revenue of the customs and the credit that could be raised from it. Early in Edward III's reign to finance his wars with France the foreign staple was revived to become a permanent feature of the wool-trade and the national system of taxation. It enabled the King to borrow money on the security of the customs and direct the export of wool to whatever city in the Low Countries suited his foreign policy of the moment. After the capture of Calais in 1347, that town became England's chief staple port and, later, when the export of cloth began to supersede that of wool, the spearhead for its sale to Europe.

The raising of wool was the concern of almost the entire rural community. Not only were the owners of the great feudal and ecclesiastical estates dependent for ready money on their fleeces, but so were knights of the shire, rich franklins and even humble villeins whose communal village flocks helped to swell the flow of wool from the manorial demesnes to the quays and warehouses of the collecting merchants. Travelling with their pack-horses to grange, village and monastery and buying up the year's produce to sell to the exporters who shipped it to Flanders or Italy, the 'woolmen', by offering credit in exchange for low prices, earned a high rate of concealed interest without infringing the Christian rules against usury. Many of the larger landowners, as well as keeping flocks, engaged in this collecting trade, buying the wool of their smaller neighbours who lacked the capital and know-how to dispose of their own produce. The Cistercian abbeys of the northern and western dales were particularly active in such business, drawing

from it and their flocks the revenues which enabled them to replace
the austere habitations of pioneer days with the magnificent buildings that still, after centuries of desolation and decay, make the
ruins of Fountains and Tintern, Rievaulx and Byland places of
aesthetic pilgrimage.

Picturing Plantagenet England, one sees the traces of this rural
industry everywhere – the open downlands nibbled close by immense flocks of tiny sheep with their shepherds, tinkling bells,
sheepcotes and dewponds; the fells and fleeces stacked in great
barns of stone and timber; the up-country towns and the market-
places of York and Lincoln, Grantham, Louth, Ludlow and
Shrewsbury, Winchester and Andover crowded with dealers and
factors; the trains of pack-horses and barges moving towards the
sea; the London merchants in their furred robes doing business
with the King's officers; the English cogs and tall Italian carracks
beating out from the Thames estuary and southern ports towards
the hungry mills of Flanders and distant Tuscany:

'The sward the black-face browses,
The stapler and the bale,
The grey Cistercian houses
That pack the wool for sale.'

The pastoral economy of shepherding and tending 'the silly
sheep', of sheep-shearing and dispatching the wool fells to their
remote destinations made a lasting impression on the nation's
character. It embraced both the solitude and meditation of the
shepherd's life, and the journeyings and bargainings involved in
selling the wool which the mills of Ghent and Arno transformed
into raiment for Europe's rich. The lonely sheepcotes and farms of
western and northern England, the epitaph in the downland
church –

'Faithful lived and Faithful died
Faithful shepherd on the hillside,
The hill so high, the field so round,
In the day of judgement he'll be found' –

are one side of the medal; Chaucer's merchant off to Bruges at
break of day and the bustling wife of Bath at her clothier's trade

the other. Wool-growing, wool-carrying and wool-mongering all tended to make men more thoughtful and resourceful than the uneventful life of communal arable agriculture by which peasant Christendom lived. They made, too, for a sense of freedom. The man who owned or tended sheep on the uplands felt himself more his own master than the husbandman of the three-field village closely bound by manorial custom and watched by prying neighbours.

*   *   *

During the last half of the fourteenth century the domestic cloth trade started to expand so rapidly that by the middle of the following century – the last of the Middle Ages – it was already absorbing most of the native wool crop. In 1353, two thousand cloths were exported; forty years later, during Richard II's reign, twenty times as many. In 1420 the export of cloth for the first time exceeded that of raw wool, and by the end of the fifteenth century, despite a halt during the Wars of the Roses, was twice as much. The introduction from the East of the fulling-mill and its exploitation by English capitalists created a new industry wherever flowing water was plentiful and good sheep pasture near. It brought an enormous accession of wealth to these localities. In the valleys of the Stroud and the Wiltshire Avon; in the upper reaches of the Aire and the Pennine streams, where the mechanisation of the fulling process laid the foundations of the prosperity of the West Riding towns; and in Suffolk along the Stour and its tributaries there occurred a rural industrial revolution. West Country broadcloths – 'Stroudwaters', 'Cotswolds' and 'Castlecombes' – and the serges and worsteds of East Anglia became as famous on the continent as the products of Ghent and Ypres. In the fifteenth century it was reckoned that nearly 25,000 workers were engaged in the trade. It was an industry based, not on cities but on villages and small towns where, free from the restrictive labour and price regulations of municipality and guild, enterprising clothiers supplied the raw material to cottage weavers from whom they later collected the spun wool, distributing it to the shearers, fullers and dyers before their pack-horses carried the finished product to London or the ports for shipment overseas. Pioneers of what was long to be the country's greatest industry, these rustic capitalists left their mark in the tall-towered churches and stone manor-houses – witnesses to their faith, wealth and enterprise – which they raised among the limestone hills that spanned England from Somerset to Lincolnshire. There, too, can be seen the brasses which preserve their likenesses – the forked beards, hawks and horses, the hall-marks of quality and honest dealing that they stamped on their bales, the fine Flemish beaver hats in which they rode out to bargain for the midsummer clip or autumn fell with Gloucestershire squires and Yorkshire abbots. Such were William Grevil, ancestor of the earls of Warwick, who was buried in 1401 in the beautiful church he built at Chipping Campden – 'late citizen of London and flower of the wool merchants of all England' – Thomas Paycocke of Coggeshall, and John Barton of Holme who had engraved on the windows of his house:

> 'I thank God and ever shall,
> It is the sheep hath paid for all.'

The success of the cloth trade and the fierce and often armed resistance it provoked from foreign competitors – especially the German Hanse in the Baltic – favoured the growth of London. Except for Bristol, with its merchant princes and shipowners like the Canynges – builders of the great Perpendicular church of St Mary Redcliffe, 'the fairest, goodliest and most famous parish church in England' – the burghers of the older provincial towns lacked the capital to finance so costly and speculative a business. The monopoly of the trade with the Low Countries, by far England's most lucrative market, was in the hands of the London Society of Merchant Adventurers. Like the older Merchants of the Staple, they formed the nucleus of a new aristocracy, marrying into the gentry, founding landed estates and playing a part in the luxurious court of Edward IV – a great patron of London merchants and their wives. It was through them and the Mercers' Company that the wealth of the cloth trade flowed into the capital, drawing with it growing numbers of tradesmen, craftsmen and artificers. By the end of the fifteenth century the city's population was nearly

75,000, and its suburbs almost joined the outlying villages of Hoxton, Clerkenwell and Shoreditch whose fields – once the Londoner's
playground – were giving way to houses. Its riches were beginning
to compare with those of the Lombard and Flemish cities; an
Italian traveller counted more than fifty goldsmiths' shops in
Cheapside; 'so rich and full of silver vessels is it,' he wrote, 'that in
all the shops of Milan, Rome, Venice and Florence put together
there would not be found so many of the magnificence that is to
be seen in London.' This was an exaggeration, but the Scottish
poet, William Dunbar, received much the same impression when
he visited it in 1501:

> 'Upon thy lusty bridge of pillars white
> Be merchantïs full royal to behold;
> Upon thy streets goeth many a seemly knight
> In velvet gownës and in chains of gold . . .
> Rich be thy merchantïs in substance that excellïs;
> Fair be thy wives, right lovesome, white and small.
> Clear be thy virgins, lusty under kellis:
> London, thou art the flower of cities all!'

CHAPTER TWENTY

Gothic Glory

'Walk there awhile, before the day is done,
Beneath the banner and the battered casque,
Where graven heraldry is bronze and stone
With lily and with cross and leopard's mask
Spandrils the arch. Thou shalt not walk alone;
There dead men walk again and dead lips ask,
"What of the isles of England and her sea?"
Till whispers fill the tower of memory.'

Muriel Stuart

WHEREVER MAN in the Middle Ages turned his eyes, he was faced by the majesty of the Catholic Church. A traveller could not approach a town in any part of western Christendom without seeing the familiar sight of its towers and spires rising above its walls and houses. For the Church did not depend for its teaching only on books and sermons or even on the candlelit mystery and drama of its Latin liturgy. In an age when not one man in a thousand could read, it drove its lessons home in sculptured stone and vaulted space, and in the carvings and paintings of artists who employed their genius to make the Christian story familiar to everyone. The supreme expression of medieval man's faith was the work of the 'engineers' or architects who, at abbot's or bishop's command, sketched on deal boards the designs of their vast buildings, and of the master-masons who carried out their conceptions with teams of travelling craftsmen. There were hewers trimming the stone with axes and dressing it with chisels, setters laying the walls and making mortar-matrixes, turners with stone-lathes shaping column and shaft; carvers and glaziers, slaters, smiths and plumbers,

411

wrights and joiners. They fashioned the timber supports from the heart of the tree, graved statues, made ironwork fittings for doors, raised with primitive cranes and pulley-wheels the baskets of stone and rolls of lead to the soaring walls and roofs, and filled the windows with geometrically patterned and brilliantly coloured glass.

During the twelfth and thirteenth centuries nearly every great cathedral and abbey church in the French-speaking lands on either side of the Channel was partly rebuilt or enlarged in the style which later became known as Gothic. The plain rounded vaulting, small windows and heavy columns of the Romanesque and Norman past were superseded by delicately pointed arches, clusters of slender pillars and tiers of long lancet-windows that flooded the vast buildings with light and lit the jewelled shrines, painted walls and stained glass within, in radiant hues. The transformation was the result, partly of revolutionary advances in engineering technique – which rendered unnecessary the unbroken masses of wall space needed to support roof and tower – and partly of new ideas introduced into northern Europe during the Crusades from the Saracen and Byzantine East. The overwhelming impression was one of height, light and energy. With their soaring pinnacles and flying buttresses – built to take the outward thrust of the immense arches and fenestrated walls – these great new buildings, glittering in white stone, looked from a distance like giants on the march.

Inside they were filled with delicate carving, with sculptured shrines, tombs and statues, and with colour and ornamentation that humanised their immense size and made them resemble gigantic jewelled boxes. In England this tendency to fine internal decoration was carried farther than in almost any other western land. Forests of airy shafts of Purbeck marble, exquisitely moulded trefoil arches, flowing leaves and flowers naturalistically carved in stone on capital and arch, elaborate and deeply carved roof-bosses were distinguishing marks of the English school. So were the compound piers that the Anglian masons, stubbornly persisting in an ancient native tradition, evolved to carry the intricate ribbed vaulting – itself partly an English invention – and which reached perfection in the nave of Wells, where dynamics and pure poetry blend and become indistinguishable. So, too were the vast traceried windows and the immense timber trusses and posts of native oak – the hardest in Europe – which, bearing the laminated stone roofs, gave a sense of illimitable height and mystery to the worshippers in choir and aisle below.

These tremendous buildings, so far transcending the apparent economic and technical resources of the time, were not raised like the architectural monuments of the East by slave-labour. They were made by craftsmen able to bargain and of the same faith as those who ordered their making. Though behind them lay the quarrymen and burners of the limestone-hills, the seamen and drovers who brought the materials to the building-sites, and the labour-services and carrying-dues of the local manorial tenants, the main work of building was done by bands of travelling masons who, under their contracting-masters, moved from one great church to another. The name of the lean-to 'lodges' which they erected against the rising walls for shelter still survive in the nomenclature of modern freemasons and trade unions.

Their services were eagerly competed for by prelates whose desire to outbuild one another was as much a stimulus to the craft of building as the later rivalry of eighteenth-century country gentlemen. So were the new fashions of Christian worship which necessitated the erection, at the eastern end of great churches, of chapels to house the shrines of saints, the tombs of benefactors and the relics which the greater religious houses accumulated to attract the offerings of pilgrims. Particularly popular were the Lady Chapels, where men and, still more, women, prayed to the Virgin Mother, whose worship afforded an outlet for a kind of sublimated chivalry and adoration of the womanly virtues of pity, tenderness and compassion. All this brought about during the first half of the thirteenth century an enlargement of the eastern ends of presbyteries of cathedrals and abbeys, later balanced by the addition of preaching-naves. This made English churches – generally inferior to those of France in height – exceptionally long.

The most complete example extant of thirteenth-century English architecture is the church which rose in the Avon water-meadows at Salisbury. Here, following quarrels between the cathedral clergy and the garrison of Old Sarum castle, Bishop Richard Poore – formerly dean – embarked in 1220 on the prodigious task of rebuilding the cathedral on a new site. Built of freestone from the Chilmark quarries twelve miles away and taking half a century to complete, Salisbury cathedral still stands as its builders designed it – save for its spire and upper tower added a century later – the only medieval cathedral in England which is all of a piece. Inside, it was brilliantly coloured, with scarlet and black scrollwork walls, white-painted vaulting and gilded capitals, across which jewels of ruby and blue in the windows cast glittering reflections with every change of sun and shadow. But, outside, in the close, and in the cloisters – the largest in England with their arches looking on to the quiet garth – one can still feel the faith that prompted men to raise such monuments to their belief in the unity of earth and heaven.

Among those who watched its rising walls was the young king Henry III from his hunting palace of Clarendon a few miles away. From his earliest days he had been brought up to venerate the Anglo-Saxon saints. In 1244, four years after the consecration of St Paul's, he started to rebuild the abbey church of Westminster in honour of its founder, Edward the Confessor, in whose name he had christened his eldest son. In doing so he drew his inspiration from the new cathedrals which, under his brother-in-law, Louis IX of France, were being raised on the other side of the Channel. From Amiens and Rheims – the crowning-place of the French Kings – and, above all, from the exquisite Sainte Chapelle in Paris, he borrowed the lofty eastern chevet and the mosaic-paved ambulatory with its semi-circle of radiating chapels and, to the west of them and St Edward's shrine, he made a raised theatre where the coronation of England's kings could be solemnised. Yet though the abbey's eastern outline was taken from Rheims and the soaring pointed arches, flying buttresses and great circular rose-windows from Amiens, its general plan, with its bold transepts and the exquisite craftsmanship of its interior, was English. The master mason who supervised its building was an Englishman, Henry of Reyns, and so were his successors – for the work took a quarter of a century – John of Gloucester and Robert of Beverley. At one time eight hundred workmen were employed on it. From the Abbey muniments we know the names of many of these craftsmen, who were settled by the Chapter in houses in Westminster: Alexander the carpenter, Odo the goldsmith and Edward his son, Henry the glazier, John of St Albans, the great master-sculptor whose twin angels, once brilliantly coloured, still swing their censers under the vast rose-window of the south transept.

By the end of the thirteenth century the lead in ecclesiastical building had passed from the monks to the canons of the 'secular' cathedrals and the 'courtier' bishops, enriched by their ministerial services to the Crown. Edward I's reign saw the culmination of the rebuilding of Lincoln's glorious cathedral – its towers crowned with three immense spires in an extension of the presbytery to house the shrine of St Hugh. The King himself was present at the translation of the saint's bones to their new resting place. With its huge traceried east window and double-banked lights extending the full width of every bay, the new choir was more brilliantly lit than any building yet erected. Beneath the windows of the clerestory, filling the spandrels of the triforium arches, thirty smiling stone angels looked down, some like those carved a generation earlier in Westminster Abbey, with musical instruments, others holding crowns, scrolls and censers. Some had their feet on monsters, others presented souls at the Judgment seat, one with stern face expelled a crestfallen Adam and disdainful Eve from Paradise. These exquisite figures, saved by their great height from the Protestant iconoclasts of a later age, were painted in vivid colours and patterned with stars.

It was light above everything else that the new architecture sought – the crying need of the sunless north. One after another the great churches of northern England followed the lead of the Angel choir. At Ripon, where every canon contributed a tenth of his prebendary income until the work was done, the east end of the choir was rebuilt during the closing decade of the thirteenth century with a huge window; at York a few years later, a new nave was begun in which, in the search for greater light and space, the upper windows of the clerestory were extended downwards to incorporate the triforium, so that the two storeys, though divided by the concealed roof of the aisle, presented a continuous double bank of light along the church's entire reach. The work took more than half a century to complete, and during that time, like almost every major church in the land, the Minster must have been full of scaffolding and of the sound of hammer and chisel. Yet this great revolution supplemented rather than superseded the country's older ecclesiastical architecture, so that everywhere, in the English mode, new Gothic mingled with old Norman and even, in places, Saxon.

As remarkable, on a smaller scale, were the beautiful polygonal chapter-houses of Salisbury and Wells, completed at the end of the thirteenth and beginning of the fourteenth century. Here, debating the business of the Chapter, the canons sat in a circle, enthroned on stone niches under traceried windows, every one an equal, facing the graceful multi-shafted central pillar which bore the vaulted roof. In the north the new chapter-houses at York and Southwell were vaulted without a central pillar, the former having a free-standing span of nearly sixty feet. At Southwell the naturalistic carving, which had recently taken the place of the more formal stiff-leaf, reached its zenith in the wonderful variegated leaves and flowers carved on the capitals during the years when Edward I was trying to subdue Scotland. Like Pygmalion's Galatea they possess all the qualities of life except movement, though made of stone.

Carved figures as beautiful, wrought in metal and stone, rose at Edward I's behest in his father's rebuilt abbey at Westminster. Soon after his return from his Welsh wars he had commissioned William Torel, the London goldsmith, to make a bronze effigy of his father to lie on his tomb at Westminster above a stone base engraved with royal leopards. Beside it a decade later he placed the effigy of his wife, Eleanor of Castile, recumbent with sceptre in hand and jewelled robe and crown under a canopy of Purbeck marble. Two other noble examples of the sculptor's art were added to the abbey's treasures in his reign – those of his brother, Edmund Crouchback, earl of Lancaster, under an elaborately carved canopy guarded by painted and gilded regal mourners and angels holding candle-sticks, and of his uncle, William de Valence. With his copperplate armour coloured with rich enamels, his mailed hands crossed in prayer and his expression of serene confidence that the aristocratic society he had adorned on earth must be mirrored in Heaven, William's effigy was the forerunner of a whole army of recumbent knights in stone, metal or brass. During the fourteenth century there everywhere appeared in the parish or collegiate church enriched by his benefaction or bequest the likeness of some local worthy, clad in the armour and heraldic trappings of his warrior craft, with his lady in long trailing mantle, kerchief and wimple at his side and his hound or supporting heraldic beast at his feet. Though those which survive constitute only a small fraction of the splendid knightly company that once glittered under the painted roofs and windows of England's churches, owing to Edward I's law of entail they proved more enduring than the statues of saints and holy personages which shared their resting places. For, when the latter were smashed as idols, in later centuries these memorials to bygone benefactors received the protection of those who had inherited their blood or lands.

The brightness of a Gothic cathedral, with its painted walls and jewelled shrines – the gleaming or *nitens* of the monkish chroniclers' phrase – is hard to visualise from the bare, grey stone interiors of today. We see the noble skeleton but not the flesh and blood with which our forefathers clothed it. The walls were frescoed with paintings, telling the Christian story by masters whose names, like their works, have been obliterated by time, though from the few which remain, faint and resuscitated from agelong layers of neglect and defacement, we can dimly apprehend their glory. The paintings on the sedilia in the sanctuary of Westminster Abbey – of the Virgin's blue robe and pink mantle and of Gabriel in mauve and green of a lovely limpidity – executed when the first masterpieces of the Italian artistic renaissance were beginning to appear at Siena, Pisa and Florence; the scenes from the life and Passion of Christ in the little Northamptonshire church of Croughton; the East Anglian figures of saints on the vaulting of the north ambulatory of Norwich cathedral and others recently discovered at Little Missenden in Buckinghamshire and in the beautiful circular room at Longthorpe Tower – once the home of the stewards of Peterborough abbey –

are among the survivors of thousands of pictures that told the Bible story to a people unable to read but able to behold and adore.

As rare today is the coloured glass which filled the windows. These, too, like the frescoes, told in picture the story of Christ and his saints and martyrs. Divided by uprights of stone or lead, each pane – medallion, lozenge, circle or square – formed part of a continuous pattern of colour and light. Most of the glass was imported, either through the Channel ports from Normandy and the Île-de-France, where the French *verriers* had given mankind the splendours of Chartres, Bourges and Rouen, or from Hesse and Lorraine by way of the Rhine and Meuse to England's eastern rivers. Owing to the very richness of this early glass, with its deep reds, blues, greens and golden yellows, some of the quality of light sought by the English Gothic window-builders was lost, and towards the end of the thirteenth century a whitish grey or grisaille glass began to be used.

In all this there was a growing elaboration unknown in western Europe since the days of imperial Rome. As the thirteenth century merged into the fourteenth a richer architectural sumptuousness began to succeed the simplicity of the Early English style, pointed arch and geometrically traceried window giving place to flowing curvilinear lines, fantastic pinnacles, crockets and finials decorated with carved globular buds known as ball-flowers. Pierced balustrades, wave parapets and foliate stone tracery radiated from the mullions of window-heads like the branches of a tree. And everywhere were niches filled with statues of the heavenly family, angels, saints and martyrs, Christian princes and prelates, brilliantly gilded and painted. Such was the passion for carving and ornamentation that the masons, working high above column and clerestory among the roof-trusses and rafters, fashioned whole legions of tiny figures on the bosses – foliage masks of men and monsters, fauns, satyrs and beasts, and the leaves and flowers of their native woods and fields – here the Lamb of God, here St George wrestling with the dragon, here a peasant with toothache or two lovers kissing, here the face of a king or bishop or of a fellow workman, here David with his harp or the Virgin crowned – all carved with a care that must have been born of creation for its own sake since, once the carver's work was done and the platform of scaffolding removed, no eye but that of some unborn craftsman repairing the roof in similar solitude would ever see them again. In Exeter alone, rebuilt between 1301 and 1338, there are more than five hundred carved bosses; in the vast late fourteenth century Bristol church of St Mary Redcliffe over eleven hundred. When the might of the medieval Church was broken and fanatics swept through every place of worship with axe and hammer, smashing and defacing the sculptured masterpieces that to them seemed only painted idols, this invisible host of carved roof-bosses remained, unknown for nearly four hundred years until the telescopic lens of the modern camera revealed their testimony to the genius of English medieval craftsmanship.

The first great cathedral to be rebuilt wholly in the decorated style was Exeter. Between Edward I's accession and that of the early years of his grandson's reign, through the zeal of five great building bishops, the old dark Norman structure was transformed into the broad graceful edifice of today with its multiple-shafted marble pillars, the flowing tracery of its windows, its pinnacled sedilia and bishop's throne, statued screen and reredos and carved roof-bosses representing every kind of man and animal, angel and demon known to the medieval imagination. Another West Country cathedral, Bristol, was rebuilt about the same time, with a feature, unique among English cathedrals, of three aisles of equal height and a vault of lierne ribs of a completely novel pattern.

During the early decades of the fourteenth century almost every great church in England was added to or partly rebuilt in this richly ornamented style. Though the greater Benedictine houses were comparatively little affected by the new style, the Cistercians, with their wealth from wool, had by now abandoned their former austerity and started to build in the grand manner on the sites of their primitive encampments in the wilderness. Fountains had already been rebuilt in Henry III's reign; Tintern, Rievaulx and Byland were refashioned in the enriched architecture of the Edwardian age. Even the friars had left their squalid abodes in the city slums and were raising great churches out of the benefactions of merchants who recalled with gratitude the days when they or their fathers had fled from villeinage to the hovels of the nearest town and were there befriended by the mendicants. As with their evangelical mission the Franciscan and Dominican friars had no need to provide for the elaborate liturgical and processional services of the monastic Orders; their churches were usually built without aisles and with naves larger than the choirs to accommodate the middle-class congregations who flocked to hear their sermons. The most celebrated of all was the vast Greyfriars church in London founded in 1306 by Edward I's second Queen, who was buried in it.

In 1321 the monks of the Benedictine abbey at Ely began to build a Lady Chapel with the largest span of vaulting yet seen in England and, under its traceried roof and wide decorated windows, arcaded niches filled with hundreds of gilded and painted statues, today mutilated and headless, telling the story of the Virgin in sculptured stone. Scarcely had the work begun when the central tower of the abbey church fell, crashing into the choir below and destroying three of its bays. Faced by the problem of revaulting so large a space, the Sacristan, Alan of Walsingham, employed a London mason to build, instead of a new tower, an octagonal lantern of revolutionary design with four traceried windows to flood the centre of the Norman church with light. And, as the seventy-foot span proved too wide to bridge with stone, the monks called in William of Hurley, the King's master-carpenter, to vault it in timber with eight gigantic hammer-posts and hammer-beam trusses. The work took twenty years to complete and, when finished, constituted, as it still does, the only Gothic dome in Europe.

Though the new style was decorative rather than structural, in its seeking for ever greater illumination it continued the trend which had begun with the evolution of the Gothic arch. Even before Edward III's accession in 1327, there were signs that English masons were beginning to feel their way towards a further architectural revolution. There was a sense of ever-growing light and unity in the many-ribbed vaults which broke through the older vaulting system of each separate bay and in the marriage between piers, vaulting and roof. The pillars of the new nave of York were like the trunks and branches of a beech wood, and the lierne vault of the choir at Ely like the stars on a winter's night.

It was the reign of this famous warrior king that saw the first flowering of the Perpendicular style, England's supreme contribution to the art of architecture. Hitherto, with their broad bases and close relationship to the earth, her cathedrals had not sought to emulate the perilous height of the Gothic churches of the Île-de-France. But now, under the leadership of William Ramsey, the King's chief mason, English architects began to evolve a technique which produced the effect of height without sacrificing structural proportion or safety. It was an art not of mass but of line, in which the vertical mullions of vast rectangular windows extended upwards and downwards to form, with the horizontal lines they crossed, continuous rectilinear panels of wall and glass. First used by the London masons in the new chapter-house and cloisters of St Paul's and the royal chapel of St Stephen's, Westminster, its end – a reaction against the excessive ornamentation of the Decorated style – was an all-embracing unity in which the separate parts, arch, pier, vault, window and wall, were subordinated to a single whole.

It is in the West Country abbey which sheltered the murdered body of Edward's father, the hapless Edward II, that the earliest surviving example of the new style can be seen. Aided by the gifts of pilgrims to the dead King's shrine, the monks of Gloucester in the 1340s began to transform the dark Norman south transept by substituting for the end wall an enormous eight-light window crowned with a lierne vault. During the next decade they rebuilt the choir, marrying the massive Norman pillars to delicate vaulting shafts and encasing the walls in a framework designed to flood the interior with light. And at its east end, in place of the Norman apse, they made the largest window in Europe, canting the walls of the last bay outwards to increase its size. This great wall of glass, seventy feet high and nearly forty wide, with over a hundred lights, was glazed, through the munificence of a local lord, with the shields and likenesses of his fellow commanders at Crécy – Edward III and the Black Prince in their midst – and, above, them, Christ, surrounded by apostles, seraphim, saints and martyrs singing the *gloria in excelsis* for the crowning of the Virgin. In the foreground, high above the choir, the masons carved on the bosses of the vault fifteen angels, each with a different musical instrument, to accompany that chant of praise sung by figures poised in painted glass between the glittering interior and the grey Gloucestershire skies.

During the years which saw England's martial triumphs in France one magnificent ecclesiastical building after another was raised by the genius of her craftsmen. The Lady Chapel at Lichfield, the cloisters at Norwich, the retrochoir and St Andrew's arches at Wells, the choir of Bristol, the exquisite decorated nave of Exeter were all completed or partly completed in the same decade as Crécy. So, in the north, was the lovely Percy tomb at Beverley and the west front and nave – finished in the year of Edward's victory – of York Minster. And at Salisbury, Richard of Farleigh crowned the thirteenth-century cathedral with a decorated tower and spire whose proportions have never been surpassed.

Even the Black Death of 1348 and 1349, carrying off probably a third of the country's craftsmen, only temporarily halted the rebuilding of its churches. Almost before the pestilence had ceased, the master-mason of Christ Church, Canterbury was summoned to Windsor to succeed the dead William Ramsey in his task of raising a chapel and college dedicated to St George to accommodate the King's new order of chivalry, the Garter. To build it five hundred masons, carpenters, glass-makers and jewellers were requisitioned by the sheriffs of the southern counties and issued with scarlet caps and liveries to prevent their absconding to rival employment.

It was at Winchester that, in the reign of Edward's grandson, Richard II, the master-mason William Wynford – designer of the western towers of Wells – started to rebuild the Norman nave of the cathedral, making it the longest in England after St Paul's. In the same city he built for its bishop, William of Wykeham, a college for boys and another for the bishop's other scholastic foundation, New College, Oxford, equipping both with Perpendicular chapels dedicated to the Virgin. In the same reign a still greater architect, Henry Yevele – for forty years the King's master-mason – rebuilt the nave of Canterbury and, earlier supervised by the Clerk of the Works, the poet Geoffrey Chaucer, reconstructed William Rufus's hall at Westminster, calling in the royal carpenter, Hugh Herland, to span its 240-foot length and 70-foot width with a hammer-beam roof of Sussex oak – the first of the great hammer-beam roofs which, with the fan-vault and the Perpendicular style, were England's most original architectural achievements.

In the century following Richard II's dethronement, when, after their victories at Agincourt and Verneuil, the English were trying to hold down the French provinces Henry V had conquered, and during the bitter years when the dynastic quarrels of York and Lancaster escalated into civil war and near-anarchy, the work of church building still went on. It was now the turn of the parish churches to be refashioned, many through the munificence of the merchant capitalists, woolmen and clothiers who continued to grow rich while the feudal princes and nobles were destroying one another in their sterile fights of the Wars of the Roses. It was an age of towers which arose everywhere above the western end of rustic churches to become the crowning glory of the English landscape. One of the loveliest was the four-staged tower of St Michael's, Coventry, begun in the reign of Edward III and completed with a soaring three-tiered steeple in that of his great-great grandson, Henry VI. Yet it was only *primus inter pares*. The towers of Lavenham, Boston and Halifax, of Magdalen and Merton Colleges in Oxford, of All Saints', Derby, and Cotswold Cirencester, Chipping Camden and Northleach, and a score of great Norfolk and Somerset churches, have equal claims to perfection of beauty and proportion. Some of the finest were raised by a few hundred parishioners, like the 300-feet steeple of Louth, begun in 1501 and finished in 1515, less than a generation before the English Reformation.

One tower of the time stands in a class by itself, the great 'Bell Harry' of Canterbury, raised during Henry VII's reign by Archbishop Morton's master-mason, John Wastell, and completed in 1497 – the year in which the Portuguese rounded the Cape of Good Hope. It was the same artist who vaulted and roofed the wonderful chapel of King's College, Cambridge, begun by Henry VI as the companion foundation to his school at Eton. By a strange irony the culmination of English Gothic was reached a generation later, in 1517, in the very year of Luther's challenge to the Roman Church, when William Vertue completed

the building of Henry VII's Chapel at Westminster, crowning
it with the canopy which, in John Harvey's words, is 'one of the
wonders of the world'.

CHAPTER TWENTY-ONE

Twilight of Holy Church

' "Holy Church I am," quoth she,
"Thou oughtest to know me,
I was the first to nurse thee,
And taught thee the Faith . . ." '

'Parsons and priests complained to the bishop
That their parishés were poor since the pestilence time,
And asked leave and license in London to dwell,
And sing *requiems* for stipends, for silver is sweet.'

William Langland

ABOVE HIS allegiance to king or lord the medieval Christian had
one loyalty transcending all others. It was to the Christian faith
and the Church which was its repository. Within that Church, set
to guide both rulers and subjects in their spiritual duties, was a vast
hierarchy – cardinals, archbishops and bishops, abbots and priors,
deans and archdeacons, monks vowed to perpetual prayer and
contemplation, parish and chantry priests, confessors and chaplains, learned doctors expounding the lore of the universe of which
the Church was the sole interpreter, wandering friars and solitary
hermits. In England, with a population of not more than four
million before the Black Death and, at most, two and a half
million after it, there were between eight and nine thousand
parishes, each with at least one priest or deacon and many with an
unbeneficed chaplain as well, some seventeen or eighteen thousand
regulars living under corporate vows and rule, and a large, though
uncertain, number of unbeneficed priests and chantry chaplains.
York, with ten thousand inhabitants at the outside, had forty-one

parish churches and over five hundred clergy; Norwich, twenty churches and forty-three chapels. Even in the over-crowded capital there was a church for every five hundred people.

In addition to priests and deacons in holy orders who were forbidden to marry and who alone, with their attendant acolytes, officiated in the presbytery or eastern portion of the church shut off from the congregation by the rood-screen, there was a huge army of clerks in minor orders. These had received the Church's initial tonsure – the small round patch cut in the centre of the hair by the officiating bishop as a reminder of Christ's crown of thorns and which, by bringing its wearer under the Church's protection, secured him 'benefit of clergy'. Among them were the acolytes who tended the church-lights and helped the priest at the altar, parish-clerks, readers who read and sang the lessons, exorcists who laid evil spirits, door-keepers who looked after the church and its bells. They included, too, the students of the two universities who numbered at least another two thousand. Probably one in every fifty of the population was a cleric. The poll-tax returns of 1381 listed more than twenty-nine thousand inferior clergy in England, exclusive of friars.

The English Church or *Ecclesia Anglicana* was part of the universal Church of western Christendom. Yet it was also part of the English State. Its bishops and abbots were not only fathers in God but feudal magnates, leaders of the local community and royal advisers. A bishop was a great territorial magnate, enjoying the revenues of numerous manors and knights' fees, who wore princely attire and lived in state. His income of two or three thousand pounds a year was fabulous compared with the yearly wage of forty of fifty shillings earned by a shepherd or ploughman. The bishop of Durham's castle above the Wear was the greatest fortress in the north; the bishop of Exeter had nine residences in Devon alone. The archiepiscopal palace of Bishopthorpe was only one of a score of similar homes owned by the northern metropolitan; the bishop of Lincoln had ten palaces and forty manor-houses including, like every other prelate, a mansion in London from which to perform his duties as a peer of the realm and attend meetings of Parliament and the royal Council. When a bishop travelled it was on horse-back or in a litter with a retinue of thirty or forty mounted clerics and attendants, including knights and men-at-arms drawn from his tenantry to guard him.

For the Church was not, as the saints had sought to make it, above the world; it was part of it. Everywhere was a tacit collusion between Church and State, in which loyalties did not so much clash as merge. Both supported one another; every re-enactment of the great Charter began by guaranteeing the freedom and rights of Holy Church, while anyone who infringed Magna Carta incurred the penalties of excommunication. Clerics administered the Chancery and Exchequer, sat on the judicial bench and headed diplomatic missions and fiscal enquiries. King and community had showered wealth on the Church yet, by doing so, they had made churchmen servants as well as spiritual leaders of the realm, subject, as owners of national land and property, to the same common law as everyone else. England was a country in which the sanctity of canonical doctrine and law was scrupulously respected so long as it did not override the legal rights of Crown and subject. Its very churches were proprietary ones, whose lay owners, having given and endowed them, retained the right to confer their emoluments on any qualified priest who conformed to the spiritual requirements demanded by the Church.

Since every worldly activity was conducted in the Church's name and with the Church's blessing, it followed that official Christianity had grown into a very wordly religion. It was one which had made existence richer and fuller, had fostered artistic and intellectual achievement and, at a time when life was harsh and precarious and death a constant visitant, had given millions a sense of hope and security. Yet many if not most of those who served the Church were very ordinary men who, without any particular sense of calling, had entered it as the only profession offering advancement for anyone not a warrior, land-owner, lawyer or merchant. It was the avenue to wealth, power and dignity and to every learned and intellectual pursuit.

For cleric and layman alike the drama of Christ's life, death and resurrection was seen as a wonderful success-story in whose honour the whole glittering edifice of medieval religion had been raised.

The splendid churches and their treasures, the processions, pageants and thrilling rites, the familiar company of tutelary angels and saints ready to help all who propitiated them, and Holy Church itself, watching over man's spiritual fortunes like a wise and far-sighted banker over his client's securities, were all there for his enrichment. And on the principle that to those that have shall more be given, it was the 'possessioners', as the richer clergy were called, to whom the Church offered most.

For though entry to the Church was open to all, and even a bondsman's son, if his lord would free him, could rise, with the necessary parts and patronage, to the glittering top of the profession, there was an unbridgeable gulf between those selected for preferment and the common ruck of poor clerks. Whether the successful aspirant owed his fortune to birth and aristocratic connections, or whether he was a youth of humble antecedents whose talents had brought him to the notice of authority, the pick of the Church's benefices were available to enable him to pay for his education and to support him for the rest of his life in comfort and even affluence. So far as it gave financial independence to men of ability the system had much to commend it and brought outstanding talents to the service of Church and State. But it was subject to grave abuses. Lords and rich landowners with younger sons unfitted for arms or with a taste for clerkhood would present them to livings before they were in their teens; a brother of the earl of Gloucester in Edward I's reign accumulated in the course of his far from edifying career no fewer than twenty-four benefices, in addition to two canonries and three other collegiate and cathedral appointments.

Nor was there any point of contact between the untutored peasant priesthood and the university-trained ecclesiastics who by the end of the fourteenth century all but monopolised the higher ranks of the Church. In their subtle labours of theological and philosophical analysis and classification, expressed in language intelligible only to those trained in dialectic, the regent masters of Oxford and Cambridge were too busy disputing with one another to have time to popularise their learning for the rustic clergy from whom nine Englishmen out of ten derived their religion. The amorphous image conjured up for superstitious parishioners by the Mass magic of bucolic priests bore little resemblance to the highly intellectualised God of the great doctors. Nor did the Church seem concerned by this double standard in its teaching. With reckless disregard of its own Canon Law it continued to dispose of parochial endowments as though the training and competence of the parish clergy were a matter of minor importance. Of the 376 rectors whom one bishop instituted to benefices in lay patronage only 135 were in holy orders; in another diocese, of 193 parishes visited more than a third were held *in absentia*.

This separation of the clerical sheep from the goats was aggravated by the Crown's demand for clerks of parts for the kingdom's growing administrative machine. It was accepted as a necessity of state that the Church should train and support in a condition of dignity its ablest sons to serve the King. One of Edward I's clerks of the Exchequer held twenty-one livings. For such pluralism seemed almost a civic virtue; 'clerks in the King's service,' it was laid down by statute, 'shall be discharged of their residence.' From time immemorial it had been the Church's task to guide and counsel the State and its rulers, and it seemed natural that part of its wealth should be used to maintain those who performed such duty, and that the descendants of the princes and lords who had endowed it should be able to call on churchmen for those administrative services which only churchmen were trained to give. During the fourteenth century more than half the English bishops were employed in offices of state. Many were chosen from the clerical administrators of the royal Household. In 1300 there had been only two civil servants on the episcopal bench; a quarter of a century later there were twelve, most of them Wardrobe or ex-Wardrobe officials. Under Edward III it was the keepers of the Privy Seal who were most favoured; in 1350 six out of the seventeen bishops had held this office. Though there was never in England an aristocratic monopoly of high ecclesiastical office as in some continental countries, about a fifth of the bishops came from the land-owning and warrior families who surrounded the throne –

Beaumont, Cobham, Berkeley, Burghersh, Arundel, Courtenay.[1]

Great nobles too, needed clerical servants, not only for spiritual, but worldly purposes. A fifteenth century earl of Northumberland had ten priests in his service as well as a clerk of the signet, a clerk of the works and a surveyor, a private secretary and a secretary of his privy council. Thanks to the pious bequests of their forefathers such territorial magnates seldom lacked advowsons to provide for them. For centuries the rich and powerful had showered wealth on the Church; and if a rich man, eager for salvation, offered to endow a chantry, a college, a hospital, a perpetual mass for the souls of himself and his relations, to give a stained-glass window, rebuild a church or provide a wayside altar or rest-house for pilgrims, the Church could not do other than accept it. Provided the rich made a show of conforming to its observances and dogma, it reserved for such benefactors a place in the heavenly as in the earthly kingdom, negotiating, as it were, a special relationship between them and the Almighty. With their endowments for obits, masses and private chantries, their benefactions to parish and collegiate churches, their gifts of gems and relics, altar-cloths, statues and painted windows, they were permitted, and encouraged, to buy themselves into Heaven. A rhyme of the time depicts them doing so:

'Thou shall'st kneel before Christ
In compass of gold,
In the wide window westward
Well nigh in the middle;
And Saint Francis himself
Shall folden thee in his cope
And present thee to the Trinity
And pray for thy sins.'

Pride and privilege not only helped to raise and sustain the Church's fabric; they penetrated the very sanctuary. Instead of having to confess to low-born parish priests, nobles were allocated confessors of rank, and the lord of the manor and his lady wor-

---

[1] W. A. Pantin, *The English Church in the Fourteenth Century*, p. 12; R. Highfield, *The English Hierarchy in the Reign of Edward III* (T.R.H.S. 5th series, VI, p. 133).

shipped with the clergy in the chancel instead of with the congregation in the nave. Even at the moment when all Christians, living
and dead, were supposed to be united in the sacrament of Christ's
sacrifice and when, before Holy Communion, the pax-brede or
picture of the crucified Saviour was passed round to be kissed in
token of brotherly love, there was jostling and shoving for prece-
dence. Such pomp and vainglory – the sin of *superbia* as theologians
called it – was most frequently to be met in the fine new town
churches raised by the merchant community and nobility. One
indignant preacher spoke of 'great lords and ladies that cometh
to holy church in rich and noble apparel of gold and silver, pearls
and precious stones and other worldly, worshipful attire before
our Lord God Almighty', each fine lady 'stirring up the dust with
her train, making the good laymen, the clerks and the priests all
drink of it and making it fall upon the altar of the Lord'.

This growing identification of the Church with wealth and
power resulted in a grave loss of spiritual influence. Since it had
inherited, and insisted on retaining, so large a share of Caesar's
goods, it was forced to render unto Caesar the things that were
God's. Because its prelates were great landowners and magnates, it
had had to concede to the Crown the right of appointing them.
They were seen by the laity as servants of the State rather than of
the Church and therefore as agents of the State's oppression and
injustice. Whatever their gain in worldly dignity, their possession
of excessive wealth and the luxurious display which accompanied
it lost them the respect of many true Christians. For the values that
attached to the pursuit of wealth were not Christian values; by the
Church's own tenets they were sometimes diabolical ones. The
bishop of Winchester was joint owner of the Southwark stews;
even the wonderful new nave of Winchester cathedral and William
of Wykeham's scholastic foundations of Winchester and New
College, Oxford, were partly and indirectly raised on the profits of
prostitution. Such confusion of worldly and spiritual values ran
through the Church's structure like an ugly flaw.

The Church's obsession with its wealth – with 'Christ's land',
'Christ's goods', 'Christ's property' – had other consequences. It
made it seem obese and conservative. It was no longer, as in the days

431

of St Bernard and St Francis, on the march; it was resting on its endowments. The 'possessioners' who enjoyed its wealth would admit of no change. Religion in their hands had become materialistic and mechanical; it was the quantitative in worship that mattered, not the spirit of the worshipper. Salvation was measured by the number of prayers and masses said – so many *Pater Nosters* an hour, so many *Ave Marias*, so many candles lit, so many benefactions to Holy Church. Great men would hurry into church just before the elevation of the Host and then hurry out again, conscience and public opinion satisfied that they had rendered homage for the day. Outward and visible signs seemed everything, inward and spiritual grace tended to be forgotten.

*   *   *

Among those to be met on the highways in the latter Middle Ages was the pardoner, a sanctified huckster licensed by papal or episcopal letter to sell indulgences at every price-range to anyone prepared to buy. These pardoners, with their wallets 'brimful of pardons come from Rome all hot', not only sold their wares but, though not themselves in holy orders, preached sermons advertising them. Sometimes they sold them on behalf of some chantry or work of piety such as a hospital, the repair of a church or a new painted glass window; sometimes they were complete charlatans, pretending they had the power to absolve from any sin and travelling with a string of forged indulgences round their necks, like the one who was sentenced to ride through Cheapside with his face to his horse's tail and a penitent's paper hat on his head. As a sideline they also peddled faked relics which were supposed to secure for their purchasers remission from punishment or protection from accident. Chaucer's pardoner had a pillow

> 'which he asserted was our Lady's veil.
> He said he had a gobbet of the sail
> St Peter had . . .
> a cross of brasse full of stones.
> and in a glass he haddë piggës' bones.'

The Church did not approve such abuses, but in practice it condoned them. In its need for ever more money to support its huge bureaucracy and magnificent court, the papacy countenanced ways of raising money which amounted to a wholesale sale of indulgences. The ecclesiastical authorities in every country did the same. The theory of an indulgence was that punishment for any venial sin could be partly remitted, with the aid of the Church's intercession, for any genuine penitent who received absolution and did penance. With the advance of civilization the Church had tended to substitute for physical penances, like flogging and fasting, such useful acts of public service and charity as the building and repair of churches, the endowment of almshouses, schools and hospitals and the provision of bridges and wayside chapels. Penance could also take the form of money payments to provide priests to say prayers and masses for an offender, securing for him, provided he had confessed his sins and shown true contrition, remission of so many days in purgatory. Such vicarious intercession by the Church could, it was held, secure earlier release from posthumous suffering. In practice, it proved a step to the tacit assumption by the unrighteous that anyone with a long enough purse to purchase the Church's indulgence could commit sin with impunity.

The sale of indulgences was not the only way of raising money for the Church which aroused criticism. Its finances, the taxation of its vast wealth, the enforcement of its rights and its relations with the temporal power and laity were all regulated by Canon or ecclesiastical Law. And Canon Law was binding, not only on every officer and servant of the Church, but on all Christians. Growing in complexity with the advance of civilization and the multiplication of bureaucratic functions, it operated through an ascending hierarchy of courts that stretched from the humblest rural deanery to the papal *Curia* at Rome or Avignon and with rights of appeal at every level up to the Holy Father himself. It sought to adjudicate between nation and nation – for the Church was traditionally the peace- and truce-maker of Christendom. It investigated and suppressed heresy; it dealt with the moral problems, offences and rights of princes and rulers. It tried – though, as capitalist enterprise grew, with diminishing success – to enforce good faith and equitable dealing in economic matters and to impose the ideal of the just price and wage. Its officers had jurisdiction over every matter that concerned the salvation of souls.

433

In many respects the Canon Law affected the lives of ordinary men and women far more closely than that of the King's courts which normally touched only criminals and men of means. The ecclesiastical courts had cognisance of marriage, bigamy and divorce, intestacy, wills and probate, provision for dower and orphans, libel, perjury and breaches of good faith, as well as sexual offences, including adultery, fornication and brothel-keeping. They dealt with sacrilege, blasphemy, failure to pay tithes and church dues or to attend Mass, and the crime of simony or trading in ecclesiastical preferments. Offences on consecrated ground also came within their jurisdiction. These ranged from poaching and cutting down trees to infringements of the right of sanctuary, for which tremendous penalties could be inflicted. In such cases the Church was both party and judge.

Since the ecclesiastical courts also possessed wide, and in some cases overriding, powers in matters affecting the individual rights of clerics, and since the term cleric included not only those who had been ordained, but anyone who could claim 'benefit of clergy' – by the simple device of translating a verse of Latin psalm known as the 'beck verse' – laymen often suffered what they regarded as gross injustice through the one-sided leniency of the ecclesiastical courts. Among those whom Canon Law protected were university students – a particularly unruly type – schoolmasters, professional men like doctors, and nearly all schoolboys.

It was the inquisitorial methods of the courts Christian and their petty interference in men's daily lives which aroused resentment. Laymen could be convicted for brawling in the churchyard, for failing to attend Mass, for irreverent behaviour in church and disrespect to the clergy, for working on Sundays and holy days. And many of the penances to which they could be subjected were of the most humiliating kind. A man might be sentenced to be whipped at the church door, to appear on consecutive Sundays barefoot in shameful garments, to stand before the high altar holding a candle whilst his crime was proclaimed to the congregation. Thus for mowing a meadow on the feast of St Oswald, two labourers were sentenced to four whippings and to perambulate the village on the next saint's day bearing bundles of hay, while two women who had washed linen on St Mary Magdalene's day were given 'two fustigations with a hank of linen yarn'.

The court which most affected the ordinary man was that of the archdeacon. Nobody much liked archdeacons – 'the bishop's eyes', as they were called – not even their fellow churchmen; it was an old ecclesiastical jest to speculate whether an archdeacon could get to Heaven. He was employed by the bishop to investigate and punish cases of embezzlement and misapplication of church funds, unchastity both of churchmen and laymen, and breaches of the Christian code. The agent, and often instigator, of such petty persecution was the archdeacon's summoner. He was the most hated of all the Church's officials. Usually a clerk in minor orders, he seems all too often to have been a man of the lowest character who kept *agents provocateurs*, including loose women, and made his living by spying and blackmail. The specimen in Chaucer's *Canterbury Tales*, with his drunken bullying ways and fiery face, carbuncles, whelks and pimples, knew the secrets of the entire neighbourhood and would

> 'allow just for a quart of wine
> Any good lad to keep a concubine
> A twelvemonth and dispense it altogether',

yet would strip anyone of his possessions who was not prepared to bribe him. 'Purse,' he used to say, was 'the good archdeacon's hell' – by which he meant that any offender could escape penance and punishment provided he paid enough. The customary rate of what was known as 'sin-rent' was £2 p.a.

*   *   *

Medieval man believed that divine justice ruled the universe and that sooner or later every breach of it would be punished. To define justice – *justicia* or righteousness – he looked to the Church. Yet, though the Church existed to teach men how to live righteously, it was all too apparent that this was what so many of its ministers failed to do themselves. Having, like all institutions with a monopoly of power, created an overstaffed profession, it was forced to sacrifice its standards to maintain it. While it admonished

435

men to be virtuous, it virtually allowed them to buy absolution
and spare themselves the trouble of trying. Official Christianity had
become a gigantic vested interest, living on pardons, indulgences,
relics, miracles, shrines, masses for the dead and almost every conceivable device for extracting money out of the faith it taught.

The growing sense of disillusion with the clergy had been in-
tensified by the terrible calamity of the Black Death. The medieval
Church, like the medieval agrarian system, never wholly recovered
from it. For too often it was those who remained at their posts who
died, and those who fled and betrayed their faith who lived. That a
priest out of fear for his life could deprive the dying of the last rites
and rob them of their hope of salvation was a thing so shattering
to the medieval mind that it struck at the roots of belief. Those
who suffered most in repute were the friars. A parish priest could
only escape the pestilence by openly running away, and most of
them, for all their natural fears, probably died at their posts. For a
friar, with his vagrant commission, it was temptingly easy to evade
his Christian duty; those who performed it were the bravest of all,
going out of their way to succour the sick and dying but almost
inevitably succumbing. This survival of the worst did the mendicants untold harm. Their very eloquence made their hypocrisy
seem the more glaring.

Nor did the damage done to the Church by the Black Death
stop there. By demoralising weak natures it drove men, including
many of the clergy, to a hectic pursuit of pleasure. 'Where,' asked a
preacher, 'will you find the priests of today? . . . Not mourning
between the porch and the altar but playing lasciviously around
the prostitute and the brothel; not praying in the choir but wandering about the market place; not in the sanctuary but in the tavern
and alehouse where sometimes they imbibe so much that they can
say neither vespers nor matins properly.' A popular rhyme put it
still more forcibly:

> 'At the wrestling and at the wake,
> And chiefe chanters at the ale;
> Market-beaters, and meddling-make,
> Hopping and hooting with heave and hale.

436

At fairë fresh, and at wine stale;
Dine and drink, and make debate;
The seven sacraments set a' sale;
How keep such the keys of heaven's gate?'

Thus in the half-century which followed the Black Death there grew up a widespread feeling that the Church was failing Christ's people. Bishops too often seemed proud luxurious lords, arch-deacons and proctors blackmailers, monks gluttons, friars scroungers and liars.[1] There was no lack of devout Christians in England, a country famed for its orthodoxy. It was the age of the mystic recluse, both clerical and lay, who, withdrawing from the world to a life of religious contemplation, found in the inner experience of the heart a new revelation. It was among such men and women that dissatisfaction with the Church was strongest. The contrast between Christ's life of poverty and the wealth and self-indulgence of so many of its leaders was too great to overlook.

As for the papacy, it was even more fatally damned by its wealth and the shameless rapacity with which its officials and agents pursued it. Its bankers and lawyers, levying toll on every country's ecclesiastical revenues, had become the chief tax-collectors of Europe. To provide for its luxurious court and ever-growing bureaucracy it employed, in Christ's name, the techniques of the lawyer, tax-collector and money-lender. In place of the theological and philosophical ferments of the twelfth and thir-teenth centuries the chief canonical controversies of the late Middle Ages centred round papal taxes, fees and subsidies, procurations to meet the expenses of legates and papal emissaries, the sale of pardons and indulgences, fines or *spolia* on the property of dead prelates, and – most resented of all – the *annates*, or first-fruits demanded of all new incumbents for provision to benefices by the

---

[1] And worse – 'When the good man is from hame
And the friar comes to our dame,
He spares neither for sin nor shame
But that he does his will . . .
Each man that here shall lead his life
That has a fair daughter or a wife
Beware that no friar them shrive.'
Political Poems and Songs (ed. Wright), 1, pp. 263–8.

Holy Father, of which the cash to pay was advanced by the papal bankers at crippling interest-rates which were subsequently enforced, in disregard of the Christian prohibition against usury, by threats of excommunication.

The English were devout Catholics and, like all western Christians, believed in the unity of Christendom. But they were growing increasingly insular and did not like to see native benefices and endowments diverted to provide for foreign papal nominees and benefice-hunters. They liked it still less when, during Edward III's wars with France, Pope after Pope was a Frenchman and the papacy itself resided in a French enclave at Avignon. The Holy See seemed to have become the preserve of their enemies, its occupant 'the French King's tame cat'.

So unpopular was the papacy with the English at this time that when, in the last year of Edward III's reign, the city of London put on a pageant 'with great noise of minstrelsy, trumpets, cornets and shawms and many wax torches', the highlight in the procession was a mock Pope accompanied by twenty-four cardinals and 'eight or ten arrayed with black masks like devils, not at all amiable, seeming like legates'. When, following an attempt to re-establish the papacy at Rome, the French cardinals in 1378 challenged the election of a fantastically irascible and autocratic Italian Pope and set up a rival one at Avignon, Christendom was confronted for forty years with the shocking spectacle of two Popes. At one time there were three. Each demanded payment of ecclesiastical taxes, excommunicated the other's supporters and hired 'crusaders' to harry the other's lands.

The 'great schism', as it was called, was the culmination of the scandals which shook men's faith in the Church at the end of the fourteenth century. It was against a background of popular indignation at simony, papal provisions, pluralism, non-residence and the sale of indulgences that the Oxford theologian and philosopher, John Wycliffe, raised his voice of protest. This radical-minded Yorkshireman – at one time Master of the little Oxford college of Balliol and 'holden of many to be the greatest clerk then living' – began by opposing papal claims on native benefices on behalf of Parliament, went on to denounce ecclesiastical wealth, and ended

438

by attacking nearly all the institutional assumptions of the Church. He based his stand on the life and teaching of Christ as revealed by the scriptures, which he maintained were alone necessary for salvation and capable of interpretation by the humblest. 'No man,' he declared, 'was so rude a scholar but that he might learn from the words of the Gospel according to his simplicity.' All that was necessary was that they should be made available in his native tongue. 'To be ignorant of the Bible,' he wrote, 'is to be ignorant of Christ.'

Wycliffe spoke with contempt of the 'possessioners': of monks with 'red and fat cheeks and great bellies' and gowns of superfine cloth big enough to clothe four or five needy men; of the blasphemous sale of papal indulgences, of the worship of relics and images, of excommunication for political and financial ends. The 'dowering of the Church with lordship of the world' had been a heresy, for 'Christ came of poor folk'. Its wealth and power were millstones round its neck, its over-elaborate conventual services 'the religion of fat cows'. Even the Pope himself was only 'a naked servant of God'.

Wycliffe's revolutionary indictment traversed the Church's whole position: that it had been exclusively entrusted with the salvationary powers won for mankind on the cross. Against its claim that God's will could only be known through its sacraments and ordinances, this gaunt, uncompromising North Country puritan set up, not only the right of every man to judge the scriptures for himself, but the direct responsibility of the individual conscience to God. The ministry was requisite for the well-being of the Church but not for its existence; its business, and sole business, was to teach the Gospel. Everything that came between the individual and Christ was evil, and that included most of the ecclesiastical establishment of the day, including episcopacy. Far in advance of his time, Wycliffe foreshadowed an age when family and congregational worship would take the place of the ritual and mystery of the candle-lit altar and what he indignantly called 'the drawing of the people by curiosity of gay windows . . . paintings and babwynerie'.

For a short time Wycliffe was the most popular man in the

country. He was supported against the papal charges of heresy by
the masters and students of Oxford – at that time, after Paris, the
most important university in northern Europe – by the royal Duke
of Lancaster and the Princess of Wales, by an anti-clerical Parliament and the London mob. The rising middle class delighted in
his defence of national rights and his opposition to foreign ecclesiastical taxation, while many applauded his proposal to confiscate the
surplus wealth of the Church and distribute it among deserving
noblemen and knights 'that wolden justly govern the people and
maintain the land against enemies'. But when he extended his
theological arguments and attacks on the institutional side of
religion to its central mysteries, repudiating transubstantiation and
insisting that the Host remained bread and wine and that it was
blasphemy to pretend that Christ's body and blood could be made
by the incantations of an ignorant and possibly sinful priest, he
lost the support of his patrons. The ordinary Englishman was
ready to support an attack on excessive clerical wealth, papal
interference and Caesarian bishops but took fright at the idea of
challenging hallowed beliefs that were the sacred preserve of the
Church. He could see no sense in incurring the risk of excommunication and eternal damnation by abstract speculations which
affected neither his personal life nor his purse.

Nor, however much he wanted to see it purged of corruption,
did he wish to destroy what was still the most valued and venerable
thing in the kingdom's polity – Holy Church. Though riddled with
imperfections, its beliefs and practices, including its very superstitions and abuses, were part of the community's continuing life.
It had created the society and civilization to which medieval man
belonged and, without it, life would have seemed bleak and unthinkable. Owning as it did something like a third of the nation's
wealth there can have been few, even of moderate means, who did
not have some interest in its survival. This was true even of the
monasteries whose widespread financial ramifications, fame and
hospitality made them centres of regional social life. Ecclesiastical
and lay society were intimately interwoven; many a local knight
was proud to act as steward to some neighbouring religious house,
and the humble ancestors of Samuel Pepys, by serving the great

abbey of Crowland for two and a half centuries as reeves, rent-collectors and granators, raised themselves from servile beginnings to respectability, yeomanry and even gentry.

For this, as well as for other reasons, Wycliffe's attack on clerical abuses failed to make any impression on the Church establishment of his day. It was too sweeping, too academic and too colourless for the ordinary unthinking man. It not only challenged vested interests, it proposed to abolish them altogether. Papacy, episcopacy, endowments, monasteries, friars, images, pilgrimages, gilds and chantries, all were to go and, with them, the outward grace and beauty of religious observance. In stripping Holy Church of its corrupting wealth, Wycliffe and his followers sought to strip it also of its charm. Had they had their way nothing would have remained but the authority of the Bible as interpreted by the individual worshipper, a parish priesthood supported by voluntary offerings, and a presbyterian system of church government under the ultimate authority of the Crown.

Forbidden to lecture in the university and banished to his rustic living at Lutterworth, where he spent his last years supervising the translation of the scriptures, Wycliffe and his heresy passed – for a time – out of the mainstream of English life. For a generation after his death in 1384, his doctrines were preached on village green and highway by the russet-clad evangelists he had trained, and received the support of many younger churchmen and knights of the shire. Even as late as 1414 they precipitated a rising against the government of Henry V on the eve of Agincourt, and the ecclesiastical authorities reacted against the 'mutterers' or Lollards, as they were called, with ruthless repression. In this they were zealously backed by the new Lancastrian dynasty which, seeking to buttress its dubious right to the throne by its orthodoxy, had procured from Parliament a statute – *De Haeretico Comburendo* – that not only forbade unlicensed preaching and the holding of views 'contrary to the faith and blessed determination of Holy Church', but empowered the civil arm to burn, 'in some prominent place', any persistent or relapsed heretic condemned by a spiritual court. In March 1401, rejecting all his persecutors' attempts to make him recant, a London chaplain, William Sawtrey, was burnt at Smithfield, the first martyr of the coming Protestant Reformation. That was still more than a century distant, awaiting the day when the introduction of printing and the growth of a literate laity could bring the forbidden vernacular scriptures to a wider public than existed in Plantagenet and Lancastrian England. Yet, though driven underground by Caesarian bishops, Wycliffe's heretic creed survived, smouldering in secret conventicles and hearth-side readings in the little towns of the Chilterns, east midlands and home counties and in the capital, until, fanned by fresh persecutions, it broke into renewed flame under the early Tudors. Nor did it survive only in England. Carried by the courtiers of Richard II's Bohemian Queen to Prague, it lit in the pyres of the Hussite martyrs a still more prophetic conflagration on the banks of the Elbe, where, a hundred years later, the Saxon monk Martin Luther challenged the Roman Church at Wittenberg.

BOOK LIST

*A short list of the chief documented
and other works on which this book is based*

M. D. Anderson, *Looking for History in English Churches*
G. W. S. Barrow, *Feudal Britain*
H. S. Bennett, *Life on the English Manor*
J. Betjeman, *Collins Guide to English Parish Churches*
H. Braun, *An Introduction to English Medieval Architecture*
A. Bryant, *Makers of the Realm*
——, *The Age of Chivalry*
——, *The Medieval Foundation*
A. H. Burne, *The Crécy War*
——, *The Battlefields of England*
H. M. Cam, *Liberties and Communities in Medieval England*
——, *The Hundred and The Hundred Rolls*
——, *Law-Finders and Law-Makers in Medieval England*
S. C. Carpenter, *The Church in England 597–1688*
C. J. P. Cave, *Roof Bosses in Medieval Churches*
M. V. Clarke, *Medieval Representation and Consent*
R. G. Collingwood and J. N. L. Myres, *Roman Britain and the
    English Settlements* (Oxford History of England)
G. G. Coulton, *Medieval Panorama*
——, *The Medieval Village*
——, *Life in the Middle Ages*
——, *Social Life in Britain from the Conquest to the Reformation*
——, *The Black Death*
A. G. Dickens, *The English Reformation*
C. W. Dickinson, *Scotland from the Earliest Times to 1603*
D. C. Douglas, *William the Conqueror*
——, *The Norman Achievement*
D. C. Douglas and G. W. Greenaway (eds.) *English Historical
    Documents* Vol. II
D. L. Edwards, *Christian England*

J. Evans, *English Art, 1307–1461* (Oxford History of English Art)

V. H. Galbraith, *The Making of Domesday Book*

V. H. H. Green, *The Later Plantagenets*

John Harvey, *Gothic England*

——, *English Cathedrals*

Jacquetta Hawkes, *A Land*

W. S. Holdsworth, *Makers of Law*

——, *History of English Law, Vols I to III*

W. G. Hoskins, *The Making of the English Landscape*

J. Huizinga, *The Waning of the Middle Ages*

E. F. Jacob, *The Fifteenth Century* (Oxford History of England)

J. J. Jusserand, *English Wayfaring in the Middle Ages*

M. D. Knowles, *The Evolution of Medieval Thought*

——, *The Religious Orders in Medieval England*

W. Langland, *The Vision of Piers Plowman* (ed. W. Skeat)

G. T. Lapsley, *Crown, Community and Parliament in the Later Middle Ages* (ed. H. Cam and G. Barraclough)

E. Lipson, *Introduction to the Economic History of England*

F. W. Maitland, *The Constitutional History of England*

——, *The Court Baron* (Selden Soc.)

——, *Collected Papers* (ed. H. A. L. Fisher)

G. Mathew, *The Court of Richard II*

K. B. McFarlane, *John Wyclif and the Beginnings of English Nonconformity*

M. McKisack, *The Fourteenth Century 1307–1399* (Oxford History of England)

Medieval England, (ed. A. L. Poole) 2 vols

R. J. Mitchell and M. D. R. Leys, *A History of the English People*

S. K. Mitchell, *Taxation in Medieval England* (ed. S. Painter)

J. E. Morris, *The Welsh Wars of Edward I*

J. R. H. Moorman, *Church Life in England in the Thirteenth Century*

A. R. Myers, *England in the Later Middle Ages*

——, (ed.) *English Historical Documents*, Vol. IV

G. R. Owst, *Preaching in Medieval England*

——, *Literature and Pulpit in Medieval England*

W. A. Pantin, *The English Church in the Fourteenth Century*

444

T. F. T. Plucknett, *A Concise History of the Common Law*
——, *Legislation of Edward I*
A. L. Poole, *From Domesday Book to Magna Carta*
M. M. Postan, *The English Medieval Economy and Society*
Eileen Power, *Medieval People*
——, *The Wool Trade in English Medieval History*
F. M. Powicke, *Henry III and the Lord Edward*
——, *The Thirteenth Century* (Oxford History of England)
——, *Medieval England*
C. W. Previte-Orton, *The Shorter Cambridge Medieval History*
E. Rickert, *Chaucer's England*
J. E. Thorold Rogers, *History of Agriculture and Prices* (Vols I
    and II)
H. Rothwell (ed.) *English Historical Documents,* Vol. III
L. F. Salzmann, *English Industries of the Middle Ages*
——, *English Life in the Middle Ages*
——, *English Trade in the Middle Ages*
G. O. Sayles, *The Medieval Foundations of England*
——, *Select Cases in the Court of King's Bench under Edward I*
    (Selden Society)
F. Seebohm, *The English Village Community*
A. L. Smith, *Church and State in the Middle Ages*
J. Maynard Smith, *Pre-Reformation England*
(ed. W. C. Dickinson, C. Donaldson and I. A. Milne) *A Source*
    Book of Scottish History
T. C. Smout, *A History of the Scottish People 1560–1830.*
F. Stenton, *Anglo-Saxon England* (Oxford History of England)
W. Stubbs, *The Constitutional History of England*
L. Stone, *Sculpture in Britain, The Middle Ages* (Pelican History
    of Art)
J. Tait, *The English Medieval Borough*
A. Hamilton Thompson, *The English Clergy and Their*
    Organisation in the Later Middle Ages
S. L. Thrupp, *The Merchant Class of Medieval England*
T. F. Tout, *Chapters in the Administrative History of Medieval*
    England
S. Toy, *The Castles of Great Britain*

445

E. W. Tristam, *English Wall Painting of the Fourteenth Century*
W. L. Warren, *King John*
D. Whitelock (ed.) *English Historical Documents,* Vol. I.
B. Wilkinson, *Constitutional History of Medieval England*
——, *Studies in the Constitutional History of the Thirteenth and Fourteenth Centuries*

ACKNOWLEDGEMENTS

In addition to all those who so generously helped me in the research and typing of my earlier books on which this comprehensive and shorter version of so many of them has been based, I have in particular to thank Mrs Judy Airy for her flawless compilation of the present volume's vast Persons and Places Index, and Mrs M. A. Shore who, with others, during the last two years has meticulously and patiently typed every word of the text at least a dozen times.

SUBJECT INDEX

Numbers in italics indicate major references

448

Numbers in italics indicate major references

449

Numbers in italics indicate major references

Using the *Curia Regis*, the inner executive of the Great Council, Henry II, the Conqueror's great-grandson, established a
COMMON LAW, 90, 92, 153–6, 166, 172, 174, 181, 332, 347, 350, 375, 376
for all England, bringing under direct royal control both the despotic and divisive power of the military feudal jurisdictions and the humble village manorial courts their Norman owners had usurped, and the old Anglo-Saxon public courts of
SHIRE AND HUNDRED, 70, 86, 87
To administer and enforce this common system of law he created a body of trained judges whose business it was "to do justice habitually", sending them out to join, and later replace, the royal Sheriffs on annual *Progresses in Eyre*, and
ASSIZES, *86–7*, 131, 157, 160, 161
Others, sitting on the royal Bench in Westminster Hall, formed with them a permanent judicial tribunal which, reinforcing the
COURT OF EXCHEQUER, 85–6, 163, 307
grew into the Courts of
KING'S BENCH, 87, 157, 161, 163, 166. 230, 256, 284, 323, 351
and
COMMON PLEAS, 87, 131, 157, 161, 163, 166, 230, 256
Writs or royal commands issued by these Judges restored possession to any

Numbers in italics indicate major references

freeman forcibly dispossessed of his land and struck at the root of the great lord's power over his feudal tenants dealing a death-blow to trial-by-battle and private law and establishing the most important of all English institutions, the RULE OF LAW, 90–2, 121–2, 127.
Such WRITS, *88–90*, 157–8, 161–2, 165, 167, 194, though strictly defined, were of many kinds, offering an ever-growing variety of remedies. Among them were – right, 162, praecipe, 88, 162, novel disseisin, 88, 162, mort d'ancestor, 88, 162, replevin, 162, trespass, 162, 164, detinue, 162, debt, 162, account, 162, covenant, 162, assumpsit, 162, case, 162.
Henry's Judges, issuing these Writs, substituted for proof-by-battle an inquest or recognition by "twelve free and lawful men" of the neighbourhood summoned to decide with whom disputed possession lay. Such JURIES, 88–9, 91, 125, 126, 143, 158–9, 160, 163, 164, 165, 166, 378 constituted the conscience of neighbours acquainted with the facts and sworn to speak the truth. Between 1166 and 1176 by the Constitutions of Clarendon and Northampton Henry extended the criminal jurisdiction of the Crown – formerly confined to *lèse majesté* and breaches of the peace on the royal domains and highways – to murder, rape, larceny, arson, forgery and harbouring criminals. Based on precedent and the verdicts of Juries determining question of fact, and of royal Judges expounding and interpreting the Law there grew up a system of CASE LAW, 90–1, 157–8.
This principle of allowing representatives of the neighbourhood to decide questions of fact in criminal, as well as land law, applied to trials, not only of Englishmen, but of Normans, and was governed by the ancient English principle, unknown to Roman law, that every case should be tried in public, as in the presence of the Anglo-Saxon tribe, 91.
The secret tribunal, that instrument of imperial tyranny, was never allowed a lodgment in English Common Law. This participation of the ordinary man in its processes proved a bulwark of both public and private liberties.

OTHER COURTS
  Curia Regis, 79, 86, 87
  Danelaw, 69, 90, 163, 373
  Feudal, 86, 87–8, 89–90, 106, 125, 159–60, 175
  Hundred, 51, 69, 86, 90, 123, 125, 126, 160, 163–4
  Manor court, leet or moot, 86, 297, 332, 373, 376–7
  Marshalsea, 316, 324
  Quarter Sessions, 157, 160
  Shire, 51, 52, 69, 86, 90, 125, 126, 157, 160, 163–4
  Tourn, Sheriff's or halimot, 21, 159, 160, 164–5, 377

LEGAL PROFESSION AND EDUCATION, 150, *166–8*
  Apprentices, 166, 167–8, 319
  Attorneys, 153, 161, 166
  Barristers, narrators and pleaders, 150, 161, 164, 166, 167, 168, 220
  Inns of Court, 167–8
  Judges, 82, 87, 89, 90–2, 125–6, 127, 128, 149, 150, 152, 153, 154, 155, *157–8*, 159, 160, 161, 163, 165–6, 167–8, 192, 193, 196, 230, 317, 323, 345, 346, 350, 351, 375, 377
  Lawyers, unpopularity of, 299, 304, 309, 314, 317, 330
  Sergeants-at-law, 153, 158, 161, 166, 167, 168, 220, 322, 350
  Year books, 167, 319

MISCELLANEOUS
  Civil Law (Roman), 158–9, 166, 347, 350, 375
  Compurgation, 163
  Copyhold, 332, 376
  Coroners, 92, 157, 160, 163, 165, 378
  Criminal Jurisdiction, 87, 91, 105, 330
  Curia Regis, 79, 86, 87
  Corruption, judicial, 165–6, 295, 300–3
  De Donis Conditionalibus, 135
  Entail, law of, 155–6
  Frankpledge, 164
  Gaols, 73, 79, 314
  Grand Assize, 89
  "Hue and cry", 378
  Inquests, 89, 92, 125, 157, 158, 163, 296
  Justices of the Peace, *156–7*
  "King's Peace", 50, 162, 165, 182, 202, 377, 391
  Law merchant, 162
  Manumission, 373–4
  Ordeal of fire and water, 85, 88, 91, 158
  Outlaws, 91, 163, 381
  Primogeniture, 156
  Prisoners, 303, 314, 315–16, 319

SUBJECT INDEX

Numbers in italics indicate major references

Taxation, 13, 31, 70, 72, 127, 131, 132,
150–1, 160, 199, 226, 239, 307, 333, 339,
356, 364, 405
Coinage and Currency, 34, 50, 226
Commissioners of Array and Taxes, 157
"Custom, Great and Ancient", 151, 406
Customs, 405
Domesday Book, 70, *72*
Feudal aids, 127, 131, 151, 155, 374
Fines, 78, 128
Inheritance, confiscation of, 365
Loans, forced, 364
Moveables, taxation on, 127, 150–1, 307
'Pleasuance, La', 364
Poll tax, *307–9*
Scutage or shield money, 86, 127, 129,
131, 132
Staple, customs, 224, 252, 405–6, 409
Tallages, 86, 127, 151, 226
Tithing penny, 165
Tonnage on wine imports, 151
Trailbasten, Commission of, 309
Wardships, 128, 131

Transport
Bridges, 35, 101, 391, 433
Cartage, 374, 382
Coaches, 392
Oxen-drawn carts, 102, 392
Pack-horses, 392, 402, 406, 407, 408
Roads, 6, 10, 11, 12, 16, 32, 35, 65, 87,
101, 209, 255, 379, *391–5*
Water, 402
travel, perils of, 391–2

Wales, 1, 9, 16–17, 18, 26–7, 40, 53, 65,
68, 74, 76, 78, 100, 104, 120, 124–5,
169–88, 189–90, 194, 195, 197, 215, 221,
222, 241, 242, 257, 311, 362, 366, 368
early history, 26–7, 83, 143
character of, *181–5*
fighting quality, *177,* 215
eisteddfod, 172
Prince of, 188, 250
Marchers, 74, 76, 118, 141, 143, 146,
170, 171–5, 178, 180, 182, 183, 217n,
218

Way of the World, passing
Ale-houses, 147
Baths, 11, 12, 98, 361
Bawdy-houses, 431
Destitution, 302–3
Fairs, 388, 395
Lepers, 312
Luxury and display, 300–2
May Day rites, 51
Pedlars and chapmen, 381, 395
Sanitation, lack of, 381, 383, 397
Sport
Archery, 221–2, 399
Football, 399
Harvest Home, 51
Hawking, 82, 275
Horse-racing 395
Hunting, 71, 78, 82, 203, 274, 398,
400
Morris dancing, 51
Rowing, 399
Skating, 399
Stone throwing, 399
Wrestling, 395, 399
Trades Unions, 413
Weather-cocks, 52

454

PERSONS AND PLACES INDEX

467

Legend
- ● Towns
- ✗ Battlefields
- ✳ Castles
- ⯗ Monastic cathedrals
- ✝ Secular cathedrals
- ▢ Monasteries, collegiate churches and nunneries

MORAY FIRTH

Urquhart

ROSS

Kinloss
Forres
MORAY

Banff
BUCHAN

Inverness

Aberdeen

BADENOCH

Montrose

LORN

Forfar
Dundee
Scone
Perth

Arbroath

ARGYLE

OCHIL HILLS
L. LEVEN

FIRTH OF TAY
St. Andrews

Stirling
Bannockburn
Cardross
Falkirk
Glasgow
Linlithgow

Dunfermline
Kinghorn
Leith
Edinburgh

Crail
FIRTH OF FORTH
Dirleton
Dunbar
Halidon Hill

CLYDE
Dumbarton
ARRAN

Newbattle
Lanark
TWEED
Dryburgh
Melrose
Jedburgh

Norham
Kelso
Roxburgh

Berwick
Lindisfarne
Bamborough
Alnwick

Ayr
Turnberry

Dalry
LOCH TROOL
CREE→
GALLOWAY
Wigtown
Kirkcudbright

Lochmaben
Dumfries
Caerlaverock
Castle
Douglas

Wark
Otterburn

TYNE
Lanercost
Carlisle
Hexham

Newcastle
Tynemouth

Hartlepool
Durham

ISLE OF MAN

Barnard Castle

Richmond
Jervaulx
Fountains
Furness

Northallerton
Ripon
Rievaulx
Bridlington

Lancaster
Boroughbridge
York
Myton
Beverley
Kingston upon Hull

Preston

Selby

Pontefract

0   50
Miles

~ARTHUR BANKS~